**select
editions**

Reader's
Digest

Reader's Digest

The condensations in this volume
are published with the consent of the authors
and the publishers © 2010 Reader's Digest, Inc.

www.readersdigest.co.uk

Published in the United Kingdom by Vivat Direct Limited
(t/a Reader's Digest), 157 Edgware Road,
London W2 2HR

For information as to ownership of
copyright in the material of this book,
and acknowledgments, see last page.

Printed in Germany
ISBN 978 0 276 44442 5

select
editions

THE READER'S DIGEST ASSOCIATION, INC.

contents

author in focus

Apartheid in South Africa was a regime that censored writers, forcing them to either write books approved by the state or flee abroad to find a publisher. In the last 20 years, since Nelson Mandela walked free from Robben Island and began to lead his people into a democracy, publishing has emerged strong and vibrant. There is a growing pool of crime and thriller writers, among whom Deon Meyer is seen as 'the king'. His novels give colourful and rare insights into modern-day life in South Africa.

in the spotlight

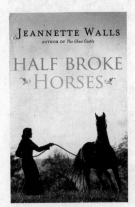

Jeannette Walls's highly praised memoir, *The Glass Castle* (2005), was a triumphant account of overcoming a difficult childhood with her dysfunctional but colourful family. Following its success, Walls decided to write a book about her mother's childhood on a cattle ranch in Arizona, but was persuaded by her that it was her grand-mother's story that should be told. Walls calls *Half Broke Horses* 'a true-life novel', saying that because she was only eight when Lily Casey Smith died, she had to draw on numerous stories and memories, and use her own imagination to fill in any gaps. 'So the only honest thing to do was to call the book a novel,' she explains.

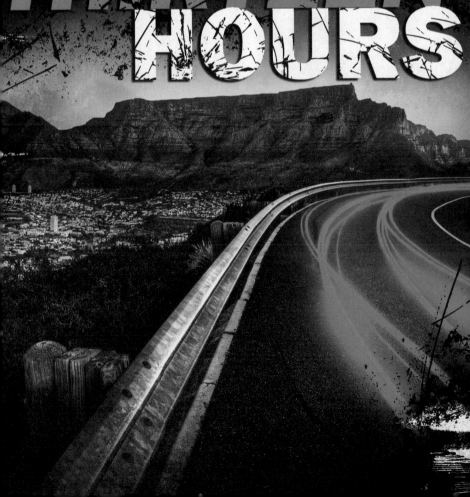

DEON MEYER

THIRTEEN
HOURS

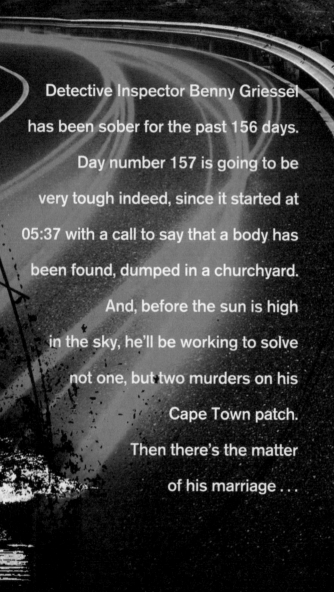

Detective Inspector Benny Griessel

has been sober for the past 156 days.

Day number 157 is going to be

very tough indeed, since it started at

05:37 with a call to say that a body has

been found, dumped in a churchyard.

And, before the sun is high

in the sky, he'll be working to solve

not one, but two murders on his

Cape Town patch.

Then there's the matter

of his marriage . . .

05:36–07:00

I

05:36: a girl runs up the steep slope of Lion's Head, the sound of her running shoes urgent on the broad footpath's gravel.

At this moment, as the sun's rays pick her out like a searchlight against the mountain, she is the image of carefree grace. Seen from behind, her dark plait bounces against the little rucksack. Her neck is deeply tanned against the powder blue of her T-shirt. There is energy in the rhythmic stride of her long legs in denim shorts. She personifies athletic youth.

Until she stops and looks back over her left shoulder. Then the illusion disintegrates. There is anxiety in her face. And utter exhaustion.

She does not see the beauty of the city in the rising sun's soft light. Her frightened eyes search wildly for movement in the tall shrubbery behind her. She knows they are there, but not how near. It is the fearsome urge to live that drives her to run again, despite the fatigue of a night without sleep and the disorientation of a foreign country.

Ahead of her the path forks. Instinct spurs her to the right, higher, closer to the Lion's rocky dome. She doesn't think, there is no plan. She runs blindly.

DETECTIVE INSPECTOR Benny Griessel was asleep. When his cellphone rang, he opened his eyes and checked the radio clock. It was 05:37.

He swung his feet off the single bed, then stumbled down the stairs to the living room where he had left his phone. His hair was unkempt, too long between trims. He wore only a pair of faded rugby shorts. His single thought was that a call at this time of the morning could only be bad news.

'Hey, Benny, it's Vusi. Sorry to wake you. We've got a . . . body.'

'Where?'

'St Martini, the Lutheran church up in Long Street.'

'I'll be there now.'

Probably just a tramp who had drunk too much. He put the phone down beside his secondhand laptop. He turned, still half asleep, and bashed his shin against the bicycle leaning against his pawnshop sofa. He grabbed it before it toppled. Then he went back upstairs.

In the bedroom he took off his shorts and the musky scent of sex drifted up from his midriff. The knowledge of good and evil suddenly weighed heavily on him. Along with the events of last night, it squeezed the last remaining drowsiness from his brain. Whatever had possessed him? He tossed the shorts onto the bed and walked through to the bathroom.

SUDDENLY SHE WAS on the Signal Hill Road and spotted the woman and dog. It was big, a Ridgeback. The woman looked about sixty, white, with a large pink sun hat. The dog was unsettled. Maybe it smelled her fear, sensed the panic inside her. She stopped three metres from them.

'Help me,' said the girl. Her accent was strong.

'What's wrong?' There was concern in the woman's eyes.

'They're going to kill me.'

The woman looked around in fear. 'But there's nobody.'

The girl looked over her shoulder. 'They're coming.'

She knew the woman and dog wouldn't make any difference against them. She would put them all in danger. 'Call the police,' she said and ran again, her body reluctant, down the road towards Table Mountain. 'Just call the police.'

She looked back once. The woman was standing there, frozen to the spot.

GRIESSEL FLUSHED the toilet and wondered why he hadn't seen last night coming. *Jissis*, he shouldn't feel so guilty, he was only human after all. But he was married. If you could call it a marriage. Separate beds and separate homes. Damn it all, Anna couldn't expect him to support two households, expect him to be sober for six months, and celibate on top of that.

At least he was sober. One hundred and fifty-six days now. More than five months of struggling against the bottle. God, Anna must never hear about last night, less than a month before his exile was served, the punishment for his drinking. If Anna found out, all the struggle was for nothing.

He stood in front of the mirror and had a good look at himself. Greying at the temples, wrinkles at the corner of his eyes, the Slavic features. He had never been much of an oil painting.

Whatever had she seen in him, that Bella?

IT WASN'T A *TRAMP*. Griessel's heart skipped a beat as he climbed over the spiked railings of the church wall and saw the girl lying there. The running shoes, khaki shorts and the shape of her arms and legs told him she was young. She reminded him of his daughter.

Inspector Vusumuzi Ndabeni stood beside her with Thick and Thin from Forensics, a police photographer and three men in South African Police Services uniform. On the pavement there were more uniforms in the white shirts and black epaulettes of the Metro Police, all very self-important. Together with a group of bystanders, they stared at the motionless figure.

'Morning, Benny,' said Vusi in his quiet manner. Lean and neat, his trousers sharply pressed, snow-white shirt with tie. His peppercorn hair was cut short, his goatee impeccably clipped. He wore surgical rubber gloves. Griessel had been introduced to him for the first time last Thursday, along with the other five detectives he had been asked to 'mentor' throughout the coming year. That was the word that John Afrika, Regional Commissioner: Detective Services and Criminal Intelligence, had used. But when Griessel was alone in Afrika's office it was, 'We're in the shit. I'm losing my best people and the new ones are totally green. Benny, can I count on you?'

An hour later he was in the Commissioner's large conference room, along with six of the best 'new' people seated in a row on grey government-issue chairs. This time Afrika toned down his message: 'Benny will be your mentor. He's been on the Force for twenty-five years and what he's forgotten, you still have to learn. But he's not here to do your work for you. He's your mentor, that is . . .' the Commissioner glanced at his notes, '"a wise and trusted counsellor". That's why I transferred him to the Provincial Task Force. Learn from him.' Griessel watched their faces. Four lean black men, one fat black woman, and one broad-shouldered coloured detective, all in their early thirties. There was not much ungrudging gratitude, with the exception of Vusi Ndabeni. The coloured detective, Fransman Dekker, was openly antagonistic. But Griessel was already accustomed to the undercurrents in the new SAPS. He told himself he ought to be grateful he still had a job after the dissolution of the Serious and Violent Crimes Unit. Grateful that his former commanding officer, Mat Joubert, had put him up for promotion. If his luck held, he would hear today whether he had made Captain. Captain Benny Griessel. It sounded right to him. He needed the raise too.

''Morning, Vusi,' he said.

'Hey, Benny,' Jimmy, the tall, skinny white coat from Forensics, greeted him. 'I hear they call you "The Oracle" now.'

'Like that auntie in *Lord of the Rings*,' said Arnold, the short, fat one. Collectively they were known as Thick and Thin.

'*The Matrix*, you ape,' said Jimmy.

'Whatever,' said Arnold.

''Morning,' said Griessel. He turned to the uniforms under the tree and took a breath, ready to tell them, 'This is a crime scene; get to the other side of the wall,' and then he remembered that this was Vusi's case; he should shut up and mentor. He hunkered down to look at the body.

The girl lay on her belly. Her blonde hair was very short. Across her back were two short horizontal cuts on her shoulder blades, but these were not the cause of death. That was the deep gash across her throat. Her face, chest and shoulders lay in the wide pool of blood. The smell of death was as bitter as copper.

'*Jissis*,' said Griessel. He looked up at the trees, searching for objectivity. This was a dreadful way to die. And his mind wanted to spool through the event as it had happened, the knife flashing and slicing. She looked so young. Eighteen, nineteen? What kind of madness did it take to cut the throat of a child like this?

He forced the images out of his mind, thought of the facts, the implications. She was white. That spelled trouble. That meant media attention and huge pressure and everyone trying to cover their ass.

'Trouble,' he said quietly to Vusi.

'I know.'

'It would be better if the uniforms stayed behind the wall.'

Vusi nodded, and asked the uniformed policemen to go out. They were reluctant, wanting to be a part of the action. But they went.

Vusi came to stand beside him. 'All the gates are locked. She must have jumped over the railings—it's the only way in here.' Vusi pointed at a coloured man standing on the pavement. 'That *ou* there . . . James Dylan Fredericks, he found her. He went past here and something caught his eye. When he saw the blood he phoned the Caledon Square station.'

Griessel nodded. He suspected Ndabeni was nervous about his presence, as though he were there to evaluate him. He would have to put that right.

'I'm going to tell Fredericks he can go; we know where to find him.'

'That's fine, Vusi. I appreciate you giving me the details, but I don't want you to . . . you know . . .'

'It's OK, Benny. I want to learn. I don't want to blow this. I was in Khayelitsha for four years and I don't want to go back. But this is my first . . . white,' he said that carefully, as if it might be a racist statement.

Griessel was no good at this sort of thing, never knowing what the proper, politically correct words were. Vusi came to his rescue. 'I tried to check if there was anything in her shorts pockets. For ID. There isn't anything. We're just waiting for the pathologist now.'

Griessel looked around. There was a white Toyota Microbus in the church grounds. 'Adventure' was spelled in big red letters along the side.

Ndabeni followed his gaze. 'They probably park here for security. I think they have an office down in Long Street.'

Long Street was the hub of backpacker tourism in the Cape—students from Europe, Australia and America looking for cheap lodgings and adventure.

Griessel squatted down beside the body. Please, don't let her be a foreign kid, he thought. Things would really get out of hand then.

SHE RAN OVER Kloofnek Road and stopped for a second. She had to decide: right, away from the city, or left, more or less back the way she had come. Her instinct was to go right, farther from her pursuers.

But that was what they would expect, and it would take her deeper into the unknown, farther away from Erin. She turned left, her running shoes loud on the downhill gradient. She kept to the road for 400 metres and then scrambled down a stony slope, to a residential area with large homes behind high walls. Hope flared that here she would find someone to help.

All the gates were locked. Every house was a fort, the streets deserted this early. She saw the open gate of the house to her right and her whole being ached for rest. She ducked through the gateway. To the right there were dense shrubs against the high wall. She crept deep into the shrubbery, to where she couldn't be seen from the street.

She dropped to her knees, the backpack against the wall. Her head drooped in weariness. Then she slid down until she was seated flat on the ground. She knew the damp in the decaying leaf mould would stain her shorts, but she didn't care. She just wanted to rest.

The scene imprinted on her brain all those hours ago suddenly played unbidden through her mind. Her body trembled with shock. She dared not think of that now. It was too . . . just too much.

At 06:27 she heard running steps in the street: more than one person, from the same direction she had come, and her heart raced again. She heard them calling to each other in a language she did not understand. She looked for a gap in the foliage and stared at the open gate. One of them was standing there, barely visible, the pieces of the mosaic showing he was black.

She kept dead still.

The mosaic moved. He walked in through the gate, silent on his rubber soles. She knew he would look for hiding places. He was approaching. Could he see her, right at the back?

'Hey!' She was shocked by the voice, a hammer blow to her chest. The dark figure moved away, but without haste. 'What do you want?' The voice came from the house, up above.

'Nothing.'

'Get off my property.'

No answer. He stood still, then moved, reluctantly, until his broken shape disappeared through the leaves.

THE TWO DETECTIVES searched the church grounds. Vusi began at the front, along the Long Street border. Griessel began at the back, along the high brick wall. He battled to concentrate on the bare ground, the grass tufts around the base of the trees. He worked his way round behind the church, and glanced up at the steeple. The church building was lovely and the garden well cared for, with big palms, pines and oleanders. In the northern corner he stood looking down Long Street. This was still the old Cape here, the buildings semi-Victorian, most only two storeys high, some painted now in bright colours, probably to appeal to the young. What was this unease he felt? Was it the mentoring? To be at the scene of a murder, able to look but not touch? He would find it hard, he knew that.

He looked south, towards the Orange Street crossing. Just before seven on a Tuesday morning and the street was busy. The energetic bustle of mid-January, schools reopening, holidays over. On the pavement the murder audience had grown to a small crowd. Press photographers had arrived, camera bags over shoulders, long lenses held like weapons in front of them.

He saw a cyclist weaving through the traffic in tight shorts, vivid shirt, crash helmet, even wearing gloves. His gaze followed the cycle to the traffic lights, knowing that he never wanted to look that silly. He felt stupid enough with the helmet. He wouldn't have worn it if he hadn't got it free, with the bicycle.

Doc Barkhuizen, his sponsor at Alcoholics Anonymous, had started the whole thing. Griessel had told Doc that the pull of the bottle was not diminishing. The first three months were over, yet his desire was as great as on the first day. Doc said, 'What do you do in the evenings?'

Evenings? Policemen had no 'evenings'. When he did get home he would write to his daughter Carla, or play one of his four CDs on the computer and pick up the bass guitar to play along.

'I'm busy in the evenings, Doc.'

'And mornings?' The trouble with Doc was that he was eloquent. And enthusiastic. One of those 'the glass is half full' guys who would not rest until he had inspired you. 'About five years ago I started cycling, Benny. It's fun. You see things from a new perspective. You have time to think . . .'

Swept up by Doc's enthusiasm, he went looking for a bicycle and found the advert—a flowery description of a Giant Alias, twenty-seven gear, super-light aluminium frame. He thought, what had he bought for himself in the past six months since his wife kicked him out? Just the lounge suite from Faizal's pawnshop in Maitland. And the bass guitar he meant to give Fritz for Christmas. Essential items. You couldn't count the laptop. How else would he keep in touch with Carla?

He bought the thing and began riding every morning. He almost gave up after a week. But towards the end of November, it suddenly became a pleasure. He found a route that he enjoyed. Just after six in the morning he would ride down to the harbour. He would look at the mountain and out over the sea and at the people, the pretty young women out jogging, mothers with babies in pushchairs, other cyclists greeting him. Then he would ride back, sixteen kilometres in total, and it made him feel good. About himself. And about the city—whose underbelly was all that he had seen for a very long time.

And about his smart purchase. Until his son came around before Christmas and said he'd decided bass was not for him any more. 'Lead guitar, Dad, that's my dream.'

Griessel had been hiding the bass guitar from Fritz for nearly two months. It was his Christmas present. So he had to go and see Faizal again and he had only one guitar available, a Fender, horribly expensive. Plus, what he gave to Fritz had to be matched by a gift to Carla in London. So he was financially stuffed, because Anna made him pay maintenance as though they were divorced. He had a strong feeling he was being milked, but when he had something to say she would reply, 'You had money for booze, Benny, that was never a problem . . .'

The moral high ground. She had it and he must pay. It was part of his punishment. But that was not the thing churning in his guts.

Griessel walked back to the murder scene. As his mind focused on the growing crowd of onlookers, he recognised the new unease he was feeling. It was a premonition. As if the day brought evil with it. He shook his head. He had never allowed himself to be bothered by such tripe.

THE METRO POLICEMEN were helping a young coloured woman over the railings with eager hands. She came across to Griessel and Ndabeni.

'Tiffany October,' she said, holding out a small hand to Benny. He saw it trembling slightly. She was slim, slight under the white coat.

'Benny Griessel,' he said. 'This is Inspector Vusumuzi Ndabeni.'

They looked at her enquiringly. It took her a second to realise. 'I'm the pathologist.'

'You're new?' Vusi asked, after an uncomfortable silence.

'This is my first solo.' Tiffany October looked down at the body.

The detectives were quiet. They watched her open her case, take out gloves and kneel beside the girl.

Vusi came closer. 'Benny, I asked the photographer to take pictures of her face. I want to show them around. We have to identify her.'

Griessel nodded. 'Good idea. But you will have to put pressure on the photographer. They're slow . . .'

'I will.' Ndabeni bent down to the pathologist. 'Doctor, if you could give me an idea of how long she has been dead . . .'

Tiffany October didn't look up. 'It's too soon . . .'

Griessel wondered where Prof. Phil Pagel, the chief pathologist, was this morning. Pagel would have prodded the corpse here and there, saying it was the small muscles that displayed rigor mortis first, and he thought she had been dead for approximately so many hours. But Tiffany did not have Pagel's experience.

'Give us a guess,' said Griessel.

'Really, I can't.'

She's afraid of getting it wrong, Griessel thought. He spoke softly to Vusi so that she would not hear. 'She's been lying there a while. The blood is black already. Four hours . . . maybe five.'

'OK. So we'll have to get moving.'

Griessel nodded. 'Get those photos quickly. And talk to the Metro people. They have video cameras monitoring the streets. There might be something.'

SHE FELL ASLEEP against the wall. She had wanted to rest for just a moment. The events of the night were demons in her mind. To escape that, she had thought about her parents, what time it would be at home. If it had been early morning in Lafayette her father would be sitting with the paper, shaking his head over the comments of the Purdue football coach. Her mother would be late, as always, and father and daughter would share their ritual smile over the kitchen table. This routine, the safety of her family home, overwhelmed her with terrible longing and she wanted to phone them right now, hear their voices, tell them how much she loved them. She carried on this imaginary conversation with her father until sleep crept up and overcame her.

DR TIFFANY OCTOBER called to them, 'I could speculate a little . . .'

Griessel wondered if she had overheard him talking.

'The blood pattern shows that he cut her throat while she lay here. I think he held her flat on the ground, on her stomach, and then he cut her. There are no splash marks to show that she was standing.'

'Oh . . .' He had already worked all that out.

'And these two cuts . . .' She pointed to the girl's shoulder blades. 'It seems as if they were inflicted post-mortem. These look like fibres here . . .' Dr October used a small pair of tweezers. 'Synthetic material, a dark colour, totally different from her clothing. I think he cut something off her back like a backpack, you know, the two shoulder straps . . .'

Vusi looked at the forensic team. 'Jimmy, here's something for you.'

Jimmy and his partner took out instruments to collect the fibres.

Vusi called the photographer over. 'How soon can I get my pictures?'

The photographer, young, curly-haired, shrugged. 'I'll see what I can do.'

'No,' said Griessel. 'We need them before eight. It's not negotiable.'

The photographer walked away, not bothering to hide his attitude. Griessel looked after him with disgust. 'Thanks, Benny,' said Vusi quietly.

'Don't be too nice, Vusi.'

'I know . . .' After an uncomfortable silence, he asked, 'Benny, what am I missing?'

Griessel kept his voice gentle, counselling. 'The backpack. It must have been robbery, Vusi. Her money, passport, cellphone . . .'

Ndabeni caught on quickly. 'You think they dumped the backpack somewhere.'

'I'll handle that, Vusi. Let's give the Metro guys something to do.' He went up to the wall and called to the uniforms. 'Who's in charge here?'

'This pavement is ours,' said a coloured Metro policeman in an impressive uniform, emblems of rank all over it. Field Marshal at the very least, Griessel mused. He felt the anger rise. He had an issue with the whole concept of the city police, traffic cops that didn't do their jobs, total absence of law enforcement on the roads.

'Are you in charge here?' Benny asked him.

'Yes.'

'What is your name?'

'Jeremy Oerson.'

'I want you to inspect every pavement and alley within six blocks of here. Every dustbin, every nook and cranny, got that?'

The man gave him a long look. Probably weighing up the implications should he refuse. Then he nodded, sourly, and began barking orders.

'You need to look at this,' the pathologist called from where she was crouched by the body. They went over to her. With a pair of tweezers, she held up a clothing label, the one from the back of the girl's T-shirt. 'Broad Ripple Vintage, Indianapolis,' she said and gave them a meaningful look.

'What does that mean?' asked Vusi.

'I think she's American,' she said.

'Trouble,' said Vusi. 'Big trouble.'

II

In the library of the big house in Brownlow Street, Tamboerskloof, the terrified screams of the maid shocked Alexa Barnard from her sleep.

She had no idea where she was, her limbs felt stiff and unwieldy, and her thoughts were as sluggish as molasses. She lifted her head and tried to focus. She saw the plump woman at the door, mouth twisted in what she at first recognised as revulsion. Then the noise penetrated to the marrow.

Alexa realised she was lying on her back on the Persian rug. As she became aware of the fact that she had spent the night on the floor in a drunken stupor, she followed the gaze of Sylvia Buys: someone was lying beside the armchair opposite her. Who could it be? She sat upright and recognised the figure. Adam. Her husband. He was wearing only one shoe. Black trousers and a white shirt smeared with black on the chest.

Then she realised that Adam was wounded. The black on the shirt was blood, the shirt itself was torn. She pressed her hands on the carpet to get up. Her fingers touched something and she saw the firearm lying next to her. She recognised Adam's pistol. What was it doing here?

Alexa got to her feet, and took a cautious step forward. Adam was dead. She knew it from the sum of the wounds and the way he was lying, but she couldn't understand it. Was it a dream?

'Why?' said Sylvia, approaching hysteria. 'Why did you kill him?'

THE PATHOLOGIST and the two ambulance men manoeuvred the corpse carefully into a black zip-up bag. Griessel sat on the stone border of a palm tree bed. Vusi Ndabeni was on his cellphone talking to the Station Commander. 'I need at least four, Sup, for legwork . . . I understand, but it's an American tourist . . . Thanks, Sup, I'll wait for them.'

He came over to Benny. 'The SC says there's a protest of some or other labour union at Parliament and he can send me only two people.'

'There's always a protest of some or other union,' said Griessel and stood up. 'I'll help with the footwork, Vusi, until the photos arrive.'

'Thanks, Benny. Would you like some coffee?'

'Are you going to send someone?'

'There's a place down the street. I'll go quickly.'

'Let me go.'

THEY FILLED the Caledon Square charge office, complainants, victims and their hangers-on, with stories of the night past. Over the protesting voices a telephone rang monotonously. A female sergeant, weary after nine hours on her feet, grabbed the receiver. 'Sergeant Nyathi speaking.'

It was a woman's voice, barely audible. 'I want to report something.'

'Yes, madam?'

'There was this girl . . . This morning, at about six o'clock, on Signal Hill. She asked me to call the police because someone wanted to kill her.'

'May I have your name, madam?'

'Sybil Gravett. I was walking my dog. She came running up and said someone was trying to kill her, and then she ran off again.'

'Did you see anybody following her?'

'I did. A few minutes later. There must have been five or six. Some were white and some were black. And they were quite young . . . I found that very disturbing, these young men, running with such intent . . .'

SHE WAS WOKEN with a start by someone shouting at her. She tried to stand up but her legs betrayed her and she stumbled against the wall.

'You fucking druggie!' He stood on the other side of the shrubbery, the same voice that had shouted from the house earlier. 'Get off my property.'

She made her way through the plants. She saw he was wearing a dark suit, a businessman, middle-aged, furious. 'Please, I need your help . . .'

'No. You shoot up somewhere else. I'm sick and tired of this. Get out.'

She began to cry. 'It's not what you think. I'm from the United—'

The man grabbed her and dragged her roughly to the gate. 'I don't care where you come from. All I want is for you people to stop using my property for your filthy habits.' He shoved her towards the road. 'Now fuck off, before I call the police.' He turned back to his house.

'Please, call them,' she said through sobs. He opened a metal gate and disappeared. 'Oh, God.' She stood crying on the pavement. Through the tears she looked up and down the street. Far off, where the road curled over the flank of the mountain, stood two of them, one with a cellphone to his ear. Frightened, she began walking in the opposite direction. She didn't know whether they had seen her. She kept against the walls of the houses, looking back over her shoulder. They were running towards her.

Despair dragged at her. One solution would be to stop, so that the inevitable could happen. Her strength was gone. For a second that option seemed irresistible. But she replayed the scene with Erin in the night, and the adrenaline gushed and she carried on, weeping as she ran.

AMBULANCE MEN were lifting the body over the wall on a stretcher as Griessel arrived with coffee. He passed a cup to his colleague.

'Thanks, Benny.'

The aroma reminded Griessel that he hadn't had breakfast yet. Perhaps he could get back to the flat for a quick bowl of Weet-Bix. He could check whether Carla had written to him.

Vusi said something in Xhosa that he couldn't understand, some exclamation of surprise. He followed the detective's gaze and saw three of the Metro policemen climbing the wall. Jeremy Oerson was carrying a blue rucksack. They marched up, full of bravado.

'Jesus,' said Benny.

'We found it,' said the Field Marshal and held out the rucksack to Vusi. The Xhosa man just shook his head and pulled his rubber gloves from his pocket.

'Next time,' said Griessel in a reasonable voice, 'it would be better if you let us know you found it. Then we would bring in the forensic guys and cordon off the area before anyone touched it.'

'It was lying in a doorway in Bloem Street. A thousand people could have touched it already. There's not much in it anyway.'

'You opened it?' asked Vusi, reaching for the bag. The two straps were cut, just as the pathologist had predicted. 'Did you handle these items?' he asked, taking out a make-up bag.

'No,' said Oerson, but Griessel could tell he was lying.

Vusi took a plastic spoon out of the backpack. Next, a small wooden carving of a hippopotamus in dark wood, and a headlamp. 'That's all?'

'That's all,' said Oerson.

'Would you go back and see if there is anything else? What I need most is some form of identification. A passport, a driver's licence . . .'

Oerson was not keen. 'We can't help you all day.'

'I know,' said Vusi, patiently. 'But if you could just do that, please.'

'I'll get some more people.' Oerson turned away.

Vusi's fingers explored the pockets on the sides of the backpack. He pulled out a card with a black and yellow logo: *Hodson's Bay Company*. In smaller type: *Backpacking, camping, climbing gear. Levee Plaza, West Lafyette, IN.* The Xhosa man studied it. 'I think the IN stands for Indiana.'

'Fax them a photo, Vusi. They might be able to identify her.'

Griessel's phone rang shrilly in his pocket. He took it out and answered.

'Benny, it's Mavis. Inspector Dekker called. He said to tell you he has a murder at 47 Brownlow Street in Tamboerskloof, if you want to mentor him.'

'I'm on my way.' He told Vusi, 'Another murder. Up in Tamboerskloof.'

'No problem. I'll call you when we find something.'

Griessel began to walk away. Vusi called after him, 'Benny . . .'

Griessel turned. Vusi came up to him. 'I just wanted to ask you . . . the pathologist . . . Would a coloured doctor go out with a darkie cop?'

It took him a few seconds to make the leap. 'Er . . . you're asking the wrong guy, Vusi . . . but yes, why not? A man can only try.'

THE TRAFFIC was bumper to bumper up Buitesingel's hill. His plan to down-load Carla's email quickly was stuffed. It would have to wait until tonight. He had been offline for a week already with that damn laptop, he could wait a few more hours. Carla would understand—he'd had problems with the stupid machine from the start. He'd bought it for a knockdown price at a police auction. Once Carla left for London, he had to know how she was—his Carla who needed to 'sort her head out' before she decided what to do with her life.

So how did vacuuming floors in a hotel in London sort out your head?

It had cost him R500 to get the laptop connected to the Internet before he could send an email to Carla:

How are you? I miss you and worry about you. An article in *The Burger* said
South African kids in London drink a lot. Don't let anyone put pressure on you.

Dear Daddy

I have a job at the Gloucester Terrace Hotel near Marble Arch. I'm a cleaner.
I work from ten in the morning to ten at night, six days a week. It's not very pleasant and the pay's not much, but it's something.

Daddy, you know I will never drink . . .

When he read those words they burned right through him. Carla would never drink because her father was an alcoholic. He might have been sober for one hundred and fifty-six days, but he could never erase the past.

It took two days before he answered, told her about his bicycle and his transfer to the Provincial Task Force. She encouraged him:

It's nice to know what you're doing, Daddy. Much more interesting things than I am. At least I was at Buckingham Palace on Monday . . .

Their correspondence found a level both were comfortable with: a rhythm of two emails a week, four or five simple paragraphs. But a week ago his Internet connection stopped working. Mysteriously, suddenly. On Friday after work he bumped into Charmaine Watson-Smith who was in her seventies and lived at number 106. She knew everyone in the block of flats, and their business.

'How's your daughter?' Charmaine asked.

He told her about his computer troubles.

'Oh, I might just know someone who can help.'

Yesterday, Monday evening at half past six, he was ironing clothes in his kitchen when Bella knocked on his door.

'Auntie Charmaine said I should take a look at your PC.'

He had seen her before, a young woman in an unattractive chunky grey uniform who had short blonde hair and looked tired at the end of the day.

He had hardly recognised her at his door: she looked pretty.

'Bella van Breda. I'm from number 64.' He shook her hand quickly. It was small and soft. She was wearing jeans and a red blouse. Her eyes were shy behind the glasses, but from the first he was aware of her wide, full mouth.

She had spotted the laptop that he kept in the open-plan kitchen, his only worktop. 'Is this it?'

'My Internet connection just stopped working. Do you know computers?'

They stood close together watching the screen as it got going.

'I'm a PC technician,' she answered and sat down in front of the tin brain.

He realised she was slimmer than he had previously thought. She was in her late twenties. He could be her father.

'Is this your connection?' She had a menu open and the mouse pointer on an icon. 'It looks like you accidentally changed the dial-up number. Do you have it somewhere?'

'I think so.' He took the pack of documents out of the cupboard. 'Here.' She typed the number in and suddenly the modem dialled up.

'Well, fuck me,' he said in genuine amazement. She laughed. With that mouth. So he asked her if she would like a cup of coffee.

'That would be nice, thank you.'

He put on the kettle and they fell into conversation. Maybe it was purely because they each had a lonely Monday evening ahead. Two cups of coffee later, he made his big mistake. Without thinking he picked up the top CD from his stack of four and pushed it into his laptop's CD player.

She said in surprise, 'You like Lize Beekman?' and he said in a moment of honesty, 'Very much.' Something changed in her eyes, as though it made her see him differently.

He had bought the CD after he had heard a song on the car radio, '*My Suikerbos*'. There was something about the singer's voice—vulnerability, or was it the melancholy of the music? He didn't know. The combination of words and music with that voice made him happy and made him sad. He couldn't remember when last music had made him feel this way. And when Bella asked him if he liked Lize Beekman, it was the first time he could express this to someone. That's why it came out, 'Very much.' With feeling.

Bella said, 'I wish I could sing like that,' and surprisingly, he understood what she meant. He had felt the same yearning, to sing of all the facets of life with the same acceptance. He had never felt that kind of acceptance. Disgust, yes, that had been with him all his life. He could never explain why he felt this low-grade disgust for everything and, above all, for himself.

He said, 'Me too,' and the conversation blossomed. She told him the story of her life. He talked about his work. Bella said she would like to open her own business one day and passion shone in her eyes. He listened with admiration. She had a dream. He had nothing. Just a fantasy or two. Maybe to have his own four-piece band again. Singing the old blues or the real old rock 'n' roll—Berry, Domino, early Elvis . . .

But he said none of this, just listened to her. About ten o'clock he said: 'More coffee?' They were close and her mouth had a small, furtive smile that showed she had an idea what was going to happen next, and she didn't mind.

So he kissed her. It had been without lust at first, more an extension of their conversation, a gentle coming together. Two people needing to be touched.

They kissed for a long time, then she took off her glasses. Her eyes suddenly looked deep-brown, defenceless. He sat in the police car remembering how her body felt—soft, warm, welcoming. He remembered the slow intensity on the sofa, seeing in her eyes the same gratitude that he felt in his own heart. That she was there, that this had happened. How could it be wrong?

His phone rang and brought him back to the present. It must be Dekker asking where he was. But the screen read *ANNA* and his heart lurched.

IT WAS THE FALL that saved her.

Instinctively, she had sprinted up the steep row of steps that led up out of the street, up a narrow twisting footpath. Table Mountain was suddenly a colossus looming over her, steep slopes of rock and *fynbos* and open stretches. She felt sure she had made a mistake. They would spot her and catch her on the slope. They would hold her to the ground and slit her throat, like Erin's.

She drove herself up the mountain. She did not look back. Above, she saw the cable car station, sun glinting off car windscreens, tiny figures of people, so close, yet so far. If only she could reach them. No, it was too steep, too far.

She saw the fork in the footpath, chose the left one and ran. Forty paces and then a sudden drop, the path unexpectedly falling to a rocky gully. Her foot landed badly and she fell downhill. Trying to brake herself with her hands, she banged her shoulder hard and was winded. She rolled over once and lay still, inhaling hoarsely. The bank of the stream came into focus and she saw the crevice carved out under the giant rock by centuries of water. Just big enough for her to creep into.

She moved like a snake towards the opening. She heard the urgent running steps of her pursuers. She realised her rucksack would not fit in. She was running out of time; they would see her. She rose to her knees to tear the rucksack off, wriggled her body into the hollow and dragged the rucksack after her. Three of them jumped over the dry stream bed three metres away from her, and she held her breath. She lay still, and shut her eyes, as if that would make her invisible.

HE SAT IN THE TRAFFIC with his phone to his ear and said, 'Hello, Anna.'

'Benny, we need to talk.'

'About what?'

'Everything, Benny. I wondered if we could talk tonight. I thought we could go out to eat somewhere.'

Jissis. What did that mean? 'That's fine. Where?'

'Canal Walk is sort of halfway. There's a Primi . . .'

'What time would suit you?'

'Seven?'

'Thanks, Anna, that would be nice.'

'Goodbye, Benny.' Just like that. As if he had said the wrong thing.

He sat with the phone in his hand. Why not at their house? Maybe she felt like going out. Like a kind of date. But when he said, 'That would be nice,' she said goodbye as if she was angry with him.

Could she know about last night? What if she had been at his door? She might have heard something and seen Bella leave and . . . But she had never been to his flat. Why would she have come last night? To talk?

If she knew . . . He was screwed. But she couldn't know.

NUMBER 47 BROWNLOW STREET was large and impressive, with two storeys, verandas and balconies with curlicued ironwork railings, cream walls and windows with green wooden shutters.

Griessel parked in the street behind a black Mercedes convertible, two police vehicles and a white Nissan with the SAPS emblem on the door and *Social Services* under it in black type. Forensics' minibus was parked across the road. Thick and Thin must have come direct from Long Street.

A uniformed policeman stopped him at the front door. He showed his identification. 'You will have to go around the back, Inspector; the sitting room is a crime scene,' he said. 'I think they are still in the kitchen, sir.'

'Thank you.'

He walked round. Another policeman was on duty at the back door. He took his SAPS ID out of his wallet again and showed it.

'The Inspector is expecting you.'

Dekker sat at the kitchen table, totally focused on the coloured woman opposite him. She wore a pink and white domestic uniform and held a handkerchief in her hands. She was plump, her age difficult to judge.

'Fransman . . .' said Griessel.

Dekker looked up irritably. 'Benny.' As an afterthought, he said, 'Come in.' He was a tall, athletic, coloured man, broad-shouldered and strong, with a face from a cigarette advert, handsome in a rugged way.

'This is Mrs Sylvia Buys. The domestic worker here. Mrs Buys arrived at work . . .' he consulted the notebook, 'at six forty-five and made coffee in the kitchen before moving to inspect the living area at seven o'clock . . .'

'Damage assessment,' said Sylvia Buys. 'That woman can make a mess.'

'. . . where she discovered the deceased, Mr Adam Barnard, and the suspect, Mrs Alexa Barnard. Mrs Buys found them in the library on the first floor. The firearm was on the carpet next to Mrs Barnard . . .'

'Not to mention the booze. She's an alkie, drinking like a fish every night, and Mr Adam . . .' Sylvia lifted the handkerchief, and dab-dabbed at her nose.

'Was she under the influence last night?' Griessel asked.

'She's as drunk as a lord every night. I went home at half past four and she was well on her way.'

'Mrs Buys says when she left the house yesterday the suspect was alone. She does not know what time the deceased came home.'

'He was a good man. Always a kind word. I don't understand it. Why did she shoot him? What for? He took all her drinking, every night he would put her in bed and what did she shoot him for?' She wept, shaking her head.

'Sister, you're traumatised. We'll get you some counselling.'

'I don't want counselling,' sobbed Sylvia Buys. 'Where will I get another job at my age?'

'IT'S NOT AS SIMPLE as that,' said Dekker as he climbed the yellow-wood stairs to the library. 'You'll see.'

Griessel could sense the man's tension. He had heard the stories. Dekker was the son of a French rugby player and a coloured woman from the poverty of Atlantis township. There had been just one encounter; shortly afterwards the rugby player returned to France, unaware of his offspring. Dekker's mother could not remember his name, so she christened her son Fransman, Afrikaans for Frenchman. The child had inherited his father's Gallic nose, build and straight black hair, and his mother's coffee-coloured complexion.

Griessel followed Dekker into the library. Thick and Thin were at work. 'We can't go on meeting like this, Benny, people will talk,' said Jimmy.

An old joke, but Benny grinned, then looked at the victim lying on the left side of the room. Adam Barnard had been tall and strong. In death his eyes were open, making him seem mildly surprised.

Dekker folded his arms expectantly. Thick and Thin stood watching him.

Griessel approached carefully, taking in the Persian carpet, the paintings, the liquor bottle and glass beside the chair. The firearm was in a transparent plastic evidence bag on the ground, where Forensics had circled it with white chalk. 'She was on this side?' he asked Dekker.

'She was.'

'Had the pistol been fired?'

'Quite recently,' said Arnold.

'But not here.'

'Bingo,' said Arnold.

'I told you he would get it straightaway,' said Jimmy.

'Yes,' said Dekker. He sounded disappointed. 'It's an automatic pistol; three rounds are missing from the magazine, but there are no casings here. No blood on the floor, no bullet holes in the walls and the shoe is missing. She didn't *klap* him here. We have to search the car in the street . . .'

'Where is she?'

'In the sitting room with Social Services. Tinkie Kellerman.'

'Jimmy, did you test her for gunshot residue?' asked Dekker.

'Not yet. But I did put her hands in paper. She didn't like that.'

'Can you do it now? I can't talk to her with paper bags over her hands.'

Jimmy took a box out of his case. It was marked 'SEM Examination'. He went to the stairs with both detectives in tow.

'Fransman, you've done a good job,' said Griessel.

'I know,' said Dekker.

THE CCTV CONTROL ROOM of the Metro Police was impressive. It had twenty flickering TV screens, a whole bank of video recorders and a control panel that looked as though it belonged to the space shuttle. Vusi stood looking at a screen, watching the grainy image of a small figure running under the street lights of Long Street. Nine seconds of material, now in slow motion: seven shadowy people in a desperate race. The girl was in front, recognisable thanks only to the dark hump of the rucksack. Here, between Leeuwen and Pepper Street, she was just three steps ahead of the nearest assailant, her arms and legs pumping high in flight. Another five people were sixteen to seventeen metres behind. In the last frame, just before she disappeared off the screen, Ndabeni could see her turn her head as if to see how close they were.

'Can you enlarge this?'

'Not really,' the operator answered. He was white, a little man, owl-like behind big round spectacles. 'If you zoom in, you just get grain.'

'Could you try, please?'

On the screen the figures ran backwards slowly and froze.

'Which one do you want to see better?'

'The people chasing her.'

The Owl used a mouse to select two of the last five figures. They suddenly filled the screen. He tapped the keyboard again and the image brightened, but neither of the figures was recognisable.

'You can at least see they are men and the one in front is black,' said the Owl. Vusi stared at the screen. It wasn't going to help much.

'Are they on only one camera?'

'I'll have a look but it will take time. There are sixteen cameras in that section but they don't all work.'

'Thanks,' said Vusi. One thing he couldn't understand. If one of the pursuers was only three strides behind her in Pepper Street, why hadn't he caught her before the church? It was 500 metres away, maybe more. Had he slipped? Fallen? Or deliberately waited for a quieter place.

GRIESSEL WALKED into the sitting room behind Dekker. It was a large room with big couches and a huge coffee table. Tinkie Kellerman of SAPS Social Services sat upright in an easy chair that dwarfed her. She was the one they sent for when the victim or the suspect was a woman, because she had compassion and empathy, but now there was a frown of unease on her face.

'Ma'am, let me take those bags off your hands,' said Jimmy to Alexa Barnard, a hunched figure in a white dressing gown. She sat on the edge of a four-seater couch, elbows on her knees, head hung low, her unwashed grey and blonde hair hiding her face. She held out her hands without looking up.

'I just have to press these discs on your hands. They are sticky, but that's all . . .' Griessel saw Alexa Barnard's hands trembling.

He and Dekker each picked a chair. Dekker opened his notebook.

Jimmy worked quickly and packed away his things.

'Mrs Barnard . . .' said Dekker.

Tinkie shook her head slightly, as if to say the suspect was not communicative. Jimmy walked out rolling his eyes.

'Mrs Barnard,' said Dekker, this time louder and more businesslike.

'I didn't do it,' she said without moving, in a surprisingly deep voice.

'Mrs Barnard, you have the right to legal representation. You have the right to remain silent. But if you choose to answer our questions, anything you say may be used in court.'

'I didn't do it.'

'Do you want to contact your lawyer?'

'No,' and slowly she raised her head and pushed the hair back on either side of her face, revealing bloodshot blue eyes and skin an unhealthy hue. Griessel saw the regular features, hints of former beauty under the tracks of abuse. He knew her, he knew a version of this face, but he couldn't quite place it. She stretched out a hand to a small table beside her and picked up a packet of cigarettes.

'Mrs Barnard, I am Inspector Fransman Dekker. This is Inspector Benny Griessel. Are you ready to answer some questions?'

She nodded slightly and lit the cigarette. She inhaled the smoke deeply, as if it would give her strength.

'The deceased was your husband, Mr Adam Barnard?'

She nodded.

'Age?'

'Fifty-two.'

Dekker wrote. 'And his profession?'

'AfriSound. It's his. It's a record company.'

'And he owns this record company?'

She nodded.

'Your full name?'

'Alexandra.'

'Age?'

'Forty-six.'

'Profession?'

She gave an ironic snort. 'I don't work.' She pushed her hair off her face. Griessel saw confirmation that she was a drinker—trembling hands, the characteristic colour of her face. But she reminded him of something else. How do I know her? Griessel wondered.

'Homemaker,' said Dekker and wrote that down. 'Mrs Barnard, can you tell us about last night's events?'

She sank back slowly into her seat. 'No.'

'Excuse me?'

'I am an alcoholic. I drink from eleven in the morning. By six o'clock usually I am mercifully drunk. From half past eight on I don't remember much.' In that instant, perhaps because the deep, rich voice resonated somewhere in his memory, Benny Griessel remembered who she was. The word sprang to the tip of his tongue: *Soetwater*. Sweet water.

She was the singer. Xandra. Lord, how old she looked.

Soetwater. The word activated a picture from memory, a television image of a woman in a tight-fitting black dress. Mid-Eighties, somewhere around there. Griessel remembered the incredibly sensual blonde singer with a voice like Dietrich and enough self-confidence not to take herself too seriously. She had four or five hits, he remembered, the big one, '*Soetwater*'. She had been this huge star and look at her now. Benny felt pity for her, also loss, and empathy.

'So you don't remember what happened last night?'

'Not much.'

'Mrs Barnard,' said Dekker. 'I get the impression that your husband's death hasn't upset you very much.'

He was mistaken, thought Griessel. He was too hasty.

'No, Inspector, I am not in mourning. But if you bring me a gin and dry lemon, I will do my best.'

Dekker said, 'Can you remember anything about last night?'

'Enough to know it wasn't me.'

'I will have to test your blood for alcohol.' Dekker stood up. 'I'll just get the technician.' Griessel followed him.

In the sitting room Thick and Thin were busy packing up. 'Can you just take a blood sample before you leave?'

'Sure, chief,' said Jimmy.

'Fransman,' said Griessel, 'you know I am an alcoholic?'

'So?' Dekker asked.

'I know how she feels.'

'She feels nothing. Her husband is lying there and she feels nothing. She killed him, I'm telling you. The usual story.'

How do you explain to a nondrinker what she was feeling now? Alexandra Barnard's whole being craved alcohol. She was drowning in the terrible flood of that morning; drink was the only lifeline. Griessel knew.

'You're a good detective, Fransman. You do everything by the book and ten to one you're right. But if you want a confession . . . give me a chance.'

Griessel's phone rang. He watched Dekker while taking it out. The coloured man didn't look too keen about his suggestion.

'Griessel.'

'Benny, it's Vusi. I'm at the Metro CCTV room. There are two of them.'

'Two what?'

'Two girls, Benny. I'm standing here, watching five guys chasing two girls up Long Street.'

'They're *chasing* the girls, you say? In Long Street?'

'The time code says it was this morning at a quarter to two. Five men, coming from Wale Street towards the church. Six blocks.'

'*Jissis*, Vusi, you don't do that to steal a tourist's purse.'

'The other thing is, the guys chasing them are black and white, Benny.'

'Doesn't make sense.' In this country criminals didn't work together across the colour lines.

'I've put a bulletin out on the other girl.'

'Good work, Vusi.'

'I don't know if it will help much,' said Ndabeni, and ended the call.

Griessel saw Dekker waiting impatiently for him. 'Sorry about that, Fransman. It's Vusi's case . . .'

'And this is *my* case.' His body language showed he was ready to argue.

Griessel hadn't expected this aggression, but the territorial urges of detectives were strong, and he was just here as mentor.

'You're right,' he said and walked towards the door. 'But it might help.'

Dekker stayed on the spot, frowning. Just before Benny left the room, he said, 'Wait . . .'

Griessel stopped.

'OK,' said Dekker finally. 'Talk to her.'

SHE COULD NO LONGER hear them. Only the birdsong and cicadas and the hum of the city below. She lay in the cool shade of the rock overhang. She considered staying there, all day, until darkness fell and she would be invisible. She could do it even though she was thirsty. If she could sleep a little, she would have new strength tonight with which to seek help.

But they knew she was there, somewhere. They would backtrack on the path and if anyone came close enough, they would see her. The hollow wasn't deep enough. She would have to move. The mountain was a poor choice, too deserted, too open. She must get down to where there were people. Somewhere someone must be prepared to help.

Reluctantly she lifted her head from the rucksack, pushed the bag ahead of her and slid carefully after it. She couldn't drag it; it would be too noisy. She rose to a crouch, swung the rucksack slowly onto her back. Then she crawled on hands and knees over the round stones.

GRIESSEL WALKED into the sitting room and whispered in Tinkie Kellerman's ear. Alexandra Barnard dragged on another cigarette; her eyes followed Tinkie as she left the room. Without speaking, Griessel went to a large Victorian cupboard and took out a glass and a bottle of gin.

'My name is Benny Griessel and I am an alcoholic. It's been one hundred and fifty-six days since my last drink,' he said and broke the bottle's seal. Her eyes were fixed on the transparent fluid that he poured carefully into the glass, three thick fingers deep. He held it out to her. She took it, hands shaking. She drank, an intense and thirsty gulp, and closed her eyes.

Griessel went back to the liquor cabinet and put the bottle away. When he sat down he said, 'I won't be able to let you have more than that.'

She nodded.

He knew how she felt at this precise moment. He knew the alcohol would flow through her body like a gentle, soothing tide, healing the wounds and quietening the voices. He realised he was staring intently at the glass at her lips, smelling the alcohol, feeling his own body straining for it. He took a deep breath, looked at the magazines on the coffee table, until she said, 'Thank you,' and he heard the voice had lost its edge.

She put the glass down and offered him the packet of cigarettes.

'No, thank you,' he said.

'An alcoholic who doesn't smoke?'

'I'm trying to cut down. My AA sponsor is a doctor.'

'Get another sponsor,' she said in an attempt at humour, but it didn't work; her mouth pulled in the wrong direction and she began to weep silently. Her shoulders shook, her head drooped, and the long hair fell over her face like a curtain. Griessel saw it was blonde and silver; most women dyed their hair. He wondered why she no longer cared. She had been a star, a major one. What had dragged her down to this?

He waited until her sobs subsided. 'My sponsor's name is Dr Barkhuizen. He's trying to get me to quit. I'm down to three or four a day.'

Eventually she looked up. 'Was it hard?' She wiped her face with a handkerchief and blew her nose.

'The drink was. Is. Still. The smoking too.'

'I couldn't.' She crumpled the hanky and picked up the glass and drank. 'It wasn't me.'

Griessel nodded.

'We didn't talk any more,' she said. 'He comes home from the office at half past six. Then he comes to the library and looks to see how drunk I am. Then he goes to his study. Or out again. Every night he puts me in bed. I have wondered if that is why I drink. So that he would still do that one thing for me. Isn't that tragic? Sometimes, when he comes in, I try to provoke him. Last night I asked him whose turn it was now. You must understand . . . it's a long story . . .' and for the first time her sobs were audible, as if the full weight of her history had come to bear on her. Pity welled up in Benny Griessel, because he saw again the ghost of the singer she had once been.

Eventually she stubbed out the cigarette. 'He just said, "Fuck you" and he left again. That's all I know. He didn't put me to bed, he left me there and this morning, he was lying there . . .'

She drained the last bit of alcohol from the glass and looked at Griessel with intense focus. 'Do you think it could have been me that shot him?'

THE PLUMP GIRL behind the reception desk of the Cat & Moose Youth Hostel looked at the photograph the constable was holding out and asked, 'Why does she look so funny?'

'Because she's dead.'

'Oh my God.' She put two and two together. 'Was she the one this morning at the church here?'

'Yes. Do you recognise her?'

'They came in yesterday, two American girls.' The girl opened the register. 'Rachel Anderson and Erin Russel, from West Lafayette, Indiana. Who killed her?'

'We don't know yet. Is this one Anderson?'

'I don't know.'

'And the other one, do you know where she is?'

'No, I work days. Let's see, they are in room sixteen.' She shut the register and went ahead down the passage saying, 'Oh my God.'

THROUGH CAREFUL questioning he got information about the firearm. It was her husband's. Adam Barnard kept it locked up in a safe. He kept the key with him, probably afraid she would do something foolish with it in her drunken state. She said she had no idea how it had landed up on the floor beside her. There were times she had wished him dead, but her true fantasy was to kill herself and then watch him finding her dead. Watch him kneeling beside her body begging forgiveness. But, she said with irony, you can't watch anything when you're dead.

Then she just sat there. Eventually he whispered, '*Soetwater*' but she didn't respond; she hid behind her hair for an eternity until she slowly held out the glass to him and he knew he would have to pour another if he wanted to hear the whole story.

08:13–09:03

III

Benny Griessel listened to Alexandra Barnard's story.

'Alexa. Nobody calls me Alexandra or Xandra.'

Now, just as he was about to open the front door of number 47 Brownlow Street to go and find Dekker, he felt a peculiar emotion pressing on his heart, a sort of separation from reality, as though he stood back a few millimetres from everything, a second or two out of step with the world.

So it took him a while to register that outside was chaos. The street was a mass of journalists and the inquisitive: photographers, reporters, a camera team from e.tv and a growing crowd of spectators. The noise washed over Griessel, along with the knowledge that he had listened so acutely to Alexa's story that he had been oblivious to all this.

On the verandah Dekker was exchanging words with a bald man, both their voices raised in argument. 'Not before I've seen her,' said the man. His head was completely shaven, and he was tall and sinewy, with large fleshy ears and one round silver earring. Black shirt, black trousers and the black basketball shoes that teenagers wear, although he seemed to be in his late forties.

Dekker spotted Griessel. 'He insists on seeing her,' said Dekker.

The man brought out a small black cellphone. 'I'm calling my lawyer; this behaviour is totally unacceptable.' He began to press keys on the phone. 'She's not a well woman.'

'He's the partner of the deceased. Willie Mouton,' said Dekker.

'Mr Mouton,' said Griessel reasonably.

'I'm on the phone,' said Mouton. His voice had the penetration and tone of an industrial meat saw.

'Mr Mouton, if you wish to make personal calls, you will do it in the street . . .' Dekker said on a rising note, '. . . and not on my crime scene.'

'Your crime scene? Who do you think you are?' Then, into the phone, 'Sorry. Can I speak to Regardt, please . . . ?' Dekker advanced in a threatening way, his temper beginning to get the better of him. 'Regardt, this is Willie, I'm standing on Adam's verandah with the Gestapo . . .'

Dekker jerked Mouton roughly off the verandah. Cameras clicked.

'They're assaulting me, Regardt,' said Mouton with less confidence.

''Morning, Nikita,' said Prof. Phil Pagel, the state pathologist, from beyond the gate. He was amused.

''Morning, Prof.,' said Benny, watching Dekker push Mouton through the gate onto the pavement.

'Regardt, I want you to sue their arses,' said Mouton. 'Alexa's in there and God knows what these storm troopers are doing with her . . .'

Pagel squeezed past and went up the stairs with his black case in hand. 'Busy morning, Nikita?'

Pagel had been calling him 'Nikita' for the past twelve years. The first time he had met Griessel he had said, 'I am sure that's how the young Khrushchev looked.' Griessel had to think hard who Khrushchev was.

'Things are hectic as usual, Prof.'

'I understand you are mentoring the new generation of law enforcers.'

'As you can see, Prof., I'm brilliant at my job,' Griessel grinned. Dekker came back up the verandah steps. 'Have you met Fransman yet?'

'Indeed I have. Inspector Dekker, I admire your forcefulness. Rumour has it that Adam Barnard is the victim. This means big trouble, gentlemen.'

IN THE LIBRARY Pagel knelt beside the body and opened his doctor's bag.

'It wasn't her, Fransman,' said Griessel. 'It's not just what she says, it's how it fits in with the scene.'

'She could have hired someone.'

That argument had merit. Women hiring others to get rid of their husbands was the latest national sport. But he shook his head. 'I doubt it. You don't hire people to make it look like you did it.'

'Anything is possible in this country,' said Dekker.

'Prof., did you know Barnard?' Griessel asked. 'What's his story?'

'Music,' said Pagel. 'And women.'

'That's what his wife says too,' said Griessel.

'You know she was a huge star?' Pagel's hands were deftly handling instruments and the body. 'Barnard "discovered" her. He was a lawyer who became involved with the pop music industry. Xandra was a singer, a very good one.'

'How long ago was this, Prof.?'

'Fifteen, twenty years.'

'Never heard of her.' Dekker shook his head.

'She disappeared off the scene. Rather suddenly.'

'She caught him with someone else,' said Griessel. 'That's when she started drinking.'

'That was the rumour. Gentlemen, unofficially I estimate the time of death at between two and three this morning. The cause of death is two shots by a small-calibre firearm. The position of the wounds and small amount of propellant residue indicates a shooting distance of two to four metres.'

'Only two wounds?' asked Griessel.

The pathologist nodded.

'There were three rounds fired by his pistol . . .'

'Prof.,' said Dekker, 'she is an alcoholic. Say she was drunk last night. I had blood drawn, but will it help, eight or ten hours after the fact?'

'Nowadays we can track alcohol levels up to thirty-six hours afterwards. But I must throw my weight behind Nikita. I don't believe it was her.'

'How so, Prof.?'

'Look at him, Fransman. He must be about one point nine metres tall, on the wrong side of a hundred and ten kilograms. You and I would battle to get his body up those stairs—and we are sober.'

'Somebody went to a lot of trouble to get him here,' said Dekker.

Pagel stood up. 'Don't write off the music industry as a potential source of conflict. There's money in Afrikaans music. The intrigues are legion. Scandals like divorce, sexual harassment, paedophilia. They fight over everything—contracts, artistic credits, royalties . . . Our Adam was in the thick of things. Would it be enough to inspire murder? As Fransman correctly pointed out, in this country, anything is possible.'

Dekker's phone rang. He checked the screen. 'It's Cloete,' he said. Cloete was the SAPS media liaison officer.

'Goodbye, colleagues,' said Pagel on the way to the door.

Griessel said goodbye and listened to Dekker give Cloete the details. Something big was brewing. Just a look outside would tell you that. His own phone rang. He answered, 'Griessel.'

'Benny,' said Vusi Ndabeni, 'I think you should come.'

RACHEL ANDERSON crept down the gully. It deepened as she progressed. The steep sides offered shelter enough for her to stand. They would have difficulty seeing her. It was just after eight, and hot. She clambered down, her throat parched, her knees threatening to give in. She had to keep moving.

Then she saw the path leading up to the right, and steps carved out of the rock and earth. She stared. She had no idea what awaited her up there.

ALEXA BARNARD watched them carry her husband's body past the door and her face twisted with emotion. Tinkie sat on the couch beside her and put a hand on her arm. Alexa felt an overwhelming urge to be held by this slender policewoman. But she just hung her head and watched the tears drip onto the white material of her dressing-gown sleeve.

RACHEL CLIMBED to just short of the top and peered over the edge of the gully with a thudding heart. Only the mountain. And silence. To her left were the roofs of houses, the highest row on the mountain. Ahead was a path running along the back of the houses, with trees offering shade and cover.

She looked back once, then stepped hastily onto the path, head down.

GRIESSEL DROVE BACK to Long Street in much lighter traffic. Vusi had said he should come to the Cat & Moose. Benny thought of Alexa Barnard. About her voice and her story, about the beauty hidden beneath twenty years of alcohol abuse. He thought of the intensity with which she had drunk the gin and knew it was a dangerous thing to see. It had unravelled his own desire, so that it dangled inside him like a thousand loose wires. The voice in his mind was saying there was a bottle store right here in Kloof Street, where all the wires could be reconnected. The electricity of life would flow strongly once again.

'God,' said Benny to himself and turned deliberately into Bree Street, away from temptation.

WHEN THE TEARS STOPPED, Tinkie said, 'Come, you'll feel better when you've had a bath.' Alexa was a bit unsteady on her feet, so the police-woman guided her up the stairs to the bedroom door.

'I think you should wait here.'

'I can't,' said Tinkie in a voice full of compassion.

Alexa stood still for a second. Then the meaning penetrated. They were afraid she would do something. To herself. And she knew the possibility was real. But first she must get to the liquor, the four centimetres of gin in the bottle underneath her underwear. 'I won't do anything.' Alexa walked into the bedroom. 'Just stay out of the bathroom.' She would take the bottle out of the cupboard along with her clothes. Her body would screen it.

THE KNOCKING wasn't going to stop. Fransman Dekker went to open the door. Willie Mouton stood on the verandah along with an equally lean man, with a full head of dark hair, painstakingly combed into a side parting. He had the appearance of an undertaker. 'My lawyer is here. I'm ready for you now.'

'You're ready for me?' Dekker's temper flared at the way the white man talked down to him.

'Regardt Groenewald,' the lawyer said apologetically and extended a cautious hand. It was a peace offering.

Dekker shook it. He had expected a Doberman, not this basset hound.

'Where is Alexa?' Mouton asked.

'She is being looked after by an officer of Social Services.'

'I want to see her.' A white man's command.

'That is not an option now,' said Dekker.

'But she's a sick woman.'

'Mrs Barnard chose to talk without a lawyer present. She is not a suspect at this stage,' said Dekker.

'That's not what Adam's maid said.'

'As far as I know, the domestic worker is not in police service.'

'You see, Regardt. That's what they're like. Smartass.'

'Willie, Mr Dekker, let's all keep calm . . .'

'I *am* calm, Regardt.'

'My client has information connected to the case,' said Groenewald. 'Perhaps we could talk inside?'

Dekker hesitated.

'My client has a strong suspicion of who murdered Adam Barnard.'

'You know who shot Adam Barnard?'

'My client has no proof, but feels it is his civil duty to share the available information with the law.'

Dekker looked at the crowd, then at Groenewald and Mouton. 'Come in.'

RACHEL WALKED along the footpath on the contour of the mountain, hurrying more now as she had left the shelter of the pine trees behind. There were only the houses below, large properties with swimming pools and high walls. Beyond them lay the city and Table Bay. It was a lie, all this beauty, she thought. A false front. She and Erin had allowed themselves to be misled by it.

Ahead the path curved to the right, skirting a reservoir. The high earthen bank would conceal her for a few hundred metres.

BEHIND THE BATHROOM door Alexa took off her dressing gown and night clothes and reached for the bottle she had hidden under her clean clothing. There wasn't much in the bottle. She brought it to her lips and drank. The movement was echoed in the tall mirror and she watched the naked body, its femininity so wasted, mouth open, bottle lifted high in a desperate attempt to catch the last drops. Who was this person standing there? Was it really her?

'*Soetwater*,' the sympathetic detective had said. 'How did you come to this?' was what he meant. She had told him, but now, in front of this sudden reflection, the explanation was insufficient.

She turned back and looked at the reflected woman again. The tall body looked so defenceless. Legs, hips, the firm breasts, the skin of the neck no longer smoothly taut. A face, worn, used, drunk up. It was *her* body, *her* face.

God. 'How *did* you come to this?' There was genuine curiosity in her own question. She stepped into the shower. Mechanically she opened the taps. Adam was dead. What was she going to do? Tonight? Tomorrow? The fear that welled up inside her was huge, so that she had to press her palms against the tiles to remain standing. She stood like that a while, the water scalding her, but she did not feel it. The sleeping pills, that's what she must get, the sleeping pills, so she could drift away from that woman in the mirror.

The pills were in the room with Tinkie Kellerman. She would have to do it with something else. She stepped out of the shower, pulled open the bathroom cabinet with shaking hands. Too hasty, she knocked bottles over, nothing of use.

'Mrs Barnard?' called the voice from the other side of the door.

Alexa spotted the gin bottle. She grabbed the neck and struck it against the wall. She examined the sharp glass blade that remained in her hand. She lifted her left arm and sliced violently, deep and desperately, from the palm to the elbow. The blood was a fountain. She sliced again.

In the sitting room Mouton and Groenewald sat side by side on the couch. Dekker was opposite them.

'Just tell him what happened, Willie.'

'This guy burst into my office and said he was going to kill Adam . . .'

'And who is this guy?'

Mouton drew a deep breath. 'It was Josh Geyser,' he said. 'The gospel singer. Josh and Melinda.'

'Never heard of them.'

'Everyone knows them. Sixty thousand of the new CD, four thousand in one day alone, when they were featured on radio RSG. They're big.'

'And why would Josh Geyser want to kill Adam Barnard?'

Mouton leaned forward conspiratorially: 'Because Adam nailed Melinda in his office. He had sex with her.'

'And Geyser caught them?'

'No. Melinda confessed.'

'To Josh?'

'No. Higher up. But Josh was with her when she prayed.'

Dekker snorted with disbelief. 'Mr Mouton, you can't be serious.'

'I am!' Indignant. 'Yesterday afternoon Josh Geyser just about broke my office door down. He said he was going to kill Adam because he raped Melinda—Melinda said so. I said, "What did she say?" and he said she'd confessed to the Big Sin in Adam's office, on the desk, she said it was the devil, but he, Josh, knew about Adam's ways. And he was going to beat him to death. He was crazy. He nearly grabbed hold of me, when I said it didn't sound like rape. He's a huge *ou*, he was a Gladiator before he was saved.'

'Adam's ways. What "ways" was Geyser referring to?'

'Adam is . . .' Mouton hesitated. 'I can't believe Adam is dead. He was my friend. My partner. I told him one day someone would . . .'

Dekker heard the high and urgent voice of Tinkie Kellerman calling, 'Fransman!' He stood up quickly.

He saw Kellerman at the top of the stairs.

'Come and help,' she said. 'Hurry.'

A HUNDRED METRES beyond the reservoir the path turned down the mountain, towards the city. Rachel Anderson walked through the pine trees, following the path. She saw a stone wall ahead with a gap in the middle and beyond it an almost completed house. She went past the garage, eyes searching, towards the street. A sawn-up pine tree filled the doorway of the double garage. She spotted the tap beside the back door of the house, walked faster, stooped and turned it. The silvery water gushed out, hot for a few seconds, then suddenly cool. She dropped down on one knee and drank directly from the spout.

FRANSMAN DEKKER had forced enough doors to know you don't use your shoulder. He took a step back and kicked. He kicked again before it broke, swinging open only about forty centimetres. It was enough to see the blood.

'Oh, dear heaven,' said Tinkie behind him.

'What?' said Willie Mouton, trying to get past her.

'Sir, you can't . . .'

Dekker was already in the bathroom. He saw Alexa Barnard lying on the floor. He stepped in the blood and turned her naked body over. Her eyes were open, but unfocused.

'Ambulance,' he ordered Tinkie. 'Now.'

He bent to examine the damage. Her left wrist was deeply cut, at least three times. The blood still flowed from it. He grabbed a garment off the floor and began to bind it as tightly as he could.

Alexa spoke, the words barely audible. 'The other arm,' she whispered.

'I'm sorry?'

'Cut the other arm, please,' and with a weary hand she held out the broken bottle to him.

SHE QUENCHED her thirst, then stood up and took a deep breath. She walked round the corner of the house, fear mellowed by the drink of water.

Then she saw them, only twenty paces away down the street. She froze, breath caught in her throat. They were standing with their backs to her. She knew them. She was turned to stone. Her heart beat thunderously in her ears.

The garage was five paces behind her. She shuffled backwards, too terrified to take her eyes off them. They must not look round. She reached the wall of the garage. One more step. Then one of them began to turn. The one who had started it all. The one who had bent over Erin with the knife.

IN THE BREAKFAST ROOM of the Cat & Moose Youth Hostel, nineteen-year-old Oliver 'Ollie' Sands sat with his head in his hands. A bit overweight, he had red hair and pale skin that had seen too much sun. His angular black-rimmed glasses lay on the table in front of him. Opposite him, close to the door, sat Inspectors Vusumuzi Ndabeni and Benny Griessel.

'Mr Sands has identified the victim as Miss Erin Russel,' said Vusi. 'He's been travelling through Africa with Miss Russel and her friend, Rachel Anderson. He does not know where Miss Anderson is. The last time he saw them was last night in Van Hunks, the nightclub in Castle Street.'

Griessel said, 'Mr Sands, you arrived in Cape Town yesterday?'

'Yes, sir. From Namibia.' The accent was American, the voice quavering, emotional. Sands placed the glasses on his nose and blinked.

'Just the three of you?' Griessel asked.

'No, sir. There were twenty-one of us on the tour. The African Adventure Tour. Overland, by truck.'

'And you and the two girls were together?'

'No, sir, I met them in Nairobi. They're from Indiana; I'm from Phoenix, Arizona.'

'But you were with the girls last night?' Vusi asked.

'A whole bunch of us went to the club.'

'But the two girls were part of the group?'

'Yes, sir.'

'What happened at the club?'

'We had a good time. You know . . .' Sands took off his glasses again. 'We had a few drinks, danced a little . . .' He replaced his glasses.

The gesture made Griessel suspicious.

'At what time did you leave?' Vusi asked.

'I . . . I was a little tired. I came back at about eleven.'

'And the girls were still at the club when you left?'

'Yes, sir.'

'Could you give us the names of the people they were with?'

'I guess . . . Jason was there. And Steven, Sven, Kathy . . .'

'Do you know their surnames?' Vusi pulled his notebook closer.

'Not all of them. It's Jason Dicklurk, and Steven Cheatsinger . . .'

'Could you spell that for us?'

'Well, Jason, you know. I'm not sure about spelling his surname . . . Sorry, I can't help. But I have pics of Rachel and Erin on my camera. I can show you.' Sands stood up. 'Is it OK if I go and get it?'

'That would be good.'

'He's hiding something,' said Griessel as Sands walked out the door. 'People who wear specs . . . they have a way . . .' Griessel hesitated. He had learned with Dekker to put his mentoring boots down carefully. 'Vusi, you learn things over the years, with interrogation . . .'

'You know I want to learn, Benny.'

Griessel got up. 'Sit here, Vusi. The person you are interviewing must always have his back to the door.' He shifted the chairs around. 'With the door behind him, he feels trapped. The signs become clearer, he will sweat, keep pulling at his collar, a leg or foot will jump. If he wears glasses, he will take them off. This one did that when he started talking about coming back early last night.'

Ndabeni had hung on every word. 'Thanks. I'll ask him about that.'

'Is he the only one here from the group?'

'Yes. The rest are somewhere else. A wine tour. Or up the mountain.'

Griessel's phone rang and he saw the name on the screen. *AFRIKA.*

He took the call. 'Benny, what the hell is going on?' the Regional

Commissioner asked, so loudly that even Vusi could hear it. 'Some lawyer is phoning me saying you all made a big cockup with Adam Barnard's wife. Now the woman has committed suicide because you intimidated her and she has nothing to do with the whole bloody thing . . .'

A hand clenched his heart. 'She's dead?'

'No, she's not bloody dead, but you are there to mentor, Benny, that's why I brought you in. Just imagine what the press are going to make of this, I hear Barnard is a celebrity . . .'

'Sir, nobody—'

Meet me at the hospital, you and Dekker. If I try to cover for him they say it's because he's a *hotnot* like me, and I only look after my own people. Where are you, anyway?'

'With Vusi, Commissioner. The church murder . . .'

'And now I hear that's an American tourist, *jissis*, Benny. At the hospital, five minutes.' The line went dead. Then Sands walked in with the camera, crying as he stared at the screen. He held it so that the detectives could see. As Benny looked he felt that ghostly hand squeeze his heart, that familiar oppression. Rachel Anderson and Erin Russel stood laughing with Kilimanjaro in the background. Young and effervescent, just like his daughter Carla.

RACHEL ANDERSON lay on her belly behind the heap of pine logs in the garage and tried to control her breathing. She heard voices right in front of the garage. 'I hope to God she's still out there.'

'The mountain is huge. But if she moves, Barry will spot her. And our cops will have the streets covered. We'll get the bitch. Sooner or later, we'll get her and this whole thing will go away.'

She lay listening to the footsteps that faded away uphill. *And our cops will have the streets covered.* These were the words that echoed in her mind, that killed the last vestige of hope.

BENNY GRIESSEL SAID in Afrikaans, 'He will talk, Vusi. Just give him a fright. I have to go.'

On the way to his car, he phoned Dekker. 'Is she still alive, Fransman?'

'Yes. Tinkie was with her but she locked the bathroom door and cut her wrists with a broken gin bottle. She lost a lot of blood, but she should be all right.'

'Where are you?'

'City Park. Did the Commissioner call you? Mouton made a huge scene. When he saw the blood, he just lost it . . .'

'We can handle it, Fransman. I'll be there now.' He climbed into his car and wondered if he had missed something in his conversation with Alexa Barnard. Had there been a sign?

VUSI SAID, 'I'm your friend. You can tell me anything,' and he saw Oliver Sands reach for his glasses and take them off.

'I know.' Sands began cleaning the glasses on his T-shirt, now with his back to the door.

'So what really happened last night?' Vusi watched for the signs Benny had talked about.

'I told you,' the voice was too controlled.

Vusi allowed the silence to stretch out. He waited until Sands put the glasses back on, then leaned forward. 'I don't think you've told me everything.'

'I did, honest to God.' Again the hands went to the glasses and adjusted them.

Benny had told him to give Sands a fright. He took a set of handcuffs out of his pocket and put them on the table. 'Police cells are not nice.'

Sands stared at the handcuffs. 'Please,' he said.

'Mr Sands, please stand up and put your hands behind your back.'

'Oh, God,' said Oliver Sands and stood up slowly.

'Are you going to talk to me?'

Sands looked at Vusi and his whole body shivered. 'Yes.'

09:04–10:09

IV

Griessel drove down Loop Street towards the harbour. There was heavy traffic. He stopped with the lights showing red as far ahead as he could see. Why couldn't the Metro Police get off their backsides and synchronise them?

That reminded him he ought to call the Field Marshall. Oerson. Perhaps they had found something. No, better to remind Vusi. This was Vusi's case. He drummed his fingers impatiently, realised it was the rhythm of '*Soetwater*' and could no longer ignore his conscience. Alexa Barnard had told him she had a suicide fantasy. 'I wanted Adam to come home and find me dead.'

He shook his head. How the hell could he have missed that? And he had given her alcohol as well. Benny the great mentor.

He had fixated on her thirst; that was the problem. He had poured her two tots and she had pushed the hair from her face and said, 'I was such a terribly insecure little thing.' And then her history had led his thoughts away from suicide; it had fascinated him. She was an only child. Her father worked for a bank and every four or five years the family relocated as her father was transferred. She left half-formed friendships behind with every move, had to start over as an outsider at every school. More and more she began to live in her own world and dreamed of becoming a singer.

The source of this dream was her paternal grandmother. Ouma Hettie was a music teacher, an energetic woman with a spotless house and a baby grand in the sitting room. Hettie loved Schubert and Beethoven, but her true joy was the brothers Gershwin. At first Alexa would sit beside her grandmother and just listen. Later she learned the words and melodies by heart and often sang along.

On a sweltering evening in Alexa's fifteenth year, Ouma Hettie suddenly stopped playing and told her, 'Stand there.' Meekly, she took her place beside the piano. 'Now *sing!*'

She did, in full voice. As the last note faded in the sultry evening air, Hettie said, 'My dear, you have an extraordinary voice. You are going to be a star.' That was how the dream began. And Ouma Hettie's official tuition.

A week before her finals she went for an audition with the Dave Burmeister Band. Stage fright nearly got the better of her but as soon as she began to sing, the demon melted away. At her first performance with Burmeister in a Johannesburg club, her grandma had been there to give her courage. 'This is what you were born for, my dear. Go out there and knock them dead.' And she had. The reviews were still beside Ouma Hettie's bed when she passed away in her sleep two months later.

OLIVER SANDS TOLD Vusi he had fallen in love with Rachel on Day Eight of the African Overland Adventure. In Zanzibar. Over a plate of seafood that he had been eating with great concentration.

'You are obviously enjoying that,' said Rachel.

He looked up. She stood on the opposite side of the restaurant table with the emerald-green sea as a backdrop, dark-brown hair in a plait over her shoulder, a baseball cap on her head and long legs in shorts. When she pulled out the chair opposite him he could scarcely believe his luck. Girls like that never noticed him. When she sat at his table and ate her own seafood with gusto, he struggled to remember her name. She asked him where he was from and what his future plans were. She told him of her dream of becoming a doctor, and that one day she would like to make a difference, here, in Africa.

And so he lost his heart to a nameless woman.

ALEXA'S STAGE FRIGHT grew worse. The loss of her grandma was a blow. Despite the glowing reviews and the enthusiastic response of audiences, the demon of self-doubt clung to her shoulders every night. One night she burst in on Dave Burmeister in tears and confessed her fear. With fatherly patience, Burmeister explained that all the great names struggled with stage fright. At first his gentle voice calmed her but every night it took a little longer before she could make the terrifying walk across the stage. One day, at his wits' end, Burmeister placed a glass of brandy in front of her and said, 'For God's sake, just drink it.'

OLIVER SANDS CONTROLLED his attraction to Rachel with an iron hand. He knew he must not reveal his burning desire. He waited for those magical moments when she talked to him spontaneously. Sometimes in the evening she would sit beside him at the campfire and say, 'So, Ollie, did we have a good day today or what?'

Day and night he was completely aware of her. He saw that she was friendly with everyone in the group, but realised he was especially privileged—he received more of her attention than anyone else. The two self-assured chief guides were very popular with the other girls, but she treated them just the same as the men in the group, while choosing to take her meals with Ollie, talk to him and share many more personal secrets.

It was like that until Lake Kariba, in Zimbabwe. On their second day there she was different, sombre and quiet, the joy and spontaneity gone.

ALEXA LEARNED to have three drinks before a performance. Four made her slur the lyrics. But two was not enough. She kept the demon under control for four years, hundreds of appearances and two recordings with Burmeister and his band.

Then she met Adam Barnard. After a show he came knocking on her dressing-room door with a bunch of flowers in his hand. He was fluent and charming, and his compliments were measured, and therefore seemed more genuine. He invited her out: a business lunch, he made it clear.

Three days later she signed a contract with Adam. It bound her to his record company and to him, as manager. He made good on his professional promises. He sought out Afrikaans compositions to suit her voice and her style. He hired the best musicians, developed a unique sound for her and introduced her to the media. He courted her with the same professionalism and married her. He even weaned her off the three pre-appearance drinks with his total support, belief in her talent and his silver tongue. For two years her life and career were everything she had dreamed of.

One day she came home unexpectedly. In the sitting room, she found Adam with his trousers round his ankles and Paula Phillips, a singer with big boobs, on her knees in front of him. That was the day Alexa began to drink in earnest.

EVEN THOUGH RACHEL had changed in her behaviour towards everyone, Ollie knew it must have been something he had said or done. The previous night in Van Hunks he had cracked under the strain. What he ought to have said was, 'I can see something is bothering you, Rachel. Do you want to talk about it?' But he had already downed too many beers. He sat down beside her and like a complete idiot said, 'I don't know why you suddenly hate me, but I love you, Rachel.' He had gazed at her with big hungry puppy eyes in the crazy hope that she would say, 'I love you too, Ollie. I've loved you since that magical day in Zanzibar.'

But she hadn't. He thought she hadn't heard him over the loud music, because she just sat there staring into the middle distance. Then she stood up, turned to him and kissed him on the forehead.

'Dear Ollie,' she said and walked away between the crush of people.

'That's why I came back here,' Sands said to Vusi. 'I knew the dorm would be empty, and I didn't want anybody to see me cry.' He did not remove his glasses. The tears trickled under the edge of the frame and down his round, red cheeks.

RACHEL ANDERSON LAY on her stomach behind the pine logs, powerless, gutted. She couldn't hold back the self-pity any longer; it overwhelmed and paralysed her. Her thoughts had stalled, all escape routes slammed shut, except this single option, to lie in the shade, a gasping, helpless fish on dry land.

She couldn't hear the voices any more. They had walked uphill. Maybe they would look at the unfinished garage and realise it offered a hiding place and then they would look behind the pine logs and one would grab her hair and slash open her throat. She didn't even think she would bleed; there was nothing left.

Oh, to be home. It was a longing that slowly overcame her—her father's voice, far off and faint. 'Don't you worry, honey, just don't you worry.' Oh, to be held by him, to curl up on his lap with her head under his chin and close her eyes. The safest place in the world.

The idea took shape, instinctive and irrational, to get up and phone her father. He would save her.

IF THERE WAS A MURDER or armed robbery in his area at night, the SAPS members of Caledon Square had instructions to call the Station Commander at home. But the more mundane affairs of the previous night had to wait until he was at his desk in the morning and could scan the notes in the register. The SC ran his pen down the list of domestic violence, public drunkenness, burglaries and various false alarms.

At first his pen slid over the Lion's Head incident but it hovered back. The reluctant woman who had seen a young girl on the mountain. Then he reached for the bulletin that a constable had brought in only minutes before. He had scanned it quickly. Now he gave it his full attention. He saw the connection.

At the bottom was Ndabeni's name. He picked up the phone. 'Vusi,' said the Caledon Square SC in Xhosa. 'I think I have something for you.'

BENNY GRIESSEL STOOD with his colleagues in one of the examination rooms of the City Park Hospital Casualty Department. Space was limited, so they were quite an intimate little group. While Fransman Dekker talked,

Benny observed the people around him: John Afrika, Regional Commissioner, in full uniform. Afrika was shorter than Dekker, but he had a presence that made him the dominant force in the room. Beside Afrika was Tinkie Kellerman. Then there was Dekker: serious, focused, voice deep and intense as he talked. They said he had a beautiful coloured wife in a senior position at Sanlam, and that's how he could afford to live in an expensive house somewhere on the Tygerberg. They also said that he sometimes played away from home.

And Cloete, the liaison officer with tobacco stains on his fingers and permanent shadows under his eyes. Cloete, with his endless patience and calm, the man in the middle, between the devil of the media and the deep blue of the police. How many times had he been through this, Griessel wondered, this kind of emergency meeting?

Dekker concluded his explanation, and John Afrika looked up. 'The press . . .' he looked at Cloete.

'It's a major story,' said Cloete. 'Barnard is a celebrity of sorts.'

'That's the problem,' said Afrika, deep in thought. When he focused on Dekker with an apologetic slant to his mouth, Griessel knew what was coming. 'Fransman, you're not going to like this . . .'

'Commissioner, maybe . . .' Griessel said, because he had had control taken away from him before, and he knew how it felt.

Afrika held up a hand. 'They will tear us apart, Benny, if Mouton puts the blame on us. You know what the papers are like. Tomorrow they will say it's because we put inexperienced people on the case.'

Dekker got it now. 'No, Commissioner . . .' he said.

'Fransman, don't let us misunderstand each other; it happened on *your* watch,' Afrika said sternly. Then more gently, 'I'm not saying it's your fault; I want to protect you.'

'Protect? But sir, if I crack this, tomorrow . . .'

'You know it's not that simple. Benny, you take charge of this one. As of now, Fransman, you work closely with Benny. Let him handle the Moutons of this world. You're a team, if you crack this—'

Griessel's phone rang.

'—then you can share the honours.'

Benny took the phone out of his pocket. 'It's Vusi,' he said meaningfully.

'*Jissis,*' said Afrika, shaking his head. 'It never rains . . .'

Griessel answered with a 'Vusi?'

'Is the Commissioner still there with you, Benny?'

'He's here.'

'Keep him there, please, just keep him there.'

THE OBSERVATION POINT with the best view of the city is a hundred metres below Mount Prospect on the northern flank of Devil's Peak. The young man was sitting just above the path, on a rock in the shade of a protea bush. He was in his late twenties, white, lean and tanned. He held a pair of binoculars to his face and scanned the ground slowly from left to right. Below him the Cape was breathtaking—from the cable car sliding past Table Mountain's rugged cliffs to the top, past the sensuous curves of Lion's Head and Signal Hill, over the blue bay, a glittering jewel that stretched to the horizon. He saw none of this, because his attention was focused only on the city's edge.

Beside him on the flat rock was a map book of Cape Town open at Oranjezicht, the suburb directly below him. The mountain breeze gently flipped the pages, so that every now and then he had to put out a hand to flatten them.

RACHEL ANDERSON STOOD up slowly. She walked out of the shadow of the garage and turned right in the direction of the city, across the tar of Bosch Avenue to where it turned into Rugby Road ten metres farther on. She was drained, she could no longer run, she would just walk slowly and go and phone her father.

THE YOUNG MAN with the binoculars spotted her instantly. The denim shorts, the powder-blue T-shirt and the small rucksack—it was her.

'Jesus Christ,' he said out loud and took out a cellphone. He called and brought the binoculars back to his eyes with one hand. 'I see her. She just walked out of nowhere.'

'Where is she?'

'Right there, in the road, she's turning right . . .'

'Which road, Barry?'

Barry picked up the map. The wind had turned the page again. Hurriedly, he turned back and ran his finger over the map, looking for the right place. 'It's right there, first road below . . .'

'Barry, what street?'

'I'm working on it. Braemar. That's it . . .' Barry lifted up the binoculars. He spotted her in the lenses for a moment. She was walking calmly, in no hurry. Then she began to disappear, as though the suburb was swallowing her feet first.

'She's . . . she's gone, she just disappeared.'

'Not possible.'

Barry trembled as he searched the map again. 'Stairs. She's taking the stairway to Strathcona Road.' He pointed the binoculars again. '*Ja.* That's exactly where she is.'

GRIESSEL STOOD OUTSIDE on the pavement with Dekker and Cloete. Through the glass doors they watched Afrika pacify Mouton and his soberly dressed lawyer. 'Sorry, Fransman,' said Griessel.

Dekker didn't reply; he just stared at the three men inside.

'It happens,' said Cloete philosophically. 'It's not Benny's fault.'

'I know,' said Dekker. 'But we're wasting time. Josh Geyser could be in Timbuktu by now.'

'*The* Josh Geyser?' asked Cloete.

'Who?' asked Griessel.

'The gospel guy. Barnard pumped his wife yesterday in his office and she went and confessed the whole thing to Geyser.'

'Melinda?' asked Cloete urgently.

'That's right. Are you a gospel fan?'

Cloete nodded. 'I've got all their CDs. I can't believe it. Melinda is a sweet thing. And she and Josh are born-again—she would never do a thing like that.'

'Born-again or not, that's what Mouton says.'

'Fransman, wait. Explain this to me,' said Griessel.

'Apparently, yesterday Barnard screwed Melinda Geyser in his office. So her husband, Josh, pitches up yesterday afternoon saying he knows all about it and he's going to beat Barnard to death, but Barnard wasn't there.'

'Can't be,' said Cloete. 'Oh man, the press . . .'

'Benny!' All three turned when they heard Vusi's voice. The detective came jogging down the pavement. 'Where's the Commissioner?'

All three pointed fingers through the glass doors where a doctor had now joined the Mouton conference.

'The other girl—she's still alive, Benny. But they're hunting her down. The Commissioner will have to organise more people.'

SHE WALKED DOWN MARMION ROAD in the direction of the city. She saw a small black Peugeot reversing out of a driveway. The driver was a woman. The woman drove to the edge of the street and stopped. She saw Rachel and for an instant made eye contact, then looked away.

'Hi,' said Rachel calmly, but the woman didn't hear her. She stepped forward and softly knocked on the window. The woman turned the window down a few centimetres.

'May I use your telephone, please,' said Rachel.

The woman saw the dirty clothes, the grazed chin, hands and knees. 'There's a public telephone at Carlucci's. On Montrose.'

'I'm in real trouble.'

'It's just around the corner,' and the woman wound up the window. As she turned to drive away she looked once more at Rachel, suspicion in her face.

BARRY STUDIED THE MAP on the bonnet of the vehicle and said over his phone, 'Look, she could have gone left into Chesterfield, or she could have taken Marmion, but I can't see her.'

'Which one goes down into the city?' The voice was out of breath.

'Marmion.'

'Then keep your focus on Marmion. We're two minutes from the Landy, but you will have to tell us where she is.'

Barry took the binoculars and held them to his eyes. He followed Strathcona to where it led into Marmion, then followed the trajectory north towards the city. Marmion ended in Montrose. She ought to turn left there, if she wanted to reach the city. He found Montrose, broad and more visible from here.

'Barry? We're in the Landy. We're going to Marmion.'

'OK,' he said, still looking through the binoculars.

He saw her, far and tiny in the lenses, but unmistakable.

'I have her. She's in Montrose . . .'

'OK. Now just don't lose her.'

JOHN AFRIKA walked out of the glass doors of Casualty. 'Good news, *kêrels*,' he said as he took his place in the circle. 'Alexa Barnard is out of danger. The damage is not so bad, she's just lost a lot of blood; they're keeping her . . . Oh, Vusi, morning, what are you doing here?'

'I'm sorry, sir, I know you're busy, but I thought I should ask for help. The American girl at the church . . . there were two of them.' Vusi took out his notebook. 'The victim is Erin Russel. Her friend is Rachel Anderson. They came in with a tour group yesterday. Miss Anderson was seen on Signal Hill at approximately six o'clock this morning, pursued by assailants. Sir, she's an eyewitness, and she's in great danger. We need to find her.'

'Damn,' said Afrika. 'Pursued by assailants? What assailants?'

'Apparently five or six young men, some white, some black. The witness was walking her dog when Miss Anderson asked her to call the police. A few minutes later the young men came running past.'

The Commissioner checked his watch. 'More than three hours ago . . .'

'I know. I need more people, sir.'

'*Bliksem.* I don't have more people. We'll have to get the stations involved.'

'I've already asked the stations, sir, but Caledon Square has to police a union march and Camps Bay has only two vehicles in operation. I thought if we could get the chopper . . .'

Afrika took out his cellphone. 'Let me see what I can do . . . '

RACHEL ANDERSON WALKED through the front door of Carlucci's Quality Food Store and up to the counter where a young man in a white apron was taking change out of plastic bags.

'Is there a telephone I can use?'

'Over there, next to the ATM,' he said and then he looked. He saw the stains on her clothes, the dried blood on her face and knees. 'Are you OK?'

'No, I'm not. I need to make an urgent call, please.'

'It's not a card phone. Would you like some change?'

Rachel took the rucksack off her back. 'I've got some.' She went in the direction he had indicated.

He noticed her beauty, despite the state she was in. 'Can I help you with something?' She didn't answer. He watched her with concern.

'JESUS CHRIST,' Barry said over the phone. 'She's just gone into a restaurant or something.'

'Which one?'

'It's on the corner of Montrose and . . . I think it's Upper Orange.'

'We'll be there in two minutes. Just keep looking . . .'

THE RINGING OF THE PHONE woke Bill Anderson in his house in West Lafayette, Indiana. He knocked off the receiver, so he had to sit up and swing his feet off the bed to reach it.

'What is it?' his wife asked beside him, confused.

'Daddy?' he heard as he picked up the receiver.

'Baby?'

'Daddy!' said his daughter, Rachel, thousands of kilometres away, and she began to cry.

Bill Anderson's guts contracted; suddenly he was wide awake. 'Honey, what's wrong?'

'Erin is dead, Daddy. You have to help me. They want to kill me too.'

TO HER LEFT was a large window looking out on Montrose Avenue.

'They cut her throat last night, Daddy. I saw it . . .' Her voice caught.

'Oh my God,' said Bill Anderson. 'Where are you?'

'I don't have much time, Daddy. I'm in Cape Town. I can't even go to the police . . .' Tyres screeched on the road. A white Land Rover Defender stopped outside. She knew the occupants.

'They're here, Daddy, please help me . . .'

'Who's there?' her father asked urgently, but she had seen two men leap out of the Land Rover. She threw the receiver down and fled through the shop to a wooden door at the back. She shoved it open. As she ran out she heard the man in the apron shout, 'Hey!' She was in a long passage between the building and a high wall. The only way out was at the end of the passage—another wooden door. If that door was locked . . .

The soles of her running shoes slapped loudly in the narrow space. She pulled at the door. Behind her she heard the deli door open. She looked back. They saw her. She jerked open the door in front of her, went out and slammed it behind her. She saw the street before her, realised the door had a bolt and banged it with the palm of her hand. The bolt slid and the door was barred.

She raced down concrete steps. She was running down the long slope of Upper Orange Street, searching for a way out, because they were too close, even if they went back through the shop. They were as close as they had been last night just before they caught Erin.

BILL ANDERSON rushed down the stairs to his study, his wife, Jess, at his heels.

'They killed Erin?' she asked, her voice heavy with fear. 'You have to tell me what's going on.'

Anderson turned and put his hands on his wife's shoulders. 'I don't know what's going on,' he said. 'Rachel says Erin was killed. She says she's still in Cape Town . . . and that she's in danger . . .'

'Oh my God . . . what can we do?'

THE YOUNG MAN in the apron saw the two men who had chased the girl coming back through the store. He shouted, 'Hey!' again and blocked the way to the front door. 'Stop!'

The one in front shoved the young man in the chest, making him fall back against the counter. Then they were past him, into the street. He scrambled to his feet, saw them hesitate on the pavement.

'I'm calling the police,' he shouted. They didn't respond, but looked down Upper Orange Street, ran to the Land Rover and jumped in.

The young man realised he should get the registration number. He ran outside. The Land Rover turned the corner of Belmont with squealing tyres. He could see it was a CA number—he thought it was 412 and another four figures, but by then the vehicle was too far off. He hurried back to the shop.

ON THE SLOPE of Devil's Peak, Barry's phone rang. 'Yes!'

'Where did she go?'

'She went down Upper Orange.'

'Where is she now?'

'I don't know, I can't see the whole street from here.'

'Keep looking! Don't take your eyes off this street.'

BILL ANDERSON SAT in his study with the telephone to his ear. It was ringing in the home of his lawyer. His wife, Jess, stood behind him, crying softly.

'Is he answering?' she asked.

'It's two o'clock in the morning. Even lawyers are asleep.'

A familiar voice answered at the other end. 'Connelly.'

'Mike, this is Bill. I am truly sorry to call you at this hour, but it's about Rachel. And Erin.'

'Then you don't have to be sorry at all.'

THE CONSTABLE at Caledon Square taking the call from Carlucci's Quality Food Store was unaware of Vusi Ndabeni's bulletin. He made notes while the young man described the incident in his shop. Then he went to the sergeant in the radio control room, who contacted the station patrol vehicles. The sergeant gave cursory details of the incident and asked the vehicle closest to Upper Orange Street to investigate.

THEY SAT OUTSIDE a coffee shop, five policemen around a table for four. Cloete sat a little apart, talking on his phone. The rest had their elbows on the table and their heads together.

John Afrika's deep frown showed that his burden of responsibility was weighing heavily. 'Benny, it's your show,' he said.

Griessel had known that was coming, it always did. The men at the top wanted to do everything except make the decisions.

'Commissioner, our main problem is that we don't know where the Barnard murder took place. We need Forensics—there would have to be blood, bullets . . . and then we need to place Geyser at the scene. I'll have the man and his wife brought in to the station. We need to talk to them separately. Meanwhile Fransman can go to AfriSound. We need to know where Barnard was last night, and with whom. We have to build this case from the ground up.'

'Amen,' said Afrika. 'I want a rock-solid case.'

'We need a formal statement from Willie Mouton. Fransman?'

'I'll handle it.'

'As far as Vusi's case is concerned—he needs someone to coordinate the stations, who can bring people in from the southern suburbs.'

'The chopper can help us in an hour's time,' said Afrika.

Griessel's voice became serious. 'Commissioner, this is someone's child out there. We need feet on the ground. Vehicles, patrols. Vusi, the photo the American boy took of the missing girl—we need prints. Every policeman

in the Peninsula . . . the Metro people . . .' and Griessel wondered what had
come of the Field Marshal and his street search.

'The Metro people?' said Dekker. 'Glorified traffic cops . . .'

'It makes no difference,' said Griessel. 'We need all the eyes we can get.
I thought we should bring Mat Joubert in to coordinate, sir.'

'No,' said Afrika firmly. 'You don't know about Joubert yet?'

'What about him?'

Griessel's phone rang. The number was unfamiliar. 'Excuse me,' he said
as he answered, 'Benny Griessel.'

'This is Willie Mouton.' The voice was self-important.

'Mr Mouton,' Griessel said deliberately, so the others would know.

Afrika nodded. 'I gave him your number,' he said quietly.

Mouton said, 'I phoned Josh Geyser and told him to come to the office.
He will be here in ten minutes, if you want to arrest him.'

Griessel sighed. 'Mr Mouton, we would have preferred to bring him in
ourselves. Where is your office?'

'Sixteen Buiten Street. Our entrance is through the garden at the back.'

'We'll be there now.' He ended the call.

'Mouton asked Geyser to come to his office. He'll be there in ten
minutes.'

'*Jissis*,' said Dekker, 'what an idiot.'

'Fransman, I will talk to Geyser, but you have to find the wife. I'll get
their home address from Mouton, then I'll call you. Commissioner, none of
this helps Vusi. Is there no one who can help him?'

'We can bring in Mbali Kaleni temporarily until you are free.'

'Shit,' said Vusi Ndabeni. Immediately he added, 'I'm sorry . . .'

'She's clever. And thorough,' said the Commissioner.

'She's a Zulu,' said Vusi.

'She's a pain in the *gat*,' said Dekker.

'She's all I have available,' said Afrika, 'and she's on Benny's mentor list.
She can coordinate from Caledon Square—I'll ask them to arrange something for her.'

He saw no relief on Vusi and Dekker's faces. 'It's only temporary, until
Benny can take over.'

As an afterthought he added, 'And you should be supporting our efforts
to develop more women in the Service.'

THE YOUNG BLACK MAN jogged through the trees of De Waal Park, to the waiting Land Rover Defender in Upper Orange Street.

'Nothing,' he said as he got in.

'Shit!' said the young white driver. He pulled away before the door was even properly shut. 'We have to get out of here. He will have called the cops.'

'Well, then, we'll have to get our own cops here too.'

The white man passed his cellphone to the black man. 'Make sure they know exactly where she disappeared. And get Barry down here. He's no use up the mountain any more. Tell him to go to the restaurant.'

GRIESSEL AND DEKKER walked to Loop Street together. 'What have you got against Inspector Kaleni?' Griessel asked.

'She's the fat one,' said Dekker, as if that explained everything. Griessel remembered her: short, very fat, severe as the sphinx.

'And . . .?' he said.

'We were at Bellville together and she irritates the living shit out of everyone. Bra-burning feminist, she thinks she knows everything, sucks up to the SC like you won't believe.' Dekker stopped. 'I'm this way.' He pointed down the street.

'Come to AfriSound when you're finished.'

Dekker wasn't finished yet: 'She has this *moerse* irritating habit of appearing out of nowhere, smelling of KFC, though you never see her eating the stuff.'

'Does your wife know?'

'Know what?'

'That you have the horny hots for Kaleni?'

Dekker threw back his head and laughed.

GRIESSEL TOOK OUT his phone and called.

'Mat Joubert,' said the familiar voice.

'I suggested to the Commissioner that we bring the Senior Superintendent in and he says, "Don't you know about Joubert yet?" What don't I know?'

'Benny . . .' Apologetic. 'I have to come to the city. I'll buy you coffee.'

'To tell me what?'

'I'll tell you when I see you. I don't want to do it over the phone.'

Then Griessel knew what it was. His heart sank. He climbed into his car and slammed the door hard. He turned the ignition. Nothing ever stayed the same. Everyone went away sooner or later.

His daughter. Gone to London. He had stood beside Anna at the airport watching Carla walk away, off on the Great Adventure. And he always stayed behind. Would he stay behind again tonight? If Anna didn't want him any more? Would he cope with that?

What if she said, 'OK, Benny, you're sober, you can come home again.'? What would he do then? Over the past few weeks he had started wondering about that. His feelings were complicated, he knew that. He still loved Anna. But he suspected he had been able to stop drinking precisely because he was alone, because he no longer took the violence and death home to his family every night. Because he didn't walk in the front door and see his wife and children and be stalked by the fear that they too would be found, bodies broken, hands rigid in the terrible fear of death.

But that wasn't the whole story.

They had been happy, he and Anna. Once upon a time. Before he began drinking. They had their little family world, just the two of them at first; then came Carla and Fritz and he had played on the carpet with his children and at night he had snuggled up to his wife, carefree, because the future was a predictable utopia, even though they were poor. Then he was promoted to Murder and Robbery, and the future slipped between his fingers, little by little, so slowly he didn't realise it, so subtly that he got up from a drunken stupor thirteen years later and realised it was all gone.

You could never get it back. You could never go back; that life, those circumstances were gone. You had to start over, but this time without the naivety, innocence and optimism of before, without the haze of being in love. You were different, you were stuck with the way you were now.

He didn't know if he could do it. He didn't know if he had the energy to go back to where every day was judgment day. Anna watching him when he came home at night. Did he smell of drink? He would come through the door knowing this, and he would see her anxiety until she was sure he was sober and then she would relax. It all felt too much, a burden he wasn't ready to bear.

In the past two months, he had begun to enjoy his life in the flat. The silence of his home when he opened the door, nobody watching and judging him. He could lie on the couch with his shoes on and snooze till eight o'clock and then stroll down to buy a Dagwood burger at Steers, then home to type an email to Carla with two fingers, a bite and a swallow in between. He could strum on his bass guitar and dream impossible dreams. Or he could return a dish to seventy-something Charmaine Watson-Smith whose food was delicious. Charmaine who had sent Bella around. And he had taken advantage of Bella and he was an adulterer, but it had been incredible. Everything has a price.

Perhaps Anna knew about Bella. Perhaps Anna was going to tell him tonight that he was an unfaithful bastard and she didn't want him any more. He wanted Anna to want him. But he didn't know if that was the right thing for him now. *Jissis*, why did life have to be so complicated?

10:10–11:02

V

'No,' said Inspector Mbali Kaleni with absolute finality.

Superintendent Cliffie Mketsu, Station Commander of Bellville, did not react. He knew he must wait until she had fired her salvo, his outspoken, principle-driven, stubborn female detective.

'What about the other women who have disappeared?' she asked. 'What about the Somali woman nobody wants to help me with? Why don't we call in the whole Service to work on *her* case?'

'You're right,' Mketsu said. 'But the Commissioner specifically asked for you. It's in the national interest.'

She gave an angry snort. 'National interest?'

'Tourism. It's our biggest industry and our greatest leverage for upliftment. They need you, Mbali.'

'But what about all the other women?'

'It's an imperfect world,' he said gently.

'It doesn't have to be,' she said and stood up.

AT TEN PAST THREE in the morning, Bill Anderson sat on the old two-seater leather couch in his study, his arm round his sobbing wife.

'They should never have gone,' said his wife. 'How many times did I tell them? Why couldn't they have gone to Europe?'

Anderson had no answer for her. He hugged her tighter.

The phone rang. 'Bill, it's Mike. I just got off the phone with the Congressman and he's going to get things moving right away. He's going to call both the US Ambassador in Pretoria and the Consul General in Cape Town to get whatever facts are available. He will ask the State Department for all the help they can give. So don't you worry, we are going to bring Rachel home.'

'Mike, I don't know how to thank you. Erin's parents . . .'

'We need it to be official, Bill, before we say anything.'

THE SERGEANT WALKED OUT of Carlucci's to his patrol vehicle and called the Caledon Square charge office. He reported that a young woman had been pursued by a white and a black man, but there was no sign of any of them.

'See if you can find something on a white Land Rover Discovery, registration number CA and the numbers four, one, six, that's all he could see. We'll look around a bit,' he said. Then he saw the second Metro Police car in minutes driving down Upper Orange. He recalled the two Metro foot patrols he had seen on the way here, probably looking for traffic offenders.

His shift partner came out of the shop and said, 'If you ask me, it's drugs.'

VUSI MET THE POLICE PHOTOGRAPHER at the Cat & Moose Youth Hostel and asked them to fetch Oliver Sands.

When Sands walked into the entrance hall, he still looked broken.

'I want to use that photograph of Erin and Rachel, please,' said Vusi.

'Sure,' said Sands.

'I can just take the memory card,' said the photographer.

'OK. I need fifty prints quickly.'

'I can't get the prints to you today,' said the photographer.

Vusi stared at the man. *You have to be tough*, Benny had said. But he wasn't like that. He would have to make another plan. Vusi muffled a sigh. 'Is tomorrow OK?'

'Tomorrow is better,' the photographer nodded.

Vusi took his phone out of his pocket and pressed a number in. 'When you hear the signal,' said a woman's voice, 'it will be ten eleven and forty seconds.'

'May I speak to Commissioner Afrika, please?' said Vusi. He whispered to the photographer. 'I just want to hear if the Commissioner will be angry if the girl is dead tomorrow.'

'What girl?' asked the photographer.

'The one in the photo. She is out there somewhere and there are people who want to kill her. If we only get the photographs tomorrow . . .'

'Hang on . . .' said the photographer.

The woman's voice said, 'Ten twelve exactly.'

'I didn't know,' he said. 'Twelve o'clock, that's the best I can do.'

Vusi ended the call. 'OK. Take the prints to Caledon Square and give them to Mbali Kaleni.'

THE METRO PATROL vehicle stopped beside the Land Rover Defender. Jeremy Oerson wound the window down and asked the young white man behind the wheel. 'Do you know what she's wearing, Jay?'

'Blue denim shorts, light blue T-shirt. And a backpack.'

'OK,' said Jeremy Oerson and reached for his radio. He nodded to the driver. 'Let's go,' he said.

GRIESSEL WALKED into the entrance at 16 Buiten Street. The building was built round an inner garden with paved pathways, a fishpond and a birdbath. On the wall of the south wing was the huge logo of AfriSound, a bird singing with a gaping beak against an orange sun. Griessel had no idea what kind of bird it was. He opened the door and walked inside. There were framed gold and platinum CDs and posters of artists on the walls. Griessel recognised some of the names. Behind a desk sat a middle-aged black woman, who looked up when he came in.

'You must be Inspector Griessel. Such a terrible thing, Mr Barnard . . .' Her eyes were red, as though she had been crying. She nodded in the direction of the stairs. 'They're waiting for you on the first floor.'

'Thank you.' Griessel climbed the stairs. The first floor was multicoloured but the atmosphere was sombre. No music, just the whisper of the air conditioning and the hushed voices of five or six people sitting round a big chrome coffee table. They turned to look at him. Everyone looked distressed, but there was no sign of Mouton. Some of the faces were familiar—he guessed they were musicians.

A coloured woman stood up from a desk. She was young and beautiful with high cheekbones. 'Inspector?'

'Benny Griessel,' he said, putting out a hand.

'Natasha Abader.' Her hand was small. 'I am Mr Mouton's PA. Please come with me.'

'Thank you,' said Griessel and followed her down the corridor.

Natasha knocked on Mouton's door and put her head in. 'Inspector Griessel is here.'

Griessel went in. Mouton and his lawyer, Groenewald, sat stretched out like two magnates on either side of a large desk. The lawyer put out a half-hearted hand. 'Regardt Groenewald.'

'Benny Griessel. Is that Geyser out front?'

'No, they are in the conference room.' Mouton gestured with his head towards the far end of the corridor. 'He brought Melinda along.'

Griessel could not mask his annoyance. 'We want to question them separately.' He took out his cellphone. 'My colleague thought she would be at home. I have to call him.'

He found Dekker's number and called. 'How much does Geyser know?' he asked while it rang.

'Nothing yet. But you can see he's guilty. Sweating like a pig.'

'Benny,' said Dekker over the phone.

'Things have changed,' said Griessel.

MORE THAN 1,300 KILOMETRES to the north, in Pretoria, the telephone of the Acting National Police Commissioner made a single growling noise. He picked it up.

'The Deputy Minister wants to talk to you,' said his secretary.

He hesitated for a second before pushing the 'Line 1' button. He knew it would not be good news. 'Good morning, Minister,' he said.

''Morning, Commissioner,' she said and he could hear she wasn't over-joyed. 'I just had a call from the US Consul General in Cape Town.'

THE FRONT DOOR of Van Hunks in Castle Street was locked. Vusi found the service alley at the back and walked in past men unloading crates of beer from a lorry and carrying them into the kitchen. A white man with a short black ponytail was supervising the unloading. He spotted Vusi.

'Hey!' he said. 'What do you want?' Aggressive, with a slight accent.

Vusi held out his SAPS identity card. 'I would like to speak to the manager.'

'She is busy.'

'Can you take me to her, please? I am investigating a murder, and the victim was in this club last night.'

Ponytail weighed him up. 'Down the passage. Third door right.'

'Thank you,' said Vusi, and walked out of the room.

WILLIE MOUTON HELD the door to the conference room open for Griessel. The Geysers were seated at the long oval table, holding hands. Benny had imagined two young bubbly angelic faces but the Geysers were on the wrong side of forty. Josh was a big man with white-blond hair and a styled crew cut. Beside him Melinda looked tiny, like a doll, with her round face and red-blonde hair in a cascade of tight curls.

'Willie,' said Josh Geyser getting to his feet. 'What's going on?'

'This is Sergeant Benny Griessel of the police, Josh. He would like to talk to you.'

Griessel put out a hand. 'Inspector,' he said.

Geyser ignored Griessel's hand. 'Why?' he demanded.

'Adam is dead, Josh.'

An invisible hand wiped the scowl from Geyser's face. Griessel watched him pale. The big man's shock seemed genuine.

'He was shot yesterday at his house,' said Mouton.

'Oh heavens!' Melinda cried out.

'I would like to talk to you alone, Mr Geyser,' said Griessel.

'Melinda, won't you wait in my office?' asked Mouton.

'I'm staying with Josh.'

'Mrs Geyser, I am afraid that I must speak with him alone.'

'She stays,' said Geyser.

VUSI FOUND THE MANAGER in a small, untidy office. She was typing figures into a large adding machine, painted nails pecking at the keys with lightning speed. Forty, maybe, short black hair, strong features, but hard.

Vusi held out his identification and introduced himself.

'Galina Federova.' She shook Vusi's hand with a self-assured grip. 'Why are you here?' in the same accented English as Ponytail's.

Vusi gave her a quick outline of the case.

She found a packet of cigarettes. 'You know how many people last night? Maybe two hundred, maybe more. We are very poplar.'

'Are you the owner?'

'That is Gennady Demidov. I just manage.'

Vusi scribbled a note. 'Till what time are you open?'

'The door close at twelve on a Monday night. But those inside, they can stay. We close the bar when everybody go home.'

'This morning, at two fifteen, did you still have people?'

'I must ask the night manager. Petr.'

'Can you call him?'

'He sleeps.'

'You will have to wake him up.'

She drew on the cigarette and blew the smoke out through her nose. Then she began to rifle through invoices on her desk, searching for the phone. He wondered how on earth untidy people managed to function.

GRIESSEL WALKED CLOSER to Josh Geyser. 'Mr Geyser, let me explain your choices: we can sit here, just the two of us, and talk quietly . . .'

'Regardt and I will be here too, Josh, don't worry . . .' Willie Mouton said behind him.

'No,' said Griessel, taken aback. 'It doesn't work like that.'

'Of course it does. He has the right . . .'

Griessel turned round slowly, his patience wearing thin. The lawyer, Groenewald, came down the passage behind Mouton, seeming to know he needed to help.

Benny looked for patience and found a fraction. 'Mr Geyser, this is an interview, not an arrest. Do you want Groenewald to be present?'

Geyser looked to Melinda. She shook her head. 'He's Willie's lawyer.'

'I am available,' Groenewald said primly.

'I insist on it,' said Mouton. 'Both of us . . .'

Griessel knew it was time to tackle Mouton. He walked purposefully up to the shaven-headed man, the official words ready on his tongue, but Groenewald jumped in between the two men. 'Willie, if he locks you up for obstruction, there is nothing I can do for you. Let's go and wait in your office.'

Mouton walked to the door. He called over his shoulder, 'You have rights, Josh.' Then they were gone.

Griessel turned his attention to the duo. 'Mr Geyser, do you want legal representation?'

He looked to his wife. She shook her head slightly. She was the one with the final say.

'I don't want anybody,' said Josh. 'Let's get this over with.'

'Ma'am, please, would you wait in Mouton's office?'

'I'll be in the lounge.' She touched Josh's arm, gave him a weighted look. '*Beertjie . . .*' she said. *My little bear.* She was wearing jeans and a sea-green blouse that echoed the colour of her eyes. Ten kilograms ago her body must have been sensational.

'It's all right, *Pokkel*,' said Josh, but there was tension between them, Griessel could sense it.

She looked back once and closed the door softly behind her.

Griessel switched off his phone. 'Mr Geyser, sit, please.' He gestured to one of the chairs.

Josh didn't move. 'Tell me first: are you a child of God?'

THE PROVINCIAL COMMISSIONER SAPS Western Cape walked rapidly down the long corridor. He was a Xhosa, dressed in full uniform. He came to a standstill at the open office door of John Afrika.

'John, the National Commissioner has just phoned. Do we know about an American girl who died last night?'

'We know,' said Afrika. 'I was wondering when the trouble would start.'

The Provincial Commissioner sat down. 'The girl's friend phoned her father in America half an hour ago and said someone is trying to kill her too.'

'*Bliksem*. Did she say where she was?'

'Apparently not. The father said she had to run away before she had finished talking.'

'I'll have to let Benny and Vusi know. And Mbali,' said John Afrika as he picked up his phone.

GALINA FEDEROVA SPOKE over the phone in Russian then held it out for Vusi. 'Petr. You can talk with him.'

The detective took the phone. 'My name is Vusi. I want to know if something happened in the club this morning, between two o'clock and two fifteen. Two American girls, and some young men. We have them on video, running up Long Street, and we have people who say they were in the club.'

'There were many people,' said Petr, his accent much lighter than the woman's.

'I know, but did anybody notice anything? An argument. A fight.'

'I don't know. I was in the office.'

'Who would know?'

'The barmen and the waiters.'

'I need you to call them, sir. I need all of them to come to the club.'

Petr sighed deeply on the other end. 'It will take a lot of time.'

'We don't have time, sir. One of the girls is still alive and if we don't find her, she will be dead too.'

Vusi's mobile began to ring.

'One hour,' said Petr.

'Ask them to come to the club,' said Vusi, and passed the receiver back to Fedorova. He answered his cellphone.

'She's still alive,' said Afrika. 'She phoned her father half an hour ago. But I can't get hold of Benny.'

RACHEL SPRINTED down Upper Orange Street. Her eyes searched desperately for an escape route, but the houses on both sides were impregnable— high walls, electrified fences, security gates. Her father's voice had given her new urgency, a desire to live, to see her parents again.

She saw one house just a block from the shop on the corner, a single-storey Victorian dwelling with a white picket fence. She knew it was her only chance. She hurdled the hip-high fence but the tip of her shoe hooked and sent her sprawling into the flowerbed beyond, the damp garden soil leaving a wide muddy stripe on her blue T-shirt.

She scrambled up quickly, meaning to run round the house, away from the street before they saw her. Past the farthest corner of the house there were bougainvilleas, big and dense. A hiding place. She hesitated for only an instant, not realising the bushes had thorns. She dived inside, to the deepest shadow at the back. The sharp points scratched long bloody tracks on her arms and legs. She cried out softly in pain, and lay gasping behind the screen of leaves. 'Please, God,' she murmured and turned her face to the street. She could see nothing, only the thick curtain of green, and the tiny white flowers in each purple cup.

If they hadn't seen her, she was safe. For now.

'LET ME PHONE the American Consul,' the Provincial Commissioner said to John Afrika as he rose. 'I'm going to tell him we are doing everything in our power to track her down. Get Benny Griessel to take full control.'

'Right. But the stations are reluctant to allocate people . . .'

'Leave that to me,' said the Provincial Commissioner. 'Isn't Griessel up for promotion?'

'It's been approved; I think he'll be notified today.'

'Tell him. Tell the whole team.'

'Good idea.' Afrika's phone rang. 'John Afrika.'

'Commissioner, this is Inspector Mbali Kaleni. I am at Caledon Square, but they say they don't have a place for me.'

'Mbali, the Station Commander is going to get a call right now.'

'Yes, sir,' she said.

'The missing girl called home half an hour ago.'

'Where is she?'

'She did not have enough time to say. We need to find her quickly.'

'I will find her, Commissioner.' So self-assured.

'WOULD YOU LIKE to tell ME what happened yesterday?' Griessel sat down on the other side of the oval table, with his face towards the door. The big man was sitting down now, elbows on the table.

'It wasn't me.' He didn't look at Griessel.

'Mr Geyser, let's start at the beginning. Apparently there was an incident—'

'What would you do if a son of Satan messed with your woman?'

'Mr Geyser, how did you find out that Adam Barnard and your wife . . .'

'We're all sinners. But he had no remorse. Idols. Mammon. Whoring.'

'Mr Geyser, how did you find out?' With infinite patience.

'Yesterday when she came home, she didn't look well, so I asked what was wrong. First she said "nothing". She couldn't look me in the eye. That's when I knew something was very wrong . . .'

'What time was that?'

'Three o'clock, round about. I held her hands and she started crying.

Then she said, "Let us pray, *Beertjie*, Lord, forgive me because Satan got into my life today." So I said, "*Pokkel*, what happened?" Then she said she had sinned in Adam Barnard's office, because she couldn't stop the devil, and I said what kind of sin, and she said, "of the flesh, *Beertjie*, the big sin of the flesh . . ."' Geyser stopped, with both hands over his face.

Griessel sat there suppressing the urge to console. In twenty-five years he had learned to be sceptical. People could lie with astonishing skill; sometimes it led to total self-deception, so that they clung with absolute conviction to an imaginary innocence.

So he did nothing. He just waited for Josh Geyser to finish crying.

GALINA FEDEROVA PRESSED a switch and neon lights flickered on near the roof of the club, enough to cloak the large space in twilight. 'You can wait here,' she said to Vusi and pointed at the tables and chairs around the dance floor. 'Would you like something to drink?'

'Do you have tea?'

He walked between the tables and sat down. Against the wall was the long bar counter. Right at the back was a bank of turntables and electronic equipment, with a dance floor in front. High up against the ceiling hung bunches of lasers and spotlights, all dark now. Giant speakers were mounted on every wall.

He tried to imagine how it had been last night. Hundreds of people, loud music, dancing bodies, flickering lights. And now it was empty and spooky.

He felt uneasy in this place. In this city too. It was the people, he thought. Khayelitsha had often broken his heart with its pointless murders, the domestic violence, the terrible poverty. But he had been welcome there, people respected him, stood by him, supported him. In this city it was all antagonism and suspicion. As if he was some intruder.

'No respect,' his mother would say. 'That's the problem with the new world.' Vusi thought of Tiffany October, the slim young pathologist. She had the same soft eyes as his mother, the same gentle voice.

He thought of phoning her, but his guts contracted. Would she go out with a Xhosa? He looked for the mortuary number in his notebook. It rang for a long time before the switchboard answered. He took a deep breath to say, 'May I speak to Dr October?' But his courage failed him; he cancelled the call in panic.

He cursed himself and immediately phoned Vaughn Cupido, the only member of the Organised Crime Task Force that he knew. Vusi asked if they knew anything about Gennady Demidov. Cupido whistled through his teeth. 'Brother, the city belongs to him—prostitution, drugs, money-laundering. . .'

'I have an American tourist, about nineteen, whose throat was cut last night up in Long Street. But earlier she had been in his club, Van Hunks.'

'It's drugs, Vusi. Sounds to me like a deal that went wrong. They do that, the Russians. Show your network you don't take shit.'

'But the girl arrived here only yesterday, first time in Cape Town. She's no dealer.'

'She must be a mule. They bring the drugs in. On planes, fishing trawlers, any way they can.'

'Ah,' said Vusi. 'So she probably didn't deliver what she was meant to.'

'Something like that. I can't say what happened, but it's drugs . . .'

THE STATION COMMANDER of Caledon Square walked down the passage behind Inspector Mbali Kaleni, unable to hide his displeasure. Ten minutes ago his police station had been functioning normally. Then she waddles in, orders everyone around, demanding an office that he didn't have. Next minute he was being *kakked* on by the Provincial Commissioner, accusing him of bringing the Service into disrepute.

They walked into the charge office. She looked like an overstuffed pigeon—short, with a big bulge in front and a big bulge behind in her tight black trouser suit. Large handbag over her shoulder, service pistol in a thick black belt around her hips.

She stopped in the middle of the room and clapped sharply, twice. 'Listen up, people,' she said loudly, in her Zulu accent. Silence descended, everyone paid attention: complainants, their companions, uniforms.

'My name is Inspector Mbali Kaleni. There is an American tourist missing in the city, a nineteen-year-old girl, maybe in Camps Bay. There are people trying to kill her. We must find her. I am in control of the operation. So I want you to get every vehicle out there, and make sure they get the message. They must come and collect a photo of the girl after twelve o'clock. The Provincial Commissioner has made a personal call to your Station Commander. . .'

'Inspector . . .' said the constable who had taken the Carlucci's call.

'I am not finished,' she said.

'I know where she is,' he said, not intimidated, making his commanding officer proud. 'She's not in Camps Bay, she's in Oranjezicht.'

VUSI PHONED BENNY GRIESSEL, but the detective's phone was on voice-mail. 'Benny, it's Vusi. I think the two girls brought drugs in that they were supposed to deliver to Van Hunks. I'm waiting for the barmen and waiters, but I know they're not going to talk. I think we must bring Organised Crime in. Call me, please.'

He looked at his notes again. What else could he do?

The video cameras.

He phoned the Metro Police video control room and was eventually put through to the Owl.

'I can tell you they came from the lower end of Long Street. The camera on the corner of Longmarket and Long shows two girls walking past at 01:39.'

'*Walking* past?'

'They were walking fast, but definitely not running. But at time code 01:39:42 you can see the men coming past. I can see five of them running in the same direction, north to south.'

'After the girls?'

'That's right.'

So, 200 metres from the club, they were still walking, unaware of the men chasing them. He made a note in his book. What else? They must search Rachel Anderson's luggage for drugs. But would it help? The laboratory was six months behind. Understaffed.

Later. First they must find Rachel Anderson.

FRANSMAN DEKKER hesitated in AfriSound's reception until the beautiful coloured woman got up and approached him.

'Inspector Fransman Dekker.' He held out his hand. 'I am sorry for your loss.'

She lowered her eyes. 'Natasha Abader. Thank you.' Her hand felt small and cool in his. 'Inspector Griessel is in the conference room.' Her inspection of his fingers for a ring was smooth and practised. She gave nothing away when she saw the thin gold band, but looked him in the eye.

'Can I offer you some coffee? Tea? Anything.' The last was said with a measured smile, perfect white teeth.

'No, thank you,' he replied and looked away. He didn't want to start something now.

'I'M SORRY,' said Josh Geyser. 'It's just . . . she's everything to me.'

'I understand,' said Griessel.

'I was nothing. Then she took me . . .' Geyser started at the beginning. Griessel let him talk.

Geyser had been on the wrong road, he said. He had been a Gladiator on TV—women, drink, cocaine and steroids. A celebrity. Then the SABC cancelled the show. Seven months later he could no longer afford the rent, the bank took back the BMW and his friends weren't his friends any more. Then he found the House of Faith, the big charismatic church in Bryanston, Johannesburg, and his whole life changed. Because it was genuine. Everything. The friendships, the love, the compassion, the concern, the forgiveness for what he had been.

One day the pastor said they needed baritones for the church choir. Josh could always sing, since he was a boy. He had the feel for harmony, but his life had taken other directions. So he became a Praise Singer—and on the first day he saw Melinda, this pretty woman with the angel face.

After practice she came to him and said, 'I know you, you're White Lightning.' He said not any more, and then her eyes went all soft and she said, 'Come' and took his hand. In the church coffee bar they exchanged stories. She was a former singer in her ex-husband's band, with a life full of sin. After the divorce she had been rudderless. The House of Faith was her salvation. They both knew it straightaway that night. But when you've been so down, you are careful; you talk first, long hours in the safety of the church social spot.

One day, three weeks later, they were there after choir practice when she asked, 'Do you know "Down to the River to Pray", the Negro spiritual?' and she began to sing the melody until he had it and began to sing in harmony. They sang quietly, just the two of them, looking into each other's eyes, because they knew these two voices were perfectly matched. 'It was magic,' said Josh. 'Like a shaft of light from heaven. That's where it all began.'

'I see. Mr Geyser—'

'Our first CD came out on a small gospel label. Then Adam Barnard came to talk to us, said we were too good to be hidden away. So we signed and came to Cape Town. I heard about his ways only then.'

'What ways?'

The door opened. Dekker put a head inside.

Griessel stood up. 'Excuse me just a moment.' He went to the door and pulled it shut behind him. He didn't want interruptions like this now.

'I just wanted to tell you I'm here. They're looking for a place where I can talk to Melinda.'

Natasha, the beautiful personal assistant, came down the passage. 'Fransman, you can sit in the studio. Give us ten minutes.'

Griessel raised his eyebrows. 'First-name terms already . . .'

Dekker shrugged, 'Story of my life.'

PONYTAIL BROUGHT in a tray with a teapot and the necessary tea things. He put it down three tables away from Vusi and walked out again.

Vusi stood up and went over to the tray. They would all be like this, the Van Hunks employees. Aggressive and unhelpful. It was a waste of time, because the theory of the drug mules made sense.

He poured tea into a cup, then carried the whole tray over to his table.

Sands had said that Anderson had suddenly changed at Lake Kariba. That must have been when they got the drugs. Or realised they had gone? That might be it. She and Erin were to bring the drugs, because tourists were waved easily through the border posts. It might not be their first time.

And then something happened, or they sold it somewhere else, and then they came and told Demidov here at the club, or Galina or Petr. Then they walked back to the youth hostel and a minute or two later Demidov sent his thugs to make an example of them. They caught Erin and cut her throat.

It was Demidov's people hunting Anderson now. The question was, how did he stop them? He must try Griessel again. He picked up his phone and punched in the number. Voicemail again.

JOSH GEYSER told Griessel he had just let go of Melinda's hands, right there in the sitting room, because from then on he was like a man possessed. He drove here and rushed in, ready to break Adam Barnard's neck, he couldn't deny it.

'You admit that you went into Willie Mouton's office and threatened to kill Adam Barnard?'

'I went to Adam's office first. But he wasn't there. Then I went to Willie's and told him I was going to kill Adam. But Adam wasn't there. What could I do?'

'What *did* you do?'

'I went looking for him. Café Zanne and the Bizerca Bistro. That's where he hangs out at lunch times.'

'Did you find him?'

'No, thank the Lord.'

'And then?'

'Then the devil left me. It was the traffic. I got stuck in the traffic. That's when the devil left me.'

'Josh, did you go straight home?'

Geyser just nodded.

'Do you own a firearm?'

He shook his head. No.

'Where were you from midnight last night?'

'With Melinda. We went to church last night. The Tabernacle.'

'Until what time?'

'Half past ten. After the service we went to see the pastor for counselling. Then we went home.'

'Josh, did you leave the house last night?'

'No. I went out again only this morning. When Willie phoned.'

Griessel looked at Geyser intently. He recognised the simplicity of this giant, the childish honesty. He didn't know if he could believe him. He got up and said, 'You will have to wait here, Josh, if you don't mind.'

DEKKER ASKED Melinda Geyser to sit on one of the chairs in the recording studio, but when he closed the door and turned round she was still standing.

'Ma'am, this will take a while. It's better if you sit.'

'You don't understand . . . I can't talk to you about yesterday . . .'

The way she said it made him suspicious. 'To me?' His voice cut like a knife. She couldn't look at him, confirming his suspicion. 'Is it because I'm coloured?'

'No, no, I can't talk . . . to a man.'

Dekker heard the way she said it, like someone who had been caught out. He saw the flicker in her eyes. 'You're lying,' the anger flaring quickly in him. He rose from the chair. 'Your kind . . .' he said, other words welling up behind the rage, but somehow he found control.

'Please . . .' she said.

He despised her. He walked out of the door. Benny was in the passage with his phone to his ear saying, 'Vusi, I trust the guys from Organised Crime as far as I can throw them.'

BARRY SAT on the verandah of Carlucci's and listened to the sirens approaching through the city below. He saw a young man in an apron who heard them too, and came outside.

The four patrol vehicles raced up Upper Orange and stopped in front of the restaurant with a screech of tyres. A short, fat, black woman with a large handbag over her shoulder and a pistol on her hip came quickly across the street, a horde of blue uniforms in her wake.

The young man in the apron waited for them.

'Are you the man who called in about the girl?' Barry heard the black woman ask. 'Tell me everything.'

AT SEVENTEEN MINUTES to four in the morning, American Eastern Standard time—seven hours behind Cape Town—Bill Anderson sat at his desk reading Internet articles about South Africa. His wife, Jess, sat on the couch behind him, her legs covered with a blanket. She jumped when the phone rang.

He grabbed it. 'Bill Anderson,' he said.

'Mr Anderson, my name is Dan Burton. I am the US Consul General in Cape Town.' The voice rang as clear as crystal despite the distance. 'I know what a difficult time this must be for you.'

'Who is it?' Jess asked, coming to stand close to her husband. He held a hand over the receiver and whispered, 'The Consul General in Cape Town.' Then he held the phone so she could also hear.

'I can tell you that I've just got off the phone with both the National and Provincial Commissioners of the South African Police Services, and although they have not found Rachel yet . . .'

Jess Anderson made a small noise and her husband put his arm round her shoulders.

'. . . they are allocating every available resource to the search and think it is only a matter of time.'

'Thank you, sir. Our biggest concern is that Rachel said something about the police when she called.'

'Oh?'

'She said that she could not even go to the police.'

The Consul General was quiet for a moment. 'Did she say why?'

'She did not have time. But the way she spoke about the police . . . it was my impression that she could not trust them. And I've been doing some reading on the Internet. It says here the man in charge of the whole police force over there is being charged with corruption . . .'

'Well, I know how it looks, Mr Anderson, but I have every reason to believe the law enforcement people in Cape Town are competent and trustworthy. I will call the Commissioner right away to get some answers. I've taken the liberty of giving your phone number to the authorities. The Commissioner has assured me the officer in charge of the investigation will call you as soon as he can. His name is Ghreezil, an Inspector Benny Ghreezil.'

'Ask about Erin,' whispered Jess Anderson.

'Mr Burton. . . Is there any news about Erin?'

'It is with great sadness that I have to tell you that Miss Russel was killed last night.' His wife pressed her face into his neck and wept.

INSPECTOR MBALI KALENI told the uniformed policemen that Carlucci's was to be treated as a crime scene. She had the area cordoned off, then she cleared the restaurant and had the employees and clients wait while two constables took statements. She asked the young man in the apron to confirm in what direction the girl and her assailants had run. She led the way out of the restaurant, to the corner of Upper Orange and Belmont. The young man pointed towards the city centre. 'You saw her run that way?'

'I didn't see her run in any other direction, so she must have gone down Upper Orange. The guys came back through the shop, ran down to the corner, and then came back for the Land Rover. They went that way too.'

She looked at the street again. Why would they come back for the Land Rover? Two young men, chasing a girl from two o'clock that morning. She must be exhausted, but they didn't run after her, they came back for a vehicle? Made no sense.

She turned round slowly, looking down every street. They couldn't see her any more; that was it. The two attackers would have pursued her on foot if they could see her. She had disappeared; that was why they fetched the vehicle.

Kaleni called two young constables who were leaning against a police van. She told them to go out the back of the restaurant as far as the wooden door, which was still bolted shut.

'And when I say "go", you run back through the shop, out through the front door, until you get to me. Ask that guy with the apron exactly where they ran, then you follow the same route. You understand?'

'Yes, Inspector.'

'OK.' Kaleni walked round the outside to the wooden door. She waited until she could hear the constables' footsteps in the alleyway on the other side of the door. 'Are you right next to the door?'

'Yes.'

She checked her watch, waited until the second hand was close to the twelve o'clock mark. She counted down from five to one, then barked, 'Go!' She heard them take off. She watched the second hand travel ten, fifteen, twenty, then the constables came round the corner. Twenty-four seconds to reach her.

'OK. Now, I want you to start from this door and run down the streetas fast as you can,' she said, her eyes on the watch. She waited for the twelve mark again and shouted, 'Go!' They sprinted away and she kept an eye on them and the watch. The young man had said the attackers had pushed him over. Add one second for that, maybe two. They might have run outside and, not knowing in which direction the girl had gone, stopped and looked up Upper Orange and to the right down Belmont. Another two or three seconds.

She marked the constables' progress at twenty-four and thirty seconds, then yelled at them, 'OK!', but they were out of earshot and kept on running, two blue uniforms in full flight down the long hill.

'*Isidomu,*' she muttered and began to walk down the street herself, keeping her eyes on the thirty-second mark.

RACHEL ANDERSON HEARD the sirens racing up the street only twenty metres from where she lay in the bougainvillea bush. She knew they were for her because the man in the restaurant would surely have called the police.

And she could hear how the wailing stopped nearby, just up on the corner.

She lay still. They wouldn't be able to see her, even if they came into the garden. She would wait until they stopped looking. Until they went away. Then she would decide what to do.

MBALI KALENI WALKED to the corner of Upper Orange and Alexandra Avenue—more or less the twenty-four-second mark. She walked slowly across the road to the opposite pavement. The girl must have turned left here into Alexandra. That was why the men couldn't see her.

Something wasn't right.

She stared up Alexandra Avenue. The slope. A very tired girl. She was on her way down, to the city. So would she get here and choose a street that led away from her destination? It was uphill, steep; it would be hell on tired legs.

Deep in thought, Kaleni rested her hand on the white picket fence of the single-storey Victorian house on her left. She looked for the two running uniformed idiots. Yes, there they were, walking back, chatting happily.

Rachel Anderson had to have turned this corner. Or . . . Kaleni considered the Victorian house, looked at the fence. It was the only house in this part of the street without high walls or fences—the only alternative.

That's when she saw the damage to the flowerbed. The ground cover was scraped away in a broad swathe. The palm prints were there, footprints beyond. She judged the distance between the fence and the damage. Could someone climb over here? And land *there*?

She walked on, looking for the garden gate, and found it. She jogged over to it, an odd, hurried figure with a handbag over her shoulder and pistol on her hip.

'I'M NOT WHITE enough for her,' Fransman Dekker said when Griessel concluded his call with Vusi.

'What?' said Griessel, his attention on the phone. 'Sorry, Fransman, I have four more messages . . .' He put it to his ear again. 'I'll be finished soon.'

Dekker took two steps down the passage. 'It's because I'm a *hotnot*. Hypocritical gospel singers . . .'

'I have to phone the Commissioner back,' Griessel said apologetically. 'The girl phoned her father in America . . . Commissioner, it's Benny . . .'

Dekker stopped at the studio door and pressed a palm against it.

Griessel said 'Yes, sir' and 'No, sir' over the phone, until at last, 'I'm on my way.' He switched off the phone again. 'She won't talk to you because you're coloured?' he asked Dekker.

'That's not what she says, but it's what she means.'

'She can get a lawyer, and she can ask for a woman to be present, those are her choices . . .'

'You tell her.'

'That's exactly what I'm going to do,' said Griessel.

And then the lights went out.

VUSI WAS RESTLESS. He drank the last of the tea. How long would it be before Petr had his staff awake? What was Mbali doing with his case up at the restaurant? That was where the action was. There was nothing going on here.

Then the big room went dark. Another power cut. Yesterday it had lasted for three hours. Pitch black. He could see nothing. He had to get out. He felt for his cellphone, pressed a key to light up the screen and got up. He walked carefully between the tables and chairs, down the passage. A faint yellow band of light shone out of Galina Federova's office. She had lit a candle.

'I'm sorry,' he said. 'I will have to go. The girl was seen.' Vusi took a business card out of his pocket and put it down in front of her. 'Please, would you call me when the people from last night arrive?'

Using his cellphone as a torch, he walked back through the kitchen, into the alley, where the sunlight was blinding. His car was up in Long Street, more than ten minutes' walk. He wanted to talk to Mbali at the restaurant, he wanted . . . There was something he could do, even if Benny said he didn't want Organised Crime involved. He chose Vaughn Cupido's number.

'Do you have photos of Demidov's people?'

'I'm just an Inspector. You will have to ask higher up.'

'Vaughn, we have a man who saw two of the attackers in Oranjezicht just now. If he can ID Demidov's people . . . It could save the girl's life.'

'Let me get back to you . . .'

RACHEL HEARD the click-click of a woman's shoes on the garden path just metres away from her. The noise stopped abruptly, then she heard someone knocking loudly. 'Hello, anybody home?' in an African accent, a woman, urgent. What did it mean? 'Hey, guys!' the same voice barked, authoritarian. 'I called you back, but you did not hear.'

A man's voice answered from the street, then the same African woman, 'No, stay on the pavement, this might be a crime scene. Tell them I need Forensics. Shoe imprints, I want them cast and identified.'

Then there was the sound of a door opening and a man's voice, 'Can I help you?'

'I am Inspector Mbali Kaleni of the SAPS. We are looking for a girl who is running away from assailants and I think she was in your garden. I want to know if you saw her.'

'When did this happen?'

'About forty minutes ago. Can you please come and look at your garden? You did not see her?'

'No. But I heard her . . .' Rachel's heart went cold. 'I heard her run to the wall there, I think she jumped over, to the next house. By the time I looked through the window, she was gone.'

'Take a look at the tracks,' said the policewoman.

There was a moment of relief as the voices faded, but then she remembered falling in the flowerbed when she jumped over the wall. She had stepped in damp ground; mud might have stuck to the grass or the slate of the path. She heard the woman's footsteps on the path again. She kept dead still and closed her eyes.

GRIESSEL OPENED THE DOOR of the AfriSound recording studio angrily. John Afrika had told him to hurry; they were waiting for him. The room was pitch dark, as it had no windows. The shaft of light from the open door illuminated Melinda; she stood with big, frightened eyes, her hands folded across her breast. Bambi in Danger. He said, 'The power is off,' and she dropped her hands. Had she thought the darkened room was a ploy?

He went up to her and said with all the patience he could muster, 'Madam, you will have to talk to Inspector Dekker. With or without your lawyer. That is your choice. You can request that a female officer be present.'

She thought for a moment. Then she said, 'He misunderstood me. I meant only it would be easier to talk to a woman about it. I just want to be sure it's confidential.'

He explained to her that if she or Josh were charged, nothing could be confidential.

'But we didn't do anything.'

'Then it will all be confidential.' So she agreed and Natasha brought in a gas lamp. Griessel and Dekker watched Natasha walk away.

Then Benny pulled his colleague by the arm as far as Adam Barnard's empty office. 'John Afrika says I must bring Mbali Kaleni in to help you.'

Dekker exploded. He stood up straight, his eyes wild, his mouth opening and closing and he hammered his fist against Adam Barnard's door.

'Fransman! It stays *your* case.'

The coloured detective stopped, eyes staring, arms still up in the air.

'I've got a son in Matric,' said Griessel. 'He's always telling me, "Pa you must chill" and I think that is what you must do now, Fransman. You let everything wind you up. It doesn't help.'

'You would never understand. You're white.'

'What is that supposed to mean?'

'It means you're not coloured,' he said. 'Did you see last week with the Commissioner? How many coloureds were there?'

'You were the only one.'

'Yes, just me. Because they push the darkies. That's why they are sending Kaleni. I'm just a statistic, Benny, I'm just there to fill their quota. Did you watch the Commissioner on Thursday? He had eyes only for the bloody Xhosas, he didn't even see me. Eight per cent coloureds. That's how many of us they want. Do you know how many brown people that has ruined? Thousands, I'm telling you. Not black enough, sorry, brother, off you go, get a job with Coin Security. But not me, Benny. It's my *fokken* life.'

Griessel said, 'I do understand, Fransman, but . . .'

'You think so? Have you been marginalised all your life? We weren't white enough then, we're not black enough now; it never ends, stuck in the middle of the colour palette. Now this white Christian lady says no, she's not talking to a man, but I can read her like I can read all the whiteys.'

'Can you read *me*, Fransman?' Griessel was growing angry too. 'They say you've got ambition. Now listen to me, I threw my career away because I let the shit get to me. That's why I'm standing here now. I didn't have any more options. Do you want options, Fransman? Or do you still want to be an inspector at forty-four, with a job description that says "mentor" because they don't know what to do with you? Do you want to be the best policeman you can be? Then take the case and solve it, never mind how they talk to you or who John Afrika sends to help you. In any case, it won't change. I have been a policeman for over twenty-five years and I'm telling you now, they will always treat you like a dog, regardless of whether you are black, white or brown. Unless they're phoning you in the middle of the night saying "there's someone at the window"—then you're the hero. But tomorrow when the sun shines, you're nothing again. The question is: can you take it? If you can't, get another job. Or put up with it, Fransman, because it's never going to stop.'

Dekker stood still, breathing heavily. Griessel stepped away from him, his brain at work, shifting his focus. 'I don't believe it was Josh Geyser. If he's lying, he deserves an Oscar. Melinda is the only alibi he has. Let her talk, get her to give you more detail about yesterday, then phone me and we can compare their stories. I have to go and see the Commissioner.'

Dekker didn't look at him. Griessel walked away down the passage.

'Benny,' said Dekker when he was almost in the reception area. Griessel turned. 'Thank you,' Dekker said, with reluctant frankness.

Griessel gestured with his hand and left.

He jogged down the stairs, across the grass to where his car was parked. There was a parking ticket stuck to the windscreen. Frustration surged over his wall of self-control. More paperwork that he didn't need. Metro Police had time to write parking tickets, but don't ask them to help with anything else. He left the ticket right where it was, climbed in, started the engine and reversed out.

He was going to ask the Commissioner for a clear job description. Benny Griessel, Great Mentor, just didn't work for him. He had asked Afrika last Thursday exactly what this job entailed. The answer: 'Benny, you're my safety net. Just keep an eye, check the crime scene management, don't let them miss suspects. We train them until it's coming out of everybody's ears, but the minute they stand on the scene, either it's stage fright or just plain sloppiness, I don't know. Look over shoulders, Benny, give a gentle nudge where necessary.' A gentle nudge? He had to brake suddenly for the traffic jam up ahead, two rows of cars, ten deep. The power cut meant all the traffic lights were down. Chaos. He leaned back against the seat. It wouldn't help to get angry. But what were you supposed to do? From one case to the next.

That was a recipe for a disaster. He suddenly had a desire to smoke. He opened the cubbyhole, found a half-packet of Chesterfields and lit one.

This morning Alexa Barnard had offered him a cigarette and he had said no. He was trying to cut down because his AA sponsor was a doctor. Then she said get another sponsor. He liked her. He should never have given her the alcohol.

And then he remembered that he wanted to atone for his mistake. He found the phone and pressed the keys with his thumb. It rang for a long time, as usual.

'Benny!' said Doc Barkhuizen, always upbeat. 'Are you persevering?'

'Doc, you ever heard of the famous singer Xandra Barnard?'

'THEY'RE TAKING a lot of interest in a house here,' said Barry over the cell-phone. He drove slowly down Upper Orange in his beat-up bakkie—a red Toyota pick-up. 'There's a thousand uniformed Constables on the pavement, and this fat woman detective standing in the garden with a geriatric guy.'

'So find out what it's about.'

Barry looked at the houses on the street. On the right, a hundred metres down and opposite, the Victorian house was a possibility. A long driveway to a single garage. 'Yeah . . .' He saw the uniforms watching him. 'Maybe. But right now there are too many eyes. Let me give it ten minutes.'

11:03–12:00

VI

The hissing gas lamp that stood on the bench threw an absurd shadow of Melinda Geyser onto the opposite wall. She stood with her face only cen-timetres from the glass. Dekker leaned forward in a leather chair. He was perspiring. Without air conditioning it was getting hotter.

'Sorry about the misunderstanding,' she said, folding her arms under her breasts. Her figure was not without its attractions. But it wasn't what he expected from a gospel artist; the clothes were just that little bit too tight. They made him think of the kind of women most blatantly interested in him—late thirties, early forties, looks just starting to fade, and wanting to make the most of the last years of their sensual prime.

'Maybe I overreacted,' he said, the sincerity in his voice a surprise to him.

'Adam had never asked me to come on my own before. Yesterday morning he phoned to say he *had* to see me. "I have to see you. Just you." Like a headmaster sending for a naughty child.'

Then she sat down on a leather couch opposite Dekker. She looked him in the eye, and said, 'If you have done things in your life that might catch up with you, then you don't argue. You lie to your beloved husband, and you go to Adam Barnard's office and ask him what is going on.'

The usually jovial Adam was serious, she said. He had pushed a DVD across his desk to her. Someone had written on the white surface, *Melinda 1987*. She had known right away what it was.

She took a deep breath. 'You need to know about my background, Mr Dekker. If you are a person who by nature struggles to conform, you're called a rebel when you're young. I was a so-called rebel. At school I was disobedient. I wanted to do everything my way. I had a craving for the things a good little Afrikaans girl was not supposed to do. For many years I picked men who represented a certain amount of risk. It was instinctive, not conscious. Sometimes I wonder if it would have turned out differently if *that* had been my only weakness. But it isn't. I had a need for recognition. It's not necessarily a search for fame, just a need for attention, I think. It is this combination that makes me who I am.'

She was not stupid, he thought. She was a woman who could easily deceive people. 'I was never terribly pretty. If I use what I have I can attract attention, but I don't take men's breath away. I was smart enough to study, but there is no degree in what I wanted to do. All I had left to me was my voice. Then I crossed paths with Danny Vlok. Danny was cool, ten years older than me. He had a music shop and a four-piece band in Bloemfontein. I saw his ad for a singer and went for an audition. Afterwards we went to his flat and had a *zol* and then sex. Two months later we got married. Four years later we were divorced.' She stopped and looked around. 'There's usually some water here.'

'I'll ask Natasha,' he said. When he went out of the door he saw Josh down the passage, looking restless and worried.

'Are you finished?'

'Not yet, Mr Geyser.'

The big man nodded and went back into the conference room.

Rachel heard the voices farther off, but not the words. They went on for so long that she grew increasingly convinced that there were no tracks leading to her. Her heartbeat steadied. Until she heard the click-clack of a woman's shoes, right up close to her, just two or three steps away.

'I hope you find her,' said the man's voice.

'She can't be far. We will search the park.' She heard the woman walk away. Moments later the door closed and then she knew she would be safe.

Melinda gulped down half a glass of water and kept it in her hand.

'We went to play for a wedding at Lake Athlone. After the reception we stayed over. The place was empty. We made a fire outside and sat in the dark, drinking. Danny said he was going to sleep, he was tired and drunk. By then we had been married for three years and things weren't going so well. The other three and myself stayed outside. They were young, like me. We kept on drinking. Too much. The bass guitarist had a video camera and he was filming us. At first it was innocent fun, then we started saying things to the camera about Danny. We mocked him. We knew if he got to see the video it would make him furious but it was the risk that made it such fun.

'The guitarist said he knew what would make Danny totally crazy and came over and kissed me on the mouth. It wasn't a big leap from there. I don't have to give you the detail. The video shows how they undressed me, how two of them had sex with me and how I enjoyed it.' She was quiet for a while and her eyes dropped. 'I never regretted it. Until yesterday. Until I realised my sins could catch up with Josh. It would hurt him so much to know all that.'

When she fell silent, Dekker asked, 'Was that on the DVD?'

She nodded.

'Barnard wanted to blackmail you.'

'No. He was being blackmailed. He said he had to pay sixty thousand for it. It arrived with a note saying: *Watch this when you are alone. Or Melinda's career is over.* The call came three days later, from a man wanting fifty thousand or he would put it on the Internet. I asked Adam why he had paid sixty then. He told me the other ten thousand was to make sure it was the only copy.'

'How did he manage that?'

'He said this wasn't the first time he had had to protect one of his artist's interests. He had people who help with that, an agency. They followed the trail of the money transfers, until they found the man.'

'Was it the bass guitarist?'

'No. Danny Vlok.'

'Your ex?'

'You have to admit there is some kind of justice in it.'

'How did they make sure it was the only copy?'

'I don't know. I tried to phone Danny when I left here. Someone at his shop said he was in hospital. He was assaulted in his flat on Sunday night.'

Dekker digested this information. This thing was getting big. And complex. 'But why did Barnard tell you this, if it was sorted out?'

'I think Adam spotted an opportunity. He put the DVD in the player. I could have walked out. But I wanted to see it again. We watched it together. When it was over he asked if he could kiss me. I said yes.'

She saw Dekker's expression and she said, 'I was very grateful to Adam. He was discreet. He went to a lot of trouble and expense. Seeing that video again . . . yourself. Young . . . so randy. You must be wondering how a born-again woman could do something like that. Bishop Tutu said, "God has a soft spot for sinners. His standards are quite low." He understands. He knows it brings us closer to Him, knowing how weak we are. He just wants us to confess.'

Dekker was speechless. They sat there in silence, listening to the hiss of the gas lamp.

'You want to know why I told Josh. That's the thing I can't really explain. I walked out of here with the DVD in my handbag. I went and sat in my car. I took a pair of tweezers and scratched the DVD until I was sure it would never work again. I phoned Danny at his shop then drove home and threw the DVD in the rubbish. When I went into the house there was dear, sweet Josh, who loves me so unconditionally. Josh must have felt the tension. I was faced with the difference between his image of me and who I really was. I believed he had the right to know the truth, but the words wouldn't come out. Josh would find it impossible to recover from the whole truth.'

WHEN VUSI NDABENI parked opposite Carlucci's, the police helicopter was overhead, the *wap-wap* of its rotor blades deafening. He spotted Mbali Kaleni standing next to a patrol vehicle with a radio microphone in her hand. She had a map book of Cape Town open on the car's bonnet.

Vusi crossed the street, and heard her saying loudly, 'This is the centre point, where I am standing. You must search from here. First, look at all the houses, then look at the parks. De Waal Park is just down the road.'

'Roger.' The helicopter swung north towards De Waal Park. Kaleni stretched through the window to replace the microphone. She couldn't quite reach—she was too short and too wide. Vusi opened the door and replaced the microphone.

'We will find her,' said Kaleni.

Forensics' white bus pulled up. Thick and Thin got out and walked over, carrying their cases.

'Where have you been?' Kaleni scolded them.

HE WAS 200 METRES away from the corner of Riebeek Street when Griessel realised he would have to leave the car and walk to Alfred Street. To get across Buitengracht in this traffic chaos would take at least forty minutes. He found a parking space, locked his car and jogged through the motionless traffic. It was only four blocks on foot. On the way he took out his phone.

'Vusi, I'm on my way to the Commissioner; I just want to know what's happening. Where are you?'

'At Carlucci's. She's missing, Benny, but the helicopter is searching and we have nine vehicles now, another on the way, but the traffic jam . . .'

'I know. Have you talked to Metro?'

'I haven't had time.'

'Leave it to me. I'll call you as soon as I am finished with the Commissioner.'

'Benny, Organised Crime has photos of Demidov's people. I want the guy at the restaurant to look at them.'

'If you can manage it, Vusi. It can't do any harm.'

JOHN AFRIKA'S OFFICE, on the fourth floor of 24 Alfred Street, was hot without the air conditioning. He was opening a window when he heard the Provincial Commissioner's urgent steps approaching.

Afrika sighed. More trouble. He waited for his boss to arrive. This time, the little Xhosa did not knock; he was in too much of a hurry and too worried.

'They say she's afraid of the police,' he said, barely through the door.

'Commissioner?' Afrika enquired, because he had no idea what he was talking about.

'The Consul General says Rachel Anderson told her father that she could not go to the police. Her father said it sounded as though she didn't trust them.'

'*Bliksem*,' said John Afrika and sat down behind his desk.

'My sentiments exactly,' said the Provincial Commissioner.

BUITENGRACHT WAS a nightmare. The traffic was gridlocked in all five lanes. Griessel darted between the cars, grateful to be on foot. His phone rang. Probably the Commissioner wanting to know where he was. But it was Dekker.

'Benny, this is a soap opera,' said Dekker and outlined Melinda's story for Griessel all the way to the corner of Alfred.

'What did she say about where they were last night?' Griessel said.

'At the church until eleven. The Tabernacle in Parklands. Then they went home. They were at home until this morning. Nor do they own a gun.'

'That's what he said too . . .' Geyser might be lying about the firearm—he had had since last night to get rid of one. 'Fransman, tell Josh you want to search his house . . .'

'I asked that they check the national register. There is no firearm . . .'

'No, I'm not saying we must search it. Just gauge their reactions.'

'OK. But the ex, Benny, it might have been him. This thing is a circus. I'm going to phone Bloemfontein, see if they can find something. I'm going to let Josh and Melinda go . . .'

'You can do that. Or you can let them wait in the conference room. Let them sweat until you hear from Bloemfontein. And talk to your sexy girl-friend at reception. Where was Barnard last night? Look at his diary, search his office, check his email . . . Sorry, Fransman, I'm taking over again.'

'I'm trying to chill, Benny. Trying to chill.'

OVER THE PHONE, Vusi said to Vaughn Cupido, 'Let me get their email address,' and he went over to the young man in the apron, 'Do you have email here? Our Organised Crime Unit will mail photos of people I want you to look at.'

'The address is info at Carlucci's dot co-za. But there's no electricity. The PC doesn't work.'

Vusi's shoulders sagged, but he told Cupido, 'Send it anyway, Vaughn, here's the address . . .'

Mbali Kaleni came to stand next to Vusi and asked the young man, 'Are you sure about the Land Rover's registration? They say there is no Land Rover Discovery with a CA, a four, one . . .'

'It wasn't a Discovery. I told the guy it was a Defender. And new.'

'The fools I have to work with,' said Mbali shaking her head. She called Caledon Square. 'It wasn't a Land Rover Discovery, it was a Defender. You will have to search again.'

'I can't,' said the Constable. 'The power is down.'

GRIESSEL WAS PANTING and perspiring when he walked into Afrika's office—from the heat, from the four sets of stairs because the lifts wouldn't work and from the sense of urgency building inside him.

The Provincial Commissioner was seated opposite Afrika. The little Xhosa stood up, very serious, and put out a hand, 'Congratulations, Captain Griessel.'

That caught him off guard. In confusion he looked at Afrika, who winked and said, 'Congratulations, Benny.'

'Uh . . .' Benny said and wiped the sweat from his brow. 'Uh . . .'

The Xhosa laughed. 'You had better sit down, Captain. I suspect you are going to earn your promotion today.'

IN THE GARDEN of the Victorian house, beside the three prints of running shoes in the soft earth, tall, skinny Jimmy from Forensics held open the plastic bag of dental cement and watched as fat Arnold poured in some water.

'If only she wasn't so bloody bossy,' said Jimmy, zipping up the bag and shaking it. 'All I want to know is what the heck she wants to do with these casts. They know they are the girl's footprints.'

'That stuff is ready. Knead it.'

Jimmy kneaded the plastic bag of green goo between his hands. 'Get the mould ready.'

Arnold took a long mould, adjusted it to fit over the footprint and carefully pressed it into the soil. He picked up a bottle of talcum powder and sprinkled it over the print. 'Pour,' he said.

Jimmy opened the bag and held it over the centre of the mould. The paste dribbled out.

Inside the Victorian house, behind his net curtains and only ten metres from where Thick and Thin knelt, the old man could not hear their conversation. But he could see them. Just as he had seen the girl jump over the fence, the Land Rover driving past soon afterwards, those young men, searching. And the constables who had run down Upper Orange Street with such purpose, and the black lady detective who had stopped in thought at the picket fence and then investigated the flowerbed.

He knew who they were looking for. And he knew where she was hiding.

CAPTAIN BENNY GRIESSEL. Could you believe that? He sat there savouring the glow of his promotion. Tonight he would walk into Primi and say to Anna, 'Captain Benny Griessel, pleased to meet you,' and she would look up at him in surprise and say 'Benny!' and kiss him on the mouth.

'How did Dekker take the news of Mbali Kaleni?' Afrika broke through his reverie.

'I told him it was still his case, Commissioner,' said Griessel. 'He accepted it.'

Afrika looked sceptical, but merely nodded. 'Have you told her yet?'

He had forgotten. Totally. 'I haven't had the chance yet.'

'Do you know what Mbali means?' the Provincial Commissioner asked. 'Flower. It means flower in Zulu.'

Afrika grinned. 'She speaks five languages and has an IQ of a hundred and thirty-seven. Not bad for a flower.'

'She'll be sitting in my chair one day,' said the little Xhosa.

'She thinks she's sitting there already,' said Afrika, and the two officers laughed congenially. Griessel grinned, not sure whether it was proper for a Captain to laugh with them.

The Regional Commissioner suddenly went serious. 'Benny, there's a new development. Rachel Anderson's father said she can't go to the police. He thinks she means she can't trust us.'

'Can't trust us?' queried Griessel. The two senior officers nodded in unison. 'Wait a bit. Vusi has a theory that she is a drugs mule, she and the deceased. It would fit with a lot of things—the nightclub, the Russians, the rucksack that was cut away, the whole chase. It's not that she can't trust the police—it's because she can't walk into a police station and say, "Help me, I've brought in a half a million worth of drugs and then cheated Demidov."'

Afrika frowned. 'We can hardly say that to the Consul General or her father. Not without proof.'

'We promised her father we would call him,' said the Provincial Commissioner, and when Benny didn't look very enthusiastic he added 'Captain' expressly.

'Immediately,' said John Afrika. 'It would relieve a lot of pressure.'

'I'll get you the number,' said the Provincial Commissioner and rose to his feet. Then the power came on with a shudder that travelled through the entire building.

'AREN'T YOU GOING to arrest him?' Willie Mouton asked in disbelief, as the fluorescent light above his bald pate began to flicker.

'At the moment there are no grounds for arrest,' said Dekker, standing at the door. 'Could I ask you a few questions about Adam Barnard?'

'Of course. Please, take a seat . . .' said Mouton without much sincerity.

'This morning, at Barnard's house. You spoke about Adam's "ways". . .'

He saw Mouton glance at Groenewald for approval. 'The newspapers have written about some of this already, Willie . . .' the lawyer said slowly.

Mouton cleared his throat. 'Sexual harassment,' he said warily. 'I don't believe that has anything to do with his death.'

'Let them decide on that, Willie.'

Mouton leaned forward, a decision made. 'Everyone knows Adam had a thing for women. Fifteen years ago I was promoting and managing tours for pop bands and I heard the stories way back then: Adam had Xandra at home, but that wasn't enough. He came and asked me to join AfriSound, as full partner, to do production and promotion. He told me, "Willie, just so you know—I like women." He wasn't ashamed of it. Of course he had a go. But he never told a woman he would offer her a contract if she slept with him. Never.'

'What about the harassment?' Dekker said.

'A year ago, Nerina Stahl had a huge offer from Centre Stage and all of a sudden the papers were full of how Adam had harassed her . . .'

'I'm not sure I understand.'

'Nerina Stahl . . . the star. Adam *made* her. She sang in an Abba tribute, one of those shows that come and go. Adam went one evening. Pretty girl, cute voice. Adam took her out to lunch and told her she could have a solo career. She signed that very afternoon. Adam translated a bunch of German pop songs and we spent a bit on a music video. That CD went to twenty-five thousand, and two years later she was huge. She still had a year to go on her contract with us when a rival label, Centre Stage, offered her more and she went to the papers with the sexual harassment story, because that was the only way she could get out of her contract. Then there were others who jumped on the bandwagon.'

'And did they also accuse Adam Barnard of sexual harassment?'

'It was for the publicity. Front page of *Rapport*. Singers Speak Up Against Sexual Harassment, or something. We told Nerina she could go and the storm was over.'

'When last was there any talk of this?'

'It's been quiet for the past five or six months,' Groenewald said. 'But now that Adam is dead . . .'

'Can you imagine what a circus it's going to be? And no one will remember that he saved the Afrikaans music industry.'

'How so?' asked Dekker.

'It was before your time,' said Mouton, 'early Eighties. Adam was working for one of those gigantic legal firms, but he wasn't happy and he was crazy about music. He listened to everything, the pubs, the small clubs, and he noticed there was all this raw talent, but the big record labels were not interested; they wanted only the big stars. Then he discovered Xandra. He resigned his job and started AfriSound, signed Xandra and a few others. He got hold of the best songs and he marketed them cleverly. Then came *Voëlvry*—protest music in Afrikaans, you know, against Apartheid. Have you ever heard of Johannes Kerkorrel and Koos Kombuis?'

'Yes.'

'They were a part of it. That's where I began, touring with those guys. We didn't have a studio or a label. We sold tapes out of the back of a minibus. I did everything from driving the van to building sets, fixing the amplifiers. The students bought into that like you wouldn't believe. It was then that Adam came to see me. We were the men who made *Voëlvry* legit. We gave them a label that took them mainstream, with management and marketing and promotion. It got bigger and bigger and just look at Afrikaans music now. In the past five or six years it has exploded. And all the papers can write about is harassment.'

Dekker said, 'Did Adam say anything during the past week about a DVD he received in the post?'

'Why would anyone send him a DVD? Production and promotion is my department. If he did receive anything he would have passed it on to me.'

'Did he open his own post?'

'Yes. Natasha is PA to both of us, but she wouldn't open our post. We do almost everything electronically. What was on this DVD?'

'I can't divulge details at this stage. Who can I speak to about payments that Mr Barnard would have made during the past week or so?'

'Adam was in charge of finance and admin. But Wouter would know. He's the accountant. Next door down.'

'Thank you,' said Dekker and rose. 'I will also have to search Mr Barnard's office. Has anyone been in his office since yesterday night?'

'Ask Natasha, I don't know,' said Mouton.

GRIESSEL SAT in the absent director's office and studied the sheet of paper the Provincial Commissioner had given him. *Bill Anderson* was written on it. Plus a number with overseas codes.

He was reluctant to make the call. He wasn't good at this sort of thing. He would try too hard to reassure and that would spark false hope, and he knew how the man felt. If Carla were to phone him from London and say there were people trying to kill her, he would go out of his mind.

Griessel lifted the receiver. He would say, 'This is Captain Benny Griessel.'

At least that would feel bloody good.

VUSI, MBALI and the young man in the apron stood at the computer in the small office at Carlucci's. They watched the email download.

Mbali's cellphone rang. 'Yes,' she answered, and listened for a long time. 'Hold on.' She took her handbag off her shoulder and brought out a notebook and pen. 'Give it to me.' She made a note and ended the call. 'Vusi, I am going to Parklands. They have a hit on the registration number.'

'The Land Rover?'

'A Mr J. M. de Klerk registered a Land Rover Defender in September. Registration CA four-one-six, seven-eight-eight-nine. He was born in 1985. A young guy.'

'Must have a rich dad,' said the young man in the apron as he opened an email. 'Those Landies cost three hundred grand.'

GRIESSEL HEARD the phone ring on another continent. He wondered what time it was in West Lafayette, Indiana.

'Anderson,' said the voice on the other end.

'Mr Anderson, my name is Benny Griessel. I am a captain in the South African Police Services and I'm in charge of the search for your daughter. I'm very sorry for your circumstances, but I can tell you we are doing our absolute best to find her and protect her.'

'Thank you, Captain, for taking the time to call. Is there any news?' The voice was polite and American.

'We have a police helicopter searching the area where she was last seen, and we have more than ten patrol units looking for her in the streets, with more coming. But so far, we have not located her.'

There was a silence over the phone.

'Captain, this is a difficult thing for me to ask. When Rachel spoke to me she said that she could not go to the police. I am very concerned. Do you know why she said this?'

'Mr Anderson, we have been thinking about this . . . it could mean different things and I am investigating all the possibilities.' It didn't seem enough. 'I want to tell you, I have a daughter the same age as Rachel. My daughter is in London at the moment. I know how you feel, Mr Anderson. I know this must be very difficult for you. Our children are all we have.'

'Yes, Captain. That is why I am so concerned. Tell me—can I trust you?'

'Yes, Mr Anderson. You can trust me.'

'Then I will do that. I will trust you with my daughter's life.'

Don't say that, thought Griessel. He had to find her first. 'I will do everything I can. I'm going to give you my cellphone number. You can call me any time. If Rachel calls again, please give her my number, and tell her I will come to her, just me, if she is worried. And I will call you if there is any news.'

'We were thinking . . . We want to fly out there . . .'

'Let me find her, Mr Anderson. Let me find her first.'

'Will you, Captain?' There was a desperate note in his voice.

'I will not rest until I have.'

BILL ANDERSON put the phone down carefully and sank back into his chair. His wife stood beside him, her hand on his shoulder. 'It's all right to cry,' she said.

He dropped his head. His shoulders shook. 'I heard him,' said Jess Anderson. 'He will find her. I could hear that in his voice.'

GRIESSEL SAT with his elbows on the desk and his chin in his hand. He shouldn't have said it. He didn't want to make promises. But Rachel Anderson's father had pleaded with him. And he had said he would not rest until he found her.

Where the hell did he begin? The helicopter and patrols were not going to find her. She was hiding, afraid of the police. And he didn't know why. The solution was to find out who was hunting her. Vusi's plan looked better and better. He must check on their progress.

He reached for his cellphone, but then it rang.

'Griessel.'

'This is Inspector Kaleni.' Her Zulu accent was strong, but every Afrikaans word was enunciated with care. 'We traced a Land Rover Defender that fits the number to a man in Parklands, a Mr J. M. de Klerk. I am on my way.'

'Very good work, but the Commissioner asked if you would help with another case. Fransman Dekker's investigation.'

'Fransman Dekker?'

Griessel ignored the disdain in her voice. 'Call him, please.'

'I don't like it,' said the Flower, 'but I will call him.'

'ON JANUARY THE 11TH we electronically transferred an amount of fifty thousand rand into an ABSA account, on Adam's instructions,' said the accountant of AfriSound, Wouter Steenkamp.

A short man in his early thirties, he was ensconced behind a large flat-screen computer monitor.

'Who was it paid to?' Dekker asked.

'According to Adam's note the account holder was "Bluegrass". The branch code was in the Bloemfontein city centre. The transaction was successful.'

'Did Mr Barnard say what the payment was for?'

'In his email he asked me to put it under "sundry expenses".'

'Was there also a payment of ten thousand?'

Steenkamp scanned the spreadsheet on his screen. 'Not on my records.'

Dekker leaned forward. 'According to my information, Adam Barnard used an agency to determine who was behind the Bluegrass account. At a fee of ten thousand rand.'

'Aah . . .' said Steenkamp, reaching for his neat in-tray. He lifted documents and pulled one out. 'Ten thousand exactly. Jack Fischer and Associates.'

Dekker knew the company—former senior white police officers who had taken fat retirement packages and set up their own private investigation business. The document was an invoice. Under *Item* and *Cost* was printed: *Administrative enquiries, R4,500. Personal interview, R5,500.*

'Do you often use Jack Fischer?'

'Now and then.'

'You know they are private investigators?'

'The music industry is not all moonlight and roses . . . But Adam usually handled that sort of case.'

'I will have to keep this account.'

'May I make a copy first?'

'Please.'

GRIESSEL JOGGED down Buitengracht again. The traffic jam had cleared as though it had never existed. His mind was on Rachel. Where was she heading? The only possibility was the Cat & Moose; that was where her luggage was, and her friend Oliver Sands. Where else could she go?

He phoned Caledon Square and asked the radio operator to send a unit to Long Street. 'But they must not park in front of the Cat & Moose. Tell them to wait inside. If she does come, she mustn't see them.'

That was all he could do. According to Vusi, the eyewitness at Carlucci's had looked at the photos of Demidov's troops and said it was none of them. But Organised Crime might not have sent all the pictures. Or the pictures could be out of date. Or they didn't have photos of all of Demidov's people.

Either he or Vusi would have to go back to Van Hunks again. But first he would see what the house in Table View produced. He had to give the whole search some direction. He would use Caledon Square as the base; it was central, that was where the radio connection with the patrol cars was.

He ran the last 200 metres to his car, aware of the heat now smothering the city like a blanket.

'I DON'T KNOW what it was for,' said Willie Mouton, and passed the Jack Fischer invoice back across the desk to Dekker. 'I don't think they will tell you. 'It's sensitive. Client privilege.'

'What is?'

'No, Willie,' said Groenewald, the lawyer.

'Of course it is. They guarantee confidentiality. That's why we use them.'

'Privilege counts only for doctors, psychologists and legal practitioners, Willie. If the police have a warrant, they can get the information.'

'Is there anyone specific that you deal with at Jack Fischer?' Dekker asked.

'We work with Jack himself. But you're barking up the wrong tree, I'm telling you.'

RACHEL ANDERSON could no longer hear the helicopter. At first the silence was eerie, but gradually it became reassuring. She had evaded them.

She made up her mind. She would stay here until dark. She checked her watch. Another eight hours before the sun went down. She would have to make herself comfortable if she were going to lie here that long. The rucksack would have to come off. She could use it as a pillow.

She loosened the clips, pulled the straps off her shoulders and lowered the sack. She turned on her back slowly and let her head rest on the bag. The ground underneath her was not too uncomfortable. The dense shade would protect her from dehydration. She would have to find a telephone. She had to tell her father where she was.

She drew a deep breath and looked up through the dense leaf cover to where patches of sky shone through. Her eyes closed. Then she heard the front door of the house open.

BARRY DROVE UP in his Toyota bakkie from the city side. Upper Orange was quiet now, the police vehicles and uniforms gone. He wondered if it would be worthwhile to watch the Victorian house.

He looked for the driveway that he had noted earlier, turned up it and drove to the back against the garage door. He picked up the binoculars that lay beside him on the worn seat cover and realised he couldn't see the house from here. The wall on the left was too high.

He climbed onto the load bed of the Toyota and leaned back against the cab with the binoculars to his eyes. It was barely a hundred metres to the Victorian house. He let the binocular lenses sweep across the house. It was dead still. He checked the garden. Back to the house. A waste of time.

Then the front door opened. An old man appeared. Barry focused on him and waited.

JOSH AND MELINDA GEYSER were sitting close together at the big oval table in the conference room when Dekker opened the door. They looked at him expectantly.

'Inspector Griessel and I don't believe you are suspects in the case at this stage . . .'

'We didn't do it,' Josh said emphatically.

'Then give us permission to search your house, so we can make sure there is nothing that connects you with Barnard's death.'

'Such as?'

'A firearm. You can refuse, and we would obtain a search warrant. But if you give permission . . .'

Josh looked at Melinda. She nodded. 'Go ahead. There isn't anything.'

Dekker looked at her intently. He saw only the decisiveness. 'Wait here, please. I will be back as soon as possible.'

WHEN MBALI KALENI walked through the double ground-floor doors of AfriSound there were four white people standing in front of the black receptionist, in animated conversation.

'Excuse me,' said Mbali and held up her identity card. 'Police.'

All four turned to her. One had a camera slung round the neck.

'Are you here about the Barnard case?' a young woman with very short blonde hair asked.

'Are you from the newspapers?'

'*Die Burger*,' the woman said. 'Is it true that Josh and Melinda Geyser are being questioned in there?'

'I don't talk to the media,' Mbali said and directed herself towards the receptionist.

RACHEL LAY STOCK STILL. There were footsteps, scarcely audible: one, two, three. Then silence. 'The policewoman told me you are an American,' said the same voice she had heard earlier. She tensed as she realised he was speaking to *her*.

'I saw you when you jumped over the fence. I saw how scared you were. And then, the men in the Land Rover . . .' There was compassion in the voice, but the fear that he knew she was there paralysed her.

'The policewoman told me those men are hunting you. You must be very frightened. I suppose you don't know who to trust. I will leave the door unlocked. I am alone. My wife died last year. There is food and drink inside, and you have my word that no one will ever know you were here.'

Emotion welled up in her. Self-pity, gratitude, the impulse to leap up. No! She heard feet shuffling. 'I will be inside.' It was quiet for a moment before she heard his footsteps moving away. The door opened and shut. Then there was the roar of a cannon and her whole body jerked in alarm.

12:00–12:56

VII

Dekker stopped for a second in the passage of AfriSound, deep in thought. He should phone Bloemfontein and find out what they had, he must go to Jack Fischer and Associates, he must search Barnard's office, he must talk to Natasha about Barnard's schedule yesterday. He didn't know which of these to do next and he was not keen on Jack Fischer or Natasha Abader. The detective agency was full of white ex-policemen who loved to sing to the press if they could show the SAPS in a bad light. Natasha was a temptation he did not need. The story of Adam Barnard, womaniser, was a mirror held up to him.

He didn't want to be like that; he had a good, pretty and clever wife who trusted him.

The cannon roared the noonday shot from Signal Hill, breaking his train of thought. He glanced up and saw Mbali Kaleni's stormy face approaching through the reception area.

'Shit,' he said softly to himself.

BENNY GRIESSEL HEARD the cannon as he crossed the threshold of the Caledon Square police station. Was it really only twelve o'clock? He saw the police photographer trotting across with a pack of photos in his hand.

'Are you looking for Vusi? You're late.'

'How am I supposed to make copies without electricity?' The photographer angrily held out the prints.

Griessel looked at the print on top. Erin Russel and Rachel Anderson, laughing and alive. Light and dark, blonde and brunette. Erin had the face of a nymph, a small pretty nose, big green eyes. Rachel was sultry, her beauty more complex, dark plait over her shoulder, wide mouth, the line of her jaw determined. But both still children, eyes bright with excitement.

Drug mules? He knew anything was possible, he had seen it all before. Greed, recklessness, stupidity. But his heart said no, not these two.

RACHEL WAS TORN between her fear of trusting anyone, and the decency in the man's voice. The knowledge that the door was open just a few steps away, offering a safe haven, overcame her.

She got up slowly and crawled to the edge of the leaf curtain. There was a small stretch of paved garden path, a single step, a low verandah, and the wooden door, its varnish faded with age.

She hesitated then stood erect, straightening legs stiff from lying so long. She walked fast over the path and opened the door.

BARRY WASN'T LOOKING through the binoculars. They were too heavy to hold up permanently without a prop. He was looking up the street towards Carlucci's. He saw movement in the periphery, more than a hundred metres away at the house. His head turned and he saw the figure for an instant; the blue of a garment was the shade he was looking for. He lifted up the binoculars. Nothing.

Was he imagining things? No, he had seen it. He blinked, concentrating. Small figure, blue . . . Where had she come from? For the first time he recognised the potential of the bougainvilleas, the old overgrown arbour. He studied the depth of it, the possibility slowly dawning in his mind.

He reached for his phone in the pocket of his denims.

THE HOUSE WAS QUIET and cool. Rachel stood in the hallway and listened to her own breathing. One step forward. The floorboard creaked and she stopped. To the left a large room opened up between two plain pillars: a table with a laptop almost lost between piles of books and papers. Shelves crammed with books, three big windows, one looking out on the street. An old, worn Persian carpet.

'I'm in the kitchen.'

She walked in the direction of the voice. Through a white-painted door-frame was the kitchen. He stood with his back to her. He looked like an aged monk with thinning grey hair around a bald spot that shone in the fluorescent light.

He turned slowly from his work at the table. 'I'm making an omelette. Would you like some? He was older than she had thought at first, with a slight stoop and a kind face. He wiped his hands on a dishcloth and held one out towards her. 'My name is Piet van der Lingen.'

'Pleased to meet you,' she said automatically and shook his hand.

'Omelette? Perhaps some toast?'

'That would be wonderful.'

'You are most welcome to hang the rucksack on the pegs at the door,' and he pointed to the hall. She stood there, unwilling to accept the relief. 'And the bathroom is down the passage.'

'I SAW HER,' said Barry over the phone, sounding more certain than he felt. 'She went into a house just a block from the restaurant.'

'Jesus. When?' ,

'A few minutes ago. I caught just a glimpse, but it was her. No doubt.'

MBALI AND DEKKER sat in the recording studio. Dekker talked, gave her the details of the Barnard case. She knew her male colleagues did not like her, and she knew why. The men felt threatened by her talent and were intimidated by her integrity. She didn't drink, smoke or curse. She didn't hold her tongue either. She said what she thought about their incessant sexism and racism. She told them straight out it was inappropriate. But Dekker had an extra reason to hate her. She'd caught him out, cellphone to his ear, whispering words of lust to a Tamaryn, when his wife's name was Crystal. She had said, 'A man should be faithful to his wife.' Since then she had seen the hatred in his eyes. Because she knew, and despised him for it.

But there was work to be done here. So she listened attentively. She answered him only in English, although he spoke Afrikaans. Because she knew he hated that too.

RACHEL CLOSED THE BATHROOM DOOR, feeling an urgent need to pee. The relief was great. When she was finished she washed the dried blood and mud off her hands, and splashed her face. Only then did she look in the mirror. Her hands reached for her hair and brushed it back from her face.

She looked dreadful. Her eyes were bloodshot and there were lines of fatigue around her mouth. There was a cut on her chin, surrounded by a light purple bruise and another small graze across her forehead. Her neck was grimy, like her powder-blue T-shirt.

But you are *alive*. She was filled with gratitude. Then came the guilt, because Erin was dead. The emotion washed over her like a tidal wave. It broke down her defences and let her relive it fully for the first time: the two of them fleeing in terror, Erin jumping over the church railings. A fatal error.

'No!' she had screamed, yet followed blindly. Erin had stopped on a narrow path in the churchyard. Rachel realised they were trapped; she had run on desperately looking for a way out. She was already behind the building, out of sight, when she realised she couldn't hear Erin's footsteps. Where was Erin? Reluctant and afraid, she had run back to the corner of the church building.

Erin was on the ground and all five were round her, bending over, kneeling, yowling like animals. The knife had flashed. Erin's desperate scream, abruptly cut off. Black blood in the dark.

That moment was petrified in the synapses of her brain, surreal, overwhelming. She had run for her life.

Relief. Gratitude. She was alive. In front of the bathroom mirror it was all too much for her. The emotion was physical, a nausea rising from her stomach, a dry retching. She bellowed once, shuddered, then began to cry.

Vusi Ndabeni sat in the front seat of one of the patrol vehicles between a constable and an inspector. Behind them was another police van. They had wanted to put the sirens and lights on but he had said no. He wanted to arrive at J. M. de Klerk's house without fanfare, surround it quietly and then knock on the door. The inspector said he knew where the address was, one of the crescents in Parklands, a new residential area where the white and up-and-coming black middle classes lived shoulder to shoulder in apparent harmony.

At a set of traffic lights they turned right into Park Road. Vusi looked at the inspector.

'It's just up front here.' Houses all neat and new, gardens in development.

'We mustn't park in front of the house,' said Vusi. 'I don't want to scare him.' Townhouses. Big complexes behind high walls. 'Are they all townhouses?' asked Vusi.

'I don't think so.'

But number 24 was. They stopped some way off and got out. There was a high white wall and a large motorised iron gate. There was a panel at the gate with a grid for a speaker, call buttons, some with names alongside. Vusi saw no de Klerk. On the top left was one labelled *Administrator*. He pressed it.

A monotone woman's voice said, 'What do you want?'

Sixteen storeys above the bustling crowds of Adderley Street, the man stood at the window with his back to the luxury of the apartment behind him. He looked out over the city. The man's hair and beard were trimmed short—he didn't look fifty yet. He was fit and lean in denim shirt and khaki chino trousers.

He had one hand in his pocket; the other was holding a slim cellphone. He typed in a number and heard it ring once before Barry answered. 'Mr B.'

'I'm taking control,' the man said. 'Describe the house to me.'

'Right.' Relief. Barry did his best, describing the single storey, the corner site and the position of the front door.

'Does the house have a back door?'

'I don't know.'

'If it has, it should be towards Belmont Avenue. I'm going to send Eben and Robert to cover that angle. I am working on the assumption that she does not know that we are watching the house.'

'Yes, sir.'

'Let's keep it that way. I hear you saw only one occupant, an old man.'

'Right.'

'Good. Now listen carefully. You, Eben and Robert will have to be ready to move in case of an emergency. If you get the call, go in and get her, no matter what it takes. Do you understand me?'

'Yes, sir.'

'But that would be second prize, and only if she calls the cops. It can happen at any moment, which means you will have to be very quick. Whatever you do, get the bag. And we don't need witnesses.'

'I don't have a gun.'

'Barry, Barry, what did I teach you?'

'Adapt, improvise and overcome.'

'Exactly. But it might not be necessary, because we are working on first prize. It will take twenty or thirty minutes to put together. In the meantime, you are my main man. If we call, go in. If she leaves, get her. Do you understand that?'

'Yes, sir.'

As he put the phone in his pocket he saw the police helicopter flying across Table Bay directly towards him. He kept his eyes on it until it flew past, low over the city.

THE UNIFORMS STOOD OUTSIDE. Vusi was inside with the complex administrator. She reminded him of bread dough, pale and shapeless.

'De Klerk is in A-six. He is not a renter; he owns. I don't see him often.'

She had fitted out one room of her townhouse as an office. She sat at a small melamine desk in front of white melamine shelves for files, one of which was open on the desk. Vusi stood at the door.

'Is he here now?'

'I don't know.' A bald statement of an uninteresting fact.

'Can you describe him?'

'He's young. Twenty-six. Tallish. Brownish hair.'

'Where does he work?'

The index finger moved across the file. 'It just says "consultant" here.'

'Do you have a key to his place?'

'I do.'

'Could you open up for us, please?'

'The regulations state I must have a search warrant on file.'

BENNY GRIESSEL sat in the radio room of the Caledon Square station with a map of the city. He listened to the young sergeant talk to every patrol vehicle about the streets they had covered. He tried to form an image of where she might be and struggled to get his head around it all—too many permutations.

His phone rang. He checked the screen and answered, 'Vusi?'

'Benny, we need a warrant to get into the house.'

'We don't have enough for a warrant, Vusi.'

'I thought so. OK. I'll call again . . .'

Griessel put down the phone and studied the map, moving the tip of his pen towards the Company Gardens. His instinct told him she was there. He knew Upper Orange. It was his cycling route. If he had to run from there, aiming for Long Street, he would run that way.

'I want two teams in the Gardens,' he told the Sergeant. 'But first they must come and collect photos.'

PIET VAN DER LINGEN heard sobbing. He stood outside the bathroom door. He didn't want to frighten her. 'Rachel,' he said softly.

The sobs stopped abruptly. 'How do you know my name?'

'The policewoman told me. You are Rachel Anderson, from Lafayette in Indiana.' There was a long silence before the door slowly opened and he saw her with tears on her cheeks.

'West Lafayette, actually,' she said.

FRANSMAN DEKKER told Mbali about the money that had been paid to Jack Fischer and Associates. At that moment he realised how he could solve a whole number of problems. He must be careful how he held out the carrot. She was known for her ability to smell a rat.

'The Bloemfontein affair is the key,' he said, careful to keep his voice neutral. 'But Fischer and Co. are clever. Are you up to it?' He had chosen the words with care.

She made a derisive noise in her throat. 'Clever?' She rose to her feet.

'They're just men,' she said, already heading for the door.

He felt relieved but gave nothing away. 'They're old hands,' he said.

She opened the door. 'Leave Bloemfontein to me.'

AFTER VUSI HAD TRIED knocking, he sent the uniformed police to ask the neighbours if anyone knew de Klerk. He stayed behind on the back patio, peering through the gap in the curtains. He saw an open-plan room with a kitchen at the back. There was a sofa and, ahead of him, the corner of a huge flat-screen TV.

The administrator told him these townhouses cost a fraction under a million rand apiece. A new Land Rover was more than three hundred thousand. Big new TV. How could a twenty-six-year-old afford all this?

Drugs, thought Vusi.

He saw the policemen returning. He could tell they had nothing to report. Suddenly he was in a hurry to get back to the city, to Van Hunks, because that was where the key to this puzzle lay.

IT FELT SURREAL, the old man in his impeccably white shirt pulling out a chair for her. The delicious aroma of fried bacon made her hunger flare up. The table neatly laid for two.

He walked over to the stove, asked whether she would like cheese and bacon on her omelette. 'Yes, please,' she said.

He always set for two, he said, ever since his wife died. It made him feel less alone. It was a great privilege to have someone at the table now. He didn't get much company. Just the books; they were his companions now.

The books, she said, half a question, to make conversation.

I used to be a historian, he said. Now I'm just an old man with too much time on my hands and a doctor son in Canada who emails me and tells me to keep busy, as I still have a lot to give.

He slid the omelette onto a snow-white plate and brought it to her.

'This looks lovely.' She picked up her knife and fork, cut through the puffed egg and brought it to her mouth. She was incredibly hungry and the flavour was heavenly. She felt like getting up and hugging him.

He slid a second omelette onto his plate. He brought it to the table, sat down and took a mouthful.

'West Lafayette. You're a long way from home, my dear.'

ON THE SIXTEENTH FLOOR of the apartment block, the man with the trimmed beard stood etched against the city panorama, his hands behind his back.

In front of him were the six young men. Three black, three white. They looked at him, expectant.

'Mistakes have been made,' the man said in English, but with a distinctive accent. 'Learn from them. I am taking charge now. Time is our enemy so I shall keep it short. Our friend in Metro will provide a vehicle, a panel van that has been unclaimed in the pound for four months. Go and get it. Oerson is waiting at the gate. Leave the bus at the Victoria Junction Hotel.'

He picked up a metal case from the floor and put it on the table in front of him. 'Four Stechkin APS's. As you can see, they come with a silencer. These weapons are the most reliable automatic pistols on the planet. The silencers don't mean that the weapon is completely silent. It makes a sound equal to an unsilenced point-two-two pistol, enough to attract attention, which we do not want. Use it only in an emergency. Is that clear?'

Everyone nodded, greedy eyes on the guns.

'Very well. This is how we're going to do it.'

INSPECTOR FRANSMAN DEKKER was on his way over to where Natasha was sitting when the tall white man intercepted him.

'Are you from the police?'

'I am,' said Dekker. The face seemed familiar.

'I'm Ivàn Nell,' he said with an inflection of the powerful voice that said the name meant something.

'Weren't you on that TV show? *Superstars*? Pleased to meet you. You must excuse me—we're a little busy this morning,' said Dekker and began moving again.

'That's why I'm here. Because of Adam,' said Nell. 'I think I was the last person to see him alive.'

'Last night?' The singer had his full attention now.

'We were eating at Bizerca Bistro until ten o'clock. Then I went home.'

'And Barnard?'

'I don't know where Adam went. But this morning when I heard on the radio . . .'

Nell looked around at the people who were sitting too close for his liking. 'I think his death has something to do with our conversation last night. Is there somewhere we could talk?'

Dekker looked at Natasha waiting patiently only steps away from them. 'Just give me a moment.'

BENNY GRIESSEL was not good at waiting. He left the radio room, walked out onto Buitenkant Street. They were not going to find her. He had fourteen patrol vehicles driving in a grid pattern, ten foot patrols, two of them searching the Company Gardens. The helicopter had covered the entire city. There was no sign of her. Where could she be?

He walked to his car and took out the Chesterfields. He stood on the pavement, holding the packet of cigarettes.

Was there something he had missed? It was a familiar feeling. On the day a crime took place, there was so much information. It took time for the subconscious to sort and file. He took out a cigarette. He was missing something.

The Field Marshal. Jeremy Oerson and the search for the rucksack.

He began to walk hastily back along the pavement, putting the cigarette back in the packet. He went into the police station. Was that the only item knocking at the door of his consciousness?

In the radio room he phoned the Metro number and asked for Oerson.

'Jeremy is not here. Do you want his cellphone number?' The man recited the number and Griessel wrote it down. He rang off and phoned it. Oerson answered instantly.

'Benny Griessel, SAPS. We talked this morning in Long Street. Did you find anything?'

'Where?'

'In the city. The girl's rucksack. You were supposed to be looking . . .'

'Oh. Yes.' A total lack of enthusiasm. 'No, there was nothing.'

Griessel was not impressed by his attitude. 'Can you tell me exactly where you searched?'

'I'll have to check. Your case isn't the only one we are working on.'

No, indeed, they had parking tickets to write, but he limited himself to the subject at hand, 'And you are absolutely sure you found nothing?'

'The streets are full of stuff. There's a bag of junk in my office, but there is no passport or a purse or anything that would belong to an American woman.'

'Tell me where your office is and I'll have it fetched.'

NATASHA ABADER unlocked Adam Barnard's office and said, 'I will have to give you the password if you want to check his laptop.' She went in and Dekker followed. There were large framed photographs on the walls, Barnard and stars, one after another. Every photo had a signature and a message in thick black marker. *Thank you, Adam!*

He looked at the desk on which Melinda Geyser had been screwed. Apart from the laptop there was nothing else on it. His imagination ran riot, Melinda lying on her back on the wide wooden surface, stark naked.

Dekker looked at Natasha guiltily. Her attention was on the laptop, eyebrows raised. 'Adam left his laptop on. He wouldn't usually do that.'

She bent down to type in a password, her neckline gaping. Dekker could not look away. Her breasts were small, firm and perfect.

She stood up suddenly. His eyes slid away to the screen.

'I will have to look at his emails.'

She nodded and bent down again to work the mouse. Why couldn't she sit down? Did she know he was looking?

'You can use Alt and Tab to change between email and calendar,' she said, and moved away so he could sit down in the large comfortable chair.

'Thanks. Can I ask you a few questions?'

She went over to the door and shut it. She looked him in the eyes. 'I know what you want to ask. You want to know whether Adam and I, you know . . .'

'Why would I want to ask that?'

She shrugged dismissively. 'You're going to interview everyone.'

Now he did want to know, but for another reason. 'Did you?' His head was screaming, Fransman what are you doing? But he knew what he was doing—looking for trouble and he could not stop himself.

'Yes.' She dropped her eyes.

'Here?' He gestured at the desk.

'Yes.'

'There are stories about him and women. Did he force women?'

'No.' With an attitude that said she objected to the question.

'Do you know who shot him?'

It took a while for the answer to come, reluctantly, more of a question, 'Josh Geyser? He was angry enough. And he's weird. Gladiator turned gospel singer. Don't you think that's weird? Look at him.'

'I can't lock him up because of the way he looks. Who else was angry enough with Adam Barnard to shoot him?'

'I really don't know.'

He asked the question that fascinated him, 'Why were the women so crazy about him? He was over fifty . . .'

'It's not about age, it's about aura. Women like the power of money. And he was the gateway to the stars. He could introduce them to celebrities. But there is another power that is totally irresistible—the power to empower.'

'Now you've lost me.'

'Second prize is to have a powerful man in your life. First prize is to have the power yourself, so you don't need a man. That was the kind of power Adam Barnard could give.'

'To the artist? He could give them fame and fortune?'

'Yes.'

'But you're not a singer,' he said.

She walked to the door. 'Second prize is not so bad.'

'Send Nell in, please,' he called after her, but he couldn't tell if she had heard.

ALEXA BARNARD became aware of someone beside her bed. She tried to focus but closed her eyes.

'My name is Victor Barkhuizen, and I am an alcoholic,' said a voice quietly. She opened her eyes. He was an old guy, with large eyes behind thick spectacles. 'Benny Griessel asked me to look in on you. The detective. I am his AA sponsor.'

'The doctor?' she asked, but her lips were stiff and the words wouldn't form.

'You don't have to speak. I'm just going to sit here with you a while and I will leave my number with the ward sister. I will come again tonight.'

She turned her head towards him, and slowly put out her right hand. He took it and held it tight. 'Thank you,' she said and closed her eyes again.

'No problem.'

Then somewhere through the haze she had a thought. 'The detective . . . tell him to come. I need to tell him something. About Adam.'

'I'll tell him.' She wanted to add something, something that evaded her now, like silver fish slipping from her grasp into dark water. She felt Victor Barkhuizen's hand and pressed it slowly to make sure it was still there.

'I'D LIKE TO CALL my dad. I'll pay, of course,' said Rachel as she helped carry the plates to the sink.

'No need for that,' he said. 'The phone is on the table, where I work. Go, I will clear the dishes.'

'The least I can do is to wash up. I love washing up.'

'Then we'll do it together,' he said, as he squirted dish-washing liquid over the plates and opened the taps. 'You do the washing, I'll dry and put them away. Do you still live with your parents?'

'Oh, yes, I just finished high school last year. This is supposed to be a gap year, before I go to college.'

'And where would you go for your studies?'

'Purdue. My parents work there.'

'They're academics?'

'My dad has tenure in English Lit. My mom's at the School of Aeronautics and Astronautics. She's a scientist. I love her to death, but I don't understand anything she does. I think I take after my dad. I miss them very much.'

'Go and call your father.'

'Thank you.' She hesitated. 'You've been so very kind . . . Would it be rude if I . . .?'

'I don't think you have a rude bone in your body, my dear. Please, just ask.'

'I'm dying for a bath; I don't think I've ever been this dirty, I'll be quick, I promise . . .'

'Good heavens, of course. Take all the time you need.'

GRIESSEL FOUND VUSI waiting at the front door of Van Hunks.

'This door is locked. We have to go round the back.'

'I sent for the eyewitness from Carlucci's, Vusi. And Oliver Sands from the hostel,' Griessel said as they turned into the service alley. Griessel's phone rang: the screen said *MAT JOUBERT*.

'Hey,' said Benny, answering.

'Is that *Captain* Benny Griessel?' Joubert asked. 'Congratulations, Benny. It's high time. Where are you?'

'Nightclub in Castle Street. Van Hunks.'

'I'm just around the corner. Would you like some Steers?'

'*Jissis*, that would be great.' He had last eaten the previous night. His belly rumbled in expectation. 'A Dagwood burger, chips and Coke. Wait, let me ask Vusi if he wants something too . . .'

ON THE THIRD FLOOR of a recently restored office building in St George's Mall, the fat woman walked purposefully across the thick, light brown carpet to the coloured receptionist.

'Inspector Mbali Kaleni, SAPS. I need to talk to Jack Fischer.'

The woman was unimpressed. 'I doubt he is available,' she said, putting a reluctant hand out to the telephone. She typed in a number and said, 'There is a woman from the police who wants to talk to Jack . . . I see,' she said with an air of satisfaction, and replaced the phone. 'Mr Fischer's diary is full. He can see you only after six.'

'Tell him it is in connection with the murder of his client, Adam Barnard. I want to talk to him within the next fifteen minutes.'

The receptionist opened her mouth to respond but saw Mbali turn and waddle to one of the large easy chairs against the wall. She sat down and made herself comfortable. She placed her handbag on her lap and took out a white plastic bag with the letters KFC on it.

The receptionist's frown deepened as Mbali took out a red and white carton and a tin of Fanta Grape out of the bag. She watched the policewoman put her handbag on the ground and the Fanta on the table beside her. 'You can't sit there and eat,' she said with more astonishment than authority.

Mbali lifted a chicken drumstick out of the packet. 'I can,' she said, and took a bite.

The receptionist shook her head and made a little noise of despair. She picked up the phone without taking her eyes off the munching policewoman.

GALINA FEDOROVA WALKED down the passage with Vusi and Griessel behind her. Benny smelled the alcohol even before they entered the nightclub—that familiar, musty smell of drinking holes that for more than ten years had offered him a refuge. As he went through the door, he felt a powerful wave of nostalgia for the days and nights of drinking with forgotten booze buddies.

'These are the night-shift staff,' Vusi said.

'OK.' Griessel looked around the room. Some of the staff were seated at tables, others were busy arranging chairs and wiping down tables.

'Can you ask them to sit, please?' he said to Fedorova.

The woman clapped her hands to get everyone's attention. Griessel noted that they were all young and good-looking—mostly men, nine or ten of them, four women.

'Good afternoon,' he said. 'Last night, two American girls visited this club, young tourists. This morning, the body of one of them was found at the top of Long Street. Her throat was cut.'

He ignored the subdued sounds of dismay. 'I'm going to pass round a photograph of the victim and her friend. If you remember them at all, put up your hand. We believe the other girl is still alive, and we have to find her.'

Griessel gave the photographs to Vusi, who began to hand them out. In front of him the young workers' heads were lowered, busy studying the photos.

Then two or three slowly looked up, with that tentative expression that said they recognised the girls but didn't want to be first to raise a hand.

MBALI KALENI was aware of the disapproval of the receptionist, but didn't understand it. A person had to eat. It was lunch time and here was a table and chairs. That was the problem with this country, she thought, all these little cultural differences. A Zulu eats when she must eat; it was normal and natural.

As usual, she thought while she ate. Not about the murder of the music man. It was the American girl who haunted her. She had been so sure she would find her. Her colleagues had been running around like headless chickens, but that was the way men were. This situation called for calm, for logic. That was how she had found the trail in the flowerbed.

And then, nothing. That was what she found perplexing. The girl would not have jumped the picket fence only to clamber over the next wall and run down the street again. The way it seemed to Kaleni was that there were only two options for a fugitive woman trying to stay off the streets: get inside a house, or hide somewhere in a garden where nobody could see her. Had she climbed over the next wall? The helicopter would have spotted her sooner or later.

When she was finished here she would go back to Upper Orange. Have another look. She owed that to the girl: a woman's calm, logical thought.

IVÀN NELL SAT opposite Dekker in Adam Barnard's office and said, 'I wanted to see Adam, because I believe they are cheating me of my money.'

'How's that?' Dekker pulled his notebook and pen nearer.

Nell leaned forward in his chair. 'Last night I told Adam I wanted to bring in an auditor, because things didn't look right. And when I heard over the radio this morning that he was dead . . .'

'What made you think things were not right?'

'To get sales figures had become like pulling teeth. Then, last year, the money I received for some songs in compilations by independent labels was a lot more than I expected. I starting doing my own sums . . .'

'So AfriSound is not your label?'

'No, they were, until February last year. Then I started my own label.'

'Because AfriSound cheated you?'

'No, I was not aware then that they were robbing me. There were many reasons but in the end it's about margins. From a record company you get twelve per cent, sometimes less. But on your own you get everything less input costs, eighty, eighty-five per cent once you've recouped your studio expenses. That is one heck of a difference.'

'Now how did AfriSound cheat you?'

'I don't know. That's why I want to bring in an auditor.'

'Surely you must have a theory?'

'Last year, I did three songs for compilation albums and when I got the money it was proportionately much more than I was getting from Adam. So I looked carefully at the statements, at the deductions and sales and royalties, and the more I looked, the less sense it made. Then I started getting suspicious.'

'And you spoke to Adam Barnard?'

'I phoned him and said I wanted to see him. He said let's go and have a relaxed dinner.'

'And that was last night?'

'That's right. He said that as far as he knew, they had nothing to hide. When I said I wanted to bring in my own auditor, he said, "no problem". And that was that. At about half past nine, he said he had to make a quick phone call, and he went and stood outside to phone, and when he came in he said he had to leave. We got the bill and we left about ten o'clock.'

Dekker wondered what had happened to Barnard's cellphone, because it wasn't on the scene that morning. 'You have no idea who he called?'

'No. But he wasn't the sort of guy who would leave the table to phone. He would just talk, never mind who it was. When I heard this morning he had been shot, once I got over the shock, I started to wonder.'

RACHEL STOOD with one foot in the hot foam bath and considered just lying back and letting the pain and the fatigue melt away. She couldn't. She had to phone her father. They would be insane with worry. But if she phoned her father, he could get someone to fetch her from the embassy, maybe, and they could question her. It would be a long process. That meant it would be hours before she could wash off the blood and sweat. She must take the opportunity now.

She got into the bath and sat down. The hot water stung the scratches and cuts, but the satisfaction was immense. Hurry. She picked up the soap and washcloth and began to scrub her youthful body.

12:57–14:01

VIII

A waitress, two waiters and a barman remembered Erin Russel and Rachel Anderson. Griessel had them sit at a separate table with Vusi. He took a seat with his back to the bar.

'Who would like to start?' he asked.

'They were sitting right here,' said one of the waiters, pointing at a table close by, then he suddenly looked up at the door behind Griessel. Mat Joubert stood there, a bag of takeaways in each hand.

'Carry on,' said Joubert, joining them at the table. 'I'm with Captain Griessel.' He pushed boxes towards Vusi and Benny.

'This is Senior Superintendent Mat Joubert of the Provincial Task Force,' Griessel told the waiters, as he saw they were intimidated by the size of his colleague. He looked at the waiter who had spoken first. 'Where were we?'

'Those two in the photo were sitting alone at first. I served them. This one, the blondie, she was partying hard. The other one only had four or five, the whole evening. The backpackers usually booze it up.'

'How did you know they were backpackers?' he asked, spearing chips.

'I have been working here for two years now. You get to know them. The tan, the clothes, the accents . . . and they don't tip much.'

'When did they arrive?'

'Um, let's see . . . before my first smoke break, about nine, say.'

Griessel speared more chips. 'And they were sitting on their own at first?'

'For a while. Then the place filled up. They were dancing; lots of guys asked them. At one time there were five at the table—friends, it seemed. You have to understand it's chaos here when the place is full. I remember the girls, because they were pretty, but that's about all.'

'So you don't remember the men who sat with them?'

'No.'

'And you?' Griessel addressed the rest.

'I just saw them dancing together,' said the waitress, 'which isn't that strange, but they looked as though they were arguing, you know, they were standing there arguing and dancing. But that's all I can tell you.'

'This one . . .' the barman said, identifying Erin Russel. 'My post is the top end of the bar. Two guys were standing there drinking, and she came up there at one stage and talked to them.'

'Tell me about the men,' Griessel said.

'One I sort of remember, he's been here before . . . the other I don't know. They were drinking together, just standing at the bar and chatting. But then she was gone. And the men left suddenly too.'

'Wait. She stood and talked with them? How long was she with them?'

He thought about that. 'Look, all I know is that I saw her standing there. She might have been there for five minutes. Or ten . . .'

'When they left, were they in a hurry?'

'Absolutely . . . it was some time after one o'clock.'

Griessel and Vusi looked at each other. 'You have seen one of them here before,' Griessel said. 'Describe him.'

'A white guy, early twenties, short darkish hair, very tanned . . .'

'And the other one?'

'Black guy, also early twenties . . .'

The waiter suddenly pointed a finger at the door behind Griessel's back and said excitedly, 'That *oke* was at their table last night.'

The detectives turned quickly. Waiting patiently were three SAPS men in blue uniform. One had a large rubbish bag. Between them stood Oliver Sands and a young man Griessel hadn't seen before. 'Yes, we know,' said Griessel.

'The other man is the guy from Carlucci's,' said Vusi, and stood up.

'Is that the bag for me from Metro?' Griessel asked one of the uniforms.

'Yes, Inspector.'

'It's Captain now,' said Mat Joubert from the table.

'Genuine, Benny?' asked Vusi, and there was real happiness in his voice.

BEFORE LEAVING ADAM BARNARD'S OFFICE, Dekker phoned Forensics. 'About the Barnard case—have you found his cellphone anywhere?'

'No, Fransman.'

'Thanks.' Dekker stood still for a second in thought, then opened the office door and walked over to Natasha Abader's desk. Natasha was on the phone, but when Dekker approached she held a hand over the receiver.

'Adam Barnard's cellphone number?'

She recited the number and he keyed it in. He walked down the passage—perhaps Barnard's phone was in his office, in which case he would hear it. But the only ringing was in his ear. It went on and on. Just when he expected it to go over to voicemail, a familiar voice said, 'Hello?'

'Who is this?' Dekker asked in surprise.

'This is Captain Benny Griessel of the SAPS,' said the voice.

'Captain?' said Dekker, completely bewildered.

GRIESSEL AND VUSI were hoping that the young man from Carlucci's would identify one of the Van Hunks personnel when a cellphone began ringing shrilly. A policeman said, 'It's in the bag.'

Griessel ripped open the refuse bag and began scratching around frantically. He grabbed something, fished the phone out of it. The conversation was surreal until the puzzle was solved. 'Benny, it's Fransman. I have just dialled Adam Barnard's number.'

'You're joking. You will never believe where this phone was. Inside a black shoe, in a bag of stuff Metro picked up this morning in the streets around the churchyard murder scene.'

'A shoe? Unbelievable. Where did they find it?'

'I don't know; you'll have to ask Jeremy Oerson at Metro.'

'Can you look up Barnard's call history for me? He called someone last night, just before ten.'

Eventually Griessel found the right icon. *NO RECORDS*, read the screen.

'There's nothing here,' he told Dekker.

WHILE BARRY ANSWERED HIS PHONE, his eyes were on the delivery vehicle parked in front of Carlucci's.

'Why haven't they gone in yet?' said the man with the beard.

'They can't. There's a delivery truck parked in Upper Orange and the driver is looking right down the street. They've been unloading for a while now, so it shouldn't be long.'

'Call me when it's clear. I want to know exactly when they go in.'

'OK, Mr B.'

HIS MOUSTACHE was as big as his ego, thought Mbali Kaleni.

She was sitting with Jack Fischer at a round table in his luxurious office. Fischer was approaching sixty with a full head of hair painstakingly combed into a side parting. And that wide, extravagant moustache.

She did not like him. His heartiness was false and condescending, the kind of attitude towards black people that was typical of many Afrikaner men of a certain age. He had opened the conversation with, 'I would offer you refreshments but I understand you brought your own.'

She did not react.

'You realise I am not obliged to release the information without a warrant.'

She settled herself in the expensive chair and nodded.

'Nonetheless, we *are* former members of the Force.'

'I was relying on the fact that former members would appreciate the urgency of a murder investigation.'

Fischer deployed a superior smile under his moustache. 'We understand only too well.' He opened the file. 'We tracked the AfriSound payment of fifty thousand rand to the account of one Mr Daniel Vlok, and subsequently contacted a subcontractor in Bloemfontein to talk to Mr Vlok.'

'So the subcontractor assaulted him.'

'Absolutely not.' Indignant.

She looked at him with an expression that said she might be a woman in a man's world but that didn't mean he should think she was stupid. 'The name and contact details of the subcontractor?'

Slowly he took the address book out of a drawer of his giant desk.

MAT JOUBERT said he had to get going. Griessel walked with him to the door. Once they were out of earshot of the others, the big detective said, 'Benny, I'm going to join Jack Fischer's company.'

'*Jissis*, Mat,' said Griessel. 'Why? For the money?' He was angry with Joubert, now he was practically the last white man left in the SAPS, and they had come a long way together.

'You know I wouldn't leave just for the money. I'm not enjoying it any more, Benny. With SVC I could contribute, but now . . .'

Joubert had been commanding officer of the former Serious and Violent Crimes Unit and he was good, the best boss Griessel had ever worked for. So he nodded now with some understanding.

'I've been with the Provincial Task Force for four months and I still don't have a portfolio,' said Joubert. 'No people, no job description. They don't know what to do with me. John Afrika has told me I have to accept that I will not be promoted—that is simply the way it is now. That wouldn't bother me so much, but just sitting around . . . And if Zuma becomes President, the Xhosas will be out and the Zulus will be in and everything will change again—a new hierarchy, new agenda, new troubles.'

And where does that leave me? Griessel wanted to ask.

'I've done my bit, Benny. Everything I could for the new country. What are my options at this age? I'll be fifty in July.'

'OK,' said Griessel, because he could see how serious Joubert was.

'I just wanted to let you know.'

'Thanks, Mat . . . Isn't Jack Fischer a bastard?'

Joubert smiled. Only Benny would say it like that. 'How many bastards have we worked for?'

Griessel grinned back. 'A lot.'

RACHEL ANDERSON sat at the table where Piet van der Lingen's myriad books and papers were strewn across the table. In her ear the phone kept ringing—too long, she thought, what was her father doing?

'Rachel?' Her mother said suddenly.

'Mom!'

'Oh my God, Rachel, where are you, are you all right?' She could hear the underlying hysteria and fear.

'Mom, I'm fine, I'm with a very kind man, I'm safe for now . . .'

'Oh, thank God. We've spoken to the police over there, we've spoken to the Ambassador, it's going to be all right . . . Bill, she's safe, she's with somebody. Rachel, this is such wonderful news, I love you, honey. Now, I'm going to put your father on.'

Her father came on the line, 'Honey? You're OK?'

'Yes, Dad, I'm with a very kind gentleman, I'm sitting in his house, I'm perfectly safe.'

'I can't begin to tell you what a great relief that is.' Her father's voice was calm. 'I've spoken to the Consul General in Cape Town, they are standing by. I'm going to give you their number, but first I'm going to give you the number of a police captain. He's in charge of your case and he gave me his word that he'll make sure you are safe, OK?'

'Are you sure?'

'Absolutely, their Police Minister knows about you, the Consul General is talking to them, so this is very high level, nothing can happen to you. So can you take down the numbers?'

She looked across the desk, spotted a pencil, and turned over one of the typed sheets. 'I'm ready,' she said with relief. The nightmare was nearly over.

'JUST EXPLAIN one thing to me,' said Griessel to Oliver Sands. 'Why did the girls bring backpacks to the club?'

'They never went anywhere without them. You know, make-up and stuff.'

Griessel considered the bag that Oerson had brought. Small and compact. That made sense. He would have to sort through the plastic refuse bag, but not here. He would have to go back to Caledon Square.

'JEREMY SPEAKING,' Oerson answered his phone and Dekker could tell he was a coloured man.

'Bro', my name is Fransman Dekker, I'm SAPS. Listen, there was a helluva surprise in that bag of stuff your people found, a shoe. If I can just find out where it was picked up.'

'No idea, bro', but I'll get the men to tell me. Give me ten minutes.'

'Many thanks, it's a murder case. I have to run—will you call me?'

'*Daatlik*, bro'.'

Dekker rang off and opened the door of the accountant's office. Wouter Steenkamp was on the phone. He saw Dekker and said, 'The press are blocking reception. You'll have to help control them.'

'OK.'

'They'll help,' Steenkamp said into the phone. 'What a mess.'

'We need to talk some more,' said Dekker.

'Now what?'

'New information. There are some who say you are cheating them.'

'YOUR PEOPLE CAN GO,' Vusi told Galina Fedorova. 'They've been a big help.'

Griessel had to get out of here, away from the smell of alcohol. The thirst was just below the surface. He had absolutely no idea what he was going to do next. They knew the girls had been here, they knew there had been arguments. They knew two men had left shortly after the girls and they knew there had been a chase down Long Street, but all of that could not tell them where she was. And then his cellphone rang: 'Benny Griessel.'

'I've been to see Alexa Barnard,' Doc Barkhuizen said. 'She's pumped full of medication, but she's a strong woman, Benny. Beautiful too. I can see why you're so concerned about her.'

As Doc Barkhuizen chuckled on the other end, he heard the beep of another incoming call.

'She said when you have a chance, she would like to talk to you. Something to do with her husband.'

'Doc, I've got another call. Thanks for going to see her. We'll talk later,' he said and accepted the other call.

A woman with an American accent asked, 'Is that Captain Benny Ghreezil? My name is Rachel Anderson. My dad said I should call you.'

The name burned right through him, through the disappointment over Mat Joubert, through the frustrations of the day and the desire to drink, jolting his body as he said, '*Jissis*.' Then, 'Are you safe? Where are you?' Adrenaline and relief washed through him.

'I'm with a Mr Pete van der Lingen, number 6 Upper Orange Street . . . in Orainisiegh?'

'Yes, yes, Oranjezicht, 6 Upper Orange. Just stay there, I'm on my way, don't open the door for anybody, please, Miss Anderson,' he pleaded. 'I will call when I get there.' Dear God, this was good news. Griessel gestured to Vusi that they must go, jogged out the door and headed for the alley, hearing Vusi's shoes on the floor behind him.

'I'm not going anywhere,' said Rachel and her voice sounded cheerful, as if she was looking forward to his arrival, and Benny was out the back door, into the alley and running as fast as he could.

BARRY WATCHED the driver of the delivery vehicle get in and start the engine. He looked to the right where the silver Peugeot Boxer panel van stood waiting. He pressed the call button and held it up to his ear.

'Yes?' said the man with the grey beard.

'The truck is leaving.'

'Good. Can you see the panel van?'

Barry looked at the dusty Peugeot. 'Yes, they're moving.'

'Jay is going to call Eben; they will cover the back door. Then he'll turn the van round and come back to the front gate in Upper Orange, so the nose is pointing towards the city. When they go through the front gate, you tell me.'

'Right. Stand by.'

PIET VAN DER LINGEN stood next to his big worktable. 'The police are on their way,' Rachel said, 'Captain Benny Ghree-zil.' The old man smiled at her and said, 'We will have to teach you proper Afrikaans pronunciation—it's Griessel.'

'Gggg . . .' she tried it, sounding as though she was clearing phlegm from her throat.

'That's it,' he said. 'And roll the "r" as well. G-riessel.'

'Ghe-riessel.'

'Almost. Ggg-rrriessel.'

'Griessel.'

'Very good.' They laughed together.

She said, 'How will I ever be able to thank you?'

'For brightening an old man's day?'

'For saving my life,' she said.

'Well, when you put it that way . . . Come and have lunch again, before you go home.'

'I would love to.' She saw him look at the window, with sudden concern shadowing his face. Her eyes followed his, and she saw four men coming up the garden path. 'Oh my God.' she said because she knew them. She got up from the chair. 'Don't open the door! They want to kill me—they killed my friend last night.' She ran a few steps down the passage, a dead end.

Then the leaded glass of the front door shattered. She sprinted back across the hall on the way to the kitchen, the back door. 'Come on!' she shouted at van der Lingen. The old man stood frozen, as though he planned to stop them.

'No!' she screamed.

The door opened. She had to get away and ran through the kitchen, hearing a shot in the hall. She reached the back door and spotted a long carving knife in the drying rack. She grabbed it, tugged open the back door, and stepped outside in sudden dazzling sunlight. There were two more men between her and the little gate in the corner, charging at her. She had only one choice. She ran at the one in front of her, the white man whose arms were spread wide to seize her. She whipped up the knife, stabbing at his chest with hatred and terror. He tried to pull away, too late, the knife piercing his throat.

'Bitch!' the black man yelled and hit her with his fist. A cascade of light exploded in her head. She fell to the right, onto the grass, hearing their shouts. She struggled to get up, but they were on her. Another fist slammed into her face, arms pinned her down. She heard their short, brute grunts, saw an arm lifted high, something metallic swinging at her face, and then the darkness.

GRIESSEL RACED. He pressed long and hard on the hooter, saying to Vusi, 'I should have taken a car with a siren.' They sped up Long Street through one red traffic light after another. Every time he had to stick his arm out of the window and wave frantically at the crossing traffic. Vusi did the same.

'At least she should be safe,' said Vusi warily, ever the diplomat. Griessel knew that what he really meant was, 'We needn't drive so madly.'

'She should be,' Griessel said and waved wildly, hooting continuously, 'But I can't afford a fuck-up.' He put his foot down hard, and the Opel's tyres squealed.

MBALI KALENI was driving serenely down Annandale in dense traffic near the turn into Upper Orange. She put on her indicator light to change lanes, waiting patiently, but no one would give her a gap. She shook her head: Cape Town drivers. Eventually the stream thinned and she swung the Corsa over, keeping the indicator on.

IT LOOKED LIKE a hornet's nest, Dekker thought, the crowd abuzz, with microphones poised to sting you. He stood on the stairs, and shouted loudly, 'Attention, everyone.'

They swarmed on him; there must have been twenty people, all talking. He could hear only snatches of the questions '. . . Ivàn Nell shot him?'

'Is Josh Geyser under arrest?'

'. . . Xandra dead?'

He held up his right hand and just stood there. He knew they would quieten down eventually.

KALENI SAW THEM.

She spotted the panel van in front of the house, thinking at first it was those clowns from Forensics.

There was movement on the other side, as she approached.

People were carrying something. What was going on?

Closer still she saw there were four men in a hurry, each holding onto a piece of something. They moved crablike along the pavement, but the picket fence hid their burden, heading for the panel van. Strange.

They were carrying a person, she saw as they came around the corner and out from behind the fence. She kept her eyes on them: it was the girl, lifeless, they were gripping her arms and legs. Mbali accelerated and her hand reached for her pistol. She swung across the road and aimed for the front of the panel van, going too fast. In front of her one man jumped out of the van, holding a pistol. She wrestled with the steering wheel and came to a standstill just a metre from the Peugeot.

She saw a pistol aimed at her, the windscreen starred and the bullet slammed against metal behind her. She wanted to dive down, but the safety belt held her.

'*uJesu*,' she said quietly and reached a hand to unclip it.

He shot her. She felt the dreadful blow to her body, but the safety belt was loose; she flattened herself, right hand reaching for her pistol. She lifted it and fired off three blind shots through the windscreen. The pain was an earthquake that rippled through her. She checked the wound. A hole below her left breast, blood trickling into a pool on the upholstery. She fired off more shots and sat up quickly. The pain ripped through her torso. Quickly she scanned for him through the windscreen. He wasn't there. Here he was, just beside the door, pistol in both hands aimed at her eye. She saw a kind of African necklace around his neck, the beads spelling out a word. She jerked back her head, swung her pistol around in the certain knowledge of death. Fleeting sadness, so short, this life, as she saw his trigger finger tighten with purpose.

GRIESSEL BLASTED A PATH through the traffic with his hooter and turned into Upper Orange. They were nearly there. A madman in a big silver panel van came racing downhill in the middle of the road. Benny swerved out of the way. He caught a glimpse of the driver's face, a young asshole with a fierce expression. He changed down a gear, charged up the hill. Then Vusi said, 'It's just up there,' and they crested the rise. They both saw the Corsa at the same time, and neither spoke, because from the angle it had stopped, something was not right.

The Toyota bakkie drove right in front of him, reversing out of a driveway. Griessel slammed on the brakes and the Opel nosedived, just missing the Toyota's front bumper. He swung across the road and stopped behind the Corsa, leaped out and heard the Toyota racing away towards the city. Trouble here, bullet holes in the windscreen and the driver's window and there was someone behind the wheel.

'It's Mbali,' Vusi shouted as he pulled open the other door.

Griessel saw her head on her chest. He pulled open the door, trying to feel her neck for a pulse. His fingers slipped in the blood. He saw the wound below her ear, a pulsing vein pumping out thick red fluid.

'Get an ambulance! She's alive!' Carefully he pulled her out of the car and laid her on the pavement. Two wounds, but the one in the side of her head was bleeding the most. He felt for his handkerchief, bent beside Mbali and pressed the hanky against the hole. He heard Vusi talking urgently over the phone.

'Benny, they're on their way. They know it's a policewoman.'

Griessel pressed the hanky harder. She opened her eyes. 'The ambulance is coming, Mbali. You're going to make it.'

She made a noise. Vusi picked up Mbali's hand. He talked quietly to her in an African language. Griessel noted the small Xhosa man's calmness and thought Vusi might not be a hardass, but he was strong.

Mbali was trying to say something. He felt her jaw moving under his hand, he saw the blood running out of her mouth. 'No, no, don't talk now.'

He looked up at the house. 'Vusi, you will have to see what's going on inside there.' The black detective jumped up and ran.

Griessel looked at Mbali. Her eyes closed.

AT FIRST she was aware only of voices shouting, the revving of an engine. Then she felt the pain in her face and she wanted to put a hand over it, but she couldn't. Then she remembered everything and she jerked.

'The bitch is waking up,' one of them said. She tried to open her eyes, but she could not. One eye was swollen shut, the other would not focus. Four people were holding her down.

A cellphone rang shrilly. 'It's the Big Guy,' said a voice she knew.

'Tell him.' Another familiar voice.

'Mr B, it's Steve. The bitch stabbed Eben . . . It's bad, Chief . . . He's with Rob in the bakkie. OK, yes, it's here, hang on . . . The boss wants to know what's in the bag . . .'

The one holding her leg let go. 'Here, take it,' he said and then she kicked him with all her might.

A heavy blow against her head, her leg clamped fast again, and she screamed. She fought wildly, straining to break free, but it was no good.

VUSI CAME RUNNING; Griessel could hear his hasty steps. 'Benny, there's an old man inside. He's been shot, but he's alive.'

'Nobody else?'

'Nobody.'

Then suddenly and clearly, the wail of an ambulance.

'YOU DO THAT AGAIN, I'll shoot you in the leg, you hear me?'

His face was right up against hers, his voice crazed. She closed her eyes and went limp.

'It's not in here,' said Steve up front. 'Mr B, it's not in the bag.' A long silence, then the sound of the vehicle slowing to a more regular speed. Then, 'There was no time. This fat cop turned up, but Jay shot her, she's a goner . . . OK . . .' The sound of a cellphone snapping shut. 'The Big Guy says to take her to the warehouse.'

ONCE HE HAD MANAGED to get the last member of the press out of the door and locked it, Fransman Dekker heard a voice behind him, 'When will you be finished?'

Mouton stood on the stairs, looking displeased.

'When I have asked all my questions,' said Dekker.

'How many questions do you still want to ask? And you're talking to my employees without a lawyer being present. It can't go on like this.'

They walked through the spacious seating area. Dekker stopped in his tracks and shoved his face close to Mouton's. 'I have the right to talk to every member of your staff without your lawyer sitting in.'

Mouton's skin flooded crimson. 'What did Nell say to you? He's not one of our artists any more. He has no say here.'

Dekker stalked off down the corridor and opened Steenkamp's door without knocking. He wanted to shut it before Mouton came through, but then he saw the legal 'undertaker' sitting across from the accountant.

'Please, take a seat, Inspector,' Groenewald said.

THE PARAMEDICS ran from the front door with the stretcher. Griessel jogged after them. 'Will she make it?'

'Don't know,' said the front one, holding out the bag of plasma to Griessel. 'Hold that while we load.'

'And the old man?'

'I think so,' the paramedic said. They lifted the old man up in the stretcher and pushed him in beside Mbali. One paramedic ran round to the driver's door, the other jumped in the back. The ambulance's sirens began to wail as it pulled away just as the first of a convoy of patrol vehicles appeared over the hump of the hill.

'Vusi,' Griessel said, 'get them to seal off the streets.'

Griessel surveyed the scene—Mbali's car, the strewn bullet casings, the shattered front door. The old man had been shot inside there and they had grabbed Rachel . . . It would take hours to process everything. Hours that he did not have. The hunters have caught their prey. How long would they let her live? Why hadn't they killed her here, like Erin Russel?

He needed help. Between Vusi and himself they didn't have enough manpower. He called Mat Joubert's number. He knew it would piss off John Afrika. But in the big picture that was a minor issue.

WOUTER STEENKAMP, the accountant, laughed, and Mouton gave a snort of derision. The lawyer, Groenewald, shook his head ruefully.

'Why is that so funny?' Dekker asked.

Steenkamp leaned back in his throne behind the PC. 'Do you really believe Nell is the first artist who believes he is being fleeced?'

'It's the same old story,' said Mouton. 'In the beginning, with the first cheque, they come in here and it's, "Thanks, guys, I've never seen this much money." We're the heroes and they are pathetically grateful.'

'But it doesn't last,' said Steenkamp. 'Two years, *pappie*, you can set your calendar to it, then they come in saying, "What is that deduction and why is this so little?" and suddenly they have forgotten how poor they were when we signed them.'

'Ivàn Nell says he compared your figures with the amounts he made from compilations with independents.'

This time even the lawyer sang in the choir of indignation.

GRIESSEL STOOD in the hallway, the urgency hot in him. He didn't want to get too involved with this part of the investigation; he had to focus on Rachel and how to get her back. He looked fleetingly at the blood on the blue and silver carpet where the old man had been shot. He would have to phone her father.

How the hell had they found her? She had talked to her father and then with him. How long had it taken him to get here? Ten minutes? Twelve at the most. How could they have driven here, shot Mbali and the old man and carried Rachel off in twelve minutes?

How was he going to explain this to Rachel's father? The man who had asked him, *Tell me—can I trust you?*

And he had said, 'Yes, Mr Anderson. You can trust me.'

How had they found her? That was the question that mattered, because the 'how' would supply the 'who' and that was what he needed to know.

Had she phoned anyone else? That was the place to start. He would have to find out. He took his phone out of his pocket to phone Telkom.

No, phone John Afrika first. He knew what the Regional Commissioner was going to say. He could already hear the consternation. *How, Benny? How?*

Griessel sighed. That feeling he had had this morning—that there was trouble brewing . . .

And this day was far from over.

'LET ME EXPLAIN to you about a compilation first,' said Steenkamp. 'Some clown decides he wants to make money out of Valentine's Day or Christmas or something. He phones a few people and says, "Have you got a song for me?" There are no studio costs because the recording has already been done. All he has to do is market the CD a bit, and make a few TV ads.'

'He does his accounts on the back of a cigarette box,' said Mouton.

'No overheads,' said Steenkamp. 'We sit here with an admin department, a financial department and marketing and promotions departments. We carry forty per cent of a distribution wing, because we are full service. We stand by the artist for the long term. We build a brand, we don't just flog a few CDs.'

'Let me tell you another thing,' said Mouton. 'Half of the hits in this country are German pop songs or Dutch or Flemish or whatever. Adam had guys in Europe and as soon as there was a song that stood out they would email it in MP3 format and Adam would sit down with a pen and write Afrikaans lyrics. And we have to administer it all. That money has to go to Germany; the songwriter and the publisher have to get their cut. But here comes this independent and he gets someone to do a cover of Adam's translation of this German song . . . you get it?'

'I think so,' said Dekker, engrossed.

'. . . and now Adam must be paid, the German and his publisher must be paid, but the independent says, no, we made only five thousand, but he's lying, because there's no control over distribution, the independents do their own now and nobody keeps track.'

'That's why the cheques are so big.'

'Then the bastard comes along and says we are bloody cheating him.'

'Amen,' said Groenewald. 'Tell him about the passwords and the PDFs.'

'There are only three or four big CD distributors in South Africa,' Steenkamp said. 'They keep sales records of every CD and send a pass-word-protected PDF file of every artist's sales to me. We transfer the money to the artist. I email him the same PDF, just as I received it, so he can see everything. Nobody can fiddle with the statement because we don't have the password.'

'So tell me, how can we rip them off?' said Mouton.

'Impossible,' said Groenewald.

JOHN AFRIKA HAD RANTED and raved over the telephone, 'You phone the father in America, Benny, I can't do it. How the hell, I'm on my way, *jissis*, how did it happen?' He slammed the phone down and Griessel was left wondering whether Jack Fischer had a job for an alcoholic who was stuffing up two cases in a single day. Then Vusi ran in and said, 'Benny, it was the delivery van that nearly hit us—we have an eyewitness.'

So now they were on the pavement with a woman, early thirties, a little pale and shy—unimpressive until she began to talk. Her name was Evelyn Marais and she had seen everything.

She had come out of Carlucci's on the way to her car, a red Toyota Tazz. She had heard shots and stopped in the middle of the street. She spoke calmly and clearly. 'The first shots didn't even sound like gunshots, more like firecrackers. Then I looked. There were four of them carrying a girl.'

'The girl, how were they carrying her?'

'Two had her by the shoulders, two carried her legs here behind the knees.'

'Could you tell if she was resisting?'

'No . . . I think there was blood on her hands. I thought maybe she was hurt and they were helping her to the van. Then other shots went off, much louder. But I couldn't see who was shooting. I saw them only when they came running around the van. One man, the driver, had a pistol with a silencer in his hand.'

This was the moment that Griessel began to suspect she was not just your average eyewitness. 'A pistol with a silencer?'

'Yes.'

'Ma'am, what work do you do?'

'I'm a researcher for a film company. And it's Miss, actually.'

'Can you describe the men?'

'They were young, in their twenties, I'd say. Three were white, one was black. Three of them were in jeans and T-shirts, no, one was wearing a golf shirt, light green, almost lemon. The other one was in brown chinos and a white shirt with some writing over the pocket. It was too far to see . . .'

Griessel and Vusi looked at her in amazement. 'You are most observant, Miss.'

She shrugged shyly. 'It's just what I saw.'

'The girl, Miss, you said the girl had blood on her hands?'

'Yes, her hand, wait a bit, her right hand and her arm up to here,' she indicated her elbow.

'Nowhere else?'

'No.'

'Did it look as though she was . . . unconscious?'

'I . . . perhaps. No. I don't know. But she wasn't struggling.'

'And the panel van?' Vusi asked. 'You don't know what make it was?'

'A Peugeot. Only when it drove off did I see the logo. The one with the little lion, you know. . .'

Griessel just nodded. He thought, this woman is a genius.

'A silver Peugeot, but quite dirty,' she said. 'And the registration number if you want it, of course.'

'You got the registration number?' Griessel was astonished.

'CA four-oh-nine, then a little hyphen,' and she drew a line horizontally in the air with her finger, 'and then three-four-one.'

'Miss,' said Griessel, 'would you like to come and work for us?'

'IN ANY CASE,' Willie Mouton said, 'Adam phoned me last night, some time after nine, to tell me about Ivàn Nell's stories.'

'And?' Dekker asked.

'We laughed about it. Adam said, let him bring in his auditor, let him run up some overheads himself.'

'That's it?'

'Adam said he was going home because Alexa wasn't well. And that's where Josh Geyser was waiting for him. I don't care what he's telling you. You can see in that man's eyes he is capable of anything.'

'VUSI, WE'RE WORKING against the clock,' Griessel told him at the garden gate. 'I want you to follow up on the Peugeot. It might be a false number plate, but let's try. Forget everything, the panel van is your baby.'

Vusi nodded enthusiastically, fired up by Griessel's urgency.

'I've sent for Mat Joubert. He can deal with the scene. I just want to make a quick pass through the house, see if there is anything significant, then I am going to try to work out how they knew she was here.'

He turned and walked into the house, trying to reconstruct the event quickly. In the hallway they had smashed the glass and gained entry. They shot the old man here. On the left was a study, the table covered with documents and a telephone. Had she phoned from here?

He crossed the hall into the kitchen. He spotted the open back door, ran out, careful to watch where he stepped. He saw blood outside, a long trail over a paved pathway. Fear gripped his heart. He squatted down to examine the splashes. God, had they cut her throat? The thought was a blade in his guts.

No, not possible. He had asked Evelyn Marais if the blood was only on her hands. *Yes, her hand . . . her right hand and her arm up to here.*

But the blood pattern outside told a different story.

Hoping she hadn't left yet, he jumped up and ran out through the back gate to where the growing crowd stood behind the yellow tape on the corner. His eyes searched out the Tazz. There it was still, the woman seated inside, about to drive off. 'Sorry, sorry,' he said, to get through the crowd. 'Miss,' he gasped, out of breath, standing at her door while she wound down the window.

'The girl . . . are you absolutely sure about the blood . . . just on her arm?'

She shut her eyes. She sat like that for about half a minute.

The eyes opened. 'Yes,' she nodded decisively.

'There was no blood anywhere else?'

She shook her head, absolutely certain. 'No, just the arm.'

'Thank God for that,' said Benny. 'Thank you.'

It wasn't Rachel Anderson's blood.

FRANSMAN DEKKER'S FIRST INSTINCT was to blame Mouton and Steenkamp for his frustrations, for the anger that was bottled up inside him. It was the way Mouton had said Josh Geyser did it, as though Dekker were an idiot. It was the way Steenkamp leaned back in his chair, smug, *windgat* whitey . . .

He stood behind the closed door of Adam Barnard's office and glared at his photo. Big man, full of confidence. He was the very image of success, Mr Beloved, not an enemy in the world. Impossible.

And that, Dekker knew, was the source of his frustration. He was in a dead-end street. The whole investigation was slowly but surely sinking into a swamp of improbabilities. Nothing made sense and the whiteys were laughing at him.

And where was Mbali Kaleni?

He sat down and rubbed his eyes. He would have to think it all through from the beginning, because none of the pieces fitted together. Josh and Melinda Geyser. Both were lying. Or neither. The video? The blackmailer? Where *was* Mbali? She was going to solve the case and he would look like a fool. He took his phone out of his pocket and called her number. It rang and rang and rang. She was ignoring him on purpose. His temper flared up again, like a wildfire.

Wait, wait. Calm down. Concentrate: Adam Barnard was carried into his house, up the stairs to his drunken wife.

That meant someone who knew his wife passed out, blind drunk, every night. Someone strong enough to carry the dead weight of Barnard. Someone who knew Barnard had a pistol in the house—and knew where to find it. Forget Bloemfontein and the blackmailer. The knowledge of the pistol was key.

Who would know? Josh Geyser? Perhaps. But Griessel had said it wasn't Josh. Griessel was nobody's fool. Was he mistaken? How much of the new Captain's attention was on the churchyard murder? He was only human after all. Knowledge of the pistol. How many people would know that? Alexa Barnard, another one pronounced innocent by Griessel, an alcoholic woman. As a sister-in-drink, had she pulled the wool over his eyes? Did she have help? A lover?

He would have to phone Griessel, tell him he had doubts about Alexa, about the Geysers. Where was Mbali?

Someone knocked. Natasha put her head round the door. 'There is a policeman at the door. He says he wants to show you where they found a shoe.'

'Thank you,' he said. 'I want to talk to you again, please.'

She didn't look too ecstatic about that.

IX

Dekker and the young black Metro policeman had to shoulder their way through the journalists at the front door.

'Up there, around the corner,' the Metro man said and they walked in silence. Dekker realised the southeaster had picked up and the perfect summer day was gone. By late afternoon the wind would be gale force; but then it was January, there was nothing you could do about that.

They turned left into New Church Street and crossed the road. The Metro man pointed with his baton.

'The shoe was lying here?'

'Just there. Almost in the gutter.'

'You didn't look inside it?'

'Inside the shoe?' The man screwed up his face, as if he wasn't completely convinced of Dekker's intelligence.

'I wouldn't have either,' said Dekker. 'Thanks a lot.'

'Can I go now?'

'Wait. I just want to know, did they ask you to pick things up?'

'Yes, Inspector Oerson sent us. We had to pick up anything that might have been in a rucksack. I saw the shoe. I found a hat too, over there on the corner. I put it in the big rubbish bag. Abrams took the bag to Inspector Oerson, because he said he wanted to see everything.'

'Thank you. That's all I wanted to know.'

Dekker considered the spot where the shoe had lain. Then the corner of New Church and Buiten. About 200 to 300 metres from AfriSound. What was the significance of that?

He took out his phone.

It was time to call Benny Griessel.

THE METRO POLICE licensing department told Vusi the Peugeot Boxer panel van, CA 409–341, belonged to CapSud Trading, contact Frederik Willem de Jager, La Belle Street in Stikland. 'But there's a tag on it,' the woman said. 'The vehicle is in the pound in Greenpoint.'

'Is it there now?'

'That's what the system says.'

Vusi thought it over. 'Do you have a phone number for de Jager?'

GRIESSEL STOOD at the big table holding a sheet of paper with two numbers on it. One was his cellphone number, the other a Cape number he did not recognise. He studied the handwriting, comparing it to the notes on the documents on the table. The numbers were written in larger, rounder script.

Rachel Anderson?

He dialled the Cape number. 'United States Consul, how may I help you?'

'Sorry, wrong number,' he said and terminated the call.

'CAPSUD TRADING, good afternoon,' a woman's voice answered.

'Could I speak to Mr de Jager, please?'

'Who is this speaking?'

'Inspector Vusi Ndabeni of the South African Police Service.'

'Mr de Jager is deceased, Inspector.'

'I'm sorry. When did he pass away?'

'Four months ago.'

'I am calling to enquire about a Peugeot Boxer panel van, registration CA four-oh-nine, three-four-one, registered in the name of CapSud Trading.'

'That must be the stolen one. We bought it in early October last year, then we sent it to the sign writers to have our logo applied. It was stolen that night.'

'Are you aware that the vehicle was in the Metropolitan Police pound?'

'Yes, they recovered it in a Fire Service parking spot, so they impounded it. That was mid-October.'

'Why have you never collected it, Ma'am?'

'Because when Frik died everything was frozen. Nobody could draw money or sign a cheque, and the estate will only be wound up in two months' time. This is the New South Africa, you know, you have to wait.'

'You are. . .?'

'I am Saartjie de Jager. Frik's wife.'

'May I ask how Mr de Jager died, ma'am?'

'Cholesterol. The doctor warned him, I warned him, but Frik wouldn't listen. He was like that all his life. Now I'm the one trying to clear up the mess.'

EVERYTHING HAPPENED at once. Griessel waited impatiently for his contact at Telkom to get back to him, John Afrika walked past the blood in the hallway, looking at it in horror, Vusi came through the front door with an excited 'Benny!' and Griessel's phone began to ring. He thought it was the Telkom man, and answered it. Through the window he saw Mat Joubert walking up the garden path.

'Benny, it's Fransman. How sure are we that Barnard's wife and Josh Geyser are not involved?'

He needed to tell Afrika that he had asked Joubert to come. 'Don't know,' he said, his mind not on the conversation.

'So I can question them some more? I'll get Mbali to talk to Alexa . . .'

The female detective's name forced him to focus. 'Don't you know yet?'

'What are you doing here?' he heard Afrika say behind him. He turned. Joubert had entered the room. He put his hand over the receiver as Dekker asked, 'Don't I know what yet?'

'Commissioner, I'll explain,' said Griessel and then to Dekker, 'Mbali was shot, Fransman. Here in Upper Orange, the American girl . . .'

Dekker was dumbfounded.

'She's in hospital,' Griessel said.

'The American girl? What was Mbali doing there? I sent her to Jack Fischer. They did some work for AfriSound. Is Mbali OK?'

'We don't know. I'm sorry, I have to run. Talk to Geyser again if you think you should. I'll call you later.' He ended the call and said, 'Commissioner, I asked Mat to come and help.' Afrika's face began to screw up in protest but Griessel didn't give him the chance. 'All due respect,' he began, 'there's a manpower problem. Mat is underutilised at PT, he's the best detective in the Cape and I have a girl I have to find, whatever it takes. There's no time to waste. Vusi is working on the panel van they took Rachel away in, I'm going to find out who knew she was in this house. We don't have time to process the scene and I need someone who knows what he's doing. I must phone Rachel's father but not before I know what is going on. So, please, let's get the girl.'

Conflicting emotions passed like the seasons across Afrika's face. He nodded slightly. 'Get her, Benny,' he said, and walked out, careful not to step in the pool of blood.

Griessel's phone rang again and the man from Telkom said, 'Benny, between twelve and two there were only two calls made from that number. The first was to West Lafayette in Indiana, the second was to you.'

'What time was the first one made?'

'Thirteen thirty-six. It lasted for two minutes, twenty-two seconds.'

'Thanks a lot.' He ended the call and thought. He tried to piece the thing together, the thousands of loose strings in his head.

'Benny . . .' Vusi said, but he held up a hand, checked his cellphone for the record of Rachel's call to him. He received it at thirteen forty-one. Then they had raced here. If her attackers had intercepted her first call, they had only had five minutes more. They must have arrived just after he had finished speaking to Rachel. That was some quick reaction. Too quick. . . What if they had been in the area somewhere nearby?

A spark lit up in his brain. 'Vusi, was it here on the corner that she went into the café?'

'The deli,' Ndabeni nodded.

'And then she ran down here,' Griessel indicated Upper Orange. 'They were waiting somewhere, Vusi. They must have seen her, but with all the police around . . .'

'Benny, the panel van . . .'

But Griessel did not hear him. Why hadn't they shot her? Just the old man. They had cut Erin Russel's throat. But they allowed Rachel to live when they could easily have killed her. Here in this house. But they abducted her?

Another revelation.

'The rucksack,' he said. They had cut Erin's sack off her shoulders. 'See if you can find a rucksack.' He walked down the passage. 'Mat, can you look in the kitchen and outside?'

'What does the rucksack look like?'

'I have no idea,' said Griessel. But a thought occurred to him and he phoned Caledon Square. He identified himself and asked if there were still uniforms at the Cat & Moose.

'They are still there.'

'Tell them to ask where the American girls' luggage is. They must guard it with their lives.'

Griessel said to Vusi, 'They're looking for something the girls have. That's why Rachel is still alive.'

'WHAT NOW?' Natasha asked as Dekker closed Barnard's door behind her.

'Sit down, please,' said Dekker. 'Can I trust you, sister?'

'I'm not your sister.'

'Why not, sister? Are you too la-di-da working here with the whiteys?'

'Do you think that's what it's about?' Her eyes flashed. 'You can't stand it that I slept with a white man, can you? It's no use, shaking your head, I saw how you changed when I said he did it here with me too. Let me tell you, he wasn't the first white man and he won't be the last. But I don't discriminate, I sleep with whoever I want, because it's the New South Africa, but you want to "brother" and "sister" us all. You want us to be a separate tribe, us coloureds; you're the kind who goes around complaining how hard it is to be a coloured. And, just for the record, how many white women have you slept with?'

He looked away, towards the window. 'What makes you think I have?'

'What woman can look at you and not think of sex?' she said.

Now he looked her in the eyes, and she looked back, angry.

'I'll take that as a compliment.' Knowing he had lost the battle.

'Why am I here?'

'Because I trust you. I am going to tell you things you can't repeat. The people who shot Adam Barnard know his wife passes out every night and where he keeps his pistol. You are the only one I can trust. Tell me who knows him that well. The Geysers?'

'I don't think so. I don't think they have ever been to his house. Adam was ashamed of Alexa. A few times she'd made a scene when he took people to his house. He lived here. He would go home about seven o'clock, but he would come back, often. Eight o'clock, nine o'clock, then he would work till twelve.'

'So who would have known that?'

She considered before she answered. 'I knew about his wife . . .'

'Who else?'

'Willie and Wouter and Michèle . . .'

'Who's Michèle?'

'She does the PR.'

'And she knows Adam well?'

'They've worked together for years. They say Adam and Michèle were lovers years ago.'

'How many years ago?'

'From when Alexa began drinking, apparently. He went and cried on Michèle's shoulder.'

'Damnit, sister,' he said indignantly. 'My list keeps getting longer.'

MAT JOUBERT walked back to the hall where Griessel and Vusi were watching him expectantly. He shook his head. No rucksack. He watched Benny process the information silently, and waited patiently until he knew he could speak.

'You know about the blood out there?' he asked.

'Yes.' Benny was scratching the thick, unruly hair just behind his ear.

A feeling of compassion swept over Joubert for this colleague, this friend, this man he had known for a lifetime. Griessel's frame had always been too small for all his energy. That face—twenty years ago it had an elfish quality. You could barely see it now; life had eroded it away in a network of tiny furrows. But Joubert knew that in that brain the synapses were firing. Benny had the brain of a detective, always faster and more creative than his. Joubert had always been methodical but Griessel had natural flair.

'It might be drugs,' said Griessel, but to himself. 'I think the . . . the rucksack . . .'

'Benny, the panel van was in the Metro pound,' said Vusi.

Griessel stared into nowhere. 'Maybe they stole the drugs. Or took them but didn't pay . . .'

Joubert asked, 'Is it the girl's blood?'

'No.' Then Benny focused sharply on Joubert, with sudden insight. 'It's not Rachel's. It's the blood of one of those bastards.' He grabbed his phone.

Joubert said, 'Benny, let me phone the hospitals.'

'No, Mat, let Caledon Square do it,' and he called their number and gave the order to the radio room sergeant, 'Any young man between the age of, say, eighteen and thirty-five, any colour, any race, any language, Sarge, every one with blood on him, I want to know about.' Then Griessel looked at Vusi. 'Metro's pound?'

'That's right. The same Peugeot. It was stolen and Metro recovered it. It has been parked in the pound since October, because the owner died of a heart attack and the estate is frozen. I'm going to find out what's going on. How did they get it out of the pound?'

'Vusi, excellent work, go and find out. Let's get the van, because that's about all we have.'

Vusi jogged away and Griessel hung his head while Mat watched him. The two of them were the dinosaurs of the SAPS, he thought, a dying breed, but still not completely ineffective.

Griessel scratched at the bushy hair behind his ear. He grunted, 'Hu . . .' turned and went outside. Joubert followed him down the slate pathway. Griessel opened the garden gate and went and stood in the street. He turned to face Lion's Head. Joubert stood behind him, watching how the wind ruffled Benny's hair. The day was being overtaken by the southeaster.

'Before six this morning, up there,' said Griessel, pointing at Lion's Head, 'she told a woman to call the police. Those young men had been chasing her since two in the morning. At eleven at the deli there, she told her father that she couldn't talk to the police. Five hours after she was on Lion's Head she arrives at the café. And the fucker parks in the street and comes in after her. How did they know, Mat?'

They stared at Table Mountain. Then Joubert realised what Griessel obviously already had. They had been sitting on the mountain and watching the whole city. 'Could be,' he said. 'But you can't see this house from the mountain.'

'That's true.' Griessel's head jerked, a tumbler dropped, and he began walking down the street. A hundred metres farther on, he stopped in a driveway. 'He sat here, in a bakkie . . . he nearly drove us off the road.'

Griessel jogged up the drive and looked back at Piet van der Lingen's house. 'No . . . Mat, come and stand here. What can you see of the house?'

The big man came and stood there. 'Just too low to see everything.'

'He drove out of here, a guy in a bakkie. Toyota four-by-four, faded red, the old model. In a hell of a hurry.'

'He could have stood on the bakkie,' Joubert said. 'He would have been able to see everything then.'

'*Jissis*,' said Griessel. 'He was young, just like the others.' He looked at Joubert. 'I will recognise him, Mat, if I see his face again.' He was quiet for a heartbeat. 'An old Toyota . . . that's not a drug dealer's car, Mat.'

Griessel's phone rang. 'Sarge?' He listened for about forty seconds and looked at Joubert. 'About ten minutes ago someone dropped off a young white guy at City Park Casualty, and then left in haste. Victim was stabbed in the throat with a blade; they might be able to save him.' Griessel began to run.

'I'll do the scene,' shouted Joubert. 'Get her, Benny.' But he couldn't tell if Benny had heard him.

IT WAS JESS ANDERSON who broke the silence in the study and put words to their anxiety. 'Why doesn't he call? It's almost forty minutes.'

Bill Anderson sat beside her on the brown leather couch. 'We don't know how far he had to travel.'

'We could call him . . .'

'Let's give it a little more time.'

THEY HELD HER DOWN on the concrete floor, four of them. A fifth put a blade under her T-shirt and cut it away, then her shorts, then her underwear. The same knife that had cut Erin's throat stripped her naked. They pushed her against the narrow steel pillar, her arms bent backwards and tied round the pole. She sank down as far as her bonds allowed, so that her gaze fixed on her running shoes.

'Where is it?'

She didn't answer. She heard him coming, footfalls on the floor, two steps only. He grabbed her hair and jerked her head up. He knelt in front of her.

'Where is it?' the question was repeated.

Her left eye was swollen shut. She focused the other on him. His handsome face was against hers, calm as ever. His voice carried authority, control.

Her revulsion for him was greater than her fear of death. It brought with it the impulse to do something, to kick, to spit. But she reconsidered. She was not powerless. They could not kill her yet. She could buy time. She was not alone. *I'm on my way, don't open the door for anybody*, the policeman's voice. He was somewhere now, looking for her, he would find her.

She answered the man by shaking her head.

'I'm going to hurt you,' he said. In his practical way.

'Go ahead.' She tried to keep her voice as even as his.

He laughed. 'You have no idea.' He stood up. 'Their luggage is still at the Cat & Moose.'

'We should have taken that long ago.'

'We didn't know, Steve. Where's Barry? Call him, go and get their stuff.'

'They're not going to just give it to us, Jay.' She saw them looking at each other. There was tension between them.

Steve, the black guy, eventually nodded and left. Jay spoke to another one, one she didn't know, 'There's a hardware shop one block up. I want pruning shears. We'll cut off her toes.'

MICHÈLE MALHERBE was blonde, attractive. Dekker found her age hard to pin down until he looked at her hands and realised she must be in her late fifties.

'It's a great loss, Inspector,' she said. He could see she had been crying.

'It is,' he said. 'You knew him well?'

'Nearly twenty-five years.'

'I understand you know the industry well, too.' She nodded, her face serious and focused. 'Why would someone want to . . .' he searched for a euphemism '. . . do away with him?'

'I don't think Adam's death has anything to do with the industry. We may be an emotional lot—music is emotion, after all, is it not? But there is no great difference between the music industry and any other. I can't think of a single reason why anyone in Adam's world would want to murder him. I can't think of anyone who would be capable of that.'

'The way this happened points to someone who had information about Adam's domestic situation. They knew about his wife, for example . . .'

Her smile was sympathetic. 'Unfortunately, Alexa's situation is general knowledge. The press makes this seem like an environment where nobody cares, but that is a false impression. There are many of us who have contact with Alexa in the hope that she will recover. She is a wonderful person.'

'Are you one of them?'

She nodded.

'But I understand you were more than just friends with Adam Barnard?'

She looked at him in disappointment. 'I will leave my lawyer's number with Natasha,' she said and walked slowly, with dignity, to the door, opened it and closed it quietly behind her.

He sat staring at the closed door. He had no idea what to do next.

THE NURSE at Casualty told Griessel he would have to talk to the superintendent and he asked her to phone him. It's not a man, the nurse bridled, and Griessel said he didn't care what it was, she had better phone. She dialled a number, whispered over the phone and said the superintendent was in a meeting.

'Miss, I have a female detective in that operating theatre with two gunshot wounds and I don't know if she is going to make it. I have a nineteen-year-old American girl who has been abducted by people who cut her friend's throat in Long Street this morning. That man in there is my only chance of finding her before they kill her. Let me tell you now, if anything happens to her because you are obstructing the law, you will all sleep in the dirtiest, most crowded cell I can find in the Peninsula.'

She picked up the phone again. 'I think Dr Marinos should come to ICU immediately,' she said.

AT THE GATE of the Metropolitan Police vehicle pound the young traffic officer in a gleaming uniform opened a fat green file.

'Yes, that vehicle was booked out at twelve thirty-four. And here . . .' he rotated the file so that Vusi could read it '. . . is the release form, stamped and signed.'

'Who signed it?'

The traffic officer studied the signature. 'I can't say. You would have to ask Administration.'

'Where is Administration?'

'There. In the licensing building. I'll give you the case number.'

MAT JOUBERT pulled on rubber gloves and picked up the bullet casings in the foot well of Mbali Kaleni's Corsa. He heard Thick and Thin of Forensics on the tar beside him circling the other casings with chalk.

Kaleni's big black handbag lay on the front passenger seat. On top was an A5 notebook, the pages folded back, blood on the top page, fine drops, something written down. He picked the notebook up and stared at three letters written in a shaky hand: *JAS*.

He called Jimmy, the skinny forensic technologist. 'I need an evidence bag.'

JAS. The Afrikaans for 'coat'. Unfathomable.

Jimmy brought him a transparent bag and Joubert put the notebook inside.

Joubert bent again at the open door and peered under the seat. There was a pen, but nothing else. On the navy-blue shaft of the pen were two faint blood prints. The blood on the notebook was not necessarily significant. But the bloody fingerprints on the pen were. Mbali had written the letters after she had been wounded. JAS? A perp wearing a coat? Or was it Zulu?

He reached for his phone. He would have to find out.

THE SUPERINTENDENT of the City Park Hospital nodded her head while Griessel was talking. She said, 'Captain, one moment, please,' and walked quickly through the operating theatre doors.

Benny could not stand still. Let him live, please, just long enough to get what he needed. He looked at his watch. Nearly twenty-five to three. Too much time had elapsed since they took her. At the periphery of his consciousness something flitted past—what was it? He must go back to the beginning. This morning, what had happened? At the churchyard?

The superintendent burst through the doors. 'Captain, his carotid artery was cut and they are still trying to close the wound. There is no chance of you talking to him in the next five or six hours. Even then I doubt whether communication will be meaningful. His vocal chords have been damaged.'

He digested the information. 'Doc, I want his clothes, anything he had on him.'

'I'M GOING TO CALL,' said Bill Anderson decisively. He looked at the number he had written down, picked up the receiver and keyed it in. He stood listening to the crystal-clear ring on another continent.

GRIESSEL'S PHONE RANG and he looked at the screen: *MAT JOUBERT*. 'Mat?'

'Benny, I don't know what this means, but Mbali wrote the word "jas" in her notebook, and I am reasonably sure it was after she was shot. There are bloody fingerprints on the pen. I thought it might be Zulu, but it doesn't seem to be.'

'Jas?' Then he heard the soft ring tone of another incoming call. 'Mat, hold for me.' He saw the long number, the unfamiliar code, and knew who it would be. God. He couldn't talk to them now, he couldn't, what would he say?

They would be worried because he hadn't phoned. This was their child. They had the right to know.

'Mat, I'll call you back.' He switched calls and said, 'Mr Anderson?'

'Oh, thank god, Captain, we were getting very worried. Is Rachel OK?'

'Mr Anderson, Rachel was not at the address she gave me. We are still trying to track her down, but we are making good progress.'

'She wasn't there? How is that possible?'

'I don't know, sir. I honestly don't know.'

TWO YOUNG MEN full of self-confidence walked into the Cat & Moose Youth Hostel, up to the plump woman at the reception desk.

'Hi,' said the black one and smiled. 'We've come for Rachel's stuff.'

'Who?'

'Rachel Anderson, the American girl. You know, the one who was missing.'

'Are you from the police?'

'No, we're friends.'

'Don't I know you?' asked the girl.

'I don't think so. So where is her luggage?'

'Down there, in their room, with the police. Did they find her?'

'With the police?' The friendliness wavered.

'Yes. You'll have to talk to them. Did they find the girl?'

They didn't answer her. They looked at each other. Then they walked out.

'Hey!' the girl shouted, but they didn't even look back. She ran out through the door onto Long Street. She saw them walking fast. They looked back once and disappeared round the corner.

'I know you,' she said, and hurried off to find the two men who were guarding the luggage.

HE WANTED TO PULL off her running shoes. She pressed her feet against the cement floor with all her strength and he kicked her feet out violently from under her with his boots. Her legs shot forward and she fell hard.

'Jesus, you're a piece of work,' Jay said to her.

She spat at him, but missed. Jay pulled her shoes off. 'You had better hold one leg,' he said to the third man. 'This is going to drive her nuts.'

He stretched to reach the pruning shears. 'OK, one last time: where is the video?'

'Dead and buried,' she said.

Now there were two of them holding her legs, pressing down with their full weight so that her heels pressed painfully against the concrete floor.

He grabbed her right foot and brought the shears closer. He put the blades round her little toe. She jerked with all her might. They were too strong for her. He closed the handles. The pain was immediate and immense. She screamed against her will, a sound she did not know she could make.

'Where's the video?' Jay asked and gripped her foot again.

'In my big bag,' she shrieked, because the pain, the brutality and the humiliation were too much.

'Good. Where is the bag?'

'At the youth hostel.'

Then Jay's cellphone rang and they all jumped in fright.

The superintendent came back through the glass doors with bloodied clothing in a large transparent plastic bag. Griessel told Bill Anderson, 'I am really sorry, but I have to go. If there is any news, I will call you, I promise.'

Silence over the line. 'I don't think your promises mean all that much.' Then an audible click as the American put down the phone. Griessel stood frozen, torn between the injustice and the knowledge that, as a father, he would have felt the same.

The superintendent held out the bag to him. 'Captain, this is everything.'

He replaced the phone in his pocket and took the bag. 'Have you got a pair of rubber gloves around here?'

'Miss, get the captain a pair of surgical gloves,' the doctor ordered. The nurse trotted off down the corridor. 'Will that be all, Captain?'

'My colleague, Inspector Kaleni. Any news?'

'Her chances are better than the young man's in there. Apparently she received treatment on the scene to control the bleeding.'

'Will she make it?'

'It's too early to say.'

The nurse returned with the gloves. 'Thank you,' he said and pulled them on. He opened the bag and took out a white T-shirt, dark with blood. Then jeans, with a worn leather belt. He felt in the pockets and took out a bunch of keys. Car keys with Mazda on them, four others—two that would open a house door and two smaller ones. The back pockets were empty. But there was something on the belt, heavy, a leather pouch with a flap folded over. A Leatherman. The multitool was not new. He could get fingerprints off it. He lifted up the flap. Three letters were written on it in permanent ink marker: A.O.A. Initials? It made him think of the word Mbali had scribbled: *Jas*.

'Miss,' he said to the nurse, 'do you perhaps have a small plastic bag?'

She searched under her desk and produced an empty pill packet.

'That's perfect,' said Griessel. He placed the Leatherman in the packet then put in his shirt pocket. He pushed the clothing back into the big bag, then pulled off the rubber gloves, hesitating.

'You can give them to me,' the nurse said softly.

He nodded his thanks, passed them to her, took out his cellphone and called Mat Joubert. '*Jas?*' said Griessel.

'J. A.S. Just the three letters. Did you find anything?'

'Another three letters. A.O. A. I think they are initials.'

'Or an abbreviation.'

'J.A.S. Could also be an abbreviation, I don't know.' A spark lit up in the back of Benny's mind, two thoughts coming together, then it collapsed.

His cellphone rang softly in his ear. Now what? He checked. It was the Caledon Square radio room. 'Mat, I've got another call.' He manipulated the phone's keys, said, 'Griessel.' The Caledon Square Sergeant said, 'Two men just tried to collect the girl's luggage at the Cat & Moose.'

'Did you get the bastards?'

'No, Captain, they ran away, but the manager says she knows one of them.'

'*Jissis*,' said Griessel. 'I'm on my way.'

THE WOMAN at Metropolitan Police Administration frowned and paged through a file, searching. 'I can't find the receipt,' she said. She put the file aside and began pulling documents out of a basket. 'The form says the pound and traffic fines were paid but there is no receipt . . .'

'Would it help if we knew whose signature that is?'

She stared at the scrawl at the bottom of the form. 'These people, they sign like crabs. Looks like . . . I'm not sure, could be Inspector Jeremy Oerson.'

'Could we try to find out?'

'*You* can, I'm swamped. He's on the second floor.'

FRANSMAN DEKKER saw Griessel run round the corner of City Park Hospital and called out Benny's name, but the white detective had gone. Probably better that way, Dekker thought, because he wanted to go over the ground that Griessel had covered that morning. He wanted to talk to Alexa again; from whatever angle he studied the case, it had to be someone close to Adam Barnard.

He took out his SAPS identity card, held it up so the woman at City Park reception could read it and said, 'I want to see Alexa Barnard.'

'Oh,' she said, 'just a moment,' and picked up the phone.

GRIESSEL JUMPED into his car and pulled away. His cellphone rang. *FRITZ*. His son. His feelings about tonight descended, the date with Anna at seven. Should he phone and say tonight was going to be difficult?

'Fritz?' he said, wondering whether his son knew anything about Anna's intentions.

'Dad, I'm done with school.'

'What do you mean?'

'We got this fat gig.'

'We?'

'The band, Dad. Wet & Orde. That's our name, like your job, Law and Order, it was my idea. We're opening for Zinkplaat on a tour. They are talking about twenty-five thousand for a month, that's more than six thousand per guy.'

'And now you're leaving school?'

'I don't need school any more, Pa.'

THE CALL CAME through at 14:48 to the office of the Provincial Commissioner: Western Cape. The little Xhosa answered, forewarned by his secretary. It was Dan Burton, the American Consul.

'Commissioner, could you please tell me what's going on?'

'We have every available police officer in Cape Town looking for the girl and the best detective in the Peninsula leading the task force. They are doing everything in their power to find the young lady.'

'I've just had a call from her parents, and they are very, very worried. Apparently, she was safe, she called this Captain Ghree-zil, but he took his sweet time to get there, only to find her gone.'

'That's not the information I have, sir . . .'

'Do you know who these people are? Why are they hunting her like an animal?'

'No, we don't know that. All I can tell you is that we are doing everything we can to find her.'

'Apparently, sir, that is not enough. I am really sorry, but I will have to call the Minister.'

The Commissioner stood up from his desk. 'Well, sir, you are most welcome to call the Minister. But I am not sure what else we can do.' He put the phone down and walked out, down the passage to John Afrika's office. On the way he said one word in his mother tongue; the click of the word echoed off the walls.

SHE DID NOT HEAR them arguing on the other side of the wooden door. She sat with her naked back against the pillar, dreadful pain in her foot, blood still running from the stump and the severed toe lying on the cement floor. Her head drooped and she wept.

She had nothing left. Nothing.

THEY TOLD VUSI that Oerson was out. He could reach him on his cellphone. He took the number but before he could phone they said, 'Here he is now.'

Vusi turned, recognised the man; he was the one who had been at the church this morning—dreadful uniform, face shiny with perspiration.

'Inspector Oerson?' he asked.

'What?' Hurried, irritated.

'I am Inspector Vusumuzi Ndabeni of the SAPS. I am here about a vehicle that was booked out of the pound at twelve thirty-four, a Peugeot panel van.'

'So?' Oerson kept on walking towards his office. Vusi followed, amazed by his attitude.

'They say you signed the form.'

'Do you know how many forms I sign?' Oerson stood at an office door.

Vusi took a deep breath. 'Inspector, you were at the scene this morning, the American girl . . . the vehicle was used to abduct her friend. It is our only clue. She is in great danger.'

'I can't help you, I just signed the form,' said Oerson, placing a hand on the door handle. 'Every day those girls come running in here, wanting someone to sign. I check only that everything is in order.' Behind the door a telephone began to ring. 'My phone,' he said and opened the door.

'But they say there is no receipt or anything.'

'Everything was correct when I signed,' said Oerson, going into the office and closing the door. Vusi stood there. How could people be like that? He sighed, ready to turn away, when he heard Oerson's voice say something inside that sounded familiar. *Cat and Moose . . . Wait, hold on . . .*

Vusi stood spellbound.

The door opened suddenly; Oerson's face accused him. 'What are you still doing here?'

'Nothing,' said Vusi and left. He heard the door shut. He stopped at the stairs. The Cat & Moose? What did Oerson have to do with that?

Coincidence?

Oerson had been there this morning, very early. A Senior Inspector from Metro. He was the one who had found the rucksack. He was the one who had rummaged in it before handing it over. In the club, Griessel had talked to Dekker, he had told Dekker to call Oerson about the bag of stuff they had picked up. Oerson had signed the form. His attitude, arrogance.

Cat & Moose. Snake in the grass.

Vusi turned and went back to Oerson's closed door.

THEY TOLD DEKKER he could not see Alexa Barnard now.

'When will I be able to see her?' he asked.

'Doctor says some time after four; the medication should have worn off by then.' He checked his watch. Ten to three. He might just as well get something to eat. It would give him a chance to think—and what else could he do, he had let Josh and Melinda go home? 'I want to know if you leave the city,' he had threatened. Then he had gone over to Natasha and said, 'Can you give me the contact details of all the staff?' and she gave him a look that said she knew why he wanted them.

He left the hospital feeling ravenous.

VUSI LISTENED at Oerson's door. He heard English spoken. *If they don't know what we're looking for, let's wait. Sooner or later they'll move the stuff.* A long silence. And then the words that stopped Vusi's heart: *Let's make sure, then kill the bitch. But wait for me . . .*

Vusi's hand dropped to his service pistol and pulled it out. He lifted his left hand to open the door.

No, I'm fine. They have nothing, no proof. Oerson inside so smug.

It gave Vusi pause; he froze. Because all he had were suspicions and a conversation overheard. He could arrest Oerson and he would demand a lawyer; it could take hours and the girl would die. It was Oerson's word against his.

I'm coming, Oerson had said in there. *Wait for me.*

Vusi whispered a prayer. What should he do?

He shoved the pistol back in the holster, turned and ran down the passage. He would have to follow Oerson. While he was contacting Benny.

Oh God, he must not let this man slip away.

GRIESSEL LOCKED the car and jogged to the entrance of the Cat & Moose. The plump girl was behind the desk, in animated discussion with one of the Caledon Square patrols. He ran up to them. She did not recognise him. He had to say, 'Benny Griessel, SAPS, I was here this morning. I hear you recognised one of the men.'

Her face changed from insecure receptionist to indignant witness. 'I've just been telling your colleagues, they just waltzed in here and said they were taking the luggage, can you believe it?'

'And you recognised one of them?'

'I don't know him, but I've seen him.'

'In the hostel?'

'Well, he might have been in here, but I've seen him around, you know, he's in the industry, I'm sure.'

'The industry?'

'The tourist industry,' as though it went without saying.

'Look,' said Griessel, 'a girl's life depends on the fact that we identify this guy, that you remember where you've seen him, so please . . .'

'Really?' The indignation evaporated and enthusiasm took its place. 'OK, look . . . I know I've seen him at the Long Street Café. He's black, tall, skinny . . . like all the guides . . .'

But Griessel wasn't listening to her because the elusive, slippery thing in his mind was rushing at him. He scratched behind his ear, thoughts jumbled, he must get them in order. This morning . . . Griessel looked to the right where they had talked to Oliver Sands this morning, that's what his head had been trying to tell him all afternoon, it was that conversation. He tried to recall it, groping in the dark. Ollie had talked about the girls in the club. No. Nothing. Wrong track.

He watched the girl behind the reception desk. She'd said *he's skinny, like all the guides*, that was the trigger. The guides. Vusi had wanted to know who was with Sands and the girls at the club. Sands said a whole bunch. And he had said the guides were there too.

He whispered to himself. '*Jissis.*' The thing was almost within his grasp, if he could only see it. His phone began to ring. He ignored it. He stood at the desk, put his palms flat on it and dipped his head. The girl stepped back half a pace.

VUSI LISTENED to Griessel's number ringing while he watched Oerson hurry out of the Metro building.

'Answer me, Benny,' he said as Oerson climbed into a Nissan Sentra with a police badge on the door.

The phone continued to ring.

'Please, Benny,' but the call diverted to Griessel's voicemail just as Vusi got his car unlocked.

'ARE YOU ALL RIGHT?' the Cat & Moose girl asked Griessel. One of the uniforms realised what was going on and hushed her with a finger to his lips.

Benny stood still. He, Vusi and Oliver Sands. At the table, Sands telling them about last night at the club. Who was with them? Vusi had asked. Do you know the names? And Sands said . . .

The answer came like a hammer blow. Sands had given them the names, that was the spectre that had been running though his head the whole afternoon. He heard one name now in Ollie's voice: Jason Dicklurk. *Dicklurk.* This morning Griessel had thought to himself, what a funny name. Dick Lurk. But the pronunciation had been the problem. *Jissis*, he should have made the connection. Only the Afrikaners could say their own names. And one Zulu. Mbali Kaleni. She had phoned him while he was sitting with the Commissioner. A Zulu accent, but her pronunciation was flawless. *We traced a Land Rover Defender that fits the number. It belongs to a Mr J. M. de Klerk.*

Dicklurk was de Klerk. J. M. de Klerk. Jason de Klerk. One of the guides.

He said to the girl. 'Which tour company were the girls with?'

For a second there was a frown, then her face brightened, 'African Overland Adventures. That's where he works, the black guy, that's where I've seen him—'

'Where are they?'

'Just one block down.'

'Show me,' said Griessel and ran to the door. She came after him, stopped on the pavement, pointed across the street. 'On the corner.'

'Come, *kêrels*,' said Benny to the uniforms as another insight lit up his head. A.O.A. *African Overland Adventures*. On the spur of the moment he kissed the girl on the cheek before he ran off.

She watched him speechlessly.

FRANSMAN DEKKER took a bite of the chicken mayonnaise sandwich while he scribbled in his notebook.

Alexa Barnard. A woman hiding in her house all day long. Lonely. Drinking. Lots of time to think about her husband who was chronically unfaithful. A man who couldn't keep his hands off anything in a skirt.

Don't expect me to believe that she had never wondered what life would be like without the bastard, he thought. Consider the national sport: hire a coloured to do your shooting. Three or four cases in the past year alone.

Come on, Sylvia, come and have a chat with the madam, tell me where I can find someone to knock the master off. Or: *the master has a fat life insurance policy, my dear. What sort of share are we looking at if you find us a gunman?*

Only one problem. *You don't hire people to make it look like you did it*, in the words of Captain Benny Griessel. But, what if she thought, I'll make it look like a frame-up. The music business is a war zone, they'll look at them before they look at me. And when they do look at me, hey, I'm an alkie, how could I drag this man's big body up the stairs?

What do you say to that, Captain?

IN HIS DASH to African Overland Adventures, Griessel thought that was what Mbali must have been trying to write. *Jason*. How had she known? What made her go back to Upper Orange Street?

Just before he burst through the doors, his phone started ringing again. He wasn't going to answer it. He was going to get Jason de Klerk and then find Rachel Anderson.

She had to live.

JOHN AFRIKA sat with the receiver in his hand listening to Griessel's phone ringing. Opposite him stood the Provincial Commissioner.

'If we are making a mistake . . .'

'Benny is clean,' Afrika said.

'John, we're talking about my career.'

Afrika sighed and replaced the receiver. 'He's not answering.'

'They are going to clean up when Zuma gets in. They will use any excuse. You know how it is. Zulus in, Xhosas out.'

'Commissioner, I understand. But what am I supposed to do?'

'Is there no one else?'

Afrika shook his head. 'Even if there were, it's too late now.' He looked at the phone. 'Benny is clean.' He didn't sound so sure of himself any more.

JEREMY OERSON turned left into Ebenezer. Vusi gave him a gap, then pulled away himself: don't let the man get away. The Metro Nissan was on the way to the Waterfront under the Western Boulevard Freeway. Vusi drove cautiously, not daring to get too close, or too far. He had to see where he turned off.

Oerson drove into the harbour road traffic circle and then out to the right. He was heading for the N1.

Vusi relaxed fractionally. That would make it easier.

GRIESSEL BANGED OPEN the double glass doors with the two constables behind him. The lobby of African Overland Adventures was spacious—a long counter with two young women and a man behind it, a flat-screen TV against the wall, coffee tables and easy chairs. Nine young people standing or sitting. Everyone looked up, startled. Griessel pulled out his service pistol before he reached the desk. His cellphone was still ringing in his pocket.

'SAPS. Nobody's leaving and nobody is going to make a phone call.'

'Can we see some ID?' a girl asked from behind the desk. He pulled out his identity card.

'Which one of you is Jason de Klerk?'

The girl answered, 'Jason isn't here.'

'Where is Jason de Klerk?'

'We don't know.'

'All the men, I want you to show us your IDs.' To the constables he said, 'Check them.'

'Jason hasn't been in since yesterday,' said the girl.

Griessel walked up to the counter and stretched over it. 'Now you listen to me: Jason and his friends cut the throat of one of your clients last night, and they are going to kill again if I don't stop them. Right now, I'm thinking you don't know anything about it, but that can change very quickly, and you don't want that. So where can I find him?'

She swallowed audibly. 'He might be at home. He might be at the offices or the warehouse.'

'The offices?'

'Second floor. You use the entrance next door.'

'And the warehouse?'

'Stanley Road in Observatory.'

ALL THREE CAME back through the door. Rachel did not even look up.

'Hold her legs,' said Jason de Klerk and picked up the pruning shears from the floor. The other two squatted down beside her and took hold of her legs.

'Rachel,' said de Klerk, but she did not respond. 'Rachel!'

'She's fucked, Jay,' one of the others said.

'We have to make sure.' He knelt at her foot. 'Rachel, listen to me. We have to make sure you're telling the truth about the video. This is a matter of life and death, do you understand?' He put the blade round the second toe of her right foot. 'So tell me again, where is it?'

'She's not even hearing you.'

'Please,' she said so they could barely hear. 'It's in the big bag.'

'Are you sure?' Jason's voice was still calm. 'Are you very sure?'

'Yes, yes, yes, yes . . .'. A primeval sound erupted from her.

'Jay, what more do you need?' the other young man asked.

Jason, furious, hit him with the back of his hand. 'Do you know what's at stake here? Do you want to spend the rest of your life in prison?'

VUSI FOLLOWED OERSON as he took the off-ramp to the N2. He kept his distance, just over 400 metres, with seven cars between them. He picked up his phone and called Benny Griessel again.

THE 'OFFICES' of African Overland Adventures were behind a steel security door. Griessel pressed the intercom button.

'Police. Open up.'

The locks clicked and the door opened. He looked to see if there was another exit. But he saw none, only three women, desks, computers, filing cabinets. He kept his ID card handy.

'I'm looking for a Jason de Klerk?'

'He's not here.'

His cellphone rang. Who the hell wanted him so badly? He pulled it out. *VUSI.*

'Vusi, this is a bad time.'

'Benny, I'm sorry, but things happened. I think I'm following someone on his way to Rachel. Jeremy Oerson. I overheard him. He's involved.'

Griessel froze. Jeremy Oerson? What the hell? 'Where are you?'

'On the N2, just before Groote Schuur. He's just taken the off-ramp to Main Road.'

Observatory. The warehouse. 'Vusi, I think he's going to Stanley Road, there's a warehouse, African Overland Adventures. Stay with him, I'm on my way.' Griessel's feet clattered down the stairs.

'Benny!' said Vusi, afraid he would ring off. 'They're going to kill her, Benny. As soon as Oerson gets there.'

15:12–16:14

X

Griessel told the constables to let no one out of the adventure shop; they were to seal off the offices, no records were to leave the place, no calls were to be made. They didn't know who was involved.

'Do you have a patrol vehicle with a functioning siren?'

'Yes, Captain.' A constable flung his keys in an arc to Griessel.

THERE WAS ONLY ONE VEHICLE between Vusi and Oerson when they stopped at the traffic lights. Vusi pulled the sun visor down to hide his face. Oerson's indicator light was on, ready to turn right.

Where was Stanley Road?

African Overland Adventures? And the Metro police? He couldn't see any connection. The light changed to green. Vusi gave him a lead then pulled away intending to turn right as well, but a car approached and he had to wait. When he did turn he couldn't see Oerson's Sentra. Vusi accelerated. Where could he have gone? He passed the Scott Road turnoff on the left. He saw the Sentra, in the distance, a long way down Scott.

Vusi braked, slammed the car into reverse and turned left, just in time to see Oerson turn right half a kilometre away.

Was it really him?

GRIESSEL FLIPPED the switches for the siren and blue lights and pulled away with screeching tyres. The traffic opened up in front of him, past the Lutheran church where everything had begun that morning. It felt like a week ago. He turned left into Upper Orange. More traffic. It took precious seconds to get across and then he put his foot down. He picked up his cellphone.

Vusi answered on the second ring. 'Benny.'

'Where are you?'

'Stanley Street, Benny, I don't want to talk too loud. I can see the warehouse. Their trucks are parked there. African Overland Adventures.'

'Tell me how to get there, Vusi, I haven't got a map.'

'Will you find Main Road in Observatory?'

'Yes.'

'Then turn down Scott eastwards. All the way down over Lower Main, then first right and you will see them.'

'I'm coming.'

'Oerson has gone in, Benny, hurry.'

JEREMY OERSON pushed the big sliding door wide enough for him to enter. The warehouse was quiet: tents, water cans, tools, sand shovels, all in tidy piles. On one side was a white Land Rover Defender.

'Halloo,' he said.

To the left and right, two men stood up from behind piles of goods, each with a Stechkin APS pistol aimed at him. 'Christ,' he said and lifted his hands high. 'It's me.'

They slowly lowered the weapons. Jason de Klerk came out from behind the Land Rover. 'I tried to call you, Jeremy.'

'I'm a senior police officer. I can't answer my cell when I'm driving.'

'You're a traffic cop.'

He ignored the remark. 'Where is she?'

'Mr B wants to know: can you get to the luggage?'

Oerson walked deeper into the warehouse and looked about. Behind a pile of tents sat another one, sulky, with blood on his upper lip. 'Not now,' he said. 'What happened to him? She get rough?'

'I didn't mean now, Jerry,' said Jason irritably. 'But you can get it, right?'

'Don't worry, as long as they don't know what they're looking for, we're fine. They'll take it to an evidence room and I'll grease a few palms. Little videotape, slip it in your pocket, easy-peasy. Next week this will be old news, girl's gone, pressure's off. Relax. Where is she?'

'You're absolutely sure?'

'Of course. For a thousand bucks they'll be standing in line to do it.'

'OK,' said Jason and took out his phone.

'She's alive, isn't she?' Oerson asked. 'Because you guys owe me a favour.'

WHEN THE ROODEBLOEM turnoff flashed past, Griessel realised he should have taken it. He cut through to the Eastern Boulevard. The traffic was dense; there was no time to think. What was Jeremy Oerson's connection with the whole affair? Then he was round the bend on the N2 and swung over into the left-hand lane. He stomped on the accelerator. Oerson? Metro? African Adventures?

He entered the Liesbeeck off-ramp too fast, the turn sharper than he remembered, and the red light unexpected. Cars were crossing the road in front of him. Too late to brake. He was going to hit someone. Then he was through between two cars, wrenching the wheel, accelerating out the other side. He turned off the siren only when he turned onto Lower Main.

BENNY WAS TAKING too long. Vusi was parked halfway between Scott and Stanley on the pavement, his pistol on his lap. He could see the warehouse—a long building, brick walls, galvanised zinc roof. She was in there. Where was Benny? Perhaps he should go inside. But how many were there?

He got out, walked round, opened the boot and looked up. They wouldn't be able to see him. There were no windows on this side. He took off his jacket and picked up the Kevlar bulletproof vest. He put it on and checked his watch: 15:22. He would have to do something.

He came to a decision; the girl's life was the priority. He was going in.

Then he heard the squeal of rubber behind him. A SAPS patrol van stopped in a cloud of dust on the pavement. A figure jumped out with unkempt hair and a gun in his hand.

Benny Griessel had arrived.

'HEY!' SAID JEREMY OERSON, but she didn't look up. She just lay slumped against the pole, stark naked.

He stood with his feet planted wide in black boots, the pistol in both hands aimed at her head.

'Get her to look at me,' he said to one of them.

'Just get it over with.'

'No. I want to see her face. Hey, Yankee, look at me.'

Slowly she lifted her head. Hair hung over her forehead in strings. He saw the eye swollen shut, black and purple, dried blood on her temple. Her head was raised, but the eyes were still somewhere else.

'Look at me,' he said to her, saw the eyes rise to meet his. He pressed the safety off with his thumb.

'TAKE THE BACK, Vusi. I'll give you time,' said Griessel as he ran. He reached the sliding door and pressed his back against the wall, pistol in both hands in front of him. He counted, thousand-and-one, thousand-and-two, wanting to give Vusi twenty seconds. He prayed. Dear Father, let her be alive.

Thousand-and-twelve. He heard a shot, jumped, dragged the door open and ran in. He saw a young man directly in front of him with a silencer aimed at his heart. He knew in that instant that it was all over, his own pistol was degrees too far to the right.

The shot cracked and blew Griessel off his feet. His back slammed into the door and pain exploded in his chest. He fell to the ground. That unease he had had all day, that expectation of evil, here it was.

OERSON WAITED for her eyes. He wanted his to be the last face she would see. He wanted to know what mortal fear looked like, he wanted to see the light of life fade out of her. But above all he wanted to know how it felt to take a life. They said the power was indescribable.

She looked into his eyes. He saw no fear. He wondered if they had drugged her. Then he heard the shot. He looked round, at the door. Another shot.

'Shit,' he said.

VUSI SPRINTED round the corner. High windows, two metres off the ground. A single steel door with a big padlock on it. He did not hesitate. He aimed and the 9mm projectile blew the padlock to bits. He tugged the door open. It was gloomy inside, a small kitchen, with another closed door.

He heard a shot, not loud, a small calibre, perhaps. Benny! He ran to the inner door and opened it. It was a large open space. A beam of light shone through the big sliding door. Someone was lying still. Oh God, it was Benny. Movement, a young white man to the left of Vusi, a weapon in his hand. 'Don't move!' The young man swung round. Vusi fired. The man fell in slow motion.

A bullet smacked into the wall from the right. Vusi dived behind drums and rolled, stood up, pulled the trigger, once, twice, three times. The man fell. He stood up slowly, eyes on the still figure, watching the blood run out of the body. Life blood. He had killed a man, he realised. He had had no choice.

A shadow moved on his right; he came back to reality too late. The pistol pressed against his head.

AWFUL PAIN in his chest, Griessel could not move, could not breathe. He was lying on the cement floor. Death would come, it was all over. At the periphery there was movement. Vusi. A thundering shot, someone fell, farther to the right. Everything in slow motion, unreal, vague, detached. This was the beginning, the tumbling away from life. Why wasn't he afraid? Why this . . . peace, an intense longing for his children, his wife. Now he knew he wanted Anna back, too late. Movement. He could see. Not dead yet. Vusi fired again, three times. His breath came more easily now. Why? Benny's hand moved slowly to his chest. Dry. No blood. He looked and felt. A hole in his breast pocket. No blood. He felt the hard object, gripped it.

The Leatherman. The bullet had struck the Leatherman. Relief burned through him. He looked up. The one who had shot him stood there, with a gun to Vusi's head.

Griessel reached for his pistol on the floor, raised it, no time to aim. Pulled the trigger, saw the man's arm jerk, saw Vusi fall, fired again, missed. The man just stood there. His silenced pistol had disappeared.

Griessel got to his feet, his ribcage on fire, pain burning white. He aimed his pistol at the man. 'Don't move,' he said. The man was holding his arm. The elbow was shattered, lots of blood, a mess of tendons and fragmented bone.

Vusi stood up. 'Benny . . .' His voice was faint, Griessel's ears were deafened by the shots.

'I've got him, Vusi.'

'I thought you were dead.'

'So did I,' said Griessel. He jerked the man by the collar. 'Lie down.' he said. The man sank to his knees. 'Where is Rachel?'

The man looked at the closed door behind him. 'There.'

'Is she alone?'

'No.'

'Where is Jason, Jason de Klerk?' Griessel prodded him with the pistol. A moment of silence. 'I'm Jason.'

Rage swept over Griessel. He grabbed de Klerk by the hair. 'You fucking rubbish,' he said, and felt a powerful desire to shoot him, for Erin, for everything. His finger tightened round the trigger.

'Benny!'

There was a noise behind them, a door closing. Both detectives spun round.

'Don't shoot!' Another young man stood there, hands in the air.

'Where is Rachel?' Benny asked.

'She's in there.'

Griessel strode towards the door.

'Look out,' said the man. 'Oerson is with her.'

SHE WAS AWARE of the gun pointed at her, of the man in his uniform above her. He spoke her name. Did he know her? She raised her eyes, trying to focus. Why was the other one still standing here, one of those who had held her legs?

A shot cracked. The man in uniform swore. He turned away from her and pointed his pistol at the door. The other man crept towards the wall. Another shot. He moved quickly to the door and again it boomed in there.

Then it struck her: the policeman. Griessel. He had found her. She wanted to sit up. The pain in her foot was incredible, but she didn't care, she drew her heels back. Another shot. He was shooting them, Benny Griessel, he must kill them all. If only she could stand up. The uniform and the young man were frozen, petrified. Another two shots. Silence.

'I'm going out,' said the young man and opened the door, and shut it immediately.

'Shit,' said the uniform.

'He's going to kill you,' she said to him, hatred in her voice.

He moved suddenly, came to her, a boot left and right of her knees, and pushed the gun into her cheek. 'Shut up. You're going with me.' Then he looked round at the door, wild-eyed.

She kicked him. She brought up her knee, her sore right foot's knee, and struck him between the legs with everything she had left. 'Now!' she shrieked. Her voice was a desperate command. The uniform shouted something and fell onto her. A booming noise as the door was kicked in, and then a single shot and the man fell away from her. In the doorway, she saw a figure with a pistol in his hand, hair needing a cut and strange Slavic eyes.

'Benny Griessel,' she said, with perfect pronunciation.

He grabbed her clothes off the floor and hastily covered her, put his arms round her and held her tight.

'Yes,' he said. 'I have found you.'

JUST AFTER FOUR, the nurse came out of the hospital room and said to Dekker, 'Fifteen minutes.' She held the door open so he could enter.

Alexa Barnard was sitting up against the cushions. He saw the bandage on her forearm, then the look of dawning disappointment. 'I was expecting the other detective,' she said slowly. The medication had not wholly worn off.

'Afternoon, ma'am,' he said neutrally, because he could use her drowsiness; he must avoid conflict and win her trust. He dragged a chair up to the bed and sat down. She stared at him with vague interest.

'Captain Griessel is not on the case any more,' he said.

She nodded slowly.

'I understand better now,' he said quietly and sympathetically. 'Your husband was not an easy man.'

He saw the moisture collect gradually in her eyes, her lower lip's involuntary tremble. With her healthy right arm she wiped the back of her hand over her cheek in slow motion.

Better than he'd hoped. 'He hurt you so much. All those years. He kept on hurting you over and over.'

'Yes.' Barely a whisper. He wanted *her* to talk. He waited. She said nothing.

'You blamed yourself. You thought it was your fault. But it wasn't. There are men like that,' he said.

She nodded, agreeing, as though she wanted to hear more.

'It's a drug for the soul. I think they have an emptiness inside here, a hole that is never filled. They don't like themselves, it's a way of . . .'

'Gaining acceptance,' she said.

'Yes . . .'

She would not fill the silence that he had created. He said, 'He loved you, in his way. I think the problem was that he didn't want to do it, but every time he did he thought less of himself. If a woman showed she wanted him, it meant he wasn't so bad. It was like a fever coming over him, you can't stop it. You want to, but you can't, however much you love your wife . . .'

He watched her, wondering if she had caught on. He saw that she was somewhere else. Heard her say, 'I asked him to get help.'

She wiped her eyes with a tissue. 'There was a time when I tried to understand. He would never talk about it, I could never work out where it came from. But where does anything come from? Where does my alcoholism come from? The problem is, it comes from inside me.'

He had an idea where she was headed.

'Nobody can help . . .' he encouraged her.

'Just yourself.'

'He couldn't change.' She shook her head. He wanted to prompt her, *So you did something about it*, but gave her the chance to say it herself.

She slowly sank back against the cushion. 'I don't know . . .' A deep sigh. 'If I were stronger . . . Or he was. Our tragedy lay in the combination. We were . . . an unfortunate chemical reaction . . .'

His fifteen minutes expired. 'And something had to give,' he said. 'Someone had to do something.'

'No. Past a certain point there is nothing you can do.'

'There is always something you can do.' He needed more than this. He took a chance, gave her something to work with: 'When the pain is bad enough. When he starts cursing and threatening you. When he assaults you . . .'

She turned her head slowly towards him, at first expressionless, so that he couldn't tell if it was going to work or not. Then the frown began, initially as though she was puzzled, then with increasing comprehension. 'I don't blame you. You're just doing your job.'

He leaned forward, desperate, trying another tack. 'We know enough, Mrs Barnard. It was someone with inside knowledge. Someone who knew where he kept his pistol. Someone who knew about your . . . condition. Someone with enough motive. You qualify. You know that.'

She nodded thoughtfully.

'Who helped you?'

'It was Willie Mouton.'

'Willie Mouton?' He couldn't keep the astonishment out of his voice.

'That's why I asked the other detective . . . Griessel to come. I must have been thinking like you. About the pistol. Only four of us knew where it was, and only Adam had the key.'

'What key?'

'To the gun safe in the top of his wardrobe. But Willie installed that. Four, five years ago. He's good at that sort of thing. In the old days he did stage work for the bands. Adam didn't want to bring outside people in; he didn't want anyone to know about the gun, he was afraid it would be stolen. This morning Willie was here, he and the lawyer; it was a strange conversation, I realised only once they left . . .' She stopped suddenly, having second thoughts.

'What did you realise?'

'Willie always wanted more. A bigger share, more money. Even though Adam was very good to him.'

'Ma'am, what are you trying to tell me?'

'Willie stood here at my bed. All he wanted to know was what I could remember. I last saw Willie more than a year ago and then here he was, as though he actually cared. He said he was so sorry about Adam, but then he wanted to know if I remembered anything. When I said I didn't know, he asked again, "Can you remember?" Only when they left, a while later

I heard his words again. Why was he so keen to know? And why was his lawyer here? That's what I wanted to tell Griessel, that it was strange.'

'Ma'am, you said he helped you.'

She looked at him in surprise. 'No, I never said that.'

'I asked you who helped you. And you said Willie Mouton.'

'You misunderstood me,' said Alexa Barnard.

The door behind Dekker opened. 'Inspector,' said the nurse.

'Another five minutes,' he said.

'Inspector, if the doctor says fifteen minutes, that is all I can give you.'

He knew he was close; she was confused, he wouldn't get another chance, but the nurse was a witness to this statement. He stood up. 'We'll talk again,' he said and walked down the passage to the lift. He pressed the button.

The door whispered open, the lift was empty. He went in. Now she wanted to point at Willie Mouton. He wasn't going to fall for that.

The lift began to descend. He would go and talk to the maid, Sylvia Buys.

The lift doors slid open. He walked out slowly, thoughtfully. He stopped in the entrance hall.

Willie Mouton? He recalled the chaos this morning in the street, the militant Mouton. Mouton, who was desperate for him to arrest Josh and Melinda.

His phone rang. He saw it was Griessel.

'Fransman, are you still at AfriSound?'

'No, I'm at City Park Hospital. At the entrance. Why?'

'Stay there, I'll be with you in a minute. You're not going to believe this.'

WITH THE LEATHERMAN that had saved his life, Griessel cut Rachel's hands free. Then he asked Vusi to call for medical support and covered her shivering body with sleeping-bags.

'Don't leave me,' she said.

'I won't.' He called John Afrika. 'Commissioner, we got Rachel Anderson. I'm sitting with her now. I just want one thing: send us the chopper, she needs medical assistance.'

There was a heartbeat of silence before Afrika said, 'Hallelujah! The chopper is on its way, just give me the address.'

'I'M SORRY, MR BURTON, but I just don't believe you,' said Bill Anderson over his cellphone. 'There's a warning right here on the US consulate's web site, stating that fourteen Americans have been robbed at gunpoint after landing at the OR Tambo International Airport in the past twelve months.'

'It sounds worse than it is, I can assure you,' the American Consul reassured him.

'Mr Burton, we are flying out this afternoon. All I want you to do is to recommend someone to protect us.'

Just then the house phone on Anderson's desk began to ring. 'Excuse me for one second,' he said and picked up the receiver. 'Bill Anderson.'

'Daddy.' He heard the voice of his daughter.

'Rachel! Oh God, where are you?'

'I'm with Captain Benny Griessel, Daddy . . .' and then her voice broke.

GRIESSEL SAT with his back to the wall, both arms round her. She leaned heavily on him, her head on his shoulder, while she spoke to her father. When she was finished, she looked up at him and said, 'Thank you.'

He didn't know how to answer her. He heard the sirens approaching, wondering how long it would take the helicopter to get here.

'Did you find the video?' she asked.

'What video?'

'The video of the murder. At Kariba.'

'No,' he said.

'That's why they killed Erin.'

'You don't have to tell me now,' he said.

'No, I have to.'

SHE AND ERIN had shared a tent the whole tour.

Erin had adjusted easily to the new time zones, slept well, got up with the sun and said, 'Another perfect day in Africa.' Rachel struggled to sleep. Every night, somewhere between one and three, her body clock woke her.

At Lake Kariba the moonlight had taken her by surprise. Some time after two in the early hours, she had become aware of the glow and opened her eyes. She thought someone had switched on a floodlight. In her imagination she saw the moon over Kariba, the beauty of it. She realised she must capture it for her video journal.

Carefully, so as not to disturb Erin, she crawled out of her sleeping-bag, took her video camera and went out into the sultry summer night. The camp was quiet. She walked between the tents to the edge of the lake. The view was breathtaking—the moon a jewel of tarnished silver sliding across the carpet of a billion stars, all duplicated in the mirror of the lake. She switched the camera on, folded out the small screen and chose 'Sunset & Moon' on the panel. She spotted the rocks on the edge of the lake about a hundred metres away. It would give her height, a reference point and perspective. From the top of the rocks she tried again, until she heard the sounds below, scarcely fifteen metres away.

Two figures in the dark. A muffled argument. She sat down slowly, instinctively, and knew it was Jason de Klerk and Steven Chitsinga at one of the trailers.

She smiled to herself, aimed her camera at them and began to film. Her intention was mischievous. These were the chief guides who mocked the European and American tourists about their love of comfort, their inability to deal with Africa. Now she had evidence that they were not perfect either. She smiled, thinking she would reveal it at breakfast.

Until Steven pulled open one of the large storage drawers under the trailer. He jerked roughly and suddenly the shape of another person stood between them, a smaller figure.

A man's voice called out one word. Steven grabbed the smaller figure from behind and put a hand over his mouth. Rachel looked up from the screen now, dumbstruck; she wanted to be certain the camera was not lying. She saw something shiny in Jason's hand in the moonlight. She saw him drive it into the small figure's chest and how the man slumped in Steven's grip.

Jason picked up the feet, Steven took the hands and they dragged the figure away into the darkness.

She sat there a long time. At first she denied it; it could not be real. A dream, a complete fantasy. She turned off the sound and played it back. The image quality was not great, but the truth struck home: she had witnessed a murder, committed by two people to whom she had entrusted her life.

The next day passed in a haze. She realised she was traumatised, but didn't know what to do. She withdrew. Again and again Erin asked her, What's wrong? She just said, I'm not feeling well.

Rachel wanted to report the murder, but to whom? There were so many rumours about the police in Zimbabwe, so many stories of corruption that she hesitated. They passed into Botswana and then there was no more opportunity. Just the knowledge that the murder in Zimbabwe by Zimbabweans was not the concern of another country's police. Not on this continent.

In Cape Town they went with a few others to the Van Hunks nightclub, unaware that Jason would turn up later. They had both been drinking, Erin with great fervour. She began to scold Rachel in an escalating flood of complaints—about friendship and trust.

Alcohol had weakened Rachel's resolve. Eventually she told Erin everything. Erin said it couldn't be true, it must be a misunderstanding. Not Jason and Steven. Impossible. Rachel said she had watched the video many times over in the early-morning hours. There was no mistake.

Let's ask them, let's clear this thing up. This was the reasoning of a fairly intoxicated, naive arch-optimist who never saw evil in anyone. No, no, no, Rachel had protested, promise me you won't say anything.

Erin had promised. They danced. Erin went off somewhere, came back to the table. She said Jason and Steven were here, she had asked them about it, they said she was dreaming. Rachel looked up across the sea of faces and found Jason's eyes on her. He had a cellphone to his ear, and an expression of chilling determination. She had grabbed her rucksack and told Erin, 'You come with me. Now!'

They were a few hundred metres from the club down Long Street when Jason and Steven emerged. They looked left and right, saw them and began to run. The other three had joined them from somewhere: Barry, Eben and Gary.

She knew they were running for their lives.

IN THE TOYOTA BAKKIE, Steven Chitsinga and Barry Smith turned into Speke Street and saw the police vehicles in front of the warehouse, a horde of blue lights flashing and uniforms everywhere.

Steven said a word in Shona. Barry braked sharply. He jerked the gear lever into reverse and shot backwards into something. It was a SAPS patrol vehicle. With an ambulance behind, blocking the road. He ground through the gears and shot forward. If he could go left into Stanley . . . but Stanley was closed, police vans blocking the street. Uniforms came running with guns in hand.

Barry stopped the bakkie and lifted his hands off the steering wheel and held them above his head.

'HE'S COMING WITH ME,' said Rachel as they carried her to the helicopter on a stretcher. She pointed at Griessel, who walked beside her holding her hand.

They loaded her into the helicopter and Griessel shifted in beside her with difficulty. 'Wait a bit,' the paramedic said and ran back into the building. He returned with the toe in a little bag and passed the gruesome cargo to Griessel. 'They can sew it back on,' said the man.

Once they had landed on the roof of the hospital and when they were ready to wheel her into theatre, she asked them to wait. She told Griessel there was another thing last night. After they had cut Erin's throat.

'We'll talk later,' he pleaded, because he had to get back to Vusi.

'No. You have to know. They killed another man.'

SHE HAD SEEN THEM cut Erin's throat and she had run blindly in fear and shock back to the street. Somewhere not long after that she had seen a building on the left with an entrance through to an inner garden. She wanted to get out of sight. She ran in there.

A big, middle-aged man in a suit was standing at a fishpond, watching two other men walk away. He shouted something angrily before they opened a glass door and disappeared inside. On the wall was a logo of a bird, she could remember that. 'Please, help me,' she said.

The big man had looked at her and the anger on his face had quickly changed to concern. 'What's wrong?' he asked.

'They want to kill me,' she had said and went to stand with him.

'Who?' They heard running steps and looked at the entrance, where Jason and the others had appeared. Jason had a gun in his hand now.

'We just want her,' he said to the man.

The man had put his arm protectively round Rachel and said, 'Not before we call the police.'

'She stole from us. We just want our stuff back, we don't want trouble.'

'Even more reason to call the police,' and he had started to feel in his pocket for his phone.

Jason pointed the pistol at the man. 'Then I'll have to shoot you.'

The man took out a cellphone.

She realised she was not going to be responsible for another death and she started running again. The big man tried to stop the others.

She heard two shots. She looked back. The man in the suit fell down.

Then she was gone, around the corner. In the street a municipal lorry had pulled up, a truck transporting rubbish bags. She jumped onto it, saw them coming. The truck picked up speed so that Jason became smaller and smaller.

'TWO MEN WENT into the building just before he saw you?' Griessel asked her. 'What did they look like?'

'I can remember only one. He was very thin, his head was shaven and he had a silver earring.' Then the doctor told Griessel he would have to leave. 'He was dressed all in black,' she called before the theatre doors closed.

16:41–17:46

XI

Back at the Caledon Square police station Griessel took charge of Bobby Verster, the last man to come out of Rachel's torture chamber. They suspected he was the weakest link.

Bobby told Griessel he hadn't been on the tour. Last night he had been with Barry and Eben at The Purple Turtle when Jason had phoned. Outside they had seen Jason and Steven chasing two girls. So they joined in the chase.

Griessel's body was sore, but he was filled with euphoria at finding Rachel. He stood up and looked at Bobby. 'You didn't get tired of all the chasing?' Griessel asked. 'Not even when they cut an innocent girl's throat?'

Bobby said he was shocked when Jason did it. He had protested. But Steven told him, 'You're next if you don't shut your mouth and help.'

'So were you forced?'

'Yes.'

'So, actually, you are innocent?'

'Yes!'

'Would you make a statement to that effect? Just so we can close your part of the case?' Griessel asked him.

'I will,' he answered eagerly.

Benny shifted pen and paper closer. Bobby wrote. 'Sign it,' said Benny.

Once Bobby was finished, Griessel read the statement out loud to him. He asked, 'All this is the truth?'

'It is.'

'Then you are an accessory to murder. You are going to jail for a very long time.'

Bobby's eyes widened. 'But you said I was innocent!'

'No, I asked you if you were. Come, there's a police van outside that will take you to Pollsmoor.'

'Pollsmoor?'

'Just until the bail hearing. In about a week or two. Three.'

'Wait . . .' Bobby thought for a long time. Then he said, 'You're looking for Blake.'

'Who is Blake?'

'Do I still have to go to Pollsmoor?'

'Everything is negotiable.'

'Blake is the owner. Of Overland. We bring the people in for him.'

'What people?'

'The blacks they put in the bins under the trailer. From Zimbabwe.'

'Illegal immigrants?'

'Something like that. I've been helping only about a month. They won't tell me everything yet.'

'What is Blake's name?'

'Duncan. We call him Mr B. He lives in the city, that's all I know.'

'Thank you very much.'

'Do I still have to go to Pollsmoor?'

'Yip.'

FRANSMAN DEKKER brought two uniforms along with him to AfriSound. They walked as far as Mouton's office. He didn't knock, he just walked in.

'What now?' Mouton asked.

'The best thing about my job, the thing I enjoy most of all, is arresting a whitey bastard,' said Dekker.

Mouton's Adam's apple bobbed wildly up and down, but he couldn't get a word out. Dekker opened Wouter Steenkamp's door. The accountant was seated behind his computer.

'We know all about last night,' he said. Steenkamp didn't bat an eyelid. 'He doesn't phone anyone, he doesn't move, he just sits here,' said Dekker to the two uniforms. 'I'll be back soon.'

VUSI FINALLY LOST his professional cool in the interrogation room. Griessel had told him what Bobby Verster had said. Vusi told Barry Smith, 'We're bringing in Mr B. We know everything. Murder. Life sentence.'

Barry said, 'Fuck off you black bastard,' and Vusi's temper exploded over him like the mighty breakers on the Wild Coast. In one lightning move he reached the young white man, and his fist struck his temple with all the power in the lean, neat body behind it.

Barry toppled backwards. His head hit the floor with a dull thud. Vusi realised his knuckles hurt and saw that Barry's eyes had trouble focusing. Barry got unsteadily to his feet and sat down. He put his hands on the table in slow motion and dropped his head onto them. It was a while before Vusi realised that the young man was crying. He pulled out a chair and sat down. He said nothing, not trusting his voice; his rage had not subsided.

'My mother is going to kill me,' said Barry.

'I can help you,' said Vusi.

Barry sobbed, making his whole body shake. Then he began to talk.

DEKKER SAT OPPOSITE MOUTON. He said, 'I know you didn't shoot Adam Barnard. I know about the girl and the five guys chasing her.'

'I want to phone my lawyer,' said Mouton.

'Later. Let me tell you what happened. Barnard phoned you last night, just after nine. He didn't phone you to tell you how silly Iàn Nell's accusations were. He was worried. He knew someone was mucking with the money. He said he wanted to see you. So you came in here, probably very worried, because you *are* guilty. What time was that, Willie? Did he tell you to come at eleven so he could look at the figures first? I know he worked on his computer last night. He was so upset by what he saw that he never turned his laptop off. He confronted you. You argued and fought from eleven o'clock to half past one in the night. Adam must have said something like, 'Leave it, we'll talk more tomorrow.' And you and Steenkamp followed him out into the garden. Argued some more. You went in just when the girl arrived. You got lucky, in more than one way. Because if you had been standing there, you might also have been shot. But then they shot Adam. Problem number one solved. There you two were, looking out of the window at the body, and you thought, what now? Your big problem was Iván Nell. Because if Iván told us there was a snake in the grass, you were in trouble.

'So you wondered how you could make it look different, as though you had never been here. Then you remembered about Josh and the Big Sin. And Alexa and the pistol. So you carried Barnard to the car. If he was in your or Wouter's car there will be blood and hair and fibres and DNA, and we'll find it.

'I couldn't figure out the shoe and the cellphone until about half an hour ago. The shoe came off when you picked up Adam to carry him to the car. And the phone was in his hand when he was shot. You remembered that he had phoned you, so you deleted his call history and you put the phone in the shoe. When you reached the car and opened the boot, you put the shoe on the roof, just for the meantime. Then you forgot about it and drove off. And on the corner, as you turned, the shoe fell off and you didn't even know it. How am I doing, Willie? I had a really hard time figuring out that shoe, until I went up there to the corner again. It came to me in a flash.'

Mouton just stared at Dekker.

'You and Wouter carried him up the stairs and you put him down there with Alexa. And you got the pistol out of the safe that you installed in the house. Somewhere you fired off three shots. I'm guessing you couldn't do it in the house. You must have driven somewhere, Willie. Then you went back and put the pistol down there. Clever. But not clever enough.'

'I want to call my lawyer.'

'Call him, Willie. Tell him to come to Green Point station. Because this is a warrant for your arrest, and this is a warrant to search these premises. I will be bringing smart people, Willie. Auditors, computer boffins, guys who specialise in white-collar crime. You stole Adam Barnard's and Iván Nell's money, and I'm going to find out how you did it and that lawyer of yours won't be able to do a thing about it. Or is he also a part of your little scheme?'

GRIESSEL PUSHED THE MAN through the front door of Caledon Square. His beard and hair were trimmed short. He looked fit and lean, his face expressionless, only the handcuffs on his wrists showed he was in trouble. Vusi was waiting.

'May I introduce you to Duncan Blake?' Griessel asked, with great satisfaction.

Vusi looked the man up and down, as though measuring him against newfound knowledge. Then he said, 'Benny, this thing is ugly. We will have to send a team to Camp's Bay, to a hospital. A big team.'

Only then did a shadow of emotion cross Duncan Blake's face.

17:47–18:36

XII

They sat in the Station Commander's office—Griessel, Vusi and John Afrika.

'Commissioner, this thing is big,' said Vusi.

'How big?'

'They smuggled people in through Zimbabwe. Somalians, Sudanese, Zimbabweans. People who have nothing, who want to make a new start, who will do anything . . .'

'They must have charged bags of money to bring them to this honey pot.'

'No, Commissioner, not much. We thought it was just illegal immigrants at first. But Barry Smith, one of the guides, told me the rest. The hospital, the whole thing . . .'

'What hospital?' Afrika asked.

'We should start at the beginning. Benny talked to Blake, Commissioner.'

Griessel nodded. 'Duncan Blake, a Zim citizen, fifty-five years old. For thirty years he farmed the family farm in Mashonaland-West. He was married, but his wife died of cancer. His sister was a surgeon at the hospital in Harare. In May 2000, the leader of the Veterans' Movement, Chenjerai 'Hitler' Hunzvi, occupied Blake's farm. Apparently, Blake's foreman, Justice Chitsinga, tried to stop the squatters and was shot dead. For two years, Blake tried to regain possession but in 2002 he gave up and he and his sister moved to Cape Town. He brought Steven Chitsinga, his foreman's son, with him and started African Overland Adventures. Most of his staff were young men and women from Zimbabwe, children of dispossessed farmers, or their workers. De Klerk, Steven Chitsinga, Eben Etlinger, Barry Smith . . .'

'And the Metro man you shot dead? Oerson?' the Commissioner asked.

'That's another story, Commissioner,' said Vusi. 'Smith said Oerson was with Provincial Traffic. Two years ago he pulled one of their Adventure lorries off the road. It was overweight. De Klerk was immediately ready to pay something under the table. Oerson took it and let them go. But he began to wonder why the Adventure people paid so much. He waited for them to pass through again a month later. He said he wanted to have a look in the lorry and the trailer, in all the cavities. Then de Klerk said that wouldn't be necessary, how much did he want? And Oerson said, "Cut me in, because I smell big money." So they put Oerson on the payroll on one condition, Oerson must apply to Metro, because they needed another man to keep an eye on the Somalis and Zimmers who had donated organs in the city . . .'

'Donated organs?'

'I'm getting to that, Commissioner. Lots of the people who have already donated have opened street-vendor stalls in the city with the money they were paid. There were a few who threatened to talk if they didn't get more money. It was Oerson's job to shut them up.'

'As in permanently?'

'Sometimes. But never personally, he had other contacts for that.'

'*Jissis*,' said Afrika. Then he looked at Vusi. 'And the organs?'

'Blake and his sister bought the old Atlantic Hotel in Camps Bay in 2003, and fixed the place up and started a private hospital. She is the "director" now . . .'

Vusi pulled the keyboard on the desk towards him, clicked on the web browser icon and typed in a web address. A web site loaded, showed a white building, with a banner headline: ATLANTICARE: *Exclusive International Medical Centre*. 'This is the place, Commissioner. They do organ transplants.' Another web page opened up with the heading: *Transplants you can afford*. Vusi read out loud. 'The average cost of a heart transplant in the United States is three hundred thousand dollars. A lung transplant will cost two hundred and seventy-five thousand, an intestine almost half a million dollars. Impossible to afford without health insurance, but even if you are covered, there is no guarantee that you will receive a donated organ in time.'

'Don't tell me they . . .?'

'That's right, Commissioner,' Vusi said, and he read from the web pages again. 'With the most modern medical facilities available, you can receive your transplant within three weeks of arriving, at a fraction of the cost.'

'That's what they smuggled the people in for,' said Griessel.

'For the organs,' said Vusi. 'That was the price the people were required to pay for a better life in South Africa. Apparently you can donate a lot of your organs without the consequences being too serious.'

'And the hearts?'

'We will have to see, Commissioner, because the web site talks about hearts as well. But the one Rachel Anderson saw, the man de Klerk and Chitsinga murdered at Kariba, had AIDS. Smith says they had test kits with them—they drew blood and tested it. They realised that man had AIDS. So they took him out, and they couldn't afford just to let him go.'

'What kind of people are these?' John Afrika asked.

'That's what I asked Duncan Blake,' said Griessel. 'And he said Africa took everything he had, all his dreams, Africa tore out his heart, why couldn't he do that to Africa?'

Griessel's cellphone rang. He got up and went aside to answer it.

The Commissioner leaned forward, looked at the web site, sighed deeply, listening to Griessel making noises of disbelief.

Benny came back to the desk. 'That was Mat from the hospital,' he said. 'This thing is going to get ugly. There's a government minister in the hospital records.'

'One of our ministers?'

'Yes, Commissioner. Liver transplant.'

DEKKER HAD HEARD the coloured SAPS computer specialist was a genius. So he was expecting someone like Bill Gates. What he got was a slightly built man with the face of a schoolboy, a big Afro hairstyle and no sense of humour. 'This is candy floss,' the genius said to Dekker in Steenkamp's office. 'A PDF password is useless.'

'How's that, bro'?'

'People think if you have a PDF password you're secure. But you're not.'

'So how did they do it?'

'This *ou*'—he pointed at the computer, which belonged to Steenkamp—'got the password-protected PDFs for every singer's sales from the distributor. Looks like it was his job to send it on to the singer when the money was transferred. The singer thinks only he has the password, so he thinks the record company can't change the statement of CD sales. He thinks he's getting all the money.'

'Because it comes from the distributor?'

'Yes, the distributor put the password on, but emails it to this *ou*, and this *ou* emails it to the singer. But look here.' The computer boffin opened a program. 'This is software, Advanced PDF Password Recovery, made by Elcomsoft. You can buy it from their web site, the price is just under a thousand rand, and then you can do what you like with a PDF, even if it has a forty-bit encryption. It means this is candy floss, any password protection.'

'So Steenkamp could get the singer's password and he could change the statement?'

'Exactly. The singer thinks it's the original PDF.'

'How much did they skim?'

'From ten to forty per cent, depending on how much the singer sells. The big guys, like Ivàn Nell, they took up to forty per cent off him on his last CD.'

18:37–19:51

XIII

Precisely thirteen hours since they had woken Benny Griessel in his flat, at 18:37, Griessel told John Afrika, 'Commissioner, I have to be in Canal Walk by seven o'clock. Please, will you excuse me?'

The Commissioner put a hand on Griessel's shoulder. 'Captain, I just want to say if there was ever a man who deserved promotion, it's you. I never doubted you would solve this one. Never.'

'Thank you, Commissioner.'

Then he was out of there in a rush. There was no time to change his shirt, but he could tell Anna the story of how the hole came to be there.

SHE WAS SITTING OUTSIDE where she could see the water. A good sign, he thought. He paused a moment in the door of Primi and looked at her. His Anna. Forty-two, but looking good. There was a youthfulness about her again. The white blouse, blue jeans, the little cardigan thrown over her shoulders.

Then she spotted him. He watched her face carefully as he approached her. She smiled but not broadly.

He kissed her on the cheek. She didn't turn her head away. Good sign.

He pulled out a chair. 'You must excuse the way I look, it's been a crazy day.'

Her eyes went to the hole in his breast pocket. 'What happened?'

'They shot me.' He sat down.

'Lord, Benny.'

'Luckiest break of my life. Only an hour before, I put a Leatherman in my pocket, you know, one of those plier thingies.'

'You could have been killed.'

He shrugged. 'If it's your time, it's your time.' She looked at him, running her gaze over his face.

'Benny . . .' she said.

'I'm sober,' he said. 'It's been nearly six months.'

'I know. I am very proud of you.'

Good sign. He grinned at her in expectation.

She took a deep breath. 'Benny . . . there's only one way to say this. There's someone else.'

IN HIS CAR, Dekker took out the list of names and telephone numbers. Natasha's was first on the list.

What woman can look at you and not think of sex?

Time to see if she was a bullshitter. He entered the number in his phone.

He had a wife at home. A good, beautiful, sexy, smart woman. Crystal. Waiting for him. He looked at the small green button on his phone.

He thought about Natasha's legs. That bottom. She would be a handful. In every meaning of the word.

Some time or other he'd have to stop this. He loved his wife, he couldn't live without Crystal, she was everything to him. And if she found out . . .

How would she find out? The fever was in him. He pressed the button.

'Hello, Natasha.'

'THIS IS VUSI NDABENI. The detective from this morning, at the church.'

'Oh, hi,' said Tiffany October, the pathologist. She sounded tired.

'You must have had a busy day.'

'They're all busy,' she said.

'I was wondering,' Vusi said, feeling his heart thump in his chest. 'If you would like . . .'

The silence on the line was deafening.

'If you would like to go and have something to eat. Or drink . . .'

'Now?'

'No, I mean, any time, maybe another day . . .'

'No,' she said and Vusi's heart plummeted. 'No, now,' she said. 'Please. A beer. A Windhoek Light and a plate of *slap* chips, that would be wonderful after a day like today . . .'

HE DROVE DOWN THE N1, thinking ahead. He would draw money at the ABSA autobank at the bottom of Long Street. Then to the bottle store up in Buitengracht. He would buy a bottle of Jack and a two-litre Coke and then he was going to drink himself into a coma.

There's someone else, Benny.

He had asked, 'Who?'

And she'd said, 'It doesn't matter. I'm so sorry, it just happened.'

Things don't just happen. You look for them. She demands that he give up the booze for six months, and then off she goes looking for a man. He would find out who it was. He would shoot the bastard between the eyes.

He had just stared at her, waiting for her to say she wasn't serious. They were here so she could say that, because he had quit drinking, he could come home. But she just sat there with tears in her eyes, so terribly sorry for herself. There were a thousand things in his head. He'd nearly died today. He'd fought the craving to drink for one hundred and fifty-six days, he'd paid maintenance, he'd done everything right. She couldn't do this, she didn't have the right. But her teary eyes had looked back at him with bewildering finality.

He got up and left.

'Benny!' she called after him.

Benny just kept walking to his car; he saw nothing, heard nothing, just felt this thing, this anger, it was all for nothing, all for nothing.

HE DREW OUT R500 and saw how much he had left for the rest of the month. He thought about Duncan Blake sitting there in the interview room and saying, 'How much for all of this to go away?'

'I'm not for sale.'

'This is Africa. Everybody is for sale.'

'Not me.'

'How about ten million?'

And he had laughed. He should have taken the money. Ten million would buy a lot of booze.

His cellphone rang as he walked back to his car. He didn't look at the screen, just answered. 'Griessel.' Sullen. Brusque.

'Captain, this is Bill Anderson . . . Is this a convenient time?'

His first thought was that someone had taken Rachel again. 'Yes.'

'Captain, I don't know how to do this. I don't know how you thank a man for saving your child's life. I don't know how to thank a man who was willing to be shot at to save the daughter of someone he's never met. But my wife and I want to say thank you. We owe you a debt we can never repay. We're on our way to South Africa—our plane is leaving in two hours' time. When we get there, we would like to have the honour of taking you to dinner. But right now, I just want to say thank you.'

'I . . . uh . . . I was just doing my job.' He couldn't think what else to say. The call had come too suddenly, there was too much going on in his head.

'No, sir, what *you* did went *way* beyond the call of duty. So thank you. From Jess, Rachel and myself. We would like to wish you the very best, for you and your family. May all your dreams come true.'

HE SAT IN HIS CAR in front of the autobank. He thought about Bill Anderson's words. *May all your dreams come true.* His only dream had been that Anna would take him back. Now he just had the dream of getting drunk.

He started the car.

He thought about his son Fritz's dream. *Wet & Orde.*

And Carla, who had gone to work in London, because she wanted to come back and buy a car and go to university, and both of them dreamed of a sober father.

He turned the car off.

He thought about Bella, and Bella's dream of owning her own business.

Alexa Barnard, who had dreamed so long of becoming a singer. Duncan Blake: *Africa took all my dreams.*

And Bill Anderson. *May all your dreams come true.*

He opened the cubbyhole, took out the cigarettes and lit one. He thought of many things. He sat like that for a long time while the world raced past down Long Street. Then he turned round.

BENNY GRIESSEL blew the R500 on flowers. He delivered the first bunch to Mbali Kaleni's ward. They wouldn't allow him in. He wrote a message on a card. *You are a brave woman and a good detective.*

Then he went to Rachel Anderson and put a bunch of flowers down on the bed beside her. 'They're beautiful,' she said.

'And so are you.'

'And those?' she asked about the other bunch of flowers in his arms.

'These are a bribe,' he said. 'You see, I have a dream. I'm going to start a band and we are going to need a singer. And I happen to know a great singer who's right here in this hospital,' he said.

'Cool,' she said, and he wondered whether he could introduce her to Fritz.

From: Benny Griessel [mailto: bennygriessel2@mweb.co.za]
Sent: January 16, 2009 22:01
To: carla805@hotmail.com

Subject: Today.
Dear Carla

Sorry I am writing only now: my laptop wouldn't connect with the Internet. It was a lot of trouble, but it's fixed now.

It was a long day and a difficult one. I thought about you and missed you. But I did meet a famous singer and I was promoted. Your father is a Captain today.

deon **meyer**

Deon Meyer's career has taken him from journalism to Internet branding and now, as the 'king of South African crime writing', and one of a delegation of authors from South Africa, onto the international publishing stage at London's 2010 Book Fair. As he recalls his path to success, it's clear Meyer still can't believe his luck.

'My life has been filled with wonderful chances and opportunities, and one thing has just led to another. I feel really blessed. I've been extremely fortunate. When you think I come from a small, inconsequential mining town on the Veld, and last night [at a London-based publishing event] I was meeting Julie Christie! I think maybe one day I'm going to wake up and find it's all been a dream.'

He goes on to relate how luck and a passion for motorbikes drew him away from his early plans to become a teacher and led him into journalism instead. A friend offered him a job on a Cape Town newspaper and Meyer leapt at it, finding reporting much more his style than the repetitive nature of teaching the same course, year after year. Meanwhile, in his spare time, he started a blog about his lifelong passion—BMW motorbikes. 'There wasn't anything on the Internet about them, so I started a little virtual community to see if my ideas about Internet branding were correct. And the thing just took off. I offered it to BMW, when it became too much work, and they said, "Oh, yes, we know about this, and we love it because you're doing what we're trying to do with the brand. Why don't you run it for us and we'll pay you?" That turned into me doing a five-year stint with them, putting together an Internet marketing strategy. I got to see most of South Africa as a result—a lot of it on the back of a bike. We have dirt roads leading to some very beautiful places.

'The point is,' Meyer concludes, 'the path of my career has been very unpredictable. These opportunities just popped up. So I am a firm believer in following your passions because, if you do, you probably end up doing a better job than when you do something you don't like.' With six published novels to his name, all of them originally written in his native Afrikaans, Meyer has proved his point and is about to enter a new league with *Thirteen Hours*, which has been optioned for film by a British production company.

So, what triggered the writing bug? 'From the age of about nine, I always wanted to write. I got a love of books from my mother, and I can remember finishing yet another wonderful story and thinking, One day I want to entertain like this, and the urge just got stronger and stronger. My father was a natural storyteller, too, and I learned from him. We grew up without television and so our Sunday evenings—wonderful sunny evenings— were spent out on the porch, as a family, listening to Dad. I still have a great curiosity about people and I love hearing their stories. When I do research, I prefer personal interviews to the Internet. And the journalism comes in handy for that. It taught me how to find the right people, and how to interview them to get the right information.'

For *Thirteen Hours*, which features a murder connected to the burgeoning Afrikaans music industry, Meyer talked to a record-company executive and several singers, composers and musicians. 'Not only to get their take on the industry,' he says, 'but also to hear their personal stories of how they overcame adversity to become successful. I've always followed Afrikaans music. For me it is one of the wonderful signs in South Africa that our arts in general are normalising. They are starting to resemble those of other countries again. In the bad old days, the government controlled everything, often banning albums.'

He steers clear of dwelling on politics, but clearly has strong views about the racial divisions in his country. 'We, as Afrikaners, need to get involved and to integrate. We need to forget about differences and look at what we have in common with our compatriots. Afrikaners, generally speaking, are standing on the sidelines, moaning and groaning but not getting involved. Some do, of course, but not all.'

On the positive side, Meyer loves the ebullience of South Africa, which he believes is lacking in Europe. 'It's such a dynamic country. We have to make up for lost time, working hard to fight poverty, for example, and so there's great energy and focus and hustle and bustle. It's edgy, as a society. It's why the creative arts are blossoming. Music, literature, everything . . .'

Of Select Editions, Meyer says: 'It's just the coolest thing to be in Reader's Digest! I grew up with it, and my parents subscribed to Condensed Books. I discovered so many authors that way. My mother's going to be very proud when she sees the copies!' So, too, no doubt, will Deon Meyer's wife and their four grown-up children aged fifteen, seventeen, nineteen and twenty-four. 'I miss them the moment I leave home,' Meyer says, with a wistful sigh.

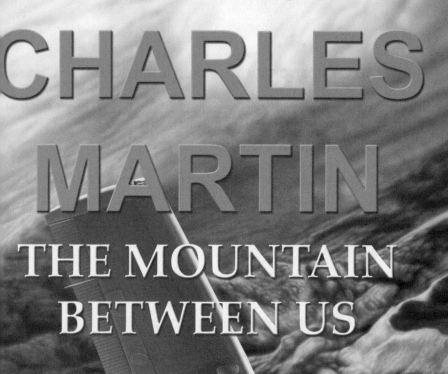

CHARLES MARTIN

THE MOUNTAIN BETWEEN US

A blizzard approaches Salt Lake City,

and the airport is about to be shut down.

Two strangers charter a small plane,

trying to outrun the storm.

Each of them needs to get home

in a hurry.

Neither will achieve that goal. Instead,

they'll find themselves fighting for

survival, their pilot dead even

before the plane hits

the ground.

Prelude

*H**ey . . .*
      *I'm not sure what time it is. This thing should record that. I woke
a few minutes ago. It's still dark. I don't know how long I was out.*

*The snow is spilling in through the windshield. It's frozen across my face.
Hard to blink. Feels like dried paint on my cheeks. It just doesn't taste like
dried paint.*

*I'm shivering . . . and it feels like somebody is sitting on my chest. Can't
catch my breath. Maybe broke two or three ribs. Might have a collapsed lung.*

*The wind up here is steady, leaning against the tail of the fuselage—or
what's left of it. Something above me, maybe a branch, is slapping the Plexiglass. And more cold air is coming in behind me. Where the tail used to be.*

I can smell gas. I guess both wings were still pretty full of fuel.

I feel like I want to throw up.

*A hand is wrapped round mine. The fingers are cold and calloused.
There's a wedding band, worn thin round the edges. That's Grover.*

*He was dead before we hit the treetops. I'll never understand how he
landed this thing without killing me too.*

*When we took off, the ground temperature was in the single digits. Not
sure what it is now. Our elevation should be around 11,500. Give or take.
We couldn't have fallen more than five hundred feet when Grover dipped the
wing. The control panel sits dark, unlit. Every few minutes the GPS will
flicker, then go black.*

*There was a dog here somewhere. All teeth and muscle. Short hair. About
the size of a bread box. Looks like he's jacked up on speed. Wait . . .*

'Hey, boy . . . Wait . . . What's your name? You scared? Yeah . . . me too.'

I'M BACK . . . was I gone long? There's a dog here. Buried between my coat and armpit. Did I already tell you about him? He's shivering and whenever the wind howls he jumps up and growls at it.

The memory's foggy. Grover and I were talking, he was maybe banking right, the dash flashed a buffet of blue and green lights, a carpet of black stretched out below us, not a light bulb for sixty miles, and . . . there was a woman. Trying to get home to her fiancé and a rehearsal dinner. I'll look.

I found her. Unconscious. Elevated pulse. Eyes are swollen shut. Pupils are dilated. Probably a concussion. Several lacerations across her face. A few will need stitches. Right shoulder is dislocated and left femur is broken. I need to set it once I catch my breath.

IT'S GETTING COLDER. I guess the storm finally caught us. If I don't get us wrapped in something, we'll freeze to death before daylight. I'll have to set that leg in the morning.

Rachel, I don't know how much time we have, don't know if we'll make it out, if . . . but I take it all back. I was wrong. I was angry. I never should've said it. You were thinking about us. Not you. I can see that now.

You're right. There's always a chance.

Always.

Chapter One

S alt Lake City Airport, twelve hours earlier. The view was ugly. Grey, dreary, January dragging on. I pressed my forehead to the glass. On the tarmac, guys in yellow suits drove trains of luggage round the planes, leaving snow flurries swirling in their exhaust.

To the west, clouds covered the runway, visibility near zero, but, given the wind, it came and went. Eastwards, snowcapped mountains rose above the clouds. Mountains have long been an attraction for me. For a moment, I wondered what was on the other side.

My flight was scheduled to depart at 6.07 p.m. but given delays was starting to look like the red-eye. If at all. I moved to a corner on the floor, against a far wall, annoyed by the flashing 'DELAYED' sign. Patient files were spread across my lap while I dictated my reports into a digital recorder. Folks I'd either seen or treated the week before I left. Years ago, Rachel, my wife, convinced me to focus on sports medicine in kids. She was right. I hated seeing them limp in, but loved watching them run out.

I had more work to do, and the battery indicator was flashing red, so I walked to the store in the terminal. I could buy two AA batteries for four dollars or twelve for seven dollars. I paid seven, replaced the two in my recorder, and slid the other ten into my backpack.

I had just returned from a medical conference in Colorado Springs where I had joined a panel on 'The Intersection of Paediatric Orthopaedics and Emergency Medicine'. The venue was beautiful, the conference satisfied several of my continuing-education requirements but, most importantly, it gave me an excuse to spend four days climbing Colorado's Collegiate Peaks. In truth, it was a business trip that satisfied my hiking addiction. Many doctors buy Porsches, big homes and country-club memberships. I take long runs on the beach and climb mountains when I can get to them.

My return trip took me from Colorado Springs to Salt Lake for the direct flight home. The crowd in the airport had thinned by this time on a Sunday.

Her walk caught my attention. Long, slender legs, purposeful gait, yet graceful. Confident, and comfortable in her own skin. She was maybe five-nine, dark haired and attractive, but not too concerned about it. Maybe thirty. Her hair was short. Think Winona Ryder. Better yet, Julia Ormond in *Sabrina*. Not a lot of fuss, yet you could find the same style up and down Manhattan with girls who'd paid a lot of money to look that way. My bet was that she had paid very little.

She walked up, spotted the crowd at the gate and chose to sit ten or fifteen feet away on the floor. I watched her out of the corner of my eye. Dark trouser suit, a leather attaché and one carry-on. She set down her bags, tied on a pair of running shoes, then sat and stretched, touching head, chest and stomach to her thigh. After a few minutes, she pulled a legal pad from her attaché, flipped to handwritten notes and started typing on her laptop.

It beeped, and she began eyeballing the wall for an outlet. I was using half. She pointed at the plug, 'Mind if I share?'

'Sure.'

She plugged in and then sat Indian-style with the computer on the floor.

I continued with my files. 'Follow-up orthopaedics consultation dated'—I studied my calendar—'January the twenty-third. This is Dr Ben Payne. Patient's name is Rebecca Peterson, identifying data follows: date of birth, 6.7.95, medical record number BMC2453, Caucasian female, star right wing on her soccer team, leading scorer in Florida, fourteen division-one offers, surgery three weeks ago, post-op normal presenting no complications, followed by aggressive physical therapy, presents full range of motion, bend test one hundred and twenty-seven degrees, strength test shows marked improvement, as does agility, movement pain-free. Rebecca is free to resume all activities . . . except she is to stay off the skateboard until she's at least thirty-five.'

I turned to the next file. 'Initial orthopaedics consultation dated January the twenty-third. This is Dr Ben Payne. Patient's name is Rasheed Smith, identifying data follows: date of birth, 19.2.79, medical record number BMC17437, black male, starting defensive back for the Jacksonville Jaguars. MRI confirms no tear in the ACL or MCL, recommend that he stay off the YMCA basketball court until he's finished playing professional football. Range of motion is limited due to pain and tenderness, which should subside given aggressive therapy during the off-season. Can resume limited strength and speed training with cessation in pain. Schedule two-week follow-up and call the YMCA and tell them to revoke his membership.'

I slid the files into my backpack and noticed she was laughing. She said, 'You a doctor?'

'Surgeon.' I held up the manila folders. 'Last week's patients.'

'You really get to know them, don't you?' She laughed again. 'Sorry, but I couldn't help overhearing you.'

I nodded at her pad. 'And you?'

'Columnist. I write for several women's magazines.'

'What kind of topics do you cover?'

'Fashion, trends, a lot of humour or satire, some relationships.'

'I can't write my way out of a wet paper bag. How many will you write in a year?'

She weighed her head from side to side. 'Forty, maybe fifty.' She glanced at my recorder. 'Most doctors I know loathe those things.'

I turned it in my hand. 'It grew on me. I'm seldom without it.'

'Take much getting used to?'

'Actually the opposite, I couldn't live without it.'

'Sounds like a story here.'

'Rachel . . . my wife, gave it to me. I was joining the staff at the hospital in Jacksonville. She was afraid of never seeing me. This was a way to hear the sound of the other's voice, to not miss the little things . . . She'd keep it a day or so, speak her mind . . . then I'd keep it and pass it back.'

'Wouldn't a cellphone do the same thing?'

I shrugged. 'It's different. Try it some time and you'll see.'

'How long you been married?'

'We married . . . fifteen years ago this week.' I glanced at the single diamond on her left hand. 'You got one coming up?'

She couldn't control the smile. 'I'm trying to get home for my rehearsal dinner party tomorrow night.'

'Congratulations.'

She shook her head and smiled, staring out across the crowd. Her charm was magnetic. 'I have a million things to do and yet here I am making notes on a story about a flash-in-the-pan fashion I don't even like.' A shrug. 'Jacksonville still home?'

'Yep. And you?'

'Atlanta, Georgia.' She handed me her card. It read, 'ASHLEY KNOX'.

'Ashley.'

'To everyone but my dad who wanted a boy. He calls me 'Asher'. Instead of ballet and softball he took me to tae kwon do.'

'Let me guess, you're one of those crazy people that can kick stuff off the top of other people's heads. What degree?'

She held up three fingers.

'I worked on a guy a few weeks ago, put a few rods and screws in his shin. His opponent's elbow sort of folded it the wrong way.'

'Competing in my teens, I broke my share of bones and joints. There was a time when my orthopaedist in Atlanta was on speed-dial.' She smiled. 'Is this trip work, play or both?'

'I'm returning from a medical conference, where I sat on a panel, and got in some climbing on the side.'

'Climbing?'

'Mountains.'

'Is that what you do when you're not cutting on people?'

I laughed. 'I have two hobbies. Running . . . it's how I met Rachel. In high school. The second is climbing mountains, something we started while I was attending medical school in Denver. There are fifty-four peaks in Colorado higher than fourteen thousand feet. Locals call them "Fourteeners". An unofficial club of folks have climbed them all.'

'Are you two members?'

'Not yet. I climbed one this trip. Mt Princeton. 14,197 feet.'

She thought about that a minute. 'Almost three miles above sea level. How long does something like that take?'

'Normally a day or less, but this time of year it's tougher.'

She laughed. 'You need oxygen?'

'No, but acclimatising helps.'

'And was it bitter cold, snowing and blowing like crazy?'

'At times.' I laughed. 'I'll bet you're a good journalist.'

One eyebrow raised. 'So, you're the "man vs wild" type?'

I shook my head. 'Weekend warrior. Most at home at sea level.'

She stared down the rows of people. 'She's not with you?'

'Not this time.' My stomach had started growling, and I stood. 'You mind watching my stuff?'

'Sure.

'Be right back.'

I returned with a Caesar salad and a plate-sized pepperoni pizza as the loudspeaker cackled, 'All passengers for Flight 1672 to Atlanta, please board. If we load quickly, we might beat this storm.'

The eight gates around me read, 'DELAYED'. Frustrated faces populated the seats and walls. I grabbed my pack and my food, and with eight other passengers—including Ashley—jogged to the plane. I found my seat, buckled in, the attendants crosschecked and we began backing up. The plane stopped and the pilot got on the intercom. 'Folks, we're in line for the deicer. By the way, there's plenty of room up-front in first class.'

Everyone moved.

The only remaining seat placed me next to Ashley. We sat for thirty minutes while the attendants served us most anything we asked for. I drank spicy tomato juice. She drank cabernet. The pilot again. His tone did not encourage me. 'Folks, the controllers tell us we've got about an hour's window to beat this storm, but the ground crew just informed me that one of our two deicing trucks is inoperative. We're twentieth in line on the runway and, long story short, we're not getting out of here tonight.'

Groans echoed round the plane.

The pilot continued. 'If you'd like a hotel voucher, please see Mark in the red coat at the gate. Once you reclaim your baggage, our shuttle will take you to the hotel. Folks, I'm really sorry.'

We walked back into the terminal and watched the 'DELAYED' signs change to 'CANCELLED'. I walked to the counter. The attendant stared at a computer screen. Before I opened my mouth, she pointed at a television tuned to the weather channel. 'I'm sorry, there's nothing I can do.'

Four screens showed a huge green blob moving east-southeast from Washington, Oregon and Northern California and announced snow, ice, single-digit temperatures and wind chills in the negatives. Mark began handing out vouchers. I had the daypack that doubled as my briefcase and one checked bag in the belly of the plane. I walked towards the baggage claim and lost Ashley when she stopped at the Natural Snack store. Standing round the conveyor belt, my eyes wandered. Through the sliding glass doors I saw the lights of the private airport less than a mile away. Painted on the side of one of the hangars, in huge letters, 'CHARTERS'.

The lights were on inside. My bag appeared, I hefted it atop my shoulder and bumped into Ashley who was waiting on hers. She pointed. 'You weren't kidding when you said you went hiking.' My bag is an orangeish Osprey 70 backpack and it was stuffed with gear for my climb. sleeping-bag, Therm-a-Rest pad, Jetboil, Nalgene bottles, a few layers of polypropylene, other odds and ends. Ashley eyed it. 'You really need all that?'

'These are just the essentials. Good to have along.'

She spotted her bag and ran it down, then turned back. Her facial expression was pained. The idea of missing her wedding was starting to sink in, bleeding away her charm. She extended her hand. 'Great to meet you. Hope you can get home.'

'Yeah, you . . .'

She never heard me. She headed towards the taxi lane where a hundred people stood in line.

I FLAGGED DOWN the airport shuttle. Normally it would be busy taxiing people between terminals and the private airport, but given that everyone was trying to leave the airport, it was empty.

When we arrived in front of the hangar the driver sat in the bus with the engine running while I ran inside. The sky was clear but the wind was picking up and the temperature was dropping.

Inside I found a red-hot space heater and a white-haired guy standing next to one of three planes, a small single-engine whose side read, 'GROVER'S CHARTER'. Below that, '*Fishing and hunting charters to remote locations.*'

He was facing away from me, aiming a compound bow at a target against the far wall. Maybe forty yards. As I walked in, he released an arrow that whistled through the air. He wore faded jeans and a shirt with snap buttons with the sleeves rolled up. '*Grover*' had been stamped across the back of his leather belt, and he carried a Leatherman multitool in a holster on his hip. A Jack Russell terrier stood at his heels, sniffing the air and sizing me up.

I waved at the man. 'Hi.'

He relaxed and turned. He was tall, handsome, and had a strong square chin. 'Howdy. You George?'

'No sir. Not George. Name's Ben.'

He raised his bow and returned to his target. 'Shame.'

'How's that?'

He came to full draw and talked while staring through his peep sight. 'Two guys hired me to fly them into the San Juans down near Ouray.' He released the arrow. 'One of them is named George. Thought you might be him.' He nocked another arrow.

I stared at his target. The evidence round the bull's eye suggested he'd spent a good bit of time shooting that bow. I smiled. 'You look like you're new at that.'

He laughed, came to full draw a third time and said, 'I do this when I'm bored and waiting on clients.' His arrow slid in with the other two. He set his bow down on the seat of his plane and we walked towards his target.

He began pulling out the arrows. 'Some guys retire to chase a little dimpled ball around only to beat the white off it with an expensive piece of metal.' He smiled. 'I fish and hunt.'

'Any chance I could convince you to fly me out of here tonight?'

He raised an eyebrow. 'You running from the law?'

A smile. 'No. Just trying to get home ahead of this storm.'

He checked his watch. 'I was fixing to close up shop, head home myself and climb into bed with my wife.' He noticed my wedding ring. 'I 'magine you'd like to do the same.' He smiled a broad smile. 'Although not with my wife.' He laughed. It was easy and there was great comfort in it.

'Yes, I would.'

He nodded. 'Where's home?'

'Florida. Thought if I could get ahead of this storm, maybe I could catch a red-eye out of Denver. Or, at least the first flight out tomorrow.'

'You in a hurry?'

'I'm scheduled for a knee and two hip replacements in'—I checked my watch—'thirteen hours and forty-three minutes.'

Grover laughed. Pulled a rag from his back pocket and rubbed the grease round his fingers. 'You might be sore tomorrow night.'

'No . . .' I laughed. 'I'm performing them. I'm a surgeon.'

'Oh. Big birds not flying tonight?'

'Cancelled. One of their deicing trucks broke down.'

'They do that a lot. You know, they can reschedule surgeries. I've done that a few times myself.' He tapped his chest. 'Bum ticker.'

'I've been gone a week. Need to get back.'

He stuffed the rag in his pocket, fed the arrows into the quiver hanging on his bow, then slid the bow into a compartment behind the back seat of the plane. Alongside the bow were three tubes extending back into the body of the plane. He tapped the ends. 'Fly rods.'

A hickory-handled something had been fastened alongside the rods. 'What's that?'

'Hatchet.' He tapped a 'stuff sack' beneath the seat, compressing a sleeping-bag. 'Where I fly, it pays to be self-sufficient.' Behind the seat hung a waistcoat with flies, small scissors and a net. He waved his hand across it. 'My clients take me to some wonderful places I couldn't afford to get to on my own, so I use them as an excuse to do things I love. My wife even goes with me from time to time.' He looked early seventies with the body of a fifty-year-old and the heart of a teenager.

I pointed at the plane. 'Yours?'

'Yep. It's a Scout. Powered by a Locoman zero-three-sixty that generates a hundred and eighty horsepower. Top speed is a hundred and forty at full throttle.'

I frowned. 'That's not very fast.'

'I gave up speed a long time ago.' He put his hand on the three-bladed propeller. 'She can land at thirty-eight miles an hour, which means I can put her down in a space about the size of this hangar. Makes me popular with my clients.' He stared at a large clock, calculating the time and hours. 'Even if I get you to Denver, you may not get out of there tonight.'

'I'll take my chances. Folks at the counter say that storm may dump enough snow to ground everything tomorrow.'

He nodded. 'Won't be cheap. One-fifty an hour and you pay my way going and coming. Cost to you is about nine hundred dollars.'

'You take a credit card?'

He squinted one eye and considered me. Like he was having a conversation with himself. Finally, he extended his hand. 'Grover Roosevelt.'

I shook it. 'Any relation to the former president?'

He smiled. 'Distant, but they don't claim me.'

I handed him my business card. 'I'm Ben Payne.'

He pulled a pipe from a pocket, packed it, and flicked open a brass Zippo lighter out of his shirt pocket. 'Orthopaedics, eh?'

'That and emergency medicine. The two often go hand in hand.'

'Give me fifteen minutes.' He thumbed over his shoulder towards the men's room. 'I need to see a man about a horse.'

'Has this place got wireless?'

'Yep.' He walked away. 'Password is "Tank".'

I flipped open my laptop, found the network, logged in and downloaded my email, which included my business and personal voicemail, which had all been forwarded as audio files. That done, I synced my recorder with my computer, then emailed the dictation file to our transcription office while copying two other servers, in the event that we needed a back-up.

Grover reappeared and I said, 'How many people do you carry?'

'Me and two more if they don't mind sitting hip to hip.'

I stared at the airport. 'You mind waiting ten minutes?'

'I'll be working through my preflight. But you need to hurry.'

My friend in the shuttle van returned me to baggage claim and offered to wait again. I found Ashley standing on the kerb waiting on the next taxi.

She had zipped up a North Face down jacket over her suit coat. I pointed over my shoulder. 'I've hired a charter to fly me to Denver. Maybe get ahead of the storm. I know you don't really know me from Adam's house cat but there's room for one more.'

'You're serious?'

'I've been through that whole wedding thing and if you're anything like my wife you won't sleep for the next two days trying to make every detail perfect. It's just an honest offer from one professional to another. No strings.'

Disbelief shaded her face. She looked me up and down.

I spun my wedding ring round my finger. 'On the back porch of my condo, where I sip coffee and stare out across the ocean, my wife placed three bowls to feed the dumpster cats hanging out in the parking lot. They drink with me every morning. I've got names for them and I've got used to that little purring thing they do.'

A wrinkle appeared between her eyebrows. 'You saying I'm a stray cat?'

'No. I'm saying that I never noticed they were there until she opened my eyes.' I paused. 'I don't want you to miss your wedding. That's all.'

'Will you let me split the fare with you?'

I shrugged. 'You're welcome either way.'

She stared down the runway. 'I'm supposed to take my six bridesmaids to breakfast, followed by a few hours at the spa.' She looked at the hotel lights in the distance. 'Getting out of here would be fantastic.'

Chapter Two

Grover was sitting in the plane, headphones on, clicking buttons and turning dials in front of him. 'You ready?'

'Grover, this is Ashley Knox, a writer from Atlanta. She's getting married in forty-eight hours. Thought we could give her a lift.'

He helped her with her bag. 'Be my pleasure.'

He stowed our luggage behind the rear seat and my curiosity got the better of me. 'Any storage space in the tail?'

He opened a small door near the rear of the tail. 'Currently in use.' He pointed to a bright-orange battery-powered gizmo. 'It's an ELT, an Emergency Landing Transmitter. If we crash-land, and that thing experiences more than thirty pounds of impact pressure, it sends out a tone on emergency frequency 122.5. Flight service picks up the signal, sends out a couple of planes, triangulates our position and sends in the cavalry.'

We climbed into the plane, and he cranked the engine while Ashley and I put on the headsets hanging above our seats. We rolled out of the hangar, where he sat flicking more switches, moving the stick between his knees and adjusting knobs. Two dash-mounted GPS units sat on either end of the control panel. I tapped his shoulder and pointed. 'Why two?'

He laughed. 'Just in case one quits on me.'

I dialled my voicemail. One message. I held the phone to my ear. 'Hey . . . it's me.' Her voice was low. Tired. Like she'd been sleeping. Or crying. I could hear the ocean in the background. That meant she was standing on the porch. 'I don't like it when you leave.' She took a deep breath. 'I know you're worried. Don't be. It'll work out. In three months, this'll all be forgotten. You'll see. I'll wait up.' She attempted a laugh. 'We all will. Coffee on the beach. Hurry . . . And don't think for a minute I love you any less. I love you the same. Even more. Don't be angry. Trust me. We'll make it. With all of me, I love you. Hurry home. Meet you on the beach.'

I clicked the phone shut and stared out of the glass. Grover glanced at me and gently rolled down the blacktop. 'Want to call her back?'

'What?'

He pointed at my cellphone. 'You want to call her back?'

'No . . .' I slid it into my pocket. I didn't know how he heard anything over the drone of the propeller. 'You've got pretty good ears.'

He pointed at the microphone connected to my headset. 'Your mike picked up her voice. Might as well have been listening to it myself.' He pointed at Ashley. 'There are no secrets in a plane this small.' She smiled, tapped her earphones, and nodded. 'I can wait if you want.'

I shook my head. 'No . . . really, it's OK.'

Grover slowed to a stop and spoke into his mike. 'Control, this is one-three-eight-bravo, request permission to take off.'

A few seconds passed and a voice spoke through our headphones. 'One-three-eight-bravo, you're cleared for takeoff.'

Two minutes later, we were airborne and climbing. Grover spoke over the microphone. 'We'll climb to twelve thousand feet and cruise across the San Juan Valley towards Strawberry Lake. Once she's in sight, we'll turn northeast, head across the High Uintas Wilderness and then descend to Denver. Feel free to move about the cabin. In-flight meal and entertainment service will begin immediately.' He reached into the door pocket, passed two bags of smoked almonds over his shoulder and began singing, 'I'll Fly Away', then cut the song midsentence. 'Ben? How long you been married?'

'We married fifteen years ago this week.'

Ashley piped up. 'Tell the truth. Is it still exciting or just ho-hum?'

Grover laughed. 'I will have been married fifty years in July, and trust me, it gets better. Not worse. Not dull. I love her more today than the day we married, and I thought that was impossible.'

She looked at me. 'How 'bout it? Got any plans?'

I nodded. 'Thought I'd bring her some flowers. Open a bottle of wine and watch the waves roll up on the sand.'

'You still bring her flowers?'

'Every week.'

She turned and lowered her head, raising one eyebrow, which pulled up one lip—doing that thing women do when they don't believe a word you're saying. 'You bring your wife flowers every week?'

'Yep.'

The journalist in her surfaced. 'What's her favourite flower?'

'Potted orchids. But if I can't get her an orchid, then I go to this shop not too far from the hospital and buy whatever is blooming.'

'You're serious? What does she do with all the orchids? Please don't tell me you just pitch them.'

'I built her a greenhouse.'

'A greenhouse? How many do you have?'

I shrugged. 'Last time I counted, two hundred and fifty-seven.'

Grover laughed. 'A true romantic.' He spoke over his shoulder. 'Ashley, how'd you meet your fiancé?'

'The courtroom, in Atlanta. I was writing a story about a celebrity trial. He served as opposing counsel, and invited me to dinner.'

'Perfect. Where're you two going on your honeymoon?'

'Italy. Two weeks. Starting in Venice and ending in Florence.'

Turbulence shook the plane. Ashley turned the questioning back to him. 'Just curious, Mr . . . ?' She snapped her fingers.

He waved her off. 'Call me Grover.'

'How many hours have you logged in the air?'

He dipped the plane hard right, then pulled back, shooting us upwards and sending my stomach into my throat. 'You mean can I get you to Denver without dipping the nose into a mountain?'

'Yeah . . . something like that.'

He rocked the wheel, left then right, dipping each wing. 'Including or not including time spent in the military?'

I latched a death grip on the handle above my head. She did likewise and said, 'Not.'

He levelled out, smooth as a tabletop. ''Bout fifteen thousand hours.' I could hear a smile in the way he spoke. 'You two feel better now?'

His dog crawled out from under his seat, hopped up on his lap and stared over his shoulder at us. Snarling and twitching like a squirrel on steroids. His body was one massive, rippled muscle but his legs were only four or five inches long. He commanded a lot of personal space, and reading his body language told me that this cockpit was his space.

Grover again, 'You two meet Tank. My copilot.'

'How many hours has he got?' I asked.

Grover's head tilted. 'Between three and four thousand.'

The dog turned, satisfied, hopped back down and curled beneath the seat.

I leaned forward slightly to watch Grover's hands. Gnarled. Meaty. Dry skin. Big knuckles. Wedding ring thin round the edges. 'How long will it take us to get there?'

He slid a silver pocket watch from his shirt, clicked it open. A woman's picture was taped to the inside of the cover. He then stared at his instruments. His GPS gave him an estimated arrival time but I got the feeling he was double-checking. 'Given our crosswind . . . right at two hours.'

The picture I'd glimpsed was tattered and cracked, but, even faded, she was beautiful. 'You got kids?'

'Five, and thirteen grandchildren. Our youngest is probably older than you.' He glanced over his shoulder. 'Ben, how old are you?'

'Thirty-nine.'

'And you Ashley?'

'Don't you know you're never supposed to ask a lady her age?'

'Well, technically I'm not supposed to put two people in that back seat but I'm old school and it's never stopped me.'

I tapped him on the shoulder, 'What's the deal with two people?'

'The FAA has stated from on high that I'm allowed only one.'

'Then why did you tell me two?'

''Cause I can fit two.'

Ashley smiled and stuck a finger in the air. 'So, this isn't legal?'

He laughed. 'Define legal.'

'When we land . . . are we going to jail or the terminal?'

He laughed. 'Technically, they don't know you're on this plane so I doubt they'll be waiting to arrest you. If they do, I'll tell them you kidnapped me and I'd like to press charges.'

She looked at me. 'I feel better.'

He continued. 'This plane is designed to fly low and slow. I fly under a VFR designation, meaning "visual flight rules". Which means, I don't have to file a flight plan as long as I plan to fly by sight. Which means, what they don't know won't hurt them. So?' He looked towards Ashley. 'Your age?'

'Thirty-four.'

He looked at his instrument panel and then eyed one of the GPS units. 'Wind drift is killing us. This is a big storm coming in. Good thing I know where I'm going otherwise we'd be way off course.' He laughed to himself. 'Youngsters. Both of you. Your whole life before you. What I wouldn't do to be thirty-something, knowing what I know now.'

The two of us sat quietly. Ashley's disposition had changed. More pensive. I wasn't all that comfortable knowing I'd put her in a precarious position. Grover picked up on it. 'Don't you worry. It's only illegal if you get caught, and I've never been caught. In a couple of hours you'll be on the ground.' He coughed, cleared his throat and laughed some more.

The night shone through the Plexiglass above my head. The stars looked close enough to touch. 'All right, you two.' Grover coughed again. 'Given that we're trying to outrun that storm and given the wind drift and given that I don't carry oxygen, we've got to stay below fifteen thousand feet or you'll land with a headache.'

Ashley said, 'I hear a "so" coming.'

'So . . . hold on because we're coming up on the Uintas.'

'You-what-as?'

'The High Uintas Wilderness. Largest east-to-west mountain range on the continent, home to 1.3 million acres of uncivilised wilderness, five to seven hundred inches of snow a year, seven hundred lakes, some of the best fishing and hunting anywhere.'

'Sounds remote.'

'Ever see the movie *Jeremiah Johnson*?' He pointed down. Nodded longingly. 'That's where they filmed it.'

'No kidding? One of my favourites.'

'No kidding.' The ride was starting to get bumpy. My stomach jumped into my throat. He rolled the stick towards his left knee. 'Feel nice and easy? Like a rolling roller-coaster ride?'

He stared out of the glass and we did likewise. The dog jumped up on his lap. 'In the middle is a national forest that's designated a "wilderness", which means there are no motorised vehicles of any kind. Hence, it's one of the more remote places on the planet. More Mars than Earth. If you robbed a bank, it'd be a great place to hide.' Another cough. Another laugh.

The wilderness spread out beneath us. 'Grover?' Ashley raised an eyebrow. 'How far can we see right now?'

'Maybe seventy miles, give or take.'

There wasn't a single light. 'You've made this run many times?'

'A hundred or more.'

'Good, 'cause if we get any closer to the snowcapped peaks, they'll scrape off the bottom of the plane.'

'Naw . . .' He was playing with us. 'We got a good hundred feet.' He pulled a sleeve of Tums from his shirt pocket, popped two, started chewing and coughed again. He tapped his chest.

I tapped him on the shoulder. 'Tell me about your bum ticker. How long you been coughing and popping antacids?'

He pulled back on the stick and we rose up over what looked like a plateau and skirted between two mountains on either side. The moon appeared out of the left glass. Shining down on a world blanketed in white. He was quiet a minute, looking right, then left. 'Beautiful, isn't it?'

Ashley answered for all of us. 'Surreal.'

'Doc,' Grover started, 'saw my cardiologist last week. He's the one recommended the antacids.'

'Did you have the cough then?'

'Yep, it's why my wife sent me.'

'They run an ECG?'

'Yep. All clear.'

'Do yourself a favour and go back. Might be nothing. But, might be something too. I think it'd be worth another look.'

He nodded. 'I live by a couple of simple rules. One is that I stick to what I'm good at and I give people credit for sticking to what they're good at.'

Ashley interrupted him. 'Tell me about your wife.'

We were rolling across mountaintops with precision. 'A Midwest girl, she married me when I had nothing but love, dreams and lust. Gave me children, stuck with me when I lost everything, believed me when I told her we'd be OK. No offence, but she's the most beautiful woman on the planet.'

'None taken. So, got any advice for a girl forty-eight hours from walking down the aisle?'

'When I wake up in the morning, she's holding my hand. I make coffee and then she sits with her knees touching mine while we drink it.' He shrugged. 'We've been married a long time, seen a lot, but loving somebody gets better the more you do it. You might think an old man like me doesn't get fired up when she walks across the bedroom in a faded flannel gown, but I do. Maybe she ain't as perky as she was in her twenties. Maybe she's got some wrinkles she don't like, but I don't look like the man in our wedding pictures. I married a woman who fits me. I'm one half of a two-piece puzzle.'

Ashley spoke again. 'What's the best part?'

'When she laughs, I smile. And when she cries, tears roll down my cheeks.' He nodded. 'I wouldn't trade that for nothing.'

The drone of the motor vibrated the plane as we rolled over mountaintop and across valley. He pointed out of the glass, waving his hand across the Earth. 'You two walked into my hangar tonight and saw a blue and yellow plane piloted by a crusty old man with a snotty dog at his heels. A quick hop to Denver so you can get on with your busy email, voicemail, text-messaged lives. I see an enclosed capsule that lifts you up above the problems of the Earth and gives you a perspective you can't get on land. Where you can see clearly. All of us spend our days looking through lenses that are fogged up, scratched and some broken. But this'—he tapped the stick—'this pulls you out from the lenses and for a few brief seconds gives you 20/20 vision.'

Ashley's tone was quiet. 'That why you love flying?'

He nodded. 'Sometimes, Gayle and I, we'll come up here and spend two or three hours. Not saying a word.'

We were quiet several minutes. Then he coughed.

GROVER GRUNTED, something low and guttural. He grabbed his chest, leaned forward, pushed off his headset and his head slammed against the side of the glass. He arched his back, then grabbed his shirt and pulled, tearing the shirt and popping off the buttons. He lunged over the stick, jerked it hard right, and then dipped the wing ninety degrees towards the Earth.

The mountain rose up to meet us. It felt like we were falling off a table. Just before we hit, he corrected her, pulled back on the stick, and the plane began to stall. Our speed slowed to almost nothing.

Then, as if he'd done it a thousand times, he pancaked the plane against the mountain.

The tail touched first, then the left wing, which hit something and snapped off. The weight of the right wing pulled on the plane, making an anchor of sorts. Somewhere in there Grover shut the engine. The last thing I remember was spinning, somersaulting, and the tail breaking off. Then I heard a loud crack, Ashley screamed, the dog barked and floated through the air. Snow peppered my face. The sound of impact followed.

HAVING JUST MET ASHLEY, who reminds me a lot of you, I was thinking about the day we met.

After school. I was standing on the track. A good bit warmer then than I am now. We were running quarters when the cross-country team came across the field, clustered behind a breakaway, single girl. You.

You were floating. Barely skimming the surface of the grass. A concert of arms over legs controlled by some unseen puppeteer. A sophomore on the team, I'd seen you before. Your hair was cut short back then. Like Julie Andrews in The Sound of Music. *You jumped a trackside bench, then the high hurdle next to me. Your breathing was deep, rhythmic, purposeful. Somewhere over the hurdle, you shot me a glance.*

Your whipping arms slung sweat across my legs and stomach. I heard myself say, 'Wow.' I tripped over a hurdle and in that single second you broke your concentration. Or, allowed it to be broken. Your eyes lit up. Then your feet touched down, and you were gone.

I must have said 'Wow' a second time because a teammate smacked me in the back of the head. 'Don't even think about it.'

'What?'

'Rachel Hunt, she's taken, and you don't stand a chance.'

'Why not?' I had yet to take my eyes off you.

'Two words. Nate Kelsey.'

Nate Kelsey played middle linebacker. Had no neck. And set the state bench-press record. You crossed the infield. 'I can take him.'

Scott smacked me in the head again. 'Boy, you need a keeper.'

But that was all it took.

Coach's wife worked in admissions. She was always trying to set me up. I asked her for your class schedule. Soon after, I discovered I had an insatiable desire to make a change in my third-period elective.

My adviser was not persuaded. 'You want to take Latin? Why?'

''Cause I think it's cool when people speak it.'

'People haven't spoken Latin since Rome fell.'

'Rome fell?'

He was not impressed. 'Ben, what's her name?'

'Rachel Hunt.'

'Good luck. You'll need it.' He signed my changed form and smiled. 'You seen her boyfriend? You got health insurance?'

'Yeah.'

I got to class early and watched you walk in. If I hadn't been seated, my knees would've buckled. You looked at me, smiled and set your books on the table to my left. Then you spun round and stuck out your hand. 'I'm Rachel.'

'Hi.' OK, OK. Maybe I stammered a bit.

I remember looking at your eyes and thinking 'I've never seen green like that.' Big, round. They reminded me of that snake in The Jungle Book that was always trying to hypnotise people.

You said, 'You're Ben Payne.'

My jaw fell and I nodded. 'You know me?'

'Fast as you run, who doesn't?' You turned your head sideways, half smiling. 'Anyone ever told you you have a nice voice?'

My finger touched my voice box. My voice rose about eight octaves. 'No.' I cleared my throat. 'I mean'—lower this time—'no.'

You opened a notebook. 'Well . . . you do. It's . . . warm.'

We spent the rest of the year as 'friends', because I didn't have the you-know-whats to ask you out. Not to mention the fact that Mr No-neck could break me in half—if he could catch me.

Junior year, I had just arrived at school, had about thirty minutes before *the first bell rang and we bumped into each other as you came out of the girl's locker room. Your eyes were wet. 'You OK?'*

You clenched your fists and began walking. 'NO!'

I took your pack and together we walked away from school, out onto the track, circling the obvious. 'What's wrong?'

You were exasperated. 'I'm not getting any faster, that's what.'

'Well. I think I can help with that.' I pointed at the cross-country coach's office. 'I'm pretty sure he can't help you. If he could, he'd have told you.'

'Oh, and you can see something he can't?'

I pointed. 'Your arms. Too much lateral movement. And'—I waved my hand over your hip flexor—'you're too tight here. Your feet are fast but you need to cover more ground with each stride.'

Your lips turned down. I was starting to look over my shoulder for your boyfriend. 'And you can fix this?'

'Well . . . I can run alongside and maybe help you find a rhythm that will cause you to lengthen it. Run with someone who has a longer stride and then let your brain kick in. Your stride adjusts.'

'And you'd do that? You haven't given me the time of day.'

I could almost hear him breathing down my back. 'What about Number fifty-four? The guy with no neck.'

'In case you haven't heard, Einstein, we stopped dating last year! You may be fast out here, but when it comes to this thing'—you tapped me in the chest—'I can run circles round you.'

You still do.

Chapter Three

It was dark and the pain had worsened. I pressed the light button on my watch. 04:47. Maybe six hours had elapsed since the crash. Another two to daylight. But in this cold, I wasn't sure I'd last another fifteen minutes. I was shivering so hard, my teeth were chattering. Grover was covered in four inches of snow.

Ashley lay on my left. I touched her neck and the carotid artery. Her pulse was strong and elevated but she was quiet. I couldn't see her in the dark. I felt around me. Snow and broken glass covered us. To my right, I found the compression sack strapped to the underside of Grover's seat. I pulled and the sleeping-bag came out slowly. I unzipped the side and spread it over us as much as I could. I could move only a little at a time because the pain in my rib cage left me breathless. I tucked the bag round Ashley, slipping her feet into the end. The dog tucked himself in with me. Several feet in front of me I saw the propeller stuck in the air. Caked in snow. Part of the blade was missing.

DAYLIGHT BROKE and I woke to the dog standing on my chest, licking my nose. The sky was grey and still dumping snow. Grover, a few feet away, had mostly disappeared beneath what looked like a foot of it. The down sleeping-bag was warming me up. But, with increasing blood flow came more pain in my ribs.

Ashley still lay unmoving. Her pulse wasn't as elevated. Meaning, her body had burned through the adrenalin that flooded her system when we crashed. I sat up and tried to examine her. Her face was swollen and caked with blood due to cuts above her eyes and on her scalp. I ran my hand along her shoulder. It looked like someone had stuffed a sock inside her down jacket. I slid my arm up her sleeve, pulled down and let the tendons pull the bone back and snap it into the socket. Once in place, I manipulated the joint. Dislocated shoulders are pretty good about going back into place if you start them in the right direction. I ran my hands along her hips. Then her legs. Her right was fine. Her left was not.

The femur had broken when the plane smashed into a rock. Probably the source of the scream. Her thigh was grossly swollen, maybe twice its normal size, and her trouser leg was taut. Fortunately, the bone had not broken the skin.

I had to set it but I needed space to work. Currently I felt like I was in an MRI machine with all the sides too close to my face. I sat up and found that we were encased in a snow and plane-fuselage cave. Which, from a certain perspective, was good.

The impact, along with the storm, had buried us in a snow bank. That formed a snow cocoon, which meant that we were more or less maintaining thirty-two degrees—better than whatever the outside temperature was. Not to mention the wind chill. The majority of the light was coming in through the Plexiglass atop the plane, filtering through the snow.

While I worked to dig away the snow to make room for me to get at Ashley's leg, the dog whined and spun in circles. Then he climbed up on Grover and started licking the snow from his face. He wanted to know when this plane was taking off. My hands got too cold, so I dug around in front of Grover and found a plastic clipboard in the door pocket. I used it like a shovel to dig a shelf in the snow long enough for Ashley to lie in.

I pulled the bag off her, laid it flat inside the shelf and slowly slid and lifted her body across the seat and onto the shelf. The effort exhausted me, so I fell back against Grover's seat and sat there breathing short and shallow, trying to lessen the pain in my chest. Thirty minutes passed before I had enough energy to return to her leg.

I spoke to her but she didn't respond, which was good, because what I was about to do was going to hurt more than the break.

I took off my belt, wrapped it round her ankle and then my wrist. Giving me an anchor to pull on. Then I took off my left hiking boot and slowly placed my foot between her legs. I straightened my leg against her, then tightened the belt and grabbed her foot with both hands. I took four or five deep breaths and felt her hand slide onto my foot. She patted it and mumbled, 'Pull . . . hard.'

I pulled, pushed with my leg and arched my back, all at the same time. The pain shot through her, her head rocked back and she uttered a muffled scream before losing consciousness. The leg popped loose, I turned it, let it straighten naturally, and then let go.

The leg 'hung' to the side in a mostly natural position that mirrored the right. With it set, I began looking for a brace. Above my head hung two mangled wing supports, both more than three feet long. I began working them back and forth, weakening the metal, and they eventually snapped off. When hiking, I carry two pocketknives. My backpack lay behind us in the snow bank. Only a corner was visible. I pulled away some snow, found the zipper, and slid my hand inside until I found the knives.

Using my Swiss Army knife, I slit Ashley's trouser leg up to her hip. Much of the thigh was a deep purple.

The belt restraints on both seats comprised an over-the-shoulder harness system with a typical quick-release buckle. I loosened ours and used both pieces of one harness to secure the 'poles' round her leg, tightened the straps and placed the buckle directly above her femoral artery. Then I took a T-shirt from my suitcase, cut it in two, and wound each piece into a taut tubelike piece that I placed beneath either side of the buckle, taking pressure off the artery and giving her leg ample blood flow. Lastly, I packed the area round the break in snow to bring down the swelling.

I reached into my backpack, pulled out a pair of long johns and a wool sweater lined with a windstopper fabric that's warm even when it's wet. I pulled off her down jacket, her suit coat, her blouse, even her bra, and checked her chest and ribs for any evidence of internal injuries. No bruises had surfaced. I slid her into my long underwear and sweater, then back into her down jacket. I pulled the sleeping-bag beneath her, wrapped her up like a mummy with only her left leg hanging out, then elevated and covered her left foot. We lose half our body heat from our head, so I pulled a wool beanie from my pack and slid it down over her ears and forehead.

Once she was dry and warm, I realised how shallow my breathing and elevated my pulse had become. The pain in my ribs had intensified. I pushed my arms into my jacket and lay down next to her trying to share warmth. When I did, the dog walked across my legs, turned in two circles while his nose stretched to find his tail and burrowed between us. He looked like he'd done that before. I stared across at Grover's snow-covered body.

IT'S DAYLIGHT. The snow is still falling heavily and I can see my breath. It's really quiet, like somebody hit the mute button on the world. Ashley may have some internal injuries. She's in bad shape. I set her leg and shoulder but she'll need X-rays, and surgery on her leg when we get out of here.

She passed out when I set her leg. She's been talking some in her sleep. Grover, the pilot, he didn't make it. Did I tell you that? He landed the plane after his heart stopped. I don't know how. Putting it down without killing us was nothing short of heroic.

Me? I broke a few ribs. Maybe three. The pain on inhaling is piercing. And, I may have a collapsed lung. Course, the elevation is above eleven thousand feet so breathing isn't easy anyway.

I can't think of any reason why we should expect a rescue. Grover wasn't required to file a flight plan. He never told anyone he had passengers, so the tower had no idea we were on the plane.

From the side, Grover sort of looked like Dad. Although kinder.

Some said Dad was a jerk. Others said I was lucky to have such a committed father. Course, they wouldn't have lasted a day in my house. He abused Mom, she crawled inside a bottle and he kept her hopping from one rehab to the next, stripped her of parental rights. I don't know the whole story. He let me talk to her by phone.

From the moment he clicked on the light at 4.55 a.m., I had five minutes to be standing at the back door. Dressed. Two pairs of sweat pants, running shorts and shoes. Most nights I slept dressed.

Six miles to the lifeguard station and back. I don't know why he chose six, but he called it my warm-up. I think it had more to do with the doughnut shop than anything else. Cheating was impossible because he'd drive to the shop, sit next to the glass, coffee in one hand, doughnut in the other, checking my time as I trudged up the beach and slapped the lifeguard's chair. If I was up a few seconds, he'd beat me home and say nothing. But if I was slow, he'd run out and shout across the sand, 'Down seven!' or 'Down twenty!'

I learned how to run within myself, monitoring and gauging output and speed. Fear does that.

When I got home, he met me on the beach, where I was allowed to pull off both pairs of sweats before I started my speed work. Mondays we ran twelve 660s. As in six hundred and sixty metres. Tuesdays were 550s, and so on. Sunday was my free day, but Monday was just around the corner.

We always finished with a speed rope, sit-ups, crunches, pushups and whatever other pain-inducing thing he could dream up. He had this piece of bamboo he'd hold out above my knees. 'Higher!' I'd lift them but they were never high enough. He'd shake his head and speak softly. 'Pain is weakness leaving your body.'

I'd stand there, thinking, 'Good . . . why don't we let some out of your body. I'm about out.' I lost a lot of pain in his house.

By 7 a.m. I'd run seven to ten miles. I'd go to school, try not to fall asleep in class and then go to track practice or run with the cross-country team—both seemed mundane in comparison. Dad was managing his firm, fifty traders, and because the stock market closed at four, he'd appear about 4.15 p.m., loosened tie, holding a stopwatch.

Yeah, he was committed all right.

My freshman year, I won the 400-metre dash in 50.9 seconds, anchored the 4x400-metre relay and won the mile in 4:28. That made me State Champion in three events. Dad drove me home in silence. No celebration. No day off. He parked the car. 'If you're going to break four minutes, you've got work to do.' Somewhere in there it occurred to me that, to my dad, I was only as good as my last time and no time was ever good enough.

When it came to school, Bs were not accepted. And an A minus might as well be a B plus. I had few friends, and if I wasn't in school, I was either running or sleeping.

Then came my sophomore year. You entered the picture and lit my world with laughter and light and wonder. You ran by me, a dart of the eyes, a quick glance, flicking sweat off your fingertips, and I wanted to take a shower, wash off Dad and bathe in you.

So much of what I am, he made. Forged it in me. I know that. But Dad used pain to rid me of pain. Leaving me empty and hurting.

You gave me love. Minus a stopwatch.

IT WAS DARK when I woke. I pressed the light button on my watch. 00:01. An entire day had passed. Then I checked the date. Make that two days. We'd slept thirty-six hours straight.

A billion stars stared down on me. Close enough to touch. The moon had appeared over my left shoulder. Big as Christmas. I squinted my eyes. If I could climb the mountain to my left, I could step right onto the moon and keep walking.

As sleep pressed in, I made a mental list, which included two things: food and water, and we needed both soon. With emphasis on water. If Ashley was fighting infection, I needed to get her kidneys working. Shock has a way of burning up your fluids, and while I'd not been conscious of it, I had been in shock and running on adrenalin since the crash.

Daylight lit a blue sky. I tried to move but I was so stiff it hurt to pick up my head. I sat up and leaned against a large boulder protruding from the snow bank. It might have been the rock that had broken Ashley's leg.

Bad news first. While Grover's plane was bright blue and yellow, all but the left wing was buried in a ten-foot snow drift. Needle in a haystack came to mind. Not to mention that the tail disintegrated when it hit the boulder. I'd found bright-orange pieces of plastic but no ELT. No ELT, no signal on 122.5, no cavalry. I didn't know how to break it to Ashley.

The only good news was this 'burial' gave us a measure of protection from the elements. Thirty degrees above zero is better than thirty below.

Ashley lay sleeping, and her face was flushed. I rolled to my backpack, pulled out my Jetboil and filled the canister with fresh powder from just outside the cave. I clicked it on, the blue flame erupted, and as it melted the snow, I added more. Either the noise of the burner or my movement woke Ashley. Her face was puffy and her eyes were slits.

I held a cup of warm water to her lips. 'Drink this.'

She sipped. I had a bottle of Advil somewhere in my pack. I desperately wanted to down about four but I knew she would need them more than I in the days to come. I found them in a side pocket and dumped four into my hand. 'Can you swallow this?'

She nodded. I placed one on her tongue and she swallowed. We repeated this three times. Slowly. The snow round her leg had long since melted so the swelling, while it might have gone down, was back. If I could reduce it, I could help reduce the pain. The Advil worked from the inside, snow would work on the outside. I repacked her leg and felt for the pulse round her ankle. She was getting good circulation. I held the cup to her lips until she finished the eight ounces. My goal for the day would be five more of those.

I refilled the cup and the Jetboil, taking some fluid myself. She forced her eyes open as much as the swelling would allow. She scanned the cave, what was left of the plane, her torn clothing, the brace on her leg. Her eyes settled on Grover's body. 'Is he . . . ?'

'He was gone before the plane touched down. I don't know how he landed it. Heart I guess.'

She reached up, walking her fingertips across her face and head. Her voice was hoarse. 'What day is it?'

I gave her the short version. She didn't say anything.

I had found monofilament in Grover's fly-fishing waistcoat behind my seat. I needed to clean Ashley's cuts and sew the few that needed stitches. I stripped one of the flies off the waistcoat and removed all the stuff that made it look like a fly, exposing a single barbless hook. I needed to straighten the hook to more of a ninety-degree angle but needed a tool. Grover's belt. I dug through the snow round his waist and found the Leatherman. I straightened the hook, threaded monofilament through the eye and tried to flatten the eye with the pliers. When I looked back at Ashley, tears were rolling down her face. She said, 'I'm sure his wife is worried about him.'

I dug out a shelf in the snow lower than the shelf on which she lay. I pulled my sleeping-bag out of my pack and spread it on the shelf next to her. I wiped a tear from her face. 'What hurts?'

She glanced at Grover's body. 'Him.'

'What about on your body?'

'Everything.'

'I'm not finished hurting you. I need to sew a few stitches.'

She nodded. Three places. The first required two stitches in her scalp, which were relatively painless. The second was along the top of her right eye running through the middle of her eyebrow. I pierced the skin with the hook and said, 'There's an older scar here.'

'Nationals. I was eighteen. Kid caught me with a roundhouse.'

I tied the first stitch. 'Knock you out?'

'No. I caught him with a spinning back kick followed by a double round and an axe kick that cockroached him.'

'Cockroached?'

'We had names for the positions people fell in when we knocked them out. The porpoise, the white man's dance, the cockroach.'

I tied the third knot and cut the line. 'What I've done is good enough to hold you until we can get to a hospital.'

'What about my two-poled brace? My leg is killing me.'

'It's the best I can do without an X-ray. When we get to a hospital, if it's not aligned, I'll recommend that they rebreak it and give you a few presents that will set off the metal detector when you pass through security. Either way, you'll be good as new.'

'You've just said "get to a hospital" twice, but do you really think anybody is coming?'

As we looked up at the blue sky through the hole created between the leaning wing and the eight-foot snow wall, we saw a commercial airliner cruising at what looked like thirty-plus thousand feet. I shook my head. 'We can see them just fine'—I pointed to the more than three feet of accumulation on the wing—'but I'm pretty certain they can't see us.'

'Don't crashed planes send out some sort of SOS signal?'

'Yes, but the thing that sends it is lying all around us in about a thousand little pieces.'

'Maybe you should crawl out and wave your shirt or something.'

I chuckled. Which hurt. I clutched my side.

Her eyes narrowed. 'What's up?'

'Couple of broken ribs.'

'Let me see.'

I pulled up my shirt. The whole left side of my rib cage was a deep purple. She looked worried but said nothing. 'Only hurts when I breathe.' We laughed.

I turned my attention to the side of her arm. Either the rock or a branch had cut the skin on her nondislocated shoulder, about four inches in length. Fortunately for her, when the plane came to a stop, and she was unconscious, pressure and snow stopped the bleeding. It would need twelve or more stitches. 'I need you to slip your arm out of your sleeve.'

She pulled slowly, wincing. 'What do you think of our chances?'

'Let me ask you a few questions. Did you tell anyone you were getting on this plane? Send anybody an email?'

She shook her head.

'No phone call?'

Another shake.

'So, nobody on planet Earth knows you stepped into a charter plane and attempted to fly to Denver? Me neither.'

She whispered, 'I imagine everyone thought I was still in Salt Lake. Now they'd be looking for me but where would they look?'

I nodded and tied off another stitch. 'Based on the way Grover was talking, there's no official record that we flew. And we two professionals with probably twenty years of college and graduate school between us never told a soul we were going.' I paused. 'It's as if this flight never existed.'

'It existed all right.' She stared at Grover. 'I just thought it'd be a quick hop to Denver and life would continue.'

I cut the line. 'Ashley, I'm really sorry.' I shook my head. 'You should be somewhere getting a manicure or something.'

'Don't beat yourself up over good intentions. I was glad you offered.' She stared around. 'Not so much now, but was then.' She laid her head back. 'I was scheduled to go to the spa for a massage. You know one of those hot rocks deals? Instead I'm lying on ice with one rock. You have any idea how much I paid for that dress?'

'It'll be waiting when you get there.' I held the cup to her lips, finishing off twenty-four ounces. 'Your sense of humour is a gift.'

'Well . . . would you think it funny if I told you I had to pee?'

'From a certain point of view, that's good.' I looked at the bag and her immobility. 'From another, it's not.'

'Which way are we looking at it?'

'Whatever way lets you go without putting pressure on that leg.' I looked around. 'What I wouldn't give for a catheter.'

'Oh no, don't let's. Those things give me the creeps.'

I grabbed one of my Nalgene travel bottles out of my pack and laid it next to her. 'All right, here's the deal. It's better than the alternative and you get to stay right there, but I've got to help.' I pulled out my Swiss Army knife. 'I'm going to finish slitting your trousers on up to the side of your hip. That way, while you're lying there, you can lay them over you. Then I'm going to dig a hole in the snow beneath you big enough for this bottle. Then we're going to ease your underwear out of the way and you're gonna go in it.'

'I'm not going to like this.'

'We need to measure your urine output and I need to see if there's any blood in it.'

'Blood?'

'Internal injuries.'

I slit her trousers, dug out the snow, held the bottle in place and she used her one healthy arm to lift herself slightly, without changing the position of her leg. 'Can I go?' I nodded.

She went. 'This has got to be one of the more embarrassing moments I've ever shared with another human being.'

'Given that I blend orthopaedics and emergency medicine, few days go by that I don't study people's urine. You OK?'

'Just my leg.' After a second, she said, 'Your fingers are cold.'

'Most of the folks I see in the ER have suffered some trauma, which usually means a substantial impact, which means internal injuries, which can mean blood in their urine.'

She looked at me. 'Are you trying to make me feel better?'

When she finished, I pulled up on the bottle, studied the colour and screwed on the cap. 'Yep. And the colour's good, too.'

I helped her dress, slid the sleeping-bag underneath her and then covered her up. The process of doing so brought her skin into contact with mine. And while I was acting as her doctor, her nakedness, her total vulnerability, was not lost on me. I thought of Rachel.

By the time we got it all finished, I felt like someone had stabbed me with a stiletto in the ribs. I lay down, breathing heavily. She said, 'You taken anything for the pain?'

I shook my head. 'No.'

'Why not?'

'To be honest, if you think you're hurting now, just give it three or four days. I've got only enough Advil to get you through a week. I've got a few prescription-strength narcotics somewhere in that pack but I thought I'd save them for tonight when you can't sleep.'

She eyed my pack. 'Got any red wine in there?'

'No, but I could make you a gin and tonic if you'd like.'

'Great. My leg's throbbing like somebody hit it with a hammer.'

I lifted the top of the sleeping-bag and repacked the snow. 'I'm going to keep doing this for several days. It'll speed recovery and help anaesthetise the pain. Only problem is you're going to be cold.'

I started crawling towards daylight. 'I'm going to take a look around and empty this bottle.'

'Good. I'm going to clean up a bit round here, maybe order a pizza or something.'

'I like pepperoni.'

'Got it.'

I crawled out of the fuselage, or what was left of it, under the wing and into the sunlight. The temperature was probably in the single digits but I'd expected worse. I took one step off the packed snow where the plane had landed and my foot submerged all the way to my groin. The impact shook my chest and I tried not to scream but I'm afraid I wasn't very successful.

Her voice rose up out of the plane. 'You OK?'

'Yeah. Just wishing I had some snowshoes.'

I dumped the bottle and looked around as best I could. Nothing but snow and mountains. We seemed to be on some sort of plateau with a few higher peaks to my left but most everything else spread out below and before us. No wonder it was tough to breathe.

I crawled back in and collapsed on the shelf next to her.

'Well?' she asked.

'Nothing. Grover was right. More Mars than Earth.'

'Really, you can tell me the truth. I can handle it. Just the facts.'

I stared up at her where she sat, eyes closed. Waiting. 'It's . . . beautiful. The view is . . . panoramic. One in a million. I've got two lawn chairs set up and a little guy with umbrella-drinks will be back around in a few minutes. Had to go and get some ice.'

'Glad to hear it's not as bad as I thought.' The first ear-to-ear grin I'd seen since we'd been in the snow.

Somewhere in there it struck me that Ashley Knox was one of the stronger human beings I'd met. Here she lay, half dead, probably in more pain than most people have felt in their lives, in the process of missing her own wedding, not to mention the fact that we had no probable chance of rescue—if we got out of here, it'd be up to us. Most people would be panicked, despondent. But somehow she could laugh. What's more, she made me laugh. And that's something I actually hadn't done in a long while.

I was spent. 'We need food but I'm in no shape to go find it. I'll go tomorrow. Right now, I'm going to try and get a fix on where we are.' I turned the mounting screws for the GPS and unplugged it. 'Rescue people will tell you never to leave the site of a crash, but we're breathing half the oxygen we're used to and we need it to heal. Especially you. I'm going to think about getting to a lower elevation.'

She stared at me. 'How do you know to do all this? I mean, what if you didn't?'

'When I was a kid, my dad realised I could run faster than most. He took that ability and turned it into his passion. But once Rachel and I were on our own, we gravitated to the mountains. We bought up gear and spent the weekends there. Course . . . there was Boy Scouts, too.'

'You're a Boy Scout?'

I nodded. 'The one freedom away from my dad. He figured it was training I needed that he didn't have to give me.'

'How far'd you get?'

I shrugged.

She lowered her head, gave me a disbelieving look. 'You're one of those Hawks, or Ospreys or . . . Come on, what's it called?'

'Eagle.' I got the sense that talking took her mind off the pain.

'Yeah . . . that's it. Eagle Scout. Guess we're 'bout to find out if you really earned all those badges.'

'Yep.' I hit the power button and the GPS unit flickered.

'Did they offer an electronics badge?'

I tapped the unit. 'No, but cold interferes with their circuits. You mind warming it up inside your bag?'

She pulled back the sleeping-bag and I set it gently on her lap. 'Vince . . . my fiancé, wouldn't know the first thing about all this. If he had been in this plane, he'd be looking for the nearest Starbucks and cussing the fact that there was no cell service.' She lay back and closed her eyes. 'What I wouldn't give for a cup of coffee.'

'I can help with that.'

'Don't tell me you have coffee.'

'I have three addictions. Running. Mountains. And good, hot coffee. And not necessarily in that order.'

'I'll pay you a thousand dollars for one cup.'

The Jetboil is one of the greatest advancements in hiking technology, maybe ever. Next to the compass. I scooped in snow and clicked it on while I dug through my pack for my Ziploc bag of coffee. There wasn't much in there, maybe a few days at best.

Ashley saw it. 'Ben Payne, will you take a credit card?'

'A fellow coffee-lover. It's amazing what we value when we're at our lowest.' Jetboil makes an accessory that allows me to convert the canister into a French press. The water boiled, I measured and dumped in the coffee, let it steep and poured her a cup. She cradled it in her good hand.

I was starting to learn that she used humour to ward off the pain. I had only a couple of Percocet but she'd need one tonight and probably the next few nights. It'd been six hours, so I poured four Advil into my palm and handed them to her. She swallowed and then hovered above her cup.

She smiled. 'It's amazing the moment a cup of coffee will allow you.' She passed the cup. I sipped. She was right. It was good.

She nodded at her attaché. 'If you reach in there, you'll find a bag of snack mix I bought in the terminal.'

Filled with dried pineapple, apricots and nuts, it probably weighed a pound. We both poured a handful and chewed slowly. I nodded. 'I believe this is the best snack mix I've ever tasted.'

I gave the dog a handful. He sniffed it, then inhaled it, wagging his tail and begging for more. He put his paws on my chest, sniffing the air. 'How do you tell a dog that he's not getting any more?'

She laughed. 'Good luck with that.'

I gave him one more small handful and when he returned a third time I pushed him off me and said, 'No.' Dejected, he turned his back on me and curled up at the foot of Ashley's sleeping-bag.

We sat in silence for a long time, drinking the entire pot. When we finished, she said, 'Save the grounds. We can use them twice and then, if we're desperate, we can chew on them.'

'You're serious about your coffee.' I touched the power button and the GPS flickered to life. 'You got paper in your briefcase?'

She nodded. 'Should be right in the front.'

I pulled out a yellow legal pad and a pencil, found the screen that showed our location and copied the map as best I could. Including the coordinates down to the minute. Once I had a relatively detailed drawing on par with a kindergartner, I said, 'Be right back.'

I climbed out of our hole and compared the picture on the screen with that before my eyes, marking mountains and making mental notes of mountain crests and where they landed on the compass. I knew the batteries wouldn't last for ever, and whatever I could copy now would pay dividends in the days ahead. But the more our predicament sank in, the more concerned I became.

'You want the good news or the bad?'

'Good.'

'I can pick a direction and stick with it.'

'And the bad?'

'Our elevation is 11,652 feet, give or take three feet; the nearest logging road is over thirty miles and something like five mountain passes that way.' I pointed. 'We're nearly fifty miles from the nearest thing that looks like a hard road. And most of the snow out there is higher than I am tall.'

She bit her lip and her eyes wandered the white-walled cave. She crossed her arms. 'You're going to have to leave me.'

'I'm not leaving anybody.'

'You can't get me out. You have a better chance alone. Give me the coffee, put those legs to work and take my coordinates with you. Bring a helicopter on your way back.'

'Ashley . . . drink your coffee.'

'OK, but you've got to recognise it's a distinct possibility.'

'Look, we need a fire, we need food and we need to lose a few thousand feet in elevation, then we'll talk about what's next. One crisis at a time.'

'But . . .' She was strong. She had toughness that matters. 'We can keep the truth on the table. It is a possibility.'

'I'm not leaving anybody.'

The dog noticed my change in tone. He stood, walked up to Ashley and dug his head beneath her hand. She scratched his ears. He looked over his shoulder at me.

'I know you're hungry.'

We sat, listening to the wind. I looked at her. 'Do you do that with all your friends? Prepare them for the worst?'

She nodded. 'If the worst is a possibility. If and when it does happen, you need to have thought about it ahead of time. That way, you're not crushed when your worst thought becomes your reality.'

I Jetboiled more snow and made us both sip. We napped on and off through the afternoon. The snack mix had taken the edge off but food was a real problem, and I needed energy to trudge through waist-deep snow to find it. And the pain in my chest was spreading.

Night fell, as did the cold. I crawled out, shimmied beneath the lower limbs of a pudgy evergreen, gathered handfuls of dead pine needles, twigs and branches and piled them up beneath the wing. Doing this took three trips and left me gasping. Ashley watched me with narrowed eyes.

Grover's door was a single piece of some sort of sheet metal hanging by a single hinge. Probably didn't weigh ten pounds. I prised it up, laid it flat beneath the wing and piled pine needles and twigs atop it. The door would keep out the melting snow a fire created.

I needed a light. I could use the Jetboil but I needed to save its butane. Then I remembered Grover's lighter. I brushed the snow from his pocket, fingered out the brass Zippo and clicked it open, making a sound that reminded me of Dean Martin and John Wayne. I thumbed the wheel. It lit.

I lit the end of a twig, let the flame climb towards my finger and then fed it beneath the pine needles. Dead and dry, they caught quickly. I fed the fire the empty snack-mix bag, adding larger sticks as the fire grew in size. Ashley watched. 'That was good snack mix.'

The dog walked down to the end of Ashley's bag, some four feet from the flame, and curled up in a puffy spot. The fire was a welcome addition. It improved our general disposition. We stared at it, letting our eyes grow lazy.

Ashley broke the silence. 'I've been thinking about what to get Vince for a wedding gift. I'm coming up blank. Got any ideas?'

'First anniversary. A cabin in the Colorado Rockies. Snowed in.' I shrugged and forced a laugh. 'A little like this. We were paying off school loans and, like our honeymoon, had agreed on a no-present anniversary.'

She laughed. 'What'd you get her?'

'A purple orchid.'

She nodded. 'Ah . . . hence the orchid and greenhouse thing. I like the way you talk about your wife. Sounds like you "do" life together.' She laid her head back. 'In my job, I work with a lot of people who treat their spouse like a room-mate. Somebody they cross paths with, split the mortgage with, maybe have kids with. How'd you two meet?'

'Tomorrow. We need to try and get some sleep.' I extended my hand. 'Here, take this Percocet.'

She held out her palm. 'What's in it?'

'A combination of oxycodone and acetaminophen.'

'How many do you have?'

'Three.'

'Why don't you take one?'

'I'm not in that much pain. Go ahead. It'll help you sleep. And, up here—where the air is half as thin—taking one is like taking two.'

'Will it help my headache?'

'Probably not. That's the altitude, mixed with the crash impact.'

'Do you have a headache?'

'Yes.'

She swallowed and her eyes fell to Grover. He sat, frozen, about five feet from her bag, covered in snow. 'Can we do anything?'

'I need to bury him, but moving is tough right now.'

'When you breathe, you sound like you're in a lot of pain.'

'Get some rest. I'll be right outside.'

'One favour? I need to go again.'

This time was faster, no red tint and a good bit of fluids. I packed snow round her leg and she said, 'You can stop doing that. I'm freezing.'

'If I let your leg warm up too much, we'll fall behind the pain curve.' I dug out some snow on her good side, creating a flat spot, and laid my bag down. 'If we share body heat, we'll both sleep better and live longer.'

She nodded. 'What time is it?'

'A little after six.'

She lay down, staring up. 'I should be walking down the aisle.'

I knelt next to her. 'Ever been married before?'

She shook her head, her eyes tearing up.

I held out my sleeve and she leaned forward, wiping her tears. I checked the stitches on her head and eye. Her face was not quite as swollen. 'We're going to get off this mountain and you're going to have your wedding—just a little later than you planned.'

She smiled and closed her eyes.

'You'll look beautiful in white.'

'How do you know?'

'We had a small wedding . . .'

'How small?'

'Me, Rachel and her folks. But the moment that door opened and she stood there, that white dress . . . It's a picture a groom never forgets.'

She turned her head.

'Sorry. Thought I was helping.'

She nodded and said nothing.

An hour later, when her breathing had slowed, I crawled out and pulled the recorder from my pocket. The sky had leaned down, fire and crimson to a sea of white etched with veins of silver as the last rays of sun disappeared. The dog followed me out. He was light enough to walk on top of the frozen snow, but he didn't like it. He walked a few circles, lifted his leg next to a small tree, kicked some snow behind him like a charging bull and then stared off across the mountaintops. After two or three seconds he disappeared back down the hole to curl up with Ashley.

I pressed 'record'.

LONG DAY HERE. *Day three I think. We're alive, but staying that way is another thing. Ashley is hanging in there but I don't know how. If I had all the breaks and pains she had, I'd be begging somebody to thump me over the head or shoot me with morphine.*

We're a long way from anywhere in terrain that's tough with two good legs. Improbable with one bad one. I haven't told her that. I know . . . I will.

I don't really know how we're going to get out of here. I can make some sort of stretcher but how far can I drag her on that? We need to find some place to rest up until help comes, which it won't, or until I can walk us out of here. And we need food.

Not to mention the dog, whose name I can't remember. I know he's hungry 'cause he's chewing on tree limbs. He doesn't like the snow and he spends all his time shivering.

I think I upset Ashley. I was trying to cheer her up. Maybe I'm out of practice.

Speaking of practice . . . you ever added up all the miles we ran together? Me neither.

Seems like every time we ran, you'd ask me about your stride and I'd act like I was paying attention, but in truth, I couldn't take my eyes off your legs. I figure you knew that, too. I loved running behind you.

When I look back on us, and our beginnings, I am reminded that we did something we loved, and shared it. We never had to think of a reason to hang out. And nothing ever divided us.

Once you got your licence, you'd drive to the beach, tap on my window at 4 a.m. and we'd take off. Long runs. Where time didn't matter. If we didn't run on the beach, I'd pick you up at the end of your drive and we'd run the bridges downtown. Over the Main Street, through the Landing, back over the Acosta, round the fountain and do it all over again. If one of us was tired or needed a break, we'd drive through Dunkin' Donuts, order two coffees and tour the town with the top down.

There was that Saturday morning. We were coming back up the beach. This kid on a surfboard caught a wave, the nose of his board dipped and he started tumbling. He washed up in front of us. The two pieces of his board surfaced a few moments later. His forehead was cut, shoulder was out of its socket and he was disorientated and nauseous. I sat him down, put pressure on his head, he pointed to his house and you ran to get his folks while I helped him set his shoulder. When you returned, he was laughing, talking about getting a new board. His folks walked him home and you said, like you'd known it all your life, 'You're going to make a great doctor some day.'

To be honest, I'd never thought about doing anything other than getting out of my dad's house. But something clicked. 'How do you know?'

'Something about the way you talk soothes people.'

'It does?'

A nod. 'I should know.'

That was the first time I clued in to the fact that you saw potential in the mundane. The insignificant. The ordinary.

The second time occurred when I came to see you at work. Volunteering after school at the children's hospital. Bald, sickly kids. Oxygen tanks. Wheelchairs. Uncomfortable smells. When I found you, you were rubber-gloved, holding a bedpan, laughing with the little girl who moments before had sat on top of it. I saw sickness and misery in every room. Not you. You saw possibility and promise. Even in the improbable.

Somewhere in my junior year, I looked around and you had taught me what it meant to smile. To live with a heart that felt alive. With every mile, you dug down into the quarry that had become me and chipped away at the rocks piled up round my soul. You put together the pieces of me. When it came to love, you taught me to crawl, walk, run and then somewhere on the beach, beneath the moon, running into a headwind, clipping away five-minute miles, you cut the ties that held my wings and taught me to fly.

Staring out across this ice-capped landscape with nothing but the impossible staring back at me, I am reminded.

I see what is. You see what could be. I miss you.

Chapter Four

Twice during the night I repacked snow round Ashley's leg. She moaned a lot in her sleep. When she woke, her eyes were slits.

'How do you feel?'

Her voice sounded thick. 'Like I've been hit by a Mack truck.' With that, she rolled on her side and vomited for several minutes. It was mostly dry heaves and stomach acid. Finally, she sat back. Trying to catch her breath. She was in a lot of pain.

I wiped her mouth and held the cup while she sipped. 'I've got to get some Advil in you but I doubt your empty stomach is going to like it.'

Eyes closed, she nodded.

I added fuel to the fire and clicked on the Jetboil. The smell of coffee opened her eyes. 'How long you been up?'

'Couple of hours. I did some looking around.'

She eyed the contraptions to my left. 'You make those?'

I'd taken the netting off the backs of the seats, disassembled the wire and metal seat frames using Grover's Leatherman, double-folded the netting, stretched it over the frames and attached the squares using Grover's fly line. I held them up. 'Snowshoes.'

'If you say so.'

I poured coffee and handed it to her, then dug Grover's flare gun out of the box in the back where he kept his fishing tackle. I loaded it and handed it over. 'I'm going to leave you for a couple of hours. Walk around a bit. If you need me, cock this, and squeeze this. And when you do, make sure it's pointed out of that hole. Otherwise you're liable to set yourself on fire. There's still gas in the tanks in the wing.'

She nodded and breathed over the cup of coffee.

'If I'm not back at dark, don't worry. I'm taking my sleeping-bag, bivvy sack, emergency blanket. Out here, conditions change quickly and I might have to wait them out. I'm going to try and find some sort of food.'

'You know how to do all this?'

'I know how to do some of it. What I don't know, I'll learn.'

I unstrapped Grover's bow from its case in the tail of the plane, along with a fly rod, his waistcoat and one of the reels stuffed in it. 'You can fly-fish?'

'I've done it once. Didn't catch anything.'

'I was afraid you were going to say that.' She eyed the compound bow. 'How about that contraption?'

'This I actually used to hit stuff with.'

'Before you go, will you help me with something?'

Ashley went to the toilet and then I got her covered up. 'Will you hand me my case?' She pulled out her cellphone. 'Just for kicks.' She turned it on but the cold had killed it, too.

I shrugged. 'You could play solitaire.' I pointed at my backpack. 'You're welcome to use my computer but I doubt it'll turn on.'

'Got any books?'

A shrug. 'Not much of a reader. Guess you're alone with your thoughts—and the dog.' I scratched his ears. He had grown comfortable with us. 'Can you remember his name?'

She shook her head. 'No. What should we call him?'

'I think we should call him Napoleon.'

'Why?'

'Just look at him. If ever an animal had a Napoleon complex, it's him. He's got the attitude of an angry bull mastiff shoved into a package the size of a loaf of bread.'

'Can we do anything for his feet?'

I looked at the back seat that was leaning over, looking half deflated after I'd robbed it of part of its frame. I opened the Leatherman and cut four squares of the vinyl covering. A half-inch of foam padding was stuck to the back. I cut slits in the corners, fed a piece of fly line through each, and tied them round Napoleon's feet. He looked at me like I'd lost my mind. He sniffed them, stood up, walked around on the snow, then leaned against me and licked my face. 'OK, I love you too.'

Ashley smiled. 'I think you made a friend.'

I held out my hand. 'The GPS.' She slid it from within her sleeping-bag and I tucked it inside my jacket. Lastly, I unzipped a small pocket on the side of my backpack, grabbed my compass and hung it round my neck.

It's lensatic, or fluid-filled. Rachel had given it to me years ago. Some of the green had given way to the dull aluminium beneath.

I shouldered my backpack, zipped up my jacket, pulled on my gloves and lifted the bow. 'Remember . . . when it starts getting dark, remind yourself that I am coming back. It may be tomorrow morning, but I'll be here. Coffee date, you and me. Deal?'

She nodded.

I knew when it got dark and I hadn't arrived, her worries would populate the shadows. 'Even if it's tomorrow morning?'

She nodded again.

I pulled out the Advil bottle. 'Take four every six hours.' I crawled out of our 'den' and strapped on the snowshoes. Napoleon followed. 'Stay here and take care of her. OK? I think she's lonely and it's not a very good day. She's supposed to be on her honeymoon now.'

I turned and began walking up the mountain.

MY SENIOR YEAR, State Championships. You watched me win the 400 in a new state record, we'd set a record in the 4x400, I'd won the two mile just seconds off a national record and I was standing at the start line of the mile. They were holding the mile last to garner media attention. Somebody had started a rumour that I could run four minutes. I had twenty division-one scholarship offers. Full rides.

You had two offers. I was more proud of yours than mine.

But I had my piles and dad had his. His prized pile centred on MBAs in finance. 'They'll pay for five years of education. Get your BA in two and a half. Then your MBA. Once you're out of school, you can write your own ticket. With your drive, you could run my agency.'

I wanted nothing to do with his agency. I just never told him.

I could see his face out of the corner of my eye. Sweat was pouring off him. I'd run 4:04 several mornings on the beach, but that was on sand. He was sure I could run 3:58. You hung on the fence. The gun sounded.

After the first lap, we were still a tight group. Some guy from down south was trying to elbow me out. By the start of the third lap, I was all alone. And I knew I had it.

People in the stands were on their feet. Screaming. Dad was stone-faced. A hundred metres to go and I was looking at 3:57. Everything I'd ever worked for was coming true in those few seconds. And it struck me that no matter what time I turned in, he'd assume I hadn't tried hard enough.

Something about his stony face cut something loose in me. I slowed. Watched the clock roll through 3:53. Then 3:57. My official time would be 4:00:37. The place went crazy. I'd done something no Florida runner had ever done. Four-year State Champion in twelve events headed to the National Championships.

I stood on the track, swarmed by my teammates. But the only face I wanted to see was yours. And you found me. I never saw my dad.

We were going out. The whole team. To celebrate. I came home to change. We walked in. He was sitting in his chair. An empty crystal glass on his thigh. The bottle half empty next to him. He considered drinking to be something weak people did. You peered round me. 'Mr Payne, did you see?'

He stood, pointed his finger in my face. 'Nobody ever gave me nothing. You son of a . . .' He balled his fist and swung. The blow broke my nose. By then, I was six-two, two inches taller than him, and I knew if I swung back

I might never stop, but when I stood up, he was raising his hand over you.

I caught it and spun him into the sliding glass door. Tempered glass, it shattered into a million pieces. He lay on the deck, staring at me.

You drove me to the hospital where they set my nose. Around midnight we drove to a twenty-four-hour pancake place, and ordered one piece of French silk pie and two forks. Our celebration. Then I drove you home. Your mom met us and we all sat at the kitchen table talking through the meet. You sat, sleep in your eyes, wrapped in a terrycloth robe and your leg touching mine.

I got home around one. A few hours later, 4.55 a.m. arrived and dad did not. He never woke me again. I lay awake. Wondering what to do. Who to be. I couldn't answer that so I dressed and went for a walk on the beach—watching the sun come up. I walked through lunch. On towards dinner. The sun was falling when I quit walking at the jetties in Mayport, some twenty miles north. I climbed on the rocks and out towards the end of the jetties.

Your voice sounded behind me. 'What're you running from?'

'How'd you get out here?'

'Walked. Followed the footprints.'

'Kind of dangerous, don't you think?'

You smiled. 'Knew I wouldn't be alone.'

You climbed up and pulled me to you. You lifted your sunglasses. Costa Del Mars. I'd given them to you. Your eyes were red. You stared out across the water, hands inside the long grey sleeves of your sweatshirt. 'You think they'll care that we cut class?'

'I don't. You've been crying. Why?'

You pounded my chest. 'I don't want it to end.'

'What?'

Your eyes welled again. 'Us, dummy. Seeing you . . . every day.'

Maybe that's what had me walking up the beach twenty miles. And I'd found no answer. We were both about to hurt a whole lot.

High-school love was one thing, but choosing your college because of that love was something everyone cautioned us against. Remember? Sometimes, I wish we'd listened to them. Then I shake my head and think. Not so. I don't blame us. I'd do it again.

I remember calling the track coach and asking him to look at your tapes and your times. He didn't skip a beat. 'Would that influence your decision to attend this institution?'

'Yes . . . it would.'

I heard some papers shuffling. 'Funny. I just happen to have an extra scholarship lying on my desk.'

Just like that.

THE STORM HAD DUMPED three feet of snow. Without the shoes, I'd have been thigh deep, the cold wet stinging my legs. Wouldn't be long before they were numb. Given that, I stopped, cut a tether, tied one end to the back of each snowshoe, then tied the other end round each ankle, like a surfer's leash.

Despite the fact that we needed to lose elevation, I needed to gain it to get a bird's eye view of where we were. The surface was covered with a slick sheet of ice and I was much weaker than I expected. I climbed through lunch and into the late afternoon before I summited a small ridge that rose up over the plateau, maybe a thousand feet above the crash site.

It was a desolate landscape, etched with jagged peaks and impossible routes that stretched sixty or seventy miles in every direction. I turned on the GPS and orientated myself, using the compass to confirm the directions and degrees the electronic unit was telling me. The only surprise was the number of lakes and streams showing on the screen. I was noting the few that were closest when it flickered to black. I tapped the GPS, but it was dead. The cold had drained the battery. I closed my eyes, tried to remember everything on the screen and added that to the sketch I'd made yesterday.

I started back after dark. It was midnight by the time I got to the plane. Napoleon heard me and poked out his head. The temperature had dropped to single digits, which meant my trouser legs were frozen. I was cold down to my bones. The snow was starting again. I'd peed only once the entire day, and even then not much. I watched Napoleon disappear again, his covered feet making small indentations in the snow. Only then did I notice the larger tracks leading to and from our cave. I'm no expert on tracks but my first thought was mountain lion. The tracks came out of some rocks above us, wound down a snowdrift and up to the entrance. I also noticed a small burrowed area where it looked like something had been lying down. As in 'lying in wait'. Didn't take long to make sense of it. Even frozen dead people smell. So do injured people and little dogs.

I snapped off some dead branches and carried them into the hole. I stoked the fire, stripped, spread out my wet clothes and climbed naked but for my underwear inside my bag. I was shivering, and my fingers were stiff, as though they'd been dipped in wax. I dropped snow in the Jetboil and clicked it on. Ashley watched me. I curled up and let myself shiver, trying to create some heat. 'Hey.'

She was suffering and it showed in her eyes. 'Hi.'

'Taken anything lately?'

She shook her head.

I placed a Percocet on her tongue and she sipped what looked like the last of her water. 'You don't look too good,' she offered. 'Why don't you take some of the Advil.'

I knew if I didn't I might not get out of my bag tomorrow. 'OK. Two.' She poured two into my hand and I swallowed.

'What'd you see?'

'There's a level-one trauma centre in just a few hundred metres. The EMTs are pulling a gurney here now. I talked to the administrator and secured a private room for you. Should have you showered, warm and pumped full of pain medication in ten minutes.'

'That bad, huh?'

I slid down farther into my bag. 'Nothing but snow, ice, rock and mountain as far as I can see.'

'And the GPS?'

I poured some warm water and started sipping. 'Same picture.'

She let out the deep breath she'd been holding all day. 'Got any ideas?'

'There are some lakes down below us. A few streams. I'm sure they're all frozen but I thought I'd see if I could make my way down tomorrow and find some fish. How's the leg feeling?'

She lay back and closed her eyes. 'Hurts.'

I slid over, packed snow round it and saw that while the swelling had gone down, her skin was a deep purple from the top of her knee to the side of her hip. I clicked on my flashlight, checked her stitches and then her pupils. They were slow, and fatigued quickly. Which meant her body was weak and the elevation was starting to take a toll. I felt her toes. They were cold. Which was bad. By treating the leg with constant ice, I was compromising the toes. I had to get some blood flow in that foot.

I turned so we were face to toes. I unzipped my bag and pressed my chest and stomach to the bottom of her foot. Then I wrapped us both in the bag and wrapped my palm across the top of her foot. 'When we get out of here, please don't sue me for putting you in danger the day before your wedding.'

She stared up through the tarp and tree limbs. 'Funny you should mention that. I've been lying here drafting my attorney's opening argument. If I were you, I'd hire a very good lawyer.'

'That bad?'

'Let's see . . . you started with good intentions, saved my life, and despite the fact that I've seen you cough up blood at least twice, you set my leg and really haven't left my side.'

'You saw that? We'll both get better when we lose a few thousand feet.'

Ashley stared at the compass hanging from my neck. 'When did she give you that?'

'Loggerhead turtles lay their eggs along our beach, leaving big mounds up in the dunes. Rachel began marking them off with stakes and tape, counting the days. She gave it to me after a particular nest hatched. She was amazed that the turtles knew every time, somehow, to head for the water.'

'This may sound stupid, but how does a compass know which way to point?'

'Actually, it points only one way. Magnetic north. The earth is magnetised, and the source of that is up near the North Pole. True north and magnetic north are not the same. But I use it mainly to walk point-to-point.'

'Point-to-point?'

'A compass can't tell you where you are. Only the direction you are headed, or have come from. A right-handed person, like me, will walk in a right-turning circle if given enough time without a compass. To walk in a straight line, you pick a direction, a degree on the compass, then pick a visual marker in front of you that lines up with that point. A tree, lake, whatever. Once you get there, you pick another, but this time you also use the point behind you as a reference point—double-checking yourself. Not difficult but takes patience.'

'What about the GPS?'

'It's dead. Cold killed it.'

'Will that compass help us get out of here?' Her tone suggested something I'd not heard. The first outward sign of fear.

'Yes.'

'Make sure you don't lose it.'

IT'S SNOWING AGAIN. Ashley's in a lot of pain and starting to show the effects of elevation. I've got to get her down or she's going to die up here. If I don't try, we'll both die.

The wind's picking up. When it blows out of the south, through the fuse-lage, it sounds a low whistle. Like a train that never arrives.

I've got to get some rest.

Grover? I need to bury him, but I'm not sure I have the strength. Plus there's something up in the rocks that's got me a bit worried.

I've been studying the compass, trying to find a way out, but it's mountains all around. If I choose the wrong degree . . . well, things are bad. Real bad.

I want to tell people that Ashley was trying to get home. I wish they knew. But chances are good they never will.

Chapter Five

I woke on day five groggy and sore with the sun. Rolled over, pulled the bag up over my face and woke again around lunch time. I finally crawled out towards sundown. No matter how hard I tried I could not get out of bed. I hurt everywhere and could barely move. Evidently my adrenalin gave out. Ashley seldom stirred. Elevation mixed with starvation mixed with a plane crash mixed with a lot of pain had taken its toll on both of us.

Daylight on day six, the fire had long since died out but my clothes were dry so I pulled them on, forced myself to pack my backpack, rekindled the fire to keep Ashley warm and dropped a few handfuls of snow in the Jetboil for her. I tried not to look at Grover.

We needed food.

I shouldered my backpack, tied the bow onto the back of it, stepped out and the sun was just coming up. The air was crisp and dry with ice crystals floating on my breath. I threw fresh snow across the tracks at the entrance to let me know if anything had been there when I returned. I tied on the snow-shoes, pulled out my compass, took a reading and set off.

For three hours, I picked points and ploughed through the dry, frozen snow. I had to keep stopping to tighten my gaiters round my knees. I walked the first lake's frozen perimeter until I found the creek that spilled out of it. The water was clear, and tasted almost sweet. I risked dropping my core temperature, but I was moving, so I kept forcing myself to drink.

A mile later, the creek made a hard turn, creating a deep pool below a rock overhang. I didn't put much faith in my ability to work the fly rod with my cold, cut-up hands. And I couldn't figure out why a fish would bite at a fly that it knows can't live in its conditions. Fish aren't stupid.

Grover had a small bottle of synthetic salmon eggs. I slid one over a hook, threaded the line and dropped it into the water.

Twenty minutes later, no bites, I packed up and looked for a bigger pool. A mile later, I found one. Same routine. Only this time, I could see little black shadows darting in and out beneath the rock into the swirling current.

Thirty minutes later, I packed up and continued trudging through the snow looking for another pool. I was tired, cold and hungry, expending calories I couldn't afford to spend. I climbed over a small rise, descended and walked down to the bank of one more stream. This one was maybe twice as wide, but more shallow and running with a good volume of water.

The black shadows reappeared. A good number, too.

I brushed away the snow and lay on the rock, a face-down snow angel, salivating at the sight of mountain trout. This time, I lowered Grover's hand-net slowly into the water below the bait, submerging one hand. The pain was excruciating until it went numb.

The shadows disappeared, then slowly returned. Swimming closer. Slowly, they approached the egg and began to nibble. Maybe it was the cold water but they too were sluggish. I slowly raised the net and caught seven finger-sized trout. I dumped them in the snow and buried my cold hand into the pocket of my down jacket. With the hatchet, I cut a branch, lashed it to the net and submerged both it and the egg, catching a couple more.

I ate everything but the heads.

When they were gone, I crept back to the bank and kept 'fishing'. I did that off and on for more than an hour. When the sun started casting my shadow on the snow, I counted my catch. Forty-seven. Enough for tonight and tomorrow. I packed up and followed my tracks home.

On the way back, I pulled an arrow from the quiver, nocked it, took a deep breath and drew hard on the string. It resisted, then gave and released all the way to my face. The pain in my ribs was sharp, but I had the bow at full draw. I set the top pin on the base of a wrist-sized evergreen some twenty yards away and released. The arrow missed by about two inches. I dug round the base and retrieved it from the snow. While I had not hit the tree, I was close. And at that distance, close was good enough.

It was well after midnight when I climbed back onto our plateau. Oddly, it was plenty light. I approached slowly, keeping my eyes peeled for anything moving. I saw nothing, but the entrance to our cave told a different story. Beneath the moonlight the tracks were parked right at the entrance, with a rounded indentation between them where it had lain resting its stomach on the snow. Chances were good that it was lying here as I walked up.

I said nothing to Ashley.

SHE WAS WEAK and her eyes hurt. Classic altitude sickness mixed with a concussion and lack of food. I found some more wood, stoked the fire, gutted several trout and fed them onto a long slender stick, piercing them like a kebab. I cooked them and made coffee at the same time. Caffeine would help her absorb the nutrients—not to mention fight the hunger. She drank and ate slowly as I held the cup to her lips, and then a fish, while she chewed. She ate fourteen like that. Napoleon sat quietly licking his face. I laid out six on the snow and said, 'Go ahead.' He stood, smelled them, wiggled his nose and devoured them. Including the heads.

I gave Ashley a Percocet, packed and elevated her leg and checked the circulation in her foot. She was asleep before I realised we hadn't said two words since I'd returned. I sat up a few hours feeding the fire, making myself eat. Much of that time I sat in my bag with her foot pressed to my stomach. Just before midnight, I walked outside. As I did, a long shadow disappeared up a rock face and into some trees. Napoleon stood next to me, snarling.

CAUGHT SOME FISH TODAY. Nothing to brag about but we're alive. Sort of like big sardines. And I shot the bow. If it came to a pinch, I think I could hit what I shoot at. Inside twenty yards. It's better than jumping around and waving my arms in the air.

I gave Ashley a Percocet, hoping she'll get some sleep. Maybe put some energy back in her tanks. I'm going to bury Grover tomorrow. Get him some place where he can see the sun come up and set. Where he can count the stars at night.

You remember that cabin in the mountains? Our daytime hikes, night-time fires, watching snow stick to the windows as a mountaintop wind whistled atop the chimney? Our honeymoon.

The second night . . . we'd finished dinner and were sitting in front of the fire. Between our student loans, we didn't have two pennies to rub together. I think we'd paid for the cabin with a maxed-out credit card. Drinking a cheap bottle of cabernet. You were wearing your robe and . . . my sweat.

The firelight was dancing across your skin as you handed me the Timex Ironman. You said, 'I set it thirty minutes fast.'

'But I thought we'd agreed "no presents"?'

'This isn't a wedding present. It's something you need if we're going to stay married for seventy years.'

'Seventy years?'

You nodded. 'You sure you're going to love me when I'm old, wrinkly and can't hear a word you're saying?'

'Probably more.'

You crossed your right leg over your left and the split in your robe climbed halfway up your thigh. I remember marvelling at how comfortable you were with me. Your smile. Flushed cheeks. Firelight. Laughter. Beauty. I remember closing my eyes for a brief second and burning the image onto the back of my eyelids because I wanted to take it with me.

And I did.

Rachel, you're still the measuring stick. No one else holds a candle.

THE GROWLING woke me. Low and different. His tone told me he wasn't kidding. I opened my eyes. Ashley's breathing had become laboured. Napoleon stood between us, staring at the entrance. Bright moonlight filtered in. He lowered his head and took two slow steps. Two eyes stared back at us, crouched low, looking like two pieces of red glass. I sat up on an elbow and Napoleon's growl grew deeper, louder. I put my hand on his back and said, 'Easy.' Evidently, he didn't understand that.

As if he'd been shot out of a cannon, Napoleon launched himself towards the thing staring back at us. The two collided, spun in an angry ball, a loud catlike roar erupted and then the thing disappeared leaving Napoleon jumping two feet straight into the air.

I crawled towards him and pulled him back. 'Easy, boy. It's gone. Easy.'

He was shaking and his shoulder was wet. Ashley clicked on the flashlight. My palm was sticky, and the snow was splattered red beneath us.

The cut was deep, from the side of his shoulder to the top of his back. I grabbed my needle and thread and Ashley held him still. I closed it with four stitches. He chased it, turning in a few circles, but gave up, stared at the entrance then licked me on the face. 'Yeah . . . you did good.'

Ashley cleared her throat. 'What was it?'

'Mountain lion.'

'Is it coming back?'

'I think so.'

She closed her eyes and didn't say anything for a while.

We slept in fits the rest of the night. I perched the bow next to my bag, nocked an arrow and left it sitting on top of the rest, and propped myself against the tail of the plane. When the sun came up I finally drifted off.

Things had turned for the worse.

REMEMBER, AFTER MEDICAL SCHOOL in Denver, how elated we were to get the job offer in Jacksonville? A chance to get home, back to the beach.

Dad had moved to Connecticut to run another firm, but he'd kept the condo. It was weird that we ended up owning the place that was the source of so many bad memories, but you just smiled. 'Honey, "paid for" and "oceanfront" are both really cool.'

So we gutted walls, repainted, retiled. Cool blues, soft tans, sliding glass doors cracked so the sound filtered through, wave upon wave. How many nights has the sea sung us to sleep?

You remember the night of that crash? Two Cadillacs filled with people were hit by a tow truck. The ER was slammed. I'd stayed until we had everybody stable. I was tired. Thinking about life and how short it is. How you're always just a breath away from being overturned in the ditch with a fireman cutting you out with the jaws of life. It was one of those moments where I knew, really knew, that life is not guaranteed.

It was maybe 3 a.m. The ocean was angry ahead of a storm. I was standing at the glass, staring out over the choppy waves. You appeared and said, 'You OK?'

I told you what happened. What I was thinking. You tucked your shoulder under mine, wrapped your arms round my waist. Minutes passed. Lightning *spider-webbed the sky. 'You owe me something and I want to collect.'*

Seemed a strange way to start a conversation when I was sharing my deepest thoughts. Sort of irritated me. 'What?'

You'd been so patient. I kept telling you, 'Just let me get through medical school.' I don't know how long you'd been waiting to bring this up. You walked to our room. At the doorway, you turned, a candle lighting one side of your face. 'I want to make a baby now.'

I remember watching you disappear into the warm glow, the flash of a shadow across the small of your back. I remember kneeling next to our bed and saying, 'Forgive me?' I remember you smiling, nodding and pulling me towards you. A while later, I remember you lying on my stomach, your chest pressed to mine, your tears trickling onto my chest, trembling arms. And I remember that moment, when I knew. That you'd broken loose in me the stuff that only love breaks loose. That you'd given me all of you. Unreservedly.

Something about the enormity of that gift touched me down where words don't live. Where expression fails. Where there are no secrets. Where there's just you and me and everything that's us.

And I remember crying like a baby.

That's when I knew for the first time what love was. Not what it felt like. Not how it made me feel. Not what I hoped it was. But what it was. And what it was when I didn't get in the way.

You showed me. It'd been there all along but something about that night, those people, the sense of gain, loss, heartbreak and joy, all those things swirled into that moment and . . . I'd lived my whole life wanting to love but never able to do so apart from the pain I'd carried. But that night was the first time I ever took a breath deep enough to fill me. All of my life, I'd struggled in the waves, tossed, turned, screaming for air. But in that moment, you held back the waves, lifted me above the surface and filled me.

GROVER WAS STIFF when I tried to move him. Frozen in a sitting position. Ashley turned her head. I popped off a section of the wing, laid him on top of it, and slid-pushed him out of the entrance.

I pulled him across the snow to a boulder covered in lion tracks. I brushed the snow off, sat him on the rock and leaned him backwards.

I backtracked, counting. Eighteen steps.

I nocked an arrow, aimed at the snowdrift a few feet from Grover and released. This time I didn't shoot over. The distance was not so far away that I couldn't hit what I was aiming at.

Napoleon kept running back and forth between Grover and me. He'd started limping and his circles had developed a hitch. He looked up at me. 'I won't let anything happen to him.'

I crawled in. Ashley's face was wet. She was breaking down. 'What're you doing?'

'Hunting.'

'Are you using Grover as bait?'

'If it works the way I'm thinking, nothing will happen to him.'

'Not to point out the obvious, but nothing has worked out the way you'd hoped since we met in Salt Lake.'

She was right. I had no response.

We didn't say much the rest of the day. Or that night. Or the next day. By the second night, I hadn't slept soundly in forty-eight hours and was running on fumes. So was Ashley.

The cold had intensified. I couldn't say for sure but it was crisp and painful, suggesting that it had fallen into the negatives. Clouds moved in, blocked out the moon, and that was bad. I needed the moon. Without it, I couldn't see the sight pin.

Midnight came and brought snow. I was sleepy. Fading in and out. I could see the outline of Grover just across the snow. Based on the layer covering him, we'd had another three inches.

I must have fallen asleep because I jerked when I woke. Napoleon lay next to me. Crouched. Something was leaning on Grover. And the thing was big. Six-plus feet in length.

My hands were cold but I drew the bow and tried to find the pin. I couldn't see it in the dark. 'Come on. Just a glimmer of light.'

Still nothing. I swung the bow knowing I had only another second or two. My arms were cramping and my chest felt like somebody had stuck me with a spike. I coughed, tasting blood. Next to me, something brushed my leg, then I heard a 'click,' and a roman candle shot out the entrance. The flare hovered a metallic orange maybe a hundred feet above us. The cat had both his paws on Grover's shirt, like they were dancing. I found the pin, levelled it on the cat's shoulder and pressed the release. I never saw the arrow.

I dropped the bow, clutched my side and coughed, and spat on the snow. Ashley lay to my right, staring out. 'It's gone.'

'Did I hit it?' I had hunched over. Nursing my rib cage.

'Don't know. It left in a hurry.'

Somewhere in the darkness my hand found hers. We lay there, catching our breath. I was too tired to carry her back to her bag, so I pulled her to my chest and wrapped us in my bag. Within minutes, her head fell to one side and her pulse slowed.

Morning woke us. Napoleon lay curled between us. I needed to check Ashley's leg so I climbed out of the bag and ran my hand gently along the skin. It was dark and the swelling had returned. Her hair was stubbly. Ten days overgrown. The pulse in her ankle was good. The problem was the swelling. Moving last night had been traumatic. She'd set herself back. The pain would be intense and I had one Percocet left.

I placed the pill on her tongue and she sipped and swallowed.

I propped her head on my bag, dressed and nocked an arrow. Grover had fallen over, and he looked like he was asleep on his side. A trail of blood led away up the rocks.

It'd been several hours. If it was mortally wounded, those hours would have given the lion time to die. If it was just sort of wounded, they would have given it plenty of time to get angry.

I turned to Napoleon and held out my palm like a stop sign. 'Stay. Take care of Ashley.' He climbed inside her bag, only his nose sticking out. My breath was a thick cloud of smoke and bit at my nose. The cold was painful.

I climbed the rocks, and followed the blood. It thinned, and a thin blood trail means a bad hit. After a hundred yards, I was following a drop here and a drop there. I stopped to think things over. The wind cut through me and blew snow into my eyes.

But at a large outcropping, the drops increased in number. After another hundred yards, a large puddle suggested the thing had stopped there. The trail continued another two hundred yards up through some smaller rocks. I saw the tail first, the black tip lying flat across the snow, sticking out from beneath the limbs of some squatty trees. I took a deep breath, drew the bow and, eight feet away, set the front pin on its head, lowered it and released the arrow. It sliced through the neck. The cat never moved.

I retrieved the arrow, hung it in the quiver and sat on the rock, staring at the cat. She was not big after all. Probably five feet from head to rump and maybe a hundred pounds. I held her paw in my hand.

Small or not, she'd have ripped me to shreds. I checked her teeth. They were worn, which explained why she'd hunted easy targets.

I retraced my steps and found Ashley shivering and on the verge of going into shock. I stripped to my underwear, unzipped her bag and pulled mine alongside. I climbed in, pressed my chest to hers and wrapped my arms round her. She shook for close to an hour.

When she was asleep, I climbed out, wrapped both bags round her, stoked the fire, fed it fuel and returned to the cat. I cut off the hide, and then gutted it. That left me dragging maybe fifteen pounds of edible meat through the snow. I cut several green branches, built a frame round the fire and began hanging strips of meat.

The smell woke her. She picked up her head and sniffed the air. I tore off a piece, tossed it between my hands like a hot potato, blew on it, and held it to her lips.

She chewed slowly, eating the entire thing. Dark circles shrouded her eyes. I tore off another piece and held it. She took small bites. 'I just had the worst dream. You would never believe.'

'Try me.'

'I dreamed my flight out of Salt Lake was cancelled but then this stranger, kind of homely looking but still a nice man, invited me to ride this charter flight to Denver. And somewhere over this interminable forest, the pilot had a heart attack and crashed our plane. I broke my leg and after a week, all we'd had to eat was some snack mix, coffee grounds and the mountain lion that had tried to eat us.'

'Homely? Nice?'

She chewed slowly. 'The strange part was that I agreed to get on a charter with a total stranger. Two, actually. What was I thinking? I need to re-examine my decision-making paradigm.'

I laughed. 'Let me know how that works out.'

In the daylight, I rechecked her leg. She was afraid to look. 'You're lucky you didn't rebreak it. The bone ends are just now getting tacky enough to hold it in place, and there you go pulling some stunt with a flare gun. The swelling's back with a vengeance.' Her skin was pale and she looked clammy. I repacked the snow, adjusted the braces, then pressed her foot to my stomach.

For the rest of the day, we ate barbecued mountain lion and sipped warm water. I kept the snow packed and monitored the amount of fluid she was drinking and expelling. She'd been lying still for ten days, breathing less than half the oxygen she was used to. I was worried about atrophy. And if she got an infection, I wasn't sure her body could fight it.

Once the protein hit my system, I rubbed down her good leg, forcing the blood flow through it, and stretched it as much as I could without jolting her broken leg. Throughout the day, I continued cutting long strips of meat and suspending them above the fire. Several times I gathered fuel. When I'd finished late in the afternoon, the colour had returned to her face and cheeks.

I looked out of the entrance and my eyes fell on Grover, lying on his side like a toppled statue. I strapped up my boots. 'I'll be right outside.'

She nodded. As I passed by her, she reached out and grabbed me by the coat. She pulled my forehead to her lips. 'Thank you.'

I nodded. This close to her face, I noticed how thin her cheeks had become. Even drawn. 'I don't know how you managed what you did last night. It's a deep-down kind of strength'—I looked away—'I've seen only one other time.' I pressed my palm to her forehead, checking for fever. 'Tomorrow morning we're getting out. I'm not sure where we're going, but we're leaving.'

She let go of my hand and smiled, 'First flight out?'

'Yeah. First class, too.'

I crawled out. My stomach was full and for the first time in ten days I was neither hungry nor cold. I scratched my head and it hit me. Something was strange. Something I'd not noticed in a long time. I was smiling.

YOU REMEMBER the turtles? I wonder how they're doing. Where they are. Did they make it to Australia? Especially your little friend.

Seems we found the female just as she was starting to build her nest. You said, 'What's that sound?' She was digging the hole. We climbed the dune, lay down and watched her. She was huge and dug a long time. Then she started laying eggs. Like she went into a trance or something. Must have laid a hundred eggs. When she finished, she covered her hole, crawled to the water's edge, then disappeared into the black water.

We slid down the dune and stared at the mound. It was one of the biggest we'd ever found. We carefully drove the spikes in a triangle, hung a line of pink surveyor's tape and then you made me cut little flags to make sure every beachcomber for a mile could see it.

Planes flying overhead could see that nest.

You counted the days like a kid at Christmas, and at fifty-five days we started camping out. 'Well, they don't know they're supposed to hatch at sixty days. What if they come early?'

'OK.'

We spread a blanket atop the dune and you wore a flashlight on a strap round your head. Looked like a misguided coal miner. I tried to climb inside your sleeping-bag but you zipped up. 'Not now. What if they start hatching?' When you get focused on something you are a piece of work.

So, we lay there. The beach was warm. One night, a cool breeze came out of the southwest so the ocean was more a lake than a raging torrent. Then came the fifty-ninth day. You were asleep. Drooling on your sleeping-bag. I tapped you on the shoulder, we hung our noses over the edge, and watched the first one shake the sand off his back and trek to the water. Wasn't long before the beach was crawling with loggerheads.

You were so excited. Counting quietly. Pointing at each one like you knew them by name. 'How do they know which way to go? How come they don't get lost?'

'They have this internal compass. Tells them where the water is.'

Then came our little friend. He crawled out, but unlike his one hundred and seventeen brother and sisters, headed the wrong way. Up the dune, towards us. He made it a few feet, then got bogged down. Burrowing. The wrinkle grew on your forehead as you watched him dig his own grave. You slid down the dune and carried him to the water. He found his sea legs and the first wave scooped him up. You gave him a little push. 'There you go, little guy. All the way to Australia.' The breeze was blowing your hair across your face. You were smiling. I think we stood there a long time, just watching him in the light, a floating black diamond swimming out to sea.

That was when you saw it. You turned round, stared at the dune where we'd been hiding and the scrub oaks and wire grass. The FOR SALE sign. You said, 'How much do you think they want?'

'Probably a good bit. It's been for sale a while.'

'It's a strange-sized lot. The area where you can build is small, while the protected dunes are big.'

'Yep. And you're surrounded by State Park so there are probably restrictions on what kind of house you can build.'

'Must be ten nests right here. Why doesn't the state buy it?'

I shrugged. 'Money, I suppose.'

You nodded. 'We should buy it.'

'What?'

You began walking up the dune. 'We could put it right over here. A beach house, back off the ocean. And we could build it with big glass windows where we could sit at night and watch the nests.'

I pointed back down the beach. 'Honey, we have a perfectly good condo right there. We can walk down here any time we like.'

'I know, but the next person to come along might not like the turtles digging up their front yard. We do. We should buy it.'

A week passed. I was back in the grind of work. I walked in, threw my stuff on the couch and the sliding glass door was open. You were standing on the beach, a white sarong blowing in the breeze. The sun had gone down. It was my favourite time. That cool bluish light that falls before the darkness comes. You waved.

I put on some shorts, grabbed my folder and walked out. You were holding a small wrapped box. The breeze was pulling at your hair again. When I kissed you, you pulled it aside with your finger.

You handed me the box. I opened the card. It read: 'So you can find your way back to me.' I opened the box. It was a lensatic compass. I turned it over. It was engraved. 'My true north.' You hung it round my neck and whispered, 'Without you, I'd be lost.'

'I got you something, too.' I handed you the folder.

You opened it, rifled through the pages. 'Honey . . . what is this?'

'That is a land survey. And this . . . is a contract on a piece of property.'

'What piece? We don't have the . . .' You stopped, turned the survey sideways and stared down the beach. 'You didn't.'

'It's just an offer. Doesn't mean they accept. I low-balled them.'

You tackled me. Laughing and screaming. 'I can't believe you did that!'

'Well, it has strong covenants. There's a lot we can't put there.'

'How much is it? Can we build a small house with a glass front?'

I nodded. 'But we won't be able to build right away.'

'I can wait.'

GROVER DESERVED a proper burial. I studied the landscape, and just above him sat a rock outcrop. I climbed it and the view stretched out for miles. He'd have liked it. I kicked away the snow, went back to the plane, pulled off a piece of the tail flap and used it like a shovel. I dug a hole, which was more pushing stuff out of the way than digging through the frozen ground. I climbed back down, lifted Grover over my shoulder and wound back up. I laid him in the hole and began collecting rocks.

I emptied his pockets and tried to take off his wedding ring but it wouldn't budge. I unhooked his pocket watch, and zipped all of that loose stuff into the pocket inside my jacket. Then I unlaced his boots, putting the laces in my pocket, pulled off his wool socks and slid his belt out of the loops in his trousers.

I stacked rocks under a cold sun that fell, turned a deep orange and then crimson. When I'd finished, I stood back. It was a good place. The wind had picked up. I suppose it would always be breezy up here. Maybe that was good. Maybe he'd feel like he was flying.

I took the wool beanie off my head. 'Grover . . . I'm sorry I got you into this mess. Guess if I hadn't hired you to fly me out here, you'd be home with your wife. If and when we get out of here, I'll go tell her what happened.' I tried to laugh. 'I don't know if I ought to be apologising to you. To be gut-level honest, you did stick us out in the middle of nowhere. Unless God wants two more dead people up here, we're going to need a change in the weather. And some help as to where we're going. Maybe you could put in a word for us. I think Ashley would like to walk down the aisle, get married. She's young. She deserves to wear white.' The light faded, giving way to a cloudless, cold sky. Overhead, maybe forty thousand feet in the air, a jet air-liner flew southeast. 'If that's your sense of humour, I don't think it's all that funny right now.' A second plane crisscrossed the trail of the first. 'Or that. By the way . . . since we're lost, won't take much to kill us out here. We're circling the drain now. I'm asking for that girl in there with the broken leg and the slowly breaking spirit. She thinks she's hiding it, but she's not. Up here . . . this'll break anybody. This is a tough place. It'll strip your hope fast.' My lip trembled. 'You and I, we never really finished our conversation, but I can tell you this . . . living with a broken heart is living half dead. And that's no way to live.' The mountains rose up around us, jagged, unforgiving, throwing shadows. Grover lay beneath me, covered in stones and ice. 'Once a heart breaks . . . it doesn't just grow back. It's not a lizard's tail. It's more like a huge stained-glass window that shattered into a million pieces and it's not going back together. A pile of broken coloured glass. And I just know that when half dies, the whole thing still hurts. So, you get twice the pain and half of everything else. That's all I wanted to say.' I held the compass, letting the needle spin and settle. 'I need to know which way to go.' The long white tails of the planes' wakes caught my eye. I corkscrewed my head. Their intersection created an arrow, pointing southeast. One hundred and twenty-five degrees. 'Given that I don't have a better option, that'll do.'

I WALKED BACK into the cave and slipped Grover's socks on Ashley's feet. They were medium-weight wool. She looked at me with suspicion. 'Where'd you get those?'

'Wal-Mart.'

'That's good to know. I thought you were going to say they belonged to Grover and that, well . . . that might just gross me out.'

She drifted off. Somewhere near midnight, she caught me staring at the compass face. The tritium dots on the dial glowed neon green. 'What if you choose the wrong direction?'

'You, me and Napoleon will be the only ones who ever know it.'

She pulled the bag up over her shoulders. 'Take your time . . .'

'Thanks, that's very helpful.'

'Don't get me started on what would be helpful at this moment.'

'Good point.'

Chapter Six

Ashley was grinding her teeth when I shook her. 'You ready?'

She nodded, sat up. 'Any coffee?'

I handed her a mug of fluid that looked more like weak tea. 'Go easy. That's the last of it.'

'It's already a bad day and we haven't even started yet.'

I sat next to her. We took care of the whole toilet thing and got her dressed. She zipped up her jacket. 'I'm going to ask a question. Can you get us out of here?'

'Honestly? No idea.'

'Phew. That's good to know. I thought you were going to say "no idea" and then we'd really be in a pickle.' She lay back. 'And I'm not even going to ask you about the direction we're headed, cause I know you've got that figured out. Right?'

'Right.'

'So you know where we're going?'

'Yep.'

'Seriously?'

'No.'

Her eyes narrowed. 'We've got to work on our communication.' I'm not asking you this stuff because I want honest answers. I want you to lie your butt off. Tell me we've only got a mile to go when there might be a hundred ahead of us.'

I laughed. 'OK. Listen, if you'll quit talking, we can get going. There's a helicopter waiting just beyond that first rise out there. They've got orange juice, couple of egg sandwiches, sausage, muffins, raspberry Danish and a dozen glazed doughnuts. And Starbucks.'

She patted me on the back. 'Now you're getting the hang of it.'

IDEALLY, I'D HAVE BUILT a sled of some sort. Something that would glide and not beat her to death. Problem was, that'd work great on the flat parts, but from what I could see, there weren't a lot of those, and given the angles we'd be traversing, I knew I couldn't handle a sled. If I got caught off balance, I'd never recover. She'd survive the plane crash only to die on the stretcher.

I decided on a hybrid between a sled and a stretcher. I started with the wing that had been ripped off. Given that its surfaces were made from some sort of cloth and plastic, it was light and slick. Its internal structure was metal, and given that the wing had been ripped away from the fuse-lage, the gas tanks had drained via gravity. The problem with a wing was that it was, well . . . wing-shaped. So, I cut a woman-sized cavity length-wise and reinforced the bottom with the support poles from the other wing and with sheet metal from the engine shroud. I eyed my creation. It might work. Given what I had to work with, it had to.

I packed everything I could find into my backpack and tied it crosswise over the wing where it could elevate Ashley's leg.

I fed her four Advil and held water to her lips. She sipped quietly as I explained my idea. 'I do know that northwest, behind us, the mountains rise up. That way'—I pointed—'the plateau rolls away southeast. We need to get lower, and that's the only way down. So, we're going to pick our way downhill. I'll have my hands on you all the time. When it's flat, I'll fix a harness with the straps and waistband from my backpack that will allow me to pull you. Any questions?'

She shook her head. I checked her leg, wrapped her warmly, zipped up her bag and pulled the wool beanie down over her ears. 'For the first time, your leg is now down below your heart. It's going to swell. Best we can do is ice at night. Now let's get you out of here.'

I put my hands beneath her arms and pulled her gently towards the stretcher. The sleeping-bag slid rather easily over the snow and ice. Then it hooked on a rock or root and jerked her leg.

She screamed at the top of her lungs, turned her head away from me and threw up. Everything she had eaten, including the Advil, splattered the snow. I wiped her mouth and then her forehead where she'd broken out in a sweat. 'Sorry.'

She said nothing. She was grinding her teeth.

I got her to the wing, slid her and her sleeping-bag onto it, and then lay Napoleon next to her. She put an arm round him, but didn't open her eyes.

I propped her head up with Grover's bag. I secured the bow and Grover's fly rods. All ridiculously overloaded but I was operating on the principle that it was better to have it and not need it than need it and not have it. Although I did leave both our laptops, cellphones and paperwork.

The first hour, we said little. The snow was knee-deep in most places. Deeper in others. Couple of times I fell to midchest and had to crawl out. I focused on my breathing and my grip on the makeshift handles, and the pain in my ribs was considerable.

We walked down off our plateau, towards the stream where I'd caught the trout and into a forested area of evergreens. The limbs were thick with snow, like icing. If you bumped one, it dumped shovelfuls down your back. After an hour she said, 'Excuse me Doc, but we're not going very fast. You need to giddy-up.'

I collapsed in the snow next to her, breathing heavy in the thin air. My legs were screaming. She tapped my forehead. 'Want me to get you a Gatorade or something?'

I nodded. 'Yeah, that'd be great.'

'You know what I was thinking?'

I felt the sweat trickling down my neck. 'There's no telling.'

'I was thinking how great a cheeseburger would be right now. Maybe two patties. Extra cheese, of course.'

I nodded. 'Of course.'

'Tomato. Got to be a good tomato. Onion. Ketchup. Mustard. Mayo.'

I opened my eyes. White, cottony clouds drifted overhead. Another commercial airliner streaked through the sky. 'Extra pickles.'

'And two orders of fries on the side.'

'I think I could eat that whole thing twice right now.'

She nodded, then looked through the trees, in the direction I'd been walking. 'You'd better get pulling. This thing's not battery-powered you know?'

'Funny, I figured that out about an hour ago. I need you to do me a favour.'

'Don't push your luck with me.'

I handed her a clean Nalgene bottle. 'We need to drink. A lot. If, while I'm pulling, you could pack this thing with snow, then slip it inside your bag and let your body warmth melt it, it'll help. You mind?'

She shook her head and took the bottle. 'Can I ask you something?'

The temperature was probably in the single digits yet sweat was pouring off my forehead. I'd taken off my jacket but my body was drenched. 'Sure. Fire away.'

'The voicemail. What's the deal?'

'What voicemail?'

'The one you were listening to as we were taking off.'

'We had a disagreement . . . a difference of opinion.'

'You're not going to tell me, are you?'

I shrugged.

She smirked. 'Is she right?'

I nodded without looking. 'Yes.'

'That's refreshing.' She watched me a minute. 'Why do you clam up every time I bring up the recorder?'

I took a deep breath that did not fill me.

'Silence does not qualify as an answer.'

'Rachel and I are . . . separated.'

'You're what?'

'We had a fight. Kind of a big one and we're working through an issue, or two. The recorder helps to do that.'

'She doesn't sound like she wants to be separated.'

'It's complicated. I said some words I can't take back.'

I stood up. I'd grown stiff. Cold filtered through my wet clothes. I backed up to the stretcher, lifted it and began pulling.

'So . . . where does she live?'

'Just two miles down the beach. I built her a house.'

'You're separated but you built her a house.'

'It's complicated. She and the kids . . . We . . .'

She pelted me with two handfuls of snow. 'Kids! You have kids?'

'Two.'

'And you're just now telling me? How old?'

'Four. They're twins. Michael and Hannah.'

She nodded. 'Good names.'

'Good kids.'

'I'll bet they keep you busy.'

'I don't . . . see them much.'

She frowned. 'You must've really screwed up. In my experience, it's usually the guy. Always thinking with your plumbing.'

'It's not that.'

'Is she dating? Come on . . . out with it. Why've you separated?'

I wanted out of this conversation.

'Still not telling me, are you?' Her tone changed. 'What if we don't make it out, what then?'

'You mean, "what good is it?" Why do I still talk into it?'

'Something like that.'

I turned round to face her. Blue skies were giving way to grey, heavy clouds threatening snow. I tapped my chest. 'I've operated on thousands of people, many in bad shape. Never once have I thought, "They're not going to make it." By design, doctors are some of the most optimistic people on the planet. We find ways to make very bad situations better. Every day's a game of chess. Most days we win. Some days we don't. And we do this because of one word. Hope. It circulates in our veins. It's what fuels us.'

She nodded, closed her eyes and laid back.

I turned to the front and began pulling. From behind me, I heard, 'You still haven't answered my question.'

'I know.'

Clouds blew in, mist covered the mountain. Pretty soon the snow was blowing sideways. Even circling. It stung my face and made walking nearly impossible. There was no place to hide. No shelter. I stared into that white darkness and made a tough decision.

I turned us round.

The walk back was disheartening. I hated giving up ground, but better to give it up and live than keep it and die. Four hours later, we were back at the crash. I could barely move. I got her comfortable. Her face was riddled in pain. She said nothing. I forced my eyes open until she fell asleep.

I WOKE UP four hours later. Shivering. I'd never pulled off my wet clothes. A costly mistake. The sleeping-bag is designed to insulate the temperature inside it, and I was cold and wet. I stripped, hung the clothes over a wing support, stoked the fire and crawled back into my bag. It took me an hour to get warm, spending energy I didn't have. Not only costly, stupid. Mistakes like that will kill you when you're not looking.

SHE DID NOT look impressed. 'So what's today's adventure?'

It took me a minute to remember where I was. 'Huh?'

'I've been trying to let you sleep 'cause I know you're tired but I've really got to go and it's not like I can just cross my legs. I tried without you but I didn't want to soak my bag. What day is this?'

I raised my watch and couldn't see anything on the face, so I pressed the Indiglo button. Nothing happened. I pushed harder. Still nothing. I shook it and held it up to the daylight. Condensation had gathered beneath a deep spider-webbing crack. 'I don't know.'

'That watch important?'

'Rachel gave it to me. Years ago.'

'Sorry.' She was quiet a minute. Her voice was softer. 'How many days have we been doing this?'

Napoleon was licking my ear. 'Twelve . . . I think.'

She nodded, calculating. 'Florence. I think we'd be in Florence now.' I sat up and she studied the purple bruise on my rib cage. 'How you doing?'

'OK. It's not as tender.' I began slipping into my cold, damp clothes.

'You're skinny.'

'It's this crash weight-loss diet I've been trying out.'

She chuckled. A good way to start the day.

I checked her leg, helped her take care of necessities and started melting snow in the Jetboil. I didn't know how much fuel we had left, but it had to be running low. At sea level, it would boil water in about seventy-five seconds. Up here, it was taking three to four times that long. The fuel in Grover's lighter had nearly evaporated. Any matches I'd had when we started were long gone and we needed fire. I needed to keep my eyes peeled for wood I could use to make a bow drill.

It was midday. The snow had frozen on top and created favourable walking conditions. Frozen snow meant that with snowshoes I could spend more time on top of the snow rather than down in it.

I laced up my boots, strapped on my gaiters and slid into my jacket. Given that we'd packed yesterday, it didn't take us long to do it again.

I gave her a few pieces of meat to chew on, along with some water, and pulled her through the opening—remembering the bump at the entrance. It felt twenty degrees colder. I looked at the sled, studied my process of the day before and realised I needed a harness to keep my hands free, let me pull with my legs and chest. I crawled back in and removed the harness from Grover's seat using his Leatherman. I attached cord to the sled from this harness, which made an X across my chest and, given the quick-release buckle, let me pop out in a hurry if I started slipping and needed to disconnect.

Dubious, Ashley tilted her head. I pulled off my jacket, picked up Napoleon and slid both inside the bag with her. A crucial decision. I strapped myself in, leaned into the weight and began pulling.

After an hour, we'd come maybe five hundred metres, dropping maybe a hundred feet in elevation. Every three steps was followed by several seconds of rest. But it was progress.

She was not impressed. 'Seriously'—she took a sip of water—'how long do you think you can do this?'

'Don't know.' I watched her out of the corner of my eye.

'We can't do this. You can't. We're in the middle of nowhere.'

I stopped, sweat dripping off me, breathing deeply. 'Ashley?'

She didn't answer.

'Ashley?'

She crossed her arms.

'We can't stay up there. If we do, we'll die. And I can't leave you. If I do, you'll die. So, we're walking out.'

Her frustration at being helpless bubbled over. She screamed, 'It's been twelve damn days and not a soul has come looking and we're maybe a mile from where we started.'

'They don't know to look.'

'What's your plan? How do you plan to get us out of here?'

This was fear talking. No amount of logic would satisfy it. 'One step at a time.'

'And how long do you think you can keep that up?'

'As long as it takes.'

'And what if you can't?'

'I can. What's my choice?'

She closed her eyes. I pulled out the compass, took a reading of one hundred and twenty-five degrees, picked a small ridge in the distance as a marker, and started putting one foot in front of the other.

We didn't speak for several hours.

My course took me slightly downhill and through the trees. I was constantly shaking snow from round my neck. I took my time. If I started to get overheated, I'd take more breaths between steps. In a little over six hours, we came what I judged to be a little more than a mile. It was nearly dark when I stopped.

I was soaking wet with sweat, and exhausted, but I knew if I didn't start making my fire bow, I'd regret it. I slid Ashley beneath the limbs of an evergreen and up alongside a rock. The ground beneath her had been protected from the snow so it was actually dirt and dry pine needles. I pulled off my sweaty shirt, hung it on a branch, gathered several handfuls of needles along with some twigs and made a small fire. When I clicked the Jetboil and started it, it hiccupped. We had maybe a day left in the tank. I gathered more sticks, laid them in a pile next to her and said, 'Tend this. Don't let it die. I'll be within shouting distance.'

I started making wide circles looking for two pieces of wood. One piece, maybe three feet long with a bit of an arc, and then a straight piece out of which I could cut a spindle. Took me about thirty minutes to find both.

I slipped through the trees, the snow crunching under my makeshift snowshoes. I stopped at a distance. Catching my breath. She was sitting up, tending the fire. The glow of the fire on her face. Even there, even then, she was beautiful. There was no denying that.

The difficulty of our situation was always on my mind. But I hadn't seen us through her eyes. Her sitting with nothing to do but tend the fire and scratch Napoleon's head. Dependent on me for movement, food, water, going to the toilet. She couldn't do a thing, other than sleep, without me. If I'd had to be as dependent on someone else for twelve days, I'd have been much more difficult to live with.

I returned to the fire, slid into my bag, chewed on some meat and made myself drink water. While the Jetboil was failing, the upper piece that we cooked in, sort of a small coffee can, was aluminium and would stand up to heat. So, I filled it with snow and leaned it against the coals.

We drank and ate for the next hour while I worked on my bow. Grover's laces were about to come in handy. I pulled out one lace, tied a knot in one end, threaded it through the groove on one end of the bow, pulled it tight and slid it through the groove on the other end and secured it with a few loops and a knot. Tight enough so that when I twisted the spindle into it, there would be enough tension to spin the spindle. It's sort of a touch thing and takes a few stringings of the bow to get it right. I cut the spindle to about ten inches, carved both ends into points—with one end wider for more friction—and cut a groove in the middle to hold the shoelace in place.

That finished, I drank the last of my water and looked up for the first time in a long time. Ashley was staring at me. 'You can be intense when you want to,' she said. 'I need an update.'

'I think we made it about a mile. Tomorrow I'm going to climb that rise over there and see if I can tell what's in the plateau on the other side. It'll help to stay as hydrated as you can, eat as much as you like and tell me when I jar you too much. I'm sorry when I do.'

She let out a deep breath. 'I'm sorry I jumped at you this morning.'

I shook my head. 'You're in a tough place. You can't do much of anything without my help. That'd be difficult for anyone.'

I placed more wood on the fire, slid close enough to be warm but not set myself aflame, and closed my eyes. Sleep was falling on me fast. Then I thought of Ashley. I forced my eyes open. She was staring at me again. 'You need anything?'

She shook her head. Tried to smile. 'No.'

She was asleep in seconds.

Chapter Seven

It was difficult to wake up knowing we'd been doing this for thirteen days. I shook off sleep and was dressed before daylight. The fire was out but a few coals remained. I blew on it, fanned a flame and fed it, scratched Napoleon and then headed up the rise.

I took my time. Studying our surroundings. Every indentation. I kept asking myself, 'Does anything look man-made?'

The answer was a resounding 'No'. Everything was pristine and untouched. A nature-lover's paradise. I loved nature as much as the next guy but this was ridiculous.

I steadied the compass, let the needle settle and took a reading, then stared across the face at several mountains in the distance. To get to them we'd have to travel all day, maybe two, through tall trees and deep snow. And once in the trees, I'd lose all perspective. Never make it without the compass. Maybe life is like that.

My bearing would take us through a gap and hopefully lower elevation. Staring out at the immense wilderness reminded me I could lose almost everything and have a chance, but not the compass. I tied it to a piece of nylon cord and tethered it round my neck.

When I returned, Ashley was sitting up, stirring the fire. She started on me before I had a chance to say good morning. 'How'd you know you wanted to marry your wife? I mean, how'd you know?'

'Good morning.'

'Yeah. Good morning yourself. Let me know when it gets good.'

'I see you're feeling better.'

I knelt next to her bag, unzipped the side, pulled it back, and examined her leg. The good news and the bad news was that there was no real change. 'Today at lunch, we need to ice that . . . OK?'

She nodded. 'Seriously. I want to know.'

I stuffed my bag in its compression sack. 'I wanted to spend every second with her. Wanted to laugh with her, cry with her, grow old with her, hold her hand, and since we'd been hanging out a couple of years, I really wanted to have sex with her. A lot of it.'

She laughed. 'Were you still pretty active before you separated?'

'The best-kept secret about the whole marriage thing is that the loving part gets better. You lose all the "I've got to prove something" or whatever it is. I guess us guys get our ideas of what it ought to be through movies. When, in fact, it's more of a sharing than a taking. Movies show the hot, sweaty side. And that's great, but that's not as good as it gets. Granted, a lot of folks' fires die out, but I also think a lot of married couples know a whole lot more about loving than we give them credit for.'

'What about when one wants to and one doesn't?'

I laughed. 'Rachel liked to call that "mercy loving" and it's ninety-nine per cent of the time her having mercy on me.'

'Mercy loving?'

'It goes something like, "Honey, I can't sleep. Help."'

'So . . . how's that work in the separation?'

'It doesn't.'

'How long have you two been separated?'

'Long enough for me to buy sleeping pills in the bulk section at Costco.' I began strapping stuff to the sled. 'Listen, I need to get you to stand up, start bearing weight on the good leg. Forcing circulation.'

She held out her hands. I unzipped the bag, she braced her good foot on mine and I lifted her slowly. I steadied her, she wobbled and then finally stood up straight. 'That feels good. Almost human.'

'How's the bad leg?'

'Tender. More of a dull pain than sharp as long as I don't flex the muscles round the break.'

I readjusted the straps on the brace. She put her arms on my shoulders, balancing on me. I steadied her by the hips. 'Let's just give this a few minutes. The change in blood pressure will be good for your heart.'

She stared up into the trees, smiling. 'My legs are cold.'

'That's what you get, walking round in socks and underwear.'

'You know, when I was in middle school, this was how we danced if we were "going" with someone. Vince hates to dance.'

'Can't say I'm much of a fan of it either.'

'OK, I've had enough. Put me down.' I settled her in her bag and zipped her up. She pointed. 'Come on. Let me see. Show me what you've got.'

'What? Dance? You've lost your mind.'

She swirled her finger at the ground. 'Go ahead. I'm waiting.'

'You don't understand. I have the hip movement of a toy soldier.'

'So, are you going to dance or what?'

I turned, did my best John Travolta and *Staying Alive* imitation followed by that weird mop-bucket thing that guys do with their arms and hips. I topped it off with YMCA, and a Michael Jackson moonwalk, spin and hat tilt. When I finished, she was laughing so hard she couldn't talk. Finally, she held out a hand. 'Stop . . . Don't . . . I think I just peed a little.'

The laughter felt good. Real good. And as much as I wanted a satellite phone, a surgical suite to fix her leg or a helicopter ride out of there, the laughter was worth all of that put together. Napoleon looked at us like we were nuts. Especially me.

She lay back, breathing. Half laughing.

I zipped up my jacket. 'Rachel made us take lessons.'

'What?'

'Yep. Swing. Tango. Waltz. Viennese Waltz. Jitterbug. Foxtrot. Even line dances. Some of the most fun we ever had on dates.'

'So, you really can dance.'

'With her.'

'If I'm lucky, I'll get one dance out of Vince at our wedding.'

'Course, after that she wanted to dance at every party.'

'And did you?'

'I did.' I nodded. 'I called it "mercy dancing" and ninety-nine per cent of the time it had to do with me having mercy on her. But, it had its tradeoff.' I raised my eyebrows.

'You need to talk to Vince when we get out of here.'

'I'll see what I can do.' I gave her my jacket to stuff in her bag and stepped into the harness. 'Come on, we're burning daylight.'

She snapped her fingers. 'I've heard that before. Where's it come from?'

'John Wayne. *The Cowboys*.'

She slid down in her bag. 'You are getting more interesting with every day that passes.'

'Trust me, my rabbit's hat is just about empty.' I strapped on my snow-shoes, leaned in and the sled gave way across the frozen snow.

'Can I see that little dance move one more time?'

I shook my hips, mopped the floor, tossed the pizza and spelled YMCA. She was howling, gently kicking her one good leg. We pulled out through the trees, bathed in the smell of evergreen and the sound of her laughter.

BY LUNCH TIME we'd walked a mile and a half and I was toast. My left foot was frozen. My gloves were full of holes and my hands were blistered. And because the last half-mile was slightly uphill, the straps cut into my shoulders and made my fingers numb.

We stopped for an hour alongside a small creek. I pulled Ashley up beneath a tree, pulled off my wet shirt and hung it to dry. Letting the shirt freeze was actually good because it was easier to shake off ice than wring out sweat in this temperature.

The tree's branches canopied out over the ground, protecting it from snow. Then I climbed into my bag where, warm and quiet, I slept for an hour. When I woke, I dressed, nibbled on some jerky, and stamped my foot five or six times. It felt wet. Wet was bad. Especially for toes.

Late in the afternoon, the sun poked through, heated things up slightly, which turned the snow towards mush. I'd take two or three steps, fall, bury myself in snow, climb out, take two or three more steps, bury myself again . . . This went on for a couple of hours.

By nightfall, we'd come maybe two and a half miles. A total of three and a half or four from the crash site. Sometimes I'd rest a minute between steps, and yet it wasn't enough. Clouds spilled over the mountains, night-time fell quickly and I could barely move. I was cold and wet but I didn't have the energy to make a fire. I needed to find a place to hole up tomorrow. The little voice inside my head was telling me I couldn't keep this up for long.

We camped at a rock outcrop. A ledge that years of use by critters had made somewhat of a cave. Good protection from the wind and snow while also offering a one-in-a-million view. I propped Ashley up against the wall, gave her the full effect. She said, 'Wow. Never seen anything like that.'

'Me neither,' was all I could mutter. I sat down. Totally zonked. 'Would it be all right with you if we didn't have a fire tonight?'

She nodded. I stripped out of my wet clothes, and tried to hang what I could along the rock. My inner layer of Capilene fabric was dripping with sweat. I pulled on my only pair of boxer shorts, slipped into my bag and only then thought of my boots. If I didn't get my boots dry, tomorrow would be a miserable day.

I climbed out. Grabbed handfuls of dead pine needles and twigs and built a teepee about a foot tall. I knew I would get only one shot at this.

I took out Grover's lighter, rubbed it between my palms for some reason I can't explain, stuck it inside the teepee and struck it. It sparked but no flame. I shook it. 'Come on, just one time.' I struck it again. Nothing. 'Last time.' I struck it, a flame appeared and was gone. But pine needles are incredibly flammable. I blew lightly at the base, slowly fed it small twigs. The fire grew, and once I felt like it had caught, I searched for larger sticks.

Dead on my feet, I found enough for a few hours, and stacked rocks along the edge. I set my boots close enough to dry but not melt the rubber. Climbed into my bag and fell asleep seconds after my head hit the ground.

My last thought was that conditions were worsening. Grover's lighter was finished. We had the cooked mountain lion, but even eating it sparingly we might have two days left. If we didn't feed Napoleon, maybe three.

Problem was, I couldn't not feed him. Intellectually and in different circumstances, say the warm comfort of my office, I might have talked about how in dire conditions I'd even eat him. Now I was in dire conditions, yet every time I looked at him, he licked my face and wagged his tail, and every time the wind blew he stood up, facing into it, and growled. Anything with that tough a spirit deserves a chance. Others might have carved him into dog steaks, but I just couldn't. He was probably tough as old shoe leather, anyway. But, to be honest, every time I looked at him, I saw Grover. Maybe that's reason enough.

SIX OR SEVEN HOURS LATER, with the first hint of daylight crawling across the grey and white mountains before us, my eyes opened to the unexpected sound of a hot crackling fire.

Ashley had been tending it for hours. My clothes were warm, dry and, oddly enough, folded on top of a rock. She was poking at the fire with a long green evergreen branch that she got from I don't know where. Anything within arm's reach had been thrown into the fire. Now, she was using the last of the sticks I'd gathered. My boots had been turned and the leather was dry. As were my socks.

I rubbed my eyes. 'I'd like some coffee, a cinnamon bun, six eggs over medium, a New York strip, some hash browns, more coffee, some orange juice, a piece of key lime pie and peach cobbler.'

'Can I have some?'

I sat up. 'You didn't sleep much, did you?'

She shrugged. 'Couldn't. You were pretty tired, even talked in your sleep. And your clothes were dripping wet. I can't do much, but this I can do.'

'Thanks. Really.' I dressed. Pulling on warm boots brought a smile to my face. I grabbed Grover's hatchet. 'I'll be back.'

I returned a half-hour later, arms full. I made three more trips. I'd heard wives and mothers in African tribes spend three to ten hours a day searching for water and firewood. Now I understood why.

I melted some snow, heated up some jerky and fed Ashley and Napoleon. We were quiet awhile. The fire felt good. 'How's the leg?'

She shrugged. I stood, knelt, unzipped her bag and ran my hand along her thigh. The swelling had decreased and the purple had quit spreading. I stared at the stitches in her face. 'I need to pull those out.' She nodded. I pulled out my Swiss Army knife, snipped each stitch and then began the unpleasant experience of pulling them out. She held out her palm. I laid each one into it. She winced. When I'd finished, she asked, 'How do I look?'

'Nothing a good plastic surgeon can't fix.'

'That bad?' She crossed her arms. 'What's the plan?'

'Shelter and food.' I unconsciously looked at my watch, forgetting it was dead, and said, 'We're on a bit of a plateau. It continues another mile or so through trees, then drops off, if I remember right. I'd like to get there tonight. If it drops off, it drops off to something. I'm thinking a lake, stream, some water source. Maybe we can hole up there a few days and give me a chance to find food.'

She eyed Grover's bow, strapped to the top of the sled. 'Are six arrows enough?'

'Don't have much choice.' I rubbed my chest. 'My ribs feel better, but if

I pull that thing all the way back, it stings a bit. And Grover's draw length was longer so it's harder for me than it should be.' I stared out at the dark clouds rolling in across the peaks. 'Looks like snow. I'd like to get through those trees before the worst of it drops on us.'

She nodded. 'I'm game.'

We packed quickly, something we'd got good at, and I was back in the harness before I had time to dread it.

The snow began dropping quarter-sized flakes in the first hour. Walking the mile through the trees took us more than three hours. We emerged where a steep slope seemed to fall off into a valley of sorts. Given total whiteout conditions, I had no real idea.

We pulled up under the limbs of an evergreen and I pulled out the sketch I'd made. In truth, I wasn't sure where we were. I knew we'd walked down a one hundred and twenty-five-degree line, but we were also dodging right and left to skirt round rocks, ledges, small peaks, downed trees. We were probably two to three miles off our original line. Walking a straight line in the wilderness is seldom possible. Walking in a straight direction is. Both will take you in the same direction but not to the same place.

People experienced with reading compasses, and who take it seriously, who engage in what's called orienteering, can overcome the side-to-side adjustments and arrive at an actual predetermined point. I wasn't that good. While we were now eight to nine miles from the crash site, we'd probably walked closer to twice that given the back and forth that conditions forced upon us. And my sketch suggested we were fifteen or twenty miles yet from the single line I'd seen on the GPS that might have been a logging road.

With the hatchet I cut into the tree that hid us and pulled down some limbs, giving us an entry on the lee side, and then laid those limbs on the windward side, giving us more protection. I cut more limbs from a nearby tree, stacking them like vertical boards against ours, and hand-shovelled snow against the base. I fed the tips inside the limbs of our tree to hold them up, them inserted more cut limbs inside, sort of like rafters in an attic. Within an hour, we had a fair shelter.

I was dreading what came next. The bow drill. I gathered tinder, needles and small twigs, even some fuzz off my socks. I strung the bow and slowly began turning the spindle on the hearth board. Once I'd developed the hole and cut the notch, I gave myself fully to working the bow. At this altitude, it took several minutes to get smoke but once I got it, I kept tugging. Five minutes in, I felt like I might have enough smoke. I set down the bow and spindle, picked up my hearth and studied my coal. I blew gently and a small red ember appeared. I blew again, too hard. It scattered like dust.

I had to start all over. This time I pulled on the bow for eight or nine minutes, making sure I had ample dust to create a coal. Anyone who's ever done this will tell you that eight or nine minutes is a long time. I set down the bow, lifted the hearth, blew gently, blew again, and this time smoke curled up. I blew some more, then placed the red coal gently inside my handful of tinder, needles and sock fuzz. I blew some more. Blew some more. Blew some more.

Finally, a small flame. I blew into it, the flame spread and I set the handful inside my teepee of sticks and twigs. We had a fire.

Ashley shook her head. 'You're better than Robinson Crusoe.'

Quiet settled round us. Our evergreen shelter was warm and comfortable, and the limbs above did a good job of providing shelter while also drawing the smoke out. But with two hours of daylight left, I pulled on my jacket, tied on my snowshoes and grabbed Grover's bow. 'I'm going to take a look about.'

'Be gone long?'

'An hour maybe.' I secured the fire, then looked at Napoleon. 'Keep her company.'

He turned in a circle and hid in her sleeping-bag.

I climbed up a small ridge. The lee side was sheltered from the wind so the snow was much less, spotted with sprigs of dead grass. My lungs told me we were still above ten thousand feet. The snow had quit. The sky was grey but the ceiling was high and I could see a large half-moon of valley below me. Maybe ten to fifteen square miles. Frozen creeks and small streams creased between the trees. Except for the occasional roll and pitch of a hill, it was mostly flat. Certainly better than where we'd been.

A couple of hundred yards from our shelter I reached a small ledge, sat and cupped my hands round my eyes to scan every square acre, asking myself if anything I saw hinted at the possibility that it might be man-made. I did this until the light started growing dim.

Just as the last light was fading, I caught a flash of something brown. It was horizontal, near the treetops. I squinted, even stared out of the sides of my vision. It was hard to make out. I opened my compass and took a reading of ninety-seven degrees.

I started back to camp. Twenty yards in front of me something white flashed across my trail. I nocked an arrow and waited for any sign of movement. Five minutes I waited. Then a small hop. Followed by another. There, a small white rabbit. Big ears, big feet, hopping beneath the trees.

I drew, settled the first pin in the middle of the rabbit, let out half a breath and squeezed the release. Just as the arrow left the bow, the rabbit hopped maybe six inches. My arrow sailed by and the rabbit disappeared.

I searched for my arrow, but digging in the snow was painful on my blistered hands. I decided to leave it until tomorrow.

ASHLEY HAD the fire crackling when I returned. She'd even managed to boil some water and heat up what was close to the last of our meat. Maybe a day left. She eyed the bow and the single arrow missing. 'What happened?'

'It hopped.'

'And if it hadn't?'

'I'm pretty sure we'd be eating rabbit tonight.'

'Maybe from now on, let me hold them still while you shoot.'

'If you catch them, I'm game for anything. Say, do you feel like taking a walk?'

She raised both eyebrows. 'Seriously?'

'Yeah. If you can lean on me, I think we could make our way up this ridge. I need your eyes.'

'See something?'

'Maybe. Looks like a horizontal in a sea of verticals. I'm not willing to risk it unless both of us look at it.'

'What are we risking?'

'I'd thought we'd keep trying to lose elevation, but this thing I'm looking at would keep us up on the valley. It's a two or three-day change in direction, then another three or four days if I'm wrong.' I didn't need to tell her we were flirting with the edge as it was.

'Is it safe for me to walk?'

'No, and the sled would never make it. We'd take it a step at a time. At first light. The rising sun may be our best chance.'

We climbed into our bags and watched the flame light the underside of the tree limbs. It was the first time I'd been overly warm and had to unzip my bag. Once I got some food in me I moved my attention to Ashley's leg. The swelling was down and knotting and scar tissue were discernible round the break. All good signs.

I sat opposite her, placed her good foot on my lap and began rubbing deep into her arch, her calf, and then her hamstring and quadriceps. She looked up at me. 'You sure you didn't study massage?'

'You've been lying prostrate for two weeks. You try to stand on these things and you're liable to look like a Weeble.'

'A what?'

'You know, "Weebles wobble but they don't fall down."' You look at someone and think one thing but put your hands on them and you get to know what they're made of. Ashley was all long, lean, limber muscle. Which probably saved her life. I moved to her left foot, careful not to torque her leg. 'I'd hate for you to get angry and kick me when your leg heals. You're nothing but muscle.'

'Don't feel like much lying here.' She flinched as I worked deep in her calf. 'When we get back, you have to teach Vince to do this.'

'Vince doesn't rub your feet?'

'Not even if I gave him rubber gloves.'

'I better talk to that man.'

Chapter Eight

Warmed by the fire I lay awake, staring at the ironic sight of another jetliner at thirty thousand feet. Ashley was out. Slightly snoring. A gentle breeze filtered through our tree, pulled on the branches above us and added extra twinkle to a sky lit by ten billion stars. Tomorrow's decision was worrying me. Had I really seen something or, after fifteen days, had I wanted to so badly that my mind convinced my eyes that I had?

In the middle of the night, the sound of heavy feet crunching snow woke us. Crunching it hard. I grabbed the bow and crouched between Ashley and the door, then heard antlers rub against tree limbs. It turned out to be a moose, and after circling it took off.

'Ben? You mind sleeping over here?' Ashley said.

'Sure.' I picked up my bag and slid it over. We both drifted off.

Some time later, I woke again. There was hair in my face. Human hair. Silky, it smelled of woman. My first tendency was to move. Respect Ashley's space. But I did not. I lay there, breathing in. Stealing the aroma. Slow inhales. Remembering what a woman smelled like.

Later she turned her head, pressing her forehead to mine. Her breath on my face. I pressed in, careful not to wake her. Then I drifted off again, feeling guilty and filled with longing.

IT WAS DARK when I woke. The moon was high and bright through the evergreen limbs. Ashley stirred.

I dressed, helped her do the same and, once I had her bundled, slid her out of the entrance. I could pull the sled only about a hundred yards before the angle grew too steep and I had to lift her to a standing position. She wrapped an arm round my neck. Her bad leg was between us.

We took our time. One step, then another. Napoleon trailed behind, hopping in our footsteps. Happy to be out. She wrapped her right arm round my neck and clung to my right hand with hers, locking us stride for stride. What had taken me twenty minutes took us nearly an hour, but we made it without incident. I sat her on the ledge, the view spread out before us, and she scanned the sixty or seventy square miles looking back at us.

I levelled the compass on my leg, let the needle settle, then pointed across the carpet of evergreens towards a distant ridge. 'See that brown-looking thing? Sort of flat, stretched left to right, sitting on top of the trees, just left of that white-capped ridge.' Napoleon hopped up in my lap, staring down in the valley.

She cupped her hands round her eyes. 'They're all white-capped.'

I waited while she studied the horizon. We were looking at a speck eight to ten miles distant. The proverbial needle. 'See it?'

She nodded. 'Yeah.' She was quiet a minute. 'How in the world did you see that in the first place? It's hard to make out.'

'Give it ten minutes. When direct sunlight comes over the ridges, we'll get some sort of unnatural reflection if it's man-made.'

So we waited. Sunlight crawled down the mountain, uncovering what lay before us. An immense valley, hemmed in on three sides by steep and jagged mountains. In the middle floated an evergreen sea crisscrossed by streams and small frozen lakes and ponds.

Just before the sun grew too bright and obscured the image we were looking at, the brown thing glimmered. Or shimmered.

I asked without turning my head. 'You see that?'

'Yeah. I'm not sure whether it was a reflection off ice or something else.'

'OK, look right. See that clearing? Could be a frozen lake.'

'What's your point?'

'Well . . . if I was to build a mountain house or camp or something, I'd build preferably near a lake.' The glare grew painful. 'What do you think?' I pointed down our original line, which would take us out of the valley we were looking into. 'Going that way is lower elevation. Probably warmer. Certainly we'd breathe easier. I just don't know where it leads.' I swung a wide arc to the image in the distance. 'Across the valley is a lot of deep snow, frozen creeks hidden beneath the surface that could swallow me. If that thing over there is nothing, it's going to cost us.'

'How much food do we have?'

'If we stretch it? Day and a half if we don't mind being hungry.'

'How long can you make it after that runs out?'

'I can keep breathing for maybe a week, but if I'm pulling the sled'— I shrugged—'I'm not sure.'

'Sounds to me like we've got enough energy to get across the valley on what's stored up inside you right now. And if we make it to the other side without finding food, then it might be a good place to curl up and go to sleep for a long time.'

'If you want to put it that way.'

'What if you left me here and scouted it out on your own?'

'I've thought about that. Granted, I could get there a lot quicker, but there's no guarantee I can do it safely or get back to you. If I fall, get hurt, get eaten by a mountain lion, then we'll both die alone with a lot of unanswered questions. I'm not willing to risk that.'

'What if I am?'

'It's not your choice. I'm the one that has to walk across and back.'

'What if I asked you to?'

'I'd refuse. Let's say I get over there, on top of that ridge and see a house or road. I've got to head for that. By the time I found help and returned, you'd never know it because you'd be dead.'

'But you'd have made it. I thought we were in this together.'

'We are.' I stared at her. 'Ashley, this is no game. We, both of us, are either going this way, or that way. It's either-or, not maybe-and-what-if.'

She closed her eyes, squeezing out tears. 'We've been at this for fifteen days. At some point, we're just prolonging the inevitable. If you can go a lot farther without me, then you've got to try it. One of us making it is better than both of us dying.'

'That's where you're wrong. I won't do it.'

'What if I won't go with you?'

'Then I'll thump you on the head, strap you to the sled and haul you out. Now, that's enough.'

We sat, side by side. Staring out over a painful future. She hooked her arm inside mine. 'Why are you doing this?'

'I have my reasons.'

'One of these days you've got to help me understand them, because they don't make any sense.'

I stood and pulled her up on two feet. 'That depends on whether you're looking at this through my eyes, or yours.'

We went back down. Gingerly. Halfway back, I dug out my arrow. Once I'd found it, we began walking again. 'We look like two people in a potato sack race,' she said through a running nose.

I nodded, watching where she put her foot.

'If Vince and I had tried walking to that ledge, we'd have ended up on our backs with me in a lot of pain, trying to shove snow down his throat for letting me fall.'

'Not to pry, but every time you talk about him, you tell me how different you two are. What's with that?'

'We're different all right. But I enjoy him. He makes me laugh. And we have a lot in common.'

'People go to the rescue shelter and choose dogs for similar reasons. Not seventy-year soul mates.'

'OK, doctor, what reason would you choose?'

'Love.'

She shook her head. 'That kind only happens to the select few. The rest of us better get what we can while we can. Otherwise we end up waiting on a fairy tale that never comes true.'

'But what if you could have the fairy tale if you waited for it?'

'I've waited, tried to be selective, but all the good ones are taken. Guys like Grover, and you . . . I've never had luck finding one of them.'

'I'm just saying, I think you're selling yourself short if you settle for a marriage that is less than what you'd hoped for. You're quite remarkable, and if Vince isn't, and he doesn't light you up, then, with all due respect to him, don't marry him.'

'Easy for you to say. You've been married fifteen years and don't have to look at shopping in a market where demand is high and supply is low. And it's not that Vince doesn't light me up . . .'

'I never said it's easy. I just think you deserve someone stellar.'

She smiled. 'Thank you. I'll remember that.' She reached up and scratched my beard. 'You've got some grey in there.'

'Time does that. Along with . . .'

'With what?'

'Hard miles on the chassis.'

We reached the shelter. I got Ashley settled back in her bag, and when I replayed our conversation my words hit me like a brick. The tables had turned. Time and mileage had done that, too.

I packed the sled. She stopped me. 'You OK? You look pale.'

I nodded but didn't look at her. My face would have betrayed me.

WE LEFT THE SHELTER and set out. The snow was frozen, hard on top, making my pulling easy. Ashley was quiet. Tired. Her eyes were sunken, and she'd lost maybe twenty pounds. Her body was working double-time trying to survive and feed the wounds inside her.

Towards lunch time we'd made maybe two miles. A good distance, but it had taken its toll on me. Ashley broke the silence. 'Hey, why don't you rest a while?'

I stopped, hands on my knees, breathing down into my belly. I nodded. 'Sounds good.' I unbuckled myself and pushed the sled to a small flat area beneath two trees.

I stepped and had no time to react. The false top gave way, bent both snowshoes nearly in two and swallowed me to my neck. The impact knocked the wind out of me, jolting my ribs. Water rushed over my knees. I grabbed for anything to stop my fall. I caught the sled. Doing so turned it on its side and threw Ashley and Napoleon out of it, screaming and whimpering.

I pulled, dragging myself from the sucking hole and the stream beneath. Every foothold gave way and whenever I pulled with my right side, the pain sent spasms through my chest. I paused, gathered myself and pulled once. Then again. Then again. Slowly inching myself from the hole. When I beached my body on top of the snow, Ashley lay several feet away, breathing deeply, knuckles white.

I crawled to study her pupils. Shock would show up there first.

She darted a glance, then returned her attention to some speck in the sky she'd focused on. Something she'd learned in tae kwon do.

I was drenched. We were hurt, had no fire, I couldn't get dry and we couldn't get across this valley of hell for at least another day. I could walk in wet clothes, but wet boots were another thing. Both pairs of socks were on my feet. And I'd caught the sled on something that tore a large hole in the area beneath Ashley's shoulders.

I propped her head up, unzipped her bag and carefully studied her leg. The throw had not rebroken it, but it had torqued all the tender attachments and tacky bones that had slowly been resettling and regrowing. It was swelling right before my eyes.

I sunk my head in my hands. If our situation had been bad an hour ago, even dire, it was now circling the bowl of unimaginable.

I didn't have a solution, but I knew we had to get moving. My teeth were chattering. I sat up, pulled off my gaiters, then my boots. 'I know you probably don't feel like talking to me right now, but can I borrow your socks?'

She nodded but didn't look. I slipped them off her feet, wrapped her feet in my jacket and zipped her gently back inside her bag.

Both sleeping-bags came inside what are called stuff sacks. It's paramount to keep down-filled bags dry, so most good ones come with waterproof sacks. I pulled both sacks out of my pack, stuffed my sleeping-bag back inside it, slid on Ashley's socks and slid my feet into the dry sacks, tightened the compression straps, slid into and laced up my boots and then put my gaiters on beneath my trouser legs. A poor solution, but the only one I could think of. I took a few steps. It felt like I was walking in moon boots.

The sled was a much larger problem. I needed to patch the hole. I had nothing but two snowshoes, nearly broken in two. The nets I'd used as their base had been double-folded to support my weight. If I unfolded them . . .

I did, and fastened both sides to either side of the sled. Doing so prevented Ashley from slipping through the hole but it didn't prevent snow from gushing through. My only option was to lift one end of the sled and tie it to me via the harness. Dragging it would make deep marks in the snow, and be bumpy and painful for Ashley.

I didn't see any other way.

I pulled out the food and split it with her. 'Here, this might take your mind off the pain. But go easy. This is the last of it.' I ate my three pieces, which only made me more hungry. I strapped the sled higher on the harness, buckled myself in, and put one foot in front of the other. Then did it again. And again.

I didn't stop until I could go no farther.

I REMEMBER stumbling a thousand times, crawling on my elbows, pulling at tree trunks with my blistered and frozen hands, and the quagmire of more snow than I'd ever hoped to see. I remember walking through the afternoon, through dusk, through the first of night when the moon rose. I remember starlight and low clouds moving in. I remember blowing bitter cold breath. The compass dangled about me. I held it in my palm, let it settle and kept following the arrow. Bright green, glowing in the dark. Rachel had paid a hundred dollars for it a decade ago. Now, it was worth ten thousand.

I woke up face down in the snow. It was pitch dark, no moon, no stars, and my right cheek was cold but, thanks to my two-week beard, not frozen. My hands had cramped from holding on to the front of the sled behind me, trying to prevent Ashley's head from beating about. The straps were cutting into my shoulders and I couldn't really feel my legs.

I stood, pushed into the snow and sank for the ten thousandth time up to my thigh. I had stayed warm because I'd kept moving. But I could move no more and my core was cold. Ashley was either asleep or unconscious. I unbuckled, lifted the harness over my head, crawled beneath an evergreen, kicked away the snow and pulled Ashley in. I rolled out my bag, stripped and climbed inside.

I realised that I did not expect to wake up.

Chapter Nine

The sun was high when I cracked open my eyes. I was sore in places I'd forgotten were part of my body. I wasn't hungry but I was so weak that I didn't want to move.

I rolled over and took a look around. Ashley was looking at me. Her eyes spoke two things: compassion and resolution. As in, resolved to the fate we faced. Even Napoleon looked weak.

My clothes lay in a crumpled, wet pile next to me.

The reality of last night returned, bringing with it hopelessness. Ashley leaned over to me, a strip of meat in her hand. 'Eat.'

Spread across her lap, wrapped in the cups of her bra, lay several strips of meat. My thinking was cloudy. 'Where'd you get it?'

She tapped my lip. 'Eat.'

I opened my mouth, she set a small bite on my tongue and I began to chew. It was tough, cold, mostly sinew, and may have been the best thing I'd ever put in my mouth. I swallowed and she tapped my lip again. We didn't have that much food yesterday. 'Where'd you . . . '

Clarity came with a rush. I shook my head.

She tapped me again. 'Eat this and don't argue with me.'

'You first.'

A tear dripped off her face. 'You need this. You have a chance.'

'We've had this discussion.' I pulled myself up on one elbow and grabbed her hand. 'You want to die out here alone? Let the cold take you?' I shook my head. 'Dying alone is no way to die.'

Her hand was trembling. 'But . . .'

'No buts.'

'Why?' She threw the gnarly piece of meat at me. It ricocheted off my shoulder and landed on the snow. Napoleon jumped up and devoured it. Her voice echoed off the mountains rising up around us. 'Why are you doing this? We're not going to make it!'

'I don't know if we're going to or not, but either WE are or WE are not.'

'If you kept going, you might get a step closer to finding a way out.'

'Ashley . . . I will not live the rest of my life staring at your face every time I close my eyes.'

She curled up, crying. I sat up, staring at my frozen clothes. The only thing dry was my jacket. I needed to figure out where we were. I pulled on my long underwear, then my trousers. Sliding my badly blistered feet into my boots was painful, but not as painful as those first few steps. I pulled my jacket on over my bare skin.

We'd slept in the open and were lucky it hadn't snowed. I turned in a circle, studying the top of the valley in which we'd walked. Dark, heavy clouds were spilling in across the mountains to the north.

I knelt next to her and touched her shoulder. Her face was buried in her bag. 'I'm going to look around.'

One unique thing about the trees around us was the limbs. They were straight, started near the ground and were spaced like ladder rungs. I found one I thought I could climb, slipped off my boots and started up, my arms telling me I weighed a thousand pounds.

At thirty feet, I took a look around. I was amazed at how far we'd come since the evergreen shelter of yesterday. The ridge off which we'd seen the valley lay maybe eight to ten miles behind us. That meant we had to be close. I cupped my hands round my eyes. 'Come on. Please be something.'

Our changed perspective was part of the reason it took me a few minutes to find it. Once I did, I actually laughed. I checked my compass reading, turned the bezel to mark the degree and climbed down.

Ashley wouldn't look at me. I stuffed my bag into the backpack, strapped everything onto the sled, and buckled myself into the harness. The first step sent pain spasms through me. The second was worse. By the tenth, I was numb. Which was good.

I hadn't peed since yesterday. I stuffed a Nalgene bottle with snow and handed it to Ashley. The snow was wet, thick, and I felt more like a plough than a man. The trees obscured my view, so every few feet I'd stop, check my bearing, pick a tree, walk to it, pick another and so on. Every ten minutes I'd take two or three sips. That continued for two or three hours.

When we finally broke through the tree line, the snow started in earnest. The frozen lake spread out before us, stretching an oval mile towards the mountains behind it. The snow obscured my vision, but the sight at the other end was one of the more beautiful things I'd ever seen. I collapsed and hit my knees. My wheezing was deep and my ribs were throbbing.

I crawled round and spun the sled. Ashley's eyes were closed. I tapped her on the shoulder. 'Hey? You awake?'

She stared at me. 'Ben . . . I'm sorry . . .'

I put my fingers to her lips and pointed across the lake.

She craned her eyes, staring through the thickening snow. When she tilted her head and the picture made sense, she started crying.

IT WAS LATE AFTERNOON. *Four seventeen, to be exact. I'd just finished in surgery when my nurses said, 'Your wife's waiting on you.'*

You never just appeared. And you never 'waited' on me. 'She is?'

They nodded but said nothing. They knew. I walked into my office and you were looking at a colour wheel. One of those things that looks like a fan, covered with rows of every shade in the spectrum. You were staring at it, hand on your chin. 'Hey,' you said.

I pulled the blue booties off my feet and threw them in the trash. 'What're you doing here?'

You held the fan thing up to the wall. 'I like this blue. What do you think?'

I scratched my head, looked at the wall. 'You like it better than this sixty-seven dollars a square yard paper we picked out last year?'

You picked up a catalogue off my desk. 'And I like this colour wood. It's not too dark. It's something we can grow with.'

I looked around at the six thousand dollars of swanky office furniture we'd bought in San Marco and began thinking about the money we'd make if we sold all that. I said nothing.

Then you pulled out a portfolio-looking thing. Like those large brief-cases that designers carry their drawings in. You flipped it open across my desk then started tapping each print. 'These remind me of Norman Rockwell. And here are a few Ford Rileys and even a Campay. Just don't know if we have wall space for them all.'

'Honey?'

You looked at me. Eyebrows raised.

'What in the world are you talking about?'

You said it so matter-of-factly. 'The nursery.'

Your words echoed through my office. Nerrrr-serrrr-ieeee. I remember thinking, Didn't they have one of those in Peter Pan?

Maybe a dumb look crossed my face. You took my hand, slid it beneath your shirt and pressed my palm to your stomach. 'The nursery.'

You took my breath away.

I COULDN'T RISK walking across the middle. I had a pretty good feeling the lake was frozen several feet deep but I kept to the shoreline. It was the easiest walking to date. It felt like we were speeding. The distance to the far shore was nearly a mile. We crossed it in a little over thirty minutes.

I pulled Ashley up the small incline and into the trees that lined the bank. Again I turned her so we could both look.

The A-frame construction rose up some forty feet in the air. Its front was entirely glass. A few roof shingles were missing, but on the whole the building was doing fairly well. The front door faced the lake and had been painted yellow. Because the prevailing winds came from behind the building, it was only half covered with snow.

I brought the sled up and spent several minutes pulling away snow and making a ramp. I pushed on the door and it swung easily on its hinges.

The supports for the A-frame were built of lodgepole pine, the floor was concrete and the inside of the building was nearly as large as a basketball court. On the sides, the roof went all the way to the floor and the only windows were at either end. A fireplace—big enough for two people to sleep in—sat off to our right. A huge iron grate filled the middle. Stacked ten feet high in the corner sat six or seven truckloads of wood. Beyond that, two dozen worn pews were mounded on top of one another. Several silver canoes lay atop them, awaiting summer. Off to the left sat a kitchen area, and at the far end, a set of stairs rose to a second floor that was open above the fireplace. Constructed along its length were fifty or sixty bunk beds, all covered with pencil drawings and every manner of lettering detailing who loved who. Along the windowsill lay a hundred dead flies, wasps and other flying insects. Dust covered almost everything, and there were no lights.

Napoleon hopped off the sled, ran into the room, barked, barked again, then turned in four circles, and returned to me wagging his tail and snotting all over my leg.

Slowly, I pulled the sled down the ramp and onto the concrete floor. We stared, awestruck. I pulled Ashley over to the fireplace and began stacking wood for a fire. I started laughing when I found a box of fat lighter next to the pile of wood. Small sticks on the bottom, larger pieces on top, strips of newspaper from an old box. Off on a side shelf, a can of lighter fluid sat next to a box of strike-anywhere matches. I grabbed the can, doused the wood, struck a match and threw it on.

When I began making a doctor's salary, I started taking longer showers. Admittedly, it's a luxury, but I loved the steam in my lungs, the hot water on my back, the way heat allowed me to relax.

We sat mesmerised and . . . bathing.

I was drenched. Every piece of clothing I had on was wet and cold. My hands were chapped and cracking. I knelt, hands held out. Neither of us spoke. I pulled off my wet jacket, sat next to her, put my arms round her shoulders and hugged her.

We'd caught a break. And in doing so, had pushed back the hopelessness that was crowding in, choking the life out of us.

AFTER THE FIRE bled out the cold, I climbed the stairs and searched the bunks. All were empty except one. One twin foam mattress lay wedged and half folded over in a corner. I beat it against the railing, dragged it downstairs and laid it in front of the fire. Napoleon immediately took his place at the end closest to the fire and curled into a ball.

I laid my bag on the mattress, then unzipped Ashley's bag and helped her slowly lift herself to mine. She was weak and needed help to get across. I propped her head on my pack, unbuckled the brace, helped her out of her clothes and hung them across a pew.

With Ashley dry and warm, I pulled off my clothes and spread them out across the pew. I dug in my pack and pulled on my only dry clothing. A pair of Jockey athletic briefs. Then I eyed the kitchen.

The kitchen contained two large black cast-iron wood-burning stoves and several preparation tables. A long stainless-steel sink lined a wall ending in a tall gas hot-water heater. The whole thing looked effective at serving large amounts of food to lots of people.

I tried the faucet but the water had been turned off. I tried to shake the hot-water heater but it was full and wouldn't budge. I lit the pilot light. I stacked the stove with wood, lit it and adjusted the damper. I filled a huge pot with snow, packed it, filled it again, then placed it atop the stove.

On the wall stood a rather menacing-looking door. Large hinges, bolt and padlock. I grabbed the steel poker from the fireplace, wedged it in, broke the hinge and opened the door. On the left side, there were a few paper napkins, a couple of hundred paper plates and maybe a thousand paper cups. On the right, a box of decaffeinated tea bags and one two-gallon can of vegetable soup. That was it.

An hour later, slowly savouring each piece of potato, Ashley looked at me, soup dripping off her chin, and mumbled, 'What is this place?'

I'd given Napoleon a bowl of soup, which he'd inhaled. He now lay at my feet, contentment on his face. 'Some sort of high alpine camp. Boy Scouts maybe.'

She took a sip of tea and turned up her lip. 'Who would make, much less drink, decaffeinated tea? I mean, what is the use?' She shook her head. 'How do you think they get up here?'

'Don't know. I'm pretty sure they didn't stick those iron stoves on their backs and just pack them up here. When my clothes dry, I'll see if I can see any other buildings. Maybe find something.'

She took another bite. 'Yeah, like more food.'

Two bowls later, we lay in front of the fire. Not hungry for the first time in days. I stared out of the window. Snow was falling thick, a total whiteout. I rolled up my jacket and placed it behind her head.

She grabbed my hand. 'Ben?'

'Yeah.'

'Can I have this dance?'

'If I move, I'll throw up all over you.'

She laughed. 'You can lean on me.' I hooked my arms beneath her shoulders and lifted her gently. She wasn't too steady, so she hung onto me. I moved to set her back down, but she shook her head. 'One dance.'

I'd lost so much weight that my underwear was hanging low on my hips. She was wearing a baggy T-shirt that needed to be burned and her underwear sagged where her butt used to be. I held her waist and we stood without moving. Her leg was badly swollen, nearly half the size again of her right leg.

I nodded.

Eyes closed, she was swaying. She put her arms round my neck, humming a tune I couldn't understand. She sounded drunk.

I whispered, 'Let's not hear any more of this nonsense about me going on alone. Deal?'

Quiet, she rested my hand between her chest and mine. 'Deal.'

The top of her head came just above my chin. I leaned in, touched my nose to her hair and breathed.

After a few minutes she said, 'What exactly are you wearing?'

The athletic briefs were bright, neon green. 'I was always making fun of Rachel's underwear. All function and no form. I wanted something with a little imagination. One year for her birthday, I bought her this awful pair of granny panties. Covered up half her torso. In retribution, she actually wore them . . . and . . . to top things off, bought me these things.'

Ashley raised both eyebrows. 'They come with batteries?'

'When she gave them to me, she addressed the card to "Kermit".'

'I don't think Kermit would be caught dead in those things.'

'Yeah . . . well, I wear them sometimes.'

'Why?'

'To remind myself that, among other things, I have a tendency to take myself a little too seriously.'

'Then I'd wear them, too.' She laughed.

When she grew tired, I laid her down on her bag and poured some more tea. I elevated her broken leg. It needed ice. I laid my bag out across the concrete, patted Napoleon, who was snoring, and as I lay back it hit me that during all that dancing, when Ashley's body leaned against mine, when the feeling of her as friend and woman warmed me, I hadn't once thought of my wife.

Chapter Ten

Dawn outside. New snow piled high. Pulling on dry clothes was worth its weight in gold. Ashley lay sleeping. Her face was flushed, and she was muttering in her sleep, but she looked warm and, for the first time in weeks, not uncomfortable. I found the lever on the wall that supplied the hot-water heater, broke it loose and turned it on. Brown, rusty water spilled into the sink. I ran it until it turned clear, then turned up the heat. A bath sounded like a good idea.

I slid the hatchet into my belt, grabbed the bow and set out in search of other buildings. Napoleon beat me to the door, jumped in the fresh powder, sank to his belly and lay there grounded. I picked him up and cradled him. He growled at the snow as we walked. Flakes landed on his face and he snapped at them. I scratched his stomach. 'I like your attitude.' The morning was bitterly cold.

There were seven buildings in all. One was a bathroom. I found a few bars of soap and rolls of toilet paper. Five were cabins, one-room A-frames, each with a wood-burning stove, carpet and a loft. One even had a reclining chair. All were unlocked.

The seventh was a two-room cabin. Maybe the Scoutmaster's. The back room had three bunks. A thick green wool blanket lay folded at the end of each foam mattress. One bed even had a pillow. In a closet I found white towels and a thousand-piece jigsaw puzzle. In the front room sat two chairs, a wood-burning stove and an empty desk. A 3-D map with white-capped plastic mountains was thumbtacked to the wall. It didn't give distances. Across the top it read, 'HIGH UINTAS WILDERNESS', and along one side, 'WASATCH NATIONAL FOREST'. And in the right-hand corner were the words, 'ASHLEY NATIONAL FOREST'.

Fitting, I thought. A small dialogue balloon with an arrow pointed to the centre of the Ashley. It read, '*Foot and horse traffic only. No motorised vehicles allowed at any time.*'

Along the bottom, the map read in large letters, '1.3 MILLION ACRES OF WILDERNESS EXCITEMENT FOR THE WHOLE FAMILY.' Round the edges were cartoon pictures of guys on snowboards, girls on horses, couples on snowmobiles. Evanston, Wyoming, sat in the top left-hand corner with Highway 150 leading due south. Small letters across the highway read, '*Closed in winter.*' Interstate 80 bordered the top, running east to Rock Springs. Highway 191 led south to Vernal. Highway 40 ambled west along the bottom before intersecting Highway 150 north to Evanston.

Somewhere in the middle of that plastic-capped mess, inside the Ashley National Forest, someone had stuck a thumbtack, marked an 'X', and written, '*We are here.*' I pulled it off the wall.

It took three trips to haul everything we needed—including the reclining chair—to the A-frame. As we were coming in the last time, Napoleon spotted something and ran off into the trees snarling, his feet spewing snow. Ashley was still sleeping, so I dumped my goods and slid the chair close to the fire. I checked the door for Napoleon but all I could hear was a distant bark. I figured that, of the three of us, he was probably most able to take care of himself. In one sense, we were holding him back.

I returned to the kitchen and built a fire in one of the cast-iron stoves. The sink had been welded out of stainless steel or zinc and sat on legs as round as my arm. It was deep and big enough to sit in. I washed it out and filled it with water as hot as I could stand. When I sat in it, steam was rising off the top. It was one of the more magnificent moments I'd had in the past few weeks.

After I bathed, I plunged our clothes in the water, scrubbed each piece and then hung them over the pew. I poured two mugs of tea and returned to Ashley, who had just begun to stir. I helped her sit up and she sipped. After her third sip, she sniffed the air. 'You smell better.'

'Found some soap.'

'You bathed?' She set down her mug. 'Take me to it.'

'OK, but we'll need to ice the swelling when you get out.'

I helped her hobble to the sink. Doing so, she caught sight of her legs. 'You didn't happen to find a razor, did you?' I helped her sit on the edge and lowered her in. Slowly, she bent her left knee, laying it flat across the prep area of the sink. She leaned her head back on the built-in dish drainer, closed her eyes, and held out her hand, her finger hooked where the mug would be. I brought her tea and she said, 'I'll be with you in a little while.'

'You'll never believe the name of the national forest we're in.'

'Try me.'

'It's called the Ashley National Forest.'

She was laughing as I walked off.

So you were four and a half months. You were lying on the table, the nurse squeezed that 'goo', as you liked to call it, and rubbed your stomach with a wand. I handed her an envelope and said, 'We'd rather you not tell us now, so if you don't mind, just write whether it's a boy or girl, then seal it. We'll open it at dinner.' She nodded and showed us the head, the legs, even a hand. It was the most magical thing.

Then she started laughing. We should have picked up on it, but she just wrote on the card and handed me the envelope saying, 'Congrats. Mom and baby are healthy.'

You kept asking as we drove, 'What do you think? Boy or girl?'

I said, 'Boy. Definitely a boy.'

'What if it's a girl?'

'OK. Girl, it's definitely a girl.' I laughed. 'I don't care. I'll take whatever kid comes out of the oven.'

Our favourite restaurant. Matthew's. We parked, I opened the door and they seated us in a booth in the back. You were glowing. I don't remember what we ordered. Matthew came out of the back, said hello, and sent us some champagne when he left. We sat there, champagne bubbles bubbling, candlelight flickering off your eyes, and the envelope lying on the table. You pushed it to me. I pushed it back and kept my hand on top. 'You do it. Honey, you've earned it.' You pulled out the note. Laughing. Neither one of us could talk. Then you read it.

I guess you read it two or three times. 'Well . . . what is it?'

You grabbed my hands. 'It's both.'

'Come on. Quit kidding. It can only be one.' Then it hit me. I stared at your tears streaming down. 'Really?'

You nodded and buried your face in your napkin. I stood and banged my champagne glass with my knife. 'Ladies and gentlemen, I'd just like to announce that my wife is giving me twins for Christmas.'

We bought champagne for the entire restaurant.

Driving home, you didn't say a word. Your head was spinning. We walked in the door and you said, 'You thought about names?'

'Not really.'

'Michael and Hannah.'

The moment you said it, it clicked. Like pieces of a puzzle snapping together. From then on, it became the four of us.

Maybe that was the moment. Maybe if I could go back and start over, bathed in the crazy thought of two of everything, I'd go there.

Because I'm pretty sure I wouldn't go much beyond that.

NAPOLEON HAD BEEN GONE awhile. When my clothes dried, I grabbed the bow, zipped up my jacket and stepped outside. I whistled but heard nothing. I followed his zigzag footprints up a hill then along a ridge. They were hard to follow as snow was filling them. I crossed a second hill and saw him down near the lake, hunkered over what looked like a red ball of fuzz. When I got close enough for him to hear me, he growled. Part of a rabbit lay beneath him. 'Hey, boy. Good job. How would you feel about finding two more and dropping them off at the big house up there?'

He looked at me, ripped, chewed and snorted. Picked up what was left and carried it farther from me. 'Suit yourself.'

Walking back gave me time to think. I took a different route. Several times I crossed moose tracks. Many times I crossed rabbit tracks.

I needed practice with the bow, but if I missed the target, the arrow could penetrate several feet into the snow and I'd never find it. Wouldn't take long to lose all the arrows.

I returned to the A-frame, stoked the fire and checked on Ashley, who was frolicking about like a dolphin and told me to go away. I went to one of the other cabins and pulled up a piece of carpet. Back at our place, I laid it over a pew and tacked a paper plate to its centre. In the centre of the plate I cut a hole the size of a dime.

The A-frame was more than forty yards long. I needed only about fifteen. I counted off the steps and drew a line in the dust with my toe. I nocked an arrow, drew, settled the sight, told myself, 'Front sight, front sight, front sight,' and then, 'Press.' I gently squeezed the release. The arrow struck the paper three inches above the hole. I nocked another and it struck just a hair to the right of the first.

I pushed down the peep sight, the little circle inside the string through which your eye looked. I shot again. It brought the arrow's impact down. Just not far enough. I adjusted it again, bringing the impact too far. I re-adjusted, and within thirty minutes I could hit the hole every third or fourth shot, if I held true and still.

Ashley had heard the commotion. 'What's all that racket?'

'Just me trying to improve our chances at getting some dinner.'

'How about helping me out of here.' She'd washed her T-shirt and under-wear and spread them across the dish-drainer grooves. She reached out her hands and I helped her climb out. She wrapped a towel round herself. 'I'm told guys are visual. How're you doing with all this?' she asked, acknowl-edging the elephant in the room.

'I'm still your doctor.' I got her to the reclining chair, which would elevate her leg, taking pressure off it. 'Ashley, I'm not blind. You're beautiful, but I still love my wife. The part of my heart that needs to be filled has been filled. And I want to get home and be able to look a guy named Vince in the eye and hide nothing.' I stared at her. 'I'm separated from my wife because of something I did. Anything that furthered that separation . . .'

She was quiet a minute. 'I envy her.'

'You remind me of her.'

'How so?'

'Well . . . physically, you're lean, athletic, muscular. I imagine you could knock me out with one kick.'

She laughed.

'Emotionally, you don't hide from anything. You put stuff on the table rather than dance round it. And you have a deep reservoir of strength, evidenced by your sense of humour.'

'What's her greatest weakness?'

I didn't want to answer.

'OK, what was her greatest weakness prior to the separation?'

'The thing that's also her greatest strength. Her love for me and the twins. She put us first. Always. Making herself a distant third.'

'What would you prefer?'

'I'd prefer she was selfish like me.' I dusted off a piece of plywood, laid it across her lap and handed her the jigsaw puzzle. 'Found this. The picture's worn off the box, but . . .'

She wiggled off the lid, dumped out the pieces and separated those with edges. 'You want to help?'

'Not a chance. Makes me dizzy just looking at it.'

'It's not that bad.' Her fingers flipped the pieces. 'Just take your time. Eventually, it'll come together.'

I stared at the mess in front of her. 'I don't have the patience.'

'I doubt that.'

I shook my head. 'No thanks.'

GIVEN THE CONTINUING SNOW, the light outside stayed dim and grey. High in the A-frame, ice crystals formed on the window.

The size of Ashley's leg did not encourage me. I carried our large pot outside and made a dozen tightly packed snowballs. I then folded a towel, set it beneath her leg and began rubbing one snowball at a time in circles round the break. She squirmed.

'Just give it a few minutes. Once it turns numb, it'll be better.'

Four snowballs later she turned her head and lay quietly, staring up through the window. I iced her leg for close to thirty minutes. Other than turning her skin bright red, the effect was minimal.

'Every hour on the hour. Got it?'

She nodded. 'Any idea where we are?'

I spread the map and showed her the 'X' that marked our spot.

About then, Napoleon pushed his way through the door and sauntered over like he owned the place. He walked to his corner of the mattress, circled it, then flopped down, tucked his face beneath one paw and closed his eyes. The sides of his muzzle were red and his stomach was rounded.

'Where's he been?'

'Eating breakfast.'

'He save any for us?'

'I talked to him about that but he wasn't having any. I'm going to see if I can't find us some dinner.'

'And then?'

'Well . . . we'll eat until we can't eat any more, then head out.'

'Where are we going?'

'Hadn't got there yet. I'm tackling one crisis at a time.'

I made more snowballs, set them on the far side of the chair and grabbed the bow. 'If I'm not back in an hour, ice that leg.'

THE WIND had picked up, swirling the snow, sending miniature twisters through the trees. I climbed up behind the camp. The ridge circled the lake. Lake on one side, another valley on the other.

I stared at the layout of the camp. People, Boy Scouts, somebody had to get here on something. They didn't just drop in out of helicopters. It was conceivable that they got here only via foot or horseback, but where were those trails? If we were in fact inside the Ashley, we couldn't be too far inside. Certainly, they didn't make boys carrying packs walk across the state. Unless this was a camp for Eagle Scouts only, and I doubted that. It was too big.

I circled south, and it didn't take me long to find it. A winding footpath, wide enough for two horses abreast, that led down from the lake, through the notch in the valley behind us.

I went back. Ashley slept most of the day. Regardless, I continued to ice her leg. Sometimes she woke. Sometimes not. Sleep was the best thing she could do. Every minute spent sleeping was like a deposit in the bank.

Late in the afternoon I slipped out with the bow and returned to the ridgeline where I'd seen the majority of the tracks. I pulled myself up into the arms of an aspen. The cold made it difficult to sit real still. Towards dark, I saw a white flash out of the corner of my eye. When it moved again, the picture came into focus.

Six rabbits sat within fifteen yards of me. I drew slowly, aiming at the closest. I came to full draw, let out half a breath, focused on my front sight and pressed the release. The arrow caught the rabbit between the shoulders. When the others didn't move, I nocked a second arrow and let it fly.

I walked in with two rabbits skewered on a green aspen limb and hung it over the fire. Ashley sat with the jigsaw across her lap. 'Just two? What's the problem?'

'One moved.'

I slow-cooked the rabbit and even happened to find some salt in the pantry. Ashley hovered over a leg, her lips greasy, rabbit in one hand, a bowl of soup in the other, a smile from ear to ear. 'You know, it doesn't really taste like chicken.'

'Who told you it did?'

'Nobody, it's just that everything tastes like chicken.' She pulled out a small bone. 'Nope. That's not entirely true. Since I've been hanging around with you, nothing really tastes like chicken.'

'Thanks.'

A WEEK LATER *we were back at the doctor's. You were throwing up in every trash can between the car and his office. Twins required more ultrasounds, and your doctor wanted to make sure we were on track. And given my place at the hospital, they were, in a sense, taking care of their own. A nice perk.*

They called us in. Another wand smearing goo across your tummy. They strapped the monitor round your stomach and we could hear both heartbeats. Duelling echoes. Everything normal. Right? The technician paused, ran the wand over you a second time and said, 'Be right back.'

Your doc, Steve, strode through the door. He studied the picture and patted you on the leg. 'Sheila here is going to run a few tests. When you finish, come see me in my office.'

I spoke up. 'Steve . . . what's up?'

'Maybe nothing. Let's run the tests.'

I'd have said the same thing if I was trying to figure out how to communicate bad news. I followed him into the hall.

He turned. 'Just let her run the tests.' His face told me plenty.

We sat down opposite him. He was in pain. He stood up, walked round his desk, and pulled up a chair. 'Rachel . . . Ben . . .' He didn't know who to look at. 'You have a partial abruption.'

Rachel looked at me. 'What's he saying?'

He spoke for me. 'It means your placenta has torn away from the uterine wall. I've seen larger tears, but it's not small either.'

'So you're saying . . . ?'

'Total bed rest. Let's give it time. If we can slow it down, everybody will be fine. No need to panic.'

On the ride home, in the car, you put your hand on my shoulder. 'So, what's this mean, Doc?'

'You need to take up needlepoint and find about a hundred movies you've been wanting to see. Maybe read several dozen books.'

'Will we make it?'

'If it doesn't tear any more.'

'And if it does?'

'We're not there, honey, so . . . one hurdle at a time, OK?'

Chapter Eleven

Daylight found me slipping along the ridge. The snow had not lessened. It was approaching three feet of powder, and moving was difficult. I walked an hour but saw nothing. Returning, I spotted a building I'd not seen before. The only thing showing was the top of a pipe chimney. The entire rest of the building was buried in snow.

I circled it, trying to decide where the door would be, and then started pulling at the snow. I found a window. I dug it out, tried to lift it and couldn't. I kicked it and the single pane shattered. I knocked off the sharp edges with the hatchet and crawled in.

It was a storage shed of sorts. Old saddles and bridles hung on one wall. Zebco fishing reels with no line, some tools, several jars of rusty nails. A fireplace with a bellows where it looked like a blacksmith could shoe a horse. On the other wall hung old tyres that looked like they could fit a four-wheeler. Some tubes, even a chain. I scratched my head. If they brought four-wheelers up here, we had to be on the outside border of the Ashley, closer to a road than I'd thought.

Part of me wanted to get excited. To let my heart race. To run down the rabbit trail of all the possibilities, but if I did, and if Ashley read it on my face, and none of my hopes were true, then . . . false hope was worse than no hope at all.

I kept looking. What actually carried everything up here? Pots, pans, food, supplies. Then I looked up.

Above my head, in the rafters, lay six or eight blue plastic sleds made for hauling equipment behind a snowmobile or four-wheeler or horse. I pulled one down. It was about seven feet long, plenty wide enough to lie in, had runners along the bottom, and it didn't weigh fifteen pounds.

I slid it out of the window and was in the process of climbing out when I looked up a final time. There, lying on top of the other sleds, were several sets of snowshoes. This time my heart did race. Someone might have used them to walk up here, and if they could do it, well . . .

Four pairs. They were old, and the bindings were cracking, but the frames were strong, as were the supports. And they were light. I strapped on a pair that fitted and returned to the A-frame, pulling the sled. Ashley stirred, stared over her shoulder. 'What's that?'

'Your blue chariot.' I pulled the harness off the old sled and anchored it to the new one. Between the wool blankets and sleeping-bags, I felt I could make Ashley a good bit more comfortable. 'You get to ride forward in this one.'

'That means I've got to look at your backside the entire time.'

It was good to hear the humour return.

I SLID THE BAG off her leg. The swelling had gone down and the skin was not as taut. Alongside her, spread across the plywood, portions of the puzzle were beginning to take shape. The picture was fuzzy but one section looked like a snow-capped mountain.

An hour before dark, I set the puzzle in her lap. 'I'll be back.'

I strapped on the snowshoes and slipped along the ridge in search of something to eat. The snow wasn't falling as heavily, but it was still falling. Silence was the loudest noise I heard.

After maybe a mile I found a lot of tracks merging into a ravine. The snow was all torn up. I set up under an aspen and waited. Didn't take long. A fox ran through the ravine and disappeared before I could draw. A doe soon followed, but it got wind of me and took off at light speed. That's about when I figured my hide wasn't all that great. Either that, or the animals were smelling the soap. This hunting stuff wasn't as easy as it looked on TV.

It was almost dark so, rather than move, I stayed put five more minutes. One rabbit appeared and hopped down into the ravine and up the other side. It stopped, and I let the arrow fly. Fortunately for us, I did not miss.

I retraced my steps to Ashley. Napoleon was gone and she was asleep in the chair. I boiled some water, steeped tea bags and sat alongside her while I turned the rabbit above the fire.

When I'd sufficiently burned it, she woke and we ate slowly. Chewing every bite longer than normal. Savouring what we could. It was barely enough to feed one, much less two.

Napoleon returned shortly after. I had really grown to like him. He was tough, tender when needed and did a pretty good job of taking care of himself. He walked, licking his red muzzle, to his section of mattress, circled, rolled over and stuck his feet in the air. I rubbed his tummy and he started involuntarily kicking one leg.

When I leaned over, my recorder slipped out of my shirt pocket. Ashley spoke without looking at me. 'Have the batteries held up?'

'Thanks to the airport, batteries are not a problem.'

'Those batteries the same size you use for your shorts?'

'Very funny.'

'So what are you telling her?'

I didn't respond.

'Is that too personal?'

'No . . . I have described the snow and the crappy situation in which we find ourselves.'

'You saying you don't like having me as a travelling companion?'

'No, other than having to haul you halfway across Utah, you're a great travelling companion.'

She laughed. 'Why don't you tell her what you miss about her?'

The moon must have been shining behind the clouds because an eerie and bright light shone. 'I've told her a good bit. Why don't you tell me what you miss about Vince.'

'Let's see . . . I miss his cappuccino maker, and the smell of his Mercedes, his sparse, clean penthouse . . . the view off the balcony at night. If the Braves are playing you can see the lights of Turner Field. Boy . . . a hot dog would be good right now. What else? I miss his laughter. And he's very good at calling even when he's busy.'

I lay awake a long time, thinking. She had told me very little about Vince.

A MONTH PASSED. *You were ready to climb the walls. Couldn't wait for the next ultrasound. We got to the hospital, and the attendant squirted the goo and waved the wand. Steve watched the screen.*

The attendant stopped circling and looked at him. A blank stare. You said, 'Somebody better start talking to me.'

Steve handed you a towel and the technician left. I helped you wipe the goo off and sat you up. Steve leaned against the wall. 'The tear has worsened. A lot. This doesn't mean you can't have more kids, Rachel. It's an anomaly. You can have more children.'

You looked at me so I translated. 'Honey, the abruption has . . . worsened. Sort of hanging by a thread.'

You looked at Steve, 'Are my babies OK?'

'For the moment, but . . . '

You held up your hands. 'But, what? What else is there to talk about? I stay on bed rest. I rent a hospital room, do something. Anything.'

'Rachel . . . if it tears . . . '

You shook your head. 'But as of this moment, it hasn't.'

'If you were in theatre right now, and I was scrubbed for surgery, and it tore, I'm not sure I'd have enough time to get them out before you bled to death. Your life is in danger. I need to take the babies.'

You looked at him like he'd lost his mind. 'I'm not letting you do it.'

'If you don't, none of you will make it.'

'What chance do I have? I mean, in per cent.'

'If I wheel you into surgery right now, real good. Beyond that, the numbers fall off a cliff. Even if we monitor you, we won't know it until

it's too late. Once it tears, the internal bleeding will . . . '

'But it is conceivable that if I can lie real still for the next four weeks, I can have a C-section? Is there a chance we'd make it?'

'Technically, yes, but you have better odds in Vegas. It's like walking round with a cyanide tablet in your stomach.'

You held a finger in the air. 'Is there a chance we could make it?'

'Technically, yes . . . but . . .'

You pointed at the screen. 'I've seen their faces. You showed them to me. I'll not sleep the rest of my life looking at their faces on the backs of my eyelids. Wondering if in reality they'd have made it and if it weren't for your dire predictions, they'd be right here.'

I piped in. 'How long do we have to make this decision?'

Steve shrugged. 'I can push it to first thing tomorrow morning.' He looked at you. 'You can have more children. This is not something you will incur again. It's a fluke. An accident of nature.'

'Steve . . . we didn't have an accident. We made babies,' you replied.

The ride home was quiet.

I parked and met you on the porch. The breeze was tugging at your hair. I spoke first. 'Honey, let me get you in bed.'

You nodded and I propped you up. We sat staring out across the waves. The ocean was choppy.

The silence was thick. 'Hey . . . your chances aren't real good.'

'Like what are they?'

'I'd say less than ten per cent. Steve doesn't think it's that much.'

'Seventy-five years ago this wasn't even an issue. People didn't have this much information.'

I nodded. 'You're right. Now technology is giving us a choice.'

'Ben . . . we made our choice. That night, about five months ago. It's the risk we took then and it's the one we're taking now.'

I bit my lip.

You placed my palm on your stomach. 'I can see their faces, Michael has your eyes and Hannah has my nose . . . I know which side of their lips turn up when they smile, whether or not their ear lobes are connected, the wrinkles in their fingers. They are a part of me. Of us.'

'This is selfish. Five per cent is nothing. It's a death sentence.'

'It's a sliver of hope. A possibility.'

'You're willing to bet on a sliver?'

'Ben, I will not play God.'

'I'm not asking you to play God. I'm asking you to let Him work it out. Let God be God.'

The tears came in earnest. 'What per cent is enough for you? If Steve had a different number, what would that number be?'

'Somewhere north of fifty.'

You shook your head. Touched my face. 'There's always hope.'

I was angry. Bitter. I couldn't change your mind. The very thing I loved about you—your laser-beamed focus, anchored strength—was the thing I was fighting. 'Rachel, you're playing God with you.'

'I love you, Ben Payne.'

'You don't love me. And you don't even love them. You just love the idea of them. If you did, then you'd be in surgery right now.'

'It's because of you that I love them.'

'Forget them. I don't want them. We'll make more.'

'Are you absolutely certain it'll tear loose?'

'Rachel . . . I've spent the past fifteen years of my life studying medicine. I come at this with some credibility. This will kill you. You will die and leave me alone. Why are you being so stubborn? Think about someone other than yourself for a minute.'

You turned, amazement in your eyes 'Ben . . . I'm not thinking about me. One day you'll see that.'

'Well, you're certainly not thinking about me.'

I changed, laced up my shoes and tore out the door, nearly slamming it off its hinges. I took off running.

A half-mile down the beach, I turned. You were on the porch, leaning against the railing. Watching me.

When I close my eyes, I can still see you.

And whenever I get to this point in our story I never know how to talk about what comes next.

Two DAYS PASSED. Three weeks since the crash. One moment, it seemed like a year. At another, like a day.

I woke and found myself groggy, holding my head in my hands. In the past couple of days we'd eaten rabbit and two ground squirrels. I needed a massive influx of calories. As soon as I strapped on that harness, all bets were off. We needed several days' worth of stored food. To set out before was to invite a cold, hungry death.

Ashley woke, stretched and said, 'I keep hoping to crack open my eyes and find that you've hauled us out of this place, back to where the smell of Starbucks lures me on my way to my office and my biggest struggle is road rage and where Advil exists and'—she laughed—'disposable razors and shaving cream are found.'

I scratched my face. The beard had come in thick and grown past the place where it itched. 'Amen to that.'

She lay back. 'I'd give a thousand dollars for some scrambled eggs, cheese grits and sausage. Book-ended by a pot of coffee and a Danish.'

I walked to the kitchen to boil water. 'You're not helping me.'

I MASSAGED Ashley's legs, and was encouraged by both the healthy blood flow and lack of swelling. I got her settled in the recliner and told her, 'I might be gone most of the day.' She nodded, pulled Napoleon up onto her lap, and I set the puzzle next to her. I packed my bag into my pack, buckled on the snowshoes, grabbed the bow and hatchet and set off round the lake.

I'd brought along both of Grover's fly reels in the event I could make a few snares. The wind had picked up and tiny flakes, thick, stung my face. I walked in the direction I'd spotted a cow moose and her yearling days before. Where tracks suggested animal traffic I cut branches and spread debris to narrow the lane of travel and hung loops just off the surface of the snow.

When I reached the other end of the lake, I found moose tracks everywhere. Standing-around-eating tracks. Wasn't hard to figure out. The moose stood on the lake, and the ice and snow allowed them to eat higher on tree limbs extending over what, during summertime, was water.

I needed a blind, a place to hide. I picked out an aspen with branches low to the ground about thirty yards downwind from where they fed. I cut branches, inserted them into the tree to thicken it so nothing could see me from behind, then dug out the snow beneath the tree and packed it up into the underside of the branches to block the wind. I cut a small 'window' in front of me to shoot through, nocked an arrow, slid into my bag up to my chest and began the long wait. Around lunch time I shot a rabbit and buried it in snow. By midafternoon, I'd seen nothing so I napped, waking before dark.

Night fell and I walked back. The first snare was untouched, the second had been moved, suggesting something had bumped it. I reset it and trudged home, realising I needed to increase my chances. Sort of like Bingo. If you really want to win, play more boards.

I cleaned the rabbit, hung it over the fire, and after an hour or so we ate. Ashley was chatty, the consequence of my having left her alone all day. I was not. I'd been left alone with my thoughts and questions I couldn't answer. She picked up on it. 'You don't want to talk, do you?'

I'd finished eating and I was stripping line off Grover's fly reels, making new snares. 'Sorry. Guess I don't multitask very well.'

'You run the ER at your hospital, right? I imagine you multitask just fine. What is it?'

'Are you interviewing me for an article?'

She raised both eyebrows. Universal women's body language for *I'm waiting.*

The fly line was light green and blended in well with the branches. It should work. I'd cut twelve pieces, all about eight feet in length, and looped the ends with slipknots. I sat on my bed, legs crossed. 'We're at a bit of a crossroads.'

'We've been at one since our plane went down.'

'True, but this one is different. We've got shelter here, warmth, maybe somebody will stumble upon us, but I think that'd be two or three months off. If we head out, we're taking our chances on shelter and food. If we increase our food stores we could probably last a week or two out there. But we're left with one big unknown.'

'Which is?'

'How far do we have to go? We don't know if we're twenty miles or fifty. There's four feet of fresh powder, and avalanches will be a constant concern. What if I walk you into that mess only to get us both killed when we might have got lucky and held out?'

'Sounds like you're in a pickle.' She lay back. 'Let's sleep on it. You can give me your decision in the morning.'

'Me? I'm not deciding for us. We are. You're not listening.'

She pulled Napoleon up under her arm and pulled the bag round her shoulders. It was dark except for the fire. 'Let me know when you get round to voicing the thing that's really bothering you.'

I scratched my head. 'I just did.'

'Nope. It's still in there.' She pointed towards the door. 'Why don't you go for a walk. And take your recorder. By the time you get back, you'll have figured it out.'

'You . . . are annoying.'

She nodded. 'I'm trying to be more than just annoying. Now go for a walk. We'll be here when you get back.'

DID YOU HAVE something to do with this? I don't know how you did it, but I'd bet you put her next to me on the plane. I'm not sure what she's talking about. Well, maybe I do a little, but that doesn't make her right. OK, it makes her right.

But what am I supposed to do? I haven't hunted seriously since Granddaddy took me in school. Well, a few deer hunts but we just hung out. Granddaddy took me hunting because he should've taken dad and dad grew up a jerk. I was the consolation prize. Which was fine, I loved him, he loved me and it got me out from under dad's thumb, but if we didn't shoot anything, neither of us died. We stopped at Waffle House on the way home.

Out here, if I miss, we die. It matters. A lot. I just didn't know when I got on Grover's plane that I was going to have to hunt my way out of this eternal wilderness. A lot of people have survived much worse conditions, but it's not like I have any idea what I'm doing and I'm scared that if I don't get it figured out, that girl in there is going to die a slow, painful death.

There. I said it. I feel responsible. How can I not? She should be back at her office, racing to meet a deadline, phoning her friends, glowing in post-wedding bliss. Not lying helpless in the middle of nowhere with a bumbling, tongue-tied idiot who's slowly starving her.

I've got nothing to offer her. And, I've got nothing to offer you. What is it with you women? Can't us guys NOT have the answer? Can't we NOT know what's going to happen next? Can't we be incapable and broken and worn down and disheartened?

But, I'm not telling you anything you don't already know.

I'm sorry for yelling at you. This time . . . and the last.

Guess I needed to get this off my chest. But I'm not telling her.

OK, I heard you. I'll tell her. I know she's lying there with a broken leg dependent upon a stranger. Although we're not as much strangers now as we once were. And NO, it's not what you're thinking. Well, of course, I find her attractive. She's incredible. Honey, she's getting married and I'm trying to get her home to her fiancé.

I'm not having this conversation with you.

No, I'm not having a tough time with all this. I'm missing you.

OK, maybe it's a little tough. There. I said it. It's not easy . . .

Honey . . . I didn't think I'd make it this far. Could it get worse? This is not the worst thing. The worst thing is being separated from you. That's ten times tougher than being stuck out here.

I'm going to bed now. I'm sorry for raising my voice at you.

Both now . . . and then.

THE FOLLOWING DAY, I was out early. Setting twelve snares took the better part of the morning. I set them up round the lake. Some on the bank, some inland a hundred yards.

I got settled in my blind in the midafternoon. I sat three hours before I saw anything. A young moose, followed closely by its mother, came waltzing onto the lake. It ran out a few feet, the snow above its knees, then ran back to the trees and began feeding. It might have been eight months old. Its mother was huge, probably eight feet at the shoulders. She could have fed us for a year. But we didn't need a year. If I took the calf, the cow would make it. If I took the cow, chances were good the calf would die anyway.

They fed to within forty yards and my heart started beating pretty fast. The snow was blowing into my face, which meant the wind was blowing that way too.

The cow moved to within twenty yards. The calf didn't let her get too far away and moved in closer. Getting within ten yards of me. Any closer and they'd hear my heart beating.

I drew slowly and the mother popped her head up. One big eye looking at me. Or rather the tree. She knew something was in here. She just didn't know what.

I settled the pin on the calf's chest, took a deep breath, let out half and whispered, 'Front sight, front sight, front sight . . . press.'

The arrow disappeared into the chest of the calf. It hopped, bucked, spun in a circle and took off running out across the lake, followed closely by the cow. The mother's head and ears were held high. Full alert. Pounding through the snow.

I caught my breath and allowed my nerves to settle. I'd intended to hit the heart area—causing the calf to die quickly—but I'd flinched and pulled the shot right. That meant the arrow had pierced the lungs which meant that the calf, afraid and in pain, would run. The mother would follow. Once the calf ran into cover, it would stop and listen for her. Seeing her and feeling safe, it would lie down and bleed to death. If I stepped out of my hide and traipsed off after it, I would scare it some more, and push it.

I waited almost an hour, nocked another arrow and stepped out. The blood trail was a red-brick road, trailing out across the lake. I was right. It had been a bad shot. The calf had run a straight path up into the trees. I followed slowly, keeping a lookout for the mother.

It quit snowing, a breeze pushed out the clouds and a full moon shone above me. It was the brightest night I'd seen in a long time. My shadow followed me into the trees. The only sound was my breathing and the sound of snowshoes crunching snow.

A mile later, I found them. The calf had begun climbing up a ridge and, too weak to continue, had toppled and rolled down. The mother stood over it, nudging it. It lay unmoving.

The cow was standing straight up, as was her tail. I hollered, raised the bow high and tried to look bigger than I was. She looked at me, then back over her shoulder. While its nose is quite good, a moose's eyesight is poor. I walked within forty yards, approaching downwind, arrow nocked. I didn't want to shoot her, but if she charged me I wasn't sure I'd have much choice.

I kept the trees close by. At twenty yards, she'd had enough. She charged as if she was shot out of a cannon. I stepped for the trees but tripped on my snowshoes. She caught me with her head and chest, launching me into the limbs of the aspen. I slammed against the trunk, then dove below, wrapping myself into a ball round the base. She snorted, made a deep bellowing sound, shook the limbs with her chest and then stood back listening.

They came all at once.

Eight wolves spilled out of the trees higher up and descended upon the calf. She didn't hesitate. Nine animals collided in a mass of fur, teeth and hoof.

I lay on my belly and watched. She was straddling the calf, kicking. I heard bones crunching and saw wolves flying twenty feet in the air. One jumped from somewhere and latched itself to her hindquarters while another clung to her windpipe and jugular. A third and fourth tore at her from underneath. Two more were atop the calf. With little regard for herself, she sent them spinning like footballs, filling the air with splattering wolf blood and shattered wolf teeth. Within seconds, the wounded wolves had retreated to the trees, whining. She stood in the moonlight, breathing heavily, her blood dripping on the snow, nudging the calf with her muzzle. Every few minutes she'd fill her stomach with air and sound a deep bellow.

The wolves circled for an hour, made one feigned charge, then disappeared over the ridge. In the hours that followed, she stood over the calf, shielding it from the snow that had returned. The field of red she had created slowly turned to white, burying the memory. At daylight, when the calf was little more than a white mound, she bellowed one last time and wandered into the trees.

Quietly, I pulled the calf into the trees. Its hams or hindquarters were gone. Its shoulders, too, had been chewed. I cut out the backstraps, pulled as much meat as I could off the tops of the shoulders and the tenderloins from between the shoulder blades. Doing so gave me enough to feed us for a week to ten days. Or more.

I tied it down in my pack and went to retrieve the bow where I'd dropped it during the charge. It lay in pieces. The limbs had shattered, cams had broken, the string lay in a bird's nest of a mess and all the arrows had snapped when she'd stepped on them. I left it.

I strapped on the snowshoes and walked back to the lake. At the far end I could see the A-frame, the fire glowing bright through the glass. I doubted Ashley had slept.

In the distance the cow bellowed. She'd probably do that all day and into tomorrow. I wasn't sad for killing the calf. We needed to eat. I wasn't sad that the cow was lonely. She'd have another calf. The thing that had my stomach in knots was the sight of the mother, standing over her young.

I reached the outline of the red road. Fresh snow had covered it. I sank my hand into the snow, ran my fingers through the clumps of red. In an hour, there would be no reminder.

Maybe it was my twenty-third morning, my weakened condition, my own weariness, the weight of the recorder pressed against my chest, the fading bellows of the cow, the thought of Ashley hurt and worried, maybe it was all of the above. I fell forward on my knees, my pack driving me into the snow. I scooped my hand beneath a red clump the size of my fist, lifted it to my nose, and breathed.

To my left stood a tall pine. Spiralling upwards maybe sixty feet. I unbuckled my pack, pulled the hatchet from my belt and with several good swings, I cut a band, maybe two feet long and an inch or two deep, round the base. Come summer, the sap would trickle out of the scar like tears.

Chances are, it would do that for years.

You were right . . . You were right all along.

Chapter Twelve

Ashley's face told me all I needed to know. I shuffled in and put down my pack. I didn't realise how drained I was until I tried to speak. 'I tried to call but the line was busy and . . .'

She smiled and fingered me closer. I knelt next to her. She raised her hand to my left eye. 'You've been cut. Deep, too. You OK?'

Next to her, the puzzle lay complete, a panoramic view of snowcapped mountains and a sun behind. I turned my head. 'Is that a sunrise or sunset?'

'I think that depends on the eyes of the viewer.'

I spent the day cutting strips of meat and slow-cooking them over the fire. Ashley held up a small mirror and flinched while I sewed up the skin above my eye.

She asked me to run her a bath, which I did. While she bathed, I packed the sled. My pack, our bags, the blankets, the hatchet, the meat. Anything that wasn't necessary, I left. I helped Ashley out of the bath, got her tucked in bed, then bathed myself.

I was asleep by nightfall and slept until just before daylight. Maybe twelve hours in all. The longest stretch in ages.

I cut the foam pad to fit into the sled, laid two blankets atop it then dressed Ashley, zipped her up in her bag with my jacket, slid her onto the sled and lifted her head onto a folded blanket. The sled was hollow in the middle, putting a pocket of air between her and the snow. I tied the tarp across her and tucked in Napoleon alongside her.

I strapped on my gaiters, grabbed the matches and lighter fluid, buckled myself into the harness, took one last look at the warm fire and pulled her out of the door, back into the never-ending snow.

Surprisingly, I felt good. Not tired and not as weak. If I had to guess I'd say I'd lost more than twenty pounds since the crash. Maybe twenty-five. A lot of that was muscle. Meaning I'd lost strength as well. The good news was that, for the snowshoes, I was a bit lighter now on my feet.

I tied a long tether from the harness round my shoulders and handed her the loose end. 'If you need me, just tug that.'

She nodded, looped the tether over her wrist, and tucked the tarp up under her chin.

Within minutes we were climbing up the ridge en route to the trail leading out of the valley and through the notch. I seldom felt much tension on the harness because the sled glided well, but the snow was blowing into my face, landing on my eyelashes, blurring my vision. Our path took us down small hills and up short rises but on the whole we were losing elevation and, thankfully, the path was mostly clear.

By lunch, I calculated we'd walked three miles. By midafternoon, we'd covered six. Towards dusk, the trail came down off a small hill and flattened out. I'd pushed it, and hard. I looked behind us, thinking back through each turn. Maybe we'd covered ten miles.

WE SPENT THE NIGHT beneath a makeshift shelter using our tarp, which had grown tattered, and some branches I cut to help shed the snow. Ashley lay snug on the sled. She shrugged. 'There's only room on here for one.'

A blanket and my bag separated me from the snow. 'I miss our fire.'

'Me too.'

Napoleon was shivering. I pulled him up close. He sniffed me and my bag, hopped across the snow and dug himself in with Ashley. She laughed. I rolled over and closed my eyes. 'Suit yourself.'

By midmorning we'd come down another four or so miles and the temperature was warmer. Maybe around freezing—the warmest it'd been since the crash. On the hillsides, small shoots shot up through the snow, suggesting that the ground rested only a few feet beneath us. While we had lost elevation, down as much as nine thousand feet, the snow was wet and pulled at the sled, increasing the workload.

Around mile five, the trail dropped down, widened again and straightened. Almost unnaturally. I stopped and scratched my head.

Ashley spoke up. 'What's wrong?'

'This thing is wide enough to drive a truck down.' That's about when it hit me. 'We're on a road. There's a road beneath us.'

To our right, I saw something flat, green and shiny sticking up through the snow. Took me a minute to figure out what it was. I brushed away the snow. It said, 'EVANSTON 62.'

'I want to see. What's it say?'

I stepped back into my harness. 'It says Evanston, this way.'

'How far?'

I shook my head. 'You really want to know?'

A pause. 'Not really.'

I leaned into the harness. 'That's what I thought.'

'Can you pull this thing as far as it says we need to?'

'Yes. We can make it.'

'You sure? 'Cause if you're not just tell me. Now would be a good time to come clean if you don't think . . .'

'Ashley?'

'Yes.'

'Shut up. Please.'

We walked five miles, most of which sloped downhill. It was relatively blissful walking. Night came, but with colder temperatures the sled slid easier so I walked a few hours more. Putting ten miles on the road. Twenty-five since the A-frame.

Some time after midnight, I saw an odd shape to my right. I unbuckled and investigated. A building, eight feet square, with a roof and a concrete floor. I dug out the door and slid the sled down into it. A laminated sign hung on the wall. I lit a match. It read: 'THIS IS AN EMERGENCY WARMING HUT. IF THIS IS AN EMERGENCY, WELCOME. IF IT'S NOT, YOU SHOULD NOT BE IN HERE.'

Ashley's hand found mine in the darkness. 'Are we OK?'

'Yeah, we're good. Except . . .' I unrolled my bag and climbed in. The floor was hard. 'I miss my foam mattress.'

She was quiet.

'How's the leg?' I asked.

'Still hurts.'

'Differently or the same?'

'Same.'

'Let me know if it starts feeling different.'

'And when it does, just what will you do about it?'

'Probably amputate it. That way it'll quit hurting.' I closed my eyes. 'Your leg is fine. It's healing nicely.'

'I want to ask you a question and I want an honest answer. Could we get back to the A-frame? I mean . . . is it still an option?'

My bag had become tattered, having lost some of its down. Sleep would not be easy. I thought through the miles since the A-frame. I was pretty sure I could not make it back. 'Yeah . . . it's an option.'

'Are you lying to me?'

'Maybe.'

'So, there's no going back? We'll never see the A-frame again?'

'Something like that.' I stretched out flat, staring up at the ceiling. After a few minutes, she quietly slid her hand inside my bag and placed it flat across my chest.

It stayed there all night.

WE STARTED AGAIN at daylight. Ashley was chatty but I was feeling the effects of yesterday. Not to mention the fact that our road was turning upwards. Gradual at first, it turned ugly four miles into the morning, slowly snaking and twisting its way up the mountain I'd been staring at for two days. Given the incline and the wet, sticky snow, pulling the sled became a lot harder. By lunch, we'd made five miles total and probably regained a thousand feet in elevation. And the road was still going up.

By dusk, we'd made a total of seven miles, but I was spent and my legs were cramping. I needed several seconds' rest between steps. I kept hoping we'd find another warming hut but we didn't.

We camped next to an aspen. I was asleep before my head hit the ground, but I woke in the middle of the night. I slipped on my boots, strapped on the snowshoes and went for a walk. The road was winding tighter towards the summit. It turned left sharply and I bent over, catching my breath.

Standing straight, I stared out across the darkness. The clouds were low, tucked down into the mountains. Cotton on a wound.

Beyond that, maybe thirty or forty miles, it cleared.

I UNTIED THE TARP and startled Ashley. 'What? What's going on?'

'I want you to see something.'

'Right now?'

'Yep.'

I buckled up and began pulling. What had taken me fifteen minutes alone now took an hour. I was winded and my stomach and neck muscles were sore. The straps were cutting into my shoulders.

We rounded the corner and we waited for the view to clear. After a few minutes I pointed. A single light bulb sparkled some forty miles in the distance. Beyond its orangeish glow, to the north, was a single trail of smoke.

She clutched my hand and neither of us said a word. I took a reading on the compass, careful to let the needle settle. Almost due north.

The sun rose. I needed to sleep but knew I couldn't. I was too excited. We trudged across the snow thinking about a world out there with electricity, running hot water, microwaveable food and coffee bars.

The mountain plateaued. We walked several miles across what felt like the top of the world. The wind, straight on, burned my face, the air was thin and the snow stung my cheeks. I leaned into it, numb, counting the miles in my head. Maybe forty-five to go.

After that, I walked counting backwards to myself. 'Forty-two to the light bulb . . . forty-one to the light bulb . . .'

When I got to forty, we came down into a saddle protected from the wind. Halfway through it we discovered another warming hut. Three bunk beds with mattresses, a fireplace and enough wood for an entire winter. Above the door, it read, 'RANGER'S CABIN'. Inside, I found the same laminated sign.

Given the lighter fluid we'd stolen from the A-frame, getting a fire going was easy. I got Ashley settled, fell into bed and don't remember falling asleep.

SHE SHOOK ME. 'Ben . . . you in there?'

'Yeah.'

The day was full. Overcast but not snowing. I didn't know what time it was, but it had to be close to lunch. 'You slept a long time.'

I looked around, trying to remember where we were.

My legs were sore. My feet felt like hamburger meat. In truth, all of me was sore. I ate, sipped and wondered how far we could get today. Thirty minutes later, I was leaning into the harness, pulling.

The road turned right and started descending. We were soon to lose several thousand feet of elevation. The problem was such drastic change meant steep pitches and the possibility of the sled getting away from me.

The first four or five miles were gradual decline, easy walking. At one point, the sun broke through and we saw blue skies. But late in the afternoon the road corkscrewed and looked like it dropped off a table top. I took it easy, winding my way so the sled wouldn't pick up speed. With an hour to go before dark, the road turned in a huge horseshoe that curved some ten miles in the distance. It bent round a valley a half mile across. I weighed the difference—ten miles versus a half mile. If I worked us slowly down with a rope, anchoring on a tree, moving tree to tree, we'd be across the valley before nightfall. With luck, we'd make the light bulb tomorrow.

I turned to Ashley and explained. She eyed the distance, then the steep quarter-mile to the valley below. 'Think we'll get down that?'

We'd been down steeper when we left the crash site, but hadn't traversed anything this long. 'If we take it slow.'

She nodded. 'I'm game if you are.'

There was a little voice inside my head, whispering, 'Shorter is not always better.' I should've listened to it.

I CHECKED the harness ropes and the sled was secure. I tied the snowshoes to the sled and began easing down. My boots cut into the snow, giving me leverage to hold the sled back. I lowered Ashley over the ledge; she slowly slid down, pulling the harness tight, then I began picking my way downhill, using the trees as my anchors. It actually worked quite well. I'd step down, dig a foot thigh-deep into the snow, grab a tree or branch, we'd move forwards then I'd do it again. In ten minutes we were halfway down. Napoleon was sitting on Ashley's chest, staring at me. He didn't like it at all.

Two weeks of constant snow meant at times I was waist-deep with another ten feet below me. It didn't take much to set it loose.

I don't remember it letting go. I don't remember tumbling and rolling. I don't remember the harness snapping. And I don't remember coming to an abrupt stop where, even though my eyes were open, all the world went black.

The blood was rushing to my head so I knew I was upside-down and the snow was pressing in on me, allowing only shallow breaths. The only part of me free of the snow was my right foot.

I tried to clench my fists. Pulling in. Pushing out. I tried moving my head back and forth. But I wasn't getting much air and knew I didn't have long. I began shoving. Jerking. Above me, I could see a faint light. Screaming was no use. I worked myself into a frenzy, but I was stuck and chances were good I was going to die upside-down, frozen and suffocating in the snow.

We were so close. Why go through it all to end here?

Something with really sharp teeth began biting my ankle. I heard snarling and began kicking, but it wouldn't let go. Finally I kicked it loose. Seconds later, I felt a hand on my foot. Then snow being pulled away from my leg. From my chest.

Her hand shot in, pulled out the snow round my mouth and I sucked in the sweetest, largest breath of air I'd ever known. She worked out one arm, and with it I righted myself, pulled myself out of that snowy grave and rolled on my side. Napoleon jumped onto my chest and licked my face.

It was almost dark. Ashley lay to my right. She was out of her bag and face down on the snow. Trying not to move. Her hands were cut and bloody. Her cheek was swollen. And then I saw her leg.

We didn't have long and I knew I couldn't move her.

The avalanche had carried us down to the base of the hillside. The harness had evidently saved my life because while the sled surfed the topside it kept me, albeit only for seconds, from being totally swallowed by the snow. When the ropes broke, Ashley shot off like a missile, careening down and colliding with a huge boulder.

She'd worked her way back up to me, crawling. Her leg had rebroken and this time the bone had pierced the skin. It was poking up underneath her trousers. She was in shock, and any movement, without drugs, could send her back into unconsciousness.

'I'm going to turn you.'

She nodded, and I did.

She screamed louder than I'd ever heard a woman scream.

I crawled out across the snow and found the sled by her bag. One blanket lay twisted round it. Everything else was gone. No pack, no food, no tarp, no water bottles, no jacket, no snowshoes, no bow drill and no fire.

I unzipped her bag and laid her in it. Blood had soaked through her trousers and painted the snow. I pulled the sled up next to her, laid the blanket across the bottom, slid her on and wrapped the blanket over her. I wanted to cut away her trousers and look at her leg but she managed a whisper.

'Don't.'

She lay still, unmoving. Her bottom lip was shaking. I'd kill her trying to set the leg in place. She'd lost blood but not much. The bone had come out the top outside her thigh. If it had gone the other way, through the femoral artery, she'd have been dead. As would I.

Snow returned, hastening darkness.

I knelt, whispering. 'I'm going for help.'

She shook her head. 'Don't leave me.'

I tucked the bag round her. 'You've been trying to get rid of me since we started this trip so I'm finally doing what you asked.' I leaned in, my breath on her face. 'I need you to listen to me. Ashley?' She turned to me. The pain was rifling through her. 'I'm going for help. I can't move you, so I'm leaving Napoleon with you and I'm going for help, but I'm coming back.'

She gripped my hand and squeezed tight. 'Promise?'

'Promise.'

She closed her eyes and let go of my hand. I kissed her on the forehead, then the lips. They were warm and trembling and both blood and tears had puddled there.

I'VE SPENT MY LIFE RUNNING. One thing I've learned is to look ahead no more than four or five steps. It helps in long distance because you're in a lot of pain and breaking it into small, do-able pieces is about all you can handle. Others will tell you to focus on the finish line but I can focus only on what's in front of me. If I do that, the finish line will come to me.

So, I put one foot in front of the other. The road wound down towards the valley in which we'd seen the orange light and single smokestack. I figured I had twenty-five to thirty miles to go and, if I was lucky, I was averaging two miles an hour. All I had to do was run until the sun rose over my shoulder.

I closed my eyes, and Ashley was all I could see.

IT WAS THREE, maybe four o'clock in the morning, day twenty-eight, I think. I'd fallen a thousand times and pulled myself up a thousand and one. The snow had turned to sand. I could smell and taste salt. I heard a seagull somewhere. My dad was standing at the guard shack, a scowl on his face.

I slapped the lifeguard's chair, cussed him beneath my breath, turned and picked up the pace. The beach stretched out before me, and every time I thought I was getting close to the house it would fade, reset and another moment would take its place. The past played before me like a movie.

I remember falling, pulling with my hands, standing and falling, again and again.

Many times I wanted to quit, lie down and sleep. When I did, I'd close my eyes and Ashley was still there. Lying quietly in the snow, laughing over a leg of rabbit, chatting from the sled, yakking from the kitchen in the tub, embarrassed over a Nalgene bottle, shooting the flare gun, sipping coffee, pulling me out of the snow . . .

Maybe it was those thoughts that got me up, and helped me put one foot back in front of the other. Somewhere under the moon, on a flat section with a concrete bridge and a river trickling below me, I fell, eyes wide open. The picture changed. I saw her.

Rachel.

Standing in the road. Running shoes on. Sweat on her top lip. Trickling down her arms. She fingered me forward. I tried to move. Snow had frozen round my feet. She held out her hand and whispered, 'Run with me?'

I reached, pulled, took a step and fell. Then again. And again. Soon I was running. Chasing Rachel. Her toes were barely touching the ground and I was back on the track with the girl I'd met in high school.

The road led up to a gate and a sign of some sort. I don't remember what it said. She ran with me, up the hill, towards the sunlight, and when it cleared the mountaintop, I fell. Face forward for the last time. My body would not go. I could run no more. I had done something I'd never done. Reached the end of myself.

She whispered. 'Ben . . .'

I lifted my head, but she was gone. I heard her again. 'Ben . . . get up.'

In the distance, a few hundred yards away, a single column of smoke spiralled above the trees.

IT WAS A LOG CABIN. Snowmobiles parked out front. Snowboards against the porch railing. Lights inside. A fire. Deep voices. Some laughter. The smell of coffee. And . . . pop tarts. I crawled up the drive and pushed open the door. All I could muster was a cracking whisper. 'Help . . .'

MOMENTS LATER, we were screaming across the snow. My driver was wiry, on the short side, and his snowmobile was not slow. With one hand, I held on for dear life. With the other, I pointed up the road. The other two guys followed us. We made it to the valley and Ashley's blue sleeping-bag lay flat against the snow on the far side. She was not moving. Napoleon barked at us and spun Tasmanian-devil circles in the snow. The kid cut the engine. In the distance I could hear the helicopter.

When I made it to her, Napoleon was licking her face and looking at me. He was whining. I knelt. 'Ashley?'

She opened her eyes to look up at me.

THE KIDS POPPED a handheld flare and Life Flight landed in the road. I briefed the medics, they got her breathing oxygen, injected her with painkillers, loaded her onto a stretcher, started an IV and slid her into the single patient bay of the helicopter. I backed out and she reached for my hand and slid something into it. The helicopter lifted and shot across the mountains, blinking red lights fading in its wake.

I opened my hand. The recorder. It was warm where she'd held it close to her. I must have lost it in the avalanche. I pushed the power button, but it would not play. The red warning light for 'low battery' was flashing, keeping time with the one on the tail of the helicopter.

Chapter Thirteen

She lay under a sheet of white, sleeping beneath a fog of sedation. Her vitals were good. Strong. Blue lights and numbers flickered above her. I turned the blinds, keeping daylight at bay. I sat, her hand resting in mine. Her colour had returned.

Life Flight had bypassed Evanston and rerouted her to Salt Lake, where in two hours the ER docs had put in a few bars and pins. When I arrived at Evanston atop a snowmobile, I was loaded in an ambulance and started on an IV. By the time we arrived in Salt Lake, camera crews were everywhere.

They put me in a room and I asked for the Chief of Surgery. His name was

Bart Hampton, and we'd met on more than one occasion at conferences around the States. He, along with the nurse feeding my IV, led me to a viewing room above the operating theatre where we observed the last hour of Ashley's surgery. The intercom allowed the doctors to talk me through what they were doing. There was no need to interfere. My body was trashed, and my hands were little more than raw meat. I was in no condition to be a doctor.

They rolled her into her room. Before my adrenaline could run out I walked in, flipped the switch on the light and viewed her pre- and post-op X-rays. I could have done no better. She'd make a full recovery.

I turned. Blue light lit her forehead, showered the sheets. I pushed her hair back, and gently placed my lips to her cheek. She smelled like soap and her skin was soft. I slid my hand beneath hers. Blister to tenderness. I whispered in her ear, *Ashley, we did it.*

All I wanted to do now was sleep.

THE NEXT THING I knew it was daylight and I was in a bed with white sheets, in a room filled with the aroma of fresh coffee. Bart stood over me holding a Styrofoam cup. The perspective was odd. I was used to standing in his shoes. 'That for me?'

It was good coffee. We talked awhile. I gave him more of the details. When I finished, he said, 'What can I do for you?'

'My dog. Actually, he's not mine but I've fallen in love with the little guy, and . . .'

'He's in my office. Sleeping. Fed him some steak. Happy as can be.'

'I need a rental car. And I need you to protect us from the media until she's ready to talk to them. I'm not.'

'I suppose you have your reasons. You know, when the details of this get out, they're going to want you two on every talk show in the country. You could be an inspiration to a lot of people.'

I stared out of the window, at the white-capped mountains in the distance. It was strange. A month ago I had stood in the Salt Lake City Airport and wondered what was on the other side. Now I knew. I imagine prison bars are the same way. Maybe a grave. 'I just put one foot in front of the other.'

'I called your people at the hospital in Jacksonville. They were elated, to say the least. What else? Seems I could do more to help you.'

'In my hospital, our best nurses tend to stand out. If you . . .'

He nodded. 'She's got them now and will have round the clock.'

'Anybody round here make a latte? Maybe a cappuccino.'

'All you want.'

LATE MORNING she stirred. I went down the hall, bought what I needed and came back. When she cracked an eye, I leaned in, whispered, 'Hey.' She turned slowly. 'I talked with Vince. He's on his way.'

Her nose twitched. 'Do I smell coffee? Can you just drip it into my IV?'

I held the cup to her lips and she sipped. 'Second best cup of coffee I've ever had.'

She laid her head back, tasting the beans. I sat next to her bed. 'Your surgery went well. I consulted your doctor. Knows his stuff. I'll show you the X-rays when you want to see them.'

Out of the window a jetliner was taking off from the airport in the distance. We watched it gain altitude, turn and bank out across our mountains. She shook her head. 'I'm never flying again.'

I laughed. 'They'll have you up and walking in hours. Good as new.'

She smiled. 'It's about time you gave me some good news. I mean, how long have we been hanging out and all you've had for me is one bad bit of news after another.'

'Very true.'

She stared at the ceiling, shuffling her good leg beneath the sheets. 'I really want to take a bath and shave my legs.'

I went to the door and motioned for the nurse. She followed me in. 'This kind lady is Jennifer. I've explained to her where you've been the past month. She'll help you in the shower.' I patted her hand. 'I'll check on you later. Vince lands in two hours.'

She pushed back the sheet, reached for my hand. How do you explain to other people what we'd been through? We'd just walked through a hell that had frozen over. Together. I didn't have the words. Neither did she. 'I know. It takes some getting used to. I'll be back.'

She squeezed my hand tighter. 'You OK?'

I nodded and walked out. I walked downstairs to the Grille. It was typical hospital short-order but it would have to do. I paid for a loaded double cheeseburger with a double order of fries, to be delivered to room 316 in an hour. Then I walked to my rental car.

IT WAS A SIMPLE HOUSE. Not too far from town. White with green shutters. Sat up on a hill. Flowers all around. The mailbox was marked by one of those hollow flags they use at airports to indicate wind direction.

She was sitting on the porch. Rocking. A tall, handsome woman. I stepped out of the car. Napoleon jumped onto the ground, sniffed the kerb, then tore up the sidewalk, flew up the stairs and jumped in her lap. She laughed, hugged him while he licked her face and said, 'Tank, where on earth have you been?'

Tank . . . So, that's his name.

I climbed the steps. 'Ma'am, I'm Ben Payne. I'm a doctor from Jacksonville. I was with your husband when his plane crashed . . .'

She shook her head. 'He didn't crash. He was too good a pilot.'

'Yes ma'am. He had a heart attack. Landed the plane up in the mountains. Saved our lives.' I opened a box and set it next to her. In it sat his watch, his wallet, his pipe and lighter. She touched each item. Her lip trembled and tears dripped off her face.

We talked for several hours. I told her everything I could remember. Where I'd buried him, what the view was like. She liked that.

She opened their album, or albums, and told me their story. It was filled with tenderness. Hearing it hurt. When I stood to leave, what could I say? I fumbled with the car keys. 'Ma'am, I want to . . .'

She inched forward on the rocker, Tank hopped off her lap and she stood slowly, then gave me her hand. I eyed her leg. 'If you need a hip replacement, call me. I'll come out here and do it for nothing.'

She smiled.

I knelt. 'Tank, you're the best. I'll miss you.' He slobbered my face then ran down into his yard and began peeing on every tree he could find. 'I know, you'll miss me, too.'

I gave her my card for if and when she ever needed me. I was unsure how to leave. I mean, what's protocol for saying goodbye to the wife of the pilot who died saving your life? Not to mention that if I hadn't hired him to charter me to Denver, he'd have been home with her when he died, and I imagine she'd thought of that too.

'Young man, thank you.' Her eyes shone a clear, bright blue. 'If Grover took you he had a reason. It was his gift to you.'

'Yes ma'am.'

She hugged me and squeezed my arms with her hands. I kissed her on the cheek. When I drove away, I glanced in the rearview mirror. Napoleon was standing on the top step, chest out, barking at the wind.

Vince was sitting with Ashley when I walked in. He stood. A warm smile, warm handshake. Even a stiff hug. 'Ashley is telling me what you did.' He shook his head. 'I can't thank you enough.'

'Remember, I'm the one who invited her onto the plane. You might consider pressing charges.'

He laughed. I liked him. She'd chosen well. He'd marry above himself— anyone would who married her. She was one in a million.

Three empty coffee cups sat on the bedside table. Her new cellphone was ringing nonstop. Media crews had called, wanting the exclusive. She asked, 'What are you going to tell them?'

'Nothing. I'm ducking out the back door, going home.' I looked at the clock on the wall. 'Leave in ninety minutes. Just came to say goodbye.' Her expression changed. I walked to the bed. 'You two have a wedding to plan. I'm sure we'll be in touch.'

She crossed her arms. 'You called your wife yet?'

'No . . . I'm going to go see her as soon as I get home.'

She nodded. 'I hope it works out, Ben.' She squeezed my hand. I kissed her forehead and she held on and smiled. 'Ben?'

Vince looked at her. 'Be right back. I'm going to get some coffee.' He put his hand on my shoulder. 'Thank you. For everything.'

He walked out. She was still holding on to my hand. I sat on the edge of the bed. Something was tugging at my insides. It most closely resembled an ache. I tried to smile.

'Can I ask you something?'

'You've earned the right to ask me anything.'

She smiled. 'Why'd you ask me to get on the plane with you?'

I stared out of the window. 'Seems like a long time ago, doesn't it?'

'It does. Then sometimes it feels like yesterday.'

'Our wedding was one of the happier days either of us ever knew. It was a launching out. A beginning. We were free to love each other without inter-ference. I think when two people really love each other . . . way down deep, like where their soul sleeps and dreams happen, where pain can't live 'cause there's nothing for it to feed on . . . then a wedding is a bleeding together of those two souls. Like two rivers running together. All that water becoming the same water. Mine did that. When I met you, I saw in your face the hope that yours might be that, too. I guess meeting you was a reminder that I knew a precious, tender love at one time. And, I think, if I'm honest, I wanted to brush up alongside that. Because . . . I don't want to forget.' She reached up and thumbed the tear off my face. 'I think that's why I invited you. And for that selfishness I'm both eternally sorry and eternally grateful. Those twenty-eight days in the mountains with you reminded me that love is worth doing. No matter how much it hurts.'

I stood, kissed her on the lips and walked out.

THE PLANE LANDED in Jacksonville just after 2 p.m. Media crews were waiting. My picture had circulated. Problem was, they were looking for a guy thirty pounds heavier.

I had no bags so I skirted the frenzy, walked to my car, which after a month and a half was still sitting there. The lady at the ticket booth told me with little or no facial expression, 'Three hundred and eighty-seven dollars.'

I had a feeling that arguing with her would have little effect. I handed her my American Express, grateful for the chance to pay my bill and go home.

The change in my environment was strange. Most striking were the things I was not doing: not pulling a sled, not staring out across snow, not starting a fire with a bow drill, not skinning a rabbit, not being dependent upon shooting an arrow to eat, not listening for the sound of Ashley's voice . . . not hearing the sound of Ashley's voice.

I drove south down I-95. Funny, I found myself driving slowly. Everybody was passing me. I crossed the Fuller Warren Bridge, and passed the hospital where I live most of my life. I stopped at a flower shop and bought a purple orchid with a white stripe. The purple was deep, almost black in the middle, and the stems must have had thirty blooms. Rachel would love it.

I drove east on J. Turner Butler Boulevard, then south on A1A. I bought a bottle of wine, drove past my condo at South Ponte Vedra, then to Rachel's house. I'd fenced the property with a tall wrought-iron fence. I grabbed the orchid, walked beneath the towering oaks and up the stone steps, dug in the rocks for my hide-a-key, and unlocked the door. Confederate jasmine vines hung down on both sides and I lifted them, stepped inside.

I talked to Rachel through the night. I poured the wine, pressed play on the recorder and we stared out through the glass, watching the waves crawl up and down the beach. I think parts were hard for her to hear, but she heard every word. I gave her the orchid, placing it on a shelf by the glass where it would draw the morning sun.

It was four in the morning when my last recording finished. I was tired and had drifted off. The silence woke me. Funny how that works. I was rising to leave when I noticed the recorder. The face plate was flashing blue. One file remained unplayed.

I always recorded in the same file, with the same file number. For the first time, I noticed a number I'd not created. I pushed 'play'.

There was wind in the background. I turned up the volume.

Rachel, it's Ashley. We were caught in an avalanche. Ben went for help. I don't know if I'll make it. I'm really cold. I wanted to thank you . . . I write a column for the paper about love. Relationships. Which is ironic because I've had my share of bad ones. I'm headed home to marry a man who is well-off, good-looking, gives me nice things, but after twenty-eight days with your husband in this cold, white-capped world, I'm left wondering if that's enough . . . what about love? Is it possible? Can I have it? Are there other Bens out there . . . I've been hurt, I imagine we all have, and I think somewhere in that pain we convince ourselves that if we don't love again, we don't have to hurt again. Take the Mercedes and the two-carat ring, give him what he wants and everybody's happy. Right? I have thought that a long time. But . . . when I met him on the plane, I was attracted to this man I now know as Ben Payne. Sure, he's good-looking, but what attracted me was something else. Something . . . tender and warm and whole. I don't know what to call it but I know it when I hear it . . . and I hear it when he speaks to you in this recorder. I've listened many nights when he thought I was sleeping. I've never had anyone talk to me like that. My fiancé's kind, but in Ben, there's this palpable thing that is rich and I just want to bathe in it. I'm talking about your husband so you need to know that he's treated me like a gentleman. Truly. And I saw it had to do with this thing I'm talking about, with you . . . and it's deep-wired into his DNA . . . like you'd

have to kill him to get it out. It's the truest thing I've ever sensed.
I have lain awake at night, listening to him talk to you, share his
heart, apologise for what I don't know and found myself aching for a
man to hold me in his heart the way Ben holds you. He says you two
are separated . . . I guess I'm just wanting to go on record to say he
can't love you any more than he already does. And if you won't have
him, then what does he do with a love like this? What . . . why? He
said you two argued. Said he said some things. What terrible words
could he possibly have said that caused this? What did he do to lose
your love? If a love like Ben's can be had, if it's real, then . . . I'm left
wondering. What can't be forgiven? . . . What can't be forgiven?

The recording ended, and I rose to leave, but Rachel beckoned me to
stay. She'd never wanted me to leave in the first place. I told her that many
times I'd wanted to return to her, but forgiving myself had turned out to be
easier said than done.

Maybe there was something different in me. Maybe something different
in her. I'm not really sure, but for the first time since our argument I lay
down, my tears dripping onto her face, and slept with my wife.

I TIGHTENED my cummerbund, straightened my bow tie, then walked round
the back of the country club. One of Atlanta's finest. I showed the guard my
invitation, he opened the gate and I walked up the winding walk. A throng
of people. Sparkly women. Powerful men. Laughter. Drinks. The rehearsal
dinner party. The night before the wedding. A happy occasion.

It had been three months. I had returned to work, put on a few pounds, told
bits and pieces of the story and deflected the attention. I hadn't contacted
Ashley. I fell back into routine, working my way through the separation. Up
before the sun, a long run on the beach, breakfast with Rachel and the kids,
work, sometimes dinner with Rachel and the kids, then home, maybe a run.
Putting one foot in front of the other.

Ashley stood on the far side of the room. The invitation had included a
note and a gift. The note read, 'Please come. We'd love to see you. Both of
you.' She went on to say that her leg had mended well and she was teaching
youth classes in tae kwon do, though she was kicking at only about seventy-
five per cent. The gift was a watch made by Suunto. Called the Core. Her
note continued, 'The guys at the store said this is what all the climbers wear.

Gives you temperature, barometric pressure, elevation. Even has a compass. You deserve it more than any.'

I stood staring from a distance. Her posture said her confidence had returned and the pain was gone. She was beautiful. And for the first time in a long time, I felt OK thinking that.

Vince stood alongside. Seemed happy. In the wilderness, I'd conjured my own idea of what he looked like, how he held himself. I was off by a good bit. Were it not for her, Vince and I could have been friends.

I stood in the shadows, just outside, staring in the windows. Nervous, I turned the plastic package in my hands. I'd bought two new recorders. One for her. One for me. I removed one from the packaging, inserted the batteries and clicked it on.

Hey, it's me. Ben. I received your invitation. Thanks for including me . . . us. I know you've been busy. It's good to see you on your feet. Looks like the leg healed well. I'm glad. There are a lot of people here. All to celebrate with you.

Just so you'll know, I went to see Rachel. Took her an orchid, number 258, and a bottle of wine. Talked long into the night. I played her the tape. The whole thing. I slept with her. It'd been a long time.

It was also the last time.

I had to let her go. She's not coming back. The distance is too great. The mountain between us is the one mountain I cannot climb.

I've been spending a lot of time lately trying to figure out how to start over. The single life is different from what I thought. And it's tough. Rachel was my first love. My only love. I've never dated anyone else. Never been with anyone else.

I never told you this because it just felt wrong but . . . even at your worst, broken leg, sitting over a Nalgene bottle, stitches lining your face, well, being lost with you is better than being found and alone.

I wanted to thank you for that.

If Vince doesn't tell you that, call me and I'll remind him. I'm an expert on what a husband should have said.

After Rachel . . . I didn't know what to do, how to live, so I gathered all the broken pieces of me, shoved them in a bag and hefted it over my shoulder like a bag of rocks. Years passed, dragging myself round

in a bag behind me, buckled into my harness and leaning into the
weight, the history of me slicing into my shoulders.

Then, I went to this conference, found myself in Salt Lake, and for
reasons I don't understand, you sat down, I heard the sound of your
voice and something emptied the bag, scattering the pieces of me.
Laid bare and broken. Now here I am, hidden in the trees. The pieces
of me no longer fit together. I am reminded of all the king's horses
and all the king's men. I cannot put me back together.

Funny, I have loved two women in my life and now I can't have
either. Wonder what that says about me? I wanted to give you a gift,
but what could I give you that would equal what you have given me?

Ashley, for that alone, I wish you every happiness.

I stared round the dogwood tree and through the glass. She was laughing. A single diamond hanging round her neck. She looked good in diamonds. She looked good in anything.

I left the recorder running, emptied my pockets of my last two batteries, put all that in the box, tied the bow, left no card, slipped through the back doors and slid it beneath the mound of a hundred other gifts. In thirty-six hours, they'd be on a plane for Italy. She'd find my gift upon their return.

I walked out through the unlit garden, started my car, and pointed the wheel south down I-75. The night was warm and I drove home with the windows down. Sweating. Which was OK with me.

When I got home, I changed clothes, grabbed the second of my new recorders and walked out onto the beach, stopping at the ocean's edge. I stood there a long time. While the waves and foam washed over my feet, I turned the thing in my hands and wrestled with what to say, where to begin.

With the sun breaking the horizon, I clicked 'record', took three steps and threw the recorder as far as I could. It spun through the air and disappeared into the daylight and the foam of a receding wave and an outgoing tide.

I WOKE to the sound of cats on my porch. They had come back in force. Bringing friends. A beautiful black cat with white feet. I named him Socks. The second was playful, always purring in my face. Long tail, long whiskers, quick ears. I named her Ashley.

I took the day off. Spent it at home. Leaning on the railing, cupping a warm mug, staring out over the ocean, listening to the waves, talking to the cats. Listening for the sound of laughter. Ashley was never far away. Neither the cat nor the memory. I thought back through the wilderness and drifted off to sleep some time after dark. I dreamed of her sitting in a gondola with Vince beneath an afternoon sun in Venice. She was tucked up alongside him, his arm round her. They were tanned and she looked happy.

I didn't like the picture.

I crawled off the couch a few hours before daylight. The moon was full and hung low on the horizon, glittering on the crest of each wave, casting my shadow across the beach. I laced up my shoes beneath a warm breeze. Pelicans in v-formation flew silently overhead, riding the updraughts.

I turned into the wind, taking me south. Low tide. I ran an hour, then two. A single path of turtle tracks led from the water to the dunes. She was laying her eggs. When St Augustine came into view, I turned for home. The sun was coming up.

Halfway back I intersected the mother turtle. Exhausted from her night's work. She was big, old, cutting deep grooves in her push to the water. The first wave reached her, she submerged, then floated and skimmed the surface, her shell glistening. After a few minutes, she was gone. Loggerheads can live to be nearly two hundred. I let myself think she was the same one.

I DIDN'T HEAR the footsteps. Felt only the hand on my shoulder. I recognised the veins, the freckles where she did not wear a watch.

I turned and Ashley stood facing me. A windcheater, running shorts, Nikes. Her eyes were red, wet. She shook her head. 'I was hopeful you would show, but when you didn't, I . . . I couldn't sleep, so I started picking through our presents. Anything to take my mind off . . . today.' She held my hands in hers, then pounded me softly in the chest with her fist. Her left hand had no ring. 'My doctor says I should start running again.'

'Be a good idea.'

'I don't like running alone.'

'Me neither.'

She picked at the sand with the toe of her shoe. She squinted against the rising sun and said, 'I'd like to meet Rachel. Will you introduce me?'

I nodded.

'Now?'

We turned and walked down the beach. Two miles. The house I built her sat up on the dunes, framed in scrub oaks and wire grass.

Since I'd returned, I'd marked ten turtle nests along the dunes with pink surveyor's tape. Ashley eyed it. 'Turtle nests?'

I nodded. We wound up through the dune and up the walkway. The sand was soft. A lot like snow.

I unlocked the door and lifted the vines. To combat the summer heat, the entire house, walls, floor, everything, was lined with marble. In the solarium above, many of the orchids were in bloom.

I led her through the door.

Rachel lay on my left. Michael and Hannah on my right.

Ashley put her hands to her mouth.

I waved my hand, 'Ashley meet Rachel. Rachel meet Ashley.'

Ashley knelt, brushing the marble with her fingertips. She ran her fingers through the grooves of Rachel's name, and the dates. On top of the marble lid, about where Rachel's hands would be folded atop her chest, sat seven digital recorders. All covered in dust. All but one. The one I'd carried in the mountains. Ashley touched it, turned it in her hand and then returned it to its place. On top, about where Rachel's face would be, lay my jacket, rolled up like a pillow.

I sat down, my back against Rachel, my feet resting against the twins. I stared up through the blooms and the glass above. 'Rachel was pregnant with the twins. She had what's called a partial abruption. The placenta began tearing away from her uterine wall. We put her on bed rest for a month, but, due to no fault of her own, it worsened. I tried to reason with her, telling her that when it ruptured completely, it would kill the twins and her. Her doctor and I wanted to take the twins. She stared at us like we'd lost our minds. I wanted us to grow old, laugh at our wrinkles. But because there was a chance . . . a very slim chance, she took a chance on the twins. I screamed, yelled, but she said, "Ben, I love you, but I'm not living the rest of my life looking at Michael and Hannah on the backs of my eyelids. Knowing they might have made it." So, I tied on my shoes, ran out the door. A midnight run on the beach to clear my head. When my cellphone rang, I sent it to voicemail. I can't tell you the number of times I . . .'

I ran my fingertips along the lettering of Michael's name. Then Hannah's. 'As best I can piece together, moments after I left, she ruptured. She managed to dial 911. Not that they could have done anything. Two hours later,

I returned. Flashing lights. Police in my kitchen, a call from the hospital. Strange people drove me to the morgue to identify her. In trying to save Rachel, they'd performed an emergency C-section. They'd laid the kids out next to her, kind of tucked them alongside. The voicemail you heard on the plane is the one she left. I've sent it to myself almost every day. To remind me that despite myself, she loved me.'

I looked at Ashley. Tears were streaming down her face. I nodded. 'You asked once, "What can't be forgiven?" It's words. Words you can't take back because the person you spoke them to took them to their grave four years, two hundred and eighty-one days and twelve hours ago.'

I waved my hand across the marble sarcophagus. 'A simple tombstone didn't seem right, so I built them this. I put the solarium up there so she can see the orchids. And at night the stars. Sometimes you can see the Big Dipper. Sometimes the moon.

'Many nights, I have come here, leaning against her, my fingertips resting on the twins, tracing their names and . . . listened to myself tell her our story.' I pointed at the recorders. 'I've told it many times, but the end is always the same.'

Ashley's lip was trembling. She held my hand between both of hers. Her tears had dripped onto the marble. Alongside ten thousand of mine. 'You should've told me. Why didn't you tell me?'

'So many times I wanted to stop dragging that sled, turn round and spill it, tell you everything, but . . . you have so much in front of you. So much to look forward to.'

'You should have. You owe me that.'

'I do now. I didn't then.'

She placed her hand flat across my chest, then wrapped her arms round my neck and buried her face alongside mine. She placed both palms on my face and shook her head. 'Ben?'

No answer.

'Ben?'

Forgiveness is a tough thing. Both in the offering and the accepting. I opened my mouth, my eyes on Rachel, and pushed out the words. A whisper. 'I'm so sorry.'

Ashley smiled and shook her head. 'She forgave you . . . the moment you said it.'

WE SAT THERE a long time. Through the glass I watched an osprey fly over. Beyond the breakers bottle-nosed dolphins were rolling.

Ashley tried to speak. Tried again and still could not find the words. Finally, she wiped her eyes, pressed her ear to my chest and whispered. 'Give me all the pieces.'

'There are a lot of them. I'm not sure they'll ever go back together.'

She kissed me. 'Let me try.'

'You would be better off to leave me and . . .'

'I'm not leaving you. Not going it alone.' She shook her head. 'Not looking at the memory of you every time I close my eyes.'

Something deep inside me needed to hear that. Needed to know I was worth that. That despite myself, love might snatch me back. Lift me from the fire. We sat for hours, staring out across the ocean.

Finally, I stood and kissed the stone above Rachel's face. The twins, too. There were no tears this time. It wasn't goodbye.

We walked out, locked the door and wound through the dunes. I held her naked left hand in mine. She stopped me, a wrinkle between her eyes. 'I gave Vince back his ring. Told him that I liked him very much, but . . .' She wiped her nose. 'I think he was relieved to know the truth.'

We stood atop the last dune, staring out over the beach. South, to our right, one of the nests had hatched. Hundreds of tiny tracks led to the water. The waves and foam were filling them. Far out, beyond the breakers and waves, shiny black circles of onyx floated atop the water. Glittering black diamonds. 'Start slow. It's been a long time since I've run with anyone.'

She took off running. Her arms swung from side to side. And her stride was too short by maybe three inches. And she favoured her left leg. And . . .

But she was a quick study. We could fix all that. Broken people just need piecing back together.

For so long I'd carried the pieces of me. Every now and then I'd drop one like a breadcrumb. So I could find my way home. Then Ashley came along and gathered the pieces and somewhere between eleven thousand feet and sea level, the picture began taking shape. Dim at first, then clearer. Not yet clear. But these things take time.

It's risky for both of us. You must hope in an image you can't see and I must trust you with me.

That's the piecing.

ASHLEY RAN UP the beach. The sun spilling down her back. Fresh footprints in the sand. Sweat shining on her thighs, condensation on her calves.

I could see them both. Rachel in the dunes, Ashley on the beach. I shook my head. I can't make sense of that. I don't know how.

Ashley returned. Breathing heavily, laughing, smiling. She raised her eyebrows, pulled on my hand. 'Ben Payne?'

More tears I could not explain. I did not try. 'Yes?'

'When you laugh I want to smile. And when you cry'—she brushed the tears off my face—'I want the tears to roll down my cheeks.' She whispered, 'I'm not leaving you . . . won't.'

I swallowed. How then does one live?

Maybe piecing is continual. Maybe the glue takes time to dry. Maybe bones take time to mend. Maybe it's OK that the mess I call me is in process. Maybe it's a long, hard walk out of the crash site. Maybe the distance is different for each of us. Maybe love is bigger than my mess.

My voice was slow in coming. 'Can we . . . walk a bit first?'

She nodded, and we did. First a mile, then two. A gentle breeze in our face. We reached the lifeguard chair and turned round.

She tugged at me. The breeze now at our backs. 'You ready?'

So we picked up a jog. Wasn't long and we were running.

And we ran a long time.

Somewhere in the miles that followed, sweat flinging off my fingertips, salt stinging my eyes, my breath deep, rhythmic and clean, my feet barely touching the ground, I looked down and found the pieces of me melting into one.

charles **martin**

RD: What gave you the idea to write *The Mountain Between Us*?

CM: A friend and I were climbing the Woody Ridge Trail in the eastern US. It gains 3,400 vertical feet in 2.2 miles. The conditions were horrible. My friend—who'd made some poor clothing choices—dehydrated a few hundred feet from the top. He started having decision-making trouble and losing fine motor skills. I'm no expert but I knew he wasn't right. The temp dropped to about zero, snow was blowing sideways, and I figured we needed to get our Florida selves into a tent fast. We did. I got him changed—out of wet and into dry—and in his bag, fed him some fluids, lied to him and told him he was fine, and we listened to the wind try to rip us off the mountaintop.

Hovering over my Jetboil stove in that tent, I began thinking, If a few variables changed, like maybe I was out west where elevation really becomes a problem, then add colder temperatures, then add being stuck in the middle of nowhere with no way out, then this could get messy. My imagination took over from there. Note: I am not Ben Payne. He's much better at all that stuff than I am. Although I can make a pretty mean cup of coffee over a Jetboil anywhere from sea level to 14,000 feet.

RD: You've said in interviews that your grandmother is convinced that all your female characters are based on your wife Christy. *The Mountain Between Us* has two women: Ashley and Rachel. Which of them is it?

CM: Both Ashley and Rachel are cut from differing parts of Christy. One of these days, my readers will tire of my female characters and tell me they all sound or look the same. In part, that's true, because I really only have experience with one woman. When I deviate from that, the characters end up two-dimensional. It's better if I stick with what I know, i.e, Christy.

RD: Ben's relationship with his father was a difficult one. Were your teen years anything like Ben's?

CM: No. My dad was/is nothing like Ben's. I had to research that character trait—and it wasn't fun to write. I've spent my life in and around athletics—whether my own or my sons' (we have three). Do that and you bump into a lot of dads like Ben's. Overbearing, trying to live vicariously through their sons' accomplishments. Trying to create the next Chipper Jones, Brett Favre or name your icon. I'm not immune to this. It's just easier to spot in other people.

RD: To what lengths did you go to do research for this book? How does your time in the High Uintas compare to Ben and Ashley's?

CM: In comparison, my time in the High Uintas (*see below*) was a cakewalk. We ate well, stayed warm, nothing too dicey. Again, I let my imagination run. In a summer trip to Colorado, I did climb my first fourteener [exceeds 14,000 feet above mean sea level], Mount Princeton. Great fun. The air sure did get thin, though. Especially for a guy who—like right now—is accustomed to breathing at sea level.

RD: Where do you live now and how long have you been married?

CM: Jacksonville, Florida. Christy and I have been married sixteen years.

RD: Do your sons take after you?

CM: Yes and no. Which is probably how it ought to be. As I said, they're athletic, but they also play piano and I'm not musical at all.

RD: How do you think they would describe you?

CM: Good question. Let's not ask them.

RD: If you could choose a place to build a dream home, where would it be?

CM: Number one: wherever Christy wants it. Two: somewhere on the high ground of the 1,000 acres I don't currently own but would like to own. A river or mountain view would be great. My favourite retreat is the woods with a bow in my hand, followed closely by the water with a fly rod in my hand. Archery is a lifelong hobby of mine. Maybe addiction is a better word. Christy might use the latter.

RD: Finally, you've done all kinds of jobs in your life: from selling insurance and dock-building to helping with despatch at UPS . . . Do you recall the moment when you realised you'd made it as a writer?

CM: Have I?

HALF BROKE
HORSES

JEANNETTE WALLS

Lily Casey Smith, the grandmother of journalist and writer Jeannette Walls, was a straight-talking, sassy woman for whom taming wild horses and beating ranch hands at poker were all in a day's work. Born in 1901, in the rolling grassland of West Texas, she left home at fifteen, barely educated, and rode her pony 500 miles to a first teaching job in a frontier town. And that was just the beginning. Readers will love and marvel at this intrepid woman, for her fearlessness, her courage, her wicked sense of humour and adventure.

I

Salt Draw

Those old cows knew trouble was coming before we did. It was late on an August afternoon, the air hot and heavy like it usually was in the rainy season. Earlier we'd seen some thunderheads near the Burnt Spring Hills, but they'd passed way up to the north. I'd mostly finished my chores for the day and was heading down to the pasture with my brother, Buster, and my sister, Helen, to bring the cows in for their milking. But when we got there, those girls were acting all bothered. Instead of milling Around at the gate, like they usually did at milking time, they were standing stiff-legged and straight-tailed, twitching their heads around, listening.

Buster and Helen looked up at me and, without a word, I knelt down and pressed my ear to the hard-packed dirt. There was a rumbling, so faint and low that you felt it more than you heard it. Then I knew what the cows knew—a flash flood was coming.

As I stood up, the cows bolted, heading for the southern fence line, and when they reached the barbed wire, they jumped over it and thundered off towards higher ground.

I figured we best bolt, too, so I grabbed Helen and Buster by the hand. By then I could feel the ground rumbling through my shoes. I saw the first water sluicing through the lowest part of the pasture, and I knew we didn't have time to make it to higher ground ourselves. In the middle of the field was an old cottonwood tree, broad-branched and gnarled, and we ran for that.

When we reached the cottonwood, I pushed Buster up to the lowest branch, and he pulled Helen into the tree behind him. I shimmied up and wrapped my arms round Helen just as a wall of water, about six feet high, slammed into the cottonwood, dousing all three of us. The tree shuddered as a great rush of caramel-coloured water, filled with bits of wood and the occasional gopher, surged beneath us, spreading out across the lowland.

We sat there in that cottonwood tree for about an hour. The sun started to set over the Burnt Spring Hills, turning the high clouds crimson and sending long purple shadows eastward. The water was still flowing beneath us, and Helen said her arms were getting tired. She was only seven and was afraid she couldn't hold on much longer.

Buster, who was nine, was perched up in the big fork of the tree. I was ten, the oldest, and I took charge, telling Buster to trade places with Helen so she could sit upright without having to cling too hard. A while later, it got dark, but a bright moon came out. From time to time we switched places so no one's arms would wear out. The bark was chafing my thighs, and Helen's too, and when we needed to pee, we had to just wet ourselves. About halfway through the night, Helen's voice started getting weak.

'I can't hold on any longer,' she said.

'Yes, you can,' I told her. 'You can because you have to.' We were going to make it, I told them. I knew we would make it, because I could see it in my mind. I could see us walking up the hill to the house tomorrow morning, and I could see Mom and Dad running out. It would happen—but it was up to us to make it happen.

To keep Helen and Buster from drifting off to sleep and falling out of the cottonwood, I grilled them on their multiplication tables. When we'd run through those, I went on to presidents and state capitals, then word definitions, word rhymes, and whatever else I could come up with, snapping at them if their voices faltered, and that was how I kept Helen and Buster awake through the night.

By first light, you could see that the water still covered the ground. In most places, a flash flood drained away after a couple of hours, but the pasture was in bottomland near the river, and sometimes the water remained for days. But it had stopped moving and had begun seeping down through the sinkholes and mudflats.

'We made it,' I said.

I figured it would be safe to wade through the water, so we scrambled out of the cottonwood tree. We were so stiff that our joints could barely move, and the mud kept sucking at our shoes, but we got to dry land as the sun was coming up and climbed the hill to the house just the way I had seen it.

Dad was on the porch, pacing back and forth in that uneven stride he had on account of his gimp leg. When he saw us, he let out a yelp of delight and started hobbling towards us. Mom came running out of the house. She sank to her knees and started praying, thanking the Lord for delivering her children from the flood.

It was she who had saved us, she declared, by staying up all night praying. 'You get down on your knees and thank your guardian angel,' she said. 'And you thank me, too.'

Helen and Buster got down and started praying with Mom, but I just stood there looking at them. The way I saw it, I was the one who'd saved us all, not Mom and not some guardian angel. No one was up in that cottonwood tree except the three of us. Dad came alongside me and put his arm round my shoulders.

'There weren't no guardian angel, Dad,' I said. I started explaining how I'd gotten us to the cottonwood tree in time.

Dad squeezed my shoulder. 'Well, darling,' he said, 'maybe the angel was you.'

WE HAD A HOMESTEAD on Salt Draw, which flowed into the Pecos River, in the rolling gritty grassland of west Texas. The sky was high and pale, the land low and washed out. Sometimes the wind blew for days on end, but sometimes it was so still you could hear the dog barking on the Dingler ranch two miles upriver.

It was hard country. The ground was like rock—save for when a flood turned everything to mud—the animals bony and tough, and even the plants were prickly and sparse. Dad said High Lonesome, as the area was known, wasn't a place for the soft of head or the weak of heart, and he said that was why he and I made out just fine there, because we were both tough nuts.

Our homestead was only 160 acres, which was not a whole lot of land in that part of Texas, where it was so dry you needed at least five acres to raise a single head of cattle. But our spread bordered the draw, so it was ten times more valuable than land without water, and we were able to keep the carriage horses Dad trained, the milking cows, dozens of chickens, some hogs and the peacocks.

The peacocks were one of Dad's moneymaking schemes that didn't pan out. Dad had paid a lot of money to import peacocks from a farm back east.

He was convinced that folks who bought carriage horses from him would also be willing to shell out fifty bucks for one of those classy birds.

Unfortunately, Dad overestimated the demand for ornamental birds in west Texas—even among the carriage set—and within a few years our ranch was overrun with peacocks. They strutted round screeching and squawking, pecking our knees and scaring the horses, killing chicks and attacking the hogs, though I have to admit it was a glorious sight when, from time to time, those peacocks paused in their campaign of terror to spread their plumes and preen.

The peacocks were just a sideline. Dad's primary occupation was the carriage horses, breeding them and training them. He loved horses despite the accident. When Dad was three, he was running through the stable and a horse kicked him in the head, practically staving in his skull. Dad was in a coma for days. He eventually pulled through, but the right side of his body had gone a little gimp. His right leg dragged behind him, and his arm was cocked like a chicken wing. Also, when he was young, he'd spent long hours working in the noisy gristmill on his family's ranch, which made him hard of hearing. As such, he talked a little funny and, until you spent time round him, you had trouble understanding what he said.

Dad never blamed the horse for kicking him. All the horse knew, he liked to say, was that some creature about the size of a mountain lion was darting by his flanks. Horses always did what they did for a reason, and it was up to you to figure it out. Dad loved horses because, unlike people, they always understood him and never pitied him. So, even though Dad was unable to sit in a saddle on account of the accident, he became an expert at training carriage horses.

I WAS BORN in a dugout on the banks of Salt Draw in 1901, the year after Dad got out of prison, where he'd been serving time on that trumped-up murder charge.

Dad had grown up on a ranch in the Hondo Valley in New Mexico. His pa, who'd homesteaded the land, was one of the first Anglos in the valley, arriving in 1868, but by the time Dad was a young man, more settlers had moved into the area and there were constant arguments over property lines and water rights. These disputes often led to brawls and shootings. Dad's pa was murdered in one such dispute when Dad was fourteen. Dad stayed on to run the ranch with his ma, but those disputes kept erupting and, twenty years later, when a settler was killed after yet another argument, Dad was convicted of murdering him.

Dad insisted he'd been framed, writing long letters to legislators protesting his innocence and, after serving three years in prison, he was set free. Shortly after he was released, he met and married my mom. The Prosecutor was looking into retrying the case, and Dad thought that would be less likely if he made himself scarce, so he and my mom left the Hondo Valley for High Lonesome, where they claimed our land along Salt Draw.

Lots of the folks homesteading in High Lonesome lived in dugouts because timber was so scarce. Dad had made our home by shovelling out a big hole on the side of the riverbank, using cedar branches as rafters and covering them with sod. The dugout had one room, a packed earth floor, a wooden door, a waxed-paper window, and a cast-iron stove with a flue that jutted up through the sod roof.

The best thing about living in the dugout was that it was cool in the summer and not too cold in the winter. The worst thing about it was that, from time to time, scorpions, snakes and moles wormed their way out of our walls and ceilings. Also, whenever it rained, the ceilings and walls turned to mud. Sometimes clumps of that mud dropped from the ceiling, and you had to pat it back in place. And every now and then the goats grazing on the roof would stick a hoof clear through, and we'd have to pull them out.

Another problem with living in the dugout was the mosquitoes. Mom was particularly susceptible to them—her bite marks sometimes stayed swollen for days—but I was the one who came down with yellow jack fever.

I was seven at the time and, after the first day, I was writhing on the bed, shivering and vomiting. Dad sat with me for days, splashing me with spirit lotions, trying to bring the fever down. When the fever finally broke, I weighed ten pounds less than I had before, and my skin was all yellow. Mom said, 'A fever that high can boil your brain and cause permanent damage. So don't ever tell anyone you had it. You do, you might have trouble catching a husband.'

Mom worried about things like her daughters catching the right husband. She was concerned with what she called 'proprieties'. She had furnished our dugout with some real finery, including an Oriental rug, a chaise longue with a lace doily, velvet curtains and a carved walnut headboard that her parents had brought with them from back east when they moved to California. Mom treasured that headboard, because it reminded her of the civilised world.

Mom's father was a miner who had struck gold north of San Francisco and became fairly prosperous. Mom—who was born Daisy Mae Peacock—was raised in an atmosphere of gentility. She had soft white skin and always wore a hat and gloves and a veil over her face when she went outdoors, which she did as seldom as possible.

Mom kept up the dugout, but she refused to do chores like toting water or carrying firewood. 'Your mother's a lady,' Dad would say by way of explaining her disdain for manual labour. Dad did most of the outdoor work with the help of our hand, Apache. Apache wasn't really an Indian, but he'd been captured by the Apaches when he was six, and they kept him until he was a young man, when the U.S. Cavalry—with Dad's pa serving as a scout—raided the camp and Apache ran out yelling, '*Soy blanco! Soy blanco!*' Apache had gone home with Dad's pa and lived with the family ever since.

To cook and wash, Mom had the help of our servant girl, Lupe, who had gotten pregnant and was forced to leave her village outside Juárez after the baby was born because she had brought shame on the family. She was small and barrel-shaped and even more devoutly Catholic than Mom. I liked Lupe. Although her parents had taken her baby from her, she never felt sorry for herself, and that was something I admired.

Even with Lupe helping her out, Mom didn't really care for life on Salt Draw. She hadn't bargained for it. Mom thought she'd married well when she took Adam Casey as her husband, despite his limp and speech impediment. Dad's pa had come over from Ireland during a potato blight; joined the Second Dragoons, where he served under Colonel Robert E. Lee; and was stationed on the Texas frontier, fighting Comanches, Apaches and Kiowa. After leaving the army, he took up ranching, and by the time he was killed, he had one of the biggest herds in the area.

Robert Casey was shot down as he walked along the main street of Lincoln, New Mexico. One version of the story held that he and the man who killed him had disagreed over an eight-dollar debt.

After his death, his children started arguing over how to split up the herd, which fostered bad blood that lasted for the rest of Dad's life. Dad inherited the Hondo Valley spread, but he felt his elder brother, who'd taken the herd to Texas, had cheated him out of his share, and he was constantly filing lawsuits. He continued the campaign even after moving to west Texas.

DAD WAS ALL caught up in his lawsuits, but for the rest of us, the constant fight on Salt Draw was the one against the elements. The flash flood that sent Buster, Helen and me up the cottonwood wasn't the only one that almost did us in. Floods were pretty common; when I was eight, we had been hit by another big one. Dad was away in Austin filing another claim about his inheritance when one night Salt Draw overflowed and poured into our dugout. Mom took Helen and Buster to high ground to pray, but I stayed behind with Apache and Lupe. We barricaded the door with the rug and started bailing the water out of the window. Mom came back and begged us to go and pray with her on the hilltop.

'To heck with praying!' I shouted. 'Bail, dammit, bail!'

Mom looked mortified. I could tell she thought I'd probably doomed us all with my blasphemy, and I was a little shocked at it myself, but with the water rising so fast, the situation was dire. The dugout was beginning to sag inward. When the ceiling started to cave, we grabbed Mom's walnut headboard and pulled it through the door just as the dugout collapsed, burying everything.

Afterwards, I was pretty aggravated with Mom. She kept saying that the flood was God's will and we had to submit to it. But I didn't see things that way. If God gave us the strength to bail, isn't that what he wanted us to do?

But the flood turned out to be a blessing in disguise. It was all too much for that tenderfoot, Mr McClurg, who lived up the draw in a two-room wooden house that he had built with timber he carted in from New Mexico. The flood washed away Mr McClurg's foundation, and the walls fell apart, so he decided to return to Cleveland. As soon as Dad got home from Austin, we drove over to scavenge Mr McClurg's lumber. We took everything: siding, rafters, beams, door frames, floorboards. By the end of the summer, we had built ourselves a brand-new wooden house and, after we whitewashed it, you almost couldn't tell that it had been patched together with someone else's old wood.

As we all stood there admiring our house the day we finished it, Mom turned to me and said, 'Now, wasn't that flood God's will?'

I didn't have an answer. Mom could say that in hindsight, but it seemed to me that when you were in the middle of something, it was awful hard to figure out what was God's will and what wasn't.

I asked Dad if he believed that everything that happened was God's will.

'Is and isn't,' he said. 'God deals us all different hands. How we play 'em is up to us.'

I wondered if Dad thought that God had dealt him a bad hand, but I didn't feel it was my place to ask. From time to time, Dad mentioned the horse kicking him in the head, but none of us ever talked about his gimp leg or his trouble speaking.

Dad's speech impediment did make it sound a little like he was talking underwater. If he said, 'Hitch up the carriage,' it sounded to most people like 'Ich'p uh urrj,' and if he said, 'Mama needs to rest,' it sounded like 'Uhmu neesh resh.'

Toyah, the nearest little town, was four miles away, and sometimes when we went there the kids followed Dad round imitating him. Once, I tried to explain to a couple of them that they were hurting people's feelings, but all they did was snicker, so I shoved them into a manure pile and ran.

What those kids didn't understand about Dad was that he was smart. He'd been taught by a governess, and he was all the time reading books on philosophy and writing long letters to politicians like William Taft and William Jennings Bryan. When it came to the written word, no one could string together sentences like Dad. His handwriting was elegant and his sentences were extravagant, filled with words like 'mendacious' and 'abscond' that most of the folks in Toyah would need a dictionary to understand.

Toyah had a one-room schoolhouse, but Dad thought he could do better tutoring me. Every day after lunch, we did lessons—grammar, history, arithmetic, science, and civics—and when we were done, I tutored Buster and Helen. Dad's favourite subject was history, but he taught it with a decidedly west-of-the-Pecos point of view. As the proud son of an Irishman, he hated the English Pilgrims, whom he called 'Poms', as well as most of the founding fathers. They were a bunch of pious hypocrites, he thought, who declared all men equal but kept slaves and massacred peaceful Indians.

I loved my lessons, particularly science and geometry, loved learning that there were these invisible rules that explained the mysteries of the world we lived in. Smart as that made me feel, Mom and Dad kept saying that I'd need to go to finishing school when I was thirteen, to acquire social graces and to earn a diploma. Because in this world, Dad said, it's not enough to have a fine education. You need a piece of paper to prove it.

Mom did her best to keep us kids genteel. While I was teaching Buster and Helen, she brushed my hair with a hundred strokes. At night, she curled it into ringlets. 'A lady's hair is her crowning glory,' she said, and she was always going on about how my widow's peak was my best feature, but when I looked in the mirror, that little V of hair at the top of my forehead didn't seem like much to bank on.

Even though we lived four miles from Toyah and days would go by without seeing anyone outside the family, Mom worked very hard at being a lady. She was dainty, only four and a half feet tall, and her feet were so small that she had to wear button-up boots made for girls. To keep her hands elegantly white, she rubbed them with pastes made from honey, lemon juice and borax. She wore tight corsets to give her a teeny waist—I helped her lace them up—but they had the effect of causing her to faint. Mom called it the vapours and said it was a sign of her high breeding. I thought it was a sign that the corset made it hard to breathe.

MOM WAS CLOSEST to Helen, who had inherited her tiny hands and feet and her frail constitution. But while she was close to Helen, she completely doted on Buster, whom she considered the future of the family. Buster was a rabbity little kid, but he had an irresistible smile, and he was one of the smoothest talkers in the county. Mom liked to say Buster could charm the sage off the brush. She was always telling him there were no limits on what he could become—a railroad magnate, a cattle baron, even the governor of Texas.

Mom didn't quite know what to make of me. She feared she might have trouble marrying me off, because I didn't have the makings of a lady. I was a little bowlegged, for one thing. Mom said it was because I rode horses too much. Also, my front teeth jutted out, so she bought me a red silk fan to cover my mouth. Whenever I laughed or smiled too big, Mom would say, 'Lily, dear, the fan.'

Since Mom wasn't exactly the most useful person in the world, one lesson I learned at an early age was how to get things done, and this was a source of both amazement and concern for Mom, who considered my behaviour unladylike but who also counted on me. 'I never knew a girl to have such gumption,' she'd say. 'But I'm not too sure that's a good thing.'

The way Mom saw it, women should let menfolk do the work, because it made them feel more manly. That notion made sense only if you had a strong man willing to step up and get things done, and between Dad's gimp, Buster's elaborate excuses, and Apache's tendency to disappear, it was often up to me to keep the place from falling apart. But even when everyone was pitching in, we never got out from under all the work. I loved that ranch, though sometimes it seemed that instead of us owning the place, the place owned us.

Electricity had yet to reach west Texas, so you had to do everything by hand, heating irons on the stove to press Mom's blouses, cooking cauldrons of lye and potash over the fire to make soap, working the pump, then toting clean water in to wash the dishes.

We'd also heard about the indoor plumbing they were installing in fancy houses back east, but no one in west Texas had it, and most people, including Mom and Dad, thought the idea of an indoor bathroom was vile and disgusting. 'Who in the Lord's name would want a crapper in the house?' Dad asked.

SINCE I GREW UP listening to Dad, I always understood him completely, and when I turned five, he had me start helping him train the horses. It took Dad six years to train a pair of carriage horses properly, and he had six teams going at all times, selling off one team a year, which was enough to make ends meet.

Of the six pairs of horses we'd have, Dad let the yearlings and two-year-olds simply run free in the pasture. 'First thing a horse needs to learn is to be a horse,' he liked to say. I worked with the three-year-olds, getting them to accept the bit, then helped Dad harness and unharness the three pairs of older horses. I'd drive each pair in a circle while Dad stood in the middle, using a whip to drill them, making sure they lifted their feet high, changed gaits in unison, and flexed their necks smartly.

Everyone who spent time around horses, Dad liked to say, needed to learn to think like a horse. The key, he said, was understanding that horses were always afraid. The only way they could save themselves from mountain lions and wolves was to run, and they ran like the wind. If you could convince a horse that you'd protect him, he would do anything for you.

Dad had a whole vocabulary of grunts, murmurs, clucks, tocks and whistles that he used to speak with horses. It was like their own private language. He never flogged their backs, instead using the whip to make a small popping sound on either side of their ears, signalling to them without ever hurting or frightening them.

I was in charge of breaking the horses. It wasn't like breaking wild mustangs, because our horses had been around us since they were foals. Most times I simply climbed on bareback, grabbed a handful of mane and gave them a nudge with my heels. Then off we went, at first in awkward fits and starts, but pretty soon the horse usually accepted his fate and we'd move along right nicely. After that, it was a matter of saddling him up and finding the best bit. Then you could set about training him.

Still, particularly with a green horse, you never knew what to expect, and I got thrown plenty, which terrified Mom, but Dad just waved her off and helped me up.

'Most important thing in life,' he'd say, 'is learning how to fall.'

Another one of my jobs was feeding the chickens and collecting the eggs. First thing every morning, I'd toss them a handful of corn and some table scraps. In the spring, when the hens were really fertile, I could collect a hundred eggs a week. We'd set aside twenty-five or thirty for eating, and once a week I drove the buckboard into Toyah to sell the rest to the grocer, Mr Clutterbuck. He paid a penny per egg, then sold them for two cents each, which seemed unfair to me since I'd done all the work, but Mr Clutterbuck just said, 'Sorry, kid, that's the way the world works.'

I also brought in peacock eggs, finally giving those showy old birds a way to earn their keep. At first I thought they'd fetch twice as much as chicken eggs, seeing as how they were twice as big, but Mr Clutterbuck would give me only a penny each for them. 'Egg's an egg,' he said. I thought that danged grocer was cheating me because I was a girl, but there wasn't a whole lot I could do about it. That was the way the world worked.

Dad said it was good for me to go into town and bargain with Mr Clutterbuck over egg prices. It honed my math and taught me the art of negotiation, all of which was going to help me achieve my Purpose in Life. Dad was a philosopher and had what he called his Theory of Purpose, which held that everything in life had a purpose.

That was why Dad never bought any of us kids toys. Play was a waste of time, he said. Instead of playing house or playing with dolls, girls were better off cleaning a real house or looking after a real baby if their Purpose in Life was to become a mother.

Dad didn't actually forbid us from playing, and sometimes Buster, Helen and I rode over to the Dingler ranch for a game of baseball with the Dingler kids. Because we didn't have enough players for two full teams, we made up a lot of our own rules, one being that you could get a runner out by throwing the ball at him. Once, when I was trying to steal a base, one of the Dingler boys threw the ball hard and it hit me in the stomach. I doubled over, and when the pain wouldn't go away Dad took me into Toyah, where the barber who sometimes sewed people up said my appendix had been ruptured and I needed to get up to the hospital in Santa Fe. We caught the next stagecoach, and by the time we got to Santa Fe, I was delirious. What I remember next was waking up in the hospital with stitches on my stomach, Dad sitting next to me.

'Don't worry, angel,' he said. The appendix, he explained, was a vestigial organ, which meant it had no Purpose. If I had to lose an organ, I'd chosen the right one. But, he went on, I'd almost lost my life, and to what end? I'd only been playing a game of baseball. If I wanted to risk my life, I should do it for a Purpose. I decided Dad was right. All I had to do was figure out what my Purpose was.

IF YOU WANT to be reminded of the love of the Lord, Mom always said, just watch the sunrise. And if you want to be reminded of the wrath of the Lord, Dad said, watch a tornado.

Living on Salt Draw, we saw our share of tornadoes, which we feared even more than those flash floods. On most occasions, they looked like narrow cones of grey smoke, but sometimes when it had been especially dry, they were almost clear, and you could see tree limbs and brush and rocks swirling at the bottom. From a distance they seemed to be moving slowly, as if underwater, spinning and swaying almost elegantly.

Most weren't more than a dust devil gone a little wild, ripping at the laundry on the clothes line and sending the chickens squawking. But once, when I was eleven, a monster came roaring across the range.

Dad and I were working with the horses when the sky turned dark and the air got heavy. You could smell and taste what was heading our way. Dad saw the tornado first, a wide funnel.

I set about unharnessing the horses while Dad ran in to warn Mom, who started opening all the windows in the house because she'd been told that would equalise the air pressure and make it less likely that the house would explode. The horses were stampeding like crazy around the corral. Dad opened the gate, and they galloped through it, heading away from the tornado. Dad said if we got through this, we could worry about the horses later.

By then the sky overhead was black and streaked with rain. Dad had us all, including Apache and Lupe, scramble into the crawl space under the house. As the tornado came closer, it roared so loud it sounded like we were right under a freight train.

Mom grabbed our hands to pray, and while I didn't usually feel the call, I was scareder than I'd ever been—and I started praying harder than I'd ever prayed. Right then, we heard a crash and the sound of splintering wood. The house seemed to groan and shudder, but the floor above our heads held fast, and quickly the tornado moved on. Everything grew quiet.

We were alive.

The tornado had missed the house, but it had plucked up the windmill and smashed it down on the roof. The house was a total wreck. Dad started cussing up a blue streak. Life, he declared, had cheated him once again. 'If I owned hell and west Texas,' he said, 'I'd sell west Texas and live in hell.'

Dad predicted that the horses would come back at feeding time, and when they did, he hitched the six-year-olds to the carriage and drove into town to use the telegraph. After some backing and forthing with folks in the Hondo Valley, Dad reckoned he was not going to be tried again on that phony murder charge. It was safe to return to New Mexico and take up life on the Casey ranch, which he'd been renting out to tenant farmers all these years.

The chickens had disappeared in the tornado, but we had most of the peacocks, the six pairs of horses, the broodmares and cows, and a number of Mom's choice heirlooms, such as the walnut headboard that we'd rescued from the dugout. We packed it all into two wagons. Dad took the reins of one, with Mom and Helen next to him. Apache and Lupe were in the second. Buster and I followed on horseback with the rest of the herd on a string.

At the gate, I looked back at the ranch. The windmill still lay toppled over the house, and the yard was strewn with branches. Life had been hard in west Texas, but that land was all I knew, and I loved it. Mom was saying, as she always did, that it was God's will, and this time I accepted it. God had saved us, but He had also taken our house from us. Maybe He was just giving us a kick in the behind to say, Time to move on.

II

The Miraculous Staircase

We travelled three days to reach the Casey ranch, which Dad, who believed in phonetic spelling, insisted should officially be renamed the KC Ranch. It was in the middle of the Hondo Valley, south of the Capitan Mountains, and the countryside was so green that I could hardly believe what I was seeing. The ranch was really more of a farm, with fields of alfalfa and orchards of peach trees and pecan trees planted a hundred years ago by the Spanish.

The house was made of adobe and stone. There were two bedrooms inside and a woodshed outside for Lupe, while Apache took over one of the barn stalls. The walls were as thick as Dad's forearm was long. 'No tornado's ever going to knock this feller down,' he said.

Dad relished the notion of being a big landowner but not the headaches that came with it. Instead of the fenced-in rangeland we had in west Texas, there were now fields to be planted and weeded, peaches picked, pecans collected, migrants hired and fed. Because of his gimp leg, some of the work was beyond Dad, and his speech impediment made it hard for the help to understand him so, even though I was only eleven, I took on the hiring and overseeing.

The fall that I turned twelve, Buster left to go to school, even though he was two years younger than me. Mom said that his education was important for his career, and they enrolled him in a fancy Jesuit school near Albuquerque. But they'd promised me that when I turned thirteen, I could go to the Sisters of Loretto Academy of Our Lady of the Light in Santa Fe.

I'd wanted to go to a real school for years, and the day finally came when Dad hitched up the buckboard and we set out on the 200-mile journey, camping at night on bedrolls under the stars. Dad was almost as excited about me going off to school as I was, and seeing as how I hadn't spent much time around girls my age, he gave me an earful of advice about how to get along. The best way, Dad said, was to figure out what somebody wanted and make them think you could help them get it. Dad admitted that, as he put it, he wasn't the best exemplar of his own creed, but if I could find some way to apply it to my life, I'd go a lot further.

SANTA FE was a beautiful old place, with low adobe buildings and dusty streets lined with Spanish oaks. The school was right in the middle of town, a couple of four-storey Gothic buildings with crosses on top and a chapel with a choir loft reached by what was known as the Miraculous Staircase.

Mother Albertina, the mother superior, showed us round. She explained that the Miraculous Staircase had thirty-three stairs—Jesus's age when he died—and that it went in two complete spirals without any of the usual means of support, such as a centre pole. No one knew what type of wood it was made of or the name of the mysterious carpenter who showed up to build it after the original builder failed to include a staircase and the nuns prayed for divine intervention.

I LIKED MOTHER ALBERTINA from the beginning. She was tall and wrinkled with thick black brows. She treated all of us students—she called us 'my girls'—the same, whether we were rich or poor, Anglo or Mexican, smart or utterly lacking in any talent whatsoever. She was firm without being stern, never raised her voice or lost her temper, but it would have been unthinkable for any of us to disobey her. She would have made a fine horse-woman, but that wasn't her Purpose.

I also really liked the academy. A lot of the girls moped around feeling homesick at first, but not me. I had never had it so easy, even though we rose before dawn, washed our faces in cold water, attended chapel and classes, ate corn gruel, swept the dorms, cleaned the privies, and attended chapel again before going to bed. Since there were no barn chores, it felt like one long vacation.

I won a gold medal for my high scores in math and another for overall scholarship. I also read every book I could get my hands on and tutored girls who were having problems. Most of the other girls came from rich ranch families. I did make friends, however, trying to follow Dad's advice to figure out what someone wanted and help her get it, though it was hard, when you saw someone doing something wrong, to resist the temptation to correct her.

About halfway into the school year, Mother Albertina called me into her study for a talk. She told me I was doing well at Sisters of Loretto. 'A lot of parents send their girls here for finishing,' she went on, 'so they'll be more marriageable. But you don't have to get married, you know.'

I'd never thought much about that before. Mom and Dad always talked as if it was a matter of course that Helen and I would marry, though I had to admit I'd never met a boy I liked. On the other hand, I knew that women who didn't marry became old maids, and were a burden on their families.

I wasn't too young to start thinking about my future, Mother Albertina continued. In this day, there were really only three careers available. A woman could become a nurse, a secretary or a teacher.

'Or a nun,' I said.

'Or a nun,' Mother Albertina said with a smile. 'But you need to have the calling. Do you think you have the calling?'

I had to admit I wasn't sure.

'You have time to reflect on it,' she said. 'But whether or not you become a nun, I think you'd make a wonderful teacher. You have a strong personality. The women I know with strong personalities, the ones who might have become generals or the heads of companies if they were men, become teachers.'

'Like you,' I said.

'Like me.' She paused for a moment. 'Teaching is a calling, too. And I've always thought that teachers in their way are holy—angels leading their flocks out of the darkness.'

For the next couple of months, I thought about what Mother Albertina had said. I didn't want to be a nurse, because sick people irritated me. I didn't want to be a secretary, because you were always at the beck and call of your boss. But being a teacher was different. I loved books. I loved learning. And in the classroom, you got to be your own boss. Maybe teaching was my Purpose.

I was still getting comfortable with that idea—and in fact, finding it mighty appealing—when one of the nuns told me that Mother Albertina wanted to see me again.

MOTHER ALBERTINA was sitting behind her desk in her study. She had a solemn expression. 'I've got unfortunate news,' she said.

Dad had paid the first half of my tuition at the beginning of the year, but when the school billed him for the rest, he'd written back to say that he was unable to assemble the funds.

'I'm afraid you're going to have to go home,' Mother Albertina said.

'But I like it here,' I said. 'I don't want to go home.'

'I know you don't, but the decision's been made.'

Mother Albertina said she'd prayed on the matter and discussed it with the trustees. Their thinking was that the school was not a charity. If the parents agreed to pay the tuition, as Dad had, the school counted on the money to meet expenses, provide scholarships, and support the order's mission on the Indian reservations.

'I could work for it,' I said.

'When? Your entire day is full as it is. We make sure of that.'

Mother Albertina told me there was one other option. I could take the cloth. If I joined the order of the Sisters of Saint Loretto, the church would pay my tuition. But that would mean going to the novitiate in California for six months, then living in the convent instead of the dormitory. It would mean marrying the Lord Jesus and submitting totally to the discipline of the order.

'Have you had any chance to reflect on whether you've felt the calling?' Mother Albertina asked.

I shook my head. Much as I wanted to stay in school, I knew I wasn't cut out to be a nun. I was too restless. And I didn't like taking orders from anyone, not even the pope.

Dad was a grave disappointment to me. Not only had he welched on the tuition commitment, but he also didn't have the guts to face the nuns: instead of coming to pick me up, he sent a telegram telling me to take the stagecoach home.

I was sitting in the common room in my home-dyed beechnut brown dress, my suitcase next to me, when Mother Albertina came to take me to the depot. The moment I saw her, my lip started quivering and my eyes welled up with tears.

'Now, don't start feeling sorry for yourself,' Mother Albertina said. 'You're luckier than most girls here—God gave you the wherewithal to handle setbacks like this.'

As we walked to the depot, all I could think was that I was going back to the KC Ranch, where I'd spend the rest of my life doing chores while Dad worked on his cockamamie projects and Mom sat on the chaise longue fanning herself. Mother Albertina seemed to know what I was thinking. Before I boarded the coach, she took my hand and said, 'When God closes a window, he opens a door. But it's up to you to find it.'

WHEN THE STAGECOACH pulled into Tinnie, the town that was six miles from the ranch, Dad was sitting in the buckboard outside the hotel, with four huge dogs in the back. As I got out, he tried to hug me, but I shrugged him off.

'What do you think of these big fellas?' he asked.

The dogs were black with glistening coats, and they sat there regarding the passersby regally, even though they were also drooling ropes of slobber. They were the biggest dogs I'd ever seen.

'What happened to the tuition?' I asked Dad.

'You're looking at it.'

Dad started explaining that he'd bought the dogs from a breeder in Sweden and had them shipped all the way to New Mexico. They were not just any dogs, he went on; they were Great Danes, dogs of the nobility. And, believe it or not, no one west of the Mississippi owned any. These four, he said, had cost 800 dollars, but once he started selling the pups, we'd make the money back in no time, and from then on it would be pure profit.

'So you took my tuition money and bought dogs?'

'Watch that tone,' Dad said. After a moment, he added, 'You didn't need to be going to finishing school. It was a waste of money. I can teach you whatever you need to know.'

'Did you take Buster out of school, too?'

'No. He's a boy and needs that diploma if he's going to get anywhere.' Dad pushed the dogs over and found a spot for my suitcase. 'And anyway,' he said, 'we need you on the ranch.'

On the way back to the ranch, Dad did most of the talking. I sat there, ignoring his prattle. I wondered if buying those dogs had simply given Dad an excuse to stop paying the tuition so I'd have to come home. I also wondered where in the blazes was that door Mother Albertina had talked about.

The ranch had fallen into a state of mild disrepair in the months I'd been gone. Fence boards had come loose in a few spots, the chicken coop was unwashed, and tack lay scattered on the barn floor.

To help out around the ranch, Dad had brought in a tenant farmer named Zachary Clemens and his wife and daughter, and they were living in an outbuilding on a corner of the property.

Mom considered them beneath us because they were dirt-poor. But I liked the Clemenses, particularly the daughter, Dorothy, who knew how to get things done. She was a big-boned, handsome young woman with ample curves. Dorothy knew how to skin a cow and trap rabbits, and she tilled the vegetable garden the Clemenses had fenced off, but she spent most of her time at the big kettle that hung over the fire pit, cooking stews, making soap, and washing and dyeing clothes she took in from the townspeople in Tinnie.

DAD LET THE GREAT DANES roam free and one day, a few weeks after I'd returned home, Dorothy Clemens knocked on the front door to report to Dad that she'd been out collecting pecans near the property line we shared with Old Man Pucket's ranch and had found all four dogs shot dead. Dad charged into the barn in a fury, hitched up a carriage and drove off to confront Old Man Pucket.

We were worried about what was going to happen. To keep busy, Dorothy and I sat on the corral fence shucking pecans until Dad drove back up. He told us Old Man Pucket had unapologetically admitted killing the Great Danes, claiming they were on his property chasing his cattle and he was afraid they were going to bring one down. Dad was cursing and carrying on about how he was going to bring down Old Man Pucket. He ran into the house and then came out with his shotgun and jumped into the carriage.

Dorothy and I raced over. I grabbed the reins as Dad kept trying to crack them. Dorothy leaped up on the seat and, being a big woman, wrestled the gun away from Dad. 'You can't go killing someone over dogs,' she said. 'That's how feuds get started.'

When her family was living in Arkansas, she went on, her brother had killed someone in self-defence when a dispute broke out during a game of horseshoes; then he'd been killed by that man's cousin. The cousin, afraid Dorothy's father was going to avenge his son's death, had come after him. They'd had to leave everything behind and take off for New Mexico.

'My brother's dead, and we ain't got two nickels to rub together because of a stupid argument over a game of horseshoes,' she said.

Dad eventually settled down, but he kept stewing over the matter and the next day went into town to file a legal case against Old Man Pucket. He prepared obsessively for the hearing, researching the law and taking statements from vets about the value of Great Danes.

On the day of the trial, we all piled into the buckboard. When the circuit judge came to town he held court in the lobby of the hotel, sitting in a wing-back chair behind a small desk. The various plaintiffs and defendants leaned against the walls, waiting their turn.

The judge was a thin man who looked at you alertly from under his bushy eyebrows, giving the impression that he didn't tolerate fools.

'Did you shoot those dogs?' the judge asked Old Man Pucket.

'Sure did.'

'Why?'

'They was on my property chasing my cattle, and from a distance I thought they was big ol' wolves.'

Dad started arguing, but the judge shushed him.

'Sir, I can't make out what you're saying, and it don't matter anyhow,' the judge said. 'You got no business keeping dogs bigger than wolves in cattle country.'

Turning to Old Man Pucket, he said, 'But those were valuable animals, and he deserves some compensation for their loss. If you're shy of cash, some livestock—horses or cattle—would do it.'

And that was that.

A few days after the trial, Old Man Pucket showed up with a string of horses. Dad refused to leave the house, so I went out to meet Old Man Pucket, who was turning the horses into the corral.

'Just like the judge ordered, miss,' he said.

'Payment acknowledged,' I said, and shook his hand. Unlike Dad, I saw no point in carrying a grudge with a neighbour.

Old Man Pucket handed me a paper listing what he claimed was the value of each horse, then tipped his hat.

After Old Man Pucket left, Dad came out and looked at the horses. When I handed him the paper, he snorted in disgust. 'None of those nags is worth twenty dollars,' he said.

It was true. Old Man Pucket's valuations were wildly inflated. There were eight horses in all, stumpy, tough little mustangs, the kind that cow-boys rounded up out in the wild and sat on for a day or two so they'd just barely accept a saddle. They were unshod, with chipped-up hooves in need of trimming, and their tails were matted with burrs. They were also scared, watching us nervously.

The problem with half-broke horses like these was that no one took the time to train them. Cowboys caught them and ran them on fear, taking pride in staying on no matter how desperately the horses bucked and fishtailed. Not properly broken, they were always scared and hated humans. They were, however, intelligent and had pluck and, if you broke them right, they made good horses.

One in particular caught my eye, a mare. A pinto, she seemed less scared and watched me intently. I cut her out from the herd, lassoed her, and then slowly walked up to her, following Dad's rule to keep your eyes on the ground around strange horses.

She stood still and when I reached her, I raised my hand to the side of her head and scratched behind one ear. Then I brought my hand down the side of her face. She didn't jerk back, and I knew she was something special, not the greatest beauty—being a patchwork of white, brown and black—but you could tell she could use her brain, and I'd take smarts over looks in a horse any day.

'She's yours,' Dad said. 'What are you going to name her?'

I looked at the mare. For the most part, us ranch folks liked to keep names simple. If a cat had socks, we called it Socks; if a dog was red, we called it Red; if a horse had a blaze, we called it Blaze.

'I'll call her Patches,' I said.

I set about breaking Patches properly. That was one smart horse, and in no time she had truly accepted the bit and was moving off the leg at the slightest touch of my spur. After a few months of that, she even started cutting cattle. I started racing Patches in little amateur races, and from time to time we even returned with the purse.

The following summer, Buster came home from school, having completed the eighth grade. Mom and Dad talked about him going on to high school, but Buster wasn't interested in high school. He knew enough math and reading and writing to run a ranch, and he didn't see much point in picking up more knowledge than that.

Not long after Buster got back, it became clear to me that he and Dorothy were sweet on each other. In some ways it was a strange match, since she was a few years older and he scarcely had hair on his chin. Mom was horrified when she found out, but I thought Buster was lucky. He was always a little unmotivated, and if he was going to run the ranch with any success, he'd need someone determined and hardworking like Dorothy beside him.

ONE DAY IN JULY, I rode Patches into Tinnie to collect the mail. To my surprise, there was a letter for me from Mother Albertina. I sat on the steps outside the general store to read it.

She continued to think about me, she wrote, and continued to believe I'd make an excellent teacher. In fact, she went on, because of the war that had started up in Europe, there was a shortage of teachers, particularly in the remote parts of the country. If I was able to pass a test the government was giving in Santa Fe, I could probably get a job even without a degree and even though I was just fifteen years old.

I was so excited, I had to resist the urge to gallop all the way back to the ranch. As I rode along, I kept thinking this was the door Mother Albertina had told me about.

Mom and Dad didn't like the idea at all. Mom kept saying I had a better chance of marriage if I stayed here in the valley, where I was known as the daughter of a substantial property owner. Dad kept throwing out one reason after another: I was too young; it was too dangerous; why would I want to be cooped up in a classroom?

Finally, after raising all these objections, Dad sat me down on the back porch. 'The fact is,' he said, 'I need you.'

I had seen that coming. 'This'll never be my ranch; it's going to Buster, and with Buster marrying Dorothy, you have all the help you need. Like you're always saying, I've got to find my Purpose.'

Dad thought about it for a minute. 'Well, hell,' he said at last. 'I suppose you could at least go and take the damn test.'

The test was easier than I expected, mostly questions about word definitions, fractions and American history. A few weeks later, I was back at the ranch when Buster came into the house with a letter for me. Dad, Mom and Helen all watched me open it.

I'd passed the test. I was being offered the job of an itinerant replacement teacher in northern Arizona. I gave a shriek of delight.

'Oh my,' Mom said.

Buster and Helen were hugging me, and then I turned to Dad.

'Seems you been dealt a card,' Dad said. 'I guess you better go on and play it.'

The school that was expecting me was in Red Lake, Arizona, 500 miles to the west, and the only way for me to get there was on Patches. I decided to travel light, bringing only a toothbrush, a change of underwear, a presentable dress, a comb, a canteen and my bedroll. I had money from those race purses I'd won, and I could buy provisions along the way, since most every town in New Mexico and Arizona was about a day's ride from the next. I figured the trip would take a good four weeks.

Mom was worried sick about a fifteen-year-old girl travelling alone through the desert, but I told her I'd keep my hair under my hat and my voice low. For insurance, Dad gave me a pearl-handled six-shooter, but the fact was, the journey seemed like no big deal, just a 500-mile version of the six-mile ride into Tinnie.

Patches and I were to leave at first light one morning in early August. After breakfast, I brought Patches into the barn. Dad followed me, and as I saddled up, he started deluging me with all sorts of advice, telling me to hope for the best but plan for the worst, neither a borrower nor a lender be, keep your head up and your nose clean and your powder dry, and if you do have to shoot, shoot straight and be damn sure you shoot first. He wouldn't shut up.

'I'll be fine, Dad,' I said. 'And you will, too.'

''Course I will.'

I swung up into the saddle and headed over towards the house. The sky was turning from grey to blue, the air already warming. It looked to be a dusty scorcher of a day.

Everyone except Mom was standing on the front porch, but I could see her watching me through the blur of the bedroom window. I waved at them all and turned Patches down the lane.

III

Promises

The dirt road running west from Tinnie was an old Indian trail, packed down and widened over the years by wagon wheels. It followed the Rio Hondo through the foothills of the Capitan Mountains. The land in those parts of southern New Mexico was easy on the eye. Cedars grew thick. From time to time, I saw antelope standing at the riverbank or bounding down a hillside. Once or twice a day, Patches and

I passed a lone cowboy on a horse or a wagonful of Mexicans. I always nodded, but I kept my distance.

Late each morning when the sun got high, I looked for a shady spot near the river where Patches could graze on the short grass. I needed rest, too. When it started to cool, we moved on again and kept going until it got dark. I'd make a sagebrush fire, eat some jerky and biscuits, and lie in my blanket, listening to the howling of the distant coyotes while Patches grazed nearby.

At each town—usually a small collection of wood shacks and adobe huts, a single store and a little church—I bought the next day's food and chatted with the storekeeper about the road ahead. Was it rocky? Where was the best place to water and camp?

Most of the storekeepers were happy to play the expert, giving me advice and directions, drawing maps on paper bags. They were also happy to have someone to talk to. At one lonely place, the store was deserted except for the owner. The shelves were lined with a few dusty tins of peaches and bottles of liniments. After paying for a bag of hardtack, I asked the storekeeper, 'How many customers have you had today?'

'You're the first this week,' he said. 'But it's only Wednesday.'

I rode from Hondo to Lincoln to Capitan to Carrizozo. I reached the Rio Grande at a small town called Los Lunas. It wasn't much of a river there, and a Zuni girl ferried me across in a raft, pulling us along with a rope that ran from one bank to the other.

I crossed into Arizona at the Painted Cliffs, red sandstone bluffs that rose straight up out of the desert floor. After another ten days of steady riding, I reached Flagstaff. Its hotel advertised a bathtub and, since I was feeling pretty ripe at that point, it was mighty tempting, but I kept going and two days later arrived at Red Lake.

I'd been on the road, out in the sun and sleeping in the open, for twenty-eight days. I was tired and caked with dirt. I'd lost weight, my clothes were heavy with grime and hung loosely, and when I looked in a mirror, my face seemed harder. My skin had darkened, and I had the beginnings of squint lines round my eyes. But I had made it, made it through that darned door.

RED LAKE was a small ranch town on a high plateau about thirty miles south of the Grand Canyon. The land here was greener than the parts of Arizona I'd passed through, with thick grass that grew so high it tickled the bellies of the cattle that grazed there. The arange round Red Lake wasn't used for much other than grazing, but farmers had recently come with their ploughs and well diggers and high hopes to do the backbreaking work that was needed to bring up crops as green as the grass that grew there. Those farmers brought big families with them, and their kids needed teaching.

Shortly after I arrived, the county superintendent, Mr MacIntosh, rode up from Flagstaff to explain the situation. Mr MacIntosh was a slight man with a head so narrow he reminded me of a fish. Because of the war, he explained, men were joining the army and women were leaving the countryside to take the high-paying factory jobs the men had left behind. But even with the shortage of teachers in rural areas, the board wanted the certified teachers to have at least an eighth-grade education, which I didn't have. So I was to teach in Red Lake until they could hire a more qualified person, and then I'd be sent somewhere else.

'Don't worry,' Superintendent MacIntosh said. 'We'll always find a place for you.'

Red Lake had a one-room schoolhouse with an oil stove in a corner, a desk for the teacher, a row of benches for the kids and a slate blackboard. A lot of one-room schools had a teacherage attached, where the teacher lived, but the one in Red Lake didn't, so I slept on the floor of the school in my bedroll.

Still, I loved my job. I got to teach exactly what I wanted, in the way I wanted. I had fifteen students of all ages and abilities, and I didn't have to round them up, because their parents, eager for them to learn, brought them to the school on the first day and made sure they kept coming back.

Most of the kids were born back east, though some came from as far away as Norway. The girls wore faded, floor-length gingham dresses, the boys had chopped-up haircuts, and they all went barefoot in warm weather. Some of those kids were poorer than poor.

We had no textbooks, so the kids brought whatever they had from home—family Bibles, almanacs, letters, seed catalogues—and we read from those. When winter came, one of the fathers gave me a fur coat he'd made from coyotes he'd trapped, and I wore it in the schoolroom during the day, since my desk was far from the oil stove. Mothers made a point of bringing me stews and pies and inviting me to Sunday dinner.

Halfway through the year, Superintendent MacIntosh found a certified teacher for Red Lake, and I was sent on to another town called Cow Springs. For the next three years, that's how Patches and I lived, moving from one town to another—Leupp, Greasewood, Wide Ruin—after a stay of a few months, never putting down roots. Still, all those rascals I was teaching learned to obey me, and I was teaching them things they needed to know, which made me feel like I was making a difference. I never met a kid I couldn't teach. Every kid was good at something, and the trick was to find out what it was, then use it to teach him everything else. It was good work, the kind that let you look forward to the next day.

Then the war ended. One day not long after I'd turned eighteen, Superintendent MacIntosh caught up with me to explain that, with the men all returning home, women were being laid off at the factories in favour of the veterans. Many of those women were certified teachers who were looking to get back their old jobs. Superintendent MacIntosh said he'd heard glowing things about my work, but I hadn't finished eighth grade, and Arizona needed to give priority in hiring to those who'd fought for their country.

'So I'm getting the boot?' I asked.

'Unfortunately, your services are no longer needed.'

I stared at the fish-faced superintendent. I'd figured this day might come, but I still felt like the floor had fallen out from under me. I knew I was a good teacher. I loved it, and I couldn't help feeling a little burned about being told by Fish Face that I was now unqualified to do something I'd spent the last four years doing.

Superintendent MacIntosh seemed to know what I was thinking. 'You're young and strong, and you got pretty eyes,' he said. 'You just find yourself a husband, and you'll be fine.'

THE RIDE BACK to the KC seemed to take about half as long as that first journey out to Red Lake, but that's the way it always is when you're heading home. The only adventure occurred when a rattler parked itself under my saddle one night, but it reared back and zipped off before I could get out my gun. And then there was the airplane. Patches and I were heading east near the Homolovi Ruins, when we heard the putt-putt of an engine in the sky behind us. I looked back, and a red biplane—the first I'd ever seen—was following the road east a few hundred feet above the ground.

Patches started to scutch about at the strange noise, but I held her in, and as the plane approached, I took off my hat and waved. The pilot dipped the plane's wings in response, and as it passed us, he leaned out and waved back. I kicked up Patches, and we galloped after the plane, me flapping my hat and shouting, though I was so excited that I had no idea what I was trying to say.

Never in my life had I ever seen anything like that airplane. It was amazing that it didn't just fall out of the sky, but for the first time it dawned on me what the word 'airplane' meant. That was what it did. It stayed aloft because it was planing the air.

I only wished I had some students to explain all this to.

ALL THAT TIME I was teaching, I had never gone home, since the trip took so long. While I was away, I did write to the family once a week and in return received long letters from Dad waxing eloquent about his latest political convictions, yet providing few details about how they were faring. But the place looked well run, the fences in repair, the outbuildings freshly whitewashed, a new clapboard wing on the main house, a supply of firewood stacked under the porch roof.

Lupe was out front scouring a pot when I rode up. She gave a shriek, everyone came running from the house and barn, and there was a whole lot of hugging and happy tears. Dad kept saying, 'You left a girl and you come back a woman.' He and Mom both had strands of grey in their hair, Buster had filled out and grown a moustache, and Helen had become a willowy sixteen-year-old beauty.

Buster and Dorothy had gotten married the year before. They lived in the new wing of the house, and it soon became clear that Dorothy was running the place. She handed out work assignments for Buster and Apache, and even Mom, Dad and Helen. Mom complained that Dorothy had gotten high-handed, but I could tell they were secretly glad to have someone doing what I used to do.

Mom's biggest concern was Helen. She had reached marrying age, but pretty as she was, that girl just lacked get-up-and-go. Helen was happy to sew and bake pies, but she hated any kind of work that made her break into a sweat, and most of the ranchers looking for wives wanted a woman who could help out with branding calves and drive the chuck wagon during round-ups. Mom's plan was to send Helen to the Sisters of Loretto—hoping that with a little polish, she'd attract a citified man in Santa Fe—but Dorothy argued that all the earnings from the ranch needed to be reinvested in machinery to raise crop yields. Helen herself was talking about how she'd like to move to Los Angeles and become an actress.

THE MORNING AFTER I returned, we were eating breakfast in the kitchen, Mom passing the teapot around. I'd developed a taste for coffee in Arizona, but Dad allowed nothing stronger than tea on the ranch.

After cleaning up, Dad and I walked out onto the porch. 'You ready to get back in the corral?' he asked. 'I got a couple of new saddlebred fillies that I know you can work wonders with.'

'I don't know, Dad.'

'What do you mean? You're a horsewoman.'

'With Dorothy in charge, I'm not sure there's a place for me here anymore.'

'Don't go talking nonsense. You belong here.'

But the truth was, I didn't feel I did. And even if there was a place for me, it was not the life I wanted. That plane that had flown overhead at the Homolovi Ruins had got me to thinking. Also, I'd seen a number of automobiles in Arizona, and they gave me a sinking feeling about the future prospects for carriage horses.

'You ever think of getting an automobile, Dad?' I asked.

'Consarned contraptions,' Dad said. 'No one'll ever look as smart in one of those fume belchers as they do in a carriage.'

That got him going about how President Taft had taken this country in the wrong direction by getting rid of the White House stables and replacing them with a garage.

As I listened to Dad, I could feel myself pulling away from him. All my life I'd been hearing Dad reminiscing about the past and railing against the future. What Dad didn't understand was that no matter how much he hated or feared the future, it was coming.

Another thing that airplane made me realise was that there was a whole world out there beyond ranchland that I'd never seen, a place where I might finally get that darned diploma. And maybe I'd even learn to fly an airplane.

So the way I saw it, I had two choices: stay on the ranch or strike out on my own. Staying on the ranch meant either finding a man to marry or becoming the spinster aunt to the passel of children that Dorothy and Buster talked about having. Striking out on my own meant going where the opportunities were the greatest. I wanted to go to the biggest, most boomingest city I could find.

A month later, I was on the train to Chicago.

THE RAILROAD RAN NORTHEAST through the rolling prairie to Kansas City, then on across the Mississippi and into the farmland of Illinois. The trip lasted only four days, whereas it had taken Patches an entire month to go less than half that distance.

When the train pulled into Chicago, I took down my little suitcase and walked through the station into the street. I'd never seen such a mass of people, nor had my ears been assaulted by such a ferocious din, with automobiles honking, trolleys clanging, and hydraulic jackhammers blasting away.

I walked around, gawking at the skyscrapers going up everywhere; then I made my way over to the lake—deep blue, flat and as endless as the range, only it was water, fresh and flowing and cold, even in the summer. Coming from a place where people measured water by the pailful, where they fought and sometimes killed each other over water, it was hard to imagine that billions of gallons of fresh water could be sitting there undrunk, unused and uncontested.

After gazing at the lake for a long while, I followed my plan: I found a Catholic church and asked a priest to recommend a boarding-house for women. I rented a bed—four to a room—then I bought the newspapers and looked at the help-wanted ads.

The next day, I started searching for a job. Finding work was considerably harder than I had expected. I had hoped to get a position as a governess or a tutor, but when I admitted that I didn't even have an eighth-grade education, people looked at me like they were wondering why I was wasting their time, even after I told them about my teaching experience. 'That may be fine for sodbusters,' one woman said, 'but it won't do in Chicago.'

The sales jobs at department stores all required experience. With all the soldiers returning home and all the girls like me pouring in from the countryside, there was too much competition. My money started running low, and I had to face the fact that my options were pretty much limited to factory work or becoming a maid.

Sitting in front of a sewing machine for twelve hours a day didn't strike me as a way to get ahead, whereas if I worked as a maid, I'd get to know people with money and, if I showed initiative, I might be able to parlay that position into something better.

I found a job pretty quickly, working for a commodities trader and his wife, Mim. They lived in a big modern house with radiator heat, a clothes-washing machine and faucets for hot water and cold water. I got there before dawn, spent the day scrubbing, polishing and dusting, and left after I'd cleaned the dinner dishes.

I didn't mind the hard work. What bothered me was the way that Mim, a long-faced blonde woman only a few years older than me, treated me as if I didn't exist. While Mim seemed very impressed with herself, acting terribly grand, she wasn't that bright.

In fact, I wondered if anyone could really be such a dodo. Once, a French woman with a toy poodle came for lunch, and when the dog started barking, the woman spoke to it in French. 'That's a smart dog,' Mim said. 'I didn't know dogs could speak French.'

Mim also did crossword puzzles, constantly asking her husband the answers to simple clues, and when I made the mistake of answering one, she shot me a short, sharp look.

After I'd been there two weeks, she called me into the kitchen. 'This isn't working out,' she said.

I was stunned. I'd kept Mim's house spotless. 'Why?' I asked.

'Your attitude. I don't like the way you look at me. You don't seem to know your place. A maid should keep her head down.'

I quickly got another job as a maid, and although it was against my nature, I made a point of keeping my mouth shut and my head down. In the evenings, meanwhile, I went to school to get my diploma. There was no shame in doing hard work, but polishing silver for rich dunderheads was not my Purpose.

Busy as I was, and pretty exhausted most of the time, I loved Chicago. It was bold and bawdy, though bitterly cold in the winter. Women were march-ing for the right to vote, and I attended a couple of rallies with one of my roommates, Minnie Hanagan, a spunky Irish girl with green eyes and black hair who worked in a beer-bottling plant. Minnie never met a topic she didn't have an opinion on or heard a comment she couldn't interrupt. After working all day as a zip-lipped maid, keeping my thoughts to myself and my eyes on the ground, it was great to unwind with Minnie by arguing about politics, religion, and everything else under the sun. We double-dated a couple of times, factory boys squiring us round to the cheaper speakeasies, but they were usually either tongue-tied or loutish. I had more fun talking to Minnie than I did to any of those fellows, and sometimes the two of us went off and danced by ourselves. Minnie Hanagan was the closest thing I'd ever had to a genuine friend.

Minnie asked me what my birthday was, and when it rolled round—I was turning twenty-one—she gave me a tube of dark red lipstick. It was all she could afford, she said, but we could make ourselves up to look like real ladies and go to one of the big department stores, where we'd have fun trying on all the things we'd be able to buy one of these days. I'd never been one for make up, but Minnie applied it for me, rubbing a dab into my cheeks as well, and darned if I didn't look a bit like a stockbroker's wife.

Minnie led me through the department store. It was as big as a cathedral, with aisle after aisle of gloves, furs, shoes and anything else you could possibly imagine buying. We stopped at the hat department, and Minnie had me try on one after another—little hats, big hats, hats with feathers, hats with veils. As the hats piled up on the counter, a salesclerk came over.

'Are you girls able to find anything in your price range?' she asked with a cold smile.

I felt a little flustered. 'Not really,' I said.

'Then maybe you're in the wrong store,' she said.

Minnie stared at the woman square on. 'Price isn't the problem,' she said. 'The problem is finding something up-to-date in this dowdy stock. Lily, let's try Carson Pirie Scott.'

Minnie turned on her heel, and as we walked off, she told me, 'When they get high-handed, all you have to do is remind yourself that they're just hired help.'

AFTER I HAD BEEN in Chicago for almost two years, I came home from work on a July evening to find one of my other roommates laying out Minnie's only good dress on her bed.

Minnie, she said, had been at the bottling plant where she worked when her long black hair got caught in the machinery. She was pulled into the massive grinding gears. It was over before anyone nearby even had time to think.

Minnie was supposed to wear her hair up in a kerchief, but she was so proud of those thick, shiny Irish tresses that she could never resist the temptation to let them down. Her body was so badly mangled that they had to have a closed-coffin funeral.

I loved that girl and, as I sat through the service, all I could think was that if I'd been there, maybe I could have rescued her. I kept imagining myself chopping her hair off, pulling her back, and hugging her as we sobbed happily, realising how close she'd come to a gruesome death.

That night at the boarding house, I got out a pair of scissors and a mirror, and although Mom always called my long brown hair my crowning glory, I cut it all off just below my ears.

I didn't expect to like my new short hair, but I did. It took almost no time to wash and dry, and I didn't have to fuss with curling irons, hairpins and bows. Long curls were a thing of the past. For us modern women, short-cropped hair was the way to go.

Indeed, with my new haircut, I felt I looked the model of the Chicago flapper. Men took more notice of me, and one Sunday while I was walking along the lakefront, a broad-shouldered fellow in a seersucker suit and a straw boater struck up a conversation. His name was Ted Conover, and he'd been a boxer but now worked as a vacuum-cleaner salesman for the Electric Suction Sweeper Company. 'Get a foot in the door, toss in some dirt, and they gotta let you demonstrate your product,' he said with a chuckle.

I knew from the start that Ted was a bit of a huckster. Even so, I liked his spirit. He had quick grey eyes and the gift of the gab. He bought me a snow cone from a street vendor, and we sat on a bench by a pink marble fountain. He told me about growing up in South Boston, catching rides on the backs of trolley cars, stealing pickles from the pickle man's wagon, and learning to throw a punch in street fights. He loved his own jokes so much that he'd start laughing halfway through, and you'd start laughing, too, even though you hadn't heard the punch line yet. Maybe I was missing Minnie and needed someone in my life, but I fell hard for that fellow.

The following week, Ted took me to dinner at the Palmer House Hotel, and after that we started seeing each other regularly, though he was often out of the city for days at a time, because his sales territory stretched all the way to Springfield. Ted always liked to be in a crowd, and we went to ball games at Wrigley Field, movies at the Folly Theater, and prizefights at the Chicago Arena. I smoked my first cigarette, drank my first glass of champagne, and played my first game of dice. Ted loved dice.

Late in the summer, he showed up at the boarding house with a bathing suit he'd bought for me at Marshall Field's, and we took the train down to Gary, where we spent the afternoon swimming in the lake and sunbathing in front of big sand dunes. I didn't know how to swim, but Ted taught me how.

About six weeks after I met Ted, he took me back to the pink marble fountain, bought me another snow cone and, as he gave it to me, planted a diamond ring on top. 'A piece of ice that I'm hoping will make you melt,' he said.

We got married in the Catholic church I'd visited when I first came to Chicago. I wore a blue linen dress I borrowed from one of the girls at the boarding house. Neither of us could take time off for a honeymoon.

That afternoon, we moved into a boarding house for married couples, and we celebrated in our room with a bottle of bathtub gin. The next day, I went back to my job as a maid, and Ted hit the road.

I FOUND that I liked being married. After so many years on my own, I was sharing my life for the first time, and it made the hard moments easier and the good moments better.

Ted always encouraged people to think big, to dream big, and when he found out that my great ambition had always been not just to finish high school but also to go on to college, he told me I might even want to think of getting a PhD. Ted was full of plenty of schemes for himself, too—how he was going to manufacture his own line of vacuum cleaners, build radio antennas out in the prairie, start a telephone company.

We decided we'd put off having kids and squirrel away money while I finished night school. When the future came into better focus, we'd be ready for it.

Ted was away a lot, but that was fine with me, because I was busy with work and night school. Busy as we were, the years passed quickly. When I was twenty-six, I finally got my high school diploma. I began looking for a better job but was still working as a maid when, one summer morning, crossing the street while carrying an armload of groceries, a white roadster came tearing round the corner. The driver slammed on the brakes when he saw me, but it was too late. The grille upended me, and I went rolling across the hood, scattering the apples, buns and tins that I'd been carrying.

I instinctively went soft as I tumbled off the hood and onto the street. I lay there for a moment, stunned, as people rushed over. The driver jumped out. He was a young man with slicked-back hair.

Slick knelt down and asked if I was OK. The accident looked worse than it was, and I could tell I had no serious injuries, only bruised bones and some nasty scrapes on my arms and knees.

'I'm fine,' I said. 'I used to break horses. One thing I know how to do is take a fall.'

Slick insisted on taking me to the hospital. I told the nurse at the emergency room I was fine, but she told me I was a little more banged up than I seemed to believe. While filling out her forms, the nurse asked if I was married and, when I said yes, Slick told me I should call my husband.

'He's a travelling salesman,' I said. 'He's on the road.'

'Then call his office. They'll know how to reach him.'

While the nurse bandaged me up, Slick found the number and gave me a nickel for the pay phone. I made the call.

A man answered. 'Sales. This is Charlie.'

'I'm wondering if there's any way you can help me track down Ted Conover on the road. This is his wife, Lily.'

'Ted ain't on the road. He just left for lunch. And his wife's name's Margaret. Is this some kind of prank?'

I felt like the floor was tilting underneath me. I didn't know what to say, so I hung up.

Slick was baffled by the way I rushed out of the phone booth past him, but I had to get out of the hospital to clear my head. I kept fighting panic as I made my way to the lake, where I walked for miles. Had I been two-timed? There was only one way to find out.

The Electric Suction sales office was in a five-storey cast-iron building near the Loop. When I got to the block, I fished a newspaper from a trash can and took up a position in a lobby across the street. At five o'clock, people began pouring out onto the sidewalks and, sure enough, my husband joined them, walking out of the door wearing his favourite hat. He'd clearly fibbed about being out of town, but I still didn't have the full story.

I followed Ted at a safe distance as he made his way through the crowded streets over to the El. I boarded the train one car behind him. At every stop, I stuck my head out to watch and saw that he got out at Hyde Park. I followed him a few blocks east to a shabby walk-up apartment building that had sagging wooden staircases.

Ted went into one of them. I waited until some kids came out, then slipped through the open door into the hallway. There were four apartments on each floor, and I stopped at every door, pressing my ear against it, listening for the sound of Ted's South Boston accent. Finally, on the third floor, I heard it.

Without knowing exactly what I was going to do, I knocked. After a couple of seconds, the door opened, and standing in front of me was a woman with a toddler on her hip.

'Are you Ted Conover's wife, Margaret?' I asked.

'Yes. Who are you?'

I looked at this woman Margaret for a moment. I figured that she was about my age, but she seemed tired, and her hair was going grey. Still, she had a wan smile, as if life was a struggle but she managed from time to time to find something to laugh about.

Behind her I could hear a couple of boys arguing, then Ted's voice saying, 'Who is it, honey?'

I had an almost overwhelming temptation to push past Margaret and gouge out that lying cheater's eyes, but something held me back—what it would do to this woman and her kids.

'I'm with the census,' I said. 'We just wanted to confirm that a family of four is living here.'

'Five,' she said, 'though sometimes it feels more like fifteen.'

I forced myself to smile and said, 'That's all I need to know.'

I WAS ON THE EL going back to the boarding house when I suddenly thought about our joint bank account. I stayed up all night, sick with worry about it, and was waiting in front of the bank when the doors opened. Ted and I had salted away almost 200 dollars in an interest-bearing savings account, but when I got to the teller, he told me there were only ten dollars left.

I got back to the boarding house and sat down on the bed. I was surprised by how calm I felt. But as I packed my pearl-handled revolver in my purse, I noticed my hands were trembling.

I took a bus to the Loop and walked up the stairs of the cast-iron building to Ted's office. I pushed open the frosted glass door. Ted and another man sat at two desks, reading newspapers and smoking.

As soon as I saw Ted, I lost every bit of ladylike decorum my mother had tried to instill in me. I became a wild woman, cursing and screaming—'You no-good low-down dirty lying scum-sucking son of a bitch!'—and whaling him with my purse, which, since I had my six-shooter in it, meant I was giving him a pistol-whipping.

I got in some solid blows by the time the other guy pulled me off. I then turned on him with my purse and whacked him good once before Ted grabbed me. 'Calm down or I'll drop you with a roundhouse punch,' he said, 'and you know I can.'

'You go ahead, buster; you hit me and I'll charge you with assault as well as robbery and bigamy.' But I stopped struggling.

The other fellow grabbed his hat. 'I see you two have a few things to discuss,' he said, and slipped out the door.

Everything came exploding out of me then: Why had he married me when he already had a wife and three children? Why had he taken the money that we were supposedly saving for our future?

As Ted listened, his eyes welled up with tears. He'd taken the money because he'd run up some gambling debts. Margaret, he said, was the mother of his children, but he loved me. 'Lily,' he said, 'lying was the only way I could have you.'

The louse was acting as if he expected me to feel sorry for him.

'It's my fault,' he said. Then he reached out and actually touched my hand, adding, 'By loving you, I've destroyed you.'

The bum sounded like he was about to blubber up. I pulled my hand away.

'You have a mighty high opinion of yourself,' I told him. 'The fact is, you don't love me, and you haven't destroyed me. You don't have what it takes to do that.'

I shoved past him, slamming the door on my way out, then turned and swung my purse against the frosted glass pane, shattering it, and all the broken little pieces fell in a shower to the floor.

I took another walk along the lake. Things looked pretty bleak right then, but I'd survived a lot worse than a brief marriage to a heel, and I'd survive this, too.

A wind was up, and as I watched it lash the water, one thing became crystal clear. It was over between me and Chicago. The city, for all its beautiful water and soaring skyscrapers, had been nothing but heartache. It was time for me to get back to the range.

That very day, I went over to the Catholic church where I married that heel and told the priest what had happened. He said that if I could prove my husband had been previously married, I could apply to the bishop for an annulment. With the help of a clerk at City Hall, I dug out a copy of Ted's other marriage certificate, and the priest said he'd set the wheels in motion.

I thought Ted's wife needed to know what had happened, and I wrote her a letter explaining it. I decided, however, not to file criminal charges against Ted. It had not been illegal for that weasel to take the money, since it was a joint account; it was just stupid of me to trust him. And if he was sent off to prison as a bigamist, his wife and kids would be worse off than their dad. I also figured the peckerhead had taken up enough of my time, and if he had to wait to get his just deserts from the Lord himself, that was OK by me.

After mailing the letter, I took the ring Ted had given me in to a jeweller. I wasn't going to keep it, but I certainly wasn't going to do something melodramatic, like throw it in the lake. I figured it would fetch a couple of hundred dollars, but the jeweller looked at the diamond with his eyepiece and said, 'It's fake.'

So I threw it in the lake after all.

ONCE I STOPPED smacking myself in the head for being so gullible, I focused on the future. I was twenty-seven years old, no spring chicken. Since I obviously couldn't count on a man to take care of me, what I needed more than ever was a profession. I needed to get my college education and become a teacher. So I applied to the Arizona State teachers' college in Flagstaff. As I waited to hear back—and waited for the annulment—I did nothing but work, scrimp and save, taking two jobs during the week and another on weekends. The time flew by, and when both the dispensation and the acceptance letter arrived, I had enough money for a year of college.

The day came for me to say goodbye to Chicago. I packed everything I had into the same suitcase I had brought with me. I was leaving the city with about as much stuff as I had arrived with. But I had learned a lot—about myself and other people.

The train pulled out of Union Station, and in a short time we were heading into the countryside. Not a single soul in Chicago would miss me. Aside from getting my degree, I'd spent these past eight years in thankless, pointless drudgery, polishing silver that got tarnished again, washing dishes day after day, and ironing shirts.

Working in those little desert towns during the war years—teaching ragamuffins how to read—I had felt needed in a way that I never had in Chicago. That was how I wanted to feel again.

IV

The Red Silk Shirt

You saw plenty of cars in Santa Fe now, and even out in the countryside, but when I got back to the ranch, I was surprised by how little things had changed, except that Buster and Dorothy had a couple of kids. Dad had completely abdicated responsibility for the place. Mom had grown more frail and complained that her teeth hurt. A couple of years earlier, Helen had moved to Los Angeles to chase her dream of making it in the movies. While she'd yet to get any roles, as she explained in letters home, she'd met a few producers and, in the meantime, was working as a clerk in a milliner's shop.

The first day back, I went out to see Patches, who was in the pasture. She seemed to have aged better than anyone else. I saddled her up, and we rode out into the valley. It was late afternoon, and the long purple shadow we cast dipped and swelled across the rolling grassland. Patches was a good seventeen years old, but she still had the juice, and at a rise I clucked her up to a gallop. I hadn't been on a horse since leaving for Chicago, and it just felt right.

Unlike the last time I came home, no one begged me to stay. Even Dad acted as if he assumed I'd be moving on, and that was fine by me. I didn't belong in Chicago, but it had changed me, so I didn't belong on the KC, either. Also, if I was going to stay, I'd need to pitch in on the chores, and after those years of maid work, mucking out stalls didn't exactly call to me. I left early for Flagstaff.

ALTHOUGH I WAS OLDER than most of the other students, I loved college. Unlike many of the boys, who were interested in football and drinking, and the girls, who were interested in boys, I knew why I was there and what I wanted to get out of it. I wished I could take every course and read every book in the library.

My only concern was how I was going to pay the next year's tuition. But after I'd been at the university for exactly one semester, Grady Gammage, president of the college, asked to see me. He said he'd been contacted by the town of Red Lake, which was looking for a teacher. The folks in Red Lake remembered me from the time I'd taught there. They were willing to sign me up, even though I had just begun college. 'It's a tough choice,' Mr Gammage said. 'If you start teaching now, you'll give up school.'

It didn't seem a tough choice at all. I could either pay money to go to classes or get paid for teaching classes.

'When do I start?' I asked.

I WENT BACK to the ranch to get Patches and, for the third time, that horse and I made the 500-mile journey between Tinnie and Red Lake. Patches was out of shape, but I eased her along, and she toned up pretty quick.

I ran into more people than I had last time, and every now and again a car would barrel past, trailing a cone of dust. But there were still long stretches of solitude, only me and Patches ambling along and, as I sat by my little fire at night, the coyotes howled just like they always had, and the huge moon turned the desert silver.

The town of Red Lake had changed since I first saw it almost fifteen years before. Arizona, with its wide-open spaces, had always been a haven for folks who didn't like the law, and there were more eccentrics around— Mexican rum-runners, hallucinating prospectors, a guy with four wives who wasn't a Mormon.

More farmers had also put down stakes, and more stores had opened, including a new automobile garage with a gasoline pump out front. The grass outside town had been grazed down to the nub, and I wondered if maybe there were more people here than the land could bear.

The schoolhouse now had a teacherage built onto the back, so I had my own room to sleep in. I had thirty-six students of all ages, sizes and breeds, and I made sure when I entered the classroom that every one of them stood up and said, 'Good morning, Miss Casey.' Anyone who talked out of turn had to stand in the corner. Kids are like horses in that things go a lot easier if you get their respect from the outset.

When I'd been in Red Lake a month, I went over to the town hall to pick up my first paycheque. A corral was next to the building, and inside it stood a small sorrel mustang, all veined up and with saddle sweat still on his back. When he saw me, he gave me a baleful look, ears flat, and I could tell right off that was one ornery horse.

Inside the hall, a couple of deputies were lounging by a desk. When I introduced myself, one of them—a skinny guy with rooster legs and close-set eyes—said, 'I hear you come all the way from Chicago to teach us hicks a thing or two.'

'I'm just a hardworking gal here for her paycheque,' I said.

'Before you get it, you needs to pass a simple test first.'

'What test?'

'Ride that there little fella out in the corral.'

I could tell from the sidelong glances Rooster Legs and his buddy were giving each other that they thought they were going to play some prank on the greenhorn schoolteacher. I decided to play along, and we'd see who got the last laugh. Fluttering my eyes, I said this test seemed unusual, but I supposed I could give the horse a try since I had ridden before, and I assumed he was a gentle creature.

'Gentle as a baby's fart,' Rooster said.

I had on a loose dress and my sensible schoolteacher shoes. 'I'm not wearing riding clothes,' I said, 'but if he is as advertised, I guess I could trot him round a bit.'

'You could ride this horse in your pyjamas.' Rooster smirked.

I followed the two comedians out to the corral, and while they saddled up the mustang, I went over to a hedge of juniper, broke off a nice limber branch, and stripped the twigs from it.

'Ready to pass your test, ma'am?' Rooster asked. He thought the impending disaster was going to be so hilarious he could barely contain himself.

The mustang was standing stock-still but watching me out of the corner of his eye. He was just another half-broke horse, and I'd seen plenty of them in my lifetime. I hiked up my skirt and shortened the reins, twisting the horse's head to the right so he couldn't swing his hindquarters away.

As soon as I got my foot into the stirrup, he moved off, but I had him by the mane, and I swung into the saddle. He immediately started bucking. By now the two guys were splitting their sides with laughter, but I paid them no mind. The way to stop a horse from bucking is to get his head up—he has to drop it to kick out with his hindquarters—and then send him forward. I popped the horse hard in the mouth with the reins, which jerked his head right up, and whaled his rump with the juniper branch.

That got that little varmint's attention—and the comedians' as well. We set off at a good gallop, but he was still throwing his shoulders around and fishtailing. I was following the motion, riding with my upper body loose and my legs clamped like a vice round his sides. Each time I sensed the small hesitation that meant a buck was coming, I popped the horse's mouth and whaled his rear again, and he soon learned that the only way out for him was to do what I wanted him to do. In no time he settled, and I patted his neck.

I walked the mustang back to the comedians, who were no longer laughing. I could tell it was killing them that I could get the best of a horse that must have given them plenty of trouble.

'Nice little pony,' I said. 'Can I have my paycheque now?'

Word about me breaking that mustang spread round Red Lake, and people began regarding me as a woman to be reckoned with. People asked for my opinion on problem horses and problem children. Rooster—whose real name was Orville Stubbs—started acting like my faithful sidekick, as if he owed me his utter devotion.

Rooster worked only part-time as a deputy. He lived above the Red Lake stable and also made a little money on the side mucking stalls, shoeing horses, and helping out on round-ups. He turned out to be a likable little guy.

Rooster introduced me to the other horsemen in Red Lake, telling folks I was a former Chicago flapper who'd given up drinking champagne and doing the Charleston to come teach the kids of Coconino County. He encouraged me to enter the mustang, which was his and which he'd named Red Devil, in local races. They were pick-up affairs on the weekends, with five to ten horses in quarter-mile heats and a purse of five or ten dollars. I started winning some of those races, and that put round the word about me as well.

I also started playing poker on Saturday nights with Rooster and his pals. Our games were in the 'café', and they involved a fair amount of inebriation. Most folks in that part of Arizona didn't pay much attention to Prohibition. All it meant was that saloon keepers started calling their establishments 'cafés' and stashed their liquor bottles under the counter instead of on the shelf behind the bar.

Rooster and the others would put away a good quantity of what they called 'panther piss', but I'd nurse a single glass all night long. I avoided the elaborate bluffing favoured by the cowboys and always just played the hand I was dealt. Still, on most nights, I'd end up ahead of the game, a nice little stack of coins in front of me.

I became known as Lily Casey, the mustang-breaking, poker-playing, horse-race-winning schoolmarm of Coconino County, and it wasn't half bad to be in a place where no one had a problem with a woman having a moniker like that.

After a while, I could tell Rooster was sweet on me, but I let him know I'd been married once, it hadn't worked out, and I had no desire to marry again. He accepted this and we stayed good friends, but one day he came by the teacherage with a shy, sober expression.

'I got something I needs to ask you,' he said.

It sounded like he was going to propose. 'Rooster, I thought you understood we were just friends.'

'It ain't like that,' he said, and hesitated. 'What I was going to ask was could you show me how to write out "Orville Stubbs"?'

And that was how Rooster became my secret student.

Rooster started dropping by on Saturday afternoons. We'd work on his reading and writing, then head out for a night of five-card stud. I was still racing Red Devil and winning often. I had spent some of my winnings on a crimson-coloured shirt of genuine silk, and I wore it whenever I raced. I just loved that brilliant, shiny red shirt, and it became my trademark.

One day in early spring, Rooster and I rode down to a race on a ranch south of Red Lake. It was a bigger meet than usual, with five heats, a final, and a fifteen-dollar purse, and it was held on an actual track, with an inside rail where the spectators had gathered.

Red Devil's legs were on the short side, but that little mustang had fire. We took the lead early in the second heat. We were still ahead, going into the first turn, when an automobile near the rail backfired with a bang. Red bucked and veered sharply to the right. I went left, and before I knew what was happening, I was rolling on the track.

I clamped my hands over my head and lay still, eating dirt, as the other horses thundered by. I'd had the wind knocked out of me, but otherwise I was fine, and when the sound of the hoofbeats faded, I got up and smacked the dirt off my behind.

Rooster had caught Red and was jogging back towards me with the horse. I climbed into the saddle. I had no chance of catching up with the others, but Red needed to learn that my taking an involuntary dismount didn't mean he got out of doing his job.

When I crossed the finish line, the judge stood up and doffed his Stetson. I raced in a later heat, but Red was off his stride, and we finished towards the back. I had felt that fifteen-dollar purse was within my reach and afterwards, as Rooster watered the horse, I was still cursing about that backfiring automobile when the judge came over. He was a big man with a weathered face and steady, pale blue eyes.

'That was quite a tumble you took,' he said. 'I was mightily impressed with how you got right back on and finished the race.'

I started railing about the backfiring jalopy, but Rooster cut me off. 'This here is Jim Smith,' he said. 'Some folks call him Big Jim. He owns the new garage in town.'

'Don't much like automobiles, do you?' Jim asked me.

'Just don't like them spooking my horse. Truth is, I always wanted to learn to drive.'

'Maybe I can teach you.'

I WASN'T ABOUT to pass up an opportunity like that, so Jim Smith taught the teacher how to drive. He had a Model T Ford with a brass radiator, brass headlights and a brass-funnelled horn. The car, which Jim called 'the Flivver,' was an ordeal to start. It helped to have two people, because otherwise you had to crank it by hand, then jump into the front seat to pull out the choke.

But once you got the Flivver started up, driving it was a hoot. I discovered that I loved cars even more than I loved horses. Cars didn't need to be fed if they weren't working, and they didn't leave manure all over the place. They also didn't buck, bite or rear, and they didn't need to be broke and trained. Cars obeyed you.

I practised driving with Jim out on the range, and I got the hang of it quickly. In no time at all, I was tootling round the streets of Red Lake at a breakneck twenty-five miles an hour. My driving lessons began to include trips to the Grand Canyon to deliver gas to a filling station near there, then picnics. After I'd learned to drive, we continued the picnics and also took horseback rides.

After a while, it became clear that Jim was courting me. He'd been married once before, but his wife had died ten years earlier. I still wasn't interested in marriage, but there was a lot about Jim Smith that I found to admire. For one thing, unlike my previous husband, he didn't lay down a smooth line of patter. He spoke when he had something to say, and if he didn't, he felt no need to fill the void with hot air.

Jim Smith was a Jack Mormon. He'd been born into the faith but didn't practise it. His father was Lot Smith, a soldier, pioneer and ranger who had been one of Brigham Young's chief lieutenants when the Mormons went to war with the U.S. government.

Lot Smith had eight wives and fifty-two children, and those kids learned to fend for themselves. When Jim turned eleven, his father gave him a rifle, some bullets and a packet of salt and said, 'Here's your food for a week.' Jim became an excellent marksman and horseman and a wrangler. He worked in Canada for a while but returned to Arizona and became a lumberjack and homesteader. After his wife died, he joined the cavalry and, during the Great War, served in Siberia, where American soldiers were protecting the Trans-Siberian Railway from the Red Russians. While he was in Siberia, his homestead was seized for failure to pay taxes, so after being mustered out of the cavalry he become a prospector, before finally opening his garage in Red Lake. The man was no slouch.

Jim Smith was going on fifty, which made him twenty years older than me, and he had some wear and tear on him. Plus, he was bald. But Jim Smith was hardly worn out. He could spend twelve hours in the saddle, lift a car axle off the ground, and cut, split and stack enough firewood to keep his stove going all winter.

Jim could see things with those pale blue eyes that other people couldn't see—the quail in the thick brush, the eagle's nest in the side of the cliff. It was what made him a crack shot. He could spot liars, cheaters and bluffers from the get-go. But while nothing escaped him, he never let on that he knew what he knew.

And nothing ever rattled Jim Smith. He was always calm, never lost his temper. He was dependable and established. He was solid. He had his own business, and it was a steady and respectable one. He fixed cars that needed fixing. He wasn't trying to sell vacuum cleaners to gullible housewives by throwing dirt on their floors.

Even so, I still wasn't prepared to marry again, but Jim hadn't yet broached the subject of marriage, so we were enjoying ourselves, having picnics, taking horseback rides and bombing around Coconino County in the Flivver, when I got the letter from Helen.

It was postmarked Hollywood. Helen had been writing to me since she moved to California, and her letters always seemed unnaturally cheerful: she was continually on the verge of breaking into the movies, narrowly missing out on being cast, taking dance lessons, and sighting stars as they drove around town in their convertibles.

Helen was also always meeting Mr Wonderful, the man with the connections, who treated her like a princess, who was going to open doors for her in this crazy movie business, and whom she might even marry. But after several letters, she'd stop mentioning that particular Mr Wonderful, and then an even more terrific Mr Wonderful would come along. I suspected that she was getting involved with a series of cads who used her and then dumped her.

I worried that Helen was in danger of becoming a floozy, and I wrote to her warning her not to count on men to take care of her. But she wrote back scolding me for being negative, explaining that this was the way girls made it in Hollywood. I hoped she was right.

In this new letter, Helen confessed that she was pregnant by the latest Mr Wonderful, who had wanted her to get a back-alley abortion. When she told him she was scared of those coat-hanger operations, he claimed the child wasn't his and cut her out of his life.

Helen didn't know what to do. She was a couple of months along. She knew she'd be fired from the millinery shop once she started showing.

She was too ashamed to go back to Mom and Dad. The whole mess made her want to throw herself out a window.

It was immediately clear to me what Helen needed to do. I told her not to get an abortion—women died from them. It was better for her to have the child, then decide whether she wanted to keep it or give it up for adoption. She could come to Red Lake, I wrote, and live with me in the teacherage until she figured out what to do.

Helen arrived in Flagstaff a week later, and Jim let me borrow the Flivver to drive over and meet her. As she stepped down from the train, I had to bite my lip. Her slim shoulders seemed thinner, and her eyes were red from crying. She'd also peroxided her hair. When I gave her a hug, I was startled by how fragile she felt.

On the way back to Red Lake, I did most of the talking. I laid out what I thought were her options. I could write to Mom and Dad, explaining the situation. I was sure they'd forgive her and welcome her home. I'd also gotten the name of an orphanage in Phoenix if she wanted to go that route.

Helen, however, seemed distracted, almost in a daze. Smoking cigarette after cigarette, she spoke in fragmented sentences, and instead of focusing on practicalities, her mind drifted all over the place. She kept returning to totally ludicrous plans, wondering if she could get Mr Wonderful back by putting the child into an orphanage, and worrying if childbirth would ruin her figure for bathing-suit scenes in movies.

'Helen, it's time to get realistic,' I said.

'I am being realistic,' she said. 'A girl without a figure is never going to make it.'

I decided this was not the moment to push the point. When someone's wounded, the first order of business is to stop the bleeding. You can figure out later how best to help them heal.

MY BED WAS SMALL, but I scooted over so Helen and I could sleep side by side, just as we had done when we were kids. It was October, and the desert nights were turning cold, so we snuggled together and sometimes, late at night, Helen would start whimpering, which I took as a good sign, because it meant that at least she understood how grim the situation was. When that happened, I held her close and reassured her that we'd get through this, just the way we'd survived that flash flood in Texas when we were kids.

'All we need to do,' I'd say, 'is find us that cottonwood tree to climb up in, and we'll make it.'

During the day, while I was teaching, Helen kept to herself in the little bedroom. She never made any noise and spent a lot of time sleeping. I'd hoped that once she'd gotten some rest, her mind would clear. But she continued to be vague and listless, talking about Hollywood in a dreamy way that, quite frankly, irritated me.

I decided Helen needed fresh air and sunshine. We went for a stroll through town every afternoon, and I introduced her to people as my sister from Los Angeles who'd come to the desert to cure the vapours.

Helen loved my crimson shirt. When she saw me in it, she smiled for the first time since coming to Red Lake. She asked to try it on and seemed so excited while she was buttoning it up that I thought maybe she had shaken off her blues. But as she was tucking the shirt into her skirt, I saw that she was beginning to show. Our story about her coming here to take the desert air wasn't going to wash much longer, I realised, and regardless of her mood, her problems weren't going to go away.

Helen and I started attending the Catholic church in Red Lake. I didn't particularly cotton to the priest, Father Cavanaugh, a humourless man whose scowl could peel the paint off a barn. But a lot of local farmers went there, and I thought Helen might meet someone.

One day about six weeks after Helen had arrived, we were in the stuffy church, standing then kneeling then standing again as we listened to the Mass. Helen had been wearing baggy dresses to hide her condition, but suddenly she fainted. Father Cavanaugh rushed down from the altar. He felt her forehead, then looked at her for a moment, and something made him touch her stomach. 'She's with child,' he said. He saw her ringless fingers. 'And unmarried.'

Father Cavanaugh told Helen she must make a full confession. When she did, instead of offering her forgiveness, he warned her that her soul was in mortal danger. The only place for her was one of the church's homes for wayward women.

Helen came back from the visit with Father Cavanaugh more distraught than I'd ever seen her. She had no intention of going to any home—and I wouldn't have let her—but now her secret was out, and the townspeople began regarding both of us differently. Women stared at the ground when they passed us in the street, and cowboys felt free to give us the eye, as if the word had gone round that we were loose women.

One evening a couple of weeks after Helen made her confession, I heard a knock on the teacherage door. Superintendent MacIntosh was standing there. He tipped his fedora, then looked past me into the room, where Helen was washing the supper plates in a tin pan. 'Miss Casey, may I have a word with you in private?' he asked me.

'I'll go for a walk,' Helen said. She wiped her hands on her apron and made her way past Mr MacIntosh, who, making a great show of civility, tipped his hat a second time.

Since I didn't want Mr MacIntosh looking at the dirty dishes, I led him through the connecting door into the classroom. He cleared his throat nervously. Then he began what was obviously a prepared speech about Helen's condition, moral standards, school policy, impressionable schoolchildren. I started arguing that Helen stayed well away from the students, but Mr MacIntosh said he was getting pressure from a lot of the parents. If I wanted to keep my job, Helen had to go. Then he put on his fedora and left.

I felt stung and humiliated. For the second time in my life, that fish-faced pencil pusher Mr MacIntosh was telling me I wasn't wanted. The parents of my schoolkids included cattle rustlers, bootleggers, gamblers and former prostitutes. They didn't mind me racing horses, playing poker or drinking whiskey, but my showing some compassion to a sister who'd been taken advantage of filled them with moral indignation. It made me want to throttle them all.

I walked back into the teacherage. Helen was sitting on the bed smoking a cigarette. 'I didn't really go for a walk,' she said. 'I heard everything.'

I spent the night trying to reassure Helen that it was all going to work out. We'd write to Mom and Dad, I told her. They'd understand. She could go and live at the ranch until the baby was born. I'd start racing horses every weekend, and I'd save all my winnings for her and the baby, and when it was born, Buster and Dorothy could raise the child as theirs and Helen would have money to start a new life.

Helen, however, was inconsolable. She was convinced that Mom in particular would never forgive her for bringing shame on the family. No man would ever want her again; she had no place to go and couldn't make it on her own.

'I just feel like giving up,' Helen said.

'That's nonsense,' I said. 'You're much stronger than you think. There's always a way out.' I talked again about the cottonwood tree. I also told her about the time I was sent home from the Sisters of Loretto because Dad wouldn't pay my tuition, and how Mother Albertina had told me that when God closes a window, He opens a door, and it was up to us to find it.

Helen finally seemed to find some comfort in my words. 'Maybe you're right,' she said. 'Maybe there's a way.'

I was still awake and lying in bed with Helen when the first grey light of dawn began to appear in the window. Helen had finally fallen asleep, and I studied her face as it emerged from the shadows. That silly platinum hair had fallen forward, and I tucked it behind her ear. Her eyes were swollen from all the crying she'd been doing, but her features were still delicate, her skin still pale and smooth. She looked to me like an angel.

All of a sudden, I felt a lot better about things. It was Saturday. I got out of bed, put on my trousers, and brewed some coffee. When it was ready, I brought Helen a cup and told her it was time to rise and shine. A new day was beginning, and we had to make the most of it. What we'd do, I said, was borrow the Flivver from Jim and go for a picnic up to the Grand Canyon. Those mighty cliffs would give us some perspective on our puny little problems.

Helen smiled as she sat there drinking her coffee. I told her I'd go and get the car while she got dressed, and we'd get an early start to make the most of the day. 'Back in a jiffy,' I said at the door.

'OK,' Helen said. 'And Lily, I'm glad you asked me to come out here.'

It was a beautiful morning, the air so clear and crisp in the sharp light of the November sun that every blade of grass stood out. I walked past the old adobe houses and the newer frame houses, past the café and the gas station, past the farm families in town for market day, and then all at once I felt like something was choking me.

I put my hand to my throat and, in that instant, I was overtaken with a horrible feeling of dread. I turned and ran back as fast as I could, the stores and houses and puzzled farmers all flying by in one big blur, but when I flung open the door, I was too late.

My little sister was dangling from a rafter, a kicked-over chair beneath her. She'd hanged herself.

FATHER CAVANAUGH wouldn't let me bury Helen in the Catholic cemetery. Suicide was a mortal sin, he said. So Jim and I drove out onto the range, far from town. We found a beautiful site at the top of a rise overlooking a shallow forested valley—so beautiful that I knew in God's eyes it must be sacred—and we buried Helen there, in my red silk shirt.

V

Lambs

W hen people kill themselves, they think they're ending the pain, but all they're doing is passing it on to those they leave behind. For months after Helen's death, pain laid so dark and heavy on me that most days I wouldn't have gotten out of bed if I hadn't had kids to teach. The idea of riding horses—much less racing—playing cards, or driving the Flivver seemed so pointless as to be repulsive.

I thought of quitting my job, but I was under contract and, anyway, I couldn't blame the kids for what the parents had done. But I was through with Red Lake, and when the school year was over, I was moving on. I wasn't even sure I wanted to be a teacher anymore. I felt like I'd given everything I had to the kids of this town, and when I'd needed a little understanding, their families hadn't cut me any slack. Maybe I should stop devoting myself to other people's kids and instead have some kids of my own. I had never particularly wanted kids, but when Helen killed herself she also killed the little baby inside her, and something about that made me want to bring another baby into the world.

As time passed, this idea of having a baby of my own eased my grief. One day in the spring I got up early, as usual, and sat on the front step of the teacherage, drinking my coffee as the sun rose. The shafts of light gliding across the plateau warmed my face and arms.

I realised that I hadn't been paying much attention to things like the sunrise, but the sun had been coming up anyway. It was going to rise and set regardless of whether I noticed it, and if I was going to enjoy it, that was up to me.

And if I was going to have a baby, I needed to find a husband. I started looking at Jim Smith in a different light. He had plenty of good qualities, but the most important one was that I felt I could trust that man inside and out. Once I'd made up my mind about this, I didn't see the need to beat around the bush. It was late afternoon in early May when I saddled up Patches and rode over to the garage. Jim was on his back underneath a car. I told him I needed to talk to him, so he slowly pushed himself out and stood up, wiping the grease off his hands with a rag.

'Jim Smith, do you want to marry me?' I asked.

He stared at me a moment and then broke into a big grin. 'Lily Casey, I wanted to marry you ever since I saw you take that fall off that mustang and then get right back on him. I just been waiting for a good time to ask.'

'Well, this is it,' I said. 'Now, I only got two conditions.'

'Yes, ma'am.'

'The first is that we've got to be partners. Whatever we do, we'll be in it together, each sharing the load.'

'Sounds good to me.'

'The second is, I know you were raised a Mormon, but I don't want you taking any more wives.'

'Lily Casey, from what I know of you, you're just about as much woman as any man can handle.'

When I told Jim how my bum of a first husband had given me a fake ring, he got out a Sears, Roebuck catalogue and we chose a ring together so I'd know I was getting the genuine article. We got married in my classroom once school was out for the summer.

The year was 1930, and I was twenty-nine. A lot of women my age had children who were practically grown, but getting a late start didn't mean that I wouldn't enjoy the journey every bit as much—maybe even more. Jim understood why I wanted to leave Red Lake, and he agreed to move his garage to Ash Fork, about thirty miles west. Ash Fork was a bustling little town on Route 66 at the base of Williams Mountain.

At the Ash Fork bank, Jim and I took out a loan and built a garage made of Coconino sandstone, laying the stones and spreading the mortar ourselves. We hung the GARAGE sign from Red Lake over the door. With money from the loan, we sent off for a tyre pump, a ball-bearing handle jack, and a stack of ribbed tread tyres from the same Sears catalogue that we'd used to order my ring.

We had also brought the gas pump with us from Red Lake. The big glass cylinder on top was filled with gasoline—dyed red so you could tell it apart from kerosene—and every time you filled a car, air bubbles gurgled up through it.

Business was brisk. Since we were partners, Jim taught me to pump gas. I also changed oil and fixed flat tyres. By that winter, I was pregnant, but was still pitching in every day.

We built a little house—also made of Coconino sandstone—right on Route 66, which was still a dirt road. We ordered the plumbing system from Sears and installed it ourselves. I was so proud of my indoor plumbing that if someone looking for directions knocked at the door, I couldn't resist the temptation to say, 'Would you like a glass of fresh tap water?' or 'Do you need to use the toilet?'

By the time I was eight and a half months pregnant, I had swelled up pretty big. Jim insisted I stay at home, where I'd be safe. But after a few days, I started getting cabin fever and headed back to the garage. 'I don't care if I only man the cash register,' I told Jim, 'but I'm working until I go into labour.'

The baby came two weeks later, on a scorching-hot July day. I gave birth at home with the help of Granny Combs, the best midwife in the county. One of Granny's legs was shorter than the other, and she walked with a worse limp than my dad. She also chewed tobacco. Still, all the women in the county swore by her.

When I went into labour, the pain started coming in waves. Granny Combs told me that I couldn't stop the pain, but she could teach me how to get the best of it. What I needed to do was separate the actual pain from the fear that something terrible was happening to my body. 'The pain is your body complaining,' she said. 'If you listen to the pain and tell your body, "Yeah, I hear you," then you won't be so afraid of it.'

My labour lasted only a couple of hours. When the baby came out, Granny Combs said, 'It's a girl,' and held her up. The baby let out a cry. Granny Combs had a sixth sense and could read minds and tell fortunes. While I held the baby and nursed her, Granny Combs tore herself a plug of tobacco and laid out cards to see what the future had in store for my newborn.

'She will have a long life, and it will be eventful,' Granny Combs said.

'Will she be happy?' I asked.

Granny Combs studied the cards. 'I see a wanderer.'

I named the baby Rosemary. Most babies looked to me like monkeys or Buddhas, but Rosemary was a beautiful thing. When her hair came in, it was so pale it looked white. By the time she was three months old, she had a wide smile to match her merry green eyes, and even early on it seemed to me she looked a lot like Helen.

Helen's beauty, as far as I was concerned, had been a curse, and I resolved that I would never tell Rosemary she was beautiful.

A BOY FOLLOWED a year and a half later. He was a big bruiser of a boy. We named him after his dad, and called him Little Jim.

It was around then that hard times hit northern Arizona. A big part of the problem was that too many farmers and greenhorn ranchers had moved into the area. They didn't understand that Arizona wasn't like the land back east, where thousands of years of decaying trees had built up a deep loam. This land had just a thin layer of topsoil that, if ploughed, would blow away with the first strong wind. When a long drought hit, stretches of countryside all round the state turned to swirling dust, which rose a half mile into the air.

At the same time, the country was a few years into the Depression. Some of the littler ranches in Arizona started going under.

A lot of people could no longer afford gas, and they began selling off the tractors and cars they'd been persuaded to buy, leaving many of them wishing they'd kept their plough horses. Business at the garage dwindled. Jim was also too generous for his own good, undercharging people who were poor and doing repairs for free.

I sat down at the kitchen table with pencil and paper, working the numbers, looking for ways to cut expenses, but the bottom line was inescapable: we had more going out than coming in, and it was just a matter of time before we went broke. With the loans we'd taken out, that meant bankruptcy. I figured there must be something else we could do to bring in a little extra cash.

One day, Mr Lee, the Ash Fork Chinaman, knocked on our door. Mr Lee ran a chop-suey joint in a tent near the garage and made enough money from it to drive a Model A that Jim repaired. Mr Lee was usually happy, but that day he was in a panic. Prohibition had ended a few years earlier, but people had gotten used to the easy money that came from selling bootleg liquor, and Mr Lee was one of them, offering his customers shots of home-brew to wash down their noodles. But he'd heard that the revenuers were onto him, and he was looking for a place to hide a few cases of booze.

Mr Lee and Jim had hit it off because Mr Lee had been a soldier in Manchuria when Jim was seeing service in Siberia, and they'd lived through the same bitter winters. Mr Lee trusted Jim. We agreed to take the booze and stashed the cases under Little Jim's crib, where they were hidden by the skirt.

That night, I lay awake thinking about Mr Lee's hooch, and a plan occurred to me. I could bring in extra money by selling bootleg booze at the back door.

When I proposed the idea to Jim the next morning, he wasn't so keen on it. He didn't have any problem with booze itself, he just didn't want to see me wind up in jail for rum-running.

I kept hammering away at Jim, pointing out that I couldn't see any other way to keep us afloat. He reluctantly agreed. Mr Lee also agreed, promising to provide me two cases a month from his bootlegger if we split the profit.

I was a good liquor lady. I discreetly put the word out, and soon local cowboys were knocking at the back door. I sold only to people I knew or those who came recommended. I kept things friendly but businesslike, inviting them in briefly but not allowing anyone to linger or drink on the premises. I began to get regular customers, including the Catholic priest, who always blessed the babies on the way out. I never sold to anyone I thought was drinking the rent money. After Mr Lee got his cut, I made a quarter on each bottle I sold. Soon I was averaging an extra twenty dollars a month, which balanced the books.

ONE DAY THAT SPRING, when Rosemary was three and Little Jim was starting to talk, the Camel brothers drove their huge flock of sheep past our house and towards the train depot. The Camel brothers had bought a big ranch west of Ash Fork in Yavapai County with the idea of raising sheep for wool and mutton. They were from Scotland and knew a lot about sheep, but precious little about conditions on the Arizona range. The Camel brothers had decided that the forage in Yavapai County was too dry for sheep, and they'd made up their minds to sell off their flock, as well as the ranch.

It was a dry, hot day and the sheep filled the streets of Ash Fork. The

ewes were bleating and the lambs were mewing as the Camel brothers'
hands rode back and forth, driving the flock towards the shipping station.

The Camel brothers weren't there—they were back at the ranch—
and when the flock reached the shipping pen, some numbskull got the
brilliant idea of separating the lambs from their mothers. As soon as they'd
accomplished that, bedlam broke loose. The lambs started scrambling
around, crying for their mothers. The ewes were frantically calling out for
their babies.

The hands, realising their mistake, opened the gate separating the ewes
from the lambs, and the sheep all mingled together, mothers looking for
babies and babies looking for mothers. That was when things got really
bad. The flock was so big and so jumbled up that none of the lambs could
find their mothers. After a couple of hours of this, the lambs grew weak
from hunger.

The hands, frantic themselves, were trying to force the ewes to let any
lamb nurse, but the ewes weren't cooperating. They were kicking and bawling, making a god-awful racket.

The Camel brothers finally showed up, but they were at a loss about what
to do, and the situation was getting desperate, with lambs starting to drop
from heat and hunger.

'You should talk to my husband,' I said. 'He knows animals.'

The Camel brothers sent for Jim, who was at the garage. When he
arrived, the hands explained what had happened.

'What we got to do,' Jim said, 'is get those ewes to accept any lamb as
her own for the time being. Then we can worry about straightening out
the flock.'

Jim sent me back to the house for an old bedsheet while he fetched two
cans of kerosene from the garage. He had the Camel hands tear the sheet
into rags, dip the rags in the kerosene, and wipe the ewes' noses with them.
That blocked their sense of smell, and they let whatever lamb was at hand
nurse their milk.

Once the lambs had been fed, Jim had the hands separate the lambs and
the ewes again. One by one, they brought each lamb into the ewe pen and
carried it round until its mother recognised it. The flock was so big that this
took the better part of two days.

Little Rosemary was riveted by the scene, and she stayed there watching the entire time. When it was finally done, there was one little lamb that no ewe had claimed. Its black eyes were frightened, and it ran round on its spindly legs, bleating mournfully.

The Camel brothers told Jim to do whatever he thought best with the lamb. Jim scooped it up in his arms and carried it over to Rosemary. He knelt down and set the lamb in front of her. 'All animals are meant for something,' he said. 'Some to run wild, some for the barnyard, some for market. This little lamb was meant to be a pet.'

Rosemary loved that creature. She shared her ice-cream cones with it, and it followed her everywhere. So we decided to name it Mei-Mei, which Mr Lee told us was Chinese for 'little sister'.

A couple of weeks after Jim straightened out the flock, I heard a knock on the back door. A man was standing outside, smoking a cigarette. He'd left his car door open, and a girl and a young woman were sitting inside, watching us. I could tell from the slightly off-balance way he was standing that he was a little potted.

'I'm a friend of Rooster's,' he said. 'And I heard this is where a man could get his hands on a good bottle of shellac.'

'Looks to me like you're already pretty shellacked,' I said.

'Well, I'm working on it.'

His smile became even more charming, but I looked over at the woman and the girl, and they weren't smiling at all.

'I think you've had enough to drink as it is,' I said.

His smile disappeared. When he realised I wasn't giving in, he really lost it, telling me I was going to regret crossing him and calling me nothing but the sister of a whore who'd hanged herself.

'Wait right there,' I said. Leaving the door open, I walked into the bedroom, got my pearl-handled revolver, walked back out, and pointed it at the man's face. 'The only reason I don't shoot you right now is because of those two women in that car,' I said. 'But you get out of here and don't ever come back.'

That night I told Jim what had happened.

He sighed and shook his head. 'We probably haven't seen the end of it,' he said.

Sure enough, two days later, a car pulled round the house, and when I opened the door, two men in khaki uniforms and cowboy hats were standing there. They had badges on their shirt pockets, guns in their holsters, and handcuffs dangling from their belts. They tipped their hats.

'Afternoon, ma'am,' one of them said. 'Mind if we come in?' he asked.

I didn't see that I had much choice in the matter, so I led them into the living room. Little Jim was asleep in the crib and, under it, behind the white cotton skirt, were two cases of bootleg hooch.

'We received a report,' he went on, 'that liquor is being illegally sold from these premises.'

At that moment, Rosemary came running into the room with Mei-Mei right behind. It must have been the sight of all that gleaming metal and shiny leather, but as soon as Rosemary saw the two lawmen, she gave out a shriek that could have woken the dead. Howling, she flung herself at my feet and grabbed my ankles. I tried to pick her up, but she'd become truly hysterical and was flailing her legs, screaming and blubbering.

Mei-Mei was bleating, and all the noise woke Little Jim, who stood up in the crib and started wailing.

'Does this look like a speakeasy?' I asked. 'I'm a schoolteacher! I'm a mother! I got my hands full just taking care of these kids.'

'I can see that,' the man said. All the screaming was discombobulating the two of them. 'We'll be on our way.'

When Jim came home, I told him about the visit from the law and how the howling youngsters had driven those deputies out of the door. It already seemed to me like a pretty funny story and it got Jim laughing, too, but then he stopped and said, 'Even so, they were putting us on warning. It's time we get out of the bootleg business.'

'But Jim,' I said, 'we need the money.'

'I'd rather see you in the poorhouse than behind bars.'

Selling liquor had kept us afloat for a year. But we shut the operation down and, six months later, the bank foreclosed on us.

FALL WAS USUALLY my favourite time of year, when the air turned cool and the hills were green from the August rains. But I didn't have much time to enjoy the September sunsets. Jim and I had decided to auction off everything. Once we'd done that, we would join the stream of Okies heading to California for work.

One morning, we were in the garage, arguing about what we should take with us, when Blackie Camel, the older of the two Camel brothers, stopped by. Ever since Jim had saved the lambs, Blackie had taken to dropping by the garage to shoot the breeze. The more he got to know Jim, the more he liked him.

That morning, Blackie told us that he and his brother had sold their ranch to a group of investors in England, who wanted to run cattle there. They had asked him and his brother to recommend someone to manage the ranch, and Blackie said that if Jim was so inclined, he and his brother would put Jim's name forward.

Jim squeezed my hand so hard that my knuckles cracked. We both knew the only jobs out in California were picking grapes and oranges, but there was no way we were going to acknowledge to Blackie Camel how desperate we were.

'Sounds like something worth considering,' Jim said.

Blackie sent a telegram to London and, a few days later, he dropped by to tell Jim the job was his. We called off the auction, and Jim kept most of his tools, but we did sell the gasoline pump and tyres to a mechanic from Sedona. Rooster brought a buckboard down from Red Lake, and we loaded our furniture onto it, put the kids and Mei-Mei in the back of the Flivver, and then, with Jim behind the wheel, Rooster on the wagon, and me bringing up the rear on Patches, we set out for Seligman, the town nearest the ranch.

Seligman wasn't as big as Ash Fork, but it had everything a ranch town needed: a building that served as both the jail and post office, a hotel, a bar and café, and a general store.

From Seligman, we headed west through rolling rangeland covered with rabbitweed, prairie grass and juniper trees. The Peacock Mountains in the distance were dark green, and overhead the sky was iris blue. It took a full day to get from Seligman to the ranch by wagon. Finally, late in the afternoon, we came to a gate where the road just ended.

To the right and left of the gate, barbed-wire fencing, held up by neatly trimmed juniper saplings, stretched away into the distance. Beyond the gate was a long driveway. We followed it for four miles and finally reached a fenced-in compound with a collection of unpainted wood buildings shaded by enormous cedar trees.

The buildings were at the foot of a hill dotted with pinyon and scrub cedar.

Facing east, you looked out over miles and miles of rolling rangeland that gradually sloped down towards a flat grassy basin known as the Colorado plateau. From where we stood, you could see to forever, and there wasn't a single other house, human being, or the slightest sign of civilisation, only the huge sky, the endless grassy plain, and the distant mountains.

The Camel brothers had let most of the hired help go, and the place was deserted except for one remaining hand, Old Jake, a grizzled coot who came limping out of the barn to greet us.

Old Jake showed us around. There was a main house with a long porch, its unpainted wood siding a sun-bleached grey. The barn was huge, and next to it were four small log buildings: the granary and the smithy; the meat house, where hides and sides of beef were cured; and the poison house, which had shelves full of bottles containing medicines, potions, spirits and solvents.

Old Jake took us into the other outbuildings, which included a toolshed, chicken coop and bunkhouse. Then we came to a garage filled with vehicles—carriages, an old Conestoga wagon, a few beat-up cars, a rusty Chevy pickup. Finally, Old Jake led us back through the barn to a double corral.

Jim walked round nodding and taking it all in. We could both see that although the buildings were weathered, they were solid and true. There was nothing fancy about the place—it was a real working ranch—but tools were hung in their place, ropes were coiled neatly, fence posts stacked in tidy bundles, and the barn floor was swept. You had to hand it to the Camel brothers. They knew the importance of keeping things shipshape.

Jim grinned and looked out across the range. 'I think we can make this work,' he said.

'I think we can,' I said.

I could tell life at the ranch was going to be a lot of hard work. We were too far from town to count on anyone else for anything. Jim and I would have to be our own veterinarian, farrier, mechanic, butcher, cook, as well as cattle driver, ranch manager, husband and wife, and mother and father of two little children. But Jim and I both knew how to roll up our sleeves.

I felt nature calling and asked Old Jake where I could find the facilities. He pointed towards a little wooden shed in the north corner of the compound. 'It's nothing fancy, just a one-holer,' he said.

For a moment, I missed my mail-order toilet with the shiny white porcelain bowl and the pull-chain flush. As I sat down, though, I realised that there was a big difference between needing things and wanting things. At the ranch, I could see, we'd have pretty much everything we'd need but precious little else.

Next to the seat was a stack of Sears, Roebuck catalogues. I leafed through one and came to a page advertising silk bodices and lacy chemises. I won't be ordering from this page, I thought, and when I was done with my business, that was the one I tore out and used.

AFTER ROOSTER LEFT the following morning, Jim said our first order of business was to tour the ranch. It was almost 160 square miles, and it would take us at least a week just to ride the outer fence line. We loaded one pony with supplies. Jim and Old Jake mounted up two others, and I was on Patches, with Little Jim in my lap, while Rosemary climbed on with her dad.

We headed west until we reached white and yellow limestone foothills, then swung south. We passed pinyon and juniper trees and now and then saw a herd of white-tailed antelope on distant slopes. Late in the afternoon, we reached a high point below the Coyote mountains. From there, we could see south toward the Juniper mountains and east to the Mogollon Rim.

'Lot of land,' Jim said. 'Not a lick of water.'

There were a few dirt ponds, small sad things dug out to collect rain, but the water disappeared during dry spells, and the ponds were now empty, cracked pits.

After ten days, we'd made a big circle, covering most of the ranch. And while we passed any number of gullies and draws that you could tell ran with water during flash floods, there wasn't a single stream or spring on the whole spread. 'No wonder the Camel brothers threw in the towel,' Jim said.

I kept thinking about all those water courses we'd passed. The only water this land would ever see was going to come from the sky. During flash floods, thousands of gallons of water would roar through all those gullies and draws. If we could figure out how to trap that water for ourselves, we'd have plenty.

'What we really need to do is build a dam,' I told Jim.

'How?' he said. 'You'd need an army.'

I thought about it for a while, and then it came to me. I'd read magazine articles about the building of the Hoover Dam. Alongside the articles were photographs of newfangled earthmoving machines used in the construction. 'Jim,' I said, 'let's rent us a bulldozer.'

At first Jim thought I was nuts, but I decided we at least needed to look into the idea. I drove into Seligman, and someone knew someone in Phoenix who had a construction company with a bulldozer. Sure enough, when I tracked him down he said that if we were willing to pay for it he could send his bulldozer and its operator up to Seligman by rail. We'd need to find a flatbed truck to haul it out to the ranch. It wouldn't be cheap, but once the bulldozer was here, it could build a good-sized earth dam in a matter of days.

Jim said we needed to present the idea to the English investors. A group of them was headed our way in a few weeks to meet us and survey their property.

THE POMS ARRIVED by wagon after taking a steamer from England to New York and a train to Flagstaff—a three-week trip. They had clipped accents and wore suits with waistcoats. None of them had ever pulled on a pair of cowboy boots or cracked a bullwhip, but that was fine with Jim and me. They were businessmen, not out to play cowboy. And they were polite and smart. You could tell from the questions they asked that they knew what they didn't know.

The first night they arrived, Old Jake built an open fire and roasted a shoulder of beef. He kept making fun of the investors under his breath, saying things like 'Rather cheeky' and 'Jolly good' in an English accent, and rolling up his cowboy hat to look like a bowler, so I had to bop him in the back of the head. I prepared a few range specialties like rattlesnake stew and prairie oysters to give them something to talk about when they got back to their London clubs.

Afterwards, we sat round the fire eating tins of sliced peaches. Jim rolled himself a cigarette, and then made his pitch.

Only two things really mattered to a rancher, he said: land and water. We had plenty of land in these parts, but not enough water, and without water, the land wasn't worth anything. Seeing as how the ranch had no natural source of water, Jim said, one had to be created if it was going to support a sizable herd.

What made the most sense, Jim went on, was to build a big dam to trap rainwater. He described my plan to bring up a bulldozer from Phoenix. When Jim mentioned the cost, the Poms raised their eyebrows, but then Jim pulled out a column of numbers I'd drawn up and explained that without the dam, they could run only a few thousand head on the ranch; with it, they could go to twenty thousand, and that meant bringing five thousand head to market every year. The dam would pay for itself in no time.

The next day, the Poms went into Seligman to cable the rest of the investors. After some backing and forthing, we got the go-ahead. The Poms wrote a cheque before they left and in no time a flatbed truck was pulling up to the ranch with a big yellow bulldozer on the back. It was the first bull-dozer to be seen in these parts, and people came from all over Yavapai County to marvel at it chugging away.

Since we had the contraption, we decided to build dams all over the ranch, the operator scraping out the sides of gullies and draws, lining the bottoms with packed-down clay, and using the fill to build up the walls that would hold back the water from the flash floods. By far the biggest dam we built—so big you needed five minutes to walk round it—was the one in front of the ranch house.

When the rains came that December, the water coursed through the gullies and draws and poured right into the ponds created by the dams. It was just like filling a bathtub. That winter was unusually wet and, by the spring, the water was three feet deep in the big pond—the finest body of water I'd seen since Lake Michigan.

Jim treated the pond like our proudest possession. He checked the dam every day, measuring the depth of the water and inspecting the walls. In the summer, folks drove from miles away to ask if they might take a dip, and we always let them. Sometimes during dry spells, neighbours would come over with barrels and ask, as they'd put it, to borrow from our pond, though there was no way they were ever going to repay us, and we never charged for it, since, as Jim liked to say, the heavens had given it to us.

The dam and its pond came to be known as Big Jim's Dam, and then just Big Jim. People around the county measured the severity of dry spells by the amount of water in Big Jim. 'How's Big Jim doin'?' people in town might ask me, or 'I hear Big Jim's low,' and I always knew they were talking about the water level in the pond, not my husband's state of mind.

THE RANCH'S OFFICIAL NAME was the Arizona Incorporated cattle ranch, but we always called it the AIC, or just 'the ranch'. A fancy name, Jim liked to say, was a sure sign that the owner didn't know the first thing about ranching.

With the Depression still going strong, owners were still going out of business. That meant more people were selling than buying cattle, and Jim travelled round Arizona picking up entire herds for rock-bottom prices. He hired about a dozen cowboys, mostly Mexican and Havasupai, to drive the cattle to the ranch and brand them before sending them out to the range. Cowboying was rough, and so were those kids—misfits, most of them, run-aways and boys who'd been whipped too hard.

When the cowboys arrived, the first thing they did was head out into open country and round up a herd of range horses, which they proceeded to break—after a fashion—in the palisaded corral. The horses bucked and fishtailed like rodeo broncs, but those boys would just as soon bust every bone in their bodies before calling it quits. They weren't much more than half-broke horses themselves.

I stood there watching them with Rosemary. 'I feel bad for the horses,' she said. 'They just want to be free.'

'In this life,' I said, 'hardly anyone gets to do what they want.'

Once the cowboys each had a string of horses, they started bringing in the cattle and branding them. They were all living in the bunkhouse, and I had my hands full cooking for everyone, in addition to helping out with the branding. The cowboys got steak and eggs for breakfast and steak and beans for dinner, with as much salt and roof water as they wanted.

I didn't particularly trust them around Rosemary, who wasn't allowed to go near the bunkhouse. Rosemary was also a little like a half-broke horse. She was happiest running around outdoors, without a stitch of clothing if I'd let her. She climbed the cedar trees, splashed in the horse trough, peed in the yard, and jumped from the barn rafters onto the hay bales. She loved spending the day on horseback, holding on behind her father. The saddles were too heavy for her, so she rode her mule, Jenny, bareback, mounting her by grabbing her mane and toe-walking up the animal's leg.

Jim once told Rosemary that she was so tough, any critter that took a bite of her would spit it out, and she just loved that. Rosemary was never afraid of coyotes or wolves, and she hated to see any animal caged, tied up or penned in.

SHORTLY AFTER THE HERD arrived, Jim set out to repair all the fencing on the ranch. The job took a month. He brought Rosemary along with him in the pickup, and they were gone for days at a time, sleeping in the bed of the truck, cooking over campfires, and returning only for resupplies of food and wire. Rosemary adored her father, and he was completely unfazed by her wild streak. They were happy to spend hours in each other's company, Rosemary talking nonstop as Jim dug holes, trimmed posts and tightened wire.

'Doesn't that kid ever shut up?' Old Jake once asked.

'She's got a lot to say,' Jim told him.

While they were gone, I settled in to life on the ranch. There was always more to do on any given day than you could get done, and I quickly established a few rules for myself. One was to dispense with any unnecessary cleaning—no maid's work. Arizona was a dusty place, but a little dirt never killed anyone. So I gave the house a going-over only once every few months.

As for clothes, I flatly refused to wash them. We wore our shirts till they got dirty; then we put them on backward and wore them until that side got dirty. When the shirts reached the point where Jim was joking about them scaring the cattle, I'd take the pile into Seligman and pay by the pound to have them all steam-cleaned.

I kept the cooking basic as well. I didn't make soufflés and sauces and garnished this and stuffed that. I made food. Beans were my speciality. I always had a pot of them on the stove, and that usually lasted two to five days, depending on how many cowboys we had around. My recipe was simple: boil beans, salt to taste.

When we weren't having beans, we had steak. My recipe for steak was also fairly simple: fry on both sides, salt to taste. With the steak came potatoes: boil unpeeled, salt to taste. For dessert, we'd have canned peaches packed in tasty syrup. I liked to say that what my cooking lacked in variety, it made up for in consistency.

Once when some milk had spoiled and I was feeling ambitious, I did make cottage cheese the way my mother made it when I was growing up. I boiled the clabbered milk and cut up the curds with a knife. Then I wrapped it in a burlap sugar sack and hung it overnight to let the whey drain out. The next day I chopped it again, salted it, and passed it out at supper. The family loved it so much they wolfed it down in under a minute. I couldn't believe I'd worked so long over something that was gone so quickly.

'Well that was a waste of time,' I said. 'I'll never make that mistake again.'

Rosemary was eyeing me.

'Let that be a lesson to you,' I told her.

THAT FIRST WINTER, Jim and I paid fifty dollars for a marvellous long-range radio, mail-ordered from Montgomery Ward. 'Brings the twentieth century to Yavapai County,' I told Jim.

Since we had no electricity, we ran the radio off two massive batteries. When the batteries were fresh, we could get stations all the way from Europe. Adolf Hitler had taken over in Germany, and a civil war was brewing in Spain, but we weren't particularly interested in European affairs. The reason we shelled out so much money was to get the weather report.

Every morning we got up before dawn, and Jim turned the radio on to listen to the weather report from a station in California. With water so scarce and severe storms so dangerous, we lived and died by those forecasts. We'd follow a storm that started out in Los Angeles and moved east. The clouds usually ended up getting caught by the Rockies, where they'd dump most of their moisture, but sometimes that storm drifted south, and that was when we got our big rains.

Rosemary and Little Jim loved the storms. When the skies turned dark and the air grew heavy, I called them onto the porch and we all watched as the storm, with its boiling clouds and thunder, its lightning and sheets of black rain, rolled across the range.

To live in a place where water was so scarce made the rare moments like this—when the heavens poured forth an abundance of water and the earth turned lush and green—seem magical. The kids had an irresistible urge to get out and dance in the rain, and I always let them go. Sometimes I joined them myself.

Afterwards, we all ran down to the draws that led to Big Jim the dam, and once the first rush of water had passed, I'd let the kids strip off their clothes and go swimming. They'd stay out there for hours, paddling round, pretending to be alligators or dolphins.

The rains usually arrived in April, August and December, but in our second year on the ranch, April came and went without rain. So did August and so did December, and by the following year, we were in the midst of a serious drought.

Every day Jim listened, grim-faced, to the weather report, hoping in vain for a forecast of rain, and then we'd go down and check the water level of Big Jim. The days were beautiful, with endless deep blue skies, but all that fine weather only gave us a desperate feeling as we stood there, watching the water level sink and sink until the bottom of Big Jim became visible. And then the water disappeared.

Early into the drought, Jim had sensed it coming on. He'd grown up in the desert, so he knew that one came along every ten or fifteen years, and he had culled the herd deeply, selling off steers and heifers and keeping only the healthiest breeding cattle. Even so, we had to bring in water. Jim and I hitched up the Conestoga wagon to the pickup and hauled it into Pica, a stop twenty miles away on the Santa Fe railroad where they were shipping in water. We loaded old fuel drums with as much water as the Conestoga could hold and hauled them back to the ranch.

We made that trip a couple of times a week. We darned near broke our backs loading those fuel drums, but we saved the herd, whereas many ranchers around us went bust.

The following August, the rains returned with a vengeance. We sat at our kitchen table listening to the rain drum on the roof. Unlike other storms, this one didn't peter out after half an hour. Instead, it kept raining. After a while, Jim started worrying about Big Jim. If too much water flooded into the dam, its walls might burst.

The first time Jim went out to check the dam, it was holding, but an hour later, with the rain still coming down in sheets, he checked it again and realised that if nothing was done, it would give. He had a plan, which was to go out in the middle of the storm and dig furrows in the draws and the wash approaching the dam, to drain off the water before it reached Big Jim. To dig the furrows, he was going to harness Old Buck, our Percheron draught horse, to the plough.

We headed out into the rain. The barn was dark from the storm, and we couldn't find the harness, which no one had used in years. What we could do, I said to Jim, was hitch the plough to the pickup. If he handled the plough, I could drive. Jim liked the idea. We brought the kids with us. The water out in the yard was more than ankle-deep by then, the rain coming down so hard that the force of it practically knocked Rosemary to the ground. Jim scooped her up in his arms. I followed with Little Jim, and we sloshed out to the Chevy.

At the equipment shed, Jim threw the plough into the pickup bed. Once we reached the wash above the dam, we rigged up the plough to the Chevy's hitch, and I got behind the wheel.

I looked in the rearview mirror, but the rain was splattering so hard on the window that Jim was just a blur. I had Rosemary stand up on the seat and stick her head out the window and take directions from him. Jim was gesturing and shouting, but the rain was making such a racket that it was hard to figure out what he wanted.

'Mom, I can't hear him,' Rosemary said.

'Do the best you can,' I said. 'That's all anyone can do.'

I needed the pickup to creep along at a walking pace, but the Chevy wasn't geared to go that slow, and it kept stalling and lurching, jerking the plough out of Jim's hands. Finally, I figured out that by engaging the clutch, easing up on it ever so slightly, then reengaging it, I could send the truck forward a few inches at a time, and that was how we got the job done, digging four furrows off the sides of the wash that drained the rising water away from the dam.

It was still raining furiously. Jim heaved the plough into the pickup bed and climbed in beside me. He was as wet as if he'd fallen into a horse trough.

'We did a good job—good as we could,' he said. 'If she breaks, she breaks.'

SHE DIDN'T BREAK. While our place was spared, not everyone fared as well. The rains washed away a few bridges and several miles of railroad track. Ranchers lost cattle and outbuildings. Seligman was flooded, and several houses were swept away. But a few hours after the rain stopped, the plateau turned bright green, and the next day the ranch was covered with the most spectacular display of flowers I had ever seen. There were crimson Indian paintbrushes and orange California poppies, white mariposa poppies, goldenrod and blue lupines and pink and purple sweet peas. All that water must have churned up seeds that had been buried for decades.

Rosemary spent days collecting flowers. 'If we had this much water all the time,' I told her, 'we might have to break down and give this ranch some greenhorn name like Paradise Plateau.'

VI

Teacher Lady

The water we bought during the drought cost a fortune, but the Poms knew that ranching was a long-term proposition only for people with wallets fat enough to tough out the bad times and then make a killing in the good. They actually saw the drought, and all the bankruptcies it was causing, as a buying opportunity. So did Jim. He realised that we needed even more land—land with its own water. He convinced the investors to buy the neighbouring ranch, called Hackberry. It had some hilly terrain with a year-round spring, and out on the flat range there was a deep well with a windmill that pumped water up to the cattle troughs.

Jim's plan was to move the herd back and forth between the two ranches, keeping the cattle in Hackberry during the winter and bringing them back to the high plateau around Big Jim in the summer. When the two ranches were combined, they totalled 180,000 acres. It was a big spread, and in good years we could bring some 10,000 head of cattle to market. When the Poms saw those numbers, they were more than happy to pony up for Hackberry.

The first time we rode out to Hackberry, I flat-out fell in love with the place. The house, nestled in a hollow, was a former dance hall that had been taken apart, moved to the spot, and reassembled. The walls were painted with signs saying NO ROUGH STUFF and TAKE THE FIGHT OUTSIDE.

The first time I saw the windmill, I took a drink of its well water. That water tasted sweeter than the finest French liqueur. Some folks, when they struck it rich, like to say that they are in the money, and that was how I felt—rich—only we were in the water. Our days of hauling fuel drums over dirt roads were gone for good.

After the Poms bought Hackberry, Jim drove to Los Angeles in the Chevy and returned with a truckload of half-inch lead pipe. It was a mile from the spring to the house, and we laid pipe the entire length. It brought a supply of water to our back door.

Next to the spigot, we kept a metal cup, and few things were finer than coming back from a hot, dusty ride and filling that cup with a cold, wet drink, then pouring what was left over your head.

We moved the herd over to Hackberry in the fall and stayed there until the spring. I always loved bright colours and at Hackberry I painted each room a different colour—pink, blue and yellow—put Navajo rugs on the floors, and got some red velvet curtains for the windows, using several books of S&H green stamp coupons that I'd saved.

Rosemary loved the colours even more than I did. She was already showing some artistic talent, tossing off perfect little line drawings. Both kids were crazy about Hackberry. There were several deep canyons running down out of the mountains and, after it rained, I'd rush with the kids up to the lip of one of them and we'd cheer as the flash floods came thundering down the dry creek beds.

Ever since moving to the ranch, Jim and I had talked on and off about buying it, but we'd had our hands full getting the ranch up and running. Now that I'd spent time at Hackberry—a beautiful spread with good water—I wanted to turn my dream into a plan.

We needed cash. We were never going to go into debt again, I swore; we were not going to lose this place the way we'd lost the house and the filling station in Ash Fork. I worked up the figures and decided we might be able to swing it in ten years if I started bringing in money and we scrimped and saved.

We'd always been frugal—Jim made the Poms a lot of money, but he made it a nickel at a time, reusing nails, saving old barbed wire, building fences with juniper saplings rather than milled posts. We never threw away anything.

But now I came up with additional ways to save money. We made the children chairs out of orange crates. Rosemary drew on used paper bags—both sides—and painted on old boards. We drank from coffee cans with wire tied round them for handles and, whenever possible, I drove behind trucks so their slipstream gave us an easier ride.

I also came up with all sorts of moneymaking schemes. I sold encyclopedias door-to-door, but that didn't go over well, since there were not a lot of bookish ranch hands in Yavapai County. I did better visiting neighbours to solicit orders for Montgomery Ward. I also started playing poker with the hands, but Jim put a stop to that after I cleaned a couple of them out. 'We don't pay them enough as it is,' he said. 'We can't go taking what little they get.'

By THEN I WAS closing in on my thirty-ninth birthday, and there was still one thing I'd never done and had always wanted to do. One summer day, Jim and the kids and I had driven the Flivver over to Mohave County to look at a breeding bull Jim was interested in buying when we passed a ranch with a small plane parked near the gate. A sign in the windshield read: FLYING LESSONS $5.

'That's for me,' I said.

I had Jim pull into the driveway, and we stopped to look at the plane. It was a two-seater, one behind the other, with an open cockpit, a faded green paint job and a rudder that creaked in the wind.

A fellow came out of a shack behind the plane and sauntered up to the Flivver. He had a windburned face and a pair of aviator goggles pushed up on his forehead. He rested his elbows on Jim's open window and said, 'Looking to learn her?'

I leaned across the gearbox. 'Not him,' I said. 'Me.'

'Whoa,' Goggles said. 'Ain't never taught a woman before.' He looked at Jim. 'Think the little lady's up to it?'

'Don't you "little lady" me,' I said. 'I break horses. I brand steers. I run a ranch with a couple dozen of crazy cowboys on it, and I can beat them all in poker. I'll be damned if some nincompoop is going to tell me I don't have what it takes to fly that heap of tin.'

Goggles stared at me for a moment; then Jim patted him on the arm. 'No one's ever won betting against her,' Jim said.

'That don't surprise me,' Goggles said. 'Ma'am, I like your spirit. Let's take 'er up.'

Goggles brought out a flight suit for me, along with a leather aviation helmet and a set of goggles. As I pulled them on, he walked me round the plane, explaining basics such as lift and tailwind, and showing me how to operate the co-pilot's stick. Soon Goggles was climbing aboard and having me climb in behind him.

Then we were taxiing down the driveway, bumping along, gathering speed. The bumping stopped, but at first I wasn't even aware that we were airborne—it was that smooth—then I saw the ground falling away beneath us, and I knew I was flying.

We circled around. The kids were running back and forth waving like mad, and even Jim was flapping his hat. I leaned out and waved. As we gained altitude, I saw the Arizona range rolling away in all directions, the Mogollon Rim to the east and, in the distant west, the Rockies. Route 66 threaded its way like a ribbon through the desert. The sight of the earth spread out far below made me feel like I was beholding the entire world, seeing it all for the first time, the way I figured angels did.

Goggles operated the controls for most of the lesson, but by keeping my hand on my stick, I was able to follow the way he banked, climbed and dived. Towards the end, he let me take over and, after a few heart-stopping jerks, I was able to put the plane into a long, steady turn that brought us right into the sun.

Afterward, I thanked Goggles, paid him, and told him he'd be seeing me again. As we walked back to the car, Rosemary said, 'I thought we were supposed to save money.'

'Even more important than saving money is making it,' I said, 'and sometimes, to make money, you have to spend it.' I told her if I got a pilot's licence I could bring in cash dusting crops and delivering mail and flying rich people around. 'This lesson was an investment,' I said. 'In me.'

Working as a bush pilot struck me as one glorious way of earning a living, but it would take a while to get my pilot's licence, and we needed money now. The smartest way for me to bring in the bucks was to teach. I wrote to Grady Gammage, the college president in Flagstaff who had helped me get the job at Red Lake, to ask if he knew of any opportunities.

He replied that there was a town called Main Street with an opening. It was up in the Arizona Strip, and I'd be welcome there, he said, because Main Street was so remote and peculiar that no teacher with a college degree wanted the job. The people in the area were almost all Mormon polygamists, he said, who'd moved all the way out there to escape government harassment.

Neither remoteness nor peculiarity troubled me, and as for Mormons, I'd married one, so I figured I could handle a few polygamists. I wrote back telling Grady Gammage to sign me up.

WHAT MADE MOST SENSE was to take Rosemary and Little Jim with me, so one day late in the summer, we packed the Flivver, which was still running but on its last legs, and headed for the Arizona Strip. Jim followed in the Chevy to help us get settled.

The Arizona Strip was in the northwest corner of Mohave County. It was desolate but beautiful country. There were grassland plateaus where distant mountains sparkled with mica, and sandstone hills and gullies that had been carved into wondrous shapes—hourglasses and spinning tops and teardrops—by wind and water.

The town of Main Street was so small that it didn't appear on most maps. In fact, the main street of Main Street was the only street, lined with a few ramshackle houses, one general store and the school, which had a teacher-age. It was one tiny room with two windows and a single bed that Little Jim, Rosemary and I would share. The water barrel outside the kitchen was swimming with pollywogs. 'Just drink with your teeth closed,' Jim said.

Many of the people in the area herded sheep, but the land had been over-grazed, and it was startling how threadbare the local folks were. None of them had cars. Instead, they drove wagons or rode horses. Some lived in chicken coops. The women wore bonnets, and the children came to school barefoot and in overalls or dresses stitched from feed sacks.

When we first arrived, the people around Main Street were polite yet guarded, but after they found out my husband was the son of the great Lot Smith, who fought the federals with Brigham Young and founded Tuba City, they warmed right up.

I had thirty students of all ages, and they were a sweet and well-behaved lot. Because they were polygamists, they were almost all related in one way or another and talked about their 'other mothers' and 'double cousins'. The girls were all listed in the 'Joy Book', meaning they were eligible for mar-riage and were waiting for their 'uncle' to decide whom they would marry.

The houses they lived in were essentially breeding factories where as many as seven wives were expected to churn out a baby a year. The girls were raised to be docile and submissive. In the first few months I was there, a couple of my thirteen-year-old girls simply disappeared, vanishing into their arranged marriages.

In class, I spent the bulk of my time on the basics of reading and writing and arithmetic, but I also peppered my lessons with talk of nursing and teaching, the opportunities in big cities, and the doings of Amelia Earhart and Eleanor Roosevelt. I told them how, when I was no older than they were, I was break-ing horses. I talked about going to Chicago and learning to fly an airplane. Any of them could do all that, too, I said.

Some of them—both boys and girls—looked shocked, but more than a few seemed genuinely intrigued.

I hadn't been in Main Street for long when I got a visit from Uncle Eli, the patriarch of the local polygamists. He had a long, greying beard, scraggly eyebrows, and a beak-like nose. His smile was practised, and his eyes were cold. As we talked, he kept patting my hand and calling me 'Teacher Lady'.

Some of the mothers, he said, had told him their little girls were coming home from school talking about suffragettes and women flying airplanes. What I needed to understand was that his people had moved to this area to get away from the rest of the world, and I was bringing that world into their schoolroom. My job, he went on, was to give them enough arithmetic and reading to manage the household and make their way through the Book of Mormon.

'Teacher Lady, you're not preparing these girls for their lives,' he said. 'You're only upsetting and confusing them. There will be no more talk of worldly ways.'

'Look, Uncle,' I said, 'I don't work for you. I work for the state of Arizona. My job is to give these kids an education, and part of that is letting them know what the world is really like.'

Uncle's smile never wavered. 'If you don't obey me, we will all shun you as the devil.'

The next day, I gave an especially impassioned lesson on political and religious freedom, talking about the totalitarian countries where everyone was forced to believe one thing. In America, by contrast, people were free to think for themselves.

That night when I went to throw out the dishwater, Uncle Eli was standing in the yard, his arms crossed, staring at me.

'Evening,' I said.

He didn't reply. He just kept staring, giving me the evil eye.

The next night, I looked up from fixing dinner, and there he was again, standing framed in the window, staring out from under his unruly eyebrows with the same baleful expression.

'What's he want, Mommy?' Rosemary asked.

'Oh, he's just hoping I'll have a staring contest with him.'

The teacherage didn't have curtains, but the next day I sewed together some feed sacks and tacked them over the window. That evening, there was a knock at the door. When I opened it, Uncle Eli was standing there.

'What do you want?' I asked.

He just stared at me, and I closed the door. The knocking started up again, slow and persistent. I went into the curtained-off area where we slept and loaded my pearl-handled revolver. Uncle Eli was still knocking on the door. I opened it and pointed the gun dead at him.

The last time I'd pointed the gun had been at that drunk in Ash Fork who'd called Helen a dead whore when I wouldn't sell him any hooch. I hadn't fired then, but this time I aimed just to the left of Uncle Eli's face and pulled the trigger.

When the shot rang out, Uncle Eli barked in fright. The bullet had whizzed by his ear. He stared at me, speechless.

'Next time I won't aim to miss,' I said.

Two days later, the county sheriff showed up at the school. He was an easygoing country fellow with a goitre. Investigating a schoolmarm for shooting at a polygamous elder wasn't something he did every day, and he seemed uncertain how to handle it.

'We received a complaint, ma'am, alleging you took a potshot at one of the townspeople.'

'There was a menacing intruder, and I was defending myself and my children. I'll be happy to explain in court what happened.'

The sheriff sighed. 'Around here, we like people to work out their differences amongst themselves. But if you can't get along with these folks, and there's many that can't, you probably don't belong here.'

After that, I knew it was only a matter of time. I continued to teach in Main Street, but I stopped getting dinner invitations, and a bunch of the parents took their kids out of the school. In the spring, I got a letter from the Mohave County superintendent saying that he didn't think it would be a good idea for me to continue teaching in Main Street come next fall.

I WAS UNEMPLOYED AGAIN, which fried my bacon because I'd been acting in the best interests of my students. Fortunately, that summer, a teaching job opened up in Peach Springs, a tiny town on a Walapai reservation sixty-five miles from the ranch. It paid fifty dollars a month but, in addition, the county had set aside ten dollars a month for a part-time janitor, ten dollars a month for a bus driver, and another ten dollars a month for someone to cook lunch for the kids. I said I'd do everything, which meant eighty dollars a month.

The old school bus had died, so the county had also budgeted money to buy another one—or at least some form of transportation—and after scouting around, I found the perfect vehicle at a used-car lot in Kingman: a terrifically elegant dark blue hearse. Since it had only front seats, you could jam a whole passel of kids in the back. I took some silver paint and, in big block letters, wrote SCHOOL BUS on both sides.

Despite my fancy sign, people in those parts, including my husband, were pretty literal-minded, and they kept calling it 'the hearse'.

'It's not a hearse,' I told Jim. 'It's a school bus.'

'Painting the word "dog" on the side of a pig don't make the pig a dog,' he said.

He had a point, and I started calling it the hearse, too.

I'd get up at four in the morning and cover 200 miles a day picking up and dropping off the kids all over the district. I'd teach the whole bunch by myself, take them all home, return to the school and do the janitoring, then head back to the ranch. I farmed out the cooking at five dollars a week to our neighbour Mrs Hutter, who made pots of stew that I took to the school. Those were some long days, but I loved the work, and the money started piling up.

Rosemary was seven by then, and Little Jim was five, so I took them with me, and they became part of the class. Rosemary hated being taught by her mother, particularly because I sometimes gave her paddlings in front of other students to show I wasn't playing favourites. Little Jim had also become a handful, and he got his share of paddlings as well, though a spanking never kept either of those rascals out of mischief for long.

Most of the money went into our savings, but I kept some aside for the occasional flying lesson.

IN MY SECOND YEAR at Peach Springs, I had twenty-five students in my one-room schoolhouse. Six of them were the children of Deputy Johnson, a rawboned chain-smoker who wore an old fedora and had a droopy moustache. For the most part, I liked Deputy Johnson. He turned a blind eye to minor infractions. But he could come down on you hard if you took issue with him. He had a total of thirteen children, and they did pretty much as they pleased, letting air out of people's tyres or throwing cherry bombs down outhouse holes.

One of the deputy's sons was Johnny Johnson, who was a couple of years older than Rosemary. He'd been a handful ever since I started teaching at Peach Springs. Johnny couldn't keep his hands off the girls—a regular tomcat in the making. He had kissed Rosemary on the mouth, something I learned a few days later from one of the other students. Rosemary said it was just a yucky thing, nothing she wanted anyone to get in any trouble over. Johnny, for his part, called Rosemary and the other student lying finks.

It wasn't worth holding a court of inquisition over, but I was still simmering about the matter a couple of weeks later when, one day during class, the little punk reached over and stuck his hand up the dress of a sweet Mexican girl named Rosita. I put my book down, walked up to him, and slapped him hard in the face. He looked at me with shock, and then he reached up and slapped me in the face.

For a second I was speechless. A smile started creeping across Johnny's face. It was then that I hauled him up and threw him against the wall, backhanding him again and again and, when he cowered on the floor, I grabbed my ruler and started whaling his butt.

'You'll be sorry!' he kept screaming. 'You'll be sorry!'

I didn't care. Johnny Johnson needed to learn a lesson he'd never forget, and you couldn't spell it out on the blackboard; you had to beat it into him. Also, he was in danger of becoming a heel like my first husband, and he needed to realise there could be consequences for mistreating girls. So I kept whaling on him and, truth be told, I got more than a little satisfaction from it.

Just as I expected, Deputy Johnson showed up at school the next day. 'I'm here to tell you to keep your hands off my boy. Got it?'

'You may think you run Yavapai County, but I run my classroom,' I said, 'and I'll discipline wayward kids as I see fit. Got it?'

Deputy Johnson couldn't get me fired outright, since they'd have trouble replacing me in the middle of the school year, but a few months later, I received another one of those blasted letters saying my contract would not be renewed. At this point, I'd lost count of the number of times I'd been fired, and I was getting sick of it.

The day the letter arrived, I sat at the kitchen table thinking about my situation. If I had to do it again, I'd have done the same thing. I was a darned good teacher and had been doing what was necessary, not only for Rosita but also for Johnny, who needed to be reined in before he wound up in serious trouble. Even so, I'd been booted.

As I sat there brooding about all this, Rosemary walked into the kitchen, and a look of alarm swept her face. She started stroking my arm. 'Don't cry, Mom,' she said. 'Stop it. Please stop it.'

It was only then that I realised tears were running down my cheeks. I remembered how disturbed I'd been as a little girl, watching my mother cry. Now, by letting my own daughter see me all pitiful, I felt that I'd failed her, and I was furious with myself.

'I'm not crying,' I said. 'I just got dust in my eyes.' I pushed her hand away. 'Because I'm not weak. You'll never have to worry about that. Your mother is not a weak woman.'

And with that, I headed out to the woodpile and went on a tear, splitting logs, setting each one up on the chopping block and using every ounce of strength I had to bring the axe down on it, sending the split pieces of white wood flying apart while Rosemary stood watching. It was almost as satisfying as whaling Johnny Johnson.

VII

The Garden of Eden

We were pretty isolated on the ranch, but Rosemary and Little Jim got along fine by themselves. In fact, those two little scamps were each other's best friend. After morning chores, if there was no school, they were free to do whatever they wanted. They loved to rummage round in all the outbuildings. They also hiked out to the Indian graveyard, collected arrowheads, and swam in the dam.

What they loved most of all was riding. Most days, Rosemary and Little Jim saddled up Socks and Blaze, two chestnut quarter horses, and set out into the range. One of their favourite pastimes was racing the train. A set of tracks for the Santa Fe Railroad cut across the ranch, and every afternoon they'd wait for the two-fifteen. When it came chugging up, they'd gallop alongside it, the passengers leaning out and waving and the engineer sounding the whistle until the train inevitably pulled ahead.

As much fun as ranch life was for the kids, I felt they needed more civilising than it could provide. Jim and I decided to send them both to boarding school. While they were away, I was going to finally earn that darned diploma, get a permanent teaching job, and join the union, so beetleheads like Uncle Eli and Deputy Johnson couldn't have me fired just because they didn't like my style.

Since the hearse was pretty dinged up by now, the county let us buy it for a song. We packed it up and I drove the kids south, first dropping Little Jim, who was eight, at a boys' school in Flagstaff, then Rosemary, who was nine, at a Catholic girls' school in Prescott. I sat in the car watching a nun lead her by the hand into the dormitory. At the doorway, Rosemary turned round to look at me, her cheeks wet with tears. 'Now, you be strong,' I called out to her. I had loved my time at the Sisters of Loretto when I was a girl, and I was sure that Rosemary would be fine.

When I got to Phoenix, I found a bare-bones boarding house and registered for a double load of courses. I figured that if I spent eighteen hours a day going to class and studying, I could get my degree in two years. Some of the other students were astonished at my workload, but I felt like a lady of leisure. Instead of doing ranch chores, tending sick cattle, hauling schoolkids far and wide, mopping the school floor and coping with belligerent parents, I was improving my mind.

Rosemary and Little Jim didn't share my enthusiasm for academic life. In fact, they hated it. Little Jim kept running away, climbing over fences and through windows, and using bedsheets to shimmy down from upper floors. He was such a resourceful escape artist that the Jesuit brothers started calling him Little Houdini.

But the Jesuits were used to dealing with untamed ranch boys, and they regarded Little Jim as one more rambunctious rapscallion. Rosemary's teachers, however, saw her as a misfit. Most of the girls at the academy were demure, frail things, but Rosemary played with her pocketknife, yodeled in the choir, peed in the yard, and caught scorpions in a jar she kept under her bed. She was behaving more or less the way she did on the ranch, but what seemed normal in one situation can seem outright peculiar in another.

Rosemary kept writing me sad little letters about her life. She liked learning to dance and play the piano but found etiquette excruciating, and the nuns were always telling her everything she did was wrong. She sang too loudly; she danced too enthusiastically; she spoke out of turn. Other classmates called her 'yokel'.

In her letters, Rosemary said she missed the ranch. She missed the horses and cattle, missed the ponds and the range, missed her brother and her mom and dad. The Japanese had bombed Pearl Harbor in December, and everyone at the school lived in fear. The nuns kept blankets over the windows at night as part of the blackout, and Rosemary said she felt like she couldn't breathe.

Be strong, was all I could think to say when I wrote back to her. I also corrected the grammar in her letters and returned them to her. I wouldn't have been doing that girl any favours to let those sorts of errors go unchecked.

Near the end of Rosemary's first year, I received a letter from the mother superior saying she thought it would be best if Rosemary didn't return. Her grades were poor and her behaviour disruptive. I had Rosemary tested that summer and, as I suspected, she was plenty bright. I wrote to the mother superior, assuring her of Rosemary's intelligence and pleading for another chance. She reluctantly agreed, but Rosemary's grades and rowdiness got even worse her second year and, when it was over, the mother superior's decision was final. Rosemary and the school were not a good fit.

Little Jim hadn't done much better. I'd earned my college degree by then, and I took both Rosemary and Little Jim with me back to the ranch. The kids were so happy to be home that they ran round hugging everything— cowboys, horses, trees—and then they saddled up Blaze and Socks and headed out to open country, whipping their horses into a gallop and whooping like bandits.

NOW THAT I HAD my college degree I was in demand as a teacher and got a job in Big Sandy, another little town with a one-room school, where I enrolled both Rosemary and Little Jim. Rosemary was delighted not to be returning to the academy. 'When I grow up,' she told me, 'all I want to do is to live on the ranch and be an artist. That's my dream.'

My mother had died back when I was studying in Phoenix. Blood poisoning got her, from her bad teeth, and it came so quick that I didn't have a chance to make it back to the KC before she passed.

During the summer after my first year at Big Sandy, I received a telegram from my dad. After Mom had died, Buster and Dorothy had put Dad in an old folks' home in Tucson. But now, Dad said, he was fading fast, and he wanted to be with his family. 'You've always been my best hand,' he wrote. 'Please come get me.'

It would be a long trip. But there was no way I was going to let my father die alone in a strange city. On a scorching Arizona day, Rosemary and I headed south in the hearse.

The old folks' home in Tucson where Dad was staying was really just a ramshackle boarding house run by a woman with a few rooms to spare. 'Ain't been able to make out a word of your pa's since he got here,' she said as she led us down the hall to his room.

Dad was lying in the middle of the bed, the sheet up to his chin. I hadn't seen him in several years, and he didn't look good. He was thin, and his eyes had sunk deep into their sockets. He spoke in a croak, but I could understand him as well as I always had.

'I've come to take you home,' I said.

'Won't make it,' he said. 'I'm too sick to move.'

I sat down next to him on the bed. Rosemary took his hand. I was proud to see that she was completely undaunted by the old man's state. She'd been sad about her grandpa on the drive down but, now that she was here, she'd risen to the occasion. Regardless of what those nuns thought, the kid had a brain, a spine and a heart.

'Looks like I'm going to die here,' Dad said, 'but I don't want to be buried here. Promise me you'll take my body back to the KC.'

'I promise.'

Dad smiled. 'I could always count on you.'

He died that night. It was almost as if he had been holding on until I got there, and when he knew he would be buried back on the ranch, he could stop worrying and just let go.

We buried Dad in the small cemetery where everyone who had ever died on the ranch was buried. At Dad's request, he was laid to rest wearing his hundred-dollar Stetson, the one with the beaded band that had rattlers from two rattlesnakes Dad himself had killed attached to it.

Dad's death didn't hollow me out the way Helen's had. After all, he'd lived a long life doing pretty much what he wanted. He hadn't drawn the best of cards, but he'd played his hand darned well, so what was there to grieve over?

Dad left the KC Ranch to Buster and the homestead on Salt Draw to me but, going through his papers, I discovered that he owed thousands of dollars in back taxes on the Texas property. As Rosemary and I set out on the long drive back to Seligman, I considered our choices. Did we sell the land to pay off the taxes? Or did we keep it and pay the taxes by digging into the money we'd saved to buy Hackberry?

WHEN I RETURNED to the ranch, Jim and I sat down to figure out what we should do about the west Texas land. Jim was of two minds, but for some reason, I became hell-bent on holding onto the land Dad had homesteaded.

'That's one unyielding patch of earth,' Jim said. He argued that we couldn't raise much of a herd on 160 acres, and paying off those taxes would make a big dent in the fund to buy Hackberry.

'We might not ever be able to buy Hackberry,' I said. 'This is a sure thing. I'm a gambler, but I'm a smart one, and the smart gambler always goes for the sure thing.'

We paid off the taxes and became bona fide Texas land barons.

THE FOLLOWING SUMMER, I received a letter from Clarice Pearl, a senior head honcho with the Arizona Department of Education. She wanted to investigate the living conditions of the children of the Havasupai, who lived on a remote stretch of the Grand Canyon. She was bringing a nurse from Indian Affairs to determine if the children met hygiene standards. She asked me to drive the two of them to the canyon and arrange horses and a guide to get us down the long trail to the Havasupai village.

Fidel Hanna, a young Havasupai ranch hand whom Rosemary, now thirteen, had a big crush on, lived on the reservation when he wasn't staying at the bunkhouse, and I asked him to set things up.

I drove the hearse into Williams, bringing Rosemary with me, to pick up Miss Pearl and the nurse, Marion Finch, at the depot. Both of them were stout and pucker-mouthed. I recognised the type—disapproving do-gooders. They always had very high standards, and they always let you know that you didn't quite measure up to them.

We headed north and, after about two hours, we reached Hilltop, a desolate spot at the canyon's rim, where the horse trail led down to the village. There was no sign of Fidel Hanna. We all got out of the hearse, my two customers clearly disgusted with the unreliability of the heathens they'd come to help. Suddenly a band of young Indians on horseback, half-naked and with painted faces, galloped up the trail and circled us, whooping and brandishing spears. Miss Pearl turned white and Miss Finch gave a shriek.

But by then I'd recognised that the ringleader was Fidel Hanna.

'Fidel, what the blazes do you think you're doing?' I hollered.

Fidel pulled up in front of us. 'Don't worry.' He grinned. 'We no scalp 'em white ladies. Hair too short!'

He and the other Havasu boys all started laughing. Rosemary and I couldn't help chuckling too, but my customers were outraged.

'You all belong in the reformatory,' Miss Pearl declared.

Fidel pointed at three of his friends, who jumped off their horses and doubled up with others. 'Those are your mounts,' he said to us. Then he held out his hand to Rosemary. 'You can ride with me,' he said. He pulled her up behind him, and before I could say anything they were galloping down the trail.

Miss Pearl, Miss Finch and I followed at a walk on our horses. The trail to the village was eight miles long, and it took most of the day to travel it. After a few hours, we came to a spot where clear, cold water gushed from an artesian spring, and that was where the stony landscape of the upper canyon gave way to lush greenery.

Rosemary, Fidel and his friends were waiting for us by the stream, letting their horses graze, and we all continued on together. The stream, fed by additional springs, gathered in strength and size the further we went. Eventually, the stream descended in a series of short falls before reaching the most breathtaking place I'd ever seen. The creek poured through a gap in a cliff wall and cascaded a hundred feet down to a turquoise pool. The air was filled with mist from the thundering fall.

It was midafternoon by the time we reached the Havasupai village, a collection of wattle huts where the stream flowed into the Colorado River. Naked Havasupai children were splashing in the water. We all dismounted, and Fidel and his friends dived into the biggest pond.

'Mom, can I go swimming, too?' Rosemary asked.

'You don't have a swimsuit,' I said.

'I could swim in my underwear.'

'Certainly not,' Miss Pearl piped up. 'It was improper enough for you to be riding behind that Indian boy.'

FIDEL SHOWED US to the guest hut. It was tight, but there was enough room for the four of us to stretch out on the mat on the dirt floor. Miss Pearl and Miss Finch were tired and wanted to rest, but Rosemary and I still had some gas left, and when Fidel offered to show us the valley, we took him up on it.

He found us all fresh horses, and we set out on a tour. Walls of red Coconino sandstone and pink Kaibab limestone rose steeply on both sides of the river. The narrow strip of bottomland was green and fertile, and we rode past rows of planted maize. Fidel pointed out a pair of red rock pillars towering above the cliff wall. Those were the Wigleeva, he told us. They protected the tribe. It was said that any Havasupai who left for good would be turned to stone.

'This place is like heaven,' Rosemary said. 'Even more than the ranch. I could live here for ever.'

'Only Havasupai live here,' Fidel said.

'I'd become one,' she said.

'You can't become one,' I said. 'You have to be born one.'

'Well,' Fidel said, 'the elders do say Anglos can't marry into the tribe, but as far as I know, none ever really tried to. So maybe you could be the first.'

AS EVENING CAME ON, the Havasupai offered us fried cornmeal cakes wrapped in leaves, but Miss Finch and Miss Pearl would have none of them, so we ate the biscuits and jerky I had packed. Miss Finch gave medical exams to the Havasupai children while Miss Pearl discussed their education with their parents, sometimes using Fidel as the interpreter. The village had a one-room school, but from time to time the state decided that the Havasupai children weren't getting a proper upbringing and swooped in and sent them to boarding school, whether their parents wanted it or not. There they learned English and were trained for jobs as porters, janitors and telephone operators.

After a morning of interpreting for Miss Pearl, Fidel sat down next to me and Rosemary. 'You people think you're rescuing these children,' he said.

'But they just end up unfit for both the valley and the world outside. Take it from me. I was sent to that school.'

'Well, at least you didn't turn to stone,' Rosemary said.

'What turns to stone is inside you,' Fidel said.

In the afternoon, Rosemary and I walked around the village. She continued to pester me about going swimming. I could tell that she could really see herself living here.

'Mom, it's the Garden of Eden,' she kept saying.

'Don't idealise this way of life,' I said. 'I was born in a dirt house, and you get tired of it pretty quickly.'

In the evening, we turned in early again, but I was wakened in the middle of the night by a commotion. Rosemary, streaming wet, was standing outside the hut wrapped in a blanket. Miss Pearl had her by one arm and was hollering about how she'd gotten up for some fresh air, heard laughter and found Rosemary, Fidel and a few other Indian kids swimming buck-naked in the moonlit pool.

'I wasn't naked!' Rosemary said. 'I was wearing underwear.'

'As if that makes a difference,' Miss Pearl said. 'Those boys could *see* you.'

What I was hearing made me blind with rage. I couldn't believe Rosemary would do this. I knew that Miss Pearl was appalled, not only at Rosemary but at me as well. She might well decide it made me unfit to be a teacher. But I was also plain furious with Rosemary. I thought I had taught her that young men were dangerous, that seemingly innocent situations could result in trouble. Plus, she'd outright disobeyed me.

I grabbed Rosemary by the hair, pulled her into the hut and threw her onto the floor, then whipped off my belt and started hiding her. Something dark came out of me, so dark it scared me, but even so, I kept at that girl, who was scrambling round on the dirt floor and whimpering, until I had the sickening feeling that I'd gone too far. Then I threw down the belt and stalked past Miss Pearl and Miss Finch, out into the night.

The next day, it was a long ride back up to the canyon rim. Whenever I glanced at Rosemary, she had her eyes on the ground.

Back at the ranch that night, I tried to put my arm around Rosemary, but she pushed me away.

'I know you're mad at me, but you needed that whipping,' I said. 'There was no other way to teach you a lesson. Do you think you learned it?'

For a minute she was silent, then she said, 'All I learned is that when I have children, I'm never going to whip them.'

That trip to the Garden of Eden turned out badly for just about everyone. After I told Jim about it, we agreed that hiring Fidel Hanna again was out of the question. That was a moot point, because when Fidel heard that Miss Pearl was threatening to turn him in to the sheriff, he joined the army.

He became a sharpshooter and fought in the Pacific Islands, but war eventually unhinged Fidel, and he was sent home suffering from shell shock. Not long after he returned, he came apart altogether and shot up a Hopi village. No one was killed, and when Fidel was freed from the state pen in Florence, he returned to the valley. But the Havasupai wouldn't allow him into the village because he'd brought shame on the tribe, and he lived by himself in a lonely corner of the reservation. He had, in the end, turned to stone.

AFTER THAT BUSINESS WITH Fidel Hanna, I decided the ranch was no place for my teenage daughter. I wrote to the mother superior at the academy in Prescott again, telling her that Rosemary had matured and was eager to try boarding school once more.

Rosemary didn't want to go, but we packed her off again. No sooner had she left, it seemed, than we began receiving letters full of homesickness as well as reports of the Ds and Fs she was earning. I was getting pretty exasperated with Rosemary, but also with those nuns, who I wished would learn to cut a fourteen-year-old daydreamer a little slack.

But by then we had something a lot bigger to worry about.

The Poms wrote us a letter saying that, with the war on, they were going to sell the ranch to put their money in the munitions industry. If we could pull together a group of investors, they'd entertain the offer we had put to them, but from that moment, the ranch was on the market.

Jim and I had been squirrelling away everything we could, and our savings were considerable, but we didn't have nearly enough to buy the ranch. Jim talked with neighbouring ranchers about forming partnerships. He also met with a few bankers but the fact was, because of the war, hardly anyone had two nickels to rub together. People were rationing cloth and growing victory gardens.

Most people.

LATE ON A JANUARY MORNING, a big black car pulled up in front of the ranch house, and three men got out. The first was wearing a dark suit, the second had on a safari jacket and leather gaiters, and the third wore a big Stetson and snakeskin boots. Suit introduced himself as the Poms' lawyer. Gaiters turned out to be a movie director famous for his westerns who was interested in buying the ranch. Boots was some cowboy Gaiters had cast in a few bit parts.

Gaiters, a beefy, red-faced man with a silver beard, was one of those people who acted as if everything that came out of his mouth was profoundly interesting. Each time he said something, he'd look at Suit and Boots, who'd chuckle appreciatively or nod sagely.

Jim and I showed them round. Gaiters and Boots kept tossing ideas at each other about how to improve the place. They were going to build an airstrip to fly in from Hollywood. They were going to install a gasoline-powered generator and air-condition the ranch house. They might even put in a pool. They were going to double the herd and breed palominos. It was clear that Boots was this rhinestone cowboy who had dazzled Gaiters with horse jargon and rope tricks when, in fact, he didn't know diddly about ranching.

In the middle of our tour, Gaiters stopped and looked at Jim as if seeing him for the first time. 'So you're the manager?' he asked.

'Yes, sir.'

'Funny, you don't look like a cowboy.'

Jim was wearing what he always wore: a long-sleeve shirt, dirty jeans, and round-toed work boots. He looked at me and shrugged.

Gaiters studied the weathered grey outbuildings. 'And this doesn't look like a ranch,' he said. 'The magic is missing. We need to goose the magic.' He turned to Boots. 'You know what I see?' he asked. 'I see everything in knotty pine.'

And knotty pine it was. After buying the place, Gaiters tore down the ranch house and built a fancy new place with exposed beams and walls of varnished knotty pine. Then he tore down the bunkhouse and built a new one in matching knotty pine. He renamed the spread the Showtime Ranch. True to his word, he put in the airstrip and doubled the size of the herd.

Gaiters also fired Jim and Old Jake. They were too old-fashioned and couldn't help him goose the magic. Then he fired all the ranch hands, who were mostly Mexicans and Indians, because they didn't look like cowboys. He hired Boots to run the place and brought in a bunch of fellows from the rodeo circuit who wore tight new jeans and embroidered shirts with pearl-snap buttons.

We had lived on that ranch for eleven years, and we loved the place. We knew every one of those 180,000 acres and respected the land. We'd never squandered the water, and we'd never overgrazed the grass, unlike our neighbours. We had been good stewards. We'd known all along, of course, that we didn't own the place, but at the same time, we couldn't help considering it ours.

'Guess I've been put out to pasture,' Jim said, after Gaiters delivered the news.

'You know you're the best at what you do,' I told him.

'Just seems like what I do don't need to be done anymore.'

'We've never felt sorry for ourselves before,' I said, 'and we're not going to start now. Let's get packing.'

We HAD OUR SAVINGS, so we weren't in a bind financially. I decided we should move to Phoenix and make a fresh start. Arizona was changing; money was pouring in. The city looked like it was going to take off.

When I called Rosemary to tell her we were leaving the ranch, she became almost hysterical. 'We can't, Mom,' she said. 'It's all I've known. It's inside me.'

'It's behind you now, honey,' I said.

Little Jim was beside himself as well and said he outright refused to go.

'It's not up to us, and it's not up to you, either,' I told him. 'We're gone.'

Since ranching was going to be in our past, I wanted to get rid of almost everything. We sold all the horses to Gaiters except Patches, who was pushing thirty. I gave her to the Havasupai.

I did keep the English riding jodhpurs and the pair of field boots I'd been wearing the day I'd fallen off Red Devil and met Jim, but that was about it. Everything we owned fit into the back of the hearse and, on a beautiful spring day, we packed it all up and headed down the drive. Rosemary was still at boarding school. She'd never returned to the ranch. Little Jim, who was sitting between me and Jim, twisted round for one last glance.

'No looking back,' I said. 'You can't. You just can't.'

VIII

Phoenix

Jim decided that we should start our new life in Phoenix by splurging. 'Name something you've always wanted,' he said.

'New choppers,' I said immediately. My teeth had been giving me trouble for years, but folks on the Colorado Plateau weren't big on dentists. I had a gap between my two front teeth where they had rotted in from the sides. I tried to keep the gap plugged with a piece of white candle wax, but when the wax fell out, I had to admit it looked a little scary. Jim's teeth were every bit as bad.

'You get yourself a pair, too,' I said.

Jim grinned. 'Two new sets of choppers. That should get us going just fine in this here town.'

We found a nice young dentist who pulled out our worn-down brown teeth, and fitted sets of new dentures to our gums. Overnight I'd gotten myself the smile of a movie star, while Jim looked about thirty years younger. The two of us walked round the city beaming radiantly.

We also bought a house on North Third Street. It was a big old place with high windows, sturdy wooden doors and adobe walls. Finally, we junked the hearse and bought a maroon Kaiser, a new kind of sedan made in California. I was proud of that house and proud of that car, too, but nothing made me prouder than my new set of choppers. From time to time, when I was in a restaurant or someplace telling someone about them, I couldn't help it; I had to pull them out and show them off.

At first I thought Phoenix was terrific. Our house was near the centre of town, and we could walk to stores and movie theatres. After all those years of sitting on orange crates and drinking from coffee cans, I went out and bought a carved mahogany dining set and Bavarian china. For the first time in our lives, we got a telephone.

Little Jim, however, hated Phoenix. 'You feel puny,' he said.

And when Rosemary's boarding school closed for the holidays and she joined us in the city, she hated it, too.

'You can't even see the ground,' Rosemary complained. 'It's all covered up with pavement and sidewalks.' She added that living in Phoenix was making her question her faith. 'I've been praying daily to go back to the ranch,' she said. 'Either God doesn't exist or He doesn't hear me.'

'Of course He exists, and of course He hears you,' I said. 'He has the right to say no, you know.'

But I did begin to worry about the effect Phoenix was having on that girl. She had no use for indoor plumbing, questioned the existence of God, and even acted embarrassed when, the next day at a luncheonette, I took out my dentures to show them to the waitress.

I DIDN'T CARE to admit it to the kids, but after a few months, I started feeling a little penned in myself. The traffic drove me crazy. Back in Yavapai County, you drove wherever you wanted at whatever speed you wanted. Here, there were all manner of signs ordering you to do this and forbidding you from doing that.

Nothing had ever made me feel as free as flying, so I decided to take up lessons again. The airport had a flying school, but when I showed up one day, the clerk passed me an entire sheaf of forms and started yammering about eye exams, physicals, takeoff slots and no-fly zones. I realised that these city folks had boxed off and chopped up the sky the same way they had the ground.

One thing about Phoenix: there were a lot more jobs available than in Yavapai County. Jim was hired as the manager of a warehouse stocking airplane parts, and I landed a teaching position in a high school in south Phoenix.

I found myself worrying about a number of things in Phoenix. We had bought ourselves a radio that we could listen to all day long. At first I thought that was grand, but it meant that, for the first time, I was also listening to the news every day. People were always getting robbed, raped, shot or stabbed. So I kept my pearl-handled revolver under my bed. Every night I made a point of bolting the doors, which we had never done at the ranch.

'Mom, you've become such a worrywart,' Rosemary said.

Rosemary was right. On the ranch, we worried about the weather and the cattle and horses, but we never worried about ourselves. In Phoenix, people worried about themselves all the time.

People also worried about bombs. Every Saturday at noon, the air-raid siren was tested, and an earsplitting whoop-whoop-whoop blared throughout the city. Rosemary couldn't abide the siren and when it went off, she buried her head under a pillow. 'I can't stand that noise,' she said. 'All it's doing is scaring me.'

The girl was developing a pronounced contrarian streak. One morning that August, when Rosemary and I were walking down Van Buren Street, we passed a storefront where a bunch of people were gathered, gawking at an automatic doughnut-making machine. Next to it was a newsstand, and it was when I glanced down at the headlines that I first learned about the atom bomb falling on Hiroshima. I bought the paper and as I read I tried to explain to Rosemary what had happened. Rosemary couldn't believe that a single bomb had obliterated an entire city—not only soldiers but also grandparents, mothers, children, as well as dogs, cats, birds, every living thing. 'Those poor, poor creatures,' she kept sobbing.

She also decided there was something sick about Americans who would stand there gawking at a doughnut maker while there was so much agony on the other side of the world.

Rosemary's feelings got even darker that fall. We'd enrolled her at St Mary's, a Catholic school a few blocks from the house, and the nuns showed some newsreels of the devastation at Hiroshima and Nagasaki. The scenes of flattened city blocks, incinerated corpses and babies deformed by radiation gave Rosemary nightmares. I told her to stop thinking about Hiroshima. She stopped talking about it, but one day I looked under her bed and found a folder full of drawing after drawing of animals and children, all with Japanese eyes and angels' wings.

Rosemary started drawing and painting more obsessively than ever. As far as I could tell, it was her one talent. Her grades were still terrible. 'What are we going to do with you?' I asked her.

'I'm not worried about me,' she said. 'And no one else should be, either.'

What Rosemary really wanted to do was be an artist.

'Artists never make money,' I said, 'and they usually go crazy.'

Rosemary pointed out that Charlie Russell and Frederic Remington had both gotten rich painting western scenes. 'Art's a great way to make money,' Rosemary said. 'For the cost of a piece of canvas and paint, you could create a picture worth thousands of dollars.'

I finally arranged for her to take lessons with Ernestine, an art teacher who wore a beret just in case you couldn't tell from her accent that she was a Frog.

Ernestine taught Rosemary that white wasn't really white, that black wasn't really black, that every colour had other colours in it, that every line was made up of more than one line, that you should love the weeds as much as the flowers, because everything on the planet had its own beauty and it was up to the artist to discover it.

This all struck me as hogwash, but Rosemary really lapped it up.

'You know what's the greatest thing about painting?' she said.

'What?'

'If there's something about the world that you don't like, you can paint a painting that makes it the way you want it to be.'

With Ernestine's lessons, Rosemary's paintings became less and less about the thing she was painting and more about what she was feeling at the moment. Around this time, she started spelling her name Rose Mary because she thought it made for a prettier signature. I continued to remind her that art was an iffy proposition; that most women still had to choose between being a nurse, a secretary or a teacher.

The funny thing was, even while telling Rosemary this, I was not, for the first time in my life, enjoying my job. I was teaching math and English at a large high school. A lot of the kids came from highfalutin families, wore fancy clothes, and refused to obey me if they didn't feel like it. It was also the first time I wasn't on my own, teaching in a one-room school. I had principals and other teachers second-guessing me, forms to fill out and committees to sit on.

There were more rules for teachers than for students. Once when I opened my purse in the teachers' lounge, one of the other teachers saw my little pistol and just about had a fit.

'That's a gun!' she gasped.

'Barely,' I said. 'It's only a twenty-two.'

Still, she reported me to the principal, who warned me that if I ever brought a gun to the school again, I'd be fired.

JIM NEVER COMPLAINED, but I could tell his job chafed him as much as mine did me. He was bored—a big, broad-shouldered guy sitting behind a metal desk, checking his inventory list and watching the Mexican workers boxing up airplane parts. Jim wasn't a desk man.

The simple truth was, he missed the outdoors. He missed the sweat and dust and heat of ranching. He missed the way that ranch life forced you to study the sky and the land, trying to anticipate nature's intentions. As fall came on that year, he noticed that the birds were migrating south earlier than usual, and that squirrels were storing extra nuts.

'Going to be a hard winter,' he said. The signs were all there. He hoped other people were reading them, too.

And that winter was hard. It came on early, and in January it snowed in Phoenix for the first time in most folks' memory. Back on the ranch, a blizzard like that would have been a call to action, forcing us to run around collecting firewood, bringing in the horses, and carting hay to the range. Living in the city, all we did was turn up the radiator and listen to the hiss and clank of the pipes.

The snow kept falling, and the next day the governor declared a state of emergency. School was cancelled, and most businesses were closed. Jim said he hoped that Boots and Gaiters knew what they were doing. He hoped all the cattle had been moved off the plateau down to the winter range and the hands had broken the ice on the ponds. 'The first thing you got to do is break the ice,' he said. 'The cattle'll die of thirst before they starve.'

On the third day of the storm, we got a knock on the door. It was a man from the Arizona Department of Agriculture. Cattle were dying across the state, he said. Ranchers needed help, and the name that kept coming up was Jim Smith. It had taken them a while to track him down, the man said, but he was needed.

Jim threw some heavy clothes into his old army duffle bag, grabbed his hat, and was out the door in less than five minutes.

The first thing he did was organise drops of hay. He had a cargo plane filled with round bales, and they took off into the storm. When they reached the range, the crew rolled the bales out of the back of the cargo bay and watched as the hay bounced on the ground.

Since the roads were impassable, Jim asked the government for a small plane and a pilot, and they flew across the state, touching down at isolated ranch houses. Jim explained to the ranchers what to do. You got to break the ice on the ponds, he told them, and cut down the fence wire. Let the cattle roam. They need to move to keep their blood circulating, and they'll instinctively move south. Let them get into big herds and huddle for warmth. You can sort them all out by the brands later.

At one ranch up in the hills, there was no place to land. Jim had never put on a parachute before, much less jumped, but he strapped one on. 'Count ten, pull the cord and roll into the fall,' the pilot said, and Jim heaved himself out of the plane.

THE STORM HAD STOPPED, but the temperatures were still frigid when Jim reached the Showtime Ranch. Even before he landed, he could see from the air that no one had broken the ice on Big Jim. Carcasses of frozen cattle lay along the pond's edge. When he got to the ranch house, he found Boots and the new hands sitting round Gaiter's fancy propane stove, their feet up, drinking coffee.

Any muttonhead can run a ranch during good times. You only find out who the real ranchers are when calamity strikes. I would have lit into that fool Boots and those other chumps, but that was not Jim's way. He did, however, get their sorry butts out and mounted up to cut wire, break ice, and start the cattle moving.

There were thousands of dead cattle lying rock-hard in the snow. Some of the surviving cattle were so weak they couldn't walk, so Jim had the men bring hay and water and hand-feed them. He massaged their legs and helped them stand again. If he could get them moving, they'd live.

Jim was gone two weeks. That whole time I didn't know where he was, and it was the longest two weeks of my life. When he finally came back, he'd lost twenty pounds. His face and hands were raw. He hadn't slept for days. But he was happy. He hadn't felt this useful since leaving the ranch. He was Big Jim again.

A few days after Jim returned, he got a call from Gaiters. He was so impressed that he offered Jim his old job as ranch manager. He'd even build us our own knotty pine caretaker's cabin.

Jim and I discussed it, but we agreed that it was not for us. Before, we had been the ones running the ranch, making all the decisions. The storm had humbled Gaiters somewhat, but he still had his cockamamie notions for goosing up the Showtime. Jim didn't want to do Gaiters's bidding or have to spend his time arguing the man out of foolish ideas. I told Jim I didn't want to live in a caretaker's cabin, even a knotty pine one, waiting for the owner to fly in with his Hollywood friends for weekend parties. I'd been a servant before, and once was enough.

Still, as the days went by, I couldn't help wondering if it was time to leave the city.

One day, Jim said, 'Maybe this city's making us a little crazy.'

'Then maybe we should leave,' I said.

'Maybe we should.'

'So that's settled.'

'Now we just got to find us a place to go.'

IX

The Flyboy

Horse Mesa was a flyspeck of a place, a glorified camp really, built for the men who worked at Horse Mesa Dam, which held back the waters of Salt River, formed Lake Apache, and generated electrical power for Phoenix. Only thirteen families lived in Horse Mesa, but those families had kids and the kids needed a teacher, and that summer I got the job.

We traded in the unreliable Kaiser for a good old Ford and, one day in July, packed our suitcases in the trunk and headed east, first to Apache Junction, then up to Tortilla Flats, where the asphalt ended. From there, we followed the Apache Trail, a winding dirt road, up into the Superstition Mountains, which for my money were even sweeter on the eyes than the Grand Canyon.

After several miles on the Apache Trail, we came to an even narrower road leading off to the north. Jim made the Ford crawl along, hugging the mountainside, as there was no guardrail and the ground fell away so abruptly that with one miscalculation, we would plunge into the abyss. The road was called Agnes Weeps, after the town's first schoolteacher, who had burst into tears when she saw how plunging and twisting the road was and realised how remote the town must be. But from the first moment I laid eyes on it, I loved that road. I thought of it as a winding staircase taking me away from the traffic jams, bureaucrats and locked doors of city life. Jim said we should rename the road Lily Sings.

We followed Agnes Weeps all the way to the bottom of the canyon, then came round a bend and saw a deep blue lake with red sandstone cliff walls rising on all sides around it. Across a short bridge, perched up on one of the cliffs, was Horse Mesa. It was just a cluster of stucco houses, and it was remote—Agnes had been right about that. A truck brought in groceries twice a week. There was only one telephone, in the community centre.

But we were all darned happy to be at Horse Mesa. Since it was summer, the kids spent the entire day at the lake, diving off the cliffs into the cool water. The lake attracted all sorts of animals, and we saw bighorn sheep, coatimundi cats and chuckwallas.

Jim got a job with the Bureau of Land Reclamation driving a gravel truck—he filled potholes and rebuilt eroded washes along the length of the Apache Trail—and the work made him content. He was on his own, out in the open.

And I was back where I belonged, in a one-room schoolhouse, with no fish-faced bureaucrats second-guessing me, teaching my students what I thought they needed to know.

The school at Horse Mesa went only through the eighth grade, so that fall, for the third time, we had to send the kids off to boarding school. We enrolled Rosemary at St Joseph's, a small, fancy school in Tucson. I knew that a lot of the other girls came from rich families, so before Rosemary left, I gave her a present.

'Pearls!' she exclaimed. 'They must have cost a fortune.'

'I got them with S&H green stamps,' I said. 'And they're fake.' I told her for the first time about my heel of a first husband and his other family. 'The louse gave me a fake ring,' I said. 'But for years I thought it was real and acted like it was, and so did everyone else.' I fastened the pearls round her neck. 'The point being,' I said, 'if you hold your head up high, no one will ever know.'

With the kids away at school, our life in Horse Mesa settled into a pleasant routine. Part of it was the setting itself. Living there was like living in a natural cathedral. Waking up every morning, you walked outside and looked down at the blue lake, then up at the sandstone cliffs—those awe-inspiring layers of red and yellow rock with dozens of crevices that became waterfalls after rainstorms.

Just as important, everyone in Horse Mesa got along. We had to. Since we all worked together and depended on one another, arguments were a luxury none of us could afford. No one complained or gossiped. In the evening, while the children played, the grown-ups strolled about visiting one another. None of us had much money, so we didn't talk about the things people with money talked about. Instead, we talked about what mattered to us—the weather, the level of the lake, the mountain-lion scat someone else had seen along Fish Creek. It may have seemed to city folk that we had little to do, but none of us felt that way, and the quiet routine contributed to the tranquillity of our little cliffside camp.

AFTER THEY FINISHED high school, both Rosemary and Little Jim went off to Arizona State. At six foot four and 200 pounds, Little Jim was now bigger than Big Jim. He played college football and ate half a box of cereal every morning, but he'd never be much of a student. During his first year in college, he met Diane, a full-lipped beauty whose father was a big cheese at the Phoenix postal system. They got married, and Jim dropped out of college and became a police officer. One down, I thought, and one to go.

I felt I had come to an understanding with Rosemary. We agreed that she could study art in college as long as she majored in teaching and got her certificate. After the war, young men had poured into Arizona, and Rosemary was always being pestered for dates. In fact, several men had already proposed to her. I told her to hold out; she wasn't ready yet. But I did have a good notion of the type of man she needed—an anchor. That girl still had a tendency to be flighty, but with a solid man beside her, I could see her settling down, teaching, raising kids and painting on the side.

There were plenty of solid men out there—men like her father—and I knew I could find her the right one.

THE SUMMER AFTER Rosemary's third year in college, she and her friends started driving over to Fish Creek Canyon to swim. One day she came home with what she thought was a funny story. A group of young air force pilots had been at the canyon. When she'd dived off the cliffs into the water, one of them had been so impressed that he'd jumped in after her and told her he was going to marry her.

'I said that twenty-one men had already proposed to me and I turned them all down, so what made him think I'd say yes to him. He said he wasn't proposing; he was telling me we were going to get married.'

Someone with that sort of moxie, I thought, was either a born leader or a con artist. 'What was he like?' I asked.

Rosemary considered the question. 'Interesting. Different. He wasn't a very good swimmer, but he jumped right in,' she said.

The jumper's name was Rex Walls. He had grown up in West Virginia and was stationed at Luke Air Force Base. Rosemary came back from her first date with him practically giggling with glee. They'd met at a restaurant in Tempe, and when some guy had flirted with her, Rex had started a fight that became a general brawl, but she and Rex had ducked out and run off before the cops arrived.

'He called it "doing the skedaddle",' she said.

Just what she needs, I thought. A hellraiser. 'That sounds promising,' I said.

Rosemary ignored the sarcasm. 'He talked all night,' she said. 'He has all sorts of plans. And he's very interested in my art. He actually asked to see some paintings.'

The following weekend, Rex showed up at Horse Mesa to look at Rosemary's art. He was a rangy fellow with narrow dark eyes and a devilish grin. He had courtly manners, sweeping off his air force cap, shaking Jim's hand vigorously, and giving mine a gentle squeeze. 'Now I see where Rosemary gets her looks,' he told me.

'You do know how to spread it,' I said.

Rex threw back his head and laughed. 'And now I also see where Rosemary gets her sass.'

'I'm just an old schoolmarm,' I went on. 'But I do have a nice set of choppers.' I slipped out my dentures and held them up.

Rosemary was mortified. 'Mom!' she said.

But Rex laughed again. 'Those are fine, indeed, but I can match you there,' he said, and slipped out his own set of dentures. He explained that when he was seventeen his car had hit a tree. 'The car stopped,' he said, 'but I kept going.'

This fellow did have a way about him, I thought. And at the very least, you knew anyone who could laugh off a car accident that took out all his teeth had to have a little gumption.

Rosemary had brought in some of her paintings—desert landscapes, flowers, cats, portraits of Jim—and Rex held each one up, praising it to the skies for originality, brilliance of colour, sophistication of technique and on and on. More horsecrap, as far as I was concerned, but Rosemary lapped it up, just the way she did that hogwash from the Frog art teacher, Ernestine.

'Why aren't any of these hanging on the walls?' Rex asked.

In the living room, we had two woodland prints that I had bought because the blue of the sky perfectly matched the blue rug on the floor. Without so much as a by-your-leave, Rex replaced them with two of Rosemary's paintings that didn't have any blue at all.

'There,' he said. 'On display, where they belong.'

'Well, they're nice, but they don't match the rug,' I said. 'It took me a long time to find prints with exactly the right shade of blue.'

'To hell with matching,' Rex said. 'You got to mix things up every now and then.' He pointed at my prints. 'Those are just reproductions,' he said, and then gestured toward Rosemary's paintings. 'These are originals, and not just that, they're masterpieces.'

I looked at Rosemary. She was glowing.

BY THE END of the summer, Rex and Rosemary were dating regularly. I couldn't tell how serious she was, but that polecat Rex was sure persistent. I felt I could read the man like a book. He was charming, but most con men were, since before they fleeced you, they needed to gain your trust. Rex always had a joke on hand, could talk about any subject, passed out compliments like candy, but you couldn't trust him further than you could throw him.

He also had all sorts of grand plans and was always talking about new energy sources—solar, thermal, wind. Jim thought Rex was all talk. 'If we could harness the hot air coming out of that gasbag,' he said, 'we could power the whole of Phoenix.'

I didn't actively discourage Rosemary from getting serious, since there was no more surefire way to make her want something, but I did point out that he might not make an ideal mate for the long haul.

'He's not exactly a rock,' I said.

'I don't want to marry a rock,' she said.

What she liked about Rex, Rosemary told me, was that when he was around, things always happened. He loved to start conversations with absolute strangers. He loved to act on whims. He loved pranks and surprises. Once he sneaked one of Rosemary's smaller paintings into an art museum in Phoenix, hung it in an empty spot, then invited Rosemary to come to the museum with him. She'd never been so startled—or tickled— than when Rex led her over to it and, feigning surprise, said, 'Well, lookie here. Best painting in the whole damned building.'

Early one Saturday morning that fall, when Rosemary was home from college, Rex showed up at Horse Mesa. He was wearing cowboy boots and a ten-gallon hat. Rosemary, Jim and I were finishing our Cream of Wheat at the kitchen table. I asked Rex if he wanted me to fix him a bowl.

'No, thank you, ma'am. I got a big day planned and I don't want to weigh myself down.'

'And what are your plans?' I asked.

'Well, you're all horse people,' he said. 'And I figure that since I'm going to marry this daughter of yours, I gotta show you that even though I've never been on a horse, I got what it takes to ride one. So I'm off to find myself a horse today, and if you want to come and give this hillbilly a few pointers, I'd be most obliged.'

Jim and I looked at each other. This fellow just was not going to go away. Meanwhile, Rosemary was saying that the Crebbses, who lived on a ranch at the foot of the mountains, had some quarter horses that they'd be happy to let us ride. So we all dug out our boots and set off in the Ford for the Crebbs place.

Ray Crebbs told us the horses were in the corral, and we were free to saddle up, but the horses hadn't been ridden for a couple of months and might be a bit fresh. We picked out four.

Rosemary always had to have the most spirited horse in the herd, and she chose a hot little bay. I had my eye on a quiet gelding for Rex, but he said there was no way in hell he was riding a horse whose balls had been cut off, so I gave him the mare I'd picked out for myself, even though she was acting a tad scutchy and head-shy.

After we saddled up, we headed out to the corral. Rosemary and Jim started trotting around to limber up their horses, and I sat on mine in the middle to give Rex some tips. The poor fellow was being game about it, but you could tell he was not a natural horseman. He was trying too hard. He was tensed up and leaning forward, which put all his weight in his shoulders. I told him to relax and take his hands off the horn, since it wasn't going to save him.

Instead of relaxing, Rex kept up a steady patter about what a cinch this riding was and how he wanted to put this old nag through her paces. 'How do I get her out of second gear?' he asked.

'First you got to learn to keep your fanny in the saddle,' I said.

After a while, I let Rex trot, but he kept popping out of his seat and jerking leather. Still, he insisted that he wasn't getting off until he'd galloped.

'You want to make her gallop, just kick her,' Rosemary called.

And that was what Rex did, whacking the mare in the ribs. The horse started but didn't break into a gallop, probably figuring that it wasn't a good idea with this unbalanced rider. Rex was nonetheless surprised, and he started shouting, 'Whoa! Whoa!' and sawing at the reins. All that noise spooked the poor mare, and she took off.

As the horse tore round the corral in a big circle, I yelled at Rex to sit back and grab her mane, but he didn't hear a thing. He kept shouting at the horse and jerking the reins, but the horse just galloped on.

Jim and Rosemary scooted into the centre of the corral to get out of her way. The mare had made a few circuits without slowing down, and I could tell that Rex was starting to come unglued. I could also tell by looking at the mare's eyes that she was frightened, not angry, and that meant she wanted to stop but needed permission.

I jumped off my horse and walked into the path of the galloping mare. I was prepared to dive to the side if she didn't stop, but as she got close, I slowly raised my arms, looked her in the eye, and in a quiet voice said, 'Whoa.' And right in front of me, she stopped.

In fact, she stopped so suddenly that Rex pitched forwards, clung to her neck for a moment, then fell to the ground.

Rosemary slid off her horse and ran over. 'Are you OK?' she asked him.

'He's fine,' I said. 'He just had the lace knocked off his panties.'

Rex got to his feet and dusted off his jeans. I could tell he was shaken up, but he took a deep breath and ran his fingers through his hair. Then a big grin spread across his face. 'I found the gas,' he said. 'Now all's I need to do is find the brake.'

Rex insisted on getting back on, which I was glad he did, and we had ourselves a nice little ride. It was late afternoon by the time we got back to Horse Mesa. I heated up some beans and, after we'd eaten, suggested we play a few hands of poker.

'You won't ever hear me say no to that,' Rex said. 'I got a bottle of hooch in the car. How's about we have ourselves a pop or two?'

Rex got the bottle, Jim set out glasses—including one for himself, just to be polite—and we all took a seat at the kitchen table. Rex poured everyone two fingers of whiskey. I dealt. There was no better way to read a man's character than to watch him play poker. Some played with the aim of holding on to what they had, others to make a killing. For some it was gambling pure and simple; for others it was a game of skill involving small calculated risks. For some it was about numbers; for others it was about psychology.

Rosemary, for example, was a terrible poker player. It didn't matter how many times I explained the rules, she was always asking questions that revealed her hand. No sooner had I dealt the cards than she asked, 'Does a straight beat a flush?'

'You'll never win if you give yourself away like that,' I said.

'Winning's not all it's cracked up to be,' Rosemary said. 'If you win all the time, no one wants to play with you.'

I let that one pass.

As we got deeper into the game, I could tell Rex was a good player. To him, the game was not about reading your cards; it was about reading your opponents, and at first he seemed to know exactly when to fold and when to raise the stakes.

But he'd kept the bottle of hooch at his elbow. Jim and Rosemary hadn't touched their whiskeys, and I'd taken only a few sips of mine. Rex kept refilling his glass and, as the evening wore on, he started playing too grandly, overbluffing, overbetting, losing pots he never should have tried to win, and getting mad at his cards.

After a while, he stopped pouring himself shots and started swigging straight from the bottle. That was when I knew I could take him to the cleaners. I waited until I had a solid hand—a full house, eights over fours—and then I let him think he was bidding me up, but I never called him, and soon he was in deeper than he realised.

I laid my cards on the table. Rex studied them, his expression turning sour, then threw his own cards facedown at the pot. After a few seconds, he chuckled. 'Well, Lily,' he said, 'that gelding didn't have any balls, but you sure got yourself a pair.'

Rosemary giggled. I had the feeling she liked the way her boyfriend had just gotten cheeky with her mother.

Jim looked at Rex. 'Watch yourself, flyboy,' he said.

'No offence, pardner,' Rex said. 'I was paying the lady a compliment.'

Jim shrugged. 'She's taken many a ranch hand's paycheque that very same way,' he added.

Rex reached for his bottle to take another swig, but it was empty. 'Guess we polished that off,' he said.

'You polished it off,' I said.

'Maybe we've played enough,' Rosemary said.

Rex nodded. He stood up, then lurched to one side.

'You're drunk,' I said.

'Just got a little buzz,' Rex said. 'But I do believe I'll be taking my leave.'

'You can't drive that road in the condition you're in.'

'I'm fine,' Rex said. 'I drive like this all the time.'

'You can sleep in the garage,' Jim said.

'I said I'm fine.' Rex started fishing in his pocket for his keys.

'Listen, you boneheaded boozer,' I said, 'you're too drunk to drive, and I'm not allowing it.'

Rex leaned both his fists on the table. 'Listen, lady, Rex Walls don't take orders from anyone, certainly not some old leather-faced, hard-assed biddy. And with that, I will bid you goodnight.'

We all sat there in silence as Rex staggered out, slamming the screen door. We heard him gun the engine, and then he drove off into the darkness, down the mountainside on Agnes Weeps.

THE NEXT DAY, I felt I needed to have a serious talk with my daughter about her boyfriend.

'That scallywag might be fun,' I said, 'but he's also a danger to himself and others.'

'Nobody's perfect,' Rosemary said.

'True enough,' I said, 'but Rex is unstable. You'll never have any security with him.'

'I don't really care about security,' she said. 'And I don't believe I'll ever really have it with anyone. We could all be killed by an atom bomb tomorrow.'

'So you're telling me the future's not important? That you're going to live your life like there's no tomorrow?'

'Most people spend so much time worrying about the future that they don't enjoy the present.'

'And people who don't plan for the future get ambushed by it. Hope for the best but plan for the worst, my dad always said.'

'You can't prepare for everything that life's going to throw at you,' she said. 'And you can't avoid danger. It's there. If you sit around wringing your hands, you'll miss out on all the adventure.'

I felt there was a lot more I could say about the subject of danger. I could have given her an entire lecture on it, talking about my dad getting his head staved in by a horse when he was three; about my Chicago friend Minnie getting killed when her hair got caught in machinery; about my sister, Helen, taking her own life after getting pregnant. Life came with as much adventure and danger as any one body needed. But the fact was, Rosemary hadn't listened to what I had to say ever since we visited the Havasupai and I gave her the whipping for swimming with Fidel Hanna.

Later that day, there was a knock on the door. When I answered it, Rex Walls was standing outside. He had a big bouquet of white lilies in one hand, and he held it out to me.

'Lilies for Lily, by way of apology,' he said. 'Though they're not as lovely as their namesake.'

'That's not exactly the tune you were whistling last night.'

'What I said was inexcusable, and I'm the first to admit it,' he said. 'But I was hoping you'd cut a fellow some slack.' He'd had a tough day, he went on, falling off a horse in front of the woman he loved, then getting beat by her mother in poker, all of which led him to take a few nips too many.

I shook my head and looked at the lilies. 'I could cut you all the slack in the world, but I still think my daughter needs an anchor.'

'The problem with being attached to an anchor,' he said, 'is it's damned hard to fly.'

What a scoundrel, I thought. Always having to have the last word. But the lilies were pretty. 'I'll go put these in water.'

'You like to fly,' Rex added. 'If it would get me back into your good graces, I'd be honoured to take you up for a spin.'

I HADN'T BEEN up in a plane for years, and though I was still steamed at that hooligan, the idea thrilled me, so of course I agreed. When Rex arrived to pick me up the following Sunday, I was standing outside in my aviator's jumpsuit, carrying my leather helmet, which I'd gotten cheap from my instructor in Mohave County when he'd sold up.

Rex leaned out the window of the sedan he was always borrowing from a friend. 'Amelia Earhart!' he called. 'You're alive after all!'

Rosemary wanted to come along, but Rex told her the plane was only a two-seater. 'This trip's just me and Amelia,' he said.

Rex drove like a demon, the way I liked to and, in no time, we had hurtled down Agnes Weeps and then along the Apache Trail.

I asked Rex a little bit about his background.

'Ma'am,' he said, 'if you're looking for pedigree, you're going to find more in the local dog pound.' His mother had been an orphan, he said; his father had worked as a clerk for the railroad. His uncle made moonshine and as a teenager Rex had sometimes run the hooch into town.

I told him about my days selling hooch stored under the baby's bassinet and how Rosemary had saved me by bawling at the sight of the cops who'd come to investigate. We got along just fine, chatting away until we reached the flats and came to a beat-up trailer surrounded by junk: car axles, metal sinks, old fuel drums and a rusting truck up on cinder blocks.

Rex slammed on his brakes and swerved into the yard in front of the trailer. 'Look at all that crap!' he exclaimed. 'Being from West Virginia, I'm a mite touchy about white-trash eyesores, and I'm going to give that fellow a piece of my mind.'

He got out and pounded on the door. 'Will the low-life who lives in this heap of rubble have the balls to show his ugly face?'

A scrawny fellow with a crew cut opened the door.

'My future mother-in-law's in that car,' Rex hollered, 'and she's sick of driving past this pigsty. So the next time I come down this road, I want to see it cleaned up, understand?'

The two men stared at each other for a moment, and I was certain one was going to deck the other, but then they both started laughing and slapped each other on the back.

'Rex, you ornery son of a bitch, how you been?' the fellow said.

Rex brought him over to the car and introduced him as Gus, an old air force buddy. 'You may think I've got the long-lost Amelia Earhart here, but she's Lily Casey Smith. She is the mother of my future bride.'

'You're going to let this jackass marry your daughter?' Gus cried. 'Keep the bullwhip handy!'

They both thought that was just hilarious.

Rex explained that, strictly speaking, it was against regulations for air force pilots to take civilians up in military planes, though everyone did it all the time on the QT. Since they couldn't take off from the airbase, in front of the controllers, the pilots picked up the civilians at the different grass fields outside the base where they practised landings. One of those fields was right behind Gus's trailer, so Rex was going to leave me with Gus, take off from the base, and fly the plane back to the trailer. I didn't mind a man who ignored stupid regulations, so Rex got another check in the plus column—though the minus column was still well in the lead.

I sat in the back of the trailer, shooting the breeze with Gus. Finally, the plane appeared. It was yellow, a single-engine two-seater with a glass canopy that Rex had shoved back. He landed and taxied toward us. After Rex stopped, Gus pointed out the footstep below the flap, and I scrambled onto the wing. Rex had me sit in the front while he got in the back. I plugged in my headphones and watched Rex throttle up, and we bumped across the field into the air.

As we gained altitude, I again had the sensation that I was an angel, gazing towards the earth's distant curve with that infinity of blue space behind it.

We flew toward Horse Mesa, and Rex dropped down to buzz the house a couple of times. Rosemary and Jim came running out waving like maniacs, and Rex dipped the wings.

Rex climbed, and we followed the spine of the mountains to Fish Creek Canyon. Then we dropped down into the canyon itself, flying above the winding river with the red stone cliff walls sweeping in and out on either side of us.

When we came up out of the canyon, we circled back over the flats and Rex let me take the controls. I banked left, brought her level again, banked right in a circle. Nothing was finer than flying.

Rex took the controls again. He sent the plane on a big rolling loop, and we went upside down. Coming out of the loop, we dived steeply and then went skimming along, barely fifty feet above the ground. Trees, hills, rock formations flashed by.

'We call this flat-hatting,' Rex said into the comms. 'A friend of mine was doing it over the beach and, when he leaned out to wave at the girls, his plane went right into the drink.'

Then we were flying towards a road with a string of telephone poles alongside it. 'Watch this!' Rex shouted. He dropped the plane even lower until we were practically touching the ground.

I realised he was going to try to fly under the telephone wire. 'Rex, you fool! You'll kill us!' I yelled.

Rex just cackled and before I knew it, we were lining up to shoot between two poles. They zipped past, with the blur of the wire overhead.

'You're a crazy man!' I said.

'That's what your daughter loves about me!' he hollered back.

He climbed again and headed north until he found what he wanted, grazing cattle. He dropped down behind the herd and approached it, once again almost skimming the earth. The cattle started stampeding away from us at their lumbering gallop, streaming out to the sides as we came onto them, but Rex banked right and then left, driving the cattle toward the centre. Only when he had them back together did he pull up and away.

'Can't do that on a horse, can you?' he asked.

THAT SPRING, Rex and Rosemary decided to get married. She gave me the news one day after dinner while we were doing the dishes.

'You need someone solid,' I told her. 'Haven't I taught you anything?'

'You sure have,' she said. 'That's all you've been doing my whole life. "Let this be a lesson," and "Let that be a lesson." But all these years, what you thought you were teaching me was one thing, and what I was learning was something else.'

We stood there, staring at each other. Rosemary was leaning against the kitchen sink, her arms crossed.

'So you're going to marry him even if I don't approve?' I asked.

'That's the plan.'

'I always liked to think I'd never met a kid I couldn't teach,' I said. 'Turns out I was wrong. That kid is you.'

AT THE SAME TIME, Rex announced that his tour of duty was coming to an end and he'd decided not to re-enlist. He didn't want Rosemary to waste her life raising a brood of kids in a trailer on a desert air base. Besides, he had other plans. Big plans.

The whole idea was half-baked.

'Where are you going to live?' I asked Rosemary.

'I don't know,' she said. 'It doesn't matter.'

'What do you mean, it doesn't matter? Your home is one of the most important things in a body's life.'

'I haven't really had a home since I left the ranch. I don't think I'll ever have a home again. Maybe we'll never settle down.'

Jim was philosophical about Rosemary's decision, figuring we'd only turn her against us by arguing with her.

'I feel like I failed,' I said.

'Don't beat yourself up,' Jim said. 'She might not have turned out like you planned, but that don't mean she turned out wrong.'

We were sitting on the front step of our house. It had rained earlier. The red rock cliffs round Horse Mesa were wet, and run-off was pouring over crevices, creating dozens of temporary waterfalls.

'People are like animals,' Jim said. 'Some are happiest penned in; some need to roam free. You got to accept her nature.'

'So this is a lesson for me, then?'

Jim shrugged. 'Our daughter's found something she likes, this painting, and someone she wants to be with, this Rex fellow, so she's way ahead of a lot of folks.'

'I guess I should try to let it go.'

'You'll be happier if you do,' Jim said.

I TOLD REX AND ROSEMARY I'd pay for everything if they'd get married in a Catholic church, and we'd do it in style. I was hoping that a big traditional wedding would get them off on the right foot.

We rented a banquet hall at the Sands Hotel, in downtown Phoenix. I invited practically everyone I knew: ranchers and ranch hands, teachers and former students, people from my past.

'What are you going to do for a honeymoon?' I asked Rosemary as the day approached.

'We're not going to plan one,' she said. 'We're going to get into the car after the wedding and go where the road takes us.'

'Well, honey, you're in for a ride.'

Rosemary looked beautiful at her wedding. Her dress reached the floor, with layers of lace over white silk, a long lace veil and matching gloves. In her white heels, she was almost as tall as Rex, who looked rakish in his white dinner jacket and black bow tie.

Rex and his buddies were nipping from their pints all day, and things got a little wild at the reception. Rex gave a big speech, calling me 'Amelia Earhart', Jim 'The Parachutin' Cowboy' and Rosemary 'My Wild Rose'. When the music started, he twirled Rosemary round the room, dipping and spinning her. She was having the time of her life. Then Rex led everyone in a conga line, and we all snaked round the room, swaying our hips and kicking out.

At the end, when the newlywed couple came out of the hotel, Rex's Ford was waiting for them at the kerb. It was a late afternoon in May, and that golden Arizona light filled the street. We all crowded onto the steps to wave goodbye. When they reached the sidewalk, Rex grabbed Rosemary by the waist, leaned her backward, and planted a long, deep smooch on her mouth. They almost fell over, and that set them laughing so much it brought tears to their eyes. As Rosemary climbed into the car, Rex patted her behind like he owned it, then got in beside her. They were both still laughing as Rex gunned the motor the way he always did.

Jim put his arm round me, and we watched them take off up the street, heading out into open country like a couple of half-broke horses.

Epilogue
The Little Critter

Jim and I lived on in Horse Mesa. Jim soon retired, though he stayed busy as the unofficial mayor—giving one neighbour's wayward child the talking-to he needed, helping another neighbour patch a roof or unclog his carburettor. I kept teaching. Like Jim, I was never one to lounge around.

Little Jim and Diane settled into a tidy ranch house in the Phoenix suburbs, and they had a couple of kids. Their life seemed pretty stable. Rex and Rosemary, meanwhile, drifted round the desert, Rex taking odd jobs while working on his various harebrained schemes, sipping beer as he drafted blueprints for machines to mine gold and giant panels to harness the sun's energy. Rosemary was painting like a fiend, but she also started dropping babies right and left, and every time they visited us, she was either expecting another one or nursing the one that had just popped out.

Rosemary's first two babies were girls, though crib death got the second before she was one year old. The third was also a girl. Rex and Rosemary were living in Phoenix at the time she was born, in our house on North Third Street, but they didn't have the money to pay the hospital bill, so I had to drive down with a cheque and some choice words for that reprobate Rex. Rosemary named the baby Jeannette and, probably still under the influence of her old art teacher, spelled it with two Ts the way the Frogs do.

Jeannette was not a raving beauty—and for that I was thankful—with carroty hair and a long, scrawny body. But she had smiling green eyes and a strong jaw just like mine and from the outset, I felt a powerful connection to the kid. I could tell she was a tenacious thing. When I took her in my arms and stuck out a finger, that little critter grabbed it and held on like she'd never let go.

With the way Rex and Rosemary's life together was shaping up, those kids were in for some wild times. But they came from hardy stock, and I figured they'd be able to play the cards they'd been dealt. Plus, I'd be hovering round. No way in hell were Rex and Rosemary cutting me out of the action when it came to my own grandchildren. I had a few things to teach those kids, and there wasn't a soul alive who could stop me.

jeannette **walls**

Like her grandmother, Lily Casey Smith (*pictured opposite*), the dominating figure in *Half Broke Horses*, Jeannette Walls had a most unconventional childhood. American readers of her best-selling autobiography, *The Glass Castle*, which took the country by storm in 2005, were bowled over by her recollections of her vibrant but dysfunctional upbringing, which she looked back on and wrote about with an unflinching eye and razor-sharp memory for detail.

She takes the same approach in *Half Broke Horses*, once again mining her family history, and this time drawing upon her grandmother Lily's remarkable life. Because, she explains, she couldn't possibly record the story in Lily's exact thoughts and words—not having been there to witness them—she was reluctant to label the book nonfiction, preferring instead to call it a 'true-life novel'.

Born in Phoenix, Arizona, in January 1960—the second of four children—Jeannette grew up in the shadow of her father, Rex, a brilliant yet volatile alcoholic who had trouble holding down a job, and who moved his family from place to place so often that there was barely time to unpack. He was a dreamer, of sorts, always believing that success lay round the next corner, in a new venture, and so he dragged his family with him across the USA, sharing with his children visions of the 'glass castle' that he would one day build for them.

Jeannette's mother, Rosemary, was an artist and teacher, but also unstable in her way, struggling with the basic requirements of raising a family. 'Mom always said people worried too much about their children. She said suffering when you are young is good.'

Given all this, it's no surprise that Jeannette and her siblings grew up in grinding poverty. Creditors were always on the family's tail, and there were times when there was no food in the house and Jeannette had to resort to stealing from classmates' lunch boxes.

Eventually, when they settled in Welch, West Virginia, her father's hometown, they had to make do in a shack with no running water and a very unreliable supply of electricity. The roof leaked, and rainwater would drip on the children while they tried to sleep.

Fortunately, there is a brighter to side to this terrible tale, in that Jeannette's parents valued learning and were intelligent, despite their unconventionality. Rosemary Walls taught Jeannette to read at an early age, and her father radiated enthusiasm for all matters scientific, sharing with her everything that he knew. As a result, she excelled at school. At seventeen, however, she fled the family home in West Virginia for New York City, where she moved in with her elder sister, Lori. There, she finished high school and was eventually accepted at Barnard College, somehow managing to scrape together the tuition fees and graduating with honours.

Jeannette had been a fledgling journalist since becoming a contributor to her high-school newspaper, and now managed to get a job as general office helper at *New York Magazine*. She was soon transferred to the periodical's business section, before being hired by *USA Today* as a news reporter. And then, finally, she was lured back to *New York Magazine*, to take over its gossip column. 'I was a little insulted at first,' she once said in an interview. 'I always wanted to be a serious journalist. But I just loved [gossip]. It was such a departure from just taking the news that was fed to you.'

She moved on to do a gossip column for *Esquire*, before leaving to write her first book, *Dish: The Inside Story on the World of Gossip* (2000). While writing it, word reached her that MSNBC.com, a US cable channel, was looking for an online gossip columnist and so Jeannette took her talents to the World Wide Web where her 'Scoop' column soon became hugely popular.

Lily Casey Smith, Ashfork, Arizona, 1934

Walls had married her first husband in 1988. After nearly a decade, they divorced, and she married author John Taylor in 2002. Taylor encouraged her to finally 'come clean' about her past—she had been keeping it from colleagues and friends—as rumours were beginning to fly in journalism circles. Jeanette agreed and wrote the autobiographical *The Glass Castle*, which turned her into a world-wide phenomenon.

From Cradle To Grave

Patricia MacDonald

Morgan and Claire have been friends since childhood, but Claire is suffering from severe post-partum depression and, after her new baby's christening, she is arrested for a shocking crime. The evidence is damning, but Morgan knows, in her heart, that Claire must be innocent, and she immediately launches her own investigation to unravel the dark mystery.

ONE

Morgan Adair rang the bell at the reception desk of the Captain's House. While she waited for the owner to appear, she walked across the antique-filled parlour to the French doors that led to the side porch. The day was unseasonably mild and the doors were open. She stepped outside, and inhaled the autumn air redolent of burning leaves and the tang of salt spray. Morgan lived and worked in New York, but she often felt assaulted by city life, and it sometimes seemed to her that she had been born in the wrong era—that she would have been better suited to life in the countryside in the late nineteenth century. This oceanside guesthouse had a little of that feeling of another time, another era.

A graduate student at Hershman College in Brooklyn, Morgan would be travelling next week to the beautiful English Lake District to finish the last of her research for her PhD thesis on Harriet Martineau, the essayist and feminist. Martineau had lived the last years of her life in Ambleside on the shores of Lake Windermere and Morgan planned to spend some time at the Victorian house the writer had called home. She could hardly wait.

The prospect of the trip was made all the more exciting by the fact that she would be spending much of her time there with Simon Edgerton, a poet who had guest-lectured at Hershman last spring. During Simon's time at Hershman, Morgan had been assigned to work as his assistant. Their academic relationship became an ever-escalating flirtation. When she told him that she would be coming to England to do her research, he offered to accompany her to the Lake District. Morgan was already imagining a scenario worthy of Jane Austen—their old-fashioned courtship consummated in that romantic setting. She was counting the days.

In the meantime, it was undeniably pleasant to be in this seaside town on an autumn weekend, in this quaint guesthouse she had found on the Internet—one of the few still open in late October. West Briar was one of three towns referred to as the Briars on New York's Long Island shoreline. Without the same cachet as the neighbouring Hamptons, the Briars were nonetheless a coveted summer haven. Now, the season was over, and West Briar had resumed its sleepy, rural character.

'Hello,' called a voice from inside the house. Morgan came back in and smiled at the tall woman with a stylish bob, half-glasses and a cardigan draped over her shoulders, who was now behind the desk.

'Hi there,' said Morgan. 'I'm on my way out, but I brought down my card.' She held out the plastic credit card.

The innkeeper reached for it, looking sheepish. 'I should have made an imprint when you arrived, Miss Adair. I'm just scattered. My help's gone back to college and I'm expecting company today, the daughter of an old friend, so I'm a little distracted. How's the room?'

'Very comfortable. It's charming. Are you open all year?'

'Actually, this is our last weekend. My husband and I go down to Sarasota for the winters. Is this your first visit to West Briar?'

'No. I usually stay at my friend's house. I just thought they didn't need a house guest this weekend.'

The innkeeper pointed to the box wrapped in pale blue with a white ribbon under Morgan's arm. 'Ah, I see. Wedding?'

'Baptism, actually. I'm the godmother,' said Morgan proudly.

'Oh. Well, congratulations. And you look very pretty.'

Morgan glanced into the mirror behind the desk. She wore her shiny, chestnut-hued hair in long, loose waves, and had forgone a tailored jacket and trousers for a short, swingy dress that showed off her legs. 'Thanks. It's an important day.'

The innkeeper handed back her card and smiled. 'A christening,' she said. 'It certainly is.'

THE MAILBOX at the end of the Boltons' driveway was festooned with blue and white balloons tied to the post with long, curling ribbons. Colourful leaves from the trees in the yard twirled through burnished sunlight down onto the long front lawn. Claire's grey cat, Dusty, sat on the front step of the brown cedar-clad cottage. Morgan opened the white gate and started up the stone pathway to the front door. Dusty jumped off the step as she approached and watched from his hiding place in a bed of zinnias beneath the window. As Morgan raised her fist to knock she heard the sound of a baby's cry.

Although it was the most normal of sounds, Morgan felt a knot in her stomach. This was her third visit since the birth, early in September, of Claire and Guy's son, Drew. The first visit she had come bearing gifts and a heart full of happiness. It had been a shock to see the anxiety in her best friend's eyes. 'I don't know how to take care of him,' Claire had whispered. She looked exhausted.

Although clueless about babies, Morgan had peppered Claire with reassurances while she took over every chore she could manage, including getting up at night with Drew. The second visit had come weeks later, when Guy, a chef who ran a catering business in the Briars, called her in a panic.

'Claire doesn't bathe. She won't get out of bed,' he said. 'Morgan, maybe you can talk to her. I don't know what to do.'

Morgan had posted a notice on the door of her shared office at Hershman, saying that she wouldn't be available for tutorials, and rushed out to West Briar. Guy had not been exaggerating. For four days Morgan helped out with the chores, and tried to reassure Claire that everything would be fine. She had gently urged her friend to see a doctor, get some medication for her baby blues.

Now the baby was six weeks old, and the day of his christening had arrived. But the persistent sound of his wails made Morgan uneasy. It doesn't necessarily mean anything is wrong, she told herself. Babies cry. She knocked on the door. The moment it opened, the strain in Guy's face told her that the situation had not improved.

'Morgan,' he said. 'I'm glad you're here. Come on in.'

Morgan followed him into the house. It was cosy and charming, a seaside cottage decorated with flair, now clearly ready for a party. The dining-room table was covered with wineglasses, utensils, plates and napkins. The rich aroma of a *pot-au-feu* emanated from the kitchen, and there were flowers arranged on every surface.

Parties were Guy's business. He had trained in France and worked for six years at a highly respected restaurant in Lyon. Once back home, he had many offers to be the head chef at fine restaurants. He decided instead to open a catering business that served the Briars and it was a great success. Clearly, he had brought all his culinary skills to bear in preparing for his son's baptism.

'Guy, everything looks wonderful. The food smells fantastic.'

He ran a hand through his dark, wavy hair. 'I think we're ready,' he said. He was a slim, handsome man with sensuous dark eyes and full lips. He wore a blue shirt, dark trousers and a patterned silk tie, with a white chef's apron tied round his narrow waist. Eighteen months ago, when Morgan first met him, he'd just fallen head over heels in love with Claire. In those days, his joy was catchy and intoxicating.

'Is there anything left to do?' Morgan put her offering on a pile of presents on the sideboard. 'It looks like you've done it all.'

'Maybe you could get through to Claire,' he said grimly. 'She doesn't want to come.'

'Oh, Guy, I'm sorry. I'd hoped . . .'

'Yeah, me too.' He rubbed the heels of his hands against his eyes. 'I don't know what to do.'

'Has she seen her doctor? Did she get some medication?'

'She doesn't want to leave the house. She makes the appointments and then she breaks them.'

'It's hard. I know it. But these blues aren't uncommon for new mothers. It'll pass.' Alarmed by Claire's mental state, Morgan had done some Internet research on postpartum depression.

'Will it?' he said in a flat tone.

A kitchen timer dinged. 'Excuse me,' said Guy. 'I have to get that. I'm trying to get everything on the table before we leave. I probably should have arranged to have Drew christened at home. But you know Claire. She wanted to do it at the church.'

Morgan understood. Her own turbulent, disrupted childhood had made her cynical, but Claire had retained her faith despite the impoverished life she and her single mother had known. When Claire had asked Morgan to be her baby's godmother, Morgan had felt bound by conscience to remind her friend that she was not the best person to entrust with religious upbringing. Claire had brushed off her objection. 'I want him to have a godmother who will care for him if anything happens to me. And that's you.'

Those late days of pregnancy had been such a happy, optimistic time for

Claire and her husband. Now, Morgan's heart ached at the bewilderment in Guy's voice, the misery in his eyes. 'It'll work out fine,' she said. 'We'll get her over there. Leave Claire to me.'

Guy looked at her. Hope and scepticism fluctuated in his gaze.

'Go on. I'll just go tell her I'm here,' Morgan said firmly. As he returned to the kitchen, she went down the hall to Guy and Claire's room and tapped gently on the door. 'Claire? It's me. Morgan. Can I come in?' Without waiting for an answer, she opened the door.

The smell of unwashed linen and sour milk hung in the stale, still air. Morgan frowned, trying to adjust her eyes to the darkened bedroom. She could hear the baby's cries of misery. Claire, who had worked before her pregnancy as an edgy computer graphics artist in Manhattan, was clad in a stained grey T-shirt and knickers. She was sitting up in bed, the bedclothes wadded round her slender hips, absently rocking the wailing baby in her arms.

'Hi, honey,' Morgan said. 'Do you mind if I let a little light in?'

Claire shrugged. 'I don't care.'

Morgan pushed open the curtains. The pale autumn light crept into the room. She walked over to the bed, and sat down on the edge. Now she could see that Claire's dark eyes were bright with tears, and there were tears rolling down her elegant cheekbones.

Morgan's heart sank. 'Oh, Claire. Not any better?'

'It's no use,' said Claire.

'Come on, now.' Morgan gave her shoulders a brief squeeze. 'It just takes some getting used to.'

'You don't know. I'm a bad mother. Nothing I do is right. I feed him. I change him. He just keeps crying.' Claire shook her head.

'Here, let me hold him,' said Morgan. She reached for the baby, and pressed the trembling little body gently to her shoulder. The force of his protests diminished. 'Hey, little guy,' she crooned.

'You see,' said Claire. 'He'd rather be with you.'

Morgan frowned. 'Don't be silly. I'm just a novelty.'

Claire closed her eyes and slid back down under the covers. Morgan had known Claire since their first day of junior high school in a small farming community in upstate New York. Morgan, whose father was a diplomat, had been raised in Malaysia. Her parents died in a hotel bombing and she was sent back to live with an aunt and uncle who clearly didn't want her. On

Morgan's first day of school, a skinny girl with glasses, who stood a head taller than anyone else in the class, sat down beside her in the lunchroom and asked if she liked *Lord of the Rings*. Claire. It was a moment of relief that Morgan would never forget—the revelation of a kindred soul.

They had shared innumerable experiences in the years since then, from the triumphant to the devastating. But even when Claire's mother died during her last year in college, Morgan thought, she hadn't seemed so hopeless. 'Guy's got everything ready,' Morgan said.

'I know. He's been a saint,' said Claire. 'I don't know how he stands it. I'm sure he wishes he'd never met me.'

'How can you even say that?' Morgan asked. 'He adores you.' As she spoke, she could hear the wistful pang in her own voice. When she'd told Claire about her flirtation with Simon, Claire had said gently, 'This doesn't seem right. I don't know of a guy who wouldn't have made a move by now.' Morgan had protested that as a guest lecturer, Simon wouldn't want to violate protocol. She'd proudly pointed out that they'd spend time together in England.

Claire and Guy had met when Guy catered Claire's engagement party to another man—Sandy Raymond, a dot-com mogul who got rich from Workability, the Internet employment site he founded. Sandy had hired Claire to do graphics for his site, and began to woo her soon thereafter, proposing during a vacation in Spain. Their engagement party took place at his summer home in West Briar. It had been bittersweet for Morgan. She and Claire shared an apartment, and she knew that this night marked the end of an era as room-mates and travellers, sharing exotic adventures. The event was glamorous. All the trees were lit with fairy lights, a jazz combo played and the champagne flowed.

At some point in the evening, Morgan stepped out onto the stone patio behind Sandy's beautiful house and saw Claire, in her blush-pink party dress, deep in conversation with a gorgeous man in a chef's jacket. The very next day, Claire told her that she was giving Sandy his ring back. It had only taken her one night to realise that she'd met the man she truly was meant to marry. Guy's proposal, their wedding and Claire's pregnancy followed in a happy whirlwind. Morgan made no secret of it—she envied Claire that commitment. 'You're the love of his life,' she said. 'You and that baby.'

'I know,' said Claire in a small voice.

'He wants this day to be perfect. Mainly for your sake. If it were up to Guy, I don't think he'd care about having Drew christened.'

'I know,' said Claire wearily. 'He avoids these family occasions. He's done it all for me.'

'It's tough, but you've got to pull yourself together for this.'

'Morgan, you just can't imagine how . . . helpless I feel.'

Morgan looked down at the baby, asleep in her arms. Carefully, she placed him in his cot by Claire's bed. 'Look, you and I have always helped each other through tough times, right? Now, this is tough. But when you put your mind to it, you can do anything. And I'm right here to back you up. You can do it. For Drew.'

Claire let out a sob. 'Oh, Morgan. Oh, I love him so much. I don't want to fail him . . .'

'You won't. Now, come on. I'll run you a bath and you soak a little bit, while I find you something beautiful to wear. You're going to be the best-looking mom in all of West Briar. Trust me.'

MORGAN SAT IN THE BACK beside the baby, who was strapped in his car seat. Claire, pale and unsteady, but clean, made-up, and wearing a short, navy silk sheath and a pair of pointy-toed pumps, sat beside her husband, who drove as if he had a car full of uncartoned eggs. Morgan could see Claire's delicate profile, and watched for changes that would indicate an imminent meltdown. But Claire was maintaining a shaky equilibrium, commenting on the beautiful day and asking about the baptism.

'Father Lawrence promised me it would be short,' said Guy.

'Good,' Claire murmured, and then lapsed into silence.

They pulled up in front of the simple, white, wooden Congregational church. It reminded Morgan of an old New England-style whaling church and it was where Claire and Guy's wedding had taken place. They all got out of the car, and made their way up the steps and down the centre aisle of the meeting house-style room. There were two banks of wooden pews, and a choir loft above. The other guests were already assembled.

Morgan recognised most of them from Claire's wedding. She handed the baby to Guy and sat beside his sister, Lucy, a short, podgy woman with fly-away blonde hair and glasses. Lucy suffered from the genetic disorder Prader–Willi syndrome, which could lead to obesity, mood disorders and mental impairment. Lucy, however, had a mild form of the condition and was of normal intelligence. She lived alone with two dogs and collected shells from the beach that she crafted into knick-knacks for a local store called Shellshack.

On the other side of Lucy, holding her hand, was Guy's stepmother, Astrid. Beside Astrid was Guy's father, Dick Bolton. Dick, though in his mid-fifties, still liked to surf in his free time, and had the tanned, fit look of a lifelong beach enthusiast. He was still handsome, and looked like a larger, more muscular version of his son. Soon after Dick was first married, he had bought a run-down beachfront bungalow and turned it into a surfers' lunch spot called the Lobster Shack. Over the years, its runaway success had spawned a retail business called Lobster Shack Seafoods. Dick affected a laid-back, 'no worries' persona, but, in truth, he was a demanding, impatient man. Astrid was his second wife whom he had met when he took Guy and Lucy to the Dutch Antilles to recuperate after their mother died from cancer. They stayed at a small hotel owned by Astrid's parents, and the lissom blonde, who wore her platinum hair even then in an old-fashioned crown of braids, worked there as a tour guide. While ten-year-old Lucy played alone on the beach and her teenage brother, Guy, learned to dive, Dick courted the lovely Astrid. After an indecently short courtship only the length of the vacation, they were married and Astrid returned to West Briar, now the stepmother of two stunned, angry youngsters.

According to Claire, everyone in West Briar was shocked by Dick's hasty remarriage. But Astrid helped out in his business and tirelessly made sure Lucy had the proper diet, physiotherapy, and medication. Guy, at fifteen, remained diffident in the face of his stepmother's kindness, but Lucy grew devoted to her.

Morgan also recognised a few of Guy and Claire's friends. She avoided the gaze of Earl Fitzhugh, universally known as Fitz, who was Guy's longtime best friend, and soon to be Drew's godfather. Even though she didn't look at him, her face flamed. Fitz, a wrestling coach at the local high school, was tousle-headed, with boyish good looks. He had been best man at Claire and Guy's wedding while Morgan was the maid of honour. He'd looked handsome in his tuxedo, and Morgan had felt seductive in her low-cut satin gown. They had flirted, drunk too much champagne and ended up in a feverish, awkward coupling in the back of Fitz's car. Morgan had not seen Fitz since. Now, she had to share the godparent title with him.

'Good morning,' said Father Lawrence, the bespectacled, grey-haired minister who had officiated at Claire and Guy's wedding. 'Good to have you all here today. Can I have the godparents come up to the font with the parents?' he asked.

Morgan edged out of the pew. As she mounted the step to the altar, she nearly bumped into Fitz, who winked at her lasciviously. How juvenile, she thought. Father Lawrence began the baptismal rite. As she responded to the ritual questions, she kept her eyes on the baby, yawning and clenching his little fists.

When at last she looked up, she noticed a movement in the choir loft. She hadn't seen anyone there when she came in. But there was definitely someone now, seated in the shadows of the last row. Morgan frowned in recognition. Although she had only met him two or three times, she was certain the man was Sandy Raymond, Claire's ex-fiancé. She didn't want Claire to look up and see him. At that moment, Father Lawrence told Claire to hold the baby, and he began to pour the water over the child's head. By some miracle, Drew did not cry, and Claire actually smiled, as the minister pronounced him baptised and the well-wishers began to clap.

'Guy and Claire want to invite you all to their house for a small celebration,' said the minister with a broad smile. Everyone stood, and Morgan glanced back up at the balcony, but Sandy Raymond, if indeed it had been Sandy Raymond, was nowhere to be seen.

THEY MADE THE SHORT drive back to the cottage. It had been Guy's house when Claire met him. Dick Bolton had given the cottage to his son, and a house to his daughter, some years earlier. Now, property in the Briars was too expensive for young people to afford. Morgan watched the houses of West Briar flash by, each more charming than the last, with expensive cars in the driveways and pools tucked discreetly in verdant back gardens.

As they pulled past the balloon-decorated mailbox, the first to arrive, Morgan noticed a black motorcycle parked behind her car in front of the house. Claire said, 'Honey, who's that?'

A pale, thin girl with a stud in her nose, her dyed black hair streaked pink, sat on the front steps. She wore a black leather jacket, filthy jeans, and heavy black boots. Her hands were festooned with rings. An overstuffed backpack was on the steps beside her as well as a black motorcycle helmet with a red rose across the visor.

Guy stopped the car and stared over the lawn at her.

'Who is that girl? What is she doing on our steps?' said Claire. She opened the car door and got out. Slowly, Guy got out of the driver's side. Morgan unhooked the baby, lifted him up to her shoulder, and emerged awkwardly from the back seat.

The girl stood up, wiped her hands nervously on her jeans. She ambled towards Guy, clearly trying to look nonchalant, but her gaze was shy and hopeful. 'Guy?' Her voice caught slightly. 'It's me.'

Claire looked in bewilderment from the girl to her husband.

'It's Eden,' the girl said. She had a soft, Southern accent.

'Eden. What are you doing here?' said Guy.

The girl's bright smile looked strained. 'I heard I had a brother. I came to see him.' Her voice sounded high and anxious. She turned to Morgan. 'Can I hold the baby?'

'I'm not his mother.' Morgan glanced at Claire. 'Claire's his mother.' The girl turned and looked questioningly at Claire.

Behind her, Morgan could hear car doors slamming as the other guests parked and began to walk towards the house. Claire's eyes widened, and she looked helplessly at her husband.

'Who told you about the baby?' Guy demanded.

'A friend saw the birth announcement. She sent it to me. Why?'

'You shouldn't be here. I'm sorry, but this is a very bad time.'

Claire began to sway slightly. 'Guy?' she said. 'Who is this?'

Eden shook her head in disbelief. 'Doesn't she know about me?'

Guy avoided Claire's panic-filled eyes. 'Claire,' he said grimly. 'This is Eden Summers. She's my daughter.'

Claire looked from Guy back to the teenager. Then she let out a little cry of anguish. Without another word, she fled into the house.

For a moment, Guy seemed torn. Then he rushed after her as the arriving guests watched, mouths agape.

'Who is this?' Dick Bolton asked, confused. He looked casually elegant in a black turtleneck and a tweed jacket.

Astrid murmured into her husband's ear.

'Oh, for God's sake,' said Dick angrily. He turned on the girl. 'Look, sweetie, if you're trying to get to know this family, this is not the way to do it, showing up here out of the blue.'

'It's not her fault,' Lucy said. 'He should have said something.'

Eden's chin trembled. 'It's my brother's baptism.'

Dick shook his head. 'I'm not trying to be cruel. But you should go back to Kentucky . . . or wherever you come from.'

'West Virginia,' the girl said bitterly. Her gaze grew steely.

'Dick, let's be nice,' Astrid pleaded in her accented voice. She offered the girl her hand. 'I'm Astrid. It's nice to meet you.'

Eden shook her hand briefly.

'This is ridiculous,' Dick said. 'Astrid, make her leave.'

Lucy turned on her father, her mild eyes ablaze. 'Dad. You act like she's a criminal. She's got a right to be here.'

'Not after all her grandparents put my son through. This is just wrong. Astrid, take the present in and meet me at the car.' Dick made a detour over to Morgan and rubbed his finger over Drew's delicate head. 'Be a good boy, Drew Bolton. I'll see you soon.'

Astrid, gripping the package, walked up the path into the house.

Eden's face was frozen into an expressionless mask. She did her best to avoid meeting the curious gazes of the guests.

'Lucy, what is this all about?' Morgan asked in a low voice. 'Who on earth is this girl?'

Lucy rolled her eyes. 'You heard her. She's Guy's daughter.'

'How come I've never heard of her before? Claire didn't know anything about any daughter.'

Lucy shook her head. 'He should have told her. That's just like Guy. He doesn't care about anyone else's feelings.'

'The girl said she was from West Virginia. Does her mother live in West Virginia . . .?'

'No. She was raised by her grandparents. Kimba, Guy's wife, died on their honeymoon.'

'Honeymoon!' Morgan exclaimed. 'Guy was married before?'

Lucy looked disgusted. 'For about one week. They got married after Eden was born.' The door of the cottage opened, and Astrid came out. She walked over to Lucy, opened her arms and squeezed her in a brief embrace.

'Poor Claire,' said Lucy. 'How's she doing?'

Astrid rubbed Lucy's small fingers in her well-manicured hand. 'I didn't see Claire. I only spoke to your brother. He's very upset. He's prepared a banquet in there. I wish your father would be reasonable . . .' Astrid's voice trailed away. She glanced back at the guests who were waiting by their cars, uncertain how to proceed.

'Why is he being so horrible to Eden?' Lucy asked plaintively.

Astrid sighed. 'He doesn't mean to be horrible. He doesn't know how to act. The situation is so . . . awkward.'

'Maybe I'll just go home,' Lucy said plaintively.

'Lucy, it's Drew's christening. Your brother needs our support. I can't defy your father's wishes. Won't you go in for me? Please?'

Lucy sighed. 'Oh, all right. But just because I feel sorry for Eden.' Lucy turned to her newfound niece, standing helplessly by. 'Eden, why don't you come on inside?'

Eden shrugged without looking up. Lucy walked over and took her gently by the arm. 'Come on. There's food in there. You look like you need to eat. I'm your aunt by the way. I'm Lucy.'

Morgan joined the other guests who, following Lucy's lead, stepped uneasily into the house. Guy was taking the lids off chafing dishes. 'Please, eat,' he said. Fitz walked over, picked up a plate and began to survey the buffet. Other guests followed suit. While Lucy filled two plates, Eden sat stiffly by the door, watching Guy, who did not meet her gaze.

Morgan slipped out of the room and took the now-squirming baby down the hallway. Drew had begun to cry. 'It's all right, baby,' she said. 'It's OK.'

She opened the door to the master bedroom. Claire was lying across the rumpled bed, still in her dress. She looked up and seemed almost frightened at the sight of her baby.

'Claire, I think he needs to nurse,' Morgan said.

Claire sat up and listlessly unbuttoned the front of her dress. Morgan handed her the baby and sat beside her, rubbing her back.

'Claire, I am so sorry about all this. What a shock.'

Claire looked stunned. Tears coursed down her cheeks as she looked at Drew's head. 'He's a liar.'

'I don't blame you for feeling that way. He should have told you.'

'He was married. He had a child,' Claire exclaimed.

'I know. It's a shock. But it's not the end of the world. I mean, everyone's got a past. It's just one of those bumps in the road . . .'

Claire gazed at Morgan in disbelief. 'Bumps in the road? He betrayed me. I can never trust him again.'

'Now, don't go ballistic. Think about it. If you'd known, would that have changed your feelings about him? It seems worse than it is because you're so down, emotionally and physically.'

'They all knew about it,' said Claire. 'And nobody told me.'

Morgan sighed. 'I guess they thought it wasn't their place.'

'They were laughing behind my back,' said Claire bitterly.

'Now, honey, that's just not so. If anything, they seemed almost as surprised as you that Guy hadn't told you. Really.'

Drew pushed away from his mother and began to fuss. Claire bent down to kiss his little round head, but he was flailing his tiny fists. 'What?' she cried helplessly. 'Oh, Drew, what is it?'

Morgan lifted the baby from her. 'Maybe he needs changing. I'll do it.' She carried him to the changing table in the corner.

Claire murmured something, which Morgan didn't hear.

'What?' Morgan asked.

'I said, I can't do it,' said Claire. 'I can't go on.'

Morgan felt as if a cold hand clutched her heart. 'Claire, don't talk like that. Don't even say such a thing.'

Claire turned her head, and gazed out of the bedroom window.

The afternoon sky had completely clouded over, and the stiff breeze blew the desiccated leaves from the trees. She shook her head. 'Fine,' Claire said softly. 'I won't say it.'

TWO

Morgan rolled her suitcase into the waiting area of her departure gate. She set the bag beside a bank of battleship-grey plastic chairs and sat down on the end seat. There were only a few other people scattered through the lounge. The flight to Heathrow was not scheduled to depart for another three hours.

She pulled the Sunday paper from her leather shoulder satchel, but she was too excited to read. She finally just sat with her eyes closed, imagining the gorgeous villages she would visit, the colleagues she would meet. Her doctoral thesis was outlined, but this trip would provide needed detail. Simon had called earlier to describe the manor house-turned-hotel he'd booked for them. Sometimes, after they talked, she worried she'd had little to say that was interesting. But they'd both been excited about the adventure ahead. All week she was so giddy she could barely sleep.

Giddy and, truth be told, a little guilty. She had checked out of the Captain's House early on the day after the christening. When the innkeeper asked how it went, she pretended enthusiasm. In fact, the party had been a disaster. Claire refused to leave her room, and the guests left as soon as they could bolt down a plate of food. Morgan felt terrible for Claire, but she also knew that she couldn't straighten out the problems in her marriage. 'By the time I come back, everything is going to seem much better. Life will be back to normal. You'll see,' she told the weeping Claire, who did not even beg her to stay as in the past. Claire let her go like a shipwreck survivor releasing her hold on a floating spar—numbly, hopelessly.

Thinking about it now, Morgan felt her spirits sinking. Let it go, she warned herself. Worry when you get back. Just enjoy the moment. You earned this happiness. You applied for, and received, a grant to do research in England. And you'll be with Simon.

This grant was the latest in a long string of scholarships and prizes she'd won for academic work. From the moment she had left the misery of her uncle's house in upstate New York, she'd found escape in university life. She'd found a place where she belonged. Once she had her doctorate, she'd have a chance at a faculty position. She wondered if Simon would ever consider seeking a position at a US university. He was well known for his poetry. Whoa, girl, she thought. You haven't even been to bed together yet. But she couldn't help daydreaming about the life they might have together.

Her contented musings were suddenly interrupted by a song by Alanis Morissette, which was the ringtone on her phone. She reached into her satchel, pulled it out, and frowned at the unfamiliar number in the window. 'Hello?'

'Morgan?' said a familiar voice, softly.

Morgan frowned and sat up in her chair. 'Claire? Is that you?'

'Yes,' said Claire. Her voice was flat. 'Where are you?'

'You caught me at the airport,' said Morgan.

'Where are you going?' Claire asked.

Morgan felt a moment of annoyance. She knew that Claire was over-whelmed by her new baby, and by all that had happened, but Morgan had told her repeatedly about this trip. 'I'm going to do my research. In England. I'm going to meet Simon. Remember?'

There was a silence at the other end. 'Right,' said Claire at last. 'That's right. Never mind. I'm sorry.'

'It's all right. I'm not leaving for hours. I have time to talk.'

There was silence at Claire's end.

'Claire? What's going on?'

'No. I shouldn't have called you. I always call you.' There was a note of real regret in Claire's voice.

'That's all right,' said Morgan. 'What's up?'

'Something has happened.'

It was an innocuous statement. But Morgan instantly felt alarm, though she couldn't say why. 'What?'

'Guy,' said Claire. 'And . . .' Her voice cracked. 'Drew.'

'What about Guy and Drew?'

'They're dead.'

'THEY'RE DEAD!' Chills crisscrossed Morgan's arms and legs. 'Oh my God. Claire . . . Oh my God.'

A couple across the way from Morgan looked up at her, their eyes filled with concern.

Morgan hunched in her seat, gripping the phone with both hands. 'Were they in an accident? Oh, Claire, I can't believe this.' Guy and Drew both dead? Drew . . . Morgan pictured the tiny, innocent baby resting in her arms only days ago. Tears filled her eyes and she felt an actual stabbing pain in her heart. 'Oh my God. No . . .'

'It wasn't an accident,' Claire said in a dull voice.

Through her own shock, Morgan suddenly realised that Claire was not crying. 'It wasn't an accident? What was it then?'

'Morgan, I need you here.'

'Of course. I'll come right away. But how . . .? What happened?'

'They were . . . killed,' said Claire. 'Murdered.'

'Oh my God. It can't be. Who? Where did this happen . . .?'

'At our house.'

'Claire, I don't understand. Were you there? Are you all right?'

Once again there was silence. Morgan realised that she needed to get a hold of herself. Claire was obviously in desperate need of someone to lean on. 'Claire, are you hurt? Where are you right now?'

'I'm at the police station.'

'OK, good. At least you're safe.'

'They've been asking me questions,' said Claire.

'Questions? My God. You should be at the hospital. You're in shock. Look, you tell the cops you'll answer their questions later. Is anyone with you who could take you to the hospital?'

'No,' said Claire.

'All right, look. Call someone to take you to the hospital.'

'I can't call them. The police told me I only get one call.'

'One call? That's ridiculous,' Morgan protested. 'Wait . . .'

'I called you,' said Claire simply.

Morgan felt as if the airport lounge was tilting. 'What? Are you saying they're questioning you . . . because they think you . . .?'

'They've arrested me,' said Claire.

For a moment it was Morgan who was silent. Like everyone else, she'd heard of innocent people being arrested, convicted. But that was an aberration. Normally the police had reason to believe you were guilty. But Claire kill her husband and her baby? It was impossible. For a moment, Morgan felt as if she was in some bizarre dream. 'Claire, I don't know how this happened, but it's some awful mistake. Oh my God . . .' She glanced at the clock on the wall. How long will it take me to get there? she thought. 'Look, you need someone with you. Do you and Guy have an attorney?'

'No,' said Claire. 'Not really.'

'Well, listen. It doesn't matter, you're innocent. We've all seen enough TV shows. You just tell the police you can't say anything more until you have a lawyer, OK? Then when the attorney arrives, you explain everything. He'll tell you what to do.'

'It doesn't matter,' said Claire.

Morgan could picture her friend, her eyes vacant, shaking her head. Morgan wished she could reach through the phone and shake her. 'It most definitely does matter. Claire, you have to listen to me. You called so I could help you, right? So, listen. You tell them to get you a lawyer.'

'It's too late.'

'It's not too late. Just tell them. I'll be there as soon as I can.'

'I already told them.'

Morgan's heart skipped a sickening beat. 'Told them what?'

'That I did it,' said Claire. 'I killed them.'

'What?' Morgan asked weakly.

There was the sound of shuffling and voices in the background. A conversation was going on between Claire and a brusque male voice, and then she returned to the phone. 'I did what you said. I told them I want a lawyer. Morgan, they're putting me in a holding cell. Please hurry. I need you.'

Morgan's mouth was so dry that she wondered if she could utter a sound. 'I'll come,' she tried to say, but the phone went dead.

She snapped it shut and put it into her satchel. She stood up on shaky legs, gripped the handle of her suitcase and went to the ticket counter. 'Excuse me,' she said to the agent. 'I'm supposed to go to London. I got a call. A death . . . in the family.'

'Do you want me to reschedule your flight?' the agent asked.

'Oh, no,' said Morgan, her mind racing. She fumbled in her jacket and handed over her boarding pass. 'I don't know what I'm doing. Just cross me off the list.'

She started to leave the lounge, and then sat back down in one of the chairs. She had to tell someone. She looked at the time on her phone and punched in Simon's number.

He answered on the third ring. His voice sounded tinny and far away. In the background she could hear sounds of music, and people talking. 'Simon,' she said, her voice shaking. 'It's Morgan.'

'Morgan,' he said, sounding pleased. 'I can hardly hear you. I'm at a drinks party in Belgravia. You'd adore these people. Here, let me step into another room . . .' The sound of his soothing English voice made her want to weep. 'There we go . . . OK.'

'I'm at the airport. But I have to leave. I . . . can't come tonight.'

'Can't come? Morgan, what's the matter? Why ever not?'

Morgan took a deep breath. 'My best friend just called me. Remember, I told you. She just had a baby. I was the godmother.'

'Oh, yes,' he said. 'Right.'

'She's been arrested. They're both dead. The baby and her husband. The police think that she . . .' She began to cry.

'What?' he said.

'They think that she was the one who killed them.'

'Good God. That's horrible. There, there, now. Take it easy.'

'It is horrible,' Morgan sobbed.

'No wonder you're upset.'

'Claire is my best friend. She's like a sister to me.'

'But, I'm not clear on why you're cancelling the trip. I mean, you're not a solicitor. There's not all that much you can do for her.'

'I can stand by her,' said Morgan angrily. 'She has no one else.'

'Well, of course,' he said soothingly. 'That's true, of course. But you realise these . . . situations can take a long time to be resolved.'

Morgan was silent.

'Well, I mean, they do. It's just that simple.'

'I shouldn't have bothered you. I have to go.'

'Now, hold it there. Steady on. That was boorish of me. I'm just a bit disappointed. I was so looking forward to our . . . journey.'

Morgan nodded, but didn't speak. Part of her wanted to say 'me too', and part of her wanted to rail at him for being so unfeeling.

'You've had a shock. Why don't you call back when you know more,' he said gently. 'We'll sort it out. Maybe we can rebook.'

Her heart felt frozen. 'As you said, it could take a long time.'

Simon was quiet, considering her reply. 'Circumstances change. Let's just see what happens,' he said finally. 'Shall we?'

IT WAS TWILIGHT by the time Morgan arrived in West Briar. The police department was headquartered in a historic building across from the fire station. But because of the uproar outside on the sidewalk, where reporters and news vans were clustered, she had to park several blocks away.

The weathered, wooden façade resembled that of its near neighbour, a whaling museum. But as Morgan pulled open the door, it was obvious that the interior included all the latest surveillance cameras, humming computers and ergonomic office furniture. The white-haired desk sergeant asked Morgan her business.

She frowned. 'I'm here to see Claire Bolton.'

The desk sergeant's ruddy face turned a shade redder. 'Are you another reporter? I already told you people. No interviews with the prisoner.'

The prisoner. Morgan turned the word over in her mind. 'No, I'm not a reporter. I'm her . . . sister. Morgan Adair.'

'You're her sister?' the sergeant said sceptically.

Morgan nodded. 'She called and asked me to come. I just arrived.'

'Wait a minute.' He picked up the phone on his desk and spoke into it. 'Yeah, she says she's the sister.' He waited. 'Allright,' he said and put the phone down. 'The van for the county jail is on its way to pick her up. You can visit until it arrives. But that's it.'

'Thank you,' said Morgan humbly.

'Hardiman, front and centre,' the sergeant bawled.

A heavyset female officer came up to the desk. 'Yessir.'

'Take this lady to see the Bolton woman. Pat her down before she goes in the cell and when she comes out. We don't want any screw-ups here till we get her moved to county.'

'Yessir.' The officer turned to Morgan. 'Come with me.'

Morgan followed the officer through a set of locked doors that she opened by putting her palm against a scanner. They entered a freshly painted room. On either side there was a lavatory without doors and then four barred cells. There did not appear to be anyone in the first two cells. Morgan submitted to a pat-down. Hardiman went to the cell on the far left. 'Your sister's here,' she said.

There was no reply. The officer unlocked the barred door with a card key, motioned Morgan in and slammed it shut behind her.

The cell was much darker than the corridor, because of the absence of windows. The walls were defaced by obscene graffiti. The cell had a small metal table, a chair and a bed. Claire, dressed in her own stained sweatshirt and jeans, was sitting on the bed. Her short, wedge-cut hair looked flat. There were dark circles round her eyes. Her flawless complexion was waxy. Her huge eyes were fixed on Morgan as she entered the cell.

Claire got up, crossed the cell, and put her arms round Morgan. 'Thank God you're here,' she whispered. Then she let out a sob.

Morgan could smell the odour of dried milk and baby sick on Claire's sweatshirt. In her mind, she saw Drew's tiny face, his rosebud lips and bright little eyes, and she felt herself stiffen as Claire's arms enfolded her. Normally, Claire's grief would have been enough to make her want to cry too. But today questions buzzed in her mind, like bees in a hive. Was Claire crying over the loss of Drew and Guy? Or was she crying because she was a prisoner in this cell? It seemed perverse for her to cry over her loved ones if she was responsible for their deaths.

Claire stepped back, folding her arms over her narrow chest and rubbing her forearms, as if she were freezing. 'Sit down,' she said.

Morgan pulled the chair out from the table and sat. She glanced up at Claire, who was watching her. 'Sorry. I'm just trying to . . .'

Claire resumed her seat on the bed. She folded her hands in her lap, kneading them together.

'Are you OK?' Morgan asked. 'Physically, I mean.'

Claire nodded without speaking.

'Did the lawyer come?'

'Yes.'

'What did he say?'

'She. It was a woman . . . She left a card. There, on the table.'

Morgan looked down and saw the card. 'Noreen Quick, Attorney at Law' it read over the address. 'Noreen, then. What did she say?'

'She's pregnant,' Claire said, and her eyes filled with tears. 'Any minute she's going to have her baby.'

'Claire! What did she say? About your case.'

Claire sighed. 'She said it was a difficult case because I confessed to the police. Honestly, I can't remember much of what she said. I'm so exhausted. I just kept wishing I had a tranquilliser or something to knock me out. They won't give me anything.'

Morgan felt an unreasoning flash of anger. Tranquillisers? That was all she could think of? How could you admit to killing your husband and your child and then forget how your lawyer advised you? How could you admit to killing at all, and just want to sleep. 'Never mind,' she said coolly. She slipped the card into her jacket pocket. 'I'll talk to her.'

Claire looked up at her gratefully. 'Would you, Morgan?'

'Yes, of course. I came here to help.'

'Thank God for you,' said Claire. 'I feel like I have no one else in the whole world. Guy's family won't help me.'

'You can't blame them,' said Morgan sharply.

Claire blushed. 'No,' she whispered. 'Of course not.'

Morgan felt a sudden, unexpected rush of tenderness. There had to be some mistake. This wasn't some crazed killer. This was Claire, with whom she had shared dorm rooms and apartments. Claire, with whom she had streaked her hair, taken long walks discussing the meaning of life, laughed till she cried. 'Oh, Claire, tell me this is some big misunderstanding. I mean, you couldn't kill anyone. Let alone your baby . . .'

Claire remained silent. A tear trickled down her cheek.

'How did it happen? Just tell me what happened . . .'

Claire gripped the sides of her head as if it were pounding. 'Don't make me say it again.'

'Why?' Morgan cried. 'Why would you ever do such a thing?'

'I don't know. I keep going over it in my mind. I mean, the baby had been so . . . fussy. And Guy—I threw him out.' Claire looked up with torment in her eyes. 'I was so angry at him for lying about his daughter. I let him come back that night to the spare room, but every time I looked at him . . .'

'So that's why you killed them?' Morgan said. Even as she said it, it seemed preposterous. 'Because of Eden?'

'Maybe. I'm not sure.'

'I don't understand,' Morgan wailed.

'It was very early this morning. It was still dark. I was in the bathroom. Drew was in the bath. I guess I was giving him a bath.'

'At that hour? In that great big, claw-foot tub? He was so little. He was barely big enough for the sink.'

Claire seemed to be staring past Morgan at the scene in her mind. 'There was water in the tub. Drew was in the water. Guy came in and I . . . we had an argument. And, I don't know. I guess, maybe, we struggled. And Guy slipped. He hit his head on the edge of the cast-iron tub. There was a lot of blood. Everywhere.'

'So, you're saying it was an accident.'

Claire looked at Morgan hopefully. 'It must have been.'

'And Drew?'

'Oh, Morgan.' Claire's voice broke. 'He drowned in the tub.'

Morgan felt physically sick. 'You let him drown? Oh my God.'

'Don't sound like that, Morgan,' Claire pleaded. 'I didn't mean to.

I know I didn't mean to. Don't you be mad at me too.'

'You didn't mean to? You sound like a child.' Morgan jumped up from the chair and began to pace the small cell like a tiger in a cage. She raked her hand through her hair, trying to imagine . . .

Officer Hardiman's walkie-talkie emitted static, and the officer responded, speaking in a low voice.

Morgan forced herself to calm down for Claire's sake. Claire had no one else to support her. No matter what she had done, their years of friendship required some kind of allegiance. Yes, it was appalling, but Claire needed her on her side. Morgan turned and looked at her, slump-shouldered on the bed. 'I'll do what I can to help you.'

Claire looked up at her, anguish and gratitude in her eyes.

'County van is here,' announced Officer Hardiman. 'Two officers are on their way down to escort the prisoner.' She slid the door partly open. 'Ma'am, you're going to have to leave.'

Claire grasped Morgan's hand. Morgan had to pull it free from her grip. She heard heavy boots approaching. 'I have to go.'

Claire nodded and wiped her eyes. 'I know. But, Morgan, one more thing. Will you be sure to feed Dusty?'

It took Morgan a moment to realise what Claire was asking. 'Your cat?' she said in disbelief. 'You're worried about your cat?'

'Please,' said Claire.

'All right. All right,' said Morgan. 'I will.'

THREE

Photographers' flashes popped in the dark as Claire was escorted, handcuffed, out of the police station. Across the street, Morgan watched as her best friend, so tall and attractive that people sometimes mistook her for a fashion model, stumbled down the walk in her filthy sweatshirt and jeans. Reporters shouted her name but Claire did not respond. She let herself be boosted up into the waiting van. A cop slammed the doors behind her.

The news people began to disperse as the van pulled away from the kerb. Morgan knew that she needed to return to her car. She needed to decide what to do next. Where she was going to stay. All of that. But instead, she remained where she stood, trying to absorb all that she had seen and heard.

A silver, ostentatiously large, late-model SUV with black-tinted windows pulled up in front of her and the passenger window descended. The driver leaned across the seat. Morgan frowned. Some rubbernecker, no doubt, wanting details on what happened.

'Morgan?'

She peered into the car. It took her only a moment to recognise him. Sandy Raymond was successful and wealthy, but no one would call him handsome. He was a stout man, not fat, but not muscular either. His longish brown hair always looked a little greasy. His face was scarred from teenage acne, his nose crooked from having been broken, and his blue eyes were small and keen.

Claire and Sandy had dated for a year before they got engaged. Although they did go out, and attended the odd charity event, Claire often told her that Sandy had a reclusive nature. Sandy divided his time among several impressive homes, but he didn't care much for entertaining. Morgan was frankly surprised that he even knew her name. 'Hello,' she said. 'What are you doing here?'

'Same thing as you,' he said. 'I'm . . . concerned about Claire.'

'Really?' said Morgan. Why would Sandy want to support the woman who had left him the day after their engagement party? The New York tabloids had had a field-day with the public humiliation of a most eligible, wealthy man dumped for a chef with a catering business. It would have been understandable if Sandy took a little satisfaction from the terrible turn of events in Claire's life.

'Yes, really,' said Sandy irritably.

'I'm just surprised.'

'Why? I almost married the woman. Naturally I'm concerned.'

He didn't know that Morgan had also seen him in the choir loft during Drew's baptism. Morgan pressed her lips together. Sandy Raymond's actions were very hard to understand. 'Right,' she said.

'Are you going to stick around town?' he asked.

'Yeah. I guess I'll stay at Claire's house.'

Sandy shook his head. 'That's a crime scene. The police probably have it closed down until they're finished in there. Look, I have that great big house. You've seen it. I've got six bedrooms and it's just me and my girlfriend. Why don't you stay at my place?'

Morgan noted the mention of his girlfriend. Clearly he had moved on. Morgan thought about Sandy's huge house, a house she had only visited once on the night of the ill-fated engagement party. It was a sprawling old mansion, tastelessly renovated. Still, the offer was tempting, if only for the luxury of it. But it didn't seem right. 'Well, that's very nice of you, but I can get a room some—'

'Look, Morgan. You've got to be blown away. It might help us both to air it out. You'd be doing me a favour if you stayed.'

'I don't know . . . I don't want to bother you.'

'No bother. Do you know the way?' he asked, as if she had already agreed. 'Do you want to follow me in your car?'

'I can find my way. Thanks.' She was weary from the shock of Claire's arrest. But she had come here to help, and Claire wanted her to feed the cat. 'There's something I have to do first,' she said.

'OK. Well, we'll be home all evening,' he said. 'I'll see you when you get there.'

Before she could thank him, the window of the SUV rose.

Morgan had no idea if there was cat food in the house, so she stopped at a minimart and bought a few cans. Then she continued on to Claire and Guy's cottage. As Sandy had predicted, it had been sealed off by the police. The balloons from Drew's christening were still tied to the mailbox, but they had lost most of their air. The dark house looked forlorn. Morgan sighed, and parked the car.

She got her flashlight out of the glove compartment and picked up the bag of cat food cans. 'Dusty,' she called softly. She scanned the yard with her flashlight, but there was no sign of the cat. Dusty was a feral tomcat that Claire had found, and she was the only one he allowed to pet him. He came and went from the house using a cat flap Guy had installed. Surely all the commotion with the police will have scared him away, Morgan thought, as she called him, circling to the back door.

Yellow crime-scene tape whipped in the night breeze. Morgan climbed the back steps and peered in the kitchen window. All she saw was darkness.

It made her shudder to look into the house, to think about the horror that had occurred there. She opened a can of food and left it outside for Dusty, and then hurried away.

It was more difficult to find Sandy's house than she'd anticipated. The huge homes along that winding stretch bordering the sea were tucked behind large trees, and there were no lettered mailboxes. After turning into several driveways only to find an unfamiliar house, she finally recognised the imposing grey stone façade.

Morgan pulled up into the gravelled parking area beside a Mercedes convertible and the silver SUV. She looked up at the symmetrical house with its tall multi-paned windows. The carriage lights bracketing the front door were not illuminated and Morgan immediately felt ill at ease.

Suddenly, the front door of the mansion opened, and Sandy, dressed in a hoodie and baggy sweatpants, came out and peered down at the circular drive. Then he ducked back in and the carriage lights were suddenly blazing. He reappeared. 'Morgan,' he called out. 'Come on in.'

Morgan frowned as she got out of the car. She went round and opened the trunk. She still had the same suitcase she had been planning to carry on the plane. Sandy watched her swing the densely packed bag from the trunk and jerk it up the stone steps. He did not descend the steps to help her.

Sandy led the way into the house. The front hallway, with its curving staircase, was flanked by two living rooms, each boasting ultrasuede sofas and chairs in shades of beige, taupe and chocolate. The window treatments were silken and formal, but they were also of neutral shades and blended into the walls. The rugs were sisal, and the appearance of the rooms was pristine, bland and safe.

A computer was set up on a blond-wood station beside the unlit fireplace. Sandy sat down in front of the screen, and began to tap at the keyboard. He indicated with a vague gesture the armless, overstuffed chairs. Morgan sat down and looked around.

'You want a beer?' he asked, lifting a green bottle from the top of the computer desk, his eyes fixed on the screen.

'Do you have any wine?' Morgan asked.

'Like, a whole cellar. Farah,' he bellowed. 'Bring a glass of wine.'

'What kind?' a faraway voice called back.

He turned to Morgan. 'Red or white?'

'Doesn't matter,' said Morgan.

'Montepulciano,' he called out.

Farah? Morgan thought. Was that his girlfriend? Judging from his tone, Morgan figured he was summoning the household help.

Sandy turned in his swivel chair. 'She'll be here in a minute. It's a big house. Any trouble finding it?'

Morgan shook her head. 'I remembered from the . . .'

'Engagement party,' Sandy said. He frowned and turned back to his computer. Then he brightened as a beautiful girl with glossy brown hair halfway to her elbows appeared. She wore a soft, form-fitting pink hoodie and grey leggings. She was barefoot, and carrying a glass of garnet-hued wine in either hand.

Sandy had, indeed, moved on, Morgan thought.

'There you are,' he said. 'This is Morgan. She's an old friend.'

The girl brought one of the glasses to Morgan and handed it to her with a sweet smile. 'Hi. I'm Farah,' she said.

'Thanks, Farah,' Morgan said.

Farah glided over to the sofa and curled up on it like a cat. 'Sandy,' she chided. 'Can't you tear yourself away? We have a guest.' Sandy sighed and swivelled round. She beckoned with one finger and he obediently picked up his beer and joined her.

'Move,' he said, draping his forearm round her shoulders.

Morgan took a sip of her wine. It had a bold, rich taste.

'So, Morgan,' said Sandy. 'What's the story with Claire and her husband? Was he beating her up or something?'

Farah looked up at him innocently. 'Who are you talking about?'

'My old girlfriend,' he said. 'Claire. She was arrested today for killing her husband and baby. Don't you ever watch the news?'

Farah shrugged and smiled at Morgan. 'Not really.'

'So what was it?' Sandy asked. 'Was he cheating on her?'

Morgan frowned. 'No. Nothing like that. They were happy.'

'They couldn't have been that happy.'

'I guess every marriage has its problems. Since the baby—'

'Don't get me wrong,' Sandy said. 'I'm not shedding any tears for Guy Bolton. I paid him a fortune to come to my house and make an engagement party, and he ran off with my bride-to-be.'

Farah looked at him in amazement. 'No way.'

'Oh, yeah. I figured you knew. It was all over the Net. They thought it was a riot the dot-com mogul got dumped.' He caressed her shiny mane. 'That's right. You don't read.'

'I read,' Farah protested, snuggling down again.

Sandy took a pull on his beer. 'So, why did she do it?' he asked.

Morgan sighed. 'I don't know. It seems . . . unbelievable.'

'But she confessed. Who's her attorney?'

'Some woman named Noreen Quick.'

'I never heard of her.'

'Claire seemed to like her.'

'What does Claire know?' Sandy demanded. 'She can't be trusted.'

Morgan felt a little put off. 'Maybe not. But it's still her choice.'

Sandy took another pull on his beer, wiping his upper lip on his sweat-shirt sleeve. 'Claire needs the best criminal attorney money can buy. Is money a problem? I can pay for it.'

'That's so nice of you,' said Farah. She looked at Morgan, wide-eyed. 'Isn't that nice of him?' She lifted her head like a baby bird and kissed his cheek. He didn't seem to notice.

'Yes, it is. I agree she needs a really good attorney, but it's not up to us,' said Morgan. 'Thank you, though. That's so generous.'

Sandy shrugged. 'It's no problem.'

Morgan studied his coarse features. He tried to appear casual, but the tension in his jaw told a different story. She thought about the fact that she'd seen him at Drew's christening, hiding in the shadows. She put her wineglass on the cocktail table. 'You know, I'm beat and I have a feeling tomorrow is going to be a long day.'

Sandy nodded. 'Farah, take her up to the middle guest room.'

Farah immediately began to uncoil herself from the couch. Sandy reached up and slapped her firm derrière. Her mouth dropped open in feigned outrage. Then she murmured something in his ear.

Sandy shoved her gently away. 'Yeah, yeah, OK,' he said.

Farah looked at Morgan brightly. 'Follow me,' she said.

THE VOICE OF ALANIS MORISSETTE invaded Morgan's sleep, and it took a moment to realise it was her phone. She opened her eyes to find herself sunk in the comfort of a king-sized feather bed. She slid out from the sheets and rummaged through her bag for the phone.

'Hello,' she murmured.

'I'm trying to reach Morgan Adair,' said a woman's voice.

'Yes,' said Morgan, 'that's me.'

'This is Noreen Quick's office calling on behalf of her client, Claire Bolton. Could you possibly come and see Ms Quick this morning? She has a few important matters to discuss with you.'

'Yes. Absolutely. I can come. I'll be there right away.'

Groggy though she was, Morgan got the directions and entered them into her phone. Then she stumbled off to the marble bathroom. She dressed quickly, grabbed her satchel, found her way downstairs in the huge, silent house and left for the attorney's office.

The offices of Abrams and Quick were located in a clapboard cottage in a narrow street off the main thoroughfare in Briarwood. Morgan parked in front of the building, opened the gate in the picket fence and walked in the door, nearly tripping on a dun-coloured Airedale stretched across the hallway.

The woman at the reception desk, whose sign read 'Berenice Hoffman', was middle-aged, with horn-rimmed glasses. Her grey hair was in a ponytail and she was wearing an Adelphi University sweatshirt. She looked up from her computer and smiled. Across from the desk, in a playpen, a toddler was playing with some foam blocks. The child looked at Morgan and made a gurgling sound.

Morgan smiled. 'Hi, yourself,' she said. Then she turned to Berenice. 'My name is Morgan Adair. You called . . .'

'Yes, right. Ms Quick is with Kyle's mother now. Take a seat.'

Morgan sat down, waggling a finger at the baby, who rewarded her with a radiant, toothless grin. 'Whose dog is that in the hall?'

'That's Rufus,' said the receptionist. 'He barks all day from loneliness if I leave him home and then the neighbours hate me.'

Morgan nodded. She was a little surprised by the informality of this office, but she liked it. 'He seems pretty calm around people.'

'He likes company.' Berenice rolled her eyes. 'Ms Abrams and Ms Quick do mainly divorce and custody work. So we get lots of kids in here. He lets them crawl all over him.'

Morgan thought about how Sandy had said that Claire needed the best possible criminal attorney. Obviously, criminal law was not Noreen Quick's speciality.

She heard a door opening out in the corridor, and a voice thanking someone profusely. A young woman came into reception, and her gaze turned to the playpen. 'Hey, Kyle,' she crooned. 'How's my sweetie? Were you a good boy for Berenice?'

'Ma . . .' cried the baby, clambering to the edge of the playpen.

The woman bent over to lift the child. 'Come on, sweetie. Thanks so much for watching him, Berenice.'

'No problem,' said the older woman. The phone rang on her desk. Berenice picked it up, nodded and looked at Morgan. 'She can see you now. Out in the hall, second door on your left.'

'Thanks,' said Morgan. She went into the hall.

A door opened and a woman appeared. She was short, with curly orange hair, freckles and no make-up. She was dressed in stretch trousers and a large, sky-blue sweater that covered an obviously pregnant belly. She extended a hand. 'Hi, I'm Noreen Quick.'

Morgan shook it. 'Morgan Adair.'

'Come on in, Morgan. Thanks for coming.'

Morgan followed her into an office that had family pictures on every flat surface. Noreen appeared to have children, but not a husband, if the pictures were any indication. On the wall there were framed newspaper articles extolling her charitable efforts on behalf of Planned Parenthood and Mothers At Work.

Noreen sat behind her desk and Morgan took the visitor's chair. 'How are you and Claire related, Morgan?' asked the attorney.

'We're old friends. More like sisters,' said Morgan.

'She has no close blood relations?'

'Some cousins in Oregon. Her mother died years ago. She and I are much in the same boat. We've come to rely on one another.'

Noreen held up a document. 'Well, she has a lot of faith in you. I saw Claire this morning and she wanted you to have general power of attorney while she's incarcerated. You'll be in charge of managing her financial affairs. Are you willing to act as her agent?'

The idea was daunting. 'Wow. Of course. Whatever she needs me to do. But I don't know exactly what her interests are . . .'

'Some things she can tell you herself. And you'll be able to access her computer and paperwork.' Noreen made a note on the pad in front of her. 'I'll call to find out when you can get in the house.'

'Oh, thank you. That would be a big help. How's Claire doing?'

Noreen spread her freckled hands. 'As well as can be expected.'

'Can we get her out of there on bail?'

'Bail's a problem. If it was just the baby, that would be one thing. The fact that the husband was also killed . . . Bail's not gonna happen. And, they have her on a suicide watch.'

Morgan blanched. 'You think she's suicidal?'

'Obviously, she's at a high risk now.'

'So that's all the more reason to get her out of there.'

Noreen frowned. 'Even if we could, she needs constant supervision. Trust me. I'm having her examined by a psychiatrist today.'

Morgan had a sudden image in her mind of Claire last night—the vacant, exhausted look in her eyes. 'That's probably a good idea.'

'Her state of mind is a cornerstone of my defence. I'm pleading temporary insanity. She is suffering from an extreme form of postpartum depression. Actually it's called postpartum psychosis.'

'Psychosis? I was with her last week,' said Morgan. 'She didn't seem that disturbed.'

Noreen gave a mirthless chuckle. 'She killed her husband and her baby. It doesn't get much more disturbed than that.'

This attorney was undeniably forceful. Morgan felt her objections being slammed down like badminton shuttlecocks. She felt both weighed down and emboldened by the fact that Claire had entrusted her with her affairs. 'You're probably right, but . . . Please don't take offence, but shouldn't she have a criminal defence attorney?'

'I offered to argue this case pro bono because I'm an expert on women's issues,' said Noreen equably. 'But if you want to try and find another attorney, by all means, feel free.'

'It's just that I've known Claire for so long,' Morgan pleaded. 'I can't imagine her ever deliberately doing such a thing.'

'Look. Women who suffer from postpartum psychosis have hallucinations, they hear voices telling them to kill their children, they have suicidal fantasies. A woman in this state of mind is not really responsible for her actions. All she wants to do is stop the pain. A woman with postpartum psychosis thinks she is doing something good for her baby by killing that child.'

'I've read about women like that, but Claire doesn't seem—'

'Crazy?' Noreen looked at Morgan with impatience. 'You don't have to take my word for it. Once postpartum psychosis is confirmed, we'll have an expert opinion. Then we proceed. I'll argue not guilty by reason of temporary insanity. No mother in her right mind would kill her baby. When her husband intervened, they struggled and she "accidentally" pushed him. According to the coroner, he cracked his skull on the tub. In other civilised countries, they'd see she got the help she needed. I want that for Claire.'

Morgan nodded, as if to agree. But she kept picturing Claire, weeping, and saying how much she loved Drew and didn't want to fail him. And if, Morgan thought, she was suffering from hallucinations, or the impulse to kill him, how could I not have noticed?

Noreen continued. 'If we win, Claire will be remanded to a mental health facility. She'll stay there for a period of years, until the judge finds that she is fit to be released.'

'A mental hospital,' said Morgan, shuddering. 'For years.'

'With any luck.'

'That's the best she can hope for?'

Noreen narrowed her eyes. 'Your friend confessed to killing two people. What did you think she was going to get? A parade?'

FOUR

Leaving the lawyer's office, Morgan felt stunned. Somehow she hadn't faced the fact that Claire was going to be put away for a long time. But the attorney's blunt assessment had brought the reality home. She sat in her car without moving, trying to imagine visiting Claire, year after year, in some hospital for the criminally insane.

When Morgan finally raised her key to fit into the ignition, she suddenly remembered that, while she knew where she was going, she did not know how to get there. She returned to the office where the helpful Berenice printed out directions. Morgan thanked her, and drove directly from the office to the county jail.

It was located forty minutes from West Briar, in a neighbourhood distinctly less upscale and scenic. The large, cinder-block building stood surrounded by a chain-link fence topped with barbed wire. Morgan was directed to the female side of the jail, waited for buzzers and passed through numerous locked doors. She was frisked by a female corrections officer, and waited in queues among weary men, women and children who seemed familiar with the procedures. After nearly forty minutes, she was told to go to the visiting area.

This was a bare room with armed guards at the doors, a few vending machines and some wooden tables and chairs, occupied by prisoners in jumpsuits and their visitors. She found an empty table. In a minute, she saw Claire at the doorway, escorted by a guard.

Morgan jumped up. 'Claire,' she called.

Claire turned. Her eyes registered recognition, but nothing more.

'Sit back down,' said a guard.

Morgan resumed her seat. When Claire sat down and folded her white hands on the table, Morgan covered them with her own. Claire's hands were icy cold. 'Are you all right?'

Claire was almost unresponsive. 'Sure,' she managed to say.

'Have you seen the psychiatrist? How did that go?'

Claire lifted one shoulder. 'All right, I guess.'

'What was the shrink's name, Claire?'

She shook her head. 'Beekman . . . Bergman . . . I don't know.'

'Don't worry, I'll find out.' Morgan leaned forward and forced Claire to meet her gaze. 'I've just been to see your lawyer. She told me you assigned the power of attorney to me. I appreciate that you trust me so much, and I'll do my very best for you. You know that.'

Claire seemed to gaze at her from a great distance. 'I do know.'

'Claire, Noreen Quick seems very bright, very capable. But I'm worried she wants to make a point with your case. She plans to use postpartum depression as your defence.'

'I have no defence,' said Claire dully.

'You told me it was an accident,' Morgan said. 'Even if you're acquitted with the postpartum defence, you'll have to live in a hospital for a long time. If it was an accident . . .'

'Oh, Morgan, how is that possible? How could I have killed them both by accident?' asked Claire hopelessly.

Morgan had the sudden impression that Claire had no idea what the truth was. 'Don't you know what happened?'

'Yes, of course,' said Claire, looking away.

'Then how can you ask that question? Claire, this is critical. You confessed. But if you don't really remember what happened—'

'Stop it, Morgan. I don't want to talk about it.' Claire squeezed her hands into fists. 'I did it. That's all you need to know.'

Morgan wanted to press her but then she thought better of it. 'I was talking to Sandy Raymond.'

'Sandy?'

'I stayed at his house last night. He's very concerned, Claire. He thinks you need a criminal attorney. We should consider that.'

Claire's gaze was unfocused. 'Listen, there's something else I need you to do. I want to attend the funeral services for my husband and my baby. Can you arrange that for me?'

The idea of Claire attending Guy and Drew's funeral was almost ghoulish. 'I don't know if that's allowed,' Morgan said.

'The assistant warden said it might be possible if the family agreed. Will you ask them? You can convince them . . .'

Morgan did not believe for a moment that Guy's family would ever agree to it. 'I'll do my best,' she said.

'And don't worry about the lawyer. It doesn't matter . . .'

'Doesn't matter!' Morgan cried. 'We're talking about your life here.'

Claire was silent for a moment. 'Will you take Dusty if I . . . Will you take him for me?'

'Let's not get ahead of ourselves,' said Morgan. 'Maybe you're going to get out of this.'

'No,' said Claire. 'No. It's over.'

Immediately, Morgan remembered what Noreen Quick had said. Claire was under a suicide watch. Morgan grabbed her hands again. 'Listen to me, Claire. Nothing is settled yet. Don't give up. You need to hang in there.'

'I don't know, Morgan. What for?'

'Well, for me, for one thing. I need you. We're each other's family, remember? Look, I'll fight for you. You hang in there.'

Claire did not smile or nod. 'I don't deserve it.'

'Time,' the guard intoned.

MORGAN STOPPED at the foot of the church steps and glanced over at the cemetery. Men with a small backhoe were digging two graves, side by side, one half as large as the other. In a sickening instant, she realised the graves were for Guy and baby Drew. She turned away, her heart aching.

Around the churchyard it seemed to be a day for maintenance. An overalled painter was standing beneath the mullioned church windows, daubing white paint on the sill from a quart can which he held in his hand. Morgan ascended the church steps, pulled open the door and looked inside. The church was silent, the warm autumn light spilling across the empty pews.

'Damn,' she whispered.

'Can I help you?' the painter asked.

Morgan turned to explain that she was looking for Father Lawrence and realised the bespectacled painter was, in fact, the minister himself. 'Oh. I didn't expect to see you there, Father,' she said.

The minister smiled sheepishly. 'I like painting,' he said. 'I find it relaxing. There's nothing to do on the new rectory, so I touch up the church. Is there something I can do for you?'

'Actually, I was hoping you might be able to help me.'

Father Lawrence set his brush down on a cloth and pressed the top back on the can. He pulled a rag from his pocket and wiped his fingers. 'If you want to go inside to talk, just give me a moment to get cleaned up.'

'No, that's not necessary. It's fine out here. It's a nice day.'

The minister looked at her. 'We've met before, haven't we?'

'Yes. Yes, we have. I was here last week.' Morgan took a deep breath. 'For Drew Bolton's christening. I was his godmother.'

The expression in his eyes grew pained. 'I'm so sorry,' he said. 'Such a tragedy.' He sat down on the steps and gestured for her to sit beside him. Morgan took a seat. 'So, you were the godmother. Were you related to the victims?'

'No. The . . .' Morgan refused to say 'killer', even if it was true. 'Claire, Drew's mother, is my dearest friend.'

Father Lawrence drew in a breath. 'I see.'

'I've come to see you because of Claire. I know she did a horrible thing. I mean, I've known her most of my life and it was just a complete shock. I haven't really been able to accept that she'd . . .'

'I'm sure it is a shock,' he murmured. 'I've spoken to the family, of course. They are suffering greatly.'

'I know,' said Morgan miserably. 'I know they must be.'

'And Claire seemed such a lovely, nice woman. She must have been tormented to do such a thing . . .'

'And she is suffering too, believe me. In fact, I'm afraid for her life. She's under a suicide watch, but if a person is determined enough . . .'

Father Lawrence nodded. 'Yes, of course,' he said.

'Look, I'm sure it sounds crazy to say this but Claire always had a lot of faith. I was thinking that maybe it would help if you talked to her. I don't know what the official church policy is when someone does something this bad, but I'm really worried.'

He smiled slightly. 'The official policy is that we're all sinners, and that no sin, no matter how terrible, is unforgivable.'

Morgan faced him hopefully. 'Could you go to the county jail and tell her that? I'm really afraid for what she might do.'

'I suppose I can do that,' said Father Lawrence. 'I think the rest of the painting can wait.'

Morgan sighed with relief. 'I was hoping you'd say that.'

THE BOLTONS' WAS the only house, built on a promontory, at the end of a cul-de-sac. It was a sprawling, modern house with a multitude of windows overlooking the sea. It was surrounded by windswept gardens and today there were cars wedged along the shoulder of the road, with several police cars parked among them. Dick Bolton was well-off now, but he had friends from all walks of life in the Briars.

Morgan parked, then sat in her car for a moment, looking up at the house, marshalling her forces. Finally, she got out and walked up the flagstone path, past Mexican labourers, dressed in jeans and sweatshirts, who were tending the gardens. Dick hired a multitude of Mexican workers to do his gardening, clean fish in his warehouse and wash dishes in the Lobster Shack. Morgan rang the bell, and Astrid Bolton opened the door.

At first, Morgan felt relieved that it was Astrid who had come to the door. Morgan knew from Claire that Guy had a testy relationship with his step-mother, and surely, she thought, a stepmother would feel less animosity towards Claire than would Guy's blood relations. But up close, Morgan could see that Astrid's lavender eyes glittered with tears. 'What is it?' Astrid asked hoarsely.

'Astrid, I'm terribly sorry . . .' Morgan began.

Astrid lifted a hand. 'Don't,' she said. 'If you're going to start making excuses for her, don't do it. Save your breath.'

'Believe me, I have no excuses. I'm as baffled as everyone else.'

Astrid was trembling. She was a quiet woman who, despite the ethereal fairness of her looks, seemed to have a solemn nature. The few times Morgan had met her, Astrid had struck her as someone who maintained an even keel. But her customary composure had deserted her. 'Please, we are just destroyed by this loss.'

'I understand. And I'm so sorry. But I have to talk to you. You and Dick both, if possible. Lucy too, if she's here.'

Astrid frowned. 'What about? Dick's in no shape to see anyone, much less friends of Claire's.'

'It's important. May I come in?'

Astrid hesitated and then, reluctantly, allowed Morgan to enter. There were clusters of people talking quietly in the living room, and the dining-room table was covered with platters of food.

'Follow me,' Astrid said grimly.

Morgan's stomach was churning and she wished she could turn and run. Astrid pushed open a door at the end of a hall.

'Astrid?' A voice called from the darkened room. Morgan could see all kinds of beach photos, surfing trophies, and electronic equipment on custom-made shelves. The plasma-screen TV was on, but there was no sound. A windowed wall overlooked the sea. Huddled in an armchair, covered by a tartan throw, was Dick Bolton, dressed in a grey sweatshirt that mirrored his complexion. Normally a robust sportsman, he had seemingly dwindled in his grief. He looked up with empty eyes.

'This is Claire's friend, Morgan,' said Astrid. 'She wanted to talk to you.'

'And Lucy, if possible,' said Morgan. 'This affects all of you.'

Astrid avoided Morgan's gaze. 'Lucy's not here. She's . . .'

'She's too busy,' Dick said bitterly. 'Too busy to be with her family when her brother has just been killed.'

'Now, darling,' Astrid chided him. 'She's terribly upset. This is very difficult for her. She has to deal with this in her own way.'

'She's spoilt. And you spoilt her,' said Dick. 'You've babied her ever since you set foot in this house. Thanks to you, she thinks she doesn't have to do the normal, decent things people do.'

Astrid's face was white. 'I've only tried to take care of her.'

Dick put his hand over his eyes and let out a sob. Then, he reached out with his other hand, groping the air, and Astrid took hold of it. 'Sorry, darling,' he whispered. 'I'm out of my mind. I'm sorry. You've been an angel with Lucy. With both of my children.'

'It's all right.' Astrid swiped her knuckles over her tears. She nodded at Morgan. 'Morgan has something to say to us.'

'Mr Bolton,' said Morgan. 'Astrid. I can't begin to tell you how sorry I am for your loss.'

'Thank you.' Dick peered dully at Morgan. 'I remember you. You were Drew's godmother.' He covered his eyes with a shaking hand and his voice was a wail. 'Why did she do this to us?'

Morgan shook her head without replying.

Dick Bolton dropped his forearms heavily to the arms of the chair. He looked dazed. Astrid looked at her husband with sorrowful eyes. She folded her arms over her chest. 'Well,' she said to Morgan. 'What is it you wanted to talk about?'

Morgan looked from one to the other. 'I wanted to say how sorry I am and I came to tell you is that the Claire I've known . . .'

'What is she talking about?' Dick asked miserably.

'Please,' Astrid said in a warning tone. 'Just be brief.'

Morgan drew in a deep breath and plunged. 'All right. I've been to see Claire today. She asked me to come here and . . . and ask for your permission . . . She wants to attend the funeral.'

Astrid's eyes widened. 'Oh no, you can't mean that.'

'It's up to you,' said Morgan. 'Whatever you say, that's what we'll do. She wouldn't be standing or seated . . . with you. She'd have to stay off to the side. With guards.'

'Are you mad?' Dick exploded. 'That woman killed my son and grandson.'

Morgan didn't offer any explanation. There was no way to make this less onerous. It was simply up to them to render a verdict.

'How could she ever think to show her face there?' Astrid said.

Suddenly, there was a tapping on the door, and Fitz stuck his head in. His eyes were red-rimmed and his face was puffy. 'Excuse me,' he said. 'Eden's grandparents just showed up from West Virginia looking for her. What do I tell them?'

Dick Bolton seemed to summon some of his old spirit. 'Those insane rednecks have the nerve to come here? Don't let them in.'

'Dick, don't,' Astrid murmured. She turned to Fitz. 'Did they try the Spauldings? That's where she was staying.'

Fitz shrugged. 'I think they did.'

'Well, then, I don't know,' said Astrid wearily. 'I haven't seen her since the night before . . . since the night of the dinner.' Eden, Morgan thought. She had almost forgotten that Eden had been the spark that ignited this tragedy.

'Tell them to go home,' Dick thundered. 'We don't know anything about that kid. Tell them they're not welcome here. After what they put us through, I don't owe them a thing.'

Astrid ignored his protest. 'No, darling, that would be rude. Fitz, offer them some food and tell them I'll be with them in a minute.'

Fitz nodded in agreement and withdrew, closing the door.

Astrid turned to Morgan. Her refined face and erect carriage seemed only sharpened by her grief. 'Look, you'd better go. Just tell Claire we said she can't come. Our lives are ruined because—'

'Wait a minute,' Dick interrupted from his chair. 'Maybe she should be there. Yes. Tell her she can come to the funeral.'

'Dick,' Astrid exclaimed.

'I want her there,' he said. 'I want to see her face.'

AT A TINY HEALTH-FOOD PLACE called Nature's Pantry, Morgan sat at one of the five tables and ordered a California sandwich. While she was waiting for her food, she called the county jail and was told that prisoners couldn't receive calls until five o'clock. Then she called Noreen Quick's office.

'I'm sorry,' said Berenice, who recognised her name right away. 'She's at the doctor's. She started having contractions.'

'Oh,' said Morgan. 'Really? Was that . . . expected?'

'She's not due for another month,' Berenice confided.

'Do you happen to know if she found out about Claire's house from the police? I don't know when they'll allow me to go inside.'

'Oh, I don't know anything about that,' said Berenice. 'Why don't you go and ask them yourself?'

'OK, I can do that. I guess you don't know if Ms Quick will be back at work tomorrow. I suppose it all depends on the baby.'

'Well, she was on bed rest for a month before her last baby. She may just have to work from her bedroom until this baby's born. Believe me, it won't slow her down much. She's a dynamo.'

'Yes, she seems to be,' said Morgan.

'Just drop by the police station and ask them about the house. Somebody there will help you.'

Morgan told Berenice that she would handle it, and tucked her phone away as the waitress appeared carrying a sandwich on brown bread stuffed with alfalfa sprouts. Morgan ate her food without tasting it, paid the cashier, and hurried over to the police station.

She asked the sergeant on duty if she could speak to someone about Claire's case. He spoke on the phone and then looked at her. 'Detective Heinz can see you for a few minutes. He's in the squad room, second door on the left.'

Morgan thanked him and followed his directions to the large, white room that took up half of the ground floor. She entered timidly and looked around. Uniformed officers and men in ties and shirtsleeves were mingling at the desks. A good-looking young man in uniform pointed her towards a large, bald-headed man scowling at a computer monitor in the corner. He was wearing a blue-striped shirt, a gold knitted tie and an elaborate-looking watch that could probably track the time in three time zones.

She approached his desk. 'Detective Heinz?' she said.

'Just a minute,' he said without looking up. He finished tapping something into his computer and then rolled his chair back about a foot. He frowned at Morgan. 'What?' he said.

'My name is Morgan Adair. I'm a friend of Claire Bolton's.' Morgan pulled papers from her bag. 'She asked me to help get her life in order. She gave me power of attorney while she's in jail.'

Heinz raised an eyebrow. 'What does this have to do with me?'

'Well, I need to get into her house to sort through her papers. And to feed her cat. And I hope to stay there while I'm in town.'

'You can go in. Your friend confessed.' Heinz waved a hand. 'The investigation's closed. We don't need anything in there.'

'You're sure? Nothing? You aren't looking into any other possibilities? I mean, don't you keep digging?'

Heinz folded his hands in a fashion that suggested he was restraining an urge to shake her. 'You've got real life confused with television shows, miss. You see these files?' He inclined his head to a tower of folders on his desk. 'These are investigations I'm still working on. Break-ins. Fraud. Domestic disturbances. Every one's got to be addressed. So, no, I don't have time to keep digging, as you say, in a case where I have a videotaped confession. That's a slam dunk in any courtroom. End of story.'

'Actually, she's going to plead not guilty, as I understand it.'

'Good luck to her,' said Heinz sarcastically.

'Claire just seems a little . . . confused to me,' Morgan persisted.

'Does she now?' A gap-toothed smile spread across his face. 'You're wasting my time, miss. Now, I'm a patient man.'

Morgan doubted that very much. For a moment she tried to imagine Claire—confused, depressed Claire—being questioned by this domineering man. 'Maybe she was frightened into confessing,' she said.

Heinz took a deep breath. Then, suddenly, his manner changed and he spoke to her slowly, and not unkindly, as if she were a small child. 'I know you're upset. None of us wants to think that the people we care for could do something like this. But innocent people don't confess to a heinous crime. Guilty people confess.'

Morgan knew in her heart that what he said was true. And Claire was not even claiming to be innocent. Claire was guilty, and Morgan was going to have to find a way to live with it. 'I understand what you're saying,' said Morgan with a sigh. 'I appreciate you letting me get into the house. Sorry I bothered you about this.'

'That's all right,' said Heinz calmly. 'I'm here to help.'

DRESSED IN THE CHICEST of workout clothes and listening to her iPod, Farah was skipping down the steps of Sandy Raymond's house when Morgan called out to her. Farah removed an earpiece, and beamed in welcome.

'I came for my things,' said Morgan. 'And to thank Sandy.'

'He's inside. Guess where?' said Farah, inclining her head towards the house. Her shining, wavy brown ponytail bobbed.

'On the computer?' Morgan guessed.

'Playing Wii games. On such a beautiful day!' Farah cried in exasperation. She glanced at her watch and waved as she broke into a trot.

Morgan thanked her and started up to the house. She entered the foyer and called out to Sandy. A voice responded from upstairs. Morgan climbed the staircase, and searched until she came to a room that looked like the control room on the Starship Enterprise. Sandy was standing with a wand in his hand, facing his virtual opponent on a giant screen. He was jumping back and forth, whacking at the air with the wand.

'Sandy,' she said.

'Yeah,' he replied without looking at her.

'I came for my things. The police said it was all right to stay at Claire's house. I just wanted to thank you for your hospitality.'

'No problem,' he said, lunging at the screen.

'I'll just go get my stuff.'

Morgan went down the hall until she found the room where she'd slept. She quickly threw her things into her suitcase. Then she hesitated, wondering whether to remove the sheets from the bed.

'Just leave it. The housekeeper will change them tomorrow.'

Morgan turned and saw Sandy at the door, arms folded over his sweaty T-shirt. 'Ah,' she said, pulling up the sheet and the duvet.

'How's Claire doing?' Sandy asked.

Morgan reached for her suitcase. 'Not too well. Very depressed.'

'Not too surprising.'

'No. Under the circumstances.'

'She shouldn't have left me,' Sandy said.

Morgan frowned. 'What do you mean?'

'You have to admit, her life would have turned out differently.'

'It's not as if her life is over.'

Sandy shrugged. 'It might as well be.'

Morgan stifled a retort. She rolled out her suitcase and headed to the stairs. 'Thank you for having me last night,' she said.

'Don't mention it,' said Sandy. 'Tell Claire I said hi.'

FIVE

Morgan glanced at the deflated balloons, and made a mental note to cut them down. Their bedraggled presence was like a reproach to Drew and Guy's memory. She continued up the path to the house while Dusty sat in front of the door and stared at her.

'Hey, Dusty. Remember me? I'm the one with the food.'

The cat's gaze was impassive.

Already Morgan had really had enough of this day. After she left Sandy's, she'd checked on funeral arrangements, then stopped for groceries and bought herself dinner at a little Italian place. While she waited for her pasta, she had called Claire again at the prison. This time she was able to get through.

Although her voice had sounded weak and fatigued, Claire had been grateful to hear she would be allowed to attend the services.

'I'm afraid Guy's father may be setting you up,' Morgan said.

Claire insisted that she didn't care. She fretted, however, that she had no black clothes to wear. Morgan told her that she was on her way to the cottage and would find clothes and bring them to the prison. Now she ran her hand along the top of the door frame looking for the key Claire said was there. She pulled it down and opened the door.

Claire's normally tidy cottage was in disarray. Every drawer and cabinet seemed to have part of its contents sticking out. Alarmed by the sight, Morgan realised all at once that this must be the result of the police search. With a sigh, she began a cursory effort to straighten up. She stacked books, files and papers back into drawers and onto shelves. After a while, she glanced down the hall to the master bedroom. The worst chore awaited her. She had to get the clothes Claire wanted, but the closet was adjacent to the bathroom where the crime had occurred.

She walked down the hall, and entered the master bedroom. The room was a mess with clothes strewn on the floor and the bed unmade. Avoiding looking at the empty cot, she rifled through the dresser for underwear, tights and a black sweater. Then she went to the closet. Beside it, the door to the master bathroom stood ajar. Morgan pulled out a slim black skirt. She tried not to look, but her gaze seemed drawn to the bathroom.

The scene of the crime.

Just last week, she had guided Claire in there, to help her get ready for the christening. Morgan had run a bath in the claw-foot tub, and filled it with bubbles, set out a fluffy white towel and even shampooed Claire's hair. Claire had finally pulled it together and at that moment, to Morgan, it had seemed to be a day full of hope. Now, that hope was over. Hesitantly, Morgan reached past the bathroom door and turned on the light.

Her gaze swept the room and she gasped. The walls and floor were spattered red with blood. A formerly white towel sat on the floor, stained rusty red. There was still water pooled in the bottom of the tub. The smell in the room was off, metallic, turning fetid.

Somehow Morgan had expected that the only sign of the tragedy would be some intangible feeling in the air. Instead, the police had left the room as it was, full of violence and its aftermath. Her stomach lurched. Turning her face from the appalling sight, she made her way blindly back to the living room. She flopped down on one of Claire's overstuffed, chintz-covered love seats, leaned her head back and took a few deep breaths.

Suddenly, she felt overwhelmed. What am I doing here? she thought. I'm a stranger in this town, going around making excuses for a confessed murderer. This isn't my battle. I'm not even related to Claire. Morgan thought longingly of her trip to England. Today, she would have been in London, poring over manuscripts in the British Museum, and having dinner with Simon. Tomorrow, they would have been setting out for the Lake District. Stately English homes, set like jewels in boulder-strewn hillsides sloping down to crystalline lakes. Their hotel was a former manor house, with a forest surrounding it. The brochure promised tea by the fire . . .

A pounding on the front door made her jump. She laid Claire's funeral clothes over the arm of the sofa and got up to answer.

The couple at the door looked to be in their sixties. The man had sparse white hair under a baseball cap, a pouchy face and rheumy eyes. He had on a plaid shirt and jeans. The woman's hair was dyed a lurid orange. She was a soft-bodied woman with a shy smile.

'I'm Wayne Summers. This is my wife, Helene,' said the man in a rough Southern drawl. 'I'm looking for Guy Bolton's house.'

Morgan cringed inside, wondering how much she had to say. 'This is his house. I'm sorry, but I'm afraid Guy's dead.'

'I know he's dead,' said the old man. 'His wife killed him and the baby. Couldn't have happened to a nicer fella. No, we jest come up here from West Virginia looking for our granddaughter. Eden? Thought she might still be here.'

'Eden is your granddaughter!' Morgan exclaimed.

'Do you know Eden?' Helene said hopefully.

'Well, not really. I did meet her when she first arrived.'

'Where'd she go?' Wayne demanded.

'I'm afraid I don't know . . .'

'You see a friend of ours saw on the CNN news what happened to Guy Bolton and that baby,' explained Helene. 'We tried to call Eden on her phone but we couldn't reach her. We knew she came up here to meet her father. We figured she might be all upset, and we better come see if she needed us to bring her home.'

Wayne sighed with exasperation. 'I told you this was a waste of time, Helene. That girl hasn't got the sense God gave an acorn . . .'

'That's not the case Wayne. She's a very smart girl,' Helene said staunchly. She turned to Morgan. 'Our Eden's highly intelligent. Her psychologist told me so. But she has emotional problems.'

'Emotional problems,' Wayne scoffed. 'That psychologist is just stealin' our money. Eden's not right, Helene. It's a fact of life.'

'Eden's been through a lot this last week,' Morgan said. 'She finally met her father . . .'

'How did that go?' Helene asked anxiously.

'I guess, not too well,' said Morgan.

'Who are you anyway?' Wayne asked suspiciously.

'My name is Morgan Adair. I'm a friend of Guy's wife, Claire.'

'The one who killed him?' Wayne asked.

Morgan looked at him coldly, trying to formulate a reply.

'Hey, don't glare at me, little lady. I have nothin' against her. In fact, I'd like to shake her hand. Guy Bolton got what was due him.'

'Why do you say that?' Morgan asked.

'Why? He killed our Kimberlee, that's why.'

Helene gave her husband a look full of warning. She turned to Morgan.

'Don't pay any attention to him. He's a mad dog on this subject.'

'Like hell. I don't care what the police said,' Wayne exclaimed.

Helene ignored him. 'Maybe Eden's back at the Spauldings by now. That's the woman who sent her the article from the paper about the baby. Our Kimba worked for them as a chambermaid one summer. They've got a hotel called the Captain's House.'

'I know the Captain's House,' Morgan said. 'I stayed there.'

'Well, then you know what a nice lady Mrs Spaulding is. She never forgot about Kimba. Or Eden. She sent Eden a Christmas card with five dollars in it every single year,' Helene said.

'Her name was Kimberlee,' Wayne said. 'Don't call her Kimba. Sounds like a name straight out of Swahililand.'

'She decided she wanted to be called Kimba back when she was going to art school,' Helene explained. 'That girl of ours won a contest and she got a scholarship. She wanted to be in—'

'When I catch up to Eden . . .' Wayne said in a threatening tone, interrupting his wife's reverie. 'Helene, come along.'

'I'm coming, dear,' said Helene, turning to Morgan. 'I just wondered, would you mind if I used your little girls' room?'

Immediately, Morgan remembered the bloodstained bathroom and shuddered. 'Yes, of course. Just up the stairs on your right.'

Helene started up the stairs as Wayne left the house. 'I'll wait in the truck,' he said.

In a few minutes, Helene returned. 'Don't mind my husband. He's just old-fashioned,' she said as she started for the door.

Morgan put her hand on the woman's sleeve. Helene's arm was as soft as a marshmallow. 'Wait. What did he mean about Guy killing your daughter? I thought she died in an accident.'

'Well, it *was* an accident. They were scuba diving. Kimba wanted to please him, no matter what. She was still real weak from having the baby. They think she panicked and went to the surface too fast. There's something called the "bends" . . .'

'Yes, I've heard of that,' said Morgan.

Helene shrugged. 'They had a . . . you know, a hearing and all. It seems the two of them were with a group, exploring some sunken ship, so there were witnesses. Guy wasn't even with her when it happened. They couldn't find nothing wrong with her equipment. She just panicked. They told us that panic is the number-one cause of accidents for scuba divers . . .'

'So why does your husband still blame Guy?'

'Well, Guy Bolton, may he rest in peace, was no gentleman. He got our daughter pregnant and he really didn't want to marry her.'

'Does Eden know about this?'

'Now she does. When she was so determined to come up here, Wayne told her all about his belief that it was no accident.'

'But you told her that it wasn't true?'

Helene sighed. 'Of course I did. There's no reason on earth for her to go thinking a thing like that about her father.' There was a loud blast of a horn. 'I've got to go. If you see my granddaughter, tell her Mom-mom loves her and wants her home. Will you do that for me?'

'Yes,' said Morgan.

'Bless you,' said Helene. She hurried out of the door.

Morgan watched until their truck was out of sight, but her mind was turning over all she had heard. There were a million questions buzzing in her head. All at once, she had an idea.

Morgan went into the kitchen to where Guy had his computer on a built-in desk. She searched his files and in no time found what she was looking for. She wrote down the information, stuffed it in her coat pocket, and picked up her car keys. Then, just as she was turning off the kitchen light, her gaze fell on a pair of scissors on the counter. She took them with her. She'd clip those balloons off the mialbox right now, on her way out. She didn't want to have to look at them again.

ON A ROAD through the wetlands to the Briarwood Marina was a row of old fishing shacks built on pilings, where, at high tide, the water rose almost to the decking. Many of these modest dwellings had been done up in recent years to be small but comfortable getaway homes. Others remained resolutely authentic, with ripped screens and patched roofs. Fitz lived in one of the latter.

Morgan checked the number she had lifted from Guy's computer, parked, marched up to the front door and banged on it. She could see the lights on inside the house, glowing warmly against the windows.

In a moment the door opened. Fitz, wearing a T-shirt and jeans, ran his hand self-consciously through his curly hair as he recognised his visitor. Caught by surprise, he smiled. 'Hi,' he said.

'Hi,' she said.

'What's up?' he asked.

'I had a few questions. I thought you might know the answers. Do you have a minute?'

'Sure. I guess so. Come on in. It's chilly out here.'

Morgan followed him into the small house. Inside it was sparsely furnished, but surprisingly neat. As she glanced around she saw bookshelves, a table with chairs, a TV and two well-worn leather chairs with an ottoman between them. The floor was warmed by an Oriental rug. It looked way too rustic for a bachelor pad.

Fitz indicated one of the chairs. 'Something to drink?' he asked.

Morgan shook her head, and sat on the edge of the cushion. Fitz settled himself opposite and put his feet on the ottoman, looking relaxed.

'I'm sorry to bother you,' Morgan said. 'I'm here because Eden's grandparents just came by Claire's house, looking for Eden. Her grandfather told me a very bizarre story about the death of Eden's mother. You've known Guy for ever. You were his best friend. I thought you might know something about it.'

Fitz gripped the armrests on his chair. 'Oh. Right,' he said in a bored voice. 'You mean that Guy was to blame for Kimba's accident? Didn't matter what the inquest said. The old man blamed Guy and he didn't want to hear anything different.'

'Yes,' said Morgan. 'I was just thinking that Eden came to town with that weighing on her mind. Maybe she wasn't sure whether or not to believe it. And then Guy blew her off at the baptism.'

'Well, yeah, but then they got together and they got along.'

'They did? When?' asked Morgan, startled by this news.

Fitz shrugged. 'After the baptism. Eden came here to see him.'

Morgan shook her head. 'Came here?'

'You didn't know that? I thought Claire must have told you.' Fitz sighed. 'After the baptism, Claire and Guy had a big argument about Eden and his marriage to Kimba, and Claire threw Guy out.'

'Oh, yes, she did tell me that,' Morgan remembered.

'Well, he came over here and stayed with me for a couple of days. But he kept calling Claire, begging for her to forgive him, going over there to talk to her. Finally, she let him come home. Unfortunately.'

'And you're saying he saw Eden during that time?'

'Yeah, he saw her,' said Fitz. 'I told him that he owed it to the kid. He knew I was right. You never really knew Guy, but he was a good man. He didn't want to hurt that kid any more than she'd already been hurt. It never was his fault that he couldn't see her. The grandfather wouldn't allow it.'

'So, he invited Eden to visit him here,' Morgan prompted.

'Right,' said Fitz. 'I told him to ask her over. She came a couple of times, before he moved back in with Claire. In fact, she may have even visited their cottage, after Guy moved back home. Anyway, they got along all right. And I know for a fact that they all went to a family dinner at Dick and Astrid's that last night.'

'Claire too?'

'Yeah. Claire was going, as far as I knew.'

'I thought Dick didn't want anything to do with Eden.'

'But Astrid felt sorry for the kid. And in the end, Dick went along with it. He loves his kids, though he has a hard time showing it. When Eden's grandfather tried to blame Guy for Kimba's death, there was nobody who defended Guy more than Dick. I always thought Guy didn't give Dick enough credit.'

'Guy treated his own daughter like an intruder.'

Fitz sighed. 'I'll grant you, that wasn't Guy's finest moment. But she ambushed him that day. He was freaked out.'

'He was the adult. He should have tried a little harder.'

To Morgan's surprise, Fitz nodded. 'You're right. He should have. And I know that he did when they got together. He took her out for a hamburger. She showed him some pictures of herself as a little girl. That kind of stuff.'

'So, I guess she didn't believe her grandfather's story.'

'I don't know. After Guy moved home we didn't get much of a chance to talk.' Fitz cocked his head. 'Why all the questions?'

Morgan felt the impulse to tell him what she'd been thinking, and she decided to risk it. 'It's just that I was thinking that no one could blame Eden for wanting revenge.'

Fitz shook his head. 'Revenge? Revenge for what?'

'I don't know. I'm just speculating. What if Eden decided to pay her father back for what he'd done to her and her mother?'

'He didn't do anything to her mother,' Fitz reminded her. 'They got married and she died in an accident. Period.'

'But what if Eden still believed he was to blame? Someone killed Guy. And his new baby.'

Fitz looked at her in disbelief. 'Someone? Claire confessed.'

'Maybe Claire knew it was Eden, but she felt guilty or sorry for the girl, and decided to take the blame.'

'Wait a minute. Are you crazy? You're really trying to blame these murders on Eden now? On that poor kid?'

'Kids can be very erratic. They can act without thinking,' Morgan said defensively. Now she regretted revealing her thoughts.

Fitz gaped at her. 'That's pathetic. I mean, I can see you're looking for excuses. Any excuse. For Claire. But to try to pin it on an innocent kid . . . And act like Claire was some kind of hero.'

'I'm just trying to look at the possibilities rationally.'

'You call that rational? It's obscene.' Fitz pushed himself up from his chair. 'You'll grab at any excuse. For Claire, and for yourself.'

'Myself?' Morgan stood up. 'What do I need an excuse for?'

Fitz's eyes narrowed. 'You're avoiding the obvious. Your friend confessed to this crime. Don't you feel a little bit responsible?'

'How am I responsible?' Morgan cried.

'Oh, I don't know. Maybe, if you'd been paying attention, you'd have figured out that your friend was off the deep end . . . And if you had, maybe *my* best friend and his child would be alive.'

Morgan blinked fast, blindsided by his accusation.

'You must have noticed that she was going nuts, but maybe you felt it served her right. Maybe you were a little bit jealous of all the good things that had happened to old Claire.'

'How dare you say that? You don't even know me.'

'You told me that yourself. At their wedding. After about your tenth glass of champagne, you said how much you envied Claire. How men fell in love with her at first sight and made fools out of themselves for her. And how that never happened to you.'

'I never said that,' Morgan protested, although she knew it might indeed have been something she'd said. It was certainly something she'd felt. 'I'll admit that I drank a lot of champagne,' she said coolly. 'Sorry. I don't really remember much of anything about that wedding, to be honest with you. It's mostly just a blur.'

Fitz held up his thumb and forefinger, almost touching, squinting through the tiny opening. 'Oh, come on. Tell the truth. Didn't you feel just a wee little bit of satisfaction that Claire was depressed?'

'You don't know what the hell you're talking about.'

'Are you sure? I do know you a little.'

Morgan ignored this reference to their brief encounter. 'Don't flatter yourself,' Morgan retorted coldly. She turned away from him and left the shack, slamming the door behind her. She got into her car and stared out at the dark wetlands, her heart pounding with anger. But beneath the anger, she felt humiliated. Her cheeks flamed at the thought of his scornful appraisal. It was so unjust. She had acted out of friendship, done all she could for Claire. But to her surprise, tears began to run down her face.

Morgan folded her arms on the wheel, and rested her head against them. Fitz was an arrogant fool, but as much as she tried to deny it, in her heart of hearts she knew she'd felt a little jealous of Claire, even somewhat abandoned by her. If Morgan was acting purely out of friendship, wouldn't she have noticed that Claire was descending into mental illness? Wouldn't she have insisted on taking her to a psychiatrist?

Guilty feelings rushed through her system. But after a few seconds she shook her head. True or not, she had to stay strong. Insufficient as she might be, she was the only one Claire had left.

SIX

The female guard behind a Plexiglas shield at the county jail visitors' desk looked up impassively. 'You're too late,' she said.

Morgan struggled to maintain a civil tone. 'I've got ten minutes.'

'Your friend already has a visitor.'

Who? Morgan wondered. 'Maybe they'll leave early. I'll wait.'

'Suit yourself. Sit over there.' The guard pointed with a pencil.

Morgan sat in one of the moulded plastic chairs, put her head back against the wall and closed her eyes. She had spent an almost completely sleepless night in Claire's guest room, startled by every sound. Every time she started to doze, images of the blood-spattered bathroom rose in her mind. She finally fell into a coma-like stupor at dawn, and did not even hear her alarm go off.

When she awoke, Morgan threw on some clothes and ran out of the house. She drove above the speed limit and squealed into the parking lot. She rushed through the security procedures, handing over a shopping bag that held Claire's black clothes. The security guard refused to assure her that they would be delivered.

'Visiting hours are over. Everybody out,' said the guard.

Morgan opened her eyes and sighed. She got up and followed the straggling queue of visitors out through the several sets of doors to the parking lot. As she got into the car, her phone rang.

'Ms Adair? This is Berenice Hoffman at Noreen Quick's office. Ms Quick's at home, on bed rest. She wants to see you asap.'

NOREEN QUICK lived far from the shoreline, in a quiet cul-de-sac of 1950s split-level homes built on a former potato field. Her garden was casually tended with a plastic climbing frame and a life-size plastic doll's house flattening the grass and turning it brown beneath them. Morgan walked up to the door and knocked.

A tall, angular woman with a wide smile and a cap of blonde-tipped, wildly curly hair answered, wiping her hands on an apron. Morgan introduced herself. 'I'm here to see Ms Quick,' she said.

The woman stepped aside. 'Follow me,' she said. She started down the hallway of the light-filled, pleasantly cluttered house and glanced into the living room at two young children with red hair watching Barney the purple dinosaur on the television. 'Turn that down,' she ordered. 'We'll all be deaf. After Barney's, come and get your lunch.'

The younger child looked up. 'Nanabutter?' she said hopefully.

'You got it, babe.' The woman continued down a hall filled with plants and opened a door at the end. 'Nonny, your client's here. Keep it short.' She turned to Morgan. 'She doesn't do resting very well.'

'I'll bet,' said Morgan.

She slipped into the room. Noreen Quick was lying in a four-poster bed, surrounded by files and papers on the counterpane, a computer glowing at her side and a Bluetooth phone in her ear. Her thermal shirt stretched out over her large stomach. She gestured to Morgan to sit down in the rocking chair beside the bed.

Morgan took a seat. 'How are you feeling?' she asked.

Noreen waved a hand. 'Fine. This is a pain, but the same thing happened last time. I hate it, but I deal with it.'

Morgan nodded.

'I'll get right to the point. 'Cause if I don't, and you're in here any length of time, Gert will kick you out.'

'That's fine with me. What's this all about?'

'I just got a call from the psychiatrist we hired to interview Claire. It's a little disappointing. He claims she doesn't have PPP. Not now. Or at the time of the . . . incident as far as he's concerned. Depressed, yes, but hell, everybody gets depressed now and then. That's not a defence. Psychosis is a defence. Delusions, compulsions, hearing orders from God. That's what we need to establish.'

Morgan's heartbeat seemed to flutter with anxiety. 'In a way, this confirms what I've been thinking. She was down, definitely, but she just didn't seem that crazy to me.'

Noreen looked at her coldly. 'Well, don't be too pleased with yourself for agreeing with his diagnosis. Unless we can prove psychosis, the prosecution is going to say that this case is not about mental illness. They're going to say that Claire was very angry at her husband, because of the daughter he never told her about who showed up out of nowhere. That she did this deliberately.' She studied the report she was holding for a moment. 'Obviously, we need to hire another expert. Someone who will recognise the PPP symptoms in a way this gentleman did not. A credible licensed psychologist. However, such services can be expensive. As the person with power of attorney over Claire's finances, I wanted to clear it with you.'

Morgan thought this over. 'If the prosecution has a psychologist interview her too, what if their expert comes to the same conclusion as this first doctor?'

Noreen rolled her eyes in exasperation. 'We have to see to it that our expert proves more convincing.'

'It seems . . . risky.'

'Risky? Morgan, try to understand. We don't have any options.'

'But what if . . . Look, I learned something. Eden—that's the long-lost daughter—had good reason to hate Guy Bolton. Her own grandfather blamed Guy for the death of Eden's mother . . .'

Noreen raised her eyebrows. 'Was Guy responsible?'

Morgan shook her head. 'No. Apparently not.'

'Where was the old man when Guy was killed?'

Morgan took a deep breath. 'In West Virginia. But Eden was here and she knew about it. She may have believed it and decided to—'

'Stop.' Noreen raised her hands. 'Try and understand something. Claire confessed. Whether you like it or not. Because our defence rests on her state of mind, we need an expert who will testify she was unbalanced as a result of postpartum psychosis. Unless you'd prefer that your friend spend the balance of her life in . . .'

'No, of course not,' said Morgan.

The door to the bedroom opened, and Gert entered carrying a steaming teacup. 'Nonny, I want you to drink this.'

Noreen looked at Morgan. 'That means "leave",' she said.

Morgan got up stiffly from the rocker.

Noreen accepted the proffered teacup. 'Morgan, let me do my job,' she said more gently. 'Trust me. I've got this under control.'

THERE WERE ONLY two cars in the sandy lot surrounded by beach plum bushes and brittle-looking shrubs. Morgan parked at the far end and got out of the car. She'd been here last summer and the lot had been filled to capacity. Autumn definitely brought a slowdown.

The path to the beach wound through grass-covered dunes. She could hear the sea pounding in the distance. The magnificent azure sky distracted her from her worries. She stepped out onto the sand, and took off her shoes and socks. She walked towards the divide between the grey wet sand and the eggshell-white dry, and stayed on the dry side as the waves rushed up and tried to reach her.

The last time she had walked here was with Claire. Claire, holding her stomach, already protective of the child inside. She had talked excitedly about the addition she and Guy would build onto the cottage, or maybe they would move back to France. This, the same woman who had confessed to killing her baby, her husband. Morgan sighed, but her sigh was drowned out by the restless tide.

A lifeguard's boat with a ragged hole in its wooden hull was overturned on the beach, slowly being buried by the sand. Morgan stopped and sat down on it. She stared along the lonely beach. A person in a blue anorak was walking in Morgan's direction, picking up shells and placing them in a bucket while two dogs gambolled about, yapping. It took her a few minutes of staring absently at the shell collector to realise that she was looking at Guy's sister, Lucy.

Morgan's first impulse was to turn away. She stood up from the boat, but before she could flee, Lucy lifted a small hand in an anaemic greeting. Morgan waved back, and walked to meet her.

Up close, Lucy looked ghostly. Her cottony blonde hair was being whipped around her face by the wind. Her glasses were dusty with sand. She said hello and gazed down at Morgan's bare feet.

'Aren't you freezing?' she asked.

'Honestly, yes. It's a little too cold for this.'

Lucy frowned. 'Astrid said Claire is coming to the funeral.'

'That's right. I took some black clothes to the jail.'

'Why did my father say it was OK? It's a mistake, her coming.'

'I agree with you.'

An awkward silence fell between them. Morgan glanced down at Lucy's shells. Lucy moved the bucket to her other hand, as if to shield the shells from Morgan's prying gaze.

'What made you start working with shells?' Morgan asked, trying to be friendly.

'I was good at jigsaw puzzles. Prader–Willi children are known for that,' said Lucy matter-of-factly. 'Astrid thought I might like putting shells together like puzzle pieces. Turned out I did.'

Morgan was about to make a comment about that fortuitous insight, when Lucy said abruptly, 'I thought you'd be gone by now.'

Morgan tried not to take offence. 'I'm going to the funeral too.'

'Right. You were Drew's godmother. Not me.'

'I'm sorry if that hurt your feelings,' said Morgan sincerely.

'Guy would never pick me. My brother doesn't care who he hurts.'

Morgan felt pained by the casual cruelty that Lucy's remark suggested.

She wanted to change the subject. 'Have you heard from Eden? Her grand-parents showed up looking for her.'

Lucy stared impassively out to sea. 'She's been at my house.'

'She has?' Morgan exclaimed. 'She's been staying with you?'

'She is my niece,' said Lucy. 'After it happened, nobody cared about Eden's feelings. I asked her to stay with me. The others all forgot about her.'

'Well, I'm sure everybody was in shock,' said Morgan sadly.

'Everybody in the whole town was in shock,' Lucy said. 'Every time I think of what Claire did to that helpless baby . . .'

Morgan noticed that she didn't mention Guy. 'Claire was seriously depressed,' said Morgan.

Lucy looked disgusted. 'So depressing, to have a beautiful new baby.'

Morgan ignored the barb. 'Fitz said that Guy and Eden were becoming close before he died.'

Lucy's gaze was as cold as the sea. 'Eden was trying so hard to make him love her. Even after he was mean to her and hurt her feelings.'

Morgan studied her pale, slack face. 'You didn't have a very high opin-ion of your brother.'

Lucy looked at her for a long minute. 'That's my business. He was still my brother.' Abruptly, she turned away and began trudging towards the beach entrance. The dogs swirled around her legs.

Morgan walked behind her until she reached the overturned boat. Then she stopped and sat down on the hull to brush the sand off her feet and put her socks and shoes back on.

Lucy turned and looked back at her. 'Are you leaving after the funeral?' she asked.

'As soon as I can,' Morgan said.

'Good.' Lucy nodded. 'You should go.'

ON THE DRIVE back to the cottage, Morgan thought about how much she dreaded the funeral tomorrow, coming face to face with all the people who had cared for Guy and rejoiced in the birth of his son. As she pulled up in front of the cottage, she saw a dark grey, late-model Jeep in the driveway. Dick Bolton was slumped in the passenger seat. Morgan got out of her car and tapped on the window. Dick jumped slightly, turning his handsome head. Before she could say anything, he looked away.

Her face reddening, Morgan straightened and went up the path to the house. Dusty was sprawled out in the fading, leaf-strewn flowerbed of dahlias and zinnias. Letting herself in, Morgan noticed a garment bag draped over a dining-room chair. 'Hello,' she called.

'In the kitchen.'

She walked in. Astrid was taking items from the counter and placing them in a cardboard box. 'Hi, Astrid. I saw Dick in the driveway.'

Astrid wore a black cape and her crown of platinum braids looked uncharacteristically out of kilter, wisps loose around her face. Her ivory complexion was deeply etched with lines. 'I see you've been staying here.'

'I probably should have asked you and Dick first,' said Morgan.

'Oh, I don't care,' said Astrid wearily. 'What does it matter?'

'I just saw Lucy at the beach,' said Morgan.

Astrid's face softened and she looked at Morgan hopefully. 'How is my little girl? Is she all right? I've been so distracted.'

'She seems kind of angry.'

'Well, it's easier for Lucy to be angry than to admit she's sad.'

'She does seem sad about the baby,' said Morgan carefully. 'I got the impression that she and Guy weren't that close.'

'It was never easy for Lucy. She had developmental difficulties and he was attractive and smart. Of course he teased her a little. As brothers do. But he was never cruel, I can tell you that . . . After all, they were my children.'

'I know. This is difficult. It must be so hard for you to even walk in this house,' said Morgan. 'A lot of memories.'

Astrid stared blankly out into the other room, and then shook her head, as if waking herself from a dream. 'Look, Morgan, you may as well know, I've got some professional cleaners coming in to take care of the bath,' she said. 'Dick said he'd send over a couple of the Mexican workers from the Lobster Shack, but I don't want them to see this.'

'Professionals are probably a good idea,' said Morgan.

Astrid closed her box. 'I've got what I need. Clothes for Guy and the baby . . .' Her voice caught. 'A few things to put in the coffin.'

'This is such a nightmare,' Morgan said sadly.

'Yes. Well . . .' Astrid lifted the box and walked into the dining room, where she picked up the garment bag. 'We must face it.'

Morgan opened the front door for her. Astrid walked out onto the step and looked over at the car where her husband waited. Dick made no move to get out. 'I can open the trunk,' Morgan offered.

Astrid lifted her chin. 'I can manage,' she said. 'I have to.'

THE TINY WHITE CHURCH, so recently the site of Drew's christening, was overflowing with mourners, who were lined up out of the door and down the sidewalk. When Morgan finally entered the church, the first person she saw was Fitz, standing among the other pallbearers at the back. She tried to remain inconspicuous in the line snaking down the side aisle, hoping he wouldn't notice her.

The people waiting to file past the open coffins at the front of the church inched along. The altar and the two coffins were banked with elaborate flower arrangements. The Bolton family formed a receiving line beside them. All except Eden. Though Morgan scanned the pews, she saw no sign of Guy's daughter. Dick, his complexion pasty, stood beside Astrid, who leaned against him, weeping. Lucy, dry-eyed, flanked her father on the other side. The sight of Guy's body seemed to cause weeping and head-shaking, but the sight of tiny Drew provoked wails and despair. Morgan felt almost overcome by the crowd's raw emotion. Why did they have to leave the caskets open? she thought. Wasn't this whole thing awful enough?

The sound of raised voices at the back of the church caused her to turn round. Eden had arrived, dressed in her black leather jacket and jeans. She and Fitz seemed to be having an angry discussion. Morgan could not make out their words. Eden started to march defiantly down the centre aisle, but Fitz caught her by the arm and held her back. Eden protested and shook off his grip, scowling at Fitz while he continued to murmur in her ear, pointing to the Bolton family and explaining something to her.

Suddenly the woman behind her poked Morgan in the ribs. 'Go on,' the woman hissed. It was Morgan's turn. She lurched forward and approached her godson's bier. Looking at his small, round face, she found herself remembering a long-forgotten religious teaching that newborns were free from sin and welcomed into heaven. She found the thought comforting. Tears began to run down her face. She kissed her fingertips and placed them briefly on his cold, plump cheek. 'Goodbye, my angel,' she whispered. She couldn't bear to gaze for long. There was a white prayer book in the corner of the coffin, and a stuffed brown bear that Claire had kept in his cot.

Weeping freely, she approached Guy's coffin. He had been dressed in a dark suit and tie, his face still handsome, even in death. These last few days had made her wonder what kind of man he really was. Only human, she reminded herself. Gazing at him now, all she wanted to remember was Guy, Claire's husband, who was exuberant and made her laugh. Who loved her best friend to distraction. His chef's toque, his red sash, and a block of carving knives he'd received as a parting gift from his master chef in Lyon were placed beside him in his coffin. Propped up against the coffin lid was a heart of white roses crossed by a ribbon, which read, 'Beloved Son'.

Morgan touched Guy's cold hand gently. As she passed the family, she murmured her regrets with a lowered gaze. Then she turned and stumbled up the aisle towards the first seat she could find.

'Morgan,' she heard someone hiss. She looked through her tears and saw Sandy Raymond gesturing to her to come and sit beside him and Farah. Gratefully, Morgan dropped down into the pew corner. Farah, in a black designer minidress with jet beads and black spotted veil, smiled brightly. Sandy was wearing a denim shirt under his blazer, and running shoes. He patted her arm. 'This is a freak show. Can't believe they have open caskets,' he whispered.

Morgan murmured some noncommittal reply. The sight of those two bodies in repose had shaken her. She wished she could close her eyes and drift away and forget about the grief in her heart.

Just then, a loud, anxious murmur raced through the church, and everyone seemed to turn at once. Plain-clothes officers and uniformed guards had appeared at the back, surrounding their prisoner. Claire, her cheeks and eyes sunken, her hair barely combed, walked with manacled hands, wearing the black skirt and sweater Morgan had taken to the jail. One officer held her arm as another, looking in every direction, led the police procession towards the biers. A gasp arose from the assembled mourners.

Morgan looked up at the front of the church. Lucy and Astrid seemed shocked, but Dick Bolton suddenly straightened. The line of mourners was held back as Claire was allowed to approach. Morgan felt her heart breaking as she watched her friend bend her head over the casket of her baby and stare at the tiny, waxen face.

Cry, Morgan thought. Let it out, Claire.

All through the church, Morgan could hear the loud murmurs of disapproval, disbelief. Claire raised her manacled hands and pointed to her baby's fingers. The guard nodded briefly. Moving her linked hands as one, Claire put her index finger on Drew's tiny hand. Her eyes closed, and her body was shaking from head to toe.

'OK,' said the guard gruffly, and Claire edged to Guy's coffin and tilted her head, her gaze still as death. Once again she lifted her manacled hands in supplication. Once again the guard nodded.

Slowly, she lifted her hands over the edge of the coffin. She put her fingers up to Guy's cold face. She studied his frozen features as if searching for some answer. Some explanation that he would now take to his grave. She whispered something, her lips moving feverishly.

Dick's voice cut through the shocked hush. 'Keep your filthy hands off them,' he thundered. 'How can you even look at them? Those two good, innocent souls. They thought you loved them. You'll burn in hell for what you've done. After you've spent the rest of your miserable life in prison.'

'All right, all right,' said the guard. 'Take it easy. Everyone take it easy.' Claire blinked several times but she did not look at Dick. The guard spoke in a low voice to Claire. 'Come on. That's enough.'

Claire nodded. Then, before anyone could stop her, she reached with her shackled hands for the block of knives in the coffin, grasping the largest handle and jerking it from its resting place. As the guard lunged for her, and the seated mourners in the church rose to their feet, crying out, Claire closed her eyes, lifted the knife and plunged it into her own chest. Morgan watched helplessly as Claire slumped forward, a gush of her blood soaking into the satin lining of the coffin as she fell across her husband's lifeless body.

SEVEN

Briarwood Hospital wasn't able to give Morgan any patient information. She asked to be connected to the Emergency Room as she tried to drive with one hand and talk on the phone. When a woman answered, 'Briarwood ER,' Morgan asked about Claire.

'She's in surgery. I can't tell you how she is,' the woman said. 'The privacy laws are very strict.' She hung up. Morgan slipped her phone in her bag and made the next left turn. She still remembered, from the days surrounding Drew's birth, the way to the hospital.

It took her a while to find the waiting room for the surgical theatre, but she knew she was in the right hallway when she spotted guards outside the double doors. She took a seat and waited. After a while, a woman in blood-spattered blue scrubs emerged. Morgan jumped up to enquire, but the woman held up a hand and kept walking. The guards looked curiously at Morgan but made no effort to speak to her. Please God, she thought, don't let Claire die.

After what seemed like an hour, a man in scrubs emerged from the operating room, pulled off his mask and gloves and spoke to the guards in a low voice. When the man, whom Morgan presumed to be a surgeon, left the guards, she summoned all her courage and approached him. 'Excuse me, Doctor,' she said.

The man slowed down and looked at her impassively.

'I'm . . . Is she alive? Is she . . .?' Morgan felt tears in her eyes.

He hesitated. 'She's alive, but critical. She tore herself up pretty well. The next forty-eight hours will determine the outcome.'

'Are they going to take her back to the prison?'

'No,' he scoffed. 'She's on a ventilator. She'll stay here.'

'Thank you. Thank you for saving her.'

Morgan whispered a prayer of thanks. Claire was still alive. People always said that where there was life, there was hope. Realising there was nothing to do now but wait, she decided to get some coffee, and made her way to the cafeteria.

Numbly, she queued up, took a cup of coffee and a roll and found a table in the corner. As she was stirring milk into her cup, Father Lawrence, in his black suit and collar, walked up and pulled out the chair across from her. 'May I?' he asked.

Morgan nodded. 'Is the funeral over?'

'Somehow, we got through it.' He took a seat and looked at her sadly through his steel-rimmed glasses. 'How is Claire doing?'

'She came through the surgery. But she's in a critical condition.'

'I'm glad to hear that she survived the surgery.'

Morgan sighed. 'That's nice of you to say.'

'I mean it. Are you all alone here?' the minister asked.

'Just me and the prison guards.' She tried to smile.

He shook his head. 'I don't understand why she did this . . .'

'Well, it was horrible for *me* to see Guy and the baby like that. Imagine what it was like for her,' said Morgan.

'I spent some time with her at the prison yesterday.'

'What did she say?'

Father Lawrence folded his hands on the Formica tabletop. 'I urged her to confess. To seek absolution. I told her that God would forgive her anything, if she was truly repentant.'

'So did she confess?'

Father Lawrence frowned.

Morgan took a sip of her coffee. 'Never mind. You can't talk about that. Even I know a confession to the clergy is sacrosanct.'

'No, that's just it. There was no confession. She said she was beginning to think she didn't kill them.'

Morgan's heart thudded. 'What? What do you mean?'

'She told me that all she could remember now was waking up and finding the baby in the bathtub.'

'But she told me she did it. Why in the world would she say that? And she confessed to the police.'

'Well,' Father Lawrence sighed, 'I'm afraid she may be starting to deny the truth to herself. It's all too overwhelming . . .'

Morgan's mind raced. 'Or maybe she's finally realised the truth.'

'Morgan, nothing's gained by clinging to false hope.'

'You don't know her, Father,' Morgan pleaded. 'Not like I do. It's never seemed possible to me.'

He looked at her balefully. 'The police knew Claire was guilty before they questioned her. Apparently, Guy was found alive.'

'That's impossible. Claire told me he was dead.'

'Claire isn't a doctor. She might have assumed he was dead. But the detectives interrogating her told her that he accused her. Claire is doing herself no favours by denying this now. When a man names his killer with his last breath, there isn't anyone who'd doubt it . . .'

Morgan was silent for a moment. 'What if he *was* dead, and he *didn't* accuse her. What if they only said he did?'

Father Lawrence grasped her forearm. 'Come now, stop it. You can't believe that. The police have no reason to lie about it.'

Morgan nodded automatically, as if agreeing, but her mind was elsewhere, nurturing a glimmer of hope, impervious to every word.

THE NURSE AT THE ER DESK looked up with a hint of impatience. 'Yes?' Given Morgan's recent reminder about medical privacy laws, she knew better than to simply ask for information. Although she wasn't in the habit of being deceptive, she'd stretched the truth on occasion to gain access to rare documents. Luckily, she was still wearing her good black suit. She pulled her university picture ID from her bag and flashed it. 'My name is Morgan Adair. I'm an investigator from the prosecutor's office. I have a question pertaining to one of your recent admissions.'

Immediately the nurse looked less hostile. 'Yes?'

'Sunday morning, a man by the name of Guy Bolton was transported here by ambulance. Was Mr Bolton alive when he arrived at the ER? Could you look it up for me?'

'This isn't about some lawsuit against the hospital, is it?'

'Oh, heavens, no,' said Morgan. 'I work for the county.'

The nurse nodded. 'OK. When was that, again?'

Morgan gave her the date and time.

The nurse punched a few keys on the computer. 'He wasn't brought here. Did the incident occur here in Briarwood?'

'West Briar,' said Morgan.

The nurse cocked her head. 'Well, they should have brought him here.' She frowned at her screen. 'You can find out from the Rescue Squad emergency medical technicians working out of the Briarwood Fire Department.'

'I will,' said Morgan. 'Thanks.'

THE BRIARWOOD FIRE STATION was housed in a small brick building adjoining the several bays where the ladders and ambulance were serviced. Morgan parked and entered the station. It looked more like a men's social club than a city service building. There was a pool table, a bunch of small tables and chairs, and a serving hatch through to a long galley kitchen. A few men wearing blue work clothes were playing cards at one table. Another man was cooking something redolent of tomato sauce in the kitchen.

The card players looked up. 'Can we help you?' a physically fit-looking man with white hair asked pleasantly.

'My name is Morgan Adair. I'm looking for an EMT from the Rescue Squad.'

The man instantly stood up. 'What's the problem?'

'I'm sorry, no, not like that.' Morgan gestured for him to sit back down. 'I just had a question for someone who was on duty on Sunday.'

He gave a little sigh of relief and resumed his seat. 'That was us. My partner and I work twenty-four hours on and forty-eight off. So, we just got back. How can we help you?'

'I was wondering. Could I ask you about a call you made on Sunday morning? A man named Guy Bolton and his infant son.'

The younger man, who had a shaved head, set down his cards. 'Are you a reporter?' he asked.

'No,' said Morgan innocently. 'I'm a friend of the family.'

The white-haired man's tone was chilly. 'We can't give out information about the calls we make.'

'Oh, I understand. The media is looking for every scrap of information. The family's pestered night and day. But, I thought if I came here, the news vultures wouldn't make the connection.'

The two men exchanged a sceptical glance. 'What are you after?' the younger man demanded.

'OK, look, the family's in shock from all that's happened, as you can imagine. It was such a . . . terrible thing . . .'

'That's for sure,' murmured the younger man.

'Nothing I can say is of any real comfort. But it occurred to me that Guy might have had some last words for them, you know? Some few words that they could take comfort from. He might have spoken to a nurse or a doctor or even an orderly. Someone. But the ER in Briarwood said he was never admitted there. The nurse told me to come over here and ask which hospital you took him to.'

The older man frowned. 'We didn't take him to a hospital.'

'I'm confused. How come?'

'There was no reason to transport him.'

'Why not? Are you saying that he was dead?' Morgan asked.

'That's correct,' said the younger man.

'But, don't you have to treat him anyway, just in case . . .?'

The older man nodded. 'Yes, of course. Even if the person appears dead, we begin treatment. And we call in a paramedic to administer an EKG. If it's a flatline the person is turned over to the Medical Examiner to determine cause of death.'

Her heart was pounding. 'And that's what happened with Guy?'

'Yes.' He nodded. 'Sorry we couldn't help you.'

Morgan remembered to look sorrowful. 'I was just hoping . . .'

The men seemed relieved that her question hadn't compromised their professional responsibilities. The white-haired man leaned back in his chair. 'No, Mr Bolton was well past the point of last words when we arrived at the scene.'

Morgan gave them a brave smile. She tried to remind herself that this was no proof of anything, other than that the police had stretched the truth. But, she couldn't help feeling that something was finally turning Claire's way. 'Well, thank you. Really. You have helped me. Believe me. It's always better to know for sure.'

NOREEN QUICK was having a bath. Morgan said she would return later, but Gert indicated that she was welcome to go into the bathroom to speak with the attorney in the tub. Reluctantly, Morgan opened the door, and a cloud of steam escaped. The room was lit by candles and smelled of verbena. Noreen was immersed to her shoulders in the Jacuzzi-style tub. Morgan didn't know where to look. 'Excuse me. Gert said it was OK to come in.'

'Sit down there on the john and make yourself comfortable.'

Slowly, Morgan did as she was bid.

'I'm glad you're here,' said Noreen. 'I was going to call to let you know that I've hired another shrink, a woman this time. She has a profound understanding of postpartum mental illness. I think we can be almost guaranteed of a favourable result. Especially after what Claire did at the funeral. What a scene. How's she doing anyway?'

'She's . . . critical,' said Morgan.

Noreen shook her head and some of the droplets landed on Morgan. 'Horrible. Tragic. But I have to say, this is becoming a no-brainer. I hate to sound ghoulish but this latest stunt is nothing if not helpful to our case. Our expert will have the jury in tears.'

'Maybe.'

'No maybe about it. This is going to work to our advantage.'

Morgan decided to be frank. 'Look, things have changed. Yesterday Claire told her minister that she didn't remember killing Guy and the baby. She now has doubts that she was the one responsible.'

Noreen smiled wryly. 'She has doubts.'

'Yes. And it turns out the police lied to her.'

'About what?'

'They told her that Guy implicated her as the killer before he died. But I asked the EMTs who were in the ambulance. They told me that Guy was dead by the time they arrived at the scene.'

'Morgan, you've got to stop this.'

'But what the police told her just wasn't true.'

'I saw the tape of her confession,' said Noreen.

Morgan was taken aback. 'You did?'

'I have a copy in my office files. The prosecution sent it as part of the discovery process. There's no mention by the detectives of Guy implicating her. This is just another thing Claire is imagining.'

Morgan's heart sank. 'But why would she tell Father Lawrence she doesn't remember killing them now?'

Noreen's eyes widened. 'Why does she say anything? Claire is mentally ill. Morgan, you have accept this. Claire is not the same gal you used to go shopping with. This woman killed her own family. Then she stabbed and critically wounded herself. She is suffering from severe postpartum depression. She told you herself that she did it. What does it take to convince you?'

Morgan sighed. 'I don't know.'

'Claire needs help. She's not a criminal, she's sick. She needs serious, professional help. That's certainly what I intend to convince the court.'

'How can you even go to court?' Morgan asked.

'By the time this gets to trial,' Noreen said, patting her stomach, 'this guy will be cutting his first tooth.' She planted her hands on the rim of the tub and began to lift herself up. 'I got to get out. I'm getting pruney. Grab me that towel. Can you help me?'

Morgan jumped up. 'Wait. Be careful. Let me call Gert.'

Noreen sank back down, parting the waters in a mighty splash. Morgan escaped from the steamy, candlelit bathroom, yelling to Gert for assistance.

HUNGRY AND WEARY, Morgan returned to the cottage, and let herself in. Dusty purred around her legs as she went into the kitchen. First she pulled out her phone, and checked to see if she might have missed a call from Simon. There were no missed calls registered. With a sigh, she called the hospital. The nurse would only say that there was no change in Claire's condition. Morgan rummaged in the refrigerator, slapped together the fixings for a sandwich, placed some food in the cat bowl and then carried her plate to the dining-room table. She had swallowed two bites when she heard a knock at the door.

Cursing beneath her breath, she went and opened it. Fitz stood there, his face drawn, his eyes wary. Startled at the sight of him, Morgan considered slamming the door.

'Morgan, I need to talk to you,' he said. 'Can I come in?'

'I'm busy,' she said.

'Look, I'm sorry about the other night . . . About what I . . .'

Morgan turned away and returned to her sandwich. Fitz stepped inside and closed the door. He walked to the table as if he were traversing a field of land mines. 'Mind if I help myself to a beer?'

'I don't care what you do,' she said, chewing, avoiding his gaze.

Fitz went into the kitchen, and then returned with a bottle of Heineken. He sat down opposite Morgan. 'How's Claire doing?'

Morgan gave him a cool, level gaze. 'Like you care.'

'Hey, it's been a tough day for all of us,' he said.

She was about to make a sarcastic remark when she remembered that Fitz had watched his best friend being buried today. The thought of offering him a sandwich crossed her mind fleetingly. 'What are you doing here?'

'I shouldn't have been so rough on you. I'm sorry,' he said.

Morgan did not look at him or reply.

'Eden said she came to the funeral to spit on her father's corpse.'

Morgan grimaced in surprise. 'Eden said that?'

'She said he deserved to die. She said he was an evil bastard. I tried to remind her of how Guy had been trying to get to know her. She told me that he was a terrible person and that I didn't really know him. I couldn't help thinking of your suspicions.'

Morgan felt as if she'd been zapped with an electric current. 'Did you ask her what she meant?'

'It was impossible to talk to her. She was very agitated, almost as if she was on drugs or something. She said she had to leave, and I told her I wanted to talk to her afterwards. I looked for her as we were leaving the cemetery. She was gone. Since then I've been ringing her, but no luck.'

'Did you try Lucy's? She was staying there.'

'She wasn't with Lucy. Lucy told me to try the Captain's House. But Mrs Spaulding hadn't seen her.'

Morgan stared at him. 'I wonder what she meant.'

He sighed. 'So do I. But I thought you should know.'

Morgan hesitated. The last time she'd trusted him he had turned on her. But in spite of her misgivings, she blurted out one thing she had learned on her own. 'The police told Claire, before she confessed, that Guy implicated her as his killer, but it wasn't true. I asked the EMTs. He was dead when they arrived on the scene.'

'Really?' said Fitz.

Morgan nodded. 'I know what you're thinking. It doesn't explain her confession. None of this does.'

He sat staring at his beer, and for one minute, she thought he was going to ask where the recycling bin was, and wish her good luck. Instead, he began to absently peel the label off, frowning.

'What?' Morgan said.

'Do you know anything about false confessions?'

'You mean, like, if you plead guilty to protect someone else?'

'No. That's . . . no. You mentioned that the other night. Nobody does that.' Fitz took a deep breath. 'When I got my master's in counselling I took a course on how to interview abuse victims. Kids.'

'I thought you were a wrestling coach.'

'Part-time. My main job at the school is in guidance. I like working with kids. I'm hoping to have my own practice someday.'

'Really,' said Morgan.

'Disappointed?' he said. 'Thought I was just a jock?'

'No,' she said, flustered.

'Anyway, in custody cases, kids are often coached to lie, or they lie because they're afraid. And sometimes, they are so suggestible that they accuse adults when nothing really occurred. This course I took was about the techniques you use to get at the truth.'

Morgan shook her head. 'What's that got to do with Claire?'

'It's just that it's difficult to get at the truth sometimes. There are inter-viewing techniques professionals use—even well-meaning doctors and social workers when they're trying to help—that can cause children to admit things that never happened.'

'Claire's not a child,' Morgan said cautiously. 'She knows the difference between reality and fantasy.'

Fitz frowned. 'I know. Look, I have to admit I'm not an expert on this. And it was last year when I took the class. But,' he said, pointing the beer bottle at her, 'my professor was an ace, and he's written a book about this. Are you interested in talking to him?'

'It might be worthwhile. How would I reach him?'

Fitz reached in his pocket for his phone and scrolled down the names in his address book. 'I still have his number.' He punched a number and waited. Morgan watched him, her eyes wide. He held her gaze as he spoke.

'Professor Douglas?' he asked. 'Yeah. This is Earl Fitzhugh. I'm sorry to bother you. I was in your class on interviewing techniques last year. Yeah. Graduate student. That's right. Look, would you have a few minutes to talk about something really important? I need the benefit of your expertise. If you had time now . . . Yeah, the sooner the better. Where can we meet? OK, and I'm bringing someone else. Great. Thanks.' Fitz flipped his phone shut.

He grinned at Morgan. 'Finish that sandwich. We gotta go.'

OLIVER DOUGLAS'S WIFE, a slim woman with short grey hair, greeted Fitz and Morgan at the door and directed them to a studio out behind the house. They picked their way across the dark back yard and knocked at the screen door on the small, brightly lit, peaked-roof building. 'Professor Douglas,' Fitz called out.

The inner door opened, and a white-haired man in stained overalls and a flannel shirt peered at them over the top of his half-glasses. He pushed open the screen door. 'Come in, come in,' he said.

Fitz went in first. 'Professor Douglas, thanks for seeing us.'

'Happy to. How are you doing, Earl?'

'Good. This is my friend, Morgan . . .'

'Adair,' said Morgan.

The old man wiped his hands on his overalls. 'I'd shake your hand but

I'm covered with glue,' he said. He pointed to a beat-up sofa against the wall. 'Have a seat.'

Fitz and Morgan sat down on the sofa. Morgan looked around the walls of the studio. They were covered with collages, odd and whimsical, fashioned from calendar pictures, leaves and pebbles, newspaper lettering. Somehow she had expected piles of books.

'What do you think of my work?' the old professor asked.

Morgan gazed at the collages. 'They're so . . . joyful.'

Professor Douglas looked fondly at his bright, fantastical creations. 'My field of expertise deals with the dark side of the moon, if you will. People who prey on the most vulnerable. One needs a break from it. Earl, how's your work at the high school?'

'It's tough, but I'm doing some good. I'm thinking about getting my PhD, so I can open my own practice. Work with adolescents.'

'Wonderful idea. There's a great need,' Oliver Douglas said, nodding. 'So, what was so important you had to see me tonight?'

'Well, I explained to Morgan that one of your books was about getting people to confess to crimes they didn't commit . . .'

'*Interrogation Techniques in False Confessions*,' said Oliver Douglas.

'Exactly. Morgan's best friend from childhood is in jail. She confessed to killing her husband and her infant son.'

Professor Douglas turned one of the worktable stools to face the sofa, and sat down on it. 'The Bolton woman?'

'That's right,' said Fitz. 'You know about it?'

'I've been reading about it. The woman with postpartum depression.' He turned to Morgan. 'What about her?'

For a moment Morgan felt tongue-tied. 'I've known Claire Bolton since we were twelve, and even though she told me herself that she did it, I couldn't believe that she'd be capable of such a crime . . .'

'I'm sure every prisoner in San Quentin has a friend who would say the same,' said Professor Douglas calmly.

Morgan hesitated, feeling chided. 'When she first confessed, I believed her, though it seemed impossible. Now, I have doubts.'

'What's changed?'

'For one thing, she's begun to say she can't remember doing it.'

'Did she confess to you in some detail?' he asked.

'Her description of the crime was . . . vague. And I now know for a fact that the police lied to her.'

Professor Douglas leaned forward. 'Really? Tell me about that.'

'Well, the police told Claire that her husband, Guy, implicated her before he died. But I talked to the EMTs who responded. Her husband was dead when they arrived on the scene.'

'You did your research.'

Morgan blushed. 'Force of habit.'

'You're sure they told her that her dying husband accused her?'

'Positive. She said so.'

'And is her confession on tape?'

'Yes,' said Morgan. 'The lawyer saw it. But she said there's no mention of Guy's accusation on the tape.'

'Well, the interrogation of a suspect begins on the scene, continues in the squad car and so on. Sometimes only a small part is actually on the tape. Tell me about the depression. How severe was it?'

Morgan shrugged. 'Her attorney wants the shrink to say it was post-partum psychosis, which is much more severe than . . .' Douglas was nodding, so she didn't belabour the point. 'One shrink has already said that she wasn't psychotic. And she never seemed out of touch with reality to me. Just depressed.'

Professor Douglas frowned and looked away.

'Does that sound like someone who would make a false confession?' Fitz asked.

'I can't say, based on what I've heard,' said Oliver Douglas. 'Normally we associate false confessions with young people, or people of low intelligence who can be easily manipulated—in almost every case, male.' He tapped his upper lip with his index finger. 'Although it's interesting. What was her home life like?'

'Well, they'd only been married a short time . . .' Morgan began.

'No, I mean childhood. Strong father?'

'No father. He left when she was tiny. She never knew him.'

The professor nodded, as if this was what he had expected to hear.

'Well,' said Fitz. 'What do you think?'

'Well, false confession is also associated with states of extreme stress. The idea of postpartum depression as extreme stress does fit a certain pattern.

Here we have a woman who already *feels* guilty because she is not the picture of happy motherhood, the way she is supposed to be. And most people are not sympathetic to this kind of depression. So, your friend is exhausted, probably sleep-deprived, and wrestling with the fact that she's not responding as expected to this great blessing in her life.' Douglas drifted off in thought. 'She's a law-abiding person? Never in trouble with the law?'

Morgan shook her head. 'Never.'

'And the police, whom she trusts, tell her that her own husband accused her, and she has no reason to doubt them. There she sits, tired, guilty, in despair. Obedient to authority. For the police she's simply the obvious suspect. They may want to clean up the case quickly, so they bend the truth to see if they break her.'

'And she confesses,' cried Fitz.

'It's a possibility,' Professor Douglas cautioned.

Morgan knew that his assessment should be comforting. But her heart felt like a stone. 'OK, everything you say makes sense except for the part where she admits to killing these people if she didn't.'

Douglas sighed. 'Everyone thinks that they would never do that. Let me tell you something. You'd be surprised at what you might do under duress. Very often, we aren't as brave or as honest or as strong as we'd like to imagine ourselves to be.'

Fitz nodded. 'There could be another suspect. Guy's teenage daughter.'

Professor Douglas shook his head. 'The police aren't going to be interested in other suspects. Unless the confession is discredited. And a confession is one of the most difficult pieces of evidence to discredit. For exactly the reason you just stated, Morgan. Jurors say to themselves, I would never confess to a crime I didn't commit. It's against human nature.'

'But it does happen,' said Morgan.

'In a perfect storm of circumstances, most certainly.

Fitz leaned forward. 'So, do you think that's what happened in this case?'

The professor shrugged. 'I couldn't say.'

Morgan and Fitz exchanged a glance. 'But I thought . . . you could help,' Morgan said.

'Well, I've tried to,' said the professor. 'Granted, that's an abbreviated summary.'

Morgan stood up. 'Would you talk to Claire's lawyer?'

'If her lawyer wanted to talk to me, of course. But I don't think she will. She dismissed your question about the taped confession, didn't she? I'm acquainted with Noreen Quick. Her expertise is in family law. She's not a criminal attorney. As I understand it from the newspapers, she wants to win on the PPP defence.'

'But if Claire didn't do it . . . If it's not true . . .'

'That confession will still remain the chief piece of evidence against her,' said Douglas. 'Believe me.'

'Isn't there anything we can do?' Morgan cried.

Douglas scattered magazine clippings onto his worktable like giant confetti. He was silent for a while, moving the pieces, frowning at the design he was making. Finally, he spoke without looking up. 'I could tell you more if I could see the confession,' he said.

EIGHT

Morgan stared out of the window of Fitz's car. In the moonlight it was possible to see the bay, its water dark and shining, but Morgan wasn't focusing on the view.

'What are you thinking?' Fitz asked.

Morgan shook her head.

'I thought he was saying that Claire probably did make a false confession,' said Fitz encouragingly.

'He was a little hard to pin down,' said Morgan.

'Still, it's a hopeful sign, right?'

'It's better than nothing,' she said.

They rode along in silence for a few moments. Then Fitz said, 'How long are you going to stay around here? I mean, don't you have classes for your PhD or something?'

Morgan was faintly surprised to realise that he knew that much about her. 'I'm supposed to be in England right now, doing research for my thesis. I was in the airport when Claire called.'

'That's a bummer.'

'Well, my . . . boyfriend wasn't too happy that he had to cancel the hotels. He was going to try and get the money back.'

'Your boyfriend was going with you?' Fitz asked.

Inwardly Morgan cringed, knowing that Simon would never describe himself as her boyfriend. It sounded as if they were teenagers. What exactly were they? she thought. She felt discouraged about Simon. He hadn't called back. 'Simon lives in London. He's a poet.'

Fitz was silent.

Morgan glanced over at him. 'What?' she said.

Fitz shrugged. 'Just thinking that it was a lot to give up. Most people wouldn't do that for a friend.'

In the darkness of the car, Morgan blushed at the compliment. 'Claire would do it for me. Besides, I'm just postponing it.'

Fitz drove with one hand on the wheel, looking casual. 'Are you in a hurry to get back? I live just up there. Next right. You want to come over for a drink or something?'

Morgan frowned. She didn't want Fitz to think she was interested in a relationship. 'Thanks, but it has been a long day. I'm really exhausted.'

'OK, I'll just run you back to Guy's place.' There was an awkward silence. 'So,' he said at last, 'what next? Do you think you can get your hands on that tape of Claire's confession?'

'I don't know,' Morgan admitted. 'There's no use in asking the police. And I don't think that Claire's attorney has any interest in pursuing this idea of a false confession.'

'Not from what Professor Douglas said,' said Fitz.

'I think I'm going to have to insist that Claire gets a criminal attorney. I mean, Noreen Quick did generously offer her services to Claire pro bono, and I was grateful. I think Noreen wanted the case because it's so high pro-file. But that may not be in Claire's best interest. I probably should have hired a criminal attorney in the first place. Her former fiancé even offered to pay for it,' said Morgan.

'That dot-commer she dumped for Guy? Why would he pay?'

'I don't know. He was worried about her.'

'That seems a little bizarre.'

Morgan glanced over at him. 'You seem to find it odd when anybody tries to help a friend.'

'No,' he said indignantly. 'Not at all.'

As soon as she had said it, Morgan regretted it. 'I didn't mean that. I know that you were a great friend to Guy.' She knew that losing him had wounded Fitz terribly.

'It's hard to picture my life without Guy in it,' Fitz admitted.

'How long were you two friends?' Morgan asked.

Fitz frowned, and Morgan saw that his eyes were glistening. 'I don't know. His mother—his real mother—and my mother were friends. There was a rodeo in Jersey somewhere and they decided to take us kids. Oh man, did we love that. Broncobusters and bull riders. That was the first time I met Guy. And Lucy. Poor Lucy.'

'Why do you say that?' Morgan asked.

'Oh, she wanted these red cowboy chaps. Nothing else would do and her mother bought them for her. They looked so comical . . .' Fitz shook his head. 'Guy and I teased her without mercy.'

'Making fun of a child with a handicap? Fond memories indeed,' said Morgan stiffly.

'Lucy's not handicapped,' Fitz protested. 'She's a little different, but she's always seemed normal to me. Besides, we weren't making fun of her. We were making fun of the chaps. Because they were stupid. The truth was that with those little glasses and her hair flying every which way, she looked kind of cute.'

'I happen to know that she's never forgiven Guy for his cruelty.'

'Cruelty?'

'What do you call it?' Morgan asked.

'Treating her like a little sister is what I call it,' he said. 'Making her laugh. I can still make her laugh if I mention those chaps.'

'That's what people do when they're being bullied. They laugh. They try to pretend they don't care,' Morgan said.

Fitz jerked the car to a halt in front of the cottage. 'Fine. You obviously know better than me. Guy and I were a couple of bullies.'

Now that they were back, Morgan dreaded going inside the cottage. And she felt faintly guilty for criticising Fitz when he had tried to help her. 'Look, I wasn't there. I just know that Lucy told me that Guy was mean and didn't care about other people's feelings.'

'If you say so,' he said.

'I'm not judging you, Fitz. I'm sorry if it sounded like I was accusing you. I'm so stressed out by everything.'

'Right,' he said. 'I'd better get home and get some rest. I'm taking ten seniors to a wrestling clinic for a couple of days.'

Morgan was surprised at the disappointment she felt. 'Really?' she said, opening the car door. 'Sounds like fun.'

'Kids always enjoy it,' said Fitz.

Morgan started to get out. She looked back at him. 'Thanks for taking me to see Professor Douglas. And I didn't mean to insult you. I'm sorry if it sounded that way.'

Fitz nodded. 'No problem,' he said without looking at her. The moment Morgan shut the door, he pulled away from the kerb and didn't look back.

SHE TOOK A QUICK BATH, and went to bed in the guest room. She was asleep before she knew it. A tinny, singing voice woke her and she groped for her phone on the night table. She felt utterly disorientated, and when she looked at the time, she understood why. It was four thirty in the morning. Her first thought was of Claire, and fear coursed through her. She had called the hospital before she went to bed. Claire's condition was unchanged. But anything could have happened in the interim.

'Morgan,' said a cheerful voice.

It took her a moment. 'Simon?' she said.

'Yes. I felt I had to call you.'

'Simon, it's four thirty in the morning here.'

'Oh, sorry. I wasn't thinking. We just arrived and I have to tell you, this place is fantastic. You'll love it when you finally get here.'

'What place? Where are you?'

'I'm at The Manor. You know, where we planned to stay?'

'What are you doing there?' Morgan asked, confused.

'Well, they absolutely refused to return the deposit. I was a little bit irritated at first, but then I decided it would be foolish to waste the money.'

Morgan was silent for a moment. 'You're at our hotel?' she said. 'You went without me?' She heard her own voice sounding possessive, pathetic. She wished she could take the words back.

'We just arrived and they're going to set us up in the breakfast room. It looks out over the most gorgeous formal gardens . . .'

'We . . .?'

'Oh, my friend, Tim, and I,' said Simon offhandedly. 'A chap I know from a literary magazine. I asked him to come along.'

Morgan's first impulse was to be glad that Simon was with a man. Not another woman. And then Claire's words came back to her. Why hadn't he ever made a move on her? Why would he take a man to this most romantic of hotels? Was this Tim a friend, or was it something else? Ask him, she thought. But it was too demeaning to have to ask.

'You called to tell me that you went without me,' she said flatly. 'Gee, thanks.'

Simon sighed. 'Perhaps that wasn't the thing to do,' he said.

Morgan loked at the time again and made up her mind. Normally, she might have stayed on the line, hoping he'd say something as proof that he did indeed have fond feelings for her. Somehow, tonight, that seemed too little to hope for. 'Perhaps not,' she said, and pressed a button to end the call.

WHEN SHE ARRIVED at the hospital in the morning, Morgan learned that Claire had been moved. She sought out the room, and tiptoed in. The bed by the door was empty. Although the patient on the window side was obscured by a privacy curtain, Morgan knew that she had the correct room because Sandy Raymond was slumped in a chair at the foot of the bed, staring at the bed's occupant.

Sandy looked up in bleary-eyed surprise. 'Oh, hi,' he said.

Morgan looked at her friend. Claire had tubes snaking out from her nose, her arms, and from under the covers. Bags full of blood and fluids hung on hooks. Her skin was waxy and her eyes were closed, sunk in her face. She was breathing in and out with shuddering gasps. 'Oh God, she looks so bad,' Morgan whispered.

'No need to whisper,' said Sandy. 'She's out of it. Completely.'

Morgan looked at him. 'I'm surprised to see you here.'

'I've been here for a while. I couldn't sleep.'

'Where's Farah?'

'I don't know. Probably having a manicure,' Sandy said.

'Sandy, I'm glad you're here. I've been thinking about what you said. I think Claire needs to get a good criminal attorney.'

'If she needs one at all,' said Sandy, a desolate note in his voice.

Morgan walked round to the side of the bed and took Claire's freezing white hand. 'She's going to get better.' She leaned down and spoke softly into Claire's ear. 'You're going to get better. Do you hear me? You have to.'

Claire's eyelids fluttered, and she licked her lips. Then, every sign of life subsided again.

Morgan looked at Sandy. 'I don't believe the postpartum depression defence is the right one. I don't think she killed them. I think she was coerced by the police into confessing.'

Sandy frowned, but he sat up. 'You have some reason to think that? This isn't just part of some misguided "best friends for ever" mantra, is it?'

'No.' Morgan decided not to elaborate. 'When I stayed at your house, you mentioned that you could find the best criminal attorney around. Is that offer still good?'

'Sure,' he said. 'I can put you together with a guy named Mark Silverman. He's the man. When do you want to meet with him?'

'Well, first I have to explain things to Noreen Quick.'

Sandy waved his hand impatiently. 'No, no. That's not a good idea. Talk to Mark first, then present it to Noreen as a done deal.'

'But we need the tape of Claire's confession. And she has it.'

'We need everything she has. But any research she did is work product. She'll dig in her heels and refuse to give it up.'

Morgan peered at him. 'You know an awful lot about the law.'

'Hazard of my job. I get sued a lot. The new attorney will demand copies of everything from the prosecutor's office, and he'll get it. Till then, we wait.'

'How long?'

Sandy shrugged. 'Could take months.'

'We can't wait for that.' Morgan brushed some hair off Claire's forehead. 'She needs some hope. Now. When she wakes up, I want to have good news for her. If she has to go back to jail with no hope, I'm afraid of what she'll do.'

'I know,' said Sandy, gazing at Claire's mask-like face. 'Look, do you want me to set up a meeting with Mark Silverman?'

'Yes. In the meantime, maybe I could get a copy of the tape.'

Sandy frowned. 'How?'

'I'm . . . not sure. I have to think about it,' said Morgan.

'Look, I don't know what you're up to, but don't go outside the usual channels. Mark can't use evidence if it's tainted . . .'

Morgan gazed down at her friend, struggling to breathe, unable to wake. 'I have to know for sure,' she said. 'We can do anything, once we know for sure.' She bent down and kissed Claire on the forehead. It was almost as cold as her hands. Morgan looked over at Sandy. 'I'm gonna go,' she said.

Sandy kept his gaze on Claire. 'I'll just stick around for a while.'

MORGAN PARKED across the street from the offices of Abrams and Quick, and stared at the building, trying to think of what she could say to get what she wanted. She knew that she needed to circumvent Noreen, but without Noreen's permission, she doubted she would succeed. As pleasant as that receptionist, Berenice, was, she would surely refuse to allow Morgan access to Claire's file without calling Noreen. Morgan began to try out lies on herself. Some sounded plausible. None would give her enough time or opportunity to do what she needed to do.

Should I just wait? she wondered. Let the process of lawyers and courts take its time? Obviously she couldn't wait in West Briar. She had classes to get back to. By the same token, she couldn't imagine leaving Claire alone here after this suicide attempt.

Morgan glanced into the rearview mirror. Her face was drawn and tired. How do I make you want to live, Claire, my friend? she wondered. How can I convince you that you're not to blame, when I've no idea what really happened? Her spirit felt mired in sludge.

All of a sudden, the front door of the law office opened and a dog came bounding out, dragging his owner. In one hand Berenice held Rufus's leash. In the other, she held a scoop and plastic bag, which indicated they were headed out on a doggy relief mission.

As she was dragged from the office, Berenice pulled the door to close it, but Morgan could see that it was standing open a few inches. She inhaled sharply. Berenice hurried behind Rufus to the corner, and turned down the next block. Before Morgan had time to talk herself out of it, she reached into the shelf beneath the CD player, stuffed one of the CDs into her bag, got out of the car and loped across the street. She looked all around and slipped inside.

There was no one in the waiting area. She went swiftly down the hall.

Noreen's door was wide open. Morgan wondered, briefly, why Abrams never seemed to be at the office. Noreen's desk had a computer, of course, but physical objects that were evidence had to be stored in the real world. Morgan went to the filing cabinet.

The volume of files was daunting. But the alphabet was on her side. She found Claire Bolton in the top drawer. Morgan carefully pulled the file out. Before she could even open it, a DVD disc in a plastic case slid out of the side. It had an official label from the prosecutor's office with Claire's name, the date and the time on it.

'Yes,' she whispered. She put the DVD into a zippered compartment in her bag. Then, quickly, she replaced the file. Just as she was sliding the drawer shut, she heard the sound of the front door opening and then, immediately, the barking of a dog. Morgan's heart, already racing, began to thud.

'What is it, Rufus? What? Who's there? Is somebody there?'

Morgan scanned the room, but there was no other exit. She was going to have to go back to the hall. She did her best to assume a cheerful demeanour. As the barking escalated, she stepped out.

At the sight of her, Berenice realised there was no masked intruder and fright turned to irritation. 'What are you doing?' she demanded. 'You're not supposed to be wandering around these offices.'

'I'm so sorry,' Morgan said innocently. 'The front door was open so I came in.'

'Was it? I thought I closed it,' Berenice said fretfully. Morgan could tell she was mentally retracing her steps. 'But what are you doing in Ms Quick's office? You know she's out on bed rest.'

Morgan could feel herself reddening. 'Well, when I was at her house, I liked the music that was playing. Gert lent me this and said to bring it back when I finished listening to it.' She reached in her bag and held out a Corinne Bailey Rae CD in its plastic case. 'I was passing by, so I thought I'd leave it on Noreen's desk.'

'I'll do that.' Berenice slipped the CD inside the desk drawer.

'Is that OK? I guess I should have brought it to the house.'

Berenice sighed. 'It'll be fine here. I send stuff over there all the time.' Now that the crisis was past, she was clearly anxious about her part in it. 'I'm very conscientious about that door as a rule. Noreen would not be very pleased if she thought I left it open.'

'It's not worth mentioning,' said Morgan in a reassuring tone. She smiled. 'She has enough to worry about.'

THE IMAGE ON THE SCREEN was flat grey and white. A woman was slumped in a chair at a desk. A male voice was questioning her, but no one else was visible on the screen. In the corner, white numbers indicated the date and time. The woman's eyes were vacant, her face slack. One of her hands rested, trembling, on the desktop.

'All right,' said the voice. 'This is Detective Roland Heinz here with Detective Jim Curry. We are interviewing Mrs Claire Bolton. Mrs Bolton, we're going to go over the events of the evening ending in the death of your baby son, Drew, and your husband, Guy. Before we begin, have you been apprised of your rights?'

'Yes.' Claire nodded.

'And you are making this statement of your own free will?'

'Yes.'

'Now, you told us earlier that on Saturday night you went to a family dinner at the home of your in-laws. And what was the purpose of this dinner?'

'My husband's . . . daughter was there. Eden.'

'So, the dinner was in her honour? Eden's honour?'

Claire grimaced. 'Sort of,' she said.

'You agreed to go even though you were angry about this long-lost daughter?'

'Yes. I didn't want to go. We weren't really speaking.'

'Who wasn't speaking?'

'Me and my husband. But it wasn't Eden's fault.'

'It was *his* fault, for not telling you about her. Is that correct?'

'I suppose,' Claire whispered.

'And how did the evening go?'

'Terrible,' said Claire.

'Now according to witnesses, your baby had been crying, and carrying on intolerably, is that correct?'

'Yes,' Claire whispered.

'You weren't able to soothe him?'

'No. Nothing I did . . . worked.'

'Were you embarrassed by this?'

'Embarrassed?' Claire asked.

'Well, you appeared to be an incompetent mother in front of your husband's family.'

Claire frowned as if she were trying to remember. 'I guess so.'

'After dinner you and your husband went home. And how were you feeling that night when you went to bed?'

'Very, very upset. And tired,' said Claire. 'Very tired.'

'You and your husband were not sleeping in the same room.'

'No. He was sleeping in the guest room.'

'Because of this ongoing argument.'

Claire nodded. 'Yes.'

'The baby woke you up again at what . . . four a.m.?'

Claire hesitated, as if balking at the question. 'I think so.'

'Is that a yes or no?'

'I'm not sure.'

'You heard the baby and got up?' the man's voice instructed her.

Claire sighed. 'Yes, I must have.'

'You took Drew, who was very small—seven weeks old—into the bathroom adjoining your bedroom, and ran water in the tub?'

Claire frowned, and a few tears ran down her face. 'I don't . . .'

'This is what you told us, isn't it?'

'Yes,' said Claire. 'I think . . . yes.'

'With the intention of drowning the baby to silence him?'

Claire shook her head in misery, and lowered it onto her arms.

'Mrs Bolton? Isn't that true?'

'I was so tired . . .' she said.

'You put the baby face down into the tub.'

Claire raised her head pleadingly. 'I don't remember doing that. I must have just wanted to wash him.'

'We've been over this, Mrs Bolton,' the voice said impatiently.

'Yes,' said Claire hopelessly. 'For some reason, I guess I did.'

'For some reason?' the man asked in a mocking tone. 'You didn't know a newborn would drown if he was placed face down in a tub?'

'Yes, of course.' Her voice choked with tears. 'Of course.'

'Now, Mr Bolton, hearing the baby's cries, came downstairs and found you drowning your own baby?'

Claire stared straight ahead, not speaking.

'Mrs Bolton?'

'He was shouting at me. He . . . pushed me away.'

'That infuriated you, didn't it? After all, he had caused the whole situation. You were so mad at him that you wanted to kill him.'

Claire started to shake her head in protest, and then she stopped.

'Weren't you, Mrs Bolton? We talked about this, remember?'

Claire began to sob. 'I didn't mean to hurt him. But he fell and hit his head on the edge of the tub. There was blood everywhere.'

'You called nine-one-one. Do you remember what you said?'

Claire shook her head. 'No.'

'You told the nine-one-one operator that they were both dead. You implied that you found them that way, didn't you?'

'Did I?' Claire asked.

'Even though that wasn't true,' said the voice, ambiguously.

Claire wept silently, wiping away the tears.

'That wasn't true, was it? Remember what we talked about?'

'It wasn't true,' Claire whispered.

'But they did both die. And it was your fault.'

Claire closed her eyes. There was a long silence.

'Mrs Bolton?'

'Yes,' she whispered. 'Yes. It was my fault.'

'Mrs Bolton, this ends our interview.'

The screen went blank.

Morgan, who was sitting at a student desk in Oliver Douglas's empty classroom, rubbed her hands against her eyes. She had tracked Douglas down, waited through his eleven o'clock class, and convinced him to skip lunch to watch the tape. As soon as the classroom had emptied, he'd popped the DVD into the player.

It had been agony to watch the tape. Morgan took a deep breath and looked over at the professor, who had been making an occasional note. 'What do you think?'

Douglas shook his head. 'This is not a confession,' he said.

Morgan's heart leaped in her chest as if she'd just learned she won the lottery. 'Really? Why do you say that?'

'Unbelievable. It's classic. They only film her—not themselves. It's a proven fact that this technique of isolating the suspect in front of the camera suggests guilt to a jury. Plus, there was no narrative on the part of the accused. She didn't actually say anything, except yes, or maybe. Her interrogator described the incident. He even described how she felt. She merely agreed with him.'

'She could have said no,' Morgan offered gingerly.

'Didn't you hear him telling her that they had gone over this before? That's virtually code for coercion. They were reminding her of her dying husband's accusations. Accusations, it turned out, that he never made. Witnesses can testify to that, correct?'

Morgan nodded. 'Absolutely.'

Professor Douglas got up and took the DVD out of the machine. He popped it back into the case and handed it to Morgan. 'I can't believe her attorney hasn't raised hell about this.'

'Is it that bad?' Morgan said hopefully.

Douglas, dressed in sports jacket, tie and corduroys, hoisted himself up on the edge of his desk, keeping one Hush-Puppied foot on the floor. 'Worse than bad. This poor woman has been browbeaten to breaking point. Not a difficult task, given her condition.'

'So, you don't think she did it,' Morgan exulted.

'I can't speak about that. But she did not confess to the crime. Any respectable judge should throw this out.'

Morgan frowned. 'You don't sound sure that they will.'

'Well, the prosecution may get it introduced, if Mrs Bolton's attorney is incompetent, or has another agenda.'

'I'm getting her a different attorney,' said Morgan. 'It's already in the works. Some fellow named Mark Silverman.'

'Oh, good. Good. He's a capable criminal attorney. Mark Silverman will have this confession suppressed. And even if the judge should decide to admit it, I'll help Mark tear it apart on the stand.'

Morgan felt tears spring to her eyes. 'Oh, thank you,' she said.

'That doesn't mean that Claire couldn't still be convicted. The circumstantial evidence is strong. And of course, there's forensic evidence. Although . . .' Douglas gazed at the DVD player. 'Some of it was true. I think she was telling the truth about her husband coming downstairs and finding her with the baby, drowned in the tub. I think it went just that way. He was yelling at her. They struggled. He fell on a wet, slippery floor and hit his head on the tub. She didn't equivocate about that.'

'This is no help. You're saying that she killed him.'

Douglas shook his head. 'It was obviously an accident. Given his size and the lack of a weapon, he could easily have overpowered her in a struggle. But she was lying about the baby.'

Morgan wanted to put her hands over her ears. 'You don't know that,' she pleaded.

'They led her by the hand through the part about the baby. That came through clearly on the tape. She wasn't recalling any of that.'

'How could she not remember it?' Morgan demanded angrily.

He shrugged. 'Trauma. And guilt. You can't discount guilt. I'm not saying she felt guilt about *killing* her baby. No. She felt guilt about being depressed after the baby's birth. Guilt because, from time to time, she was so frustrated that she had given birth to this child, and couldn't seem to care for him. Tremendous guilt about that.'

'So you think she feels guilty about what happened to the baby.'

'Of course. She's his mother. And, I think she's trying to make her perceptions consistent with the facts. But they don't agree.'

'I'm lost,' said Morgan, throwing up her hands.

The professor frowned. 'Claire agreed that the baby was in the bathtub, and that her husband must have heard the baby's cries and come running. But that doesn't make sense. People come running when they hear something unusual. Guy was used to the baby's constant crying. He had been hearing that night and day for two months solid. Why would he come running for that?'

'We know he came running. It doesn't really matter why.'

Professor Douglas smiled. 'Oh, but it does. Guy came running because he heard something unusual. It wasn't the baby he heard screaming,' he said slowly, as if visualising the scene in his mind. 'Claire was screaming. Because of what she saw in the bathroom. When Guy found her there, and the baby face down in the tub, he jumped to the obvious conclusion. Claire had snapped, and tried to drown the baby. Of course the two of them struggled. He was angry and horrified. Trying to save his son. And Claire was probably desperate, trying to make him understand.'

'I don't get it,' Morgan pleaded. 'Understand what?'

Douglas looked at her calmly. 'The truth, of course. That she found her baby like that. Drew was already drowned when Claire went into the bathroom. The baby was already dead.'

NINE

In that moment, Morgan could see it, in her mind's eye. Her baby godson's death, suddenly so brutally vivid that she thought she might vomit. Such an evil, perverse, frightening deed. But Claire had not committed it. 'If that's true . . . Oh my God, but who?'

Her thoughts again turned to Eden—the rejected child who arrived on the christening day of a cherished baby. Eden, who probably wanted to make her father suffer as she had suffered. Could she have chosen such a heartless way to retaliate?

'There's probably forensic evidence that can help determine who else was in that bathroom,' Oliver Douglas said.

'Yes, but the police would know that by now, wouldn't they?'

'You forget. They're not looking for anyone else.'

'But can't we force them to collect more evidence?'

Professor Douglas stood up. 'I don't know. It may be that Claire's attorney can request that new tests be made. Look, I've got another class. Ask Mark Silverman when you meet with him.'

Morgan shook hands him. 'I'll do just that. And I can't thank you enough, Professor Douglas. Thank you. Really. You've given me hope.'

On the ride back to town from the campus, Morgan felt both excited and sickeningly anxious. Professor Douglas's reconstruction of events made sense in a way nothing else did. But if she thought about the improbability of proving him correct, anxiety took over. She tried to force herself to focus on hope. As she turned down Claire's street, she saw a yellow van parked in front of the cottage. The name ServiceMaster was on the side of the van. As she drew close, she saw workers with vacuum cleaners, buckets and mops at the front door. Their foreman was inserting a key in the lock.

Morgan pulled up behind the van and jumped out. 'No!' she cried. 'No. Stop. Don't go in there.'

The foreman looked up at her in confusion. 'Excuse me?'

Morgan ran across the lawn. 'NO. You can't clean that house.'

The foreman reached into his pocket and pulled out a copy of a receipt. 'We have a work order,' he said. 'What's the problem?'

'The situation has changed. There's evidence that needs to be protected. I'm going to call Mrs Bolton. OK?'

The foreman glanced at his watch. 'I'll call her.' He pulled his phone from his pocket, tapped in a number from the receipt and waited. Finally he said, 'Yeah, Mrs Bolton. This is Steve. From ServiceMaster. We're at your son's house, and there's a lady here who doesn't want us to clean it.' He turned to Morgan. 'What's your name?'

'Morgan Adair.'

He repeated her name and listened. After a moment he held out the phone. 'She wants to talk to you.'

Morgan grabbed it. 'Astrid?' she said. 'Look, it's a long story but I've been talking to an . . . expert who analysed Claire's confession. He thinks that someone else may have killed the baby.'

'What?' Astrid cried. 'What are you talking about?'

'I know it sounds bizarre. But if there's any truth to it, the police need to go over the crime scene again. Once these people clean it up, every trace of evidence is going to be gone.'

'Did you speak to the police about this?' Astrid asked.

'No. Not yet,' Morgan admitted. 'I know it sounds crazy, but I need a little bit of time to take care of all this. If Claire is . . . if she didn't do what they said, I have to try and help her.'

'She admitted she did it,' Astrid said flatly.

Morgan wasn't about to say the words 'false confession' to the family of the victims. 'Astrid, she's my best friend. All I'm asking for is a little time. What difference will a day or two make?'

'It smells foul in that house.'

'I know it. I'm going to leave here myself and get a room. Please, Astrid, I'm begging you. Just a day or two.'

Astrid sighed. 'All right, let me speak to Steve.'

Morgan handed him the phone and Steve put it to his ear. 'Yeah,' he said. 'OK, I'll call you when I'm back in the office and we'll reschedule.'

Morgan closed her eyes and breathed a prayer of thanks.

'Let's go.' He turned to Morgan. 'We're going to clear out of here, for now.' He led the other workers back to their van.

Morgan sank down on the front step, relieved and exhausted. Now that they were gone, she wasn't sure what to do next. Dusty came and sat beside her. She reached out a hand and he allowed her to pet him. She rubbed a hand absent-mindedly over the soft fur. If she'd arrived back a few moments later, she thought, any trace of the baby's killer would have been removed.

She tried to imagine that night. Claire arguing with Guy, who went upstairs to sleep in the guest room. Someone sneaking into the house, past Claire who was exhausted and probaby in a deep sleep. It took nerve to think that one could get away with such a heinous act. Pick up baby Drew and . . . The idea of taking that tiny, innocent baby and holding his face down in the water. How much hate would that require? Was Eden capable of that kind of depravity simply to punish Guy?

Suddenly, Morgan realised there was another possibility—that the hate was directed at Claire. If someone wanted to hurt Claire, what better way?

A silver SUV pulled up in front of the house. The driver got out and walked across the grass towards where she sat. Sandy Raymond's T-shirt was untucked beneath his hoodie. When he saw her staring at him, he gave a brief wave. 'Hey,' he said.

Morgan nodded, and looked down at the cat, her heart pounding. She felt as if she had summoned Sandy Raymond with her thoughts. She had seen him hiding in the shadows at the christening and sitting in the congregation at the funeral. She had found him in the hospital, willing Claire to survive. Now, as he came towards her, Morgan wondered what he was really doing at Claire's bedside. Was he worrying? Or was he enjoying the results of his own vengeful acts?

'I've been looking for you,' he said. 'You never came back to the hospital.'

'No. I've been busy,' said Morgan evasively.

'Look, I called Mark . . . Silverman. The attorney.'

She found herself doubting his simplest statement. 'You did?'

'His secretary told me he's tied up in a big trial right now. I told her that I needed him to get back to me asap.'

Morgan nodded, thinking about the murder house, the crime scene, behind her. Unsealed. The crucial evidence available to anyone who might wish to destroy it. And Sandy, promising an attorney whom, it seemed, he couldn't deliver. 'Well, OK,' she said.

'OK what?' said Sandy.

'Well, if he's not available, I might need to get someone else.'

'Hey, keep your hair on,' said Sandy angrily. 'I told you. This guy is the best. He'll call me. I promise you.'

Morgan nodded. She avoided his gaze.

'What's the matter with you?' he asked. 'You're acting weird.'

'Nothing,' said Morgan defensively. 'It's been a strange day.'

'Hmmph. That's for sure.' Sandy leaned over and reached out a hand to Dusty. The grey cat hissed, and raked his claws down the back of his hand, drawing blood. 'What the hell!' Sandy cried. Dusty bolted off the step. 'That little bastard. Can I come in and wash this off?'

Morgan's heart pounded. 'I'm sorry. They changed the locks.'

'Who changed the locks?'

'Guy's parents don't want anyone in there. I was about to leave.'

Sandy looked ruefully at his bleeding hand. 'That mangy cat has been crawling around in the dirt. Isn't that how you get tetanus? From dirt?' He accompanied Morgan down the path to their cars.

'I have no idea.' Morgan also had no idea where she'd go when she got into the car, but she had to get Sandy away from the house.

'Sorry about the delay. I'll call when I hear from Mark.' He got into the SUV. 'Damn, I'm going to get blood on my leather seats.'

THERE WAS A CAR, packed with suitcases, parked in front of the garage at the Captain's House. The sign out front said CLOSED FOR THE SEASON, but the car indicated to Morgan that the owners were still there. She walked up to the door and rang the bell. It chimed through the guesthouse, but no one came to answer it. Morgan peered in at the window beside the door, but could see nothing inside. She pressed the bell again, knowing that somewhere inside, the proprietor, Mrs Spaulding, was wishing that whoever it was would just go away. Morgan was not going away.

After ten minutes of waiting, and pressing on the bell, she heard footsteps and the door was pulled open. Paula Spaulding looked out, her normally pleasant expression twisted into a frown. 'We're closed,' she said, and then managed to force a smile at the sight of a former customer. 'Oh, hi, Miss . . .'

'Adair. Morgan Adair.'

'Right. I'm sorry, Morgan. I thought I told you. Last weekend was our last available weekend. We're leaving for Sarasota today.'

'You did tell me. Actually, I'm here looking for Eden.'

Paula Spaulding looked surprised. 'You know Eden?'

Morgan quickly explained her connection to Claire.

'Oh my gosh,' said Paula. 'So, that baptism last week was . . .'

'It was for Eden's half-brother. Drew. My godson.'

'Oh dear, come in. I'm so sorry. Come in and sit down. I didn't mean to be rude. I'm just in a hurry to finish up here. My husband will be back any minute and ready to go. But oh, I'm so sorry about your godson.'

'Thank you. So am I,' said Morgan.

Paula indicated one of the wing chairs in the parlour and Morgan sat down. Paula sat down too. 'I'd offer you something to drink but I've cleaned out the refrigerator . . .'

'That's all right. I'm just wondering. Is Eden still staying here?'

'She was. And I thought she was headed back to West Virginia after her father's funeral, but her grandparents called and it seems she hasn't arrived yet. I guess she took a detour.'

Morgan nodded. Then she said carefully, 'Did Eden tell you who sent her the clipping about Guy and Claire's new baby?'

'Oh, I did. I wonder now if it was a mistake. I felt responsible because her mother was working for me when she got pregnant. And then, after Kimba's death, Eden's grandfather wouldn't allow the father near the child. I'm sure you think I should have stayed out of it, but Kimba was very dear to me. She came to work here as a chambermaid, she and her friend Jaslene, after their first year of art school. They were so much fun. Just a couple of young girls wanting to live in a beach town, work hard, and enjoy being young. Anyway, I was sure Kimba would want Eden to know her father.' Paula grimaced. 'I never dreamed it would end the way it did.'

'No. No one could have foreseen that.' Morgan shook her head. 'You know, Eden seemed very angry at Guy at the funeral.'

'Well, sometimes when you've had a lot of fantasies about people, they can be disappointing.'

'That's true,' Morgan conceded.

'Eden had a lot of information coming at her. She wanted to find out all she could about her mother, too. I thought Jaslene might be able to tell her more than I could. Jaslene is a big shoe designer in New York City now. Have you heard of Jaslene Shoes?'

'No, but I'm not that fashionable.'

'Well, I encouraged Eden to give her a call. Unfortunately, it turned out that Jaslene was in Milan. So Eden left her a message. Then she went to stay with her aunt for a couple of nights. And yesterday, after the funeral, she must have packed up and left. Those motorcycles can be dangerous,' Paula fretted.

'She seemed to be able to handle it pretty well,' Morgan said.

Paula sighed and stood up. 'I suppose. Well, I'd love to sit and talk but I've still got things to do before we're ready to leave.'

Morgan stood up as well. 'Thank you for your time. I've got to be going too. I've got to go find someplace to stay. I wish you were open until Christmas. This is such a beautiful house.'

'Oh heavens,' said Paula. 'I'd be completely burnt out if I was open until Christmas.'

Morgan smiled. 'I can understand that. Well, thanks again.' She shook hands with Paula and headed for the door.

'You know,' said Paula. 'I've got a house sitter coming next week. But I wouldn't mind having someone staying here until then. Of course, you'd have to check the heat, take in the mail, water the plants and all.'

'You mean, stay here in the house?'

'I wouldn't pay you. But I wouldn't charge you either. You'd have to wash your sheets and make sure the kitchen was spick-and-span.'

'Oh. I'd gladly do that. That would be great,' Morgan said.

Paula smiled. 'Well, that might work out for both of us. Come with me. I'll give you a quick tour.'

WHEN THE TOUR was over, Morgan thanked Paula profusely and went back to the cottage to pick up her things and feed the cat. All too aware of the sickening smell, she wondered how long she had before Astrid overruled her objections and blanketed the place in house cleaners. Morgan knew that she had to find another attorney, but short of the Yellow Pages, she had no idea where to look. She thought of calling Oliver Douglas, but she knew he'd advise her to wait for Mark Silverman. She felt alone and inadequate. She knew nothing about attorneys or the law, yet she had to do something.

Morgan stopped in at the hospital briefly. Claire's face seemed somewhat less yellow and waxy, but otherwise there was no change in her condition.

Morgan pulled up a chair, took her hand and whispered in her ear, 'Someone else killed Drew. Not you, Claire. Someone else, and we're going to find out who. I'm staying at the Captain's House for a while. So don't worry. I won't leave you.'

By the time Morgan returned to the Captain's House, Paula and her husband were already gone. A cheery note on the door told Morgan to make herself at home and enjoy her stay.

The lovely old house, so inviting when Paula was at the desk, now seemed isolated and gloomy. Morgan turned on a few lights to dispel the shadows of dusk and set her bag down in the room Paula had indicated would be hers. The maid's room, it held only a twin bed, a ladder-back chair and a small dresser. But the wallpaper was a beautiful yellow and blue pattern, and the room had a circular mullioned window that gave the tiny room a distinct charm. Morgan rummaged for a sweater to put on against the chill. Paula wanted the heat kept low, now that there were no guests, and she intended to be the perfect caretaker.

Morgan unzipped her boots and left them beside the bed. Then she padded into the kitchen and opened the refrigerator. All but empty. She went into the pantry and found a tin of chilli con carne among the foodstuffs. She was waiting for the chilli to heat in the microwave when her phone rang. She fished it out and answered.

'Morgan. It's Fitz.'

'Hey,' she said, surprised. 'How are you?'

'OK,' he said. 'Sorry I got a little testy with you about Guy.'

'That's all right. I shouldn't have said those things. And I'm really glad you called. How's the wrestling camp?'

'Bunch of knuckleheads,' he said fondly. 'Two injuries so far. What's happening there? How's Claire?'

'She's the same. But I am very grateful to you.'

'Really,' he asked, sounding pleased. 'Why?'

Briefly, she told him about Oliver Douglas's analysis of Claire's confession and her need to find a criminal attorney. Fitz listened quietly. 'Forget the other lawyer,' he said finally. 'You haven't got time. Go and tell the lawyer you've got what you just told me.'

'Noreen? She's just going to get mad at me for interfering.'

'Or she's going to admire what you're trying to do for your friend. You make a very persuasive case. I say it's worth a try. Not that my advice is worth anything.'

'As it happens,' Morgan said, 'I think your advice is just what I needed.'

'WE'RE JUST ABOUT to watch *Finding Nemo*,' said Gert.

'I realise this is probably not a good time,' said Morgan. 'But it's very important.'

'I know. It's always important,' said Gert, taking a detour into the kitchen. She waggled a finger indicating that Morgan should follow her. Morgan hesitated and then entered the kitchen.

Gert punched a button on a CD player on the counter, popped out the disc and set it back in its plastic case. She handed the CD to Morgan. 'She's good. I loved that "Let Your Hair Down" track. I figured I might as well listen to it before I gave it back to you,' said Gert wryly. 'Because it certainly isn't mine.'

Morgan avoided her accusatory gaze by looking down at the Corinne Bailey Rae disc. 'No,' she said.

'At least you're not trying to con me now,' said Gert, folding her arms over her chest. 'What are you up to anyway?'

Morgan grimaced. 'Did you tell Noreen?'

'Not yet.'

Morgan looked at Gert pleadingly. 'It's a long story and I had a good reason. Please. I need to see Noreen. I'll explain it to her.'

Gert shook her head, but she led the way down the hall to the bedroom. The two children Morgan had seen at her last visit were snuggled on either side of the flannel-pyjamaed Noreen, a bowl of popcorn perched precariously in front of them on the bedcovers.

'Get down for a minute,' said Gert. 'Nonny's got to talk to this lady.' She deftly lifted the plastic bowl as she shepherded the complaining children out and closed the door.

'Couldn't this wait?' Noreen said.

Morgan shook her head. 'I wouldn't be here if it could.'

'All right, fine. What is it?' Noreen asked.

'I need your help,' said Morgan, and took a deep breath. 'Claire did not kill her baby. Someone else did. I'm sure of it. And the evidence may still be in that house. Can you prevent them legally from having it scrubbed down? Or make the police retest the evidence? Or let us hire someone to retest it?'

Noreen stared at her without speaking.

'I took the DVD of the confession from your office.'

'What?' Noreen cried.

Morgan went on. 'I had an expert look at it, and when he pointed this out to me it was so obvious that he was right. Claire made a false confession. She didn't kill that baby, and I don't care how much you want this to be about postpartum depression—'

'Whoa, whoa. Back up. You took the DVD from my office?'

Morgan stuck out her chin defiantly. 'Yes.'

'Whatever made you think that you had a right to do that?'

'I was desperate. I took a chance.'

'Really?' Noreen glowered at her. 'Whom did you show it to?'

'A professor named Oliver Douglas. A lot of people think there's no such thing as a false confession, but he's studied this extensively.'

'I know all about Professor Douglas.'

'I shouldn't have taken it, but I had to do something. Claire's life is hanging by a thread. And she didn't commit this crime.'

'Everybody's innocent,' said Noreen sarcastically.

'If you looked at the tape with the professor you'd see. She made up the part about killing Drew. She doesn't remember it at all.'

'And her husband's death?'

Morgan sighed. 'Professor Douglas thought that probably did happen the way she said. But his theory is that Claire found the baby and started screaming. That's why Guy came downstairs from the guest room. It makes sense. Look at the tape and you'll see.'

'How can I? You have it. If you didn't like the way I was handling this, why didn't you just get another attorney?'

'I tried to. But now there's no time. My friend's life is at stake.'

'All right. Let's have it. I presume you have the DVD of the confession. You won't be needing that any more.'

'Oh, yes,' said Morgan, fumbling in her bag and pulling out the DVD. She handed it to Noreen. She pointed to a Post-it note which she had placed on the case. 'That's Professor Douglas's number. He'll be glad to talk to you. He said he would testify.'

'You've been quite the busy bee, haven't you?' Noreen chewed the inside of her mouth for a moment. Then she looked at Morgan. 'I imagine you want an answer to your question. Yes, the defence can petition for access to all materials in that house for testing.'

Morgan felt a cautious elation. 'Really? Will you do that?'

'I will, after I look at this again, with what you've said in mind.'

'You believe me?' said Morgan, amazed.

'No. Not necessarily.'

'But you're willing to consider the possibility that it wasn't postpartum psychosis? That someone else killed the baby?'

Noreen gave a slight smile. 'My plan for Claire's defence was a strategy. I'm capable of considering other possibilities.'

'Thank you so much,' said Morgan, almost faint with relief.

'This is an unorthodox way to go about it, I have to admit. Do you also have a theory about who *did* kill Claire's baby?'

Morgan wasn't ready to voice her myriad suspicions. 'I have no idea. We just need proof that there was someone else in that bathroom. If Professor Douglas can convince a jury that Claire's confession was coerced . . .'

'That's a very risky way to proceed,' said Noreen.

'Not if it's true,' Morgan insisted.

Noreen leaned forward and pointed her finger at Morgan. 'All right. Now hear me, Morgan. I appreciate that you are concerned for your friend, but you've interfered enough. It's time to butt out of this. If you're right, and someone else killed that baby, you had better not go around voicing your suspicions. Do you understand?'

'I understand.'

'All right. So go home.'

FOR THE LAST FEW MILES to the Captain's House, Morgan sang every show tune she could remember. Noreen had believed her. She felt triumphant at the thought of it. It had all been worth while, if only Claire would simply recover and end up going free.

The Captain's House looked dark and forbidding when she pulled into the drive and she wished she'd left some lights on. It was not the sort of place you wanted to stay in alone. She climbed the steps to the front door, unlocked it, and hurried in.

She did not bother to turn on the lights in the front rooms. Instead, she went through the kitchen to the tiny bedroom. She lay down on the bed, fully dressed, and the exhaustion of the day rolled over her like a wave. But it was a day of progress. She'd done all she could to help Claire today. As much as she would rather have been on her trip to England, there was comfort in that.

The thought of the trip made her think longingly of Simon. Why had she assumed the worst of him? He was unable to get the money back, and he decided to use the reservation and invite a friend to join him. That didn't mean anything. She groped in her bag for her phone and punched in his number. The moment the phone began to ring she remembered the time difference. It was three in the morning there. Oh well, she thought.

Still, she felt a little sheepish when a groggy voice answered.

'Simon?' she said apologetically.

'No,' he said, clearing his throat. 'It's Tim. Who's this?'

'I'm trying to reach Simon,' she said.

'Just a minute,' he mumbled irritably. 'Simon. Phone.'

Simon answered, 'This is Simon,' his voice blurry with sleep. Morgan could hear the other man ask who the caller was.

'Dunno,' said Simon. 'Can't see. Turn the light on and hand me my glasses, will you? They're on your side.'

Her face flaming, Morgan ended the call.

In a moment, the phone rang in her hand. She hesitated, and then answered it.

'Morgan, it's Simon. Why did you ring off? Is anything wrong?'

Everything, she wanted to say. Instead, she was mute. Frantically, she tried to create rationalisations. The two men were perhaps in a room with twin beds. The phone was on a table between them. Tim just happened to pick it up because he was a lighter sleeper . . .

'Morgan, it's three o'clock in the morning. What is going on?'

'I forgot about the time. I'm sorry I woke you up. And Tim.'

Simon sighed. 'Oh, he'll be asleep again in a minute. The man sleeps like a stone.'

'Simon . . .' She didn't want to ask him, but she had to know. 'Are you and Tim . . . together?'

She willed him to laugh, or make an excuse. 'Yes,' he said.

'I see.' She waited. 'So to you I'm just . . . a friend,' she said.

Simon said gently, 'Of course you're a friend.'

All her months of hope and fantasy seemed to blow away like a dandelion puffed on by a child's breath. Her heart felt ashamed, shrivelled. 'It's late. I'll call you back another time,' she whispered, and he did not protest.

For a long while she could not summon the strength to get up from the bed. After a while she forced herself to get up and take a shower. She walked to the den and turned on the television, but she couldn't concentrate. What a fool you are, she thought. Claire had been right all along, although she'd been too kind to say it directly. Morgan couldn't even accuse Simon of leading her on.

When she couldn't stand to think about it any more, she went back to bed. She was afraid she'd lie awake for hours. But she fell asleep quickly, and was having a complicated dream involving her dead parents, when suddenly she found herself instantly awake.

Confused at waking in an unfamiliar place, she took a moment to get her bearings. A banging noise was coming from the front of the house. For a moment she lay paralysed with fear, and then, pulling on a robe, she cautiously went down the hall and entered the main room.

The front door of the Captain's House was open. The night wind was blowing it to and fro on its hinges. Each time the door hit the frame, it banged back open. I locked that door, Morgan thought. Her heart hammered in her throat. The shadows from the bright moon made hulking creatures out of the antique furniture. Morgan stood shivering, frozen to the spot.

Full of dread, she walked to the door. As she closed it, she heard another sound. Someone on the staircase behind her gasped.

Morgan wheeled round and her heart seemed to jump out of her chest. She could see a figure gripping the banister and staring at her from the shadows. 'Who's there?' she asked.

'Who are you?' the stranger said, and descended a few steps.

Morgan instantly recognised the pink hair, the dusty leather clothes and boots, the glint of a stud in the girl's nostril. 'Eden.'

'Hey, what are you doing here?' Eden demanded angrily.

Morgan caught her breath. 'I'm watching the Captain's House for Mrs Spaulding. She left for Sarasota this afternoon. I thought you left town.'

'I did. I came back,' she said.

'How did you get in?'

'I have a key,' said Eden.

'What are you doing back here?'

'You first,' Eden insisted.

'I'm here because of Claire. She's still in the hospital.'

The girl assessed Morgan's answer silently, while Morgan studied her, trying again to imagine her stealing into Claire's house, looking for the baby. Taking it to the bathroom. Somehow, despite all her suspicions, she couldn't imagine this teenager drowning a baby.

Eden seemed to ponder her options for a moment and then she made up her mind. 'I left something here. My ring. It must have come off while I was sleeping.'

'So you came back to look for it? Did you find it?'

'No. I looked around my room but I didn't see it.'

'Oh,' said Morgan, holding on to the banister.

'You scared me,' said Eden

'You scared me,' Morgan admitted. 'I didn't expect someone to let themselves in here in the middle of the night.'

'Sorry. You can go back to bed. I'll leave.'

'Shall I help you look again? Maybe you missed it.'

'Why would you help me?' Eden asked.

'Well,' said Morgan with a sigh, 'I'm awake now. I don't think my heart will be back to a normal rhythm for an hour or two.'

Eden did not apologise. 'All right. Come on, then. I was staying upstairs in the lilac room.'

Morgan remembered the room from the tour that Paula Spaulding had given her. 'OK,' she said. 'What does the ring look like?'

'It's gold. It's got a black stone. Onyx.'

Morgan remembered seeing the ring on the girl's finger. 'I'll bet we can find it between the two of us.'

Eden started upstairs but kept her wary gaze on Morgan. It made Morgan think of Dusty. 'Go ahead,' she said. 'Lead the way.'

Down the hall, Eden entered a door on the right, and flipped a switch. A white wicker lamp was illuminated on the bedside table.

Eden looked around dejectedly. 'She cleaned the whole room.'

'She might have missed it. Let's look under the bed.'

'I looked there.'

Morgan got down on her knees beside the bed, and ran her hand under the dust ruffle. 'Get down at the end,' she said.

Eden went glumly to the end of bed and did the same. 'Nothing.'

'We need a flashlight. I think Paula pointed one out to me.' Morgan went out to the linen closet in the hall, found the flashlight and brought it in. Eden was still groping under the bed. Morgan got down beside her, and shone the light systematically in each corner.

Eden sat back on her heels. 'It's probably gone for good.'

'Oh, come on now. We just started looking,' said Morgan. 'You must have been halfway home and then you came all the way back to look for it. You can't be ready to quit so quickly.'

'I wasn't on my way home. I was in New York City.'

Morgan straightened. 'By yourself? That's pretty brave of you.'

'I went to see a friend of my mother's.'

Morgan remembered Paula mentioning the shoe designer, the friend that Kimba knew from art school. 'How did that go?'

Eden stood up, ignoring her question. 'I give up. It's not here.'

Morgan got to her feet. 'Wait. Let's look behind the headboard. It might have got wedged in there.'

Eden went round to the other side. Morgan shone the light down behind the elaborate oak headboard. 'I think I see something. Let's lift the bed up away from the wall. When I say go.'

Eden held on to the bed. 'OK.'

'OK, go,' said Morgan.

The two of them lifted, and something clattered to the floor. They lowered the bed and Eden crouched down, feeling around under it. She picked the ring up with a cry of delight.

Morgan came round and sat on the edge of the bed. Eden slid the ring on her finger, and sat beside her, displaying it proudly.

'That's a beautiful ring,' said Morgan.

'It was my mother's. It's the only thing I have of hers,' Eden said.

Morgan spoke carefully. 'You don't remember her, I guess.'

Eden polished her ring on the thigh of her dirty jeans. 'No. Just the stories my grandparents told me. She was an artist.'

'I guess your mom's friend helped fill in the blanks a little bit.'

Eden shrugged, but her gaze was closed and distant.

'There's a lot I don't know about my parents too. They died when I was twelve,' said Morgan. 'That's why I think it was good that you came here. Despite everything that happened, you met your father.'

Eden shook her head grimly. 'I found out things I wish I didn't know.'

'Well, Guy didn't give you a very warm reception, which I thought was kind of mean of him. But Fitz said you two were—'

'You don't know anything,' said Eden impatiently.

'I didn't know him well. That's true. But he married my best friend, and from what I saw of him, he seemed to be an OK guy.'

'He was a rapist,' Eden said flatly.

Morgan felt as if she'd knocked the wind out of her. 'A rapist?'

'See. You don't believe it. You think I made it up,' the girl said. 'It wasn't me,' she added scornfully.

'Thank God. Where did you hear that? Did your mother's friend tell you? What was her name? Jasmine?'

'Jaslene. It's none of your business. He can't hurt anyone else now.' Eden stood up abruptly. 'Thanks for helping me.'

'Eden, listen . . . This could be very important for Claire's court case. I need you to tell me. Who was the victim?'

'I promised not to tell. I hope Claire is OK. It wasn't her fault.' Eden strode to the door. 'He deserved to die.'

'Eden, wait,' Morgan pleaded, scrambling to her feet.

But the girl vanished as if she were made from smoke. Morgan ran down to the door and called, but the roar of the bike drowned out Eden's name.

TEN

Morgan watched as the motorcycle's lights disappeared. Finally, she went back into the house and locked the door. It was late, but Morgan doubted she could sleep now. Guy Bolton, a rapist? She tried to superimpose that loathsome image in her mind over the impression she had of a hard-working husband, a handsome partner to Claire . . . Was it true? And if it was, who had he raped? And had his victim decided to take revenge?

Morgan sat in a rocking chair in the parlour and wrapped a knitted afghan around her. She was shivering, partly from cold and partly from shock. Who knows the truth about this? she asked herself. She felt sure the key was Kimba's friend, Jaslene, but she didn't even know her last name.

The grandfather clock in the foyer chimed twelve times. Morgan forced herself to think. She knew Jaslene's company was called Jaslene Shoes. Perhaps the company phone rang on Jaslene's personal line as well. Surely, it wasn't too late to call a fashionista in the city that never sleeps. She dialed information, had the call connected and hoped the elusive Jaslene would pick up. Instead, she reached the automated service, and left a message.

The temperature in the house seemed to be dropping by the moment. After checking the locked door one last time, Morgan went into the maid's room and crawled under the bedcovers. As she lay there, she thought about Eden. Fitz had said that Eden wanted to spit on her father's body at the funeral, and now she knew why.

Morgan's eyes drooped and closed. She could feel her thoughts veering off track as sleep claimed her. All of a sudden, she jolted awake. If Eden had been furious at Guy at his funeral, she must have learned that he was a rapist before she met Jaslene.

Morgan felt as if she was rolling backwards down a hill she was trying to climb. She needed to start from zero, but in a minute her mind was foggy again, and she fell abruptly into a deep sleep.

MORGAN WAS WOKEN by a pounding on the front door. She opened her eyes to a grey autumn day, and felt a sudden loathing for whoever was insisting on her attention. In that minute, she understood why Paula Spaulding and her husband left town so early to escape to Sarasota.

Morgan pulled on her robe, muttering, 'Just a minute. Just a minute.' She shuffled to the door and turned all the locks.

Sandy Raymond was on the front porch, wearing jeans and a bleach-stained sweatshirt from some branch of the University of California. 'Good. You're up,' he said.

'Not really,' said Morgan. 'You woke me up.'

'You'd better get dressed.'

'Wait a minute.' Morgan pushed her uncombed hair out of her face. 'How'd you find me? I didn't tell you I was staying here.'

'That's true.'

'I didn't tell anybody.'

'Yes, you did,' said Sandy, a raffish gleam in his eye.

'No, I know I didn't.'

He couldn't keep from smiling. 'You told Claire. She's awake.'

Morgan let out a cry. 'She is. Oh, thank God. When?'

'When I got there this morning, she was awake. She asked about you. She said you were at the Captain's House.'

Morgan's mouth fell open. 'I was just babbling to her.'

'Hurry up. I'll take you over there if you want.'

'That's OK,' said Morgan. 'Thanks anyway. I've got to get dressed.' She started for her room, but then she looked back to Sandy who was not moving. 'Really. Don't wait for me. I can drive myself.'

'OK,' he said. 'I'll see you there.' He started to turn to leave.

Morgan peered at him. 'You know, I don't get it, Sandy,' she said. 'You're always at the hospital. Doesn't Farah mind?'

Sandy's eyes revealed nothing. 'Farah left me,' he said.

'I'm sorry,' said Morgan.

Sandy shook his head. 'I had to bribe her to leave. I gave her my Mercedes.'

'Really?' said Morgan.

'I know you think it's strange,' said Sandy. 'Me being there all the time for a woman who dumped me for another man.' Sandy's gaze was steady and impassive. 'Well, he's gone now, hasn't he? Now, she needs me.'

MORGAN DRESSED, drove in a hurry and practically ran down the hospital corridor to Claire's room. When she got there she found Sandy seated beside the prison guard on a chair in the hall, his legs crossed as he read the paper. He gave her a thumbs up as she identified herself and the guard checked his list.

'Hey, bro,' Sandy said to the guard, as he stood up and tossed his paper onto his chair. 'Watch this for me, will ya? I want to take a peek in.'

The guard nodded. 'Make it quick,' he said.

Sandy followed Morgan into Claire's room. Morgan looked across at her friend. Claire was lying still, eyes closed, just as she had been for days.

Morgan's heart plummeted. Sandy walked round to the foot of the bed to gaze at her. 'She's just resting,' he said. 'Claire. Wake up, you.'

Claire's eyelids fluttered and she looked up at Sandy. The first smile Morgan had seen on Claire's face for a long time lit up her dark eyes, her jaundiced complexion. 'Hey,' she said.

'Hey, yourself,' said Sandy, beaming. 'I brought someone.'

Claire turned her head and saw Morgan. She lifted a limp hand. Morgan reached out and grabbed it. Claire met her anxious gaze with a small smile, and then she closed her eyes again and sighed.

'Have a visit,' Sandy said. 'I'll be outside.'

Morgan sat in the visitor's chair and tried to release Claire's hand, but Claire wouldn't let go. 'Don't worry. I'm here.'

'I'm so sorry,' said Claire. 'About the funeral.'

'It's all right. It doesn't matter. As long as you're all right.'

Tears trickled down the sides of Claire's face. 'I saw the two of them lying there. They were my heart . . .'

'I know,' said Morgan soothingly, rubbing her hand. 'I know.'

For a few moments, the only sound in the room was Claire's shuddering sobs. Then, with a great effort, she took a deep breath. 'The doctor says I'll be OK,' she said dully.

'That's great.' Morgan leaned forward. 'Claire, listen to me. I have a lot to talk to you about and not a lot of time. Father Lawrence told me that you no longer believed you were guilty.'

Claire sighed. 'That's true. But what difference does it make?'

'But you meant it, that you're innocent. Right?'

Claire grimaced. 'It's complicated . . .'

'No, no. Don't start that. Claire, I've been over the tape of your confession with an expert. He thinks you were coerced.'

Claire shook her head. 'I was so confused about everything.'

'Did the police tell you that Guy had accused you before he died?'

A spot of colour appeared in each of Claire's cheeks. 'Yes.'

'Well, that's not true,' said Morgan. 'Guy was dead before the police got there. He never said anything.'

'But why would they say that if it wasn't true?'

Morgan glanced back at the door, afraid the guard might be listening. 'They tricked you,' she said.

'But, Morgan, I did . . . kill Guy. I didn't mean to . . .'

'Tell me what you remember.'

'He came in the bathroom. Drew was in the tub. I was trying to get him out. And Guy . . . He was yelling at me, trying to push me away from my baby . . .' Claire began to weep. Her chest, the bandages visible at the top of her hospital gown, began to heave with her sobs. 'The floor was wet. He slipped. There was blood everywhere. Morgan, I loved him. You know that.'

'I know. That was not a crime, sweetie. That was an accident.'

Claire pointed feebly to the Kleenex box on the bedside locker. Morgan gave her a handful of tissues. Claire dabbed at her eyes.

Morgan didn't want to put words in her mouth. 'And the baby?'

Claire began to sob harder. 'I took a pill that night to sleep. Something woke me up. I went to the cot but he wasn't there. I was frantic. I ran to the bathroom and found him . . . I don't know how it happened. What kind of a mother am I? How couldn't I have realised . . . Oh, no one will believe me. But I didn't hurt my baby. I would never hurt my baby. I couldn't . . .'

Morgan got up and leaned over the bedside bars, clutching Claire in an awkward embrace. 'I know you couldn't,' she whispered.

Claire grasped Morgan as if she'd never let go. Morgan gradually extricated herself, and sat back down in the chair, letting Claire's sobs subside. After a few minutes Claire looked up. 'Who would have wanted to hurt my baby?' she asked.

'Did Guy have enemies? Did anyone have grudges against him?'

'No,' Claire said hopelessly. 'Everyone liked him . . . well, almost everyone. Morgan, I don't want anyone else unfairly accused.'

'I'm not accusing anyone,' Morgan protested. 'I'm just asking.'

Claire sighed. Finally she said, 'Well, he and his sister didn't get along. I think she was a little jealous of him. It's understandable.'

Morgan felt appalled by her own blindness. Of course, she thought. Lucy had gone off collecting shells rather than be with her family after Guy and Drew died. Eden had stayed with Lucy before the funeral. Lucy was scornful of Claire's depression. Suddenly, Morgan remembered her face when they met at the beach and she said, 'My brother doesn't care who he hurts.'

Morgan had thought it was about being teased, being bullied.

'What are you thinking?' Claire said weakly.

Lucy, Morgan thought.

LUCY'S HOUSE WAS HIDDEN from view by overgrown trees on a quiet residential street. Morgan saw a short, dark-skinned man in the garden, cutting stems of marigolds and placing them in a basket. He looked like one of Dick Bolton's work crew of Mexicans, possibly sent to tend the yard. But when she rolled to a stop and parked her car, he was nowhere to be seen.

Morgan walked up onto the front porch and knocked. Dogs were barking frantically inside the house. As she stood waiting, she couldn't help noticing the grimy windows and broken porch light. A battered rocking chair had a filthy sheepskin dog bed beside it, and, at eye level, several hooks holding choke chains and leashes.

Morgan could hear Lucy inside the house, chiding the dogs. Lucy looked through the storm door at her uninvited guest. She was wearing a red apron over her shapeless sweatpants and matching shirt. The dogs leapt up beside her. 'Morgan,' she said. Morgan started to open the door. 'Don't do that. The dogs'll get out.'

'Can't you hold them? I really need to talk to you.'

Lucy shook her head. 'It's not a good time,' she said.

'I don't care. Eden told me about Guy. I want some answers.'

Lucy blinked owlishly behind her glasses. 'Told you what?'

'I think you know. Not something one would forget.'

Lucy sighed, and her shoulders slumped. She gazed back into the depths of her house and stood unmoving, as if making up her mind. 'Just a minute,' she grumbled, and dragged away the protesting beasts. When she unlocked the door, she didn't look at Morgan.

Morgan followed her into the house. Its stale, stuffy smell was partly doggy, but there was also a cloying odour. Incense burning. The combination of smells was suffocating.

Although Lucy was in her early thirties, the house looked as if it had been furnished by her grandmother. The fabrics that covered the furniture were dowdy, with pale watercolour flowers. Stuffing was coming out of the sofa arms. The blue shag rug was frowzy from the dogs' claws. Crafts made from shells were everywhere—a box on the table, a picture frame atop the television, a vase on the mantelpiece. There was something oddly touching about Lucy's display of her creations. The dogs had been shut behind a closed door, and were baying with displeasure. Lucy didn't offer Morgan a seat. 'All right,' she said. 'Go ahead and talk.'

Morgan looked at the small, plain woman. Lucy seemed so alone. Was it her brother's cruelty that had caused her to retreat from the world? It was one thing to lose your mother at a young age. It was altogether another to be the victim of a sexual predator. A family member.

'Well?' Lucy prompted her. 'When did you see Eden?'

'I'm house sitting right now at the Captain's House,' Morgan told her. 'Last night Eden showed up there.'

'I thought you were going to leave town after the funeral?'

'Claire is still in the hospital. Look, Lucy, there's new evidence. It's now apparent whoever killed the baby, it wasn't Claire . . .'

Lucy immediately bristled. 'That's stupid. She confessed.'

'It turns out she was tricked into making that confession.'

'Tricked?' Lucy scoffed. 'Into admitting murder? What next?'

'Somebody else drowned that baby. I don't know why. Eden told me what Guy had done and it struck me as a possible reason.'

Lucy looked at her balefully and then looked away.

'Look, if this subject is horribly painful for you, I'm sorry . . .'

'I don't know what you're talking about.'

'If he did that to you, Lucy, no one would blame you for hating him. For wanting to hurt him. Or his baby.'

'I'm not the one he raped, if that's what you're asking,' Lucy exclaimed. 'You thought I killed the baby?'

Morgan hesitated. 'I thought perhaps you were Guy's victim.'

'Well, I wasn't. Now will you leave?'

'But you're quite sure your brother did rape someone.'

Lucy's gaze flickered. Finally she said, 'Positive. I was there.'

Morgan felt shocked by the bald statement. 'My God, Lucy.'

Suddenly, there was a thud from the direction of the closed door, and one of the dogs let out a yelp. Behind the door an accented male voice called out, 'Lucía, Lucía, the dogs. Quick. They knocking it over. The altar.'

'Oh, no,' Lucy said. She hurried to the door, throwing it open. One of the dogs bolted out, yelping frantically, and tore round the living room in circles. Lucy called his name and tried to catch up with him. Morgan looked past her into the dining room and her eyes widened at what she saw.

A small, dark-skinned man with the features of a Mayan, his coal-black hair wet and combed back, as if he had just stepped out of the shower, was trying to right an elaborate construction on the dining-room floor. He was barefoot, dressed in a T-shirt and ill-fitting black trousers, and he looked bashfully at Morgan. The floor was littered with marigolds, thick sputtering candles and fruit. The man was resetting an arch made out of cornstalks against a tower of wooden boxes.

Lucy finally convinced the most frantic dog to settle down, and she was on her knees on the floor beside him, combing through his fur.

'Julio, it's wax,' she called out. 'He got hot candle wax on him when the altar collapsed. Poor baby.'

'He knock it all over,' Julio grumbled. He set a small, framed photo of a dark-haired, matronly woman on the makeshift altar.

'You're OK, you bad dog,' scolded Lucy, peeling off the wax.

Morgan looked again at the Mexican man who was carefully replacing the food, flowers, candles and incense. 'What is this?'

'It's ah . . . *Día de los Muertos*,' he said. 'This week.'

'It's an altar. For the Day of the Dead,' said Lucy, letting the dog loose. 'Julio, you'd better put them upstairs in our room,' she said. 'They didn't break the sugar skulls, did they?'

Julio glanced around and lifted a flat, narrow box from the dining-room table. Four white skulls nestled in the box.

'*Mira*. Everything's OK,' Julio exclaimed.

'Oh, good. I'd hate to have to start them all over again,' said Lucy.

Morgan had not missed the words 'our room'. But she pretended to take no notice. She looked in at the box of skulls on the table. 'These are made of sugar?' she asked.

'Yeah. You make them in a mould.' Lucy gazed at her defiantly. 'Julio wanted them. I found the recipe on the Internet.'

'I see,' said Morgan.

'I bet you do,' said Lucy.

Morgan looked at her directly. 'Look, I'm not trying to meddle in your business, Lucy. I just want to know about Guy.'

Lucy sat down heavily, and pointed to a chair. 'You may as well sit.' She did not meet Morgan's gaze.

Morgan sat down on the edge of the chair.

'Julio washes dishes at the Lobster Shack. If my dad finds out—'

'He won't hear it from me.'

Lucy sighed. 'He's got to know sooner or later,' she said.

'You're a grown woman. You can see whoever you want.'

'It's a little more than seeing. We got married a few weeks ago.' Lucy looked at Morgan wearily. 'I told Astrid, of course.'

'Astrid won't tell your father?' Morgan asked.

'He'd try to have the marriage annulled. Get his visa taken away. Astrid thinks we should head to Mexico. We don't want to, but we have to do something before my dad finds out. Astrid won't tell him.'

'Her own husband?'

Lucy sat quietly for a moment. 'Sometimes you have to keep a secret. Although I'll never know how Astrid did it all these years. How she kept it from my dad what Guy did . . .'

Morgan's eyes widened. 'Wait a minute. Are you saying that it was Astrid that Guy . . .? When did this happen?'

'A really long time ago . . .' Lucy seemed uncertain whether to elaborate. 'About a year after my dad and Astrid got married. Of course, I was freaked out when they got married so fast. But Astrid took care of me like my own mother. Guy hated them both.

'One day I skipped my swimming lesson and I was in my room. I heard somebody crying, so I went to the door and looked out, and Guy was walking down the hall, tucking his shirt in his trousers. He didn't see me. I could still hear the crying so I went down the hall, to my father and Astrid's room. Astrid was sitting on the floor, sobbing. Her clothes were all messed up.'

Morgan recoiled from the image. Guy Bolton did that? Had she ever known him at all? 'She told you that Guy raped her?'

'Not right away, but finally she did. She worried about *me* being upset. I was so mad at Guy. Next to my mother, and Julio, I love Astrid more than anyone.' Lucy shook her head. 'I wanted to tell my father. First she said, "Yes. Call him." But when I got him on the phone she told me to hang up. She said he'd kill Guy. My dad had been through enough. My mother's death and all. Astrid made me promise not to tell. She said we had to protect my dad. So, we did.'

Despite the stuffiness of the house, Morgan was shivering. 'God. What a terrible thing to live with,' she said.

'It was worse for Astrid. She did forgive him though. Somehow. So, don't go thinking she wanted some kind of revenge. Lots of times after that

I'd see Guy treat her bad or snap at her, and I'd want to strangle him. But Astrid isn't like other people.'

'And you never told.'

'Not till Eden. I wouldn't have told you, but you knew . . .'

Morgan frowned. 'Why tell Eden?'

Lucy's eyes were bitter. 'She was so sad about missing all those years. I wanted her to know that she was better growing up without him.'

'But weren't you worried it might get back to your father?'

'No one'll tell him,' Lucy scoffed. 'Guy's dead. It's too late.'

MORGAN TOOK the meandering coast road back in order to have a chance to clear her head. Her spirit was soothed by an occasional glimpse of the sea. But her heart was in a tumult over Lucy's appalling story. As she drove along, she realised she was approaching the Lobster Shack. She had assumed it would be closed, due to the family's traumatic bereavement, but there were cars in the small parking lot. Her heart did a surprising flip when she realised that the one with the Seahawks Wrestling sticker belonged to Fitz. He was back, earlier than he had intended.

Morgan impulsively pulled in and parked. The Lobster Shack was an old cottage, long ago minimally renovated to accommodate the kitchen and tables for a luncheonette. Now that she was in front of the funky old seaside spot, she realised how hungry she was. Ravenous, in fact.

She got out of the car and went inside, pretending not to look for Fitz. She hoped he would spot her. But no one called out, and she found herself a table. There were only two other customers. Where is Fitz? she wondered. A waitress arrived at her table and she glanced at the menu. 'I'll have the corn and lobster chowder.'

'We don't have the chowder. That's the weekend special.'

'Oh,' said Morgan, frowning. 'Well, this sandwich plate, to go.'

The waitress disappeared into the kitchen. Morgan gazed out of the windows to the ocean. There were a couple of tables on the patio. Morgan saw two men huddled at one of them. She recognised Fitz and Dick Bolton, both dressed in jackets, hands stuffed in their pockets, looking out to sea. The breeze had blown Fitz's curls back from his face, and Morgan noticed, with a flash of desire, the elegant curve of his cheekbone.

'Hey, Morgan,' said a gentle voice.

Morgan jumped and looked up as Astrid approached the table. Her T-shirt and jeans looked well on her slim figure, and her white-gold braids were pinned loosely to the top of her head. Morgan could not help thinking of what she'd heard from Lucy. Astrid, concealing her stepson's crime to save the family. Forgiving the unforgivable. Or had she forgiven him? Morgan wondered.

'Astrid,' Morgan said. 'I'm surprised to see you here.'

Astrid shrugged, and sat down in the chair opposite Morgan. She looked at her husband out on the patio. 'I guess Dick and I felt the need to get back to where we started.' She gazed around at the yellowed walls, the red check oilcloth on the tables. 'This is where we worked when we first got married. When the kids were young. Before Lobster Shack Seafoods took off . . .'

'I understand,' said Morgan. 'Back to basics.'

'Kind of,' Astrid agreed. 'Sorry about the chowder you wanted. I just put the pot on with the stock.'

'It doesn't matter. I'm sure everything here is good.' A little silence fell between them. 'I see Fitz is out there talking to Dick.'

'Yeah. Fitz is a good boy,' said Astrid. 'He was Guy's best . . .' Her voice broke and she struggled to control her tears.

Morgan studied her, puzzled. Her grief was hard to imagine after what Guy had done. For one moment, Morgan wondered if it was all for show, but she decided no one could fake that sort of misery.

Astrid glanced at her. 'You're looking at me in a funny way.'

'I'm sorry. I was just thinking that Lucy and Guy were lucky to have a stepmother who cared so much for them.'

Astrid raised her small chin, and her pale lavender eyes glittered. 'I didn't have any children of my own. I wasn't that lucky.'

Morgan nodded, feeling uncomfortable. Had Guy made amends somewhere along the line? Keeping an eye on the outside table, she noticed that the two men had stood up and were coming inside.

Dick opened the door and shuddered. 'It's freezing out there.'

Astrid stood. 'Come back in the kitchen. It's warm.'

Dick noticed Morgan and frowned. Before he could say anything, Fitz also noticed her. 'Morgan,' he exclaimed. 'Hey!'

Morgan smiled at his obvious pleasure. 'You're back,' she said.

Astrid nudged Dick in the direction of the kitchen, and Fitz came over to the small table, just as the waitress appeared, carrying a brown pape bag. 'What's this?' he said.

'Takeout,' said Morgan.

'Good! Take it outside to the patio. It's not that cold. I swear. Dick's just a little . . . susceptible, after all that's happened.'

Morgan nodded, pretending to be torn, but actually she was delighted by his impromptu invitation. 'OK,' she said. 'Why not?'

Fitz asked the waitress to bring him some lunch as well, and then he held the door open for Morgan and followed her out. It was, indeed, a beautiful day, and the sun was warm even though the air was chilly. From the patio, their view of the ocean was unencumbered. Morgan took a seat and Fitz sat beside her. She could feel his gaze, and tried not to blush.

'So what have you been up to while I was away?' he asked.

'I've been busy. I took your advice and asked Noreen Quick to intervene on testing the evidence.'

'Really?' he said, clearly pleased. 'How did it work out?'

'Great. She listened to me, and she agreed to file some kind of petition about testing the evidence. Thanks to you, and Professor Douglas, I think there's some hope for Claire.'

'I still can't imagine who would want to drown a baby.'

'That's the million-dollar question.' Morgan jammed her hands in her pockets to keep them warm and felt the outline of the scissors she'd taken from Claire's house. 'Those balloons from the christening were still on the mailbox, announcing that there was a baby in the house. It could have been some weirdo. A stranger.'

Fitz shook his head. 'That doesn't seem very likely.'

'Well, we don't know yet,' said Morgan.

'Do you still think it might have been Eden?'

Morgan shook her head. 'No. I really don't.'

The waitress emerged and set Fitz's lunch down in front of him. He pressed a note into her hand for both of them and told her to keep the change. The girl thanked Fitz and headed back inside. They ate in silence for a moment. Morgan wanted to tell him what she'd learned about Guy. But it was difficult to find a way to say it.

Suddenly he said, in a tone that was playfully chiding, 'You should have called me at the camp. You knew I was interested.'

She put down her sandwich. 'I . . . didn't have your number.'

'Where's your phone?' he demanded.

She smiled. 'In my pocket.'

'Give it to me,' he insisted.

'Why?' she said. But she reached in and handed it over to him.

Fitz began to fiddle with the keypad. 'Because I'm going to take care of that. There. I'm number one on your speed-dial.' He handed the phone back. 'I was thinking a lot about you while I was gone.'

'You were? What were you thinking?'

Suddenly unable to eat another bite, Morgan stuffed the remains of the sandwich back into the paper bag.

'Here, give that to me.' Fitz took the bag and tossed it into the rubbish bin on the patio. 'Let's take a little walk,' he said. He jumped off the edge of the patio, held up a hand and helped her down. When she was beside him, walking in the sand, he kept holding her hand. She was aware of his warm fingers entwined with her own and wondered what he had been intending to say, when he'd mentioned thinking about her. He did not keep her guessing.

'I was thinking that you and I kind of . . . got things backwards.'

Morgan's cheeks flamed. She knew he was referring to their wedding-day tryst in the car. 'I guess we did,' she said.

'I was thinking I'd like to get to know you now,' he said. He looked at her, waiting for her to meet his gaze. 'Hey, come on. Don't look surprised. You're beautiful and smart. And sexy. And I admire you. For the kind of friend you are.'

'Thanks,' she said, tongue-tied. 'That's . . . good to hear.'

Fitz squeezed her hand in his. 'Now that Guy's gone,' he said, 'I don't have a friend I could count on like that.'

'About Guy . . .' she said.

Fitz frowned at her. 'What about him?'

'Well, I found out why Eden was so angry with him.'

'Really? Why?'

Morgan pressed her lips together. Fitz had stopped walking.

'What was it?' he insisted.

'It turns out . . .' She felt a sudden pang of guilt, but it was too late to change the subject. 'Someone told me—and please don't ask who—that he raped someone. When he was younger.'

She wondered if he already knew. He said nothing, but he dropped her hand. 'That is completely . . . insane,' he said.

'I'm afraid I heard it from a reliable source. Believe me.'

Fitz shook his head uncomprehendingly. There was a mixture of disgust and disbelief in his eyes. 'You've got to be kidding.' Turning, he marched back through the sand towards the Lobster Shack.

Morgan hurried to catch up. 'Wait a minute,' she called. 'Wait.' He was reaching for the door handle when she scrambled onto the patio. 'Fitz, I didn't make this up. I'm telling you what I heard.'

Fitz wheeled round. 'I knew Guy. He would never do that. Never. What you're saying is a complete and utter lie,' he shouted.

Morgan saw Astrid and the waitress behind the windows, looking out, drawn by the sudden commotion on the patio.

'Keep your voice down,' said Morgan.

'I don't have to keep my voice down,' he shouted, pointing a finger at her. 'First you tried to pin this on Eden. Now, you're spreading filth about a man who can't defend himself. You're so busy trying to find a scapegoat. Why don't you pick on somebody who can fight back? Hell, pick on me. Maybe I killed the baby. I didn't want Guy to miss his poker night because the baby was crying. Why not? One fall guy is as good as another.'

Morgan stood frozen in place. She didn't meet his furious gaze.

Fitz pulled the door to the shack so hard that it banged against the patio railing. He strode inside without a backward glance.

ELEVEN

Morgan wanted to run back to the Captain's House and hide, but she forced herself to stop by the hospital instead, to see Claire. However, that proved impossible. Claire had been moved to the county jail's infirmary, and wasn't allowed visitors until the next day. Morgan arrived at the Captain's House as the late-afternoon darkness was descending, and let herself into the draughty house.

She turned one lamp on beside the sofa, and sat down, pulling the white afghan over her. Fitz's scorn still blistered her heart, all the more so because she had allowed herself to start musing about him while he was away. Why did you do that? she chided herself. It was probably a reaction to finding out about Simon. Because Fitz was straight, and had, at one point, desired her. And today she had felt that sexual current between them again when he was teasing her about her phone, holding her hand. But that was history now.

A needy part of her wanted to call him, and another part was angry at him. Have a backbone, she told herself. Why would you care what this guy thinks of you? She thought about how cruelly he had mocked her effort to find the truth. If that was how he chose to see her, so be it. She didn't need him in her life anyway. They couldn't seem to get along for more than about five minutes at a time.

Maybe it was time to go back to Brooklyn, let the legal system take its course. She was tired of digging around in people's secrets, and earning nothing but contempt for it. She thought of her apartment overlooking Prospect Park, her friends, the other grad students. But even as she longed for these things, the thought of Claire lying in the prison infirmary haunted her, and held her.

A knock on the door interrupted her thoughts. Reluctantly, she went to open it. Astrid stood on the porch, bundled in a wool coat, holding a bag from which steam and a wonderful smell was rising.

'Astrid,' said Morgan. 'What's this?'

'This is the pint of chowder you wanted.' Astrid held out the bag to her. 'I got a head start on tomorrow's batch.'

The bag was warm in Morgan's hands. 'That's so nice of you.'

'Well, you know it helps me to keep busy.'

It seemed rude not to be hospitable. 'Do you want to come in?'

Astrid shrugged. 'I guess for a few minutes.'

Morgan led the way into the kitchen. 'Cup of tea?' she asked.

Astrid nodded and Morgan turned on the kettle and pulled out a teacup. 'I'm going to get myself a bowl for this,' she said, pointing to the soup. 'Can I get you one?'

Astrid smiled. 'No. I've been sampling it while I was cooking.'

Morgan got a tea bag, and when the kettle whistled, poured Astrid a cup of tea. She removed the top from the container and inhaled the scent of the chowder. 'That smells divine. Mind if I dig in?'

'No. Please. That's what I brought it for.'

Morgan sat down on a stool across the counter from Astrid, poured the chowder into a bowl, and dipped in her spoon.

'I guess your lunch with Fitz didn't go too well,' said Astrid.

Morgan sighed. 'No. He was pretty mad at me.'

'So I gathered. How come?'

'Just oil and water, I guess.' Morgan concentrated on her soup.

'I thought he was kind of sweet on you,' Astrid said. 'How's the chowder?'

'Good,' said Morgan, eating with enthusiasm, although she found the taste a little bit off. Somewhat metallic. She wondered if the lobster Astrid had used might be turning a bit. She hoped not.

Astrid blew on her tea. 'Lucy told me that you came by.'

Morgan kept her eyes lowered. 'Yeah, I stopped by her house.'

'So you know about her marriage. To Julio,' said Astrid. 'You should be honoured that she confided in you.'

'I was a little surprised. It's a shame she has to keep it a secret.'

'If her father finds out, he'll have Julio on the next plane to Mexico,' Astrid said calmly. 'Dick wants to protect her. She's fragile, and every milestone's been difficult for her. But he doesn't get it that, if they're in love, they'll find a way to be together. Dick doesn't think that way. He's a pragmatist when it comes to love.'

'Didn't you and Dick get married a couple of weeks after you met? That was a pretty impulsive thing to do, you might say.'

Astrid sipped her tea. 'Yes, it was. But if it hadn't been me, he'd have married someone else. Some men need to be married. Besides, he had two children to raise all by himself.'

'I guess I pictured your marriage as kind of a fairy tale. It seemed like the most romantic story when Claire told me about it.'

'In a way, it was,' said Astrid thoughtfully. 'That was a long time ago.'

Morgan understood that Astrid did not mean to discuss her marriage any further. As Morgan looked at her, she suddenly felt an odd, dizzy sensation. Then the feeling passed. Her phone began to ring in her pocket, and she pulled it out and answered it.

'Morgan,' Fitz said. 'I need to talk to you.'

'Oh?' she said, reminding herself that he'd been cruel and insulting.

There was silence. 'What's the matter?' he said. 'Are you OK?'

Morgan's stomach was beginning to roil. 'Fine,' she said.

'Can I come over and see you?'

Morgan frowned, squeezing her eyes shut. A sudden cramping in her stomach made her want to cry out. But she stifled it. 'No,' she said. 'I'm tired. I need to sleep.' That seemed like the truth.

'Tomorrow?' he said.

'I don't know. Call me tomorrow.' She put the phone down.

'Who was that?' Astrid asked. 'Fitz?'

Morgan nodded. She took a deep breath, but the sudden cramping began again. She folded her arms over her stomach.

'Morgan, what's the matter? You look pale.'

Morgan was beginning to think that she'd been right about the seafood. She didn't want to insult Astrid though. 'I'm just so tired,' she said. 'I really need to lie down.'

Astrid slid off her seat, and pointed to the plastic container of chowder. 'Do you want me to put the rest of this in the fridge?'

Morgan felt a wave of nausea. She gagged and shook her head. 'I'm sorry. There's something wrong with me.'

Astrid looked at the container. 'You think it was the chowder?' Her eyes widened. She took the container and poured its contents down the sink, as well as the remaining soup in Morgan's bowl. She washed out the bowl, spoon and container as well as her teacup. 'Oh, Morgan, I am so sorry. Seafood can be tricky.'

Morgan nodded, but was feeling too ill to speak. 'I'm just going to go . . .' She gestured vaguely in the direction of her little room.

'Maybe you should go to the doctor,' said Astrid.

'I'll be fine. It just . . . came over me.' Morgan forced herself to get up from the stool. But as soon as she took a step, she collapsed in a heap on the wood floor.

'Oh, my God,' Astrid cried, rushing to her side. 'All right, that does it. You're going to the emergency room.'

'No, Astrid, really. I think if I just . . . maybe if I throw up.'

'No, I read that's not always a good idea. I forget why. We're going to the hospital. I feel so guilty. What if it was the soup?' Astrid threaded her arm under Morgan's. 'Come on. Upsy-daisy.'

Morgan staggered to her feet. She pointed toward the coat rack by the front door, and Astrid went and fetched her coat. Morgan slid her phone into her shirt pocket. 'Need my bag,' she said.

'No, you don't. They'll just take it from you at the hospital.'

'My insurance . . .' Morgan protested.

'I'll take care of all that. Now, don't worry. Just let's go.'

Morgan leaned on Astrid, and her limbs felt like she was slogging through jelly. Her mouth was dry and the stabbing pains in her stomach were growing more frequent. Astrid opened the door, and the blast of chilly air made Morgan shake all over. Slowly, Astrid guided her down the steps and into her car. Morgan collapsed into the passenger seat, and rested her head against the cold window.

'Put on your seat belt,' said Astrid. 'We'll be there in no time.'

'Astrid,' Morgan muttered, her tongue thick. 'Thank you.'

The car began to move, and they were on the road. Morgan felt torpor envelop her, while her stomach was assaulted by pains. Sleep seemed the only answer. Far away, she heard a familiar song.

She pulled her cellphone from her shirt pocket, opened it with wooden fingers and held it to her ear. 'Hello . . .' she mumbled.

'Is this Morgan Adair?'

'Yes . . . it is.'

'Did I wake you up?' asked a velvety voice, sounding puzzled.

'No. I'm . . . sick,' Morgan said.

'Oh. I'm so sorry. This is Jaslene Walker. You left a message at my company saying you're a friend of Eden's? I haven't had a free moment. I don't know if Eden told you but I have a show . . .'

Morgan felt as if she was hearing the breezy chatter from far away. The voice evoked a mental image of a vibrant black woman who spent a lot of time on the phone. 'Yes. Eden told me.'

'Should I call back when you're feeling better?'

'It's OK,' said Morgan. Her head was aching, pounding.

'What did you want to know about?' asked Jaslene.

Morgan remembered that she had wondered if Jaslene had told Eden about the rape. But now she knew it had been Lucy. 'Ah, it was nothing. Sorry I bothered you.'

'How's Eden doing? Did she get home all right?'

Morgan searched her mind. 'Yes. Fine.'

'Well, I was so glad to meet her. She just loved Manhattan. I tried to talk her into staying, but she was determined to go back to that awful West Virginia.' Jaslene laughed. 'I was only there for Kimba's funeral, but that was enough. Did you know Kimba?'

'I didn't,' said Morgan.

'Well, I got to that church, and Eden's grandfather let me know he didn't want any of my kind at the funeral. It was so insulting.'

'Terrible man,' mumbled Morgan through her pain.

'He was. I had to go right back to the hotel. I didn't tell Eden that, though. I didn't tell her about her father either, for that matter.'

Morgan felt a small window clear in her brain. 'About Guy?'

'Well,' said Jaslene, in a confiding tone. 'He was there, all alone, at Kimba's funeral, looking all hangdog. But he wasn't alone at the hotel. Of course, there's only one hotel in that miserable little town and they stuffed me in some room that used to be a broom closet. Anyway, it turns out he was getting it on with a woman in his hotel room, the very day of his wife's funeral.'

Morgan gripped the phone. 'Guy did that? At Kimba's funeral?'

'Yes, he did,' said Jaslene. 'I could see him kissing her from my window. I wasn't peeping, mind you. They had the curtains open. All she was wearing was a bed sheet round her. A skinny little blonde with braids wrapped in a crown all round her head.'

'Morgan, you're in no shape to be talking on the phone.' The streetlights filtering through the car window made Astrid's braids look like a halo. 'Who are you talking to?'

Morgan did not reply. 'Have to go. Thanks,' she said into the phone. Then, she slipped it into her coat pocket.

'Who was that?' Astrid asked. 'You were talking about Guy. What did they say about Kimba's funeral?'

Morgan couldn't think of a convincing lie with her brain in a fog. 'Wasn't important. I feel better,' she lied. 'I want to go back.'

'Tell me what they said,' said Astrid. 'I have a right to know.'

Morgan looked out of the window. The streetlights were becoming scarcer. 'Where are we?'

'On the way to the hospital. I told you. Now who was it?'

'Friend of Kimba's. Please, take me home.'

Astrid ignored her misery. 'What did they say about Guy?'

'Nothing. Guy was there.'

'Of course Guy was there. That wasn't all.'

A wave of nausea rolled over Morgan, and her head felt as if it was being squeezed in a vice. 'A woman. In his room.'

'Why are you bringing up Kimba's funeral now?' Astrid said. 'First you tell Fitz that Guy was a rapist. And now this.'

Morgan looked over at Astrid. 'Fitz?'

'As he left the Lobster Shack, he told me what you said about Guy. He was furious. He knew it for what it was—a disgusting lie.'

'Lucy told me,' said Morgan.

Astrid ignored her. 'Lucy's like a child. She doesn't know any better. You're slandering Guy when he can't defend himself.'

Morgan realised, in a dizzying moment of clarity, that what Astrid said was true. Of course the rape story had been a lie. Guy had not raped Astrid that afternoon at their home. Or any other time. She was willing. It had never been rape. That was a lie Astrid made up to tell Lucy. To cover her affair with her stepson. And ever after, the loyal Lucy kept the secret, hated her brother. Morgan swallowed the bile in her mouth. 'Take me home,' she whispered.

Astrid ignored her and continued to drive.

'Astrid?' Morgan asked. 'I want to get out.'

'You'll get out when I say you get out,' said Astrid. She put her foot down on the gas and the car began to fly down the road.

'Astrid, stop,' Morgan said.

'Oh, no. I can see your filthy mind at work. After all we've been through. I won't let you do this to me. To my family.'

All at once, Morgan realised that Astrid wasn't taking her to the hospital. Wherever they were going, it was not to get help. Morgan was a prisoner. 'Please. I'm sorry. I know you've suffered.'

'You don't know anything,' said Astrid.

All pretence seemed to have vanished. Though her brain was cottony, Morgan knew she was in danger. She thought about calling the police, but Astrid would hear the singsong beeps and rip the phone from her hand. Morgan knew she was no match for the other woman in this condition. Despite the danger, it was getting difficult to hold on to consciousness.

Number one on her speed-dial. Had Fitz actually done it? She slipped a hand in her pocket and opened the phone. Even in her numbed state of mind, she realised that the minute she pressed a button, Astrid would hear the beep. Morgan needed to mask the sound. Her stomach churned, from fear and from poison. She was sure, now, that the soup had been laced.

Don't vomit, Astrid had said in her motherly way. Morgan fingered the keypad. She had to hit the right number without looking. She clutched the phone with one sweaty hand, and with the other stuck a finger down her throat. As she coughed and gagged, she retched up a viscous mess on Astrid's centre console. At the same time, she pressed the phone's keypad.

'Stop that,' Astrid cried out in disgust as the car swerved.

Morgan retched again to cover the faraway sound of a recording.

'All right,' Astrid snarled. 'That's enough.' She pulled to the side of the road. Morgan could hear the waves crashing on the beach. 'Get out.'

'Can't,' Morgan pleaded. 'Astrid, I'm too sick.'

'Give me your phone. NOW. Or I will take it from you.'

Morgan groped in her pocket, felt an unfamiliar shape and then remembered. The scissors she'd used to cut down the balloons. Feeling a kind of vague steadying inside herself, she pulled out the phone.

Astrid shoved it in her own pocket, and then she jerked the keys from the ignition and started round to hte passenger side. Morgan locked the door. Astrid jammed the key in the lock and jerked the door open.

'No, please,' Morgan begged her.

Astrid grabbed her by the hair and Morgan let out a howl of pain. It felt as if Astrid was uprooting it from her scalp. 'Now,' Astrid said. 'You're coming with me.'

Morgan tried to do as she was told, but her legs were too weak. Astrid jerked her hair and she fell from the car to the sand.

'I've had enough,' Astrid muttered indignantly, 'of your interference and your legal strategies. You are not going to prevent Claire from being punished for what she did.'

Morgan coughed, relieved that Astrid had let go of her hair. 'She didn't kill the baby,' Morgan whispered. Even in the moonlight she could see that Astrid's eyes were electric.

'Who's talking about the baby? I'm talking about Guy.'

'Sorry. I know,' Morgan said. 'He was your son.'

Astrid slapped Morgan as hard as she could across the face.

Morgan fell on all fours. She wanted to put her head down and rest it in the cold sand. She rocked back on her heels, holding her stomach to assuage the pains.

'You don't know anything,' Astrid cried.

To Morgan's amazement, Astrid's eyes filled with tears. She looked out across the ocean, rolling in relentlessly under the impassive moon. 'He wasn't my son. He was my fate.'

'Fate?' Morgan whispered.

'From the very first minute we saw each other. When he walked into the lobby of my parents' hotel . . . He was fifteen years old and I was . . . older. But we both knew it.'

Morgan blinked at her.

Astrid sighed. 'We knew what the world would think. We had to hide what we felt.' Astrid looked pityingly at Morgan. 'You don't believe me, do you?'

Astrid's tale of love was like some opium dream that Morgan had entered into, as she felt her consciousness fading in and out. 'Yes. I . . . I do,' Morgan insisted. And at that moment, she did.

'I did what I had to. I married Guy's father and left my family. I did everything so that I could live under the same roof with Guy. And we stole every moment together that we could. For all these years.'

'Oh my God,' said Morgan. Chills were coursing through her, and she didn't know whether it was from the poison, or the cold, or the fascinated revulsion she felt as she listened to Astrid reminisce about her long affair with her stepson. She had the impression that Astrid had suddenly been released from bondage. That she was experiencing joy in finally telling someone aloud about her love.

Astrid's gaze was far away. 'Nothing could break us apart.'

'He got married . . .' Morgan remembered aloud. Her mental censor was failing her. She spoke without thinking.

'To Kimba?' Astrid laughed. 'She meant nothing to him. She trapped him with a pregnancy.' She gave a little smile. 'I freed him.'

Morgan's head was splitting. She felt as if it would soon break open, two halves facing up, under the stars.

'I told Dick I was going to a Prader–Willi conference. I knew where they were staying. I went there. I knew they would go diving. Guy loves to dive. We both do. They went out on another boat. All the boats stop in the same vicinity because the large turtles feed there. Once we were in the water, I slipped into Guy and Kimba's diving group. It was an easy matter to come up behind Kimba and turn down the air on her tank. Just enough so that she would feel the oxygen diminish. Panic. Break for the surface too fast. I knew she would. She was a novice.'

Morgan knew dimly, in spite of her misery, that this was a confession of murder, dangerous to know. But she was mesmerised.

'I never told Guy. If he guessed, he didn't say . . .'

'Claire?' Morgan whispered.

'I gave Claire a sleeping pill that night at our house. She asked me for it. Late that night, I let myself in. She never heard me. I took the baby and put him in the tub. I knew Guy would blame her.'

Something was pinging in Morgan's brain, a distant, urgent memory. 'He loved Claire,' she said dreamily.

Astrid shook her head patiently. 'No. He was just trying to change things. He said we were addicted and had to make the break. But he'd tried before. He spent years in Europe. I'd tell Dick I was going to see my grandmother in the Netherlands and I'd rush to Guy. He always came back to me.'

Morgan stared at the double image of Astrid shimmering before her eyes. Her voice slurred. ''S'over, Astrid. They'll find out.'

'It doesn't matter,' Astrid said. 'I haven't anything to live for.'

She reached into her coat pocket and pulled up a fistful of something twisted that gleamed in the moonlight. Morgan saw that it was a circular length of chain. All at once, she tossed the closed loop of chain over Morgan's head. She gave it a tug and Morgan felt the chain pulled tight against her neck. Adrenaline jolted her, too late, out of her drugged state.

'I bought this for Lucy, for those dogs of hers. She never uses it, of course. Now, if you don't get up and walk, I'll strangle you.'

Morgan gagged and tried to pull the chain away. Astrid jerked it. 'Get up. Once you get in the water, it will all be over quickly.'

The water? Morgan thought. Oh no. Her drugged-up heart began to hammer. She was in the grasp of a killer. No time left. She staggered to her feet, and as she did so, she reached into her coat pocket, fumbled around for the scissors and pulled them out. She reached out and jammed Astrid's hand with all her strength.

Still gripping the end of the chain, Astrid turned with rage in her eyes.

For one second, Morgan thought that she would let go. But Astrid didn't flinch. She batted the scissors from her hand, and began to pull with a terrible fury. Morgan had to follow, crawling and stumbling, trying to avoid being choked to death. It was no use.

Sick, weak, dying, Morgan could not move fast enough across the sand to save herself. She felt freezing water rush up and lap over her hands and recede. Astrid gave the chain a mighty tug and Morgan gagged for air, and saw black spots in front of her eyes, darker even than the darkness. And then, she saw nothing at all.

Fitz stepped out of the bahroom after his shower, wrapped in a towel. He pulled on his trousers and a T-shirt. Then he went to see if there was a game on the television. He picked up his phone, automatically checking, and saw that he had a voicemail. From Morgan.

For one moment, he thought about deleting it without listening. That was what she deserved. Tonight when he called, she'd said, 'I'm tired. I need to sleep.' To hell with her, he thought. A lot of girls liked him.

But that was her number. Maybe she'd regretted her snottiness. He knew that no matter what he told himself, he liked her much more than the other girls he knew. He liked her thick hair and great shape and keen eyes. And there was something about her that touched him. He felt protective of her.

Of course, she'd blow him off if she ever knew that he saw her that way. He had asked Claire about her, after that tumble at the wedding. Claire said that Morgan's parents were killed in a bombing in some godforsaken country and that she'd never got over it. 'Don't go after her,' Claire warned him, 'if you don't mean it.'

He'd taken the warning to heart. After all, he didn't know if he wanted something serious. So, he didn't call. And she didn't either.

Fitz stared at the number. Ironically, after all that had happened, now he did know what he wanted. Today, at the Lobster Shack, he was feeling sure that there was a spark on her side as well. She had seemed happy to see him, and let him hold her hand. It had felt like Christmas to be walking along the water's edge holding her hand. And then she started in on Guy. Surely she wouldn't have done that if she were really interested. Hell, he hadn't even kissed her during this whole miserable time.

Still, she had called him back. He wished he could put the phone down and walk away. But he played the voicemail and listened.

He had expected to hear her voice. Instead, he heard someone retching. Sick as a dog. And then shouting. Something thundering in the background. He broke out in a sweat. What was this?

Maybe it was nothing. Maybe she'd hit speed-dial by accident, and he was listening to her normal life. But it didn't sound normal.

He replayed the message. A woman's voice, harsh and strident, was demanding that she give up the phone. And Morgan, sounding as if she could barely speak, was refusing. This time he was able to place the crashing background. They were on the beach. His heart pounded as he listened again. This time he heard her say Astrid.

Astrid? Why would Astrid be with Morgan? Threatening her? She seemed like the nicest lady in the world. Always helping Dick and fussing over Lucy. Guy was the only one who hadn't seemed to buy her act. One time Fitz had remarked that she was great-looking for her age, still attractive. She knows it, Guy said bitterly. She cheats on my father. And if I ever hear you said anything . . .

It was not hard to imagine, now, that whatever Astrid was doing, Dick knew nothing about it. Fitz could call the police, play them the voicemail, but they would probably laugh. Two women fighting over a phone. Hardly a police matter.

They were somewhere by the ocean. Well, he thought. That narrows it down. To the coast of Long Island. But Morgan sounded really ill. She wouldn't have got far.

If they were on the coast road, he knew he could find them.

Once Morgan had been choked unconscious, the rest was simple, Astrid thought. They were ankle deep in water when Astrid gave that last furious tug of the chain. The waves would do the rest. The tide would carry Morgan's body out into the ocean, and by the time they found what was left of her, there would be no explaining how she got there.

Astrid gave the girl's inert form a gentle shove. Morgan's eyelids fluttered for a moment. Astrid had a moment's fear that the cold water might revive her. But her eyes closed again and Morgan began to float, little by little, away from shore. Astrid watched the first few waves start to take her.

She knew what she would say if, by chance, the body was found, and they uncovered that load of barbiturates in her system. The barbiturates that Astrid had dissolved in the chowder. Astrid would sadly suggest suicide. Say that Morgan had expressed depression, hopelessness, when Astrid visited and brought her the chowder.

Astrid took one last look at the floating body. Morgan would not be uncovering any more family secrets. And Morgan's death would torment Claire, who would be without her champion. Astrid shuddered when she recalled Fitz asking her about Guy being a rapist. All these years, Lucy had kept that secret for Astrid and now, thanks to Morgan, it was being bandied about. Astrid had to be sure that it was never exposed as the lie that it was.

For one moment, Astrid was tormented by the memory of how her plan had backfired so horribly. She had meant for Guy to find his baby murdered, and to blame Claire. All the while she planned it, Astrid imagined that Guy would banish his wife to prison and turn his back on her for ever. Instead, the finding of their dead child had caused Guy and Claire to get into a physical scuffle and he had fallen, hit his head and died. More of Astrid's endless tears seeped from under her eyelids at the thought of it. Guy. Gone for ever. She still couldn't imagine her life without him. Couldn't bear to.

Somehow, of course, she had always known that they were doomed. Their desire was fuelled by the impossibility of their situation. She knew that better than he did. Without frustration, it might end up being ordinary. She couldn't bear that. She knew that she would lose him that way.

And then he met Claire. Like an alcoholic newly committed to AA, Guy had told her that he had found a new kind of life. A life he wanted. He said he was through with their affair once and for all. Astrid expected him to falter, to come back. But a year had passed, a baby was born, and still he stayed, insisting he was devoted to Claire. And then Claire's depression over the baby had arrived, like a gift in her lap. Astrid had hatched her plan, but she had miscalculated, and now her life was hardly worth living.

Astrid dared not linger here too long. Her own shoes, socks and trousers were wet up to the knees and she had to get to the car and change into the dry clothes she had brought with her. She took Morgan's phone from her pocket and threw it into the water.

Then she turned and began to trudge back towards her car. She walked up the beach, approached the car from the back and opened the trunk. She rummaged around and pulled out the dry clothes and shoes she had brought along. She closed the lid and met the implacable gaze of Fitz, staring at her.

'Fitz,' she exclaimed breathlessly, trying to sound normal.

'Where is Morgan?' he said.

'Did you try the Captain's House? I was just out for a walk.'

'By yourself?'

'Well, yes, of course, by myself.'

'What's that for?' Fitz asked, pointing to the choke collar Astrid had rolled round her hand.

'What? Oh, I found this on the beach.'

'Your hand is bleeding,' he said.

'Is it?' she asked.

Fitz took her arm. 'Let's go back down on the beach.'

Astrid demurred. 'I think I'm going to go home.'

'No. I need you to come with me,' Fitz said in a menacing tone.

He shoved her forward, through the dunes and across the sand.

'Morgan,' Fitz called out. There was no answer. He looked at Astrid. 'Where is she?' he demanded.

Almost involuntarily, Astrid's gaze rose to the sea.

Fitz felt something cold clamp down on his heart as he turned to where she was looking, and saw the pale face drifting out on the waves.

MORGAN LAY on an iceberg in the Arctic, where she lived as a princess among the polar bears. It was a light, white world, where the rays of the sun were so bright that you could hardly stand to open your eyes. She was asleep, although she could see all around her and hear all that was said. The polar bears were talking, saying that in a very short time she would have some visitors. Morgan somehow knew it was going to be her parents, and her excitement was fantastic. She knew she had to wake up to meet them. It was difficult though. Her royal robes were as dark as seaweed and they seemed to keep her pinned to the iceberg. She had to get up. Suddenly she heard their voices in this cold, empty place.

'Morgan, Morgan.' The voice came from far away.

Morgan opened her eyes and saw nothing but darkness and felt the water enveloping her, crushing her with its coldness. She couldn't feel her limbs. Her heart stopped from fear. Started again.

'Morgan.'

It was a shout. Someone was there. She turned her eyes towards the shore. Fitz. He was coming through the water. Froth surrounded him and he pushed it away, pushed the water away, pushed everything away and willed her, with his eyes, to hang on.

She felt detached as she watched him, as if it were someone else he was trying to reach. She was already far away, going home.

As if he could divine her waning will, he shouted, 'Morgan, don't quit. Wait for me.' She wondered what he meant, but she couldn't ask him, because her face was frozen. It seemed that he was far away for a long time, and then, suddenly, he was beside her. He grabbed one sodden sleeve of her coat and pulled her until he could get his other arm round her. Then he drew her to his chest. She felt the heat of him, the warmth of him. The life.

'Stay with me, babe,' he said, and began to push towards shore. Every step was excruciating. She felt as if her limbs would break off and float away. He was gasping for breath. She felt the beating of his heart through his jacket. 'Stay awake. I'm bringing you in.'

She tried to speak but her lips wouldn't move. How did you get here? she asked him in her heart. She wasn't sure if life was leaving her, or returning. There was one thing she had to tell him. She forced her blue lips to move. 'Astrid.'

'What, babe? Did you say Astrid?' He put his ear to her mouth.

'Poisoned me,' she whispered.

Fitz threw his head back. 'That bitch,' he cried. His anger seemed to give him added strength. He pulled her closer and crashed through the waves like a ship's prow. In the distance he heard sirens, and he thanked God he had thought to call the ambulance the minute he saw Morgan in the water.

His eyes searched the dark beach but Astrid was gone. There was no one and nothing to be seen except for flashing red lights beyond the dunes.

LUCY LOOPED the two leashes round her hand and allowed herself to be pulled down the sidewalk. Sometimes she wondered what it would be like to wear roller skates and have the dogs pull her. Lucy knew what her father would say if he could hear her thoughts. Be careful. You're weak. You'll fall.

She glanced up at the house and saw Julio, framed by the front window, and it made her smile. Her father had no idea how brave she could be, but he soon would. Lucy waved and Julio nodded and smiled back, but he couldn't wave because he was in the process of putting up curtain rods. He said the house didn't look right without curtains. That was the kind of person he was. If there was something wrong, he fixed it. This house had always been such a burden, with all the chores she was always avoiding or forgetting to do. But not any more. Not since Julio.

'Lucy . . .'

Lucy jumped at the sound of a soft voice in the darkness. She looked all around but couldn't see anyone.

'I'm here, in the car.'

Lucy turned to look. She hadn't noticed her stepmother's car parked down the block. But there was Astrid at the wheel, the window open. Lucy went over. The dogs barked their displeasure at the interruption of their walk. 'Astrid. Oh, I'm so glad you're here.'

Astrid's face looked strange—wild-eyed and gaunt. 'I need to talk to you,' she said. 'I've had an idea.'

'Me too! I wanted to tell you. Why don't you come in?'

'No, listen to me,' said Astrid impatiently. 'I've been thinking about this, and there's only one thing to do. You go and get Julio, and throw your things in a bag. We'll set out for Mexico tonight.'

Lucy's face crumpled. 'We can't. Julio's hanging curtain rods.'

'Curtain rods? You don't need curtain rods if you're leaving town. Come on. Hurry. I brought lots of money.'

Lucy frowned. 'Astrid, I can't.'

'You have to. Do you understand about these temporary visas? If Dick finds out, he'll drive Julio to the airport and not leave until he's on a plane to Mexico. You will never see Julio again . . .'

'If hiding the truth from my father means leaving my dogs . . . Well, I won't just leave them. I can't. ' Lucy shook her head. 'Not for anything.'

Astrid's eyes were frantic-looking. 'We'll bring the dogs with us. We can manage somehow. But you have to hurry.'

'I can't do that,' said Lucy slowly. 'Besides, now that we're married, Julio can stay here, can't he?'

'It doesn't work that way. Lucy, you're being a fool.'

Lucy straightened up, holding the dog's leashes close to her chest. 'Don't say that to me. That's not right.' She turned away from Astrid's car, and Astrid jumped out of the driver's side and followed her back to the house.

'I didn't mean it like that, Lucy,' she said. 'Forgive me. Please.'

Lucy stopped on the front porch steps and looked at her ruefully. 'I thought you of all people would never talk to me that way.'

'Darling, I apologise,' Astrid pleaded.

'You always told Guy not to be cruel to me. But just then, you were being cruel,' Lucy accused her.

'I'm sorry,' Astrid said. 'Lucy, I just want to do this for you. Help you and Julio to get away so you can be together.'

Lucy's gaze softened. 'I know. You always did take care of me. But I don't want to leave my home, now that I have Julio. If it embarrasses my father that I'm married to a Mexican who washes dishes, too bad.'

Astrid looked at her helplessly. 'What are you talking about?'

'I'm saying,' said Lucy earnestly, 'that what I have to do is tell Dad the truth. We're always trying to protect him, but maybe we'd be better off just to tell him these things.'

'No, Lucy, you can't,' Astrid said wearily.

'Yes, I can. And I'm going to. Tell him everything.' Lucy glanced at the front window, and Julio waved at her, pointing at the curtain rods now in place. Lucy gave him a thumbs up. She looked proudly at Astrid. 'Actually, I already have.'

Tears sprang to Astrid's eyes. 'No, no,' she said. 'You didn't.'

'I called and said to come over, I had something important to tell him,' said Lucy stubbornly. 'Give me one good reason why I shouldn't.'

Astrid hesitated, and then she walked up the steps to where Lucy stood. Astrid studied her for a moment, with a wistful gaze. Then, she embraced her tenderly. 'You're right, darling. Don't listen to me,' Astrid said. 'I've done everything wrong.'

Lucy looked taken aback. 'You? You're the best person I know.'

Astrid wiped her tears away with the back of her hand. 'No. I'm not. When you realise . . . you'll hate me. I have to go now.'

'No, wait, Astrid. Dad'll be here soon. Don't you want to be here when I tell him? For a little moral support? I could use it.'

'I can't. Listen, when he gets here just tell him—'

'Tell me what?' said a voice beyond the arc of the porch light.

Astrid turned to her husband, her face alight, her lips ready with a lie. 'Dick. I'm so glad to see you. I was just on my way home.'

Dick stepped out of the darkness, flanked by a policeman on either side. His normally bronzed face was ashen. He gazed, unflinching, into his wife's eyes. 'Really?' he said. 'I would have thought you'd be trying to get away from here. Maybe flee the country.'

'Is this your wife, sir?' asked one of the cops.

'Yes, it is.'

The cop walked up to Astrid holding a pair of handcuffs and reached for her arms. 'Astrid Bolton, you are under arrest for the murder of Drew Richard Bolton and the attempted murder of Morgan Adair.' He began to recite her legal rights.

Lucy's eyes were wide. 'Drew? Wait! That's not true . . .'

Astrid looked at her sadly. 'I'm sorry, darling,' she said.

TWELVE

'She once wrote, "I am the happiest single woman in England,"' said Morgan.

'She never wanted to get married?'

'Her father wanted to force her into an arranged marriage, but Harriet wouldn't have any part of it. She wanted to read and write.'

'That took a lot of courage in those days.'

'And we're talking about a woman who had no sense of taste, or smell, and was deaf to boot. And Charles Darwin said of her, "I was astonished to find how ugly she is."'

'Ouch. You talk about her as if you know her,' said Claire.

Morgan stopped and looked out across the surface of Lake Windermere to softly wooded banks and the treeless slopes of the mountains beyond. 'Being here, seeing the house where she lived, and this countryside that she loved, I feel as if I do know her. She lived in a lot of places. But this was the home that was closest to her heart.'

Claire walked up beside her. 'Well, after two weeks in Cumbria, I feel like she's an old friend of mine, too. And I can certainly see why she loved this beautiful place. I don't know why you agreed to let me come with you.

After all, it's my fault it took you an extra six months to get here. But I'm grateful.'

Morgan smiled. 'I just wish you didn't have to leave. It's been like our travelling days of old. And it was worth the wait.'

The two friends continued on their way, crossing under a canopy of trees to see a waterfall spilling into a pool. As they walked, Morgan felt soothed by the sights around her, but her thoughts still teemed with images from the last six months. Her own recovery from hypothermia and barbiturate poisoning. Claire's eventual return to health. The day in court when Astrid admitted her crimes, including the murder of Kimba Summers, in front of her stoic husband and weeping stepdaughter. Astrid was sentenced to life in prison. Noreen Quick, newly svelte mother of three, was eloquent at the hearing in which all charges against Claire were dropped.

'What are you thinking about?' Claire asked.

Morgan glanced at her friend. 'These last six months.'

Claire nodded. 'Never far from my mind.'

'Do you ever . . . wonder why you confessed when you weren't guilty? I don't mean to remind you of something so painful, but I have such trouble, even now, imagining you doing that.'

'*You* have such trouble?' Claire said, with a short, bitter laugh. 'All I can think is that after I found Drew . . .' She pressed her lips together. 'I think a part of my mind wanted me to be punished . . . to die even. I don't think I'm stating that too strongly.'

'Probably not,' said Morgan.

'I certainly was punished. I have nothing left. Of that life.'

'I know,' said Morgan. They walked along in silence. 'Look at that little church up there.' She pointed across the road to a small stone chapel. 'That's from the Victorian period.'

'Let's go and look,' said Claire.

They left the shore and crossed to the church, which was set, like a jewel, among clipped box hedges, rhododendrons and shrub roses, all blooming in the April sunshine. They wandered up and looked inside. It was perfectly kept, but empty at the moment. Beside the church was a fenced graveyard.

'Was Harriet Martineau buried here?' Claire asked.

'She was buried with her family, in their plot in Birmingham.'

Claire opened the gate in the fence and walked inside, looking from one stone to another. Morgan felt her heart begin to thud as she watched her friend moving slowly among the graves. She stopped at one stone, and crouched down, reaching out to touch it.

'Claire,' Morgan said anxiously.

'These are so worn you can't even read them,' Claire said.

'Hey, I could use some lunch. Are you ready to head back to Ambleside?'

Claire looked up, and her eyes seemed to be swimming. She nodded and stood up, brushing her hands off against one another.

This time, they walked along the road, the tall hedgerows of wild flowers giving it the air of a secret garden. It opened out onto a hilly village with its stone unchanged by time. At one point, Morgan saw a tall, curly-headed man duck into a building and he reminded her of Fitz. Wishful thinking, she thought. She missed everything about him, and yet, when he'd asked if he could come to England with her, she'd told him that Claire was coming, even though Claire was only staying for two of the six weeks. For some reason, part of her wanted to keep him at bay.

The two women strolled along the street until they came to the local pub, where they entered and sat at a table by the window. The landlord came by and took their order. They looked out at the shoppers with their wicker baskets, and men passing on bicycles.

'Life unchanging through time,' said Morgan with a sigh. 'I know it isn't true, but it looks that way, doesn't it?'

'Deceiving,' said Claire.

Morgan nodded.

'You know, in the churchyard I could tell that you were worrying about me in the churchyard again.'

'Force of habit,' Morgan said.

'I don't want you to worry about me,' said Claire. 'I'm recovering, Morgan. I'm going to be all right. You know that, don't you?'

'Oh, sure,' said Morgan too quickly.

'I'm not just saying that. I found out that if one person stands by you, no matter what, it makes you realise that your life is worth living.'

'I agree,' said Morgan.

'You're that one person,' said Claire.

Morgan understood her friend's gratitude. Appreciated it. But didn't really want to dwell on it. She felt that she had done it for herself, because Claire was both friend and family to her. 'And don't forget Sandy,' said Morgan.

Claire smiled, and looked out of the window again.

'What's gonna happen with you two?' Morgan asked slyly.

Claire shrugged evasively. 'It's good to have my old job back.'

'That loyalty of his is worth something,' Morgan observed.

'It's worth a lot,' Claire agreed.

'And he threw over a really pretty girl for you,' Morgan reminded her. 'It cost him a Mercedes convertible.'

'I know,' said Claire, with a smile. 'Although I don't really understand him. I was so heartless to him.'

'He and I have talked about it,' said Morgan. She and Sandy Raymond had grown close in the last six months. In time she had come to realise that, despite his sloppy appearance and lack of tact, Sandy was one of the most quietly confident and tenacious people she'd ever met. Once she had told him that she saw him hiding in the choir loft during Drew's christening. He did not deny it. 'I thought maybe if I saw her there, with her baby, that it would force me to admit that I had lost her for good. Didn't work.' He was sure that, in time, Claire would love him again. Sometimes Morgan thought that he might be right.

'He doesn't see it that way,' Morgan said.

'I know. It's just too soon to say. What about you?'

'You know me,' Morgan said uneasily. 'First I think yes, and then . . . I don't know. I start to wonder.'

'Fitz is head over heels for you, Morgan.'

'I thought a break might do us good. Give us both time to think.'

'Think about what? You love each other.'

Morgan shook her head. 'Love isn't any guarantee of anything.'

Claire peered at her. 'Are you thinking about me and Guy?'

Morgan sighed. 'You have to admit. It makes you wonder.'

Claire shook her head. 'I'm not sorry that I married him.'

'You're not?' said Morgan. 'After all you went through?'

Claire nodded. 'Yes, I know. But no matter what Harriet Martineau might have thought about marriage, I just hope I'll have the courage to risk it again one day. And the opportunity.'

'Really?' said Morgan.

Claire nodded. 'Someday.'

The landlord came and set down their glasses of ale. Claire lifted hers to Morgan's and Morgan tapped hers on Claire's. 'To risk, then,' said Morgan. They smiled at one another and drank.

'And, ladies, when you've finished that, the gentleman over there would like to buy you another round.'

Morgan turned in her chair, expecting to see some dusty workman hunched over a ploughman's lunch. There, in a dark corner, sat Fitz, his elbows on the bar, and a smile on his face. When she met his gaze, he lifted his glass to her, and his eyes were merry.

'It's Fitz,' Claire exclaimed.

Morgan turned back and looked at her friend with narrowed eyes. Her heart was hammering. 'You knew about this.'

Claire smiled. 'I may have known something about it.'

Morgan shook her head. 'How could you?'

'He was so determined. And I owed him one,' said Claire.

No, Morgan thought. This isn't right. I didn't invite him here. I have work to do. My thesis research. This isn't a good idea.

'He said something about wanting a proper English wedding,' said Claire.

Morgan looked at her friend, aghast. 'He must have said "breakfast". A proper English breakfast.'

'I'm pretty sure he said "wedding". I'd consider it, if I were you,' said Claire.

Morgan looked back at Fitz, and found that she could not stop smiling. What are you doing here? she wanted to ask. He met her gaze boldly and the answer in his eyes would have made Harriet Martineau blush. Morgan tried to glare at him, but it was no use. As he got up from his bar stool and started to walk towards her, she thought, for a moment, that if she didn't put her foot down and send him home on the next plane, there would be no stopping him. He'd be arranging for the vicar, and calling her his wife, and she'd never be in complete control of her life again. They would be setting out together, into the unknown. Her heart was reacting unreasonably, somersaulting with happiness. Morgan knew what it meant. She made up her mind, and stood up to meet him.

patricia **macdonald**

It's no accident that Patricia MacDonald likes to write domestic murder mysteries with plenty of suspense but minimal graphic violence.

'What I know best is day-to-day life,' says MacDonald, a best-selling American author who resides in quaint, old-fashioned Cape May, New Jersey (*pictured opposite*). 'I live in a small town. I like to write about families.' Her thirteenth novel, *From Cradle to Grave*, fits the bill perfectly. It's a classic Patricia MacDonald tale of a horrible crime happening in a seemingly perfect suburban world.

She makes sure that, when the digging begins, things aren't so pleasant after all. Part of the fun and enjoyment of reading her books comes from seeing the nasty secrets of regular folks unearthed.

MacDonald says she has always preferred to focus on psychological suspense rather than the blood and guts scenes that saturate the pages of so many crime stories. 'I avoid gore,' she says. 'I avoid violence. I don't like to write it and I don't like to read it.' The author is particularly popular in France, where four of her novels have been made into films, and she feels that her comfortingly old-fashioned, low-violence recipe for books appeals to Gallic audiences. 'Go to any French movie and you'll notice that the French like their fiction low-tech and grounded in everyday life. That describes my books to a T.'

Prior to her career as a novelist, MacDonald worked for many years as an editor at a magazine for soap opera fans. She loved the job, but unfortunately the publication went out of business. Luckily, before that happened, she'd had a revelation that inspired her. 'So often, the work which I paid writers to do for our magazine needed almost a complete rewrite to be fit to publish. I began to wonder why I wasn't writing, instead of correcting the work of others!' Before long, MacDonald and a writer friend were collaborating on a novel about the soap opera world. They wrote fifty pages and submitted the synopsis to various literary agents. While the book was never sold, it was enough to help MacDonald find an agent to help launch her writing career. That agent represents her to this day.

With thirteen novels under her belt, MacDonald says it's tough to keep coming up with original ideas. Still, somehow she always discovers something new to write about. It's only after she comes upon the germ of an idea that she subsequently decides on the killer.

'I always know who the killer is and why,' she says. Having this knowledge firmly in place, fresh elements unfold as the story develops, with new characters created, red herrings planted, various diversionary suspects introduced and so on. 'All of my books are about the reverberations of murder. I am always searching news stories for murders in which there is some motive or relationship that is intriguing, and around which I can create a story.'

Her best editor is her husband, also an author. She often turns to him for the male point of view. 'I will ask him what a man will do in a certain situation,' she explains. After more than two decades of marriage, she says, 'I still find him the wisest, most insightful and funniest person I know.'

And how does this prolific author spend her leisure time? What does she like to do when relaxing?

'When I'm at home, my day is quite routine. I eat breakfast, read the paper, and then take a walk for an hour. After that I do laundry, emails and errands. After lunch I settle down to write and I work for about three hours. That's as long as I can concentrate these days. My favourite season is summer because I live at the seashore and I love to spend the weekend days at the beach with my sister. We chat and read and swim and soak up the sunshine. In the evening, my husband and I like to make dinner for friends or go out. We don't travel all that much. For both of us, our favourite place to be is at home, especially when Sara, our daughter, is home from college.'

And if she could go back in her life and change one thing, what would it be?

That is an irresistible question. If we could change the past, we would probably find that it changed everything that followed. I am lucky enough to feel that I wouldn't want to change my life—I've been very blessed. I do wish that my parents had lived long enough to see me become a novelist, and to have known their granddaughter. But if they had lived, would I have become a writer, or a mother? I'll never know.'